THE
FIFTH
SACRED
THING

THE FIFTH SACRED THING

STARHAWK

BANTAM BOOKS

NEW YORK TORONTO LONDON SYDNEY AUCKLAND

THE FIFTH SACRED THING
A Bantam Book/June 1993

BOOK DESIGN AND ORNAMENTATION BY SIGNET M DESIGN, INC.

Library of Congress Cataloging-in-Publication Data
Starhawk.
    The fifth sacred thing / Starhawk.
    p.   cm.
    ISBN 0-553-09522-6
    I. Title.
    PS3569.T33565F54   1993
    813'.54—dc20   92-14431
                                              CIP

Published simultaneously in the United States and Canada

Bantam Books are published by Bantam Books, a division of Bantam Doubleday
Dell Publishing Group, Inc. Its trademark, consisting of the words "Bantam
Books" and the portrayal of a rooster, is Registered in U.S. Patent and
Trademark Office and in other countries. Marca Registrada. Bantam Books, 1540
Broadway, New York, New York 10036.

PRINTED IN THE UNITED STATES OF AMERICA

BVG   0 9 8 7 6 5 4 3 2 1

DECLARATION OF THE FOUR SACRED THINGS

The earth is a living, conscious being. In company with cultures of many different times and places, we name these things as sacred: air, fire, water, and earth.

Whether we see them as the breath, energy, blood, and body of the Mother, or as the blessed gifts of a Creator, or as symbols of the interconnected systems that sustain life, we know that nothing can live without them.

To call these things sacred is to say that they have a value beyond their usefulness for human ends, that they themselves become the standards by which our acts, our economics, our laws, and our purposes must be judged. No one has the right to appropriate them or profit from them at the expense of others. Any government that fails to protect them forfeits its legitimacy.

All people, all living things, are part of the earth life, and so are sacred. No one of us stands higher or lower than any other. Only justice can assure balance: only ecological balance can sustain freedom. Only in freedom can that fifth sacred thing we call spirit flourish in its full diversity.

To honor the sacred is to create conditions in which nourishment, sustenance, habitat, knowledge, freedom, and beauty can thrive. To honor the sacred is to make love possible.

To this we dedicate our curiosity, our will, our courage, our silences, and our voices. To this we dedicate our lives.

THE
FIFTH
SACRED
THING

1

In the dry time of year, the dangerous time, the risk time, an old woman climbed a hill. Like most people in the southern part of the city, she called the season *El Tiempo de la Segadora,* the Time of the Reaper. The hills were dry, the gardens dependent on the dwindling waters of cisterns, the rains still weeks away. A time of ripening, but not yet of harvesting, when nothing was certain.

She climbed the hill as she had once climbed mountains, one step at a time, planting her stick firmly in front of her and letting it bear her weight as she hoisted herself up. She was ninety-eight years old, born at the midpoint of the twentieth century. Two more years, and she would see the midpoint of the twenty-first. In her day she had climbed many things: Sierran peaks, pyramids, chain-link fences, the way back from despair to hope. And this hill, looming up above the southern corner of the city, rising like a pregnant belly above the green patchwork of houses and gardens and paths and the blue waters of San Francisco Bay. By Goddess, she could still make it up this hill!

Maya stopped to catch her breath. Around her was a moving throng of people, dressed in the greens and golds of the season, gossiping happily or chanting solemnly according to temperament. They carried baskets of offerings: bread and fruit and cheese, fresh vegetables from the gardens.

Below stretched a panorama of sculpted hills crowned by toy houses, cradling the aging skyscrapers that rose from the low ground beside the bay. The city was a mosaic of jewel-like colors set in green, veined by streams and dotted with gleaming ponds and pools. Seen from above, blocks of old row houses defined streets that no longer existed. Instead, bicycles and electric carts and the occasional horse moved through a labyrinth of narrow walkways that snaked and twined through the green. Above the rooftops, gondolas like gaily painted buckets swung from cables, skimming from hilltop to hilltop, moving between high towers where windspinners turned. To the northeast, Maya could see a long train moving across the lower deck of the Bay Bridge, bringing early grain to the central market. Beyond, the blades of the wind generators atop the Golden Gate Bridge seemed suspended in midair, their supports invisible under a gray shroud of fog.

Beautiful, Maya thought. She had adored the city ever since her first glimpse of it in the Summer of Love, more than eighty years before. She had been seventeen then, enchanted by the fog concealing and revealing mysteries like the veils of an exotic dancer, delighted by the crowded streets where people seemed to be perpetually in costume: gypsies, pirates, Indians, sorceresses skipping down the sidewalks to the strains of the Beatles singing "Love, Love, Love."

You have been my most constant love, she told the city silently. Not monogamous but never unfaithful, sometimes a bit tawdry but never boring. And you haven't gone and died on me yet, like the others.

"Love is all you need." The song played in her mind. But the Beatles misled us, she said to the air, thick with the ghosts of her own dead lovers. It wasn't all we needed. We wanted to love, freely and without barriers. We had to remake the world in order to do it.

Sighing, she continued up the steep incline. The truth is, she admitted, this is a hell of a climb for an old hag like me. I could have spared my strength, let Madrone visit the shrines.

The shrines to the Four Sacred Things encircled the base of the hill at the cardinal directions. Maya had made a laborious circuit. She left seeds of rare herbs at the earth shrine, feathers of seabirds and roosters at the air shrine. At the fire shrine, she gave white sage and black sage and cedar, and at the water shrine, she'd left a jar of rainwater saved from the first storms of the previous autumn.

But Madrone probably wouldn't have time. I know how it goes, Maya grumbled. She's probably up to her elbows in blood and vernix, lucky if she can dash up the hill at the last minute. I'm fussy in my old age. An Orthodox Pagan, I like these rituals done right: a leisurely visit to each shrine, a walk up the processional way, time to meditate, contemplate, trance out a bit. . . .

The path wound its way above the small reservoir dug into the side of the hill. Now she could hear the little stream that tumbled down a sculpted watercourse to feed the gardens along her own street. There were so many more gardens, these days. By necessity, now that the Central Valley farmlands were baked to rock by the heat and the fires.

Look at it! Maya paused again, breathing heavily. The city was a place of riotous flowers and clambering vines and trees, whose boughs were heavy with ripening fruit.

It looks so lush. She took a long, deep breath, then another. You'd think we had plenty of everything, plenty of land, plenty of water. Whereas we've simply learned how not to waste, how to use and reuse every drop, how to feed chickens on weeds and ducks on snails and let worms eat the garbage.

We've become such artists of unwaste we can almost compensate for the damage. Almost. If we don't think about the bodies mummifying in mass graves over the East Bay hills. If we ignore the Stewards' armies that may be gathering, for all we know, just over the border.

Well, we made our choice. She started uphill again. We chose food over weapons, and so here we sit, lovely but as unarmed as the Venus de Milo.

As she neared the crest, the path wound across the west side of the hill. In the distance, she could see Twin Peaks, poking above a patch of fog like two brown breasts sticking out of a milk bath. They reminded her of Johanna.

"You hear that, Johanna? Twin Peaks remind me of your breasts."

Johanna, dead, did not answer, but thinking of her breasts made Maya think again of Johanna's granddaughter. Madrone works too hard, Maya thought. All the healers do. But since Sandy's death, she's hardly stopped. She'll be sick herself if she doesn't get more rest. I wish she'd taken the day off, like she said she would, but then something always comes up. . . . Goddess, I hope we're not in for another epidemic! Please, Mama, you wouldn't do that to us again? We're on your team, remember? We're the good guys.

Where was Madrone?

o o o

"Get some fluid in her!" Madrone called. "Aviva, check her dilation. Holy Mother, she's burning up! I swear the ice pack is smoking! We've got to bring this fever down."

"She's only about three centimeters," Aviva said. Above her white mask, her brown eyes looked worried. Her usual cloud of dark hair was tightly confined under a cap. Madrone had left her own face free. She believed a woman in labor needed to see a human face, and she had other ways to protect herself.

"Shit! How are we going to get this baby out of her?"

"C section?" Aviva suggested.

Madrone shook her head. "She'll die." She had one hand on the woman's throat, reading her rapid pulse, the other on her temple, feeding her *ch'i,* vital energy.

"She's dying anyway," Aviva said, reading the monitor. "Her blood pressure's sky high. None of the drugs have touched it."

"We can't lose her," Madrone said. "She's my neighbor, and she's Rosa's mother. I refuse to believe we're going to lose her. I won't lose her." I lost Sandy to this disease, she was thinking; that's enough. It should be enough.

"I wouldn't make statements like that on the Day of the Reaper," Aviva said.

Lou arrived at a dead run, pushing an IV cart. His narrow, delicate fingers expertly found a vein and inserted the drip line.

"Lou, work on her pressure point for dilation. I'm going to feed her *ch'i*."

"Be careful," Lou said. His own mask concealed most of his face, but his black gull-wing eyes were grim.

Madrone nodded, as she took a deep breath and repeated her own secret rhyme that took her quickly into trance. Her body was like a tree with a hollow trunk; her roots could reach down to the great stores of *ch'i* in the molten mantle of the earth and bring it up. Energy pulsed through her, moving from her hands into the woman's body, feeding her, keeping her alive. For how long? As long as I can sustain it, Madrone thought, and that could be an almost infinite time if I were rested, if I could keep myself out of its way and be nothing but a hollow tube, a wire, a vehicle. What I was born to be.

Two sparks of light flickered, mother and baby, struggling to hold on in a burning, smoldering, dark place. Madrone changed the earth fire to cool water, letting it pour through her, always reaching deeper, reaching for more. She was so deep now that the voices around her were dim murmurs, calling out their litanies of alarms and demands. Down and down. But it was like pouring water down an open drain. Nothing held.

One of the lights was wriggling out of her grasp, escaping her. She struggled to hold it, but she was starting to feel herself tire.

"She's hyperventilating!"

"Pulse weak."

Madrone made a last desperate effort, drawing on her own vital energy, hurling it at the light. But the light dimmed and dissolved into the dark.

"She's gone," Lou said softly.

"Take the baby," Madrone said. How far along was Consuelo? Thirty-five, thirty-six weeks? The baby would be small but viable, if they just hurried before the placenta crashed. Why weren't they moving, doing something?

Then she realized that no sound had come out of her mouth. She was pouring all her power into the child, and she had no energy left to speak. Still, she tried again.

"Take the baby."

"Madrone's saying something," Aviva said.

"What? What is it?" Lou asked. "You okay?"

"Take the baby," she said again, this time audibly.

Lou gave her a sharp glance and nodded.

Now she was fighting to hold on, not just to the life of the child but to her own life. *Diosa,* she had gone too far down, she was too tired for this, too weak. But the child lived, she knew that, and if she could just hang on . . .

Suddenly she felt a warm hand on the nape of her neck. *Ch'i* flooded through her. It was Aviva, backing her up, feeding her as she fed the child as Lou lifted it through its dead mother's opened womb. The baby flailed weak limbs and let out a weak cry as he suctioned its lungs.

"It's a girl," Aviva said.

"Give her to me," Madrone said, taking her hands from the dead woman's temples and pulling open her own shirt. Lou cut the umbilical cord and handed her the baby. Madrone clasped the wet and bloody child to her chest, nestling her between her breasts, continuing to pump *ch'i* through her hands. The tiny body was hot, feverish. She grabbed a cube of ice from the pan and rubbed its small back, making trails through the blood. It needed coolness and warmth at the same time, and comfort, and milk. *Diosa,* it needed so much!

"Are you okay?" Lou asked.

Madrone nodded, although she felt sick and weak herself. "No, stay," she said to Aviva, who had started to withdraw her hands. "I'm not *that* okay."

"The baby?" Lou asked.

"She's breathing on her own," Madrone said. "She's small and early, but she may be all right. Don't take her yet, let me work on her some more. In a moment you can check her and weigh her."

"Take a deep breath," Aviva said.

Madrone inhaled slowly, willing her body to relax. But her mind would not comply. "Who has milk? Who could we get to nurse this kid?"

"It'd be safer to get volunteers to pump some milk. We don't know how contagious this thing is," Lou said.

"There is that," Madrone said wearily. "It's too bad. Nursing would help her."

"You really think she'll live?" Aviva asked.

"I don't know. We don't know enough about this fever yet."

"I bet my neighbor would take her," Aviva said. "She just lost a baby and her breasts are still dripping. And I'd notice if she started showing signs of fever."

"That'd be good," Lou said. "That's a good idea."

"Wait," Madrone said, as Lou started to close Consuelo's eyes. She took one last look at the dead woman's face. "I'm sorry, Consuelo. *Lo siento. Lo siento mucho.*"

"I'll get Sister Marie for the rites," Lou said.

Aviva shook her head. "She already gave the Last Blessing, when the labor started. Just in case."

"May the air carry your spirit gently," Madrone whispered to the corpse. "May the fire release your soul. May the water wash you clean of pain and suffering and sorrow. May the earth receive you. May the wheel turn again and bring you to rebirth."

"Blessed be," Aviva murmured.

Lou raised the sheet and covered Consuelo's head.

"Let me take the baby now," Aviva said. "Madrone, you are wiped out."

Madrone considered for a moment. The child was still hot, but not burning. Her life force seemed fairly strong and stable, while Madrone's felt drained. She handed the baby to Aviva, who withdrew her hands from Madrone's neck to take the infant and cuddle her close. Unsupported, Madrone felt the full wash of her own exhaustion. There was a chair in the corner of the small bare room, and she just stumbled over to it before her legs gave way.

"You look terrible, Madrone," Lou said.

She nodded in acknowledgment. "I went a little too far."

"You take chances you shouldn't take." Lou's eyes narrowed to dark slivers. "I've told you this before."

Sandy's eyes had been shaped like that, but they had laughed and teased and seduced her into stroking his black silk hair and rooting for his lips with hers. No more.

Madrone closed her eyes. "You can't be my daddy, Lou. You're younger than me."

"You need a daddy."

"I never had one. I wouldn't know what to do with one."

"You were hatched?"

"He died fighting to free Guadalupe, where I was born. Or so my mama said. I think she lied. I believe I was a Virgin Birth."

"Hail Mary," Aviva said from the sink, where she was washing the baby.

"More like the great Goddess incarnate," Madrone corrected her. "Self-fertilizing, self-creating. That was my mother." And immortal. She should have been immortal. Not so quick to disappear and die and leave me. But enough of that. She looked up at Aviva. "Or do you think I'm Jesus, with a sex change?"

"Jesus was crucified," Lou reminded her. "If you don't do an aura repair, you'll be sick enough to wish it had happened to you."

Madrone looked up at him through her lashes. "Be an angel, Lou. Do it for me?"

"I shouldn't, you know. It only encourages you to excess."

"I didn't want to lose Consuelo," Madrone said, turning away from the white shape on the bed. Her eyes were heavy with tears she felt too tired to shed. Aviva was weighing the baby and testing its reflexes. "She was a friend. Her family lived down the walkway from mine. I grew up babysitting for her daughter. And now what's Rosa going to do? Her dad died six months ago."

"Close your eyes," Lou said. Madrone sank back in the chair, listening to Aviva croon to the child, and let him repair the breaks in the protective *ch'i* field that surrounded her. She could feel his hands moving around her head; she sighed when he dug strong fingers into the knots in her back.

"She's a cute baby," Aviva said. "I hope she lives."

"I'm going to have to tell Rosa," Madrone said. If she kept her eyes shut long enough, maybe when she opened them everything would be different. They'd be back in the Good Reality, as Maya liked to say, in *El Mundo Bueno* where none of this had happened.

"Let somebody else tell her," Aviva suggested.

"I can't do that. I'm her friend." She sighed. Really, she could almost drift into sleep for a moment, while Lou kneaded the tension from her neck. Drift back into her dream of last night, or was it yesterday morning? She couldn't remember when she had last slept, she only remembered dreaming of Bird, and the dream left a sweet taste in her mouth. They were back in the mountains, in their watershed year, the year they gave to the forests, when they were both sixteen. They'd worked so hard, clearing firebreaks and planting new species of drought-resistant spruce and fir. But they were young, and their sweat seemed only an invitation to taste all the body's salt streams.

Funny, she still hadn't dreamed of Sandy, although he'd been dead for a month. But Bird had come several times in the last few days. Maybe Maya was right; she said he was still alive somewhere. But nobody had seen him for almost ten years, since the big epidemic when he went off with Cleis and Zorah and Tom and disappeared deep in the Stewards' territory.

Most likely Bird was dead. Like the other men in my life, Madrone thought: my mythical father, Sandy, Rio. And a goodly number of the women.

Stop it! she told herself firmly. Stop wallowing in self-pity. She sighed again and then let out a squawk as Lou hit a sensitive point. "Ow! What are you doing to me?"

"That hurt?" Lou asked.

"Go easy, would you? I didn't ask to be tortured!"

"That's a point connected with the immune system. It needs strengthening."

"Is that any reason to torment the poor thing? You should call that point Lou's Revenge." His finger remained, strong and adamant, and in spite of her complaints Madrone felt some energy returning.

"All right, Madrone, answer this question correctly, and I'll let up. What are you going to do next?"

"Since I've failed to heal the sick, maybe I should learn to raise the dead. Ow! You're really hurting me! I'm not kidding!"

"What are you going to do next?"

"Rest! Sleep! I swear it! Ah, that's nice." She sighed as his fingers let up and he began massaging her shoulders. "Just as soon as I tell Rosa."

"What about the ceremony?" Aviva asked. "Aren't you representing the Healers' Council?"

"Oh, Goddess, I forgot all about it. What time is it?"

"About one o'clock in the afternoon on the first of August or, if you prefer, Third Foggy Moon," Lou said. "The Day of the Reaper. The day you are supposed to represent us, your guildmates, in the great and glorious celebrations of the twentieth anniversary of the Uprising. If you get a move on, you still have time to make it up the hill. I don't know if that's good news or bad."

"Oh, it's good," Madrone said. "Since the Council for its own unfathomable reasons has chosen me as its representative instead of Doctor Sam, I better get my ass up there."

"Sam suggested it," Lou said. "He meant it as a tribute to Sandy."

"Lou, if you get that knot out of my neck I'll . . . what'll I do for you? I'll bear you a child. I'll cook you a dinner. I'll nominate you for the next public honor."

"Those aren't promises," Lou said, kneading her shoulders expertly, "those are threats."

o o o

I look like the death hag herself, Madrone thought as she stared into the scrub-room mirror. Wisps of her curly black hair had escaped from their thick braid; there were blue circles under her eyes and a grayish tinge to her bronze skin. Streaks of blood covered her cheeks and chest. She stripped off all her clothing and threw it into the solar disinfector, loosed her hair, and stepped into the shower. The hot water felt good on her skin, restored her sense of being back in a body. She scrubbed thoroughly, down to the roots of her hair. She could protect herself from the fever, but until they knew how it was transmitted, she wouldn't risk passing it on.

Clean, her wet hair clinging to her back, she changed back into her street clothes and went to look for Rosa. The girl was waiting in the corridor with Marie, another neighbor, one of the Sisters of Our Blessed Lady of the Waters who had a community house on Madrone's block. Rosa was nestled, half asleep, in Marie's arms, and Madrone squatted down to take her hand and wake her gently.

Rosa opened her eyes, large and dark in her thin face. Her hair hung in two long braids, a little frizzy and disheveled after the sleepless night, and Madrone remembered Consuelo's hands moving deftly in her daughter's hair, weaving the black, shiny strands. Never again.

"I'm sorry, Rosa," Madrone said simply. "I'm very very sorry. *Tu mamá ha muerto.* Your mother is dead."

Marie's arms tightened around the child, and her blue eyes narrowed with concern. She too had been a patient of Madrone's; she too was someone Madrone had not been able to cure and would lose. The milk-white skin of Marie's Irish ancestors wasn't made to withstand the ultraviolet that poured through the earth's weakened ozone shield. Madrone noticed a new growth next to the older woman's nose. Her skin was papery, transparent, the look of cancer.

"I'm sorry," Madrone said again. "We did everything we could. We just don't understand this fever yet."

Now Rosa seemed to comprehend what Madrone was saying. Her eyes filled with tears. She buried her face in Marie's shoulder and began to sob.

"Pobrecita," Marie soothed her. "I'm so sorry." She looked questioningly at Madrone. "The baby?"

"She's alive. For now. I don't honestly know how it will turn out. We found a nurse for her. I wish I could be more optimistic."

Marie nodded. Madrone rested a hand on Rosa's back. She would have liked to curl up and cry herself. I hate this, she thought. I really hate this.

"You look exhausted," Marie said. "I'll take care of Rosa. You go and get some rest."

Nodding, Madrone stood up. If she hurried, she would have just enough time to run home, change into her festival clothes, and meet Maya before the ritual started.

o o o

At the crest of the hill, people were descending from the bucket-shaped gondolas. Their thick cables spanned the city like a metallic spiderweb. They reminded Maya of Rio, how he had grumbled when they were first proposed after the Uprising.

"It's beyond our resources!" he had objected. "We've still got people we can't feed; how can we afford to turn the City into an eco-Disneyland?"

"I like them," Maya said. "They'll be fun. They'll cheer people up."

"Circuses! It'd be cheaper to feed a few Millennialists to the zoo lions. That'd cheer *me* up!"

"Don't be an old crock," she'd said to him, but then she noticed that tears were gathering in his eyes. The cataracts gave them a milky blue look that reminded her of an infant's glazed stare. He was still a handsome man then, in his early eighties, just a few years older than she was. His blond hair had turned silky white and made a bushy frame for the roughly sculpted planes of his face. They could still end an argument by making love, burying in each other's flesh their sorrow at all that had been done too little, too late.

Maybe he was right, Maya thought. We were carried away by our own optimism, in the first flush of victory, still thinking in the old ways, in terms of massive projects and heroic efforts: the sea dikes, the gondolas. Yet in the end the gondolas were quite practical, given the impenetrable maze that the Uprising had made of the city. And beautiful, embellished over the last two decades with bright colors and sacred designs: spirals, interlocking triangles, moons, stars, animals, and birds.

"Hi, Maya. *¡Que nunca tengas hambre!* May you never hunger!" Passersby greeted her, smiling, with the ritual blessing, and to each she replied politely, "May you never thirst! *¡Que nunca tengas sed!*" Some of them she knew by name, others knew her by sight or through the books she had written. A few looked inclined to stop and chat, but she nodded at them and turned away. Too much admiration became wearying at her age.

The terminus was a tall sculptural tower forged out of the metal scavenged from the old microwave tower that had once crowned the hill. It shimmered with soft metallic hues, raising extended arms in welcome, the great windspinner on its top tracing moving mandalas with its blades as it generated power.

A figure emerged from the tower's entrance and waved at Maya. At last, Madrone. The way she moved, her gait as she walked briskly over to where Maya waited, brought Johanna vividly alive again for a moment. Johanna had also liked flowing pantaloons and elaborately draped blouses and overtunics, in those same colors, maroons and purples and deep blues. There wasn't a lot else of Johanna visible in Madrone, just that hint of Africa in the exuberance of her hair and a touch of chocolate under the bronze of her skin. And when Madrone turned, to regard Maya with one eyebrow raised and her lips pursed, shifting her basket of offerings from her right hip to her left, she was Johanna incarnate, and maybe more than that. Maya could, in fact, remember that expression on Johanna's mother's face, who had gotten it from some great-grandmother of her own, and so on back to the beginning of time, that first ancestress whose mitochondria swam in the cells of us all.

"Are you all right, Maya?" Madrone asked. "Did you walk up that hill?"

"I still have the use of my legs."

"And you still don't have any sense. You know I would never have let you try that alone."

"Let me? What makes you think you could stop me?" Maya said.

"Well, for one thing, I outweigh you."

"That doesn't count for much. I'm old but tough."

"Hmph. An old nut is the hardest to crack."

"What are you implying?"

"*Nada, madrina.* Not a thing."

Madrone appraised Maya with a healer's eye. The old woman could have passed for the Crone, the Reaper, herself: her skin, pale as cake flour, protected from the sun by a broad straw hat, her hair a wispy silver corona around the spiderweb wrinkles of her face. Her lips were a thin line, firm and determined, her jaw somewhat square, her brown eyes still clear and luminous. She wore a long black dress and leaned heavily on her silver-handled stick. She did, however, look tough, Madrone admitted, or, more accurately, vital. Amazing, really, that she had survived to such an age, through such times, her wits still sharp as cheddar.

"What are you looking at?" Maya asked.

"You, *abuelita*. You lookin' good."

"Now don't you *'ita'* me. I'm not little, and I'm not your grandmother."

"It's a term of affection, not size. As you well know. And as for exactly what we are to each other, I don't know of a word that covers the case."

"You don't know a word that means 'the daughter of the child one of my lovers had by my other lover when my back was turned'?" Maya asked innocently. "There isn't something in Spanish for that?"

"Better settle for *madrina*. It covers a multitude of sins. Are you really okay?"

"Better than you. How much sleep did you get, anyway?"

"Don't ask."

Maya's voice softened. "How did it go?"

"We lost Consuelo."

"No."

"I can't talk about it now, I'll start to cry."

Maya placed a hand on Madrone's shoulder. She pressed it against her cheek, taking comfort. A single blast of a conch rang out, wavering on the air.

"Half an hour warning," Maya said. "Where do you want to go?"

The upper slopes of the hill were dotted with shrines to Goddesses and Gods, ancestors and spirits. Some were elaborately sculpted and painted, some as simple as an offering basket under a tree. They encompassed an eclectic mixture of traditions. A cairn of memorial stones crowned a green mound dedicated to the Earth Goddess, who could be called Gaia, or Tonantzin, or simply *Madre Tierra,* Mother Earth. Kuan Yin had a shrine and so did Kali and Buddha and many bodhisattvas, along with devis and devas, African orishas, and Celtic Goddesses and Gods. Some formed natural clusters: The Yoruba Oshun, Love Goddess, Goddess of the River, stood near Aphrodite and Inanna/Ishtar/Astarte, in front of a small circle of cleared ground where, at the moment, a woman danced barefoot and bare-bellied. Farther down the hill, the Virgin of Guadalupe overlooked the Stations of the Cross. Up here, the sun was welcomed at dawn on the Winter Solstice, the shofar was blown to announce the Jewish New Year, gospel music was sung on Easter morning, the call to prayer was chanted five times a day, and at almost any time of day or night someone sat in silent meditation, counting breaths.

"To the cairn," Madrone said. "I brought a stone for Sandy." Nestled under the vegetables and herbs in her basket was a rock, carved with Sandy's name and the dates of his birth and death. Sandino Shen Lotus Black Dragon, born September 15, 2019. Died on the twenty-third day of Fog-Rolls-In Moon, Year 20 (June 23, 2048). She would add it to the memorial cairn at the top of the hill, a pile growing at an alarming rate. And that would be all that was left of him, her friend, lover, companion, *compañero:* a rock in a pile, some ashes buried in the garden, memories. There were some griefs no ritual could heal.

Maya touched her arm, lightly, like the brush of a tentative wing. "Shall we place it together?" she asked. "Or would you rather do that alone?"

"Come with me."

Maya reached for her hand. "Come on."

Around the mound, clusters of people were leaving their own stones, or placing fruit or flowers for their dead, or simply standing, weeping, holding each other for comfort.

Madrone took the stone from her basket and held it for a moment. She was trying to think about Sandy, but instead she was thinking about Bird. He was born on the Day of the Reaper; they should have been celebrating his birthday today. A Leo, but he'd had five planets in her sun sign, Scorpio. Sex and death. How old would he have been? She was twenty-eight, and he would be turning twenty-nine. Goddess, they'd been so young ten years ago! She could see his face on the night he went away, his dark skin so smooth and unmarked, his beard still a novelty.

They were going off with a raiding party, he and•Cleis and Zorah and Tom. Would she say goodbye to Maya for him?

"You're going to get yourselves killed," she'd said to him.

He met her eyes, steadily. *"Claro."* At the look on her face, he softened it a bit. "Well, probably."

She'd wanted to scream at him for being a fool, for abandoning her. But his eyes had frightened her. She had seen him look like that on the night of the Uprising, as he stood over his father's bleeding body, with everybody around them screaming and the cops trying to club them down. They were only children then, but the look was old, too old.

Her own eyes were suddenly wet with tears. I'm disloyal to Sandy, she thought, I'm not focusing on him, I'm escaping from fresh pain by probing old wounds. Easier to mourn Bird, after all these years, than to face Sandy's loss. Or Consuelo's. Or the others that would come.

"I'm so sorry about Sandy," Maya said.

"It's Bird I'm thinking about," Madrone admitted. "Today's his birthday, remember?"

"I should remember." Maya smiled. "I remember his birth clearly enough. Brigid went about it quite efficiently, the way she did everything. How a daughter of mine turned out like that, I'll never understand. Four hours of labor, start to finish. I wasn't even late for the ritual that night."

"Did she have a home birth?"

"Yes, my friend Alix was the midwife. I was there, and Bird's father,

Jamie, and Marley, who had just turned three. Brigid thought it would help him bond with the new baby. But he seemed much more interested in the drum I was playing than in his new brother."

"Marley was always more interested in drums than people," Madrone said.

"But what a percussionist!" Maya said. "He could drum the rain down from the sky! I had such talented grandsons, once. Bird was a genius with any instrument he touched. That's not boasting, that's just stating a fact."

"I loved his voice," Madrone said. "I loved to hear him sing." I loved him, she thought. I loved him from the very first day I spent in San Francisco, still in shock from what happened in Guadalupe, and grieving for my mother, and scared of those strangers who called themselves Grandma Johanna, Grandpa Rio, Auntie Maya. Bird gave me his favorite stone, a flat black beach rock with the white pattern of a fossilized sand dollar on its back.

"And so handsome," Maya went on. "The boys both had my eyes, set in that clear milk-chocolate skin. Do you remember chocolate?"

"We used to have it sometimes in Guadalupe," Madrone said.

"Don't outlive your descendants," Maya told her. "It's no fun. I'm only sticking it out until Bird comes back."

"You may have to live forever, then, *madrina.*"

"No." Maya shook her head. "He's not dead. If he were dead, I'd feel it. Anyway, we're here for Sandy now. Say a prayer for him, and place his stone."

Faded marigolds and wilting chrysanthemums dotted the mound. There were no cemeteries in the city, no land that could be spared for burial, so people brought their grave offerings here. Sandy's stone would lie in company with others, sharing their offerings in death as people shared food in life. He, at least, would not be lonely.

"What is remembered lives," Madrone said, stooping and placing the stone on the north side of the mound. *"Jiyi shi yongyuan bu mie de."* She stumbled over the inflections Lou had painstakingly taught her. Sandy had come from the north side of the city, where they spoke Mandarin instead of Spanish as their second language.

"He was a good man," Maya said. "So sweet to everyone, and sensitive. His passing leaves a big emptiness." Yes, she would miss him, like she missed so many others, but the ache in the back of her throat was for Madrone. She was too young to bear so many losses.

Madrone nodded without speaking. Maya could feel the earth under her, alive like a beating heart. Or perhaps, she thought, I'm feeling my own throbbing feet? Still, it was good, at the place of the dead, to acknowledge that One to whom she had pledged herself long ago, the aliveness at the heart of things, the ever-turning wheel of birth, growth, death, and regeneration. It had occurred to Maya lately that calling *that* the Goddess, even though she'd fought for the term all her life, was—what? Not so much a metaphor, more in the nature of an inside joke.

Madrone turned away abruptly. She felt a great need, suddenly, to be alone.

"I'm going to make an offering to Yemaya," she said. The Yoruba Sea Goddess was her favorite of the orishas, the old Goddesses and Gods that had come on the slave ships from Africa.

"Give me a jar of honey," Maya said. "I'll go annoy my ancestors."

"I thought 'commune with' was the operative term," Madrone said, pulling out a small jar of honey from the depths of the basket.

"Jewish ancestors don't commune. They kvetch. That means complain."

"That's one Yiddish word I know, *madrina.*"

○ ○ ○

Maya walked over to where a small crowd was gathered around the Jewish shrine, a brightly tiled and weatherproof ark under an arching pomegranate tree. A carved stone lectern provided a platform for the Torah scroll, and a young woman was chanting in Hebrew. The sounds took Maya back to her childhood, the voice of her grandfather praying in the morning, the voices of her mother and father, arguing.

"Lay off me, Betty!" she could hear her father say. "I'm not going to synagogue, I told you! I don't believe in his damn God!"

"You don't go for God, you go for him. He's an old man, Joe. For once in your life you could do something to make somebody else happy."

"Why should I? Would he do the same for me? Would he chant *The Communist Manifesto* to make me happy?"

"He's your father."

"Big deal!"

Maya slipped quietly behind the tree so as not to disturb the prayers as she placed the jar up against the slender trunk. The tree was encircled with a copper ribbon, inscribed with writing in Hebrew and English that said, *She is a tree of life to them that hold fast to her.*

"Hedging your bets, you old heretic?" whispered a crusty voice behind her. She turned and recognized Doctor Sam, one of Madrone's colleagues from the hospital. With his mane of white hair and tufted eyebrows, he reminded her a bit of her own father in his old age, an age she had now surpassed by a good three decades. Not a handsome man but interesting, she reflected, favoring him with a smile.

"Honoring my ancestors," Maya said.

"Are they impressed?"

"Who knows? If I really wanted to placate my father's ghost, I suppose I could burn some incense in front of a picture of Karl Marx."

"You *are* a heretic."

"And what about you? Don't you claim to be the last godless atheist?"

"I come for the arguments. Is the destruction of the environment the new form of the destruction of the Temple? And which tree of life should we hold to, Torah or Asherah, the Earth Goddess?"

"And did you reach any conclusions?"

"Nah, conclusions aren't the point. You of all people should know that. If we ever came to conclusions, we'd lose the fun of the argument."

There was that spark between them, Maya realized suddenly. Could she develop a father fixation on a man twenty years her junior?

The prayer was ending and the scroll was being replaced in the ark when the conch shells blasted forth again.

"It's time," Sam said, holding out his arm. "Allow me?"

° ° °

Yemaya's shrine was on the western slope of the hill, toward the ocean, although the bulk of Twin Peaks blocked the water from view. Madrone paused for a moment, beneath the statue of the pregnant fish-tailed mermaid, the great mother, Goddess of the Sea. She laid down the last of her offerings, a perfect sand dollar she had found long ago. It reminded her of the stone Bird had given her. Fossilized sand dollars were plentiful, but these days the cast shells of live ones were rare. It made a worthy offering. She hated to part with it, to lose a link to a memory: walking with Bird on the beach below the sea dikes that protected the outer neighborhoods from the rising waters of the ocean, the light playing on the waves, his songs in her ear, his hands smoothing her wind-whipped hair.

The last warning blast of the conch rang out over the hillside. Now it was really time to leave the ghosts of her old losses and get on with the ceremony. "Original mother of life, first Ancestress, accept this offering," she murmured to Yemaya. "Preserve the lives of the living. Lend me strength. And hey, *Iya, Mama,* I'm sad, I've lost my lovers and *compañeros,* old and new. I'm lonely. Turn the tide for me."

° ° °

The sun was hot on the nape of Madrone's neck as she headed back to the gathering place. To the east, shimmering waves of heat rose from the sun-scorched valleys, and ribbons of dust twisted in the air. West of the hill, blue fog lay in bands along the slopes of Twin Peaks.

At the summit, a bowl-shaped amphitheater was hollowed out. It was filled with onlookers, but Madrone saw Maya down below, in the innermost ring where those who had a part in the ceremony assembled. Sam stood beside her, and Madrone sighed softly. He'd want to know how the birth went, and she'd have to talk about it again. She left the food from her basket at the feasting site, and joined the other two. They exchanged greetings as the four *concheros,* bearing their shells aloft, walked proudly to the center of the circle. With eerie, dissonant harmonies, they saluted the four directions and then earth, sky, and center.

The musicians began to play, and everyone sang together, as the ritual fire was lit by four masked figures, bird, fish, coyote, and deer, who symbolized the four directions and the Four Sacred Things.

Next came dances and songs and invocations, to the Four Sacred Things, to the ancestors, to Goddesses and Gods of all the different people assembled. Madrone loved to watch the dancers, especially the Miwok and Ohlone troupes in their feather capes, but she found her eyes closing and her head drooping during a lengthy poem in praise of communal spirit declaimed by a very earnest young woman from the Teachers' Guild.

"They were supposed to have a five-minute limit on speeches," Maya whispered to Sam. "If they don't get on with it, my ass is going to atrophy."

Finally the last speaker finished and beckoned to Maya. She stepped forward. A young girl, very solemn with the weight of her responsibility, handed her the Talking Stick, an oak staff beautifully carved, beaded, and feathered, carrying in its tip a small microphone. Powerful speakers were hidden in the branches of the four sacred trees that stood at the four quarters around the outskirts of the bowl. On the Signers' platform, a man stood waiting to interpret as she spoke. All was ready.

She paused and looked at the crowd, letting her eyes roam over the brilliantly colored festival clothes and the faces of every hue and shade, eyes uplifted, heads set high and proud. This is good, Maya thought, this is what I worked for all my life, and you too, Johanna, you too, Rio. But how many more must we lose, like Consuelo, like Sandy? Like Brigid and Marley and Jamie and, yes, maybe Bird? What is this worth if we can't preserve it, protect it?

The drums began to beat, a trance rhythm, steady but just slightly syncopated, to lead the mind and then shift it in unexpected directions. Maya spoke, her voice rhythmic, musical, crooning an incantation.

"*Éste es El Tiempo de la Segadora,* the Time of the Reaper, she who is the end inherent in the beginning, scythe to the grain. The Crone, Goddess of Harvest. In this her season we celebrate the ancient feast of the Celtic sun god Lugh, his wake as he ages and descends into autumn. It is a time of sweet corn, ripening tomatoes, the bean drying on the vine. The harvest begins. We reap what we have sown."

Madrone sat up straighter, listening attentively. She always enjoyed hearing Maya work a crowd.

"The Crone, the Reaper, is not an easy Goddess to love. She's not the nurturing Mother. She's not the Maiden, light and free, not pretty, not shiny like the full or crescent moon. She is the Dark Moon, what you don't see coming at you, what you don't get away with, the wind that whips the spark across the fire line. Chance, you could say, or, what's scarier still: the intersection of chance with choices and actions made before. The brush that is tinder dry from decades of drought, the warming of the earth's climate that sends the storms away north, the hole in the ozone layer. Not punishment, not even justice, but consequence."

A deep hush fell over the crowd. Maya went on.

"This moon brings a time of hope and danger: fire season. We watch the dry hills anxiously, knowing that the rains are weeks or months away. Those of us who are old have seen fire destroy our drought-baked cities and smoke eclipse the sun. We've seen rich croplands shrivel into glass-hard deserts, and the earth itself collapse on its emptied water table. We have seen diseases claim our children and our lovers and our neighbors. We know it can happen again.

"We hope for a harvest, we pray for rain, but nothing is certain. We say that the harvest will only be abundant if the crops are shared, that the rains will not come unless water is conserved and shared and respected. We believe we can continue to live and thrive only if we care for one another. This is the age of the Reaper, when we inherit five thousand years of postponed results, the fruits of our callousness toward the earth and toward other human beings. But at last we have come to understand that we are part of the earth, part of the air, the fire, and the water, as we are part of one another."

She paused for a moment. Her voice dropped, becoming lighter, almost conversational.

"We have had two blessed decades to remake our corner of the world, to live by what we believe. Today is the twentieth anniversary of the Uprising. I've been asked to tell you the story of *Las Cuatro Viejas*, the Four Old Women who sparked the rebellion in '28 when the Stewards canceled the elections and declared martial law.

"On Shotwell Street, down below the slopes of this hill, which in that time was called Bernal Heights, lived a woman, María Elena Gómez García, whose grandmother grew fruit trees in the back yard from peach pits and avocado pits, and she saved her tomato seeds. While the Stewards' troops were massing down on the peninsula, commandeering all stockpiles of food, and the rest of us were debating what to do and trying to work up courage to do it, María gathered together with her neighbors, Alice Black, Lily Fong, and Greta Jeanne Margolis, four old women with nothing to lose. On the morning of the first of August, they marched out in the dawn with pickaxes over their shoulders, straight out into the middle of Army Street, and all the traffic stopped, such cars as a few people could still afford to drive.

"Some of them were honking their horns, some were shouting threats, but when María raised the pickax above her head, there came a silence like a great, shared, indrawn breath. Then she let it fall, with a thud that shuddered through the street, and the four old women began to dig.

"They tore up the pavement, blow by blow, and filled the holes with compost from a sack Greta carried, and planted them with seeds. By then a crowd had gathered, the word was carried through the streets, and we rushed from our houses to join them, bringing tools or only our bare hands, eager to build something new. And many of us were crying, with joy or with fear, tears streaming enough to water the seeds.

"But Alice raised her hand, and she called out in a loud voice. 'Don't you cry,' she told us. 'This is not a time to cry. This is a time to rejoice and praise the earth, because today we have planted our freedom!'

"Then we joined them, tearing up the streets as the cars backed away from us, piling up barricades on the freeways, smashing the doors of the locked warehouses. And those who supported the Stewards fled south with all the goods they could steal. And we who remained planted seeds, and we guarded the sources of our water in the valleys and the mountains, and the Stewards withdrew to starve us out.

"We were hungry, so very hungry, for a long time while we waited for the seeds to grow, and prayed for rain, and danced for rain. It was a long dry season. But we had pledged to feed one another's children first, with what food we had, and to share what we had. And so the food we shared became sacred to us, and the water and the air and the earth became sacred.

"When something is sacred, it can't be bought or sold. It is beyond price, and nothing that might harm it is worth doing. What is sacred becomes the measure by which everything is judged. And this is our measure, and our vow to the life-renewing rain: we will not be wasters but healers.

"Remember this story. Remember that one act can change the world. When you turn the moist earth over, and return your wastes to the cycles of decay, and place the seed in the furrow, remember that you are planting your freedom with your own hands. May we never hunger. *¡Que nunca tengamos hambre!*"

"May we never thirst! *¡Que nunca tengamos sed!*" the united voices of the listeners chorused.

"One act, and about a thousand hours of meetings," Sam whispered.

"Cynic," Madrone said. "Don't you know a good story when you hear one?"

"It's a great story. It's just that it bears so little resemblance to the actual history I remember."

"Quiet. It's my turn now."

Madrone and several others, representatives of various guilds and councils and work groups, stepped forward into the center of the circle. The same solemn child held the Talking Stick for each of them.

"We have come here to give an accounting of ourselves, calling on the Four Sacred Things to witness what we have made of this city in twenty years," said Salal from the Central Council. "This is how we have kept our pledges. This is what we have harvested."

As the stick passed around the circle, each person spoke, in turn, from the Gardeners' Guild, and the Water Council, and the Healers, and the Teachers, and all the interlocking circles that provided for the needs of the City.

"No one in this city goes hungry."

"No one lacks shelter."

"No child lacks a home."

When the stick came to Madrone, she hesitated for a long moment. "There is sickness here," she said finally, "but no one lacks care."

The stick moved on.

"See, the fruit hangs heavy on the bough, ready to feed the stranger."

"We have guarded our waters well, our cisterns will not run dry, no one thirsts, and our streams run clear."

"All the gifts of the earth are shared," they said in unison.

"May we never hunger!" the people responded. *"¡Que nunca tengamos hambre! ¡Que nunca tengamos sed!"*

The drums beat a hypnotic, insistent rhythm. The music rose and the drums pounded, and suddenly everyone was dancing, in the central space, up in the ringed tiers that climbed the hill, on the ridges. The sky gleamed indigo with streaks of pink and gold in the west, and against its glowing light loomed giant figures, *La Segadora* herself, fifteen feet high, with serpent head and serpent skirt and a basket strapped to her back in which she carried a machete. And Lugh, the gleaming paint of his solar disc set on fire by the dying rays of the sun, and others: ancestors, spirits, visions. Maya knew, looking up, that they were only cloth or paper, but in the twilight they came alive. The musicians were playing one of Bird's tunes, and Maya was suddenly shot through with pain like a ringing bell, the pain of missing him. The people sang:

> *Free the heart, let it go,*
> *What we reap is what we sow.*

The chant rose to a roar, subsided to a single harmonic tone, and ended abruptly, as if sung by a single voice. Everyone touched the earth. Silence swelled to consume all the echoes and the overtones.

"May we never hunger!" the people cried again.

Offerings of fruit and grain and cooked foods were piled in the central circle. A young child was blessing the food and drink, while others thanked the ancestors and spirits and the Four Sacred Things to end the formal part of the ritual. But the feasting would go on for a long time.

"Are you staying?" Sam asked Madrone, coming over to them. "I can walk Maya home." In his voice was a hopeful note.

Maya could feel the spark stretching like a thread between her and Sam. He was hoping for something, an invitation, a sign from her. She could feel his loneliness as she could feel her own. It was too much. She was too old, too tired, to take on the burden of it.

"I've got to get some sleep," Madrone said. "I was up all night."

"Good night, Sam," Maya said firmly, taking Madrone's arm. "It was good seeing you. *Que nunca tengas* and all that."

"Kay noonka," Sam said. "Get some rest, Madrone."

In the dark, spirits fluttered like memories, like birds. Fog lay on the city like the silver fingers of a gloved hand, as the moon lit their way down the hill.

2

When Bird awoke there was a boy in bed with him. They cuddled together with the ease of long-time lovers. Bird's knees curved into the back of the boy's knees, his arms were clasped across the boy's smooth chest, and his cock nestled limp and damp between the boy's buttocks. Tom? he thought sleepily. Sandino? He had been dreaming about Madrone, and for one moment he curled deeper into the sweetness of the dream. Her eyes met his. She forgave. What? He couldn't quite remember, and in trying to track the memory he came up from sleep to an awareness of the stink of piss and metal.

He opened his eyes to find his lips pressed against the nape of a neck he did not recognize. The room was dark but slowly it began to lighten, as if somewhere an unseen sun were rising. He heard a creak above him; he was in a metal bunk with somebody asleep on the tier above. A plastic mattress bulged down against metal springs. Now he could see tier upon tier of bunks. It was a big room, big enough to hold maybe sixty bunks, with metal tables down the center. The light came from a grid of bars that blocked the window.

He didn't know where he was or how he'd gotten there.

The boy stirred in his arms. "Charlie," he murmured. "You awake?"

"Charlie?"

"Your name is Charlie." The boy's voice was patient, as if he'd explained this many times before.

"Uh . . . I don't think so."

"Don't worry about it. You just don't remember."

He was pretty sure his name wasn't Charlie, but for a long moment he couldn't remember what it was and that scared him. Then it came back to him: Bird. It sounded right, it fit him, but he didn't say it out loud because he had been raised to know that names had power.

"Who are you?" he asked the boy.

"I'm Littlejohn. I'm your girl."

He was sure the boy wasn't a girl because he could feel his cock when he ran his hand down the smooth body, and the cock was beginning to stiffen, as was his own, as if his body remembered something his mind did not. He felt sick, confused.

"It's okay," Littlejohn said. "You don't remember so good. The bigsticks did something to your mind. But it's cool."

"I don't remember anything."

"I know. Don't worry about it. Fuck me."

"I don't know you."

The boy smiled. "Charlie, you been fuckin' me every day for the last year. You just don't remember."

"For a year? What year is this?"

"The Forty-eighth Year of the New Millennium."

"Fortieth?"

"No, Forty-*eighth*."

"That's ten years from now!"

"No, Charlie, that *is* now."

"That can't be true."

"Want me to flip on the vidnews and prove it to you? All I need's a screen."

"I've lost ten years?"

"Why not? If you can lose one, why not two? Two, why not five? Five, why not ten? Believe me, one thing we got plenty of around here is time. You could lose twenty and barely notice them."

"Shit."

"Fuck shit," Littlejohn said. "Or better yet, let's just fuck."

But Bird had rolled over on his back. He felt a sense of vertigo, as if everything around him were spinning and tumbling.

"Where are we?"

"Terminal Island. Angel City, heart of the Southlands. They call this the Pit."

Bird had one moment of sheer panic again. He had been fucking a stranger, a boy who could have anything in the way of disease, even the old immune disorders or the archaic blood cancers. He *felt* his body and the boy's; they seemed clean. And going into his body seemed to ground him a bit; the dizziness subsided, and a few memories swam into focus.

"I remember a prison doctor coming at me with a needle," he said.

"You remember that? Hey, you never remembered nothing like that before." The boy rolled over to look at him. Littlejohn had close-cropped straight brown hair, a dark face with delicately molded bones, and bright blue eyes. The effect was startling. "Maybe your mind can come back."

"Don't I remember anything?"

"You remember for about five minutes. Then I have to tell you all over again: who you are, who I am."

The vertigo was back, and the sick feeling in the pit of his stomach. What if it all went away again in five minutes? What if he had lost his mind and could never find it again?

"That must be hard for you," Bird said.

"I don't mind. There's worse things. Anyway, you always remember how to fuck. Sometimes when you fuck me once you forget that you already done it and you do it again. And you always remember how to fight. Around here that's about all you really need to know."

"How did you get here?"

"Got caught stealing water one too many times. Hell, I practically grew up in here. My whole family was Witches. They got rounded up in '43, and I landed out on the streets, right?"

"What do you mean, stealing water?"

"You know, water."

Bird was silent. There was something here he clearly didn't understand, something so obvious to Littlejohn that he couldn't seem to explain it. Was it one of the things Bird had forgotten? How could he know what he didn't know? He let the matter drop for now.

"How old are you?" Bird asked.

"Nineteen."

The boy seemed younger than that. Fourteen, fifteen maybe. Bird was nineteen himself, or he had been once, but if that was ten years ago, where had he been? He wanted to grab hold of something, quick, before he sank into an endless well of lost years, spinning his mind like a wheel, trying to remember, not being able to remember. Are five minutes up yet? he wanted to ask. Am I still here? Am I still me?

Something else was bothering him. It was like a faint voice in the back of his head, calling. When he followed it he dropped into a well of pain. Sweat broke out on his forehead.

"You okay?" Littlejohn asked.

"I don't know." He was caught somewhere between memory, reality, and something else. He couldn't tell who the pain he felt belonged to. "Can you ground me?"

"What do you mean?"

Speaking was becoming a greater and greater effort. "I thought you were a Witch."

"Yeah, but I don't know any magic. My folks all died before they could teach me anything."

Bird was trying to ground himself, trying to make contact with the earth, but she seemed miles away, imprisoned under concrete and steel. He bit his own lip hard, trying to breathe, trying to remember an image or a word that could anchor him. "Grab my hands," he whispered.

Littlejohn obeyed. The pressure on his hands was solid, was real. He could feel his hands and know they were his own and, from that knowledge, follow a trail of sensation slowly up through his body. His own body. His own dull pain of old injuries, which was different, he now knew, from the pain he *heard* inside him rather than felt. Someone was in pain. Someone was calling for help.

"Thanks." Bird withdrew his hands. "Somebody's hurt. But it's not me."

"Maybe it's the new guy they brought in yesterday," Littlejohn said. "They beat him pretty bad."

"Where is he?"

"The last bunk, over by the door."

Bird shifted his weight and sat up. The bed creaked.

"Be careful!" Littlejohn whispered. Bird nodded and got up slowly. His body felt odd, both uncomfortable and familiar. He moved slowly, for the sake of silence and because there seemed to be a time lag between each impulse of his brain and each movement of his muscles. At last he reached the bunk nearest the door. A still figure lay there, and Bird could feel pain radiate out from him. He knelt down and placed a hand on the man's abdomen. The breathing was shallow, and the life force waning quickly. He was dying.

Bird took a deep breath. He wished for Madrone, or Sandy, or somebody else who was talented at healing. Then his mind clutched at the names in a sudden attack of panic. Who was Madrone? Who was Sandy? He thought he remembered them as long as he didn't think too hard about them. But when he tried to focus on the memory he was swimming in doubt. Was he remembering or inventing? How could he know for sure?

Don't think, he told himself. Let your hands do it. His mind still felt dull, cloudy, and he couldn't feel any power moving through him. The pain was a sound in his head. If he could make sound, maybe he could change it, but that wasn't possible. Could he change the sound in his mind? He thought he remembered an old chant:

If we have courage
We can be healers;
Like the sun,
We shall rise.

The note of "rise" reverberated in his mind, and he held it, strengthened it, imagined it passing through the broken body on the bed. The pain drained away, and the man's breath became slower, deeper, more substantial. Bird's inner *hearing* grew keen. The broken ribs, the injured kidneys, were discordant sounds, a rupturing of the body's harmonics, but he could find a note to repair the worst of the damage. The man would live.

Eyelids fluttered on the man's face, their movement barely visible in the dark. His eyes opened. Bird could not see their color, only the brightness and intensity that flashed out. His lips moved as if he were whispering. Bird leaned close.

"The earth is our mother," the man said.

It was the beginning of a chant. Bird caught a sense of expectancy from the man, as if he waited for a reply.

"We must take care of her." Bird finished the line.

A faint smile moved over the man's lips. "Thanks, brother," he whispered, and then slept.

Bird crept back to his bunk and lay back down beside Littlejohn. His head hurt. He wanted to sleep but he was afraid to lose consciousness, afraid he might not find it again.

"What'd you do?" Littlejohn asked.

"He'll be okay," Bird whispered.

"Man, you better watch it. They catch you Witching somebody, they'll kill you. If you take my advice, I'd be cool if I was you. I mean, play like you're still crazy until you catch on to the scene. Right?"

"*Comprendo.*"

"Shhh. Talk English."

"*Com* . . . right. Got it. Goddess, do I have a headache!"

"You been under a powerful enchantment, maybe. Or maybe you done it to yourself. Where are you from?"

He didn't know how to answer. Images flashed out at him: faces, gardens, the gingerbread façade of a house with a peaked roof. His head wanted to split open, and he couldn't tell which of them were real.

"Far away," he said. That, at least, he was sure was true enough. "Far, far away."

A bell clanged harshly. Littlejohn jumped out of bed, pulled on gray pants and a sweatshirt, and handed a pile of the same clothes to Bird with an automatic gesture, as if it were something he was used to doing. "Put these on," he said. "Get up quick. It's count."

Bird just had time to slip his clothes on and lurch to his feet when the heavy metal door grated open. Five big guards walked in and surveyed the scene. "Everybody up for count!" one bellowed.

The room was filled with shuffling and grumbling as sixty men struggled to their feet. The man in the bed by the door still lay semiconscious. One of the guards jerked him roughly up to his feet, and he leaned against the metal rail of the bunk as the guards walked around, counting once, counting twice, counting again.

"Line up for breakfast."

Bird stood behind Littlejohn and followed what he did. He looked for the man he had healed. In the light, he could see that the man was slightly built, skinny, the brown skin on his face crisscrossed with lines that made him appear, somehow, not old but wizened, dried up like an apple left too long in the sun. But Bird didn't dare stare too hard or try to catch his eye.

The prisoners filed in a line through a long gray concrete corridor to a dining hall, where they stood in line to receive trays of food delivered by disembodied hands from behind a metal screen. They sat on benches and ate in silence. Bird found the routine strangely familiar, as if some part of him had done it a thousand times even though his mind did not remember. Or maybe it was just that he was surprised by nothing, not the orders barked out to them, not the taste of the glutinous starch that passed for breakfast. He was grateful for the enforced silence. It gave him time to observe the other prisoners and read the expectations in other minds.

They didn't expect much of him, Bird discovered. When they got back to the barracks someone handed him a broom, shoved him into another corridor, and locked the door. Automatically, he began to sweep.

At the end of the hall was the guard station, a square lighted room with heavy glass windows that allowed the guards to observe Bird and the doorway behind him. Windows on the other side of the station opened onto the dorm, which was empty at the moment. All the men must be at their work stations.

When Bird stood close to the window, he could see the three guards and hear their conversation faintly through the glass.

"So, Harris, you gonna be down here for good now? Guess A dorm decided to clean house."

"For better or worse. They thought you needed somebody with balls down here in the Pit. Shape you guys up."

"Yeah, we could use a little shape down here. Unfortunately, yours ain't exactly it."

"Not your type, Coleman?"

"King Cole likes the pretty boys. Sorry you don't qualify."

"Who's the pretty boy in the hall?"

"Him? He's the idiot. Don't mess with him, he's crazy. Anybody touches him, he'll bust your teeth out. Never seen anybody move like that before. They say he's a Witch—that's why they done something to his mind. But you touch him or that scrawny girlfriend of his, you'll believe he's the Devil himself."

"Bust my teeth? I'll bust his fucking balls for him."

"It don't do any good. He don't remember it. He don't remember who he is or who you are. You bust his ass once and he don't remember it the next time. He's got no fear of you."

"Then he's dangerous. Why the Jesus is he still alive?"

"They want him kept alive for some reason. I don't know. Maybe they think someday his mind'll come back and they can find out something. Maybe they want to do some experiment on him. Maybe they forgot why they want him kept alive. But you just stay out of his way and he don't cause no problems. He's sure as hell no instigator. There's others that're worse problems."

"Like who?"

"Like that new hillboy they brought in last night. Calls himself Hijohn."

"They all call themselves John. John something, something John. It's one of their names for the Devil," Coleman said.

"What's his problem?"

"His problem is our little problem, and that is: he's supposed to be dead. They worked him over good. Dropped him in on us as a little lesson to our boys, in case they got any funny ideas. So why is he up and walking today?"

"He's a tough little demonfucker. But we can fix that."

The first guard shook his head. "He's a Witch. Got to be. It stands to reason."

"You got Witches on the brain, man. You want the guy dead, seems to me we just work him over again tonight."

"That's easy enough to say." Coleman pulled a smokestick out of a pack in his breast pocket and tapped it on his desk. "Wait till you see the paperwork afterwards."

They went on talking, but Bird decided it would be politic to move away for a while. He swept, stopped, and pondered, then swept again. So he had managed to fight well enough to stake out some small space around himself, even without quite knowing who he himself was. *Diosa,* what had happened to him?

He was even more disturbed by the conversation about the man he had healed. There was too much he didn't understand. He felt like he'd come into the middle of a story where everybody else knew the background and the plot. He wasn't even too sure about who the main character was. One thing seemed clear: Hijohn's life was in danger. He would have to warn him, although what good it might do he couldn't say. But he owed him that. It seemed clear to Bird, now, that Hijohn's need had somehow called him back from wherever he was lost. He could have stayed lost for more years yet, maybe forever; the thought was cold in the pit of his stomach.

His body, he noticed, felt aching and clumsy, but the pain was dull and he seemed to be used to it. His left leg and hip hurt, and if he leaned too long on them, the muscles in his thigh began to shake. His hands on the broom handle seemed stiff and clumsy, the fingers somehow misshapen, as if they had been broken and not set right. That disturbed him in some way, almost more than anything else, as if it represented the loss of something so basic that he had to protect himself from the memory. It teased at the back of his mind, though, like liquid notes of music, like rippling melodies flowing off the strings of his guitar. And then it hit him, with a force almost physical that left him sweating and clutching the broom handle for balance. He could remember his fingers, deft and fluid, not so much making music as matching what existed already and poured through him, his hands one with his instrument and the great singing voice inside him.

He stared down at his broken hands, aching as they curled around the thick broom handle. What had happened to them? To him? In his mind were gardens, the smell of moist earth and roses, the muffled sounds of drums coming out of a basement in a tall painted house that felt like home. Lavender House. The name came to him. Down the street was Black Dragon House, where his grandmother lived, but he could not remember her name or picture her face. He could smell food cooking, onions and garlic and peppers, hear voices and laughter floating down from the kitchen windows. That was real. That was where he belonged. How had he come here, slipped through some crack in time and space to be trapped behind these walls and broken?

"Move that broom, boy!" He hadn't noticed the guard coming toward him down the hall. It was the big guard, the new one, Harris. As he passed, he shoved Bird roughly out of his way. "Move your godforsaken ass!"

Before Bird could react, he was gone, and that was fortunate, Bird thought, because he was suddenly so filled with rage he could easily have done something stupid. It struck him that if he wanted to die, opportunities abounded. But what he really wanted was to kick down these walls, smash the bars and the metal grates, breathe clear air again.

He could feel rage flowing through him, itself a form of vitality, and the thought came to him that in spite of his pain and his losses he was very much alive.

He might survive to live a long, long time, trapped in these blank walls and bare corridors. His chest constricted, and he labored to keep on breathing.

Where there is fear, there is power, he murmured to himself. He remembered the phrase from somewhere.

He was going to have to get out of there.

o o o

The long day passed. After a couple of hours Bird was bored enough to wonder if he was truly going to go crazy. He was struggling to catch hold of pieces of himself as he had once grabbed at finger holds on a sheer rock face. That was a memory, a physical one, real as the swishing sound of the broom brushing the concrete floor. He could smell sun-warmed granite and hear voices shouting encouragement from below, could feel in his body visceral fear and then exhilaration as he pulled himself up over a steep ledge, but he couldn't quite place the moment in any context.

He found that he could play with the edge of mindlessness, as if his memory were a balloon on a loose string that he could let run through his fingers and suddenly grab tight again. When he let go of memory, the moment became luminous, even there in the gray concrete, and the rhythmic action of his muscles and the soft sound of the broom on the floor were enough to keep him endlessly satisfied. When he brought memory back, he wanted to run away screaming.

His grandmother had brown eyes that looked at you as if she could see you down to the bone. Maya. That was her name, Maya. He could almost hear her voice whispering to him: "You're a Witch, boy. Use your magic." But he couldn't remember his magic.

Probably by now his grandmother thought he was dead, if she thought about him at all. No, *when* she thought about him, if she were still alive. He was afraid to reach too far for her, afraid to send his spirit home until he was more firmly rooted back in his body.

Another bell sounded, and he was marched back to the barracks for count. Then the men lined up and shuffled off to dinner. He could see Hijohn, moving slowly as if his body still hurt. Littlejohn fell into line behind Bird, and they received their food and found places at a table.

"Wait," Littlejohn whispered, when Bird prepared to eat. When all the men were seated, they folded their hands and bowed their heads as a voice came over a loudspeaker, intoning a prayer some part of Bird recognized.

"We utterly repudiate the Devil and all his works. . . ."

It was the Millennialist Creed. Bird had memorized it once for a performance in school, when he had played Justin Hardwick, the breakaway Fundamentalist who, just after the turn of the century, had preached the doctrine of Christ's rejection. Why did he remember that when so much else eluded him?

"In memory of Jesus Christ, who returned to earth only to repudiate the world for its sins, we abhor the earth, the Devil's playground, and the flesh, Satan's instrument. We abhor the false prophets and the false gods, those who lie with promises of salvation and those who tempt us to wallow in the worship of demons, whether they be called Goddesses, Saints, Lucifer, or the so-called Virgin Mary. For we know that Our Lord never lowered Himself to take on loathly flesh, but was, is, and ever shall be pure spirit. Amen."

The words fell off his tongue as if he had been saying them for years—which he had, he realized with a slight shiver. As kids, they had all made fun of Hardwick's name. "How hard is your wick?" He could hear the laughs quite clearly, although he couldn't remember who had been laughing. But if he focused on what he did remember, even the fragments, then more scraps of memory returned. Faces. A dark face like his own, brown eyes always looking off into the distance, hands tapping rhythms on the edge of the table. Marley. "If you boys can't keep still at the table, you can eat outside in the garden with the dogs." His mother's voice, crisp on the surface, but underneath Bird heard the harmonics of grief. Someone was dead. His father. "It's not fair! Marley's making noise, not me!" That was his own voice, and his mother's black eyes turned on him, and now her voice was sharp but there was humor in it too. "You're making noise now. It's a noise called 'whining.' " And then a girl's face popping in at the back door, her wild hair escaping from two black braids, her skin brown and gold and rosy in the warm evening light. "Can Bird come outside and play?"

Madrone. That was Madrone.

He wanted to go outside now, to run and run and run, to feel his numb feet pounding down on dirt, putting distance between him and captivity. When he thought he might never get outside again . . . but he couldn't afford to think about that. Instead, he focused on the cold, greasy noodles on his plate, forcing himself to chew and swallow, to stay focused in the here and now. There was something he had to do. Hijohn. He had to warn him.

The moment came as they lined up after supper to carry their trays back to be stacked and washed. Hijohn was in front of Bird, and when he set his tray down on the counter Bird stumbled and dropped his own. The guard yelled at him, but Hijohn bent down and helped him pick up the fragments of dishes.

"They're going to kill you tonight," Bird said softly, without moving his lips.

"Yeah."

"What can we do?"

"We?"

"We."

"I wish I knew," Hijohn said. "I sure wish I knew. Thanks, brother."

Their eyes met, just for a brief flash. "I'll try to stay with you," Bird whispered.

Hijohn's eyes acknowledged the whisper, as he moved away in silence.

∘ ∘ ∘

Back in the cell block, the men kept an uneasy territorial truce. They were divided into distinct and separate groups, Bird found. Each group had its own tables, its own section of bunks. They called themselves Blacks and Latins and Asians, whom the others called Slants. The terms seemed only loosely related to color or culture. Nobody spoke any Spanish, and whenever a few unwary words escaped his own tongue Littlejohn silenced him. Some of the Blacks looked white or Asian and some of the Latins looked black. Nevertheless, they identified each other clearly enough by hand signs, Bird guessed, or body language, or subtle differences in the way they wore the common uniform. And the identification with one group or another determined everything:

where you slept, whom you ate with, whom you could count on, whom you had to watch out for.

Bird was outside it all. No one needed an ally who couldn't remember who he was, or feared an enemy who might forget what he was doing in the middle of a battle. Littlejohn took shelter in the aura of his protection and guarded him, making sure he remembered to eat, to dress, to stand for count, shepherding him away from avoidable dangers, keeping him out of the others' way. He was tended like some big, friendly, protective, potentially dangerous dog.

Hijohn walked over to the table where a group of men were playing cards with a homemade deck. He sat down.

"Deal me in," he said.

The men didn't bother to look at him.

"Go hang with your own kind," one of them muttered.

"I am with my own kind."

"You ain't black."

Hijohn stood up. Suddenly the room was silent, everybody watching him. "All of us in here are the same kind," he said.

It seemed to Bird that the temperature of the air dropped about ten degrees. Nobody breathed.

"I come from the hills," Hijohn went on. He was breathing hard, and his wizened face seemed pressed into one wrinkled point with some inner effort he was making. "We've learned that the hard way. They set us against each other so they can rule. We've got to unite."

He reminded Bird of an apple doll, and it seemed wrong somehow. He should look grander or more heroic.

"You talk like that, they kill you, man," somebody muttered from across the room.

"We're all going to die," Hijohn said.

"Some of us quicker than others."

"When have you ever had a chance to live? Are you alive in here? For how long? Until they throw your ass out onto some work levee and you fry in toxins?"

"What do you want, man?"

But he never got a chance to answer, because the door opened and the guards took him away.

○ ○ ○

Bird lay on his bunk, staring blankly up at the wires that held the mattress above him. He could feel Hijohn, somewhere, in pain. Bird wanted to help him, but all he could manage to do was drift into his mind, feeling the blows as they came, a helpless witness. It was night, and around him men slept. His outer ears could hear muffled cries and moans through the walls, or maybe he only imagined he could hear them. Hijohn's pain weighed on him like a stone, while some memory of his own burgeoned up beneath him. Between the two of them, he was crushed, could hardly breathe, yet he kept feeling that if he could only remember something, something he knew, he would be able to help this man, even if only to help him die.

Then he was falling into a dark place, a memory, where he still floated unbounded, out of context. He was alone in a dark cell, but he didn't remember how he'd gotten there. He had no idea whether it was day or night. There was a thin blanket over him, but he felt cold. His right hand was shackled to something—he couldn't move it more than a foot or two—and his left leg felt heavy, encased in something that weighed him down. His whole body hurt more than he could believe. He wished for Madrone, wished she were there bending over him, her face grave but confident, her healing hands pouring warmth on his wounds. But she was far away, and he was alone. He had never felt so alone.

He had to piss, and he groped with his free hand in hopes of finding a bedpan, but there was nothing. If he got the bed wet, that would only make him colder. With a great deal of effort and some pain, he finally managed to shift his position to roll on his side and pee over the edge of the bed. Relieved, he began to feel thirsty and hollow inside. He couldn't remember eating or drinking or much of anything for a good long while, but he must be healing because his mind felt clear enough for him to begin to worry. What the fuck was going to happen to him now?

After a long, long time, a door opened. He smelled soup. "Stinking slime," a voice said, but hands placed a tray down near his free hand, and he heard a metallic sound, like something being dragged to the side of the bed. "Use the goddamn bucket," the voice said, and then the door slammed shut.

If he ate, he was going to have to shit someday, but he would worry about that later. There was some sort of thin soup, and bread, and a hot, bitter liquid to drink, and the fact that it seemed as good as it did told him how hungry he was. Then he slept.

In memory, he spent a long time in that cage. Alone in the dark, he'd begun to fly. He had always been good at spirit travel; now he had infinite time to explore and few outside distractions. He went to his power place in the mountains; it was winter there, and in his astral body the crystalline structure of the snow became a labyrinth of rainbow chambers where he could wander for hours or days. Every crystal was a world. He could move through them, into dark spaces that were also, somehow, the great reaches of emptiness between the stars.

His captors had made time into an instrument of punishment, but he was free of it on the star roads and they couldn't touch him. He was in the underworld, like a seed, gestating in the dark. The scraps of old myths he half remembered became actual places, where he dropped with Inanna down into the realm of the Queen of the Dead. The past was a place, too, where he rode with warriors of Queen Nzinga to defend their walled town, where he attacked cities and burned children in their houses, where he lay in a dungeon like this one and was dragged out to burn, where he stood behind an Inquisitor's mask and asked the question and ordered the torment, where if he lay in his hole long enough he could experience every single thing that had ever happened to a human being.

And there were beautiful places, orchards of fruit trees that shone with their own light, misty islands where he followed the tantalizing back of a woman who was always just beyond his reach. He moved in realms of color so pure that even sunlight could only diminish them; he heard music, chords so perfectly tuned he could dissolve in their perfection and lose all fear. If he could only hold the melody to himself and remember, he knew it would knit his bones. And when he was far enough gone, so that even the edge of his mind disappeared, she came: the Crone, the Reaper, the one whose breath you feel in your hair when the gate slides shut and there's no going back anymore, the terrible beauty, the hag who holds out withered arms and demands your embrace. In the fairy tales it was always the older brothers who rejected her. But he was the younger brother, the one who laid out his cloak for her and lay down with her to let her take him into herself, and take her in. And so he came to know in his body the power of the Reaper and the song of the stars.

Enough, Bird thought, struggling to shake free of his memories, to open his eyes. He didn't want to relive any more. But the images rolled on relentlessly.

He remembered the shock when the guards came for him. Suddenly the cast was broken from his hips; he was shoved to his feet and forced to walk on legs that didn't remember how. He was in a bare room facing a bright light that stabbed his eyes, and there were men facing him whose malevolence was palpable as his own rotting flesh.

"You ready to talk, boy?" they asked.

He wasn't ready to talk to them.

"What's your name?"

It occurred to him that being Bird of Lavender and Black Dragon, good Witch of the North, was maybe not the safest identity around here. "Paco," he said. It was an old nickname, short for *pájaro,* bird in Spanish. "Paco Negro."

A fist slammed into his jaw.

"Speak English, slime. None of that Devil's tongue around here. What's your name?"

"Uh . . . Charlie. Charlie Parker."

"Charlie, we'd like to know how you got into that power plant. Who let you in?"

He was silent. Who could he still betray? Who was alive? Who was dead? Spirit wings fanned the room. No, he wouldn't tell them anything. *Claro.* And there would be more pain, and then an end.

"Boy, you cooperate with us, we'll cooperate with you. You can make it easy on yourself. You want to stonewall, that's all right. We can deal with that too."

He stood, silent.

"Give me your hand, boy." One of the cops took his left hand, held it almost tenderly in his own. His face was round, and he had a gray stubble over his cheeks. His eyes were bright blue, and he smiled a lot. The good cop, Bird thought. There's always a friendly one.

"That's a nice hand," the cop said. "Delicate. Refined." He touched the calluses still there, though soft now, on the tips of Bird's fingers. The touch made his skin feel slimy, polluted. "Almost a girl's hand. Musician? Play guitar?"

Control. Bird willed himself not to respond, not through a breath or an eye blink or a gesture. He knew how the game was played. If they could read a "yes" from him on what they knew was true, they could read his "yes" or "no" to anything they asked, whether he answered or not.

"You a Witch, boy?" asked the second cop, who had black hair and wore mirrored sunglasses that concealed his eyes. "Answer me!" he barked.

Bird was silent. He was seeing Madrone's face, asleep on her pillow, and the needlepoint over her bed that Johanna had done long ago. *Who sees all beings in their own self, and their own self in all beings, loses all fear.*

In his own self, he saw the executioner. He remembered a gun in his own hand, a face coming toward him, snarling, raging, then falling, blood spewing from the nostrils. Like his father's face, dying by some other hand. Death moved on, and hands like these, like his, passed it along.

The men Bird faced were not alien to him, and so ultimately they could not defeat him. All they could do was kill him, and he wondered why they didn't get on with it.

The first cop held Bird's hand down on the table in a steely grip. The second cop pulled out his long nightstick, observed it almost philosophically, then suddenly smashed it down on Bird's outstretched hand.

He could feel the knuckles crunch and the bones break. Pain was like a chord, or grating dissonances. He could let it be sound, and not feel it, and stay where the fear couldn't get at him. As long as he stayed sheltered from the fear, nothing could get at him. Or so he told himself. In some other life, he would cry for his lost guitar and the lost possibilities of music.

They broke both his hands and then sent him back to his private underworld.

o o o

Maybe this was their modern version of the old test for Witches, the one where they threw you in the water. If you sank and died, you were innocent. If you floated, you were guilty and they burned you.

If he survived this, he had to be a Witch, he thought, as he went into the starsong for healing. He couldn't make the bones go back quite right, but he could knit them together and put the pain into an arrow and shoot it off to disintegrate somewhere else.

They would come for him again, he knew that. He didn't want to let the fear in because he sensed, now, that it was big enough to eat him alive. But he knew he couldn't block it out indefinitely. He needed a plan. He wanted to be able to walk through walls, to pass invisible through the corridors and out into the night air. He wanted to go home.

Well, he could walk. He had learned that much. Not easily or long or well, but part of that was lack of practice. The muscles had atrophied. But he would work on them, and he would make himself walk around this cell, three paces one way, three paces back, until he had the use of his legs again.

It was his mind that was the problem. Sooner or later they'd break him and pick it. They'd find the pain he couldn't resist or they'd get tired of cruder methods and drug him. Did it really matter, he wondered, what he told them? They asked him questions about magic. What could they do if they knew how much or how little he had? And they asked him about the North, how the city was governed and defended. Were they planning a war? If he told them the truth, that the North had not armed itself or prepared for war, would they invade?

He paced, and he worried. The fear crept in, chink by chink. He thought maybe he was going to lose his mind.

Or maybe that was the answer.

When they came for him again, he was ready. A good thing, too, he thought, when they laid him down on a hospital cot and came toward him with a syringe. He remembered a story about the stone they called the desert rose, pink, with ridged and striated surfaces. Maya had told him some people called it Witches' Brains. The legend was the old Witches had locked their secrets inside it when they were taken to be tortured, to keep them safe from the Witch burners until the Remembering time would come again. Inside his mind was a stone like an egg. He took a deep breath, let it out, and imagined that his mind and his memories were inside the rock. He set a ward, the tiniest speck of mindstuff, to watch and wait and bring him out again when it was safe or necessary. Then the fear got him, for one stark moment of absolute terror. They found his vein; the syringe emptied the drug into his arm, and he took the crystal egg of his mind and his memories, of what was in him that he believed made him, and fled. The more they came after him with drugs and questions, the farther away he hid. And the stone was buried deep, deep, underground. Where his mind had been was something opaque and resilient that memory bounced away from.

o o o

Littlejohn was in bed beside him, rubbing against him. Bird came alert instantly, the fear still clinging to him. Where was he? In the barracks. Who was he? Bird. How long had he been here?

Ten years? Ten years.

And the pain he was awash in was Hijohn's pain. Not his own.

Clarity. Boundaries. He remembered the lessons of his childhood. Always draw the magic circle before you step between the worlds. Don't get lost.

"I once was lost, but now I'm found." His father had liked to sing that old hymn.

"Fuck me," Littlejohn whispered.

"No, wait. I can't now." He could still hear Hijohn moaning, and he could still feel the power flooding through him. Funny, he had never been a healer, or much wanted to be. But his hands, broken, had found unsuspected powers. He imagined reaching out with them to Hijohn, imagined lifting him with his hands, as if he could lift the man up out of his broken body. They stood together somewhere on the slopes of a mountain. He smelled sage.

"Do you want to live or die?" Bird asked.

"I want to die. But I've got to live, if I can."

Bird's own body was an instrument of the great music; it could sing through him and charm Hijohn's life back into his broken bones, smooth his torn flesh. And then Littlejohn was doing something to Bird's body: he could dimly feel his cock rising with a hot stab of need. Cautiously, Bird lowered a barrier in his mind and *felt* for the younger man, to draw him into the link. Littlejohn drew away, with an electric shock of panic.

"Don't Witch me," he said. "Let's just fuck."

Bird felt shock ring through the harmony, like a door slamming in the middle of a symphony. He was almost thrown out of contact, but he reached for Hijohn and held on. Ground, he said to himself, letting the power run back to earth. Let the earth hold it, Maya used to say. She won't lose it for you, and you'll always know where to find her.

Ground.

"Come on," Littlejohn urged.

"That is how Witches fuck," Bird breathed in his ear. "I can't do it any other way."

"Sure you can, like you used to. Please, let's just do it like we always used to."

The boy feared him, Bird sensed. He feared Bird would reach into his mind, grab something there he didn't want to face, take it, and then hate him and discard him. Maybe he preferred Bird mindless, a force like raging nature he could submit to but that wasn't capable of controlling him. Maybe forms of control were all he'd ever known.

Bird started to draw back. He could still feel Hijohn, a spirit trapped in a shell of pain, just on the edge of bearable, now. He wanted to stay with him, not to be distracted. But then Littlejohn's mouth was on his cock and the need in him was raging and building. The boy's fingers drummed on his chest, and Bird could hear him make soft little sounds of imprecation and submission. He had never before, in his memory, used a body without opening to the mind, and the thought repelled him but something in it also excited him, seemed to fit the kind of cold comfort he needed in this place, as if the very bars around him could become erotic dreams. Hijohn moaned somewhere, and Littlejohn moaned in his ear, and then the sex and the healing and the power and the pain were all mixed up together, all building and vibrating in strange dissonances that finally peaked. He came, and then he owed it to the boy to make him come too.

In the stillness, he felt a silence where Hijohn was. Was he dead? Then the door opened and the guards dropped Hijohn's body back into the corner bunk. When they were gone, Bird slid out of bed and placed his hand lightly on the man's chest. No, sleeping. Healing. Imperfectly; all Bird had really been able to do was feed him the energy necessary for survival. He was damaged and in pain, but alive. Thank the Goddess.

Bird returned to his bunk. And then he lay awake, remembering, for a long, long time while Littlejohn curled up and slept. He was remembering tall, silent Tom, how making love to him was like falling into a mirror, as mind opened to mind and they could feel each other's pleasure and rise with each other's heat. He was remembering Sandy, the sensitive one, who could suck his sadness away from him, and he was remembering Cleis and Zorah and Madrone.

He had never imagined that sex could make him feel ashamed.

What would they do in the morning, when Hijohn still lived? Would they beat him up again the next night? How many times could Bird bring him back from the dead before they caught on? Before he wore himself out?

He had to get them out of there.

But he didn't see any way out.

3

Maya awoke most mornings surprised to find herself still alive when so many she loved were dead. Often they visited her in the early morning, as the sun's rays filtered through the upper bay window where her bed nestled. She had always loved being awakened by the sun. Many years ago she made herself curtains, beautiful curtains, balloon shades of raw silk dyed turquoise and trimmed with French lace. They disintegrated and she never replaced them. She no longer feared exposure.

From her bed, Maya could look through the south-facing bay of her window when the trees were bare and see the green winter slopes of Ritual Hill. If her door were open, she could look down the long hallway, through the glass door of the kitchen, and out the back window to the rising curve of Twin Peaks. *Los Pechos,* the young ones called them, the Breasts: Breasts of the Virgin, Breasts of the Goddess, depending on your persuasion. It didn't matter to her. The Goddess always was a virgin, complete in herself, untamed, unmated. She had been a virgin herself once, but then she met Rio.

"You were not. You were not a virgin when you met me. I remember it clearly. You were quite experienced."

Suddenly he was there, sitting on the edge of her bed, blond and bearded and sexy in his tight, faded jeans like he was when he was nineteen years old.

"You're blocking the view, you old crow," she said to him. "Move over. Where've you been the last couple of weeks?"

"Places. But don't change the subject. We were discussing your unlamented virginity, which as I recall you'd unburdened yourself of at fifteen or so."

"I'm not talking about my hymen. I'm talking about my state of being. I allowed you to mate me."

"Was that so bad?"

"Well, it had its moments. Good and bad."

"The best and the worst," Rio said. "You know I never do things halfway."

"Once I would have said it took years off my life. But I guess I can't complain on that score."

"Pure luck," Johanna said. She made a fairly substantial ghost, sitting next to Rio on the side of Maya's bed, her molasses-dark skin gleaming in the warm light, her washed-silk shirt glowing in soft shades of green. But no weight depressed the bedclothes and mattress. "Happenstance. Not for any great virtue the rest of us don't possess."

"What are you talking about?"

"You. Why you're still alive and the rest of us are dead."

"Jealous?"

Johanna snorted, a sound characteristic of her in life. "Not of you, girl-friend. There are a few pleasures that compensate for the discomforts and petty humiliations of corporeality, but I'm afraid you are long past them."

"Don't count on that. And watch out. Dwell too much on the pleasures of the flesh, and you'll find yourself reincarnating."

"I intend to, at the earliest opportunity, in your line if not my own."

"My line seems to have faded out."

"Don't give up on Bird yet," Rio said.

"Why not? Do you know something I don't know?"

"The dead are forbidden to tell all we know," Johanna informed her.

"Oh, screw you," Maya said, but her tone was affectionate.

"That, I'm afraid, is no longer possible between us." Johanna smiled, tilting her head down to look up from under raised brows, a seductive gesture Maya remembered well. "But you wait. Someday we'll both be back in young nubile bodies again, and it'll be like it was that first time, when we got stoned on all that acid and ended up surprising ourselves on the locker-room floor. Not to mention those two gym teachers who found us."

"Even dead, you're incorrigible."

"I am a daughter of the river, of Oshun, the Goddess of Love."

Maya turned back to Rio. "Do you or do you not know anything about Bird?"

"Can't say."

"Well, I'm not sure I want either of you in my line anyway."

"Why not? Didn't I act as a perfect father to your kid?"

"You were a great father to every kid except your own."

"And whose fault was that? If you or Johanna had told me she existed, I would have fathered her too."

"Never mind that," Maya said. "I'm not quarreling with your talent for paternity. The point is, as a son you were hell on wheels. Do you think I want to inflict that on my descendants? Wait for Madrone to breed, you and Johanna both. She's your granddaughter. Not that she has any plans in that direction right now, not since Sandy died."

"My line doesn't plan these things," Johanna said. "We have fortuitous accidents."

"Like the fortuitous accident you had after carrying on with Mr. Superstud here?" Maya kicked her foot toward Rio's ghost. "Who was, may I remind you, *my* boyfriend at the time?"

"That was no accident. That was an ancestor knocking at the door, wanting to be Rachel." Johanna stretched, yawned, and winked. "Maybe 'accident' isn't the operative term here. Maybe I'd better just say that my line is susceptible to intervention from the dead. Otherwise how do you explain Rachel herself, a fifty-year-old medical doctor, no doubt acquainted with the facts of life, getting knocked up by a twenty-six-year-old *combatiente* in the Guadalupano Liberation Front?"

"She was following the bad example of her elders."

"Speak for yourself, girlfriend."

"I was quite youthful when I had Brigid. In my mid-forties. And I would have had her by you"—she turned to Rio—"if you hadn't had that vasectomy in prison."

"You were practically menopausal," Johanna said. "But that's beside the point, which is that Rachel's little dalliance gave us Madrone, and your fling with—what was his name?"

"Carlos."

"Right. Anyway, he gave you Brigid and, through her, Marley, rest his soul, and Bird. And without them all, the odds would be even worse."

"The odds of what?"

"The odds that our next lifetime will be the restful, pleasurable, tropical idyll that I am in the process of planning instead of a miserable starved sojourn in some Millennialist-infested breeding pen."

"*Our* next lifetime?"

"You, me, and Rio, our little karmic trio. That rhymes, did you notice?"

Maya looked at Johanna with suspicion. For just a moment, she seemed to have a sheaf of colored brochures in her hand, as if she'd just come from some astral travel agency. Were there agents in the afterlife who could get you special deals on accommodations in the next? Did they offer group rates?

"How can you be making plans for my next life," Maya asked, "when I'm still in the middle of this one?"

"I'd say tail end, not middle," Johanna countered. "You're winding down."

"I'm not dead yet. Anyway, haven't we stored up enough karmic good points in this life to have assured some comfort in the next?"

"That is exactly what nobody seems to grasp about this karma business. It's not a simple matter of cause and effect, reward and punishment. It's a question of what's available. You see, as long as life for the majority of souls on this planet is just a long round of starvation, misery, torture, and early death— and believe me, outside this fortunate watershed that is an apt description of the state of affairs—as long as only a few live in comfort while the masses scrape along in want, then all us returning souls have to take our fair share of shifts among the hungry. You think this life you've lived was tough? Let me tell you, it was just R and R between the ones where you never get a solid meal two days running or you die before your first birthday from drinking bad water."

"Johanna, you're not cheering me up."

"I didn't come to cheer you up. I came to warn you. This next year is a pivotal time, one of those hinges that open or close the doors of fate. Watch out!"

"What do you mean?" Maya asked. She sat up and opened her eyes, but the room was empty.

o   o   o

Madrone quietly pushed open the door and entered Maya's room, bearing a very old tray commemorating the marriage of Prince Charles to Lady Diana, back in the last century. Upon it rested two of Maya's favorite Chinese cups, eggshell-thin, grass-green, with a pattern of butterflies on them, and a brown chipped teapot.

Maya observed her closely. She looked rested, but there was still a pale undertone to the hue of her warm skin that spoke of deep fatigue.

"How are you this morning?" Madrone asked.

"I'm still alive. What do you think of that?"

"I'm glad somebody is," Madrone said, carefully placing the tray and settling herself on the edge of the bed. "You've been talking to the dead again?"

"How can you tell?"

"A certain faraway look you get in your eye, a little cloudy, like cataracts." Madrone smiled and handed Maya her tea. "Any good news from the other side?"

"The dead are annoyingly cryptic."

"They're probably swamped with new arrivals."

Maya sipped her tea. It was the herb they called Mystery Mint, from some spontaneous miscegenation of peppermint and spearmint in the Black Dragon garden. She wished it were good old caffeinated black tea. Twinings English Breakfast: that was what she used to like. With a little milk. They never saw that anymore. She had outlasted Twinings too. Or maybe it still existed, out in some corner of that vast world they no longer moved in. Maybe, in some air-filtered sunless enclave, the Stewards drank it every day.

"You're really worried about this new disease, aren't you?" Maya observed.

Madrone swirled the tea in her cup, as if looking for her fate in the dregs. Her voice was soft, controlled, but Maya could hear the pain concealed in it. "It just hit me again, about Consuelo."

"How did it happen?"

"Her fever spiked up suddenly, triggered premature labor. She was fine the day before. There was nothing to indicate a problem, no fetal distress, no signs of toxemia. Just that odd low-grade temperature and the slight headache. Like Sandy had, before he fell off the roof."

"You think he fell because of the fever?"

"I know he did. I could feel it, this whatever it is. Like a presence in his blood, a certain color in his aura. I can *feel* it, but I can't *see* it or get hold of it. We don't know what it is or how it's spreading or what to expect. I'm afraid, *madrina*."

What to say? Maya wondered. Wasn't she supposed to be old and wise and comforting? When did this highly touted wisdom suddenly descend? Was it like tongues of fire, or the holy dove of the Christians? Would she ever feel its claws digging into her scalp?

"I wish I could help you," she said at last. "You carry too many burdens for somebody your age."

"I'm twenty-eight. Almost mature."

"A baby. A mere child, barely out of diapers. Far too young to do what you do. Why, the *curandera* who tried to train me in Mexico wasn't allowed to heal anyone except herself until she was thirty. And she couldn't work on anyone outside her family until she was forty."

"That sounds luxuriously sane," Madrone admitted. "But we don't live in sane times."

"At any rate, you need some time off. Or at least some stimulation besides the company of one crotchety old woman. Have you heard from Sage and Nita and Holybear? When are they coming back?"

"Not for another few weeks."

"They should be down here with you. The house is empty without them."

"They can't leave their trial ponds until their experiments are complete," Madrone said. "You should be more appreciative of their efforts."

"How do I appreciate fifty-seven new breeds of waterborne bacteria?"

"Bacteria that can neutralize toxins might mean that our descendants could eat shellfish out of the bay again someday. If any of us survive. Which I'm beginning to think is less and less likely."

"Everyone's so gloomy today," Maya complained. "Even the ghosts are intimating doom."

Madrone smiled. "Isn't that a ghost's prerogative?"

"Maybe. But it worries me to see you so down in the mouth."

"I just feel bad. About Consuelo, about Sandy. About everybody. I feel like I've failed them all."

Maya patted her arm. There was nothing to say, really. She herself still felt bad about everyone she'd ever known who'd died, from Sandy back to Cameron Graham Rosenthal, who'd died of AIDS downstairs sixty years ago when the house was still divided into two separate flats. Yes, she still missed him from time to time, missed dressing up with him and strolling through the Castro, making private comments about all the beautiful young men they passed. She'd been living off Johanna's charity then, just back from Mexico, trying to write. And the beautiful young men had not yet wasted to living skeletons, to die blotched with lesions, gasping for breath.

"I wish I could help you," Maya said.

"You do, *madrina*. You help a lot." Madrone closed her eyes. Really, she could almost sink back into trance, here in the sun with Maya's hand to soothe her. When you're tired enough, Madrone thought, the *ch'i* worlds are just an eye blink, a breath away. Like yesterday, watching beside Consuelo's closed coffin, surrounded by lighted candles in the Sisters' living room. Rosa sat, looking solemn, almost hidden behind a huge bouquet of calla lilies.

"I'm sorry," Madrone had said to her. "I'm so sorry."

"It's not your fault," Rosa had said, with tears pooling at the bottom of her eyes.

Not my fault but my inadequacy, Madrone said to herself, settling down to keep vigil. She had focused on the coffin, letting herself sink into the searching trance, moving down through the wood of the box, until she could *see,* with her inner eye, the body, shaped by light, its energy form already starting to come apart. Traces of Consuelo's spirit, shreds of personality, lingered like wisps of scent. Madrone sniffed emotion—anger, outrage, a sense of being cheated, the aggrieved surprise of the unexpectedly dead. She felt sweat on her face and willed herself to breathe deeper, to sink down further. This was the worst level, and she could only get through it by saying over and over again, "Not mine. Not my pain. Not my grief."

Down. And yes, there was something else—that elusive something she had *felt* after Sandy died. But what was it? Could a microbe have a personality, or was she just anthropomorphizing—what? If only she could see whatever it was, grab hold of it, learn how it spread and how to defeat it. She could track it, patient as any hunter, but what was there to scent but elusive traces in the air, shifts in energy? Not a flu virus, not something patterned on the old HIV series or a spirochete like syphilis or Lyme disease. They each had their characteristic signature in the energy realms, and she could recognize them as easily as she could identify mugwort or comfrey in an overgrown garden. No, this was something else, and she was beginning to recognize its *feel* but she still couldn't *see* it, only follow, down and down. . . .

"Where are you drifting to?" Maya said sharply. "Madrone! Come back!"

Maya's hand gripped her arm sharply and brought her back with a jerk. She felt a sharp sense of vertigo and fought down nausea.

"*Diosa,* Maya, don't do that to me!"

"I called your name three times."

"Really? I didn't know I went so far down."

"You shouldn't trance like that, unprotected, ungrounded. You didn't even cast a circle."

"I didn't mean to trance. I was just thinking about Consuelo again, and the virus—oh, all right, I guess I was starting to *search* for it."

"You be careful. You're becoming obsessed with the thing, and obsession opens the door to the Bad Reality. Did I ever explain the old *curandera*'s theory to you?"

Madrone smiled. "At least a dozen times."

"Well, I'd better explain it again, because you don't seem to get it. Doña Elena used to say that there was the Good Reality, or *El Mundo Bueno,* literally the Good World, and the Bad Reality, *El Mundo Malo,* and they were always vying with each other. In the Good Reality you have a mild headache; in the Bad Reality you have a fatal brain disease. In the Good Reality, you catch hold of the rail as your foot slips; in the Bad Reality, you miss, slide down the stairs, and break your neck.

"We walk in the Good Reality as if we were treading the thin skin on warm milk. It's always possible to break through and drown. When you take a foolish risk, especially in magical work, as you just did, it's like sticking out your tongue at fate, daring the Bad Reality to suck you down. And they say that *El Mundo Malo* never passes up a dare."

"Who says?"

"They. You know. The amorphous, ubiquitous 'they.' Ignore their advice at your peril."

"I always listen to your advice, *madrina.* I just don't always take it."

"There is a hopeful side of Doña Elena's teaching," Maya went on. "Even in *El Mundo Malo,* the Good Reality is always just on the other side of the surface of things. If you can learn to reach and pull yourself through, you can make miracles."

"I'll bear that in mind," Madrone said, "as more and more miracles seem to be called for." She stood up and placed her teacup back on the tray. "Have you finished your tea?"

"No, I've been talking to you. Leave it with me, I'll wash the cups later. And have you had any breakfast yet?"

"Are you hungry? I'll get you something," Madrone offered.

"No. I want *you* to eat. I'm fine."

"I will, when I'm hungry."

"Go back to sleep. Get some rest. You're worn out."

"I will." Madrone leaned over and kissed Maya's cheek. "But later. Today's my day to represent the healers at Council, and I'm already late."

○ ○ ○

The domed Council Hall nestled between the two hills of Twin Peaks. Madrone hurried out of the gondola that had brought her up the hill and dashed down the steps of the tower two by two. The session was already under way as she entered the hall through the Gate of Air, in the east.

The Council was open to everyone, but each neighborhood and each work collective picked spokespeople who attended one day each week, as gift work. All the healers took turns, so each was required to devote only a day every month or two to the meetings. Some guilds picked representatives who served for a fixed term, providing continuity. But no healer could be spared for weeks or months.

In the four corners of the room were stationed the Voices who spoke in trance for the Four Sacred Things. In the north, direction of earth, the first of the Voices wore the mask of the White Deer, the sacred fallow deer that roamed Point Reyes Peninsula and the slopes of Tamalpais. The bearer of the Hawk mask with its curved, sharp beak, guardian of the creatures of the air, sat in the east. Coyote, wearing a wooden mask painted with dots and stripes of brilliant color, sat in the south as the trickster guardian of fire, of the energy systems. In the west, in a mask with gleaming scales and geometric designs of red and black, sat Salmon, guardian of the waters, symbol of return and regeneration and hope. Long ago, the bay and the streams that flowed through the city had been the southern boundary of salmon country, receiving their yearly run of fish returning to spawn and die. But the pink salmon, the California salmon, and the great oceangoing steelhead trout no longer returned to the toxic bay. The great dream of the Water Council and the Toxics Council was to restore the salmon run. Holybear always said he would know their work was successful when he could sit on his front porch and fish. Although in point of fact, Nita would interject, by the time the fish made their way to their neighborhood, they'd be ready to drop their eggs and rot, and regular spawning runs through the city's streams might be a mixed blessing.

Among them walked the Speaker for the Voices, who was always either a man dressed as a woman or a woman dressed as a man. Today the Speaker was a tall, muscular man who wore a beautifully embroidered Japanese kimono and silver bracelets that chimed like bells whenever he moved.

The room was circular, lit by skylights and warmed by a fire in the central hearth. The four Voices each had a low pillow-covered platform to sit on in their appropriate direction. Everyone else sat in a rough circle on an assortment of pillows, chairs, and battered old couches. Council would eventually replace them with beautiful cushions and fine, crafted seats, as they had gradually recycled the old scraps of carpeting that once covered the floor and laid down rugs that were works of art, woven of handspun wool, with soft but vibrant colors and intricate patterns of the sacred symbols, the quartered circle with the double spiral in the center.

The Voices gave an aura of ceremony to what was otherwise a fairly informal gathering. As she made her way to a seat, Madrone felt their power flowing through the room. A chant began singing itself inside her head:

When we are gone they will remain,
Wind and rock, fire and rain,
They will remain when we return,
The wind will blow and the fire will burn.

She looked into the eyes of Coyote, painted spirals that seemed to draw her in and in. Maybe she was falling into trance herself. The humans around her seemed ephemeral, inconsequential, while the masked figures became eternal. And yet she could clearly remember the meeting when they established the Voices. It was only about five years before. She had been a devoted attender of meetings at that time, a stage everyone had to go through, Maya claimed. There was criticism of the meetings—they were too long, too heady; people left feeling drained and ungrounded. Of course, that was the nature of meetings, someone pointed out; but weren't we here to transform things? someone else asked. Somehow the question got around to the representation of the Four Sacred Things. Many people felt that nothing could truly be decided when the Four Sacred Things were not present. The animals, the plants, the waters had no voice in Council, and yet every decision should take them into account. After seemingly interminable argument, they had one of those unlooked-for bursts of collective creativity, or perhaps madness, and established this ritual, where masked representatives for each of the sacred elements sat in trance in Council, channeling the Voices of wind, fire, water, and earth.

"May the balance be restored," she murmured as she seated herself, because that was the appropriate thing to say in the presence of any manifestation of the Four Sacred Things, or when entering or leaving a sacred space. She said it under her breath, so as not to interrupt anything.

She slid onto a couch beside a short-haired, bony, brown woman with the muscles of a construction worker. The woman winked at her.

"I'm Surya," she said. "Carpenters' Guild."

"Madrone, of Healers'," she murmured back, feeling a little thread of attraction that she was far too tired to pursue. She was sinking into trance, and that was not appropriate for a Council meeting. But as she looked around the room, all she could see were energies, earth and air and fire and water congealing into bone and breath and nerve and blood, emerging into form and fading back into formlessness. They played through the colors of light coming through the skylights and through the forms carved into the beams and the lintels of the doorways. They played through the genetic bequests of the ancestors she saw reflected in the skin colors and bone structures and textures of hair around her, east, south, west, and north: Europe, Africa, Asia, the Islands, the Americas, all the waters of the world had flowed over this spirit-haunted land, leaving something washed ashore in their wake. Ivory, sepia, raw umber, burnt umber, ebony, charcoal, sienna—a palette of earth tones, like colors out of a paint box. Auspicious, they called it, when children of ancestors from all four directions sat together and the circle was whole.

About fifty people were present, finishing up a discussion about reconciling the solar and lunar calendars, a topic about which Madrone had nothing to say. Salal, who was Crow of the meeting for the day, nodded at Madrone to show that she was aware of her entrance. Sal was one of the most skilled facilitators, and Madrone was glad to see her there, looking calm and composed as she always did, graceful in her cross-legged posture, her hair dyed a shocking red and rising from her head in flamelike peaks, her dark eyes darting around the room, reading the mood of the group. Salal was not easily intimidated or confused, and she was unshakable under pressure.

I will just close my eyes, for one moment, to rest them, Madrone told herself. The buzz of voices and the flying hands of the speakers simultaneously translating their words into Sign were hypnotic. Although the main discussion was in English, side conversations went on around the edges of the room in Spanish, Mandarin, Arabic, Cantonese, Tagalog. Every neighborhood in the City claimed a mother tongue of its own to cultivate. With global transportation systems broken down and the Stewards still jamming the airwaves after twenty years, who knew, these days, what survived in Canton or Cairo or Manila or Mexico? The City's neighborhoods might well be the last preserves of their languages and cultures.

Lulled by the voices, Madrone dreamed the domed hall as the four-chambered heart of the City, where she could rest, feeling its pulse, taking the measure of its beat, listening for what swam hidden in its secret veins, the spirochete, the parasite, the virus. Oh, it was deceptive, this strength, this vigor. But she could hear what whined below, like one small mosquito in a large room when you were trying to sleep. . . .

"Madrone?"

The sound of her name jolted her into wakefulness. She opened her eyes. Salal was looking at her expectantly.

"Can you give us a report from the Healers' Council? What's happening with this latest epidemic? How dangerous is it?"

Madrone rose to speak. She looked around the room at eyes of every shape and color, all focused on her. That was what she did, sometimes, when she had to look into a mother's eyes and tell her her child would not live. She would focus on the shape, and the color of the iris, and the way the lid curved over the surface, and the way the lashes were set into the lid. Eye after eye, each one a small cauldron, container of water. A vessel. A lens.

"It's bad. Very bad." Madrone spoke, as they all did when addressing Council, in English augmented with Sign. "It begins as a low-grade fever, like a mild flu. Headache, muscle aches, congestion. In a small percentage of patients, that's all it is, and after a week or so they recover. But most go through a crisis, where the fever shoots up suddenly, high enough to cause brain damage or death, especially in children. And for pregnant women it's disastrous. The high fever triggers labor prematurely and can seriously damage the fetus even if it survives." These were the facts, laid out for them, but she felt compelled to add more. "We've dealt with a lot of diseases over the last ten years, one epidemic after another, if not on quite the same scale as '38. But this one scares me." She found, as always, that her spoken words could lie with their intonation, with the flat control of their delivery, but her fingers could not conceal her emotions. "I won't pretend it doesn't. It's the worst thing we've had to deal with in a decade."

There was silence. If Madrone was scared, they knew it was bad. Usually they counted on her for reassurance.

"You've tried to identify the cause?" Sal asked.

"We suspect another mutant virus, but we don't really know yet. None of our antivirals work against it, or any of our other drugs."

Silence again.

"Shouldn't we evacuate the pregnant women?" someone asked.

"Where to?" Madrone asked. "The damn thing appeared upriver almost as soon as it did down here."

"What do you suggest we do?"

What she wanted to say was, Do anything you ever wanted to do and haven't done, now, quick, while you still can. Eat the berries unripe off the vines, set your caged birds free. But she couldn't say that. Ghost eyes looked at her. Her hands, upraised in a gesture of helplessness, were all the answer she could give, but for the benefit of the blind, she added, "I don't know."

"What kind of support do the healers need from the Council?" Sal asked.

A miraculous appearance of the Virgin. A bleeding statue with healing powers. A *curandera* with herbs known only to the Indians. A wonder drug. "We're okay, I guess," Madrone said. "We could use someone else at the hospital to help with herbal preparations, now that Sandy's gone."

"I'll find someone." A woman spoke up.

"What about personal support?" asked Surya, at Madrone's side. "You look done in."

"I'm just tired. Not enough sleep. But that's what you sign on for when you become a midwife."

"Every healer I know looks about the same," a young man said. "Maybe we can't offer a miracle cure, but at least we could take some of the load of other work off you. Your gardens and your households."

Madrone opened her mouth to protest, but considering the state of Black Dragon House, the weeds in the garden, and the hundred chores she hadn't gotten around to since Sandy died, she shut it again.

A woman in a yellow headcloth who Madrone recognized from the central market spoke. "And not just the healers. The sick need help, too, and their households. I don't know about you all, but coming in this morning I noticed a fair number of raggedy-ass gardens. We should be organizing in the neighborhoods to take care of people better."

"If this becomes a full-scale epidemic, we're going to really need organization," said one of the men from the Fairies, the gay men's enclave in the center of the city.

"Let's think about that," Salal said. "Let's not shove it to the back of our minds, because we don't want to face that possibility. Who has ideas about what to do?"

"I think everyone in every work group should have a backup. Everyone who has an essential skill or piece of information should share it with at least three others. Every household should have two sister households to share in the workload if necessary," a pale blond woman said.

There was a general murmur of agreement.

"Are there concerns?" Salal asked.

"Yeah, are people going to panic about this?"

"It depends how we put it out. It doesn't have to come down as a Directive of Doom."

"Most of these things we're suggesting are just common sense. We should do them even if there weren't an epidemic. Anyone can die at any time, but the work needs to go on."

"We have done some of them. At least in the Transport Collective, we do. Every Tower Maintenance team has a backup. Every coordinator has two helpers who share all vital information and rotate into that position in turn. I thought every work group was organized that way."

"Toxics is, more or less."

They had moved into problem-solving mode, and Madrone felt her attention beginning to drift away. They were good, these people. She trusted them. If there was any best way to handle this crisis, they would find it. If there was anything to be done, they would do it. And maybe just for five minutes, she could rest her eyes. . . .

The Speaker began to pound his staff on the floor, the sign that one of the Voices had something to say. Opening her eyes, Madrone could see the energy of the room being stirred and swirled, changing. They waited, as the Speaker leaned his ear to the opening of Salmon's mouth and nodded.

"Friend Salmon says this: This matter concerns the waters. Human beings must survive to clean up the mess they've made."

"Well, that's helpful," another Fairy man murmured. "Does Friend Salmon have any ideas for us on how to do it?"

"Survival is in the rivers of your blood. So is death. Open to what you fear."

Life and death swam together through the currents in the great domed room. What could Madrone open to? Fear was not what she felt—more a leaden exhaustion, her eyelids too heavy to prop up. What did it all matter, after all? Maybe they were all going to die, but the forces around them would remain. And why should she take advice from a fish that couldn't even speak comprehensibly? Was there some reason oracles had to be obscure? *Diosa,* she needed more sleep.

"Madrone? There's a question directed at you."

"I'm sorry."

"I'm from the Defense Council," a woman said. She was an older woman, her straight hair a gleaming white over skin like wrinkled cream-yellow parchment. With a start, Madrone realized she was looking at Lily Fong, one of the almost mythic *Cuatro Viejas.* Madrone remembered her, standing with an upraised pickax on the day of the Uprising, her face calm but alight, the muscles of her arms, old even then, bunching and tensing in her shoulders as she swung.

"This is what we want to know," Lily said. "Do you think this disease is a natural thing, or do you think it is a weapon?"

Madrone looked at her in surprise. "You should know, if anyone does." Lily was a Listener, who rarely left the island in the lake in the center of the park, where the Deep Listeners maintained a constant protective vigil in the spirit world, alert for threats to the people. Couldn't they *hear* the answer to that question?

"You mean as in biological warfare?" the woman next to Madrone asked.

"That's what I mean. You work with these things directly, Madrone. We see only their reverberations in the *ch'i* worlds."

"I wish I knew." Madrone was tired, tired. Did she really have to go around with this one again? "We argue this one all the time in the Healers' Council." Actually she argued it back and forth daily with herself. "From the evidence of the computer models, some of us suspect it is engineered. But until we can find it and analyze it, there's no real way of knowing. Does it matter?"

"Of course it matters. How can we defend ourselves if we don't recognize an attack?"

"Well, it's like this," Madrone went on. "Essentially, we're living in a toxic stew," That was Nita's metaphor, and Sage and Holybear concurred. "Don't let the flourishing of the gardens and the clarity of the waters delude you. There are still chemicals in the Bay we may never be able to analyze, let alone neutralize. The atmosphere is suffering from an ozone depletion that won't begin to reverse itself for at least another twenty to thirty years—and that depends on what's happened to the rain forests and the consumption of fossil fuels on the rest of the planet, which we don't even know. There's low-level radiation left over from the last century, and who knows what's being pumped into the atmosphere now? And there were biological weapons developed years ago, and maybe some of them have been mutating ever since. Plus some pretty uncontrolled experiments in genetic engineering. Put that all together, and it's not surprising we have recurring epidemics. If anything's surprising, it's that we're doing as well as we are."

"What you're saying is that maybe we can't afford to continue our blessed isolation?" said the woman from the Transport Collective. Madrone knew how eager they were to build a ship that could sail out beyond the confines of the bay and go exploring. It had come up time and time again. Not that Council would stop them—it was just that nobody wanted to devote their scarce resources to the project yet.

"What she's saying is that we still aren't taking our toxics programs seriously enough," said one of Nita's protégés from the Toxics Council.

"Let me speak for myself," Madrone snapped. "I don't want to get caught up in political battles. The truth is, there are times when I've *seen* one of the viruses, and I can't deny that it's looked to me like something—constructed."

"And this one?"

"The problem with this one is that we haven't been able to *find* it. Not with magic, and not with a microscope. We aren't even sure it *is* a virus."

"We believe it's a weapon," Lily Fong said. "And we thought you should know that. Possibly the forerunner of a direct assault."

Complete silence fell on the group.

"Isn't it possible that the Defense Council, just by virtue of being con-cerned with Defense, might have a bias toward seeing things in terms of attack?" Cress, from the Water Council, pushed a hand through the thick black brush of his hair and stared straight at Lily. He reminded Madrone of a male dog asking for a fight. She expected to hear him growl.

Lily drew herself up. "We're not unaware of that possibility, young man. Don't you think we take that into account? All of us on the Defense Council are old, and we're all women—for that very reason. So that we'll be less likely to be led astray by our hormones and our paranoias."

"With all due respect for the members of Defense Council, may I say even old women are not infallible."

"And weren't we going to review that policy this summer?" another man asked. "How is it that Defense is the only council allowed to be restricted by gender?"

"Maybe when we've fully recovered from five thousand years of patri-archy, we can trust men enough to empower them for Defense," the blond woman said.

"And maybe we could argue that we need a few more generations to recover from thousands of years of racism before we let white people on Defense," a dark-skinned man snapped back.

"The policy came from the Voices," the woman retorted.

"The Voices aren't infallible either. There's people under those masks, and some of them have their own agendas," Cress said.

"Are you trying to say—?"

"I'm saying we work by consensus, and that has to hold for the Four Sacred Things as well," Cress said. "Otherwise it's meaningless. They can make suggestions, but I for one don't feel compelled to take orders from a bird or a fish or my great-aunt in a Coyote mask. We have an obligation to think for ourselves."

"Why don't we all just shut up for a moment," Salal said forcefully. "We're getting distracted by personal arguments."

In the quiet, the Speaker consulted with the Deer mask.

"Friend Deer suggests we remember our connection to the earth. Deer says, the earth is bigger than any one of us."

There was silence. Some rebel in Madrone wanted to consider not her relationship to earth but to this Council, her lack of patience with meetings and process, possibly stemming from her lack of sleep. Or from her sense of urgency—her feeling that even as she sat there listening to arguments, people were dying. And it wasn't that the questions weren't important, and the facilitation excellent, even if this conflict between Defense and Water had been going on for years. But was it important that *she* listen to it? Or was she just impatient, trying to set herself up as somehow special, Superhealer, exempt from ordinary responsibilities?

"Friend Deer says, 'Madrone, beware the cold place.' "

And what the hell does Friend Deer mean by that? she thought irritably, but she nodded her head in acknowledgment.

"Important issues have been raised here," Salal said. "Clearly there are some strong feelings in this Council about the way Defense has been set up. And maybe some questions about the Voices. Are we giving over too much power to them? These are things we can't ignore. We can put them on the agenda, for later or next week. But right now we're still talking about the epidemic. And I have to say that maybe none of us want to look it in the face. I don't. I'd much rather argue." This elicited mild laughter. "But we've got to face it if we're going to survive."

"I wouldn't have brought this question of germ warfare here to the Council if we hadn't examined it thoroughly," Lily said. "Unfortunately, it is not just paranoia. If I were to share our paranoias, none of you would sleep again for a week. No, we believe it is a real possibility, and one of fairly high probability."

"You believe, but how can we know?"

There was a stirring in the east. Speaker leaned to the mouth of the Hawk.

"Bird knows," he said.

"The birds?" Salal asked.

"That wasn't what Hawk said. Hawk said Bird."

"Who's Bird?"

"There was a Bird from our household," Madrone said. What was it with Bird lately? Like a haunting, he had become a presence who plagued her. "He disappeared almost ten years ago. We can't find him. Can Hawk?"

"Hawk isn't saying any more," the Speaker said.

A wave of desolation hit Madrone. Just for a moment, she had allowed herself to hope that he had been found, that the Voices or the Listeners or somebody had made contact with him. And hope was wrong and dangerous. Like allowing a little bit of atmosphere to seep into a vacuum, and then, when she felt it sucked out again, the hollow place it left seemed newly and sharply empty. Much to her own self-disgust, she began to cry.

Several people moved to put their arms around her. The woman beside her handed her a handkerchief.

"I'm sorry," Madrone said. "I'm just tired. Ignore me." Healers' Council meetings were usually awash with tears, interspersed with gallows humor, but she always hated people who cried in Full Council. It was so self-serving. But she couldn't seem to stop crying. Surya gathered Madrone up and hid her tearstained face against her skinny shoulder.

"Oh, hell," Salal said. "We all want to cry. I do. Why don't we take a little break? And Madrone, why don't you go home and get some sleep?"

Madrone made a great effort of will and raised her head. "There's so much work to do," Madrone said. "But it's my day to be here."

"Don't send her home," Lily said. "She won't rest there. Go to the beach, young woman. Take some strength from the ocean. Your work will go better."

"That's a special request of Council," Salal said. "Do we have consensus on that?"

o o o

Madrone stood outside the Council Hall, looking west. From the high peaks, she could see the ocean shining silver, invitingly. For one long moment, she let herself feel the temptation to take the Council's advice, to duck out of work, catch the gondola west, and spend the day walking beside the rushing and retreating waves, filling her pockets with shells and stones. It had been too long since she'd spent a day like that. Bird was still on her mind. He had loved the water. When he was fourteen he'd spent days and days windsurfing on the bay. She'd tried to keep up with him but kept wiping out on the board, inhaling salt water, and Johanna had yelled at her about pollution and cancer. Suddenly she had a strong sensation of Bird standing beside her, so physical she could almost have put her arm around his shoulder, let him lean on her. He seemed confused, in pain. It seemed to her that if she went to the beach, he would accompany her. They could walk beside each other, letting the waves wash their feet, and lie on the sand, holding each other. She could almost hold him now, reaching out to gather in this sense of contact, transform it into breathing physicality. The golden dome of the Council Hall gleamed behind her. Her arm moved through empty air.

4

It was strange, Bird thought, pushing his broom down the day's blank corridor, how the power that flooded through him at night ebbed by day, leaving him hollow. His reawakened intuition screamed inside him, Get out! Get out! They had left Hijohn alone for the last two nights, but it was only a matter of time before they started in on him again. And Bird wasn't sure how much longer he could maintain his façade of mindlessness. More and more of his memory returned each day, still patchy, like those early explorer's maps with vast spaces left blank. But enough detail had returned that he knew who he was and where he had come from. What would the guards do if they recognized that he was conscious again?

No, the three of them had to escape, and he would have to figure out how. Littlejohn was too resigned, Hijohn too battered, enclosed behind a wall of chronic pain. While he managed to drag himself up each day for count, for work, afterward he collapsed into sleep. But Bird was a Witch, with a Witch's will to apply to the matter. He was determined to save Hijohn; they had bonded so deeply, sharing pain, that abandoning him was unthinkable. And he was determined to save Littlejohn, for only by giving him the solidarity due a lover could Bird redeem their relationship for himself.

If they could escape, maybe they could reach the hills, where Hijohn came from. If they could escape, maybe he could somehow get back to the home that daily became more clear in his memory. His mind raced around like a fly at a windowpane. He had to get out, but he could not find a way.

"Use your magic," he could hear his grandmother say. But he only seemed to be able to find his magic in the night, stewing in a cauldron of pain. By day his power seemed drained, the cord that connected him to the source severed. Maybe he'd been locked away from the earth and the free air too long. The elements seemed shadowy to him, something invented or remembered but not quite real, as his own home seemed at times to be a made-up fantasy, too good to be true. He stood all day, a Witch with a broom in his hand, but the bristles were made of orange plastic and he didn't know how to fly.

"Does anyone ever get out of here?" he asked Littlejohn that night as they lay together.

Littlejohn shifted uneasily, rolling over to look at Bird with a slightly wary expression in his eyes. He's afraid of me, Bird realized. As accustomed as our bodies are to each other, I'm a stranger to him, now that I can remember and plan.

"Some serve their sentences and get released," Littlejohn said. "Some die. Some get taken for the work levees."

"What are they? Tell me about them."

"You don't want that, believe me. You're a hell of a lot safer here, even with Harris riding your ass. They're all the jobs no free man wants to do—because they're too dangerous. Mostly salvage, sometimes toxic cleanup. They keep you drugged all the time and guarded. Lots of accidents. Average survival time is about three months."

"How do you get picked for them? Can you volunteer?"

"Don't make me laugh. It's like everything else around here—you don't choose it; one day it just happens to you."

"Maybe it could happen to us. There might be more of a chance of escape, anyway."

"Don't bet on it."

He resorted at last to the simplest magic he could think of. He cast a spell. He lacked all materials but the most basic: a pubic hair of Littlejohn's and one of his own, some of their mingled semen, and a hair from Hijohn's head. He dipped the hairs in the sperm and rolled them into a ball, which he secreted under his left thumbnail. He hid the charm all through breakfast and waited until he was left alone to sweep the corridor.

Nobody noticed that his sweeping pattern took him in a clockwise circle, pausing at each of the four directions, not that he knew where they were in that featureless space but he made his best guess. He called in earth, air, fire, water, his allies and his helpers, not as he could remember calling, with power running through him like phosphorescent fire, but simply with words and a heartfelt sense of need.

He called the Mother, the first aspect of the Goddess every child knew, the Caring One, whose second name was abundance. The full moon was her breast; her milk poured out as light on the earth to bring life and fertility to every growing thing. He prayed to see her again, to feel that light on his face, to feel earth under his feet. He could hardly frame the prayer in words, beyond the very simplest.

"Please, help! *Santa Luna, Madre Tierra,* please, please, get me out of here!"

Then, as he swept, he built his magical image. He tried to send his mind diving for the causal plane, to pull the strings that wove the fabric of reality and reshape it according to his will. But he couldn't do it. All he could create was a simple visualization, pale and flat. He imagined himself with Hijohn and Littlejohn, outside on a hill, their feet standing on real earth, in their nostrils the pungent smell of coastal air, the smell of freedom. Holding the ball to his lips, he blew into it his images and his memories and all his passion and anguish. He bound the spell and opened the circle and, when he was called to sweep the guard station, dropped the ball inside the housing of their computer.

The whole thing felt like an exercise in futility; he couldn't raise any power, he couldn't let his mind loose in the other realms. Still, Maya used to tell them about the early days, when this kind of magic was about all they knew how to do, and sometimes it had worked. "Need generates its own power," she used to say. Goddess knew, he had need enough.

Late that afternoon, he was sweeping near the guard station again. He could hear their conversation even though he kept his head down and couldn't see who was speaking.

"What about that hillboy? Central wants a report."

"The little demonfucker's still up and walking."

"What do you mean? I thought you were going to take care of that."

"I did! I beat the Jesus out of him. Twice. But like I said, he's still up and moving. I'm telling you, it's Witchcraft."

"So work him over again tonight!"

"Hell, no. What do you think I am, man, some kind of sadist? You think I beat people up for the pleasure of it?"

"Well, yeah, I kind of got that impression."

"That's work, man. Hazardous Duty, to be exact. And it's supposed to get Hazardous Duty bonus pay."

"So put in for it."

"How many times can I put in for it on the same guy? They're going to think we're running some kind of a scam down here."

"So put a goddamned bullet in his head."

"Sure. You want to fill out the Use of Firearms report for me?"

"I don't care how you do it, just get rid of him."

"What I'd like to do is throw his ass and a couple of those other sinlickers out on a work levee. Get rid of them."

"Fine. What if Central wants to see them?"

"In ten godforsaken years, they haven't wanted to see the idiot. They just throw these guys down here and forget about them. And we clean up their crap."

"Look, I don't give a shit what you do, as long as I don't have to answer for it. If you can fix it, you can do it."

"Fair enough."

Two days later, Bird was standing in line for count when a new guard came in, carrying a computerized list on a clipboard. He read out a string of numbers. Bird recognized his own and Littlejohn's. Hijohn also stirred and looked up.

"Report for transport," the guard said. "Collect your things."

∘ ∘ ∘

They were strip-searched, their legs shackled so they could walk only in an awkward shuffle, their hands cuffed behind their backs. One by one, they were loaded onto a bus that wheezed and labored along with its archaic internal combustion engine. The windows were blocked with metal screening. They couldn't see outside, couldn't even tell if it were day or night. They rode for a long time, long enough for Bird to need to piss, for that need to grow into stabbing pain and then subside into numbness. He tried to sleep, to conserve his strength, and succeeded in dozing a bit.

Finally the bus stopped. A guard barked orders, and they filed off.

It was dawn. The horizon glowed orange and the sky lightened, as he blinked his eyes in the unaccustomed space. They stood on a patch of dusty ground outside a low, shabby building of corrugated metal, waiting while various guards did their own rituals with paper and signatures. Bird sniffed the air, all his senses suddenly so alive he ached all over, like the aching of salivary glands tasting food after long hunger. Behind the building stretched the rolling coastal hills, covered with the dry gold grasses of late summer. Whatever might happen next, he would have had this moment to stand once again on the living earth, to feel her like a vibrating body under his feet, to breathe air and feel a wind on his face that had blown free and unobstructed over the Pacific, to smell the compounded incense of leaves, dust, and ocean salt, the tang of bay laurel and sage, to see living things in their soft colors, blue and green, and umber earth below. He wanted to cry but he didn't dare. Instead, he took a deep breath, drinking in the life that flooded back into his body. And in a moment, just a moment more, the sun would rise.

Then the door opened, and they were marched into another gray locked room.

∘ ∘ ∘

"Everyone line up for count!" The guard's voice thundered through the barracks and rang against the metal walls. Wearily, Bird dragged himself up and prodded Hijohn, who lay in the bunk next to him. Above his head, in the upper bunk, he could hear Littlejohn stirring. They'd been fed some lumpy porridge and left to rest for about an hour after their exhausting journey. Bird moved slowly. His body felt heavy, clumsy, his mind dull. The blocked-off window on the end wall admitted only a thin crack of light.

The barracks held about forty men. As they stood at the ends of their bunks, the guards counted and then counted again.

"Hold out your right hand," a guard ordered when the count was done. Bird obeyed, wishing his extended hand gripped a weapon, a laser rifle to blast through these metal walls. But his fingers were empty. Around his wrist, the guards fitted a thin metal bracelet that locked tightly.

At the opposite end of the room, a tall man in a military uniform entered.

"Listen hard!" he said. "You have each been fitted with a PCD, a Prisoner Control Device. These devices let us monitor you at all times. We know where you are, we know what you're doing, we know what you're goddamned thinking. So don't get any ideas or try anything, because if you do, this is what happens."

He paused. Suddenly a searing pain flashed through Bird, beginning at his wrist and then extending through every cell of his body, ringing through him like a bell of agony. In an instant it was over, but he was left trembling.

"Try anything, and that will go on for a long, long time. Is that clear?"

"Yes, sir," the men chorused, and then they were marched out to work.

The sunlight was warm and welcome on Bird's skin, but he felt encased in some barrier that kept him from feeling or thinking. All he could focus on was his desire to avoid pain.

The guards led them down a dusty road that wound through the hills. Bird's feet were unbound, but they dragged as if they were shackled, and his head rang. They rounded a bend, and suddenly in the distance he could see the ocean, luminous and calm in the morning light. For an instant, his mind cleared. I've been drugged, he thought, and then the fuzziness was back again.

On a flat shelf of land a hundred feet above the ocean, hordes of men were swarming around the ruins of giant machinery. A huge crane stood in the center, a black skeleton against the sky, and at its top, men were working with laser torches, taking it apart piece by piece. A few hundred feet away, another group of men were dismantling the once-sleek shell of what appeared to be a giant missile.

The prisoners' job was to pick up the pieces of metal scrap dropped from above as the workers cut them loose. They sorted and loaded them onto the back of a flatbed truck. The metal was jagged and sharp, and Bird's arms were scratched raw by the end of the day. He tried to look out for the flying metal chunks, tried to avoid cutting himself, but his mind kept drifting away and he didn't care much. The sun was warm and he felt no pain.

Days passed, and he sank deeper into numbness, as did the others. There were no fights in the barracks, no more arguments, no card games with decks improvised from scraps, no moans of passion in the night. After they returned to the barracks, they ate, slept, and woke to work again, made docile at last.

Bird knew there was something he needed to remember, but it kept slipping away from him. Each time he first glimpsed the ocean as they marched over the crest of the hill, something teased his mind. But he couldn't focus long enough to track it.

Other memories came, evoked by the scent of the air, by a sound or a word, by random electrical patterns in his brain. He remembered coming down from the high place in the mountains where he had fasted for his vision quest, his hands on fire with melodies and rhythms that had snaked their way into his dreams. Madrone was naked beside a clear glacier-fed pool on a high meadow. He watched her slide under the blue waters and emerge, the wetness on her red-brown skin reflecting back the sky's blue light so that she seemed to glow, blue and silver and golden in her own newfound power. They came together, power reaching out to power on the soft green grasses of the high country, where the wildflowers of spring bloomed in August. Then she was gone, and his hands hurt dully through a haze.

Something was important, but what? His brain was too foggy, he wanted to sleep, only someone was yelling behind him and he pitched the hunk of metal he was carrying onto the back of a truck. It landed with a clang; something in the sound reminded him of barred doors slamming home behind him, of finality.

Pain shot through him from his wrist, and he jerked awake.

"Get to work, slimecrawler," shouted the guard behind him, and there was a new sheet of metal to grasp hold of and carry, cut from the side of some mammoth cylinder that might once have been a weapon, some guided missile of the old times that no one any longer knew how to guide. And who would guide him out of this place, guide him home if he could only remember how to get there? It smelled like the ocean, he sort of remembered that.

"Get hold of yourself, boy," he said out loud. But his self kept sliding away, leaving at most a phrase he would repeat over and over, like an incantation.

"The ocean is the road home. The road home is the ocean. The ocean is the road home. . . ."

The rhythm of his chant merged with his feet, with the shouts and cries of the men, and soothed him. He was too tired to ask what his own words meant. He no longer believed in home.

o   o   o

By the second week on the work levee, Bird began to wonder if they would, indeed, survive. The question seemed distant, almost unimportant. He dragged his heavy body over the hill each day to work in a stupor of heat and exhaustion, dropping things, narrowly missing cutting himself half a dozen times. The others were no better. Hijohn had a new gash along his arm that wasn't healing well, but somehow Bird couldn't rouse any energy to heal it.

Littlejohn barely spoke. There was something Bird should do but he couldn't think what. Maybe it didn't matter anyway.

Bird was stooping to pick up a chunk of metal when suddenly he heard a keen, shuddering cry in the air above him. He looked up. A red-tailed hawk was circling, its wings still against the updraft that held it. As he watched, the hawk cried again. He wished he could circle with it, rising to see the hills and the valleys and the roads all spread out under him, flying free.

But what he saw was a hunk of metal flying toward him. His mind was still blank but somehow his body responded, leaping away. The metal crashed down just a few feet from where he stood; he could feel the whine in the air and the dust of its impact. Fear rushed through him, a flood that for a moment cleansed his blood of every other chemical.

I am alive, he thought. I almost died. I will die here if I don't break out of this. He was drugged, he remembered that now, and he needed to refuse their food, if necessary, even their water, and get clear. If he could only keep on remembering. He made a chant and repeated it again and again. "No food, no water, no eating, no drinking; no food, no water, no drugs to keep from thinking." It wasn't a very good chant, but it would do.

He skipped supper, although he was hungry and the smells tantalized him. Nobody noticed: they were not strictly supervised in the barracks. He slept fitfully and woke with a headache in the morning, skipped breakfast, and went out to work with a throbbing pain behind his eyes that grew to nausea as the day wore on. He drank water only from the tanks at the site that the guards also used. His muscles ached and he wanted to vomit, but he forced himself not to.

That night he hardly slept, the pain in his muscles so bad that he bit his fist to keep from screaming. He tried to heal himself, but he couldn't channel any power. He wished for Madrone or Maya, but he hadn't seen them for so long he'd forgotten how to look for the road back to them.

Instead, he tried to distract himself by remembering stories. When he was a child his mother, Brigid, had put him to sleep with tales of shapeshifters and magicians. Now he recognized that she had been teaching him magic, telling him history in a form that kept him eager for more and more. "Once there were some children who could turn themselves into birds," she would say. He tried to imagine her there beside him, soothing his pain with cool hands. She had died a long time ago, turned herself into a bird in the big epidemic, just before he went away. He sang himself an old folk song:

> I wish I was a tiny sparrow,
> And I had wings, and I could fly,
> I'd fly away to my own true lover . . .

There was another line but he couldn't remember it, so he sang what he knew of the verse over and over in his head, until it became a droning chant that finally calmed him into oblivion.

In the morning, he woke with his body still sore but his head clear. When he walked out on the earth he could feel her life humming beneath him and and could draw her strength into his body. He could pull down power from the golden sun and let it wash away the remnants of the drug in him. He was himself again, standing on the living earth under the unfettered sky, with the hills curving around him that were part of his own land. He was ready to make a plan. And he would have to act soon; he couldn't go forever without eating.

His first problem was the others. When they returned that night to the barracks, he touched Littlejohn's shoulder and took him aside.

"Don't eat," he said. "The food is drugged."

"Yeah, sure," Littlejohn said in a dull voice and then went blankly into the dinner line. Bird took the tray out of his hands, set it down on the communal table, and took him back to the corner by their bunks.

"Wha' the fuck," Littlejohn said.

"Shut up," Bird said. "I'm telling you, don't eat. We're getting out of here."

"Yeah, sure," Littlejohn said, starting back toward the table where the other men were already devouring his dinner. "Hey, tha's my food!"

"Shut up, man. I'm telling you, we're not eating another thing, and we're getting out."

When he had Littlejohn settled on the bunk, Bird managed to intercept Hijohn, who was, as usual, shunted to the back of the dinner line while stronger men pushed ahead of him. Bird tapped him and pulled him aside.

"The food is drugged," he said. "Don't eat it. We're getting out of here."

It seemed as if his words had to penetrate a thick cloud of fog before they reached Hijohn's center, but once they did a spark of comprehension lit up in his eyes. He returned to his bunk, lay down, and slept.

Bird held Littlejohn all through the night, while the younger man twitched and jerked in withdrawal. The barracks were still, and every sound Littlejohn made seemed to rattle the metal walls, but no one disturbed them. Bird drew on all the healing power he could remember or invent, and in the morning Littlejohn seemed more lucid and slightly more comfortable. At least Bird didn't have to fight him to keep him from breakfast.

With Littlejohn demanding all his attention, he didn't know how Hijohn got through the night. In the morning, Bird could see that the lines of pain had deepened in Hijohn's wizened forehead, but his eyes were clearer, and he winked a greeting as they hung back from the breakfast line.

As they filed out to work, Bird observed the lay of the land. He felt sure that if they could just get into the hills, no one could catch them. There was cover in the ravines and the stands of live oaks. Although it was the dry time of year, they would find water, and the land would feed them.

The problem was the bracelets, the PCDs. They were electronic, and that was hopeful. Electronics were more susceptible to magic than physical locks and bars. The brain emits an electrical field; back home, they had developed entire technologies based on that principle, like the intelligent crystals in their computers that were programmed purely by visualization. Tecchies would know what to do with the damn bracelets, but they trained for years and began with special talent. Bird himself had only the minor training given to every schoolchild, and he hadn't practiced those skills for a long time.

Well, he could only try. Maya always said that magic was like riding a bicycle: once you learned how you could never forget. Nevertheless, Bird thought, when you were out of shape you were more prone to fall. He wished he could practice somehow, try making the lights flicker in the barracks, maybe, or mess with their computers. But he didn't dare do anything that might arouse suspicion. So far, no one had noticed that he and the others were refusing food, and he wanted to keep it that way.

On the sixth day of his fast, he awoke with his hunger gone, feeling light, clarified, his intention pure as a beacon. Today, he said to himself, and he whispered it to Littlejohn and Hijohn, hope and fear racing each other through his veins. "Today."

They walked the winding road to work with the same slow shuffle of the other prisoners. Bird was alert, on edge, fearful of some freak accident that could undercut their chances of escape. In the few days without drugs to take the edge off his pain, he had learned the limits of his injured body. His muscles were slack from years of disuse and now sore from unaccustomed labor. His leg had never healed correctly, and he walked with a limp that strained tendons and the muscles in his lower back. He wondered if he were going to be able to pull it off—both the magic and the running. Maybe he would fall behind, unable to sustain the pace. Maybe they were all going to die.

Time marched with its own drugged shuffle, dragging its feet interminably. But at last the sun began its slide down toward the horizon, and in the slanted light of early evening the prisoners were lined up to go back to the barracks.

Bird made sure that he and the two others positioned themselves toward the middle of the line. One guard was stationed in front, one in back. There were one or two places where the road curved and the head of the line would be out of sight of the tail, and the middle of the line out of sight of both. The guards depended mostly on the PCDs to keep prisoners in line; they wouldn't be on the lookout for trouble.

As they began the walk, Bird knew that he was going to have to act.

"*Madre Tierra,* Earth Mother, *La Llorona* who weeps for your children, help me now if you don't want to weep for me again," he prayed. "If you're out there anywhere, give me a hand." He felt the earth currents through his feet, steadied his breath, and let his mind sink back to the level he remembered from his training. "Think of it like descending into a house built underground," the teacher had said. He couldn't remember her name but he could clearly see her red jumpsuit, outlining every curve of her body. He'd had to close his eyes and look away and steady his breath to go into the trance. "One of the levels you come to will be the right one for influencing electronic fields. Imagine it like a floor of a house, with a door you can enter. Notice what pattern is on the door and remember it, so you can bring yourself back here."

His pattern, he remembered, was nothing visual; it was a riff of music, four bars of an Irish reel he'd been picking out on the guitar that morning. Funny he could remember that, but not the teacher's name. He hummed the tune to himself, and, yes, he was there, at the level where he could *see* the lines of energy running through the metal on his wrist.

Careful. Twist them wrong, and they would alert the guards. How to undo them without setting off the alarms? Breathe, he told himself. Ground. He sent his mind a little deeper, until the energy lines took on colors, red and yellow and blue. He could see a red line like a thread that extended through the line of men. So that was how it worked: when that connection was broken by somebody stepping out of line, the alarm sounded and the pain stimulation was set off. He looked more closely at the blue lines. Surely there was something here, some power source he could switch off. He took a deep breath and called back the memory of the pain he'd felt from the device that first day, watching the energy lines. Yes, there was one that glowed brighter. He noted it carefully, tracing it back to its source in a glowing sphere of power that pulsed rhythmically. Breathing deep, he pulled up a piece of earth fire from somewhere deep below and struck. Incredible, unbelievable pain shot through him, and then it was gone. The red line stretched unbroken from wrist to wrist, but he was no longer linked to it. He was free.

Sweating, he turned to Littlejohn and took his wrist. "This'll hurt," he whispered, "but only for a moment." Bird found the power source, more quickly this time, and killed it. He felt Littlejohn jerk, saw him break into a sweat, but he kept quiet.

In another moment Bird had freed Hijohn. A soft moan escaped his lips, but no one seemed to notice.

They were starting around the curve Bird had picked for their escape. He watched until the guard ahead of them was out of sight and stole a quick glance backward. The tail of the line and the second guard were hidden around the bend.

"Now!" he whispered to the others. They scrambled up the side of the hill, heading for the cover of the underbrush in the dry creek bed over the slope. Bird's heart was pounding, and the other two sounded noisy as hell behind him. They didn't have his old facility for running silently through the bush—and even Bird found himself crashing along on his bad leg, his body awkward and clumsy.

Maybe the other prisoners would shout after them, maybe they'd protect them, maybe they were all too drugged to notice. Maybe the guards had seen them go, maybe not. Maybe they'd die in the next minute, bullets sliding through their brains or laser beams blasting holes through their hearts. Or maybe they had an hour or more of freedom, until they were missed back at the barracks, at count.

Now they were in the ravine, sheltered by brush and a clump of live oaks. Bird hit the ground, motioning to the others to follow him. Forcing himself to breathe quietly, he listened. Nothing. Only their panting and his own pounding heart.

"So far so good," he said. "Let's go."

Bird kept them to the cover of the creek bed as long as he could. The sun was falling rapidly, and he debated the wisdom of remaining hidden until dark. They had open ground to cross if they were to make their way north, his direction home, if home still existed, if the home he remembered had ever existed anywhere outside his mind. The creeks ran down to the ocean, mostly east to west. To go north, they'd have to climb over the ridges, where the oaks grew more sparsely and only dry grass covered the crests. It would be safer after dark. But the need to make good use of the time before their absence was noticed outweighed in his mind the dangers of being spotted. They pressed on.

They crossed open ground as fast as they could, running in a low crouch from tree to tree, always looking for cover that could shelter them. Bird's whole body ached, and he desperately wanted to rest, but he didn't dare. He had thought nobody could catch him once he got into the hills, but now he wasn't so sure. Maybe the guards would use electronic surveillance. Maybe they'd go after them with dogs. Maybe they'd come in the night with helicopters and infrared searchlights. Maybe.

"Copter!" Hijohn called out. Bird could hear it, thrumming in the sky behind them. "Down. Keep your head down. Cover your bracelet with your body."

Bird dove into a patch of brush, lay on his right arm, and stared at the dirt, trying to surround them with invisibility. The helicopter passed over them, turned, and swept by again.

Hijohn was crouched at the base of a manzanita bush, not three feet away from Bird. He spoke in a rough whisper.

"They're trying to pinpoint our location. Don't talk—they can hear the vibrations. Just whisper."

"They can't see us, can they?"

"They don't need to. Probably they can track the bracelets. Something in them they can fix on."

"Shit." Bird closed his eyes and brought himself back down into trance, fighting the adrenaline racing through his blood. He couldn't *see* anything emanating from the bracelets, but perhaps they worked in a different way. The guards might have a scanner keyed to some alloy in them. Queen of Heaven, *La Reina del Cielo,* why don't you send down one of your famous freak winds, right now? But the sky remained clear.

They had to get the bracelets off, but how? They had no knives, so cutting off their hands wasn't even an option. The bracelets had no visible locks that could be picked. Only two hairline cracks on opposite sides showed that they were not a single fused strand of metal.

He could hear Littlejohn rustling behind him.

"Don't move," Hijohn whispered.

The helicopter returned, lower this time, stirring the air around them and scattering leaves with the wind from its blades. Bird's heart was pounding so hard he thought his whole body must be bouncing on the ground. You've got to do something. Think!

Breathing deep, he forced his mind into the calm necessary for trance. Down to the door, sing in your head the pattern, the key, open it and enter, look at the bracelets from that level. Yes, there was something, a ring, a loop of light. Break that and yes, *snap!* something opened.

"I can get the bracelets off," he hissed to Hijohn.

"Great. But we gotta get out of here, somehow."

The noise of the helicopter was so loud above them that Bird could hardly think. They were high on a ridge, too exposed. Behind them was the gentle slope they'd climbed; in front of them, another ravine dropped steeply. There were trees above them with leaves and branches that offered some cover. They would be hard to see. If only they could get down into the ravine below. Maybe, when the copter made one more pass. . . .

But it hovered above them, churning the air. Bird heard a small sound, just a whisper of something speeding through the air, and then a bullet slammed into Hijohn's tree. It was followed by others, a barrage that came so close to Bird it scattered dust in his eyes.

"Keep down," Hijohn whispered again. "If you get up and run, you're dead."

They seemed likely to be dead soon, anyway. The helicopter banked and turned, and in the split second while it faced away, Bird slipped his bracelet off and, still keeping low, tossed it back down the slope they'd come up. Luck was with him; it skidded down at least fifty feet before it stopped, and a line of bullets followed it. Bird rolled quickly and threw himself on top of Hijohn, reaching below him to touch the metal of his bracelet and release the electronic catch.

"Down the ravine," Bird whispered. "Fast as you can, when I say go. Leave the bracelet. Now!"

The helicopter was still pointed away from them. Bird grabbed Hijohn's bracelet while he scrambled for the edge of the ridge.

"Give me your hand," Bird yelled to Littlejohn, clutching at the younger man's wrist and *reaching* for the lock of his bracelet. Nothing happened. Shit. He was out of trance, too scared to concentrate, and now he could hear the copter coming back; they were both exposed, without even the mass of their bodies to provide some shielding for the bracelets. Bullets whined and thudded up the slope, coming closer. Frantically, Bird hurled Hijohn's bracelet away.

"*Santa Madre, Madre Tierra,* let them follow it, please, please!" Without waiting to see if his prayer was answered, he steadied his breathing, tried again. Nothing.

One more time. The copter was turning, now it was coming back again, bullets raking the hillside in a fan-shaped pattern, slowly, methodically. Good, that gave them one minute more, one last chance. *See* the energy, *feel* for it, calm, now, and—yes, there it went. *¡Gracias a la Diosa!*

"Over the edge," he whispered to Littlejohn. "On your belly till you get there."

He left the third bracelet there, in their hiding place, and dragged himself over the ground, squirming like a worm across the few yards to the crest. Bullets were coming closer and closer. He rolled over the edge and slid down a nearly vertical drop, his hands scrabbling at loose dirt in vain attempts to break his fall.

He landed hard at the bottom and lay there, struggling for breath, the wind knocked out of him. Littlejohn sprawled nearby; Hijohn grabbed him and dragged him under the cover of an alder thicket. Bird forced himself to crawl, gasping, to lie beside them. He was scraped and bruised, every bone in his body ached, but they were alive.

"You okay?" he asked. Hijohn grunted. Littlejohn was bleeding from a cut on his forehead where he had scraped it coming down the hill. Bird ripped the tail off his shirt and bound it around the wound. It wasn't too clean, but it would stanch the blood.

"*Tenemos suerte,*" Bird said.

"What?" Hijohn asked.

"Our luck is strong today. They damn near killed us all."

"Coulda been worse," Hijohn admitted. "If they'd used lasers, the whole damn woods would be on fire."

They could still hear shots ringing above them.

"How long before they figure out we're not up there?" Bird asked.

"Not long enough. We should get out of here," Hijohn said.

"You okay, Littlejohn? Ready to travel?"

"I'll be okay. Let's go."

The sun was already low in the sky. Hijohn took the lead, guiding them down the ravine, keeping them under cover. There was a little water in the streambed and they drank, filtering out the mud with their teeth. Maybe it's bad water, Bird thought, but we have to have it. They crawled through thickets of brush, toyon and chamise and beds of ruddy-leafed poison oak, keeping on until they rounded a bend of the stream and could make their way north up a side canyon, over another ridge. No more shots sounded behind them.

The sun slid between a crack in the hills and disappeared. Twilight deepened to darkness, giving them a sense of safety more psychological than real. They kept moving. A cold wind off the ocean was breathing down their necks, and walking kept them warm. Bird hoped they could walk all night and put some real distance between themselves and any pursuit. He was tired, and adrenaline had sharpened his hunger again. Tomorrow they'd find food, if they still lived. Now, they must simply endure and push on.

                                    ◦ ◦ ◦

They kept on all night and through much of the next day. Bird's legs felt like stones, if stones could generate pain, and after a while he was no longer thinking or worrying or doing anything but concentrating on the labor of placing one foot in front of the other, of keeping breath wheezing in and out of exhausted lungs.

Finally, in the heat of the afternoon, he let them rest. Hijohn was gray with pain and exhaustion, and Littlejohn's forehead was bleeding again. They had found very little water, but at last they came to a deep creek that still flowed strong, even in the height of the dry season. They knelt and drank. Hijohn collapsed in the center of a clump of chamise. The feathery gray-green foliage offered concealment, and Bird was tempted to join him. But he decided to scout a little, first. Where there was year-round water there might well be settlements, still peopled or maybe abandoned, promising both food and danger. He'd go now, because once he gave in to his weariness he might not rise again.

"I'm going to look for food," he said to Littlejohn. "You want to come or stay here with Hijohn?"

"Man, I don't ever want to move again. I'll stay here."

About a mile upstream, Bird found an old apple orchard. The trees were overgrown and unpruned, the ground covered with fallen apples that smelled of sweetness and decay. The air tasted of fermentation; he could get drunk on it. Light filtered through the trees; the air was hazy with dust and bees hummed as they gathered around the fallen fruit. He sensed magic in the place. Someone had done rituals here, made offerings to the spirits, he was sure of it. For the first time in as long as he could remember, he felt safe.

He sat down with his back against a gnarled old tree. Suddenly tears were welling up and spilling from his eyes. He hadn't been able to cry before. The demands of survival had been too pressing. Now he looked down at his hands and wept for the suppleness that was gone and the years he'd lost and for the sheer raw ugliness that had been imposed on the beauty of the world. He cried for his lost voice that hadn't sung a song or laughed at a joke in a decade, and he cried because he could hardly believe they had really escaped and he was headed home at last.

Hunger and exhaustion had emptied him. The humming of bees was loud in his ears, taking him somewhere, as if he had stumbled into the sacred orchard of the Shining Isles where the living and the dead walk together.

Then the gates of the worlds opened, and the dead came walking, Cleis and Zorah and Tom, not as in a vision but with the sound of leaves crackling under their feet and a scent in the air that was blossom and sage and rot all at once. They came toward him, his beloved dead, arms outstretched and eyes shining, and behind them walked Rio, Maya's partner, almost but not quite his own grandfather, who had been alive when Bird left home. Bird reached for them, opening his mouth and taking in breath to speak, to ask them what had happened and why they had abandoned him. But they were gone. Above his head circled three black cormorants and one old crow.

He looked down. At his feet were four black feathers. He looked up at the brow of the hill and saw a small herd of deer watching him with tender animal eyes. Their leader was a stag with full antlers raised high and proud, and the sun dropped behind him into the west, a flaming ball between his horns.

With his left hand, Bird made the sign of the God who gives himself away, the prey who yields to the hunter so the people may live. The stag dipped his head. A sense of strength and compassion flooded through Bird, and under it all was something else, a quiet sense of expectation.

Then a crow called, and the herd wheeled and turned and bounded off into the brush.

Bird gathered apples, eating one himself, slowly. He found a tree of ripe walnuts, stripped off his shirt, and improvised a carrying bag. And there were plenty of live oaks, heavy with brown, slender acorns. Soaking in the stream overnight would take away some of their bitterness. It was a bad time of year for water, but a good time for foraging. Berries were ripe, and there were seeds of sage and fennel they could collect. When he returned to the others, he came laden with fruit.

° ° °

Littlejohn was kneeling beside Hijohn, letting him drink from his cupped hands. The sky glowed indigo, and a bright pink cloud scudded overhead. The scene reminded Bird, for a moment, of one of the holy pictures the Sisters kept in their living room back home. The peace of the orchard remained with him; everything seemed beatified. He set down his shirt.

"I found food," he said. "Let's eat."

"Food!" Littlejohn whistled. "Man, you really are some kind of Witch."

They crunched apples and broke the nuts open between stones. The apples weren't quite as ripe as they could be, and some of the berries were sour, but to Bird they had a sweetness that was almost a pain, the sweetness of real earth and sun and wind. It had been so long since he'd eaten anything at all, and longer still since he'd tasted food that wasn't prepared as an aspect of punishment.

After the first rush of hunger was satisfied, they settled in to crack walnuts between stones and pick out the delicate meats. Bird looked thoughtfully at Hijohn. The man could use a night of rest, he decided. He'd never completely recovered from the beatings he'd received, and now his mouth was set in lines of pain. While he didn't complain, it was obvious that any movement hurt him. For that matter, Bird could use some rest himself. He closed his eyes for a moment, asking the still, deep place inside him for guidance.

"I think we're safe here tonight," he said. "I say we don't try to push on. What do you think?"

Hijohn laughed. "If you expect me to say we should move, forget it. I'm not sure I could if I wanted to."

"Let me rest just a bit, and I'll work on you," Bird said. "What do you think, Littlejohn?"

"Push on to where?"

"I'm sorry," Bird said. "I guess I just instinctively headed toward home. We should have discussed it."

"And where is your home?" Hijohn asked.

"In the north. San Francisco. And don't, for Goddess's sake, tell me to call it Saint Francis or Frankie's Place or any of that shit. Although some of us have taken to calling it *Hierba Buena,* since the Uprising."

Hijohn looked at him thoughtfully. "And just what kind of place is that?"

"It's a city," Bird said. "And the land around it, the watershed. All the way up to the High Sierras in the east. And north up the coast. It's beautiful there. Redwood country."

"I've heard about redwoods," Hijohn said. "What are they like?"

"They're like . . . guardians. When you're around them you feel protected. Watched over. They collect fog in their branches, way above your head. People say the spirits of your beloved dead hang out there."

He felt good, remembering the redwoods of Mount Tamalpais, the damp earth smell when you were down in a grove of them, the soft, rough, ridged bark, and the bay laurel trees raising graceful limbs in between and wafting their pungent perfume around you. A tune he had forgotten came back to him, and he sang it for them.

"That's the redwood song," he said. "It kind of sounds like they are."

The music sang itself inside his head, and his hands ached for an instrument to chase it with. They ached of old wounds, too, and he felt a sudden stab of loss, looking down at them. But the music is still inside me, he told himself. I will find it again, somehow. I'll have to.

The sun was gone and the indigo air began to take on the chill tang of night. Bird considered building a fire. They had no matches, but he could always make a fire drill. It was a pain in the ass, but he knew he could do it. He'd done it often enough as a kid, the year they'd studied fire. That was the way Johanna ran the schools; she believed children should be taught about things from beginning to end. So they learned to make fire from sticks, and how to put out fires, and then studied all the chemistry and physics involved as they built steam engines and solar panels and tracked the course of the sun. He supposed it was a good way to learn; certainly they had never been bored, and he was always coming across bits of useful knowledge. Thanks, Johanna, Bird said silently. I wish you were still alive for me to say that to. But she had died, the same year his mother died, in the same epidemic. What would you advise me now about fire?

"Don't tempt your luck."

Maybe the voice was Johanna's ghost, maybe just his own sense of caution, but he had to agree that a fire seemed unwise. He felt safe where they were—but not that safe.

"It's getting cold," Littlejohn said.

"Let's get close together, under this bank," Bird said. "We'll keep each other warm."

They huddled together, letting the rise in ground behind them break the force of the wind. But the earth under them was damp, and Littlejohn shivered.

"Don't think about the cold," Hijohn said. "There's nothing we can do about it. Think about something else. Tell us more about your home, Charlie. Who owns the water?"

"What do you mean?"

"I mean the water. Like, to drink and grow your food. Who owns it?"

"Nobody owns it. You can't own water where I come from."

"Somebody's got to own it," Littlejohn said. "Somebody always does."

"We believe there are Four Sacred Things that can't be owned," Bird said. "Water is one of them. The others are earth and air and fire. They can't be owned because they belong to everybody. Because everybody's life depends on them."

"But that would make them the best kind of thing to own," Littlejohn said. "Because if your life depends on it, you've got to have it. You'll pay any price for it. You'll steal or lie or kill to get it."

"That's why we don't let anybody own them," Bird said.

"So if nobody owns the water, who decides who gets it and who doesn't?" Hijohn asked.

"Everyone decides together. Four times a year, each household sends a representative to the Neighborhood Councils to discuss water issues. Water Council coordinates distribution and arranges for the work that's needed to maintain the system. Each house has its own cistern that fills with the winter rains. But that doesn't give us enough for the whole summer. We draw from the streams and reservoirs and bring down water from the Sierras."

"What if you don't agree?"

"We keep talking about it until we do agree. It works out."

"What if it doesn't?"

"It always does. It has to, because we know what the alternative is."

"What?"

"The Stewards, or something like them."

In the silence, they could hear the call of the night birds. The sun was gone but the wind had dropped.

"Well, where we come from, you pay," Hijohn said. "The Stewards control the water supplies; that's how they took control of the government in '28. The Millennialists backed them with funds and religious prophecies, and in return they put into law most everything the Millennialists believe. You've got to work for the Stewards and obey the Millennialist Purities, or you can't even buy water and you lose your right to eat."

Bird sighed. "We studied the Millennialists in school. They were part of the history that led to our Uprising. Back in the twenties they had a lot of political clout. But it's hard to imagine that people take them seriously. All that stuff about Jesus returning in 1999 and then repudiating the world because of sin."

"He came and left," Littlejohn said. "Leaving us to fight sin, which is most things worth doing."

"And people really believe that?"

"Plenty do," Hijohn said. "Or pretend to, now. They have to, if they want a job and a roof and a full belly every now and then. Or they join us up in the hills and fight."

"It's hard to imagine," Bird said. "Even after where we've been."

"It's harder to imagine a city where nobody's thirsty," Hijohn said. "That's what we're fighting for, but it's still hard to believe it might really be true."

"Nobody's thirsty in my city," Bird said. "Nobody goes hungry. Nobody's in prison." Even to him, the words sounded unlikely, an article of faith more than a solid memory. "But we were hard hit by the epidemic. I don't know what's left, now. That's why I've got to get back, to find out."

"I don't suppose you'd change your mind, come back south to the hills?" Hijohn asked. "We could sure use someone like you. I'd always heard stories about Witches from the north with supernatural powers. But now that I've met you, man, I believe them."

Bird laughed. "My powers aren't supernatural. In fact, as powers go, they're fairly mediocre."

"Then I'm not sure I want to meet the ones you'd consider well endowed."

"Tell me about the hills. Who do you mean when you say 'we'?"

"Come and see for yourself. We're fighting for what you've got. Fighting the Stewards and the Millennialists. It's not so easy down here."

"It wasn't so easy up there. People died. But we did it. We got free."

"For a while," Hijohn said.

"For a while," Bird agreed. "We know they could come back any time, and I don't know what we'd do if they came."

"What we do," Hijohn said. "Fight. Go thirsty. Die. Maybe win a few small battles, once in a while. But if we had someone like you, to teach us what you know—"

"I haven't seen my home in ten years, man. I don't know who's alive anymore or who's dead. Probably all my folks think I'm dead."

"So they're done mourning for you, years ago," Hijohn said. "Why reopen old wounds? Come south, just for a while."

"I'll think about it," Bird said, to quiet him. "But there's something else I want to know."

"What?"

"Why are you both named John?"

"It's a tradition," Hijohn said. "When you go to the hills, you leave your name behind. You become anonymous: John Doe. And it's to do honor to John the Conqueror, the spirit who came over from Africa with the slaves, who brings hope to the hopeless. Because, to be honest, we don't have too much hope of winning. But we're fighting anyway."

Bird heard what he didn't say: We are desperate. He felt Hijohn's will like a physical pull. The man's eyes were on him; even in the dark Bird could feel their glow. But he had to go home. He had to find out if he still had a home.

Hijohn was silent. Bird could smell the sage wind off the land rise and blow out to sea.

Littlejohn yawned. "I'm wiped out. You two must be really beat."

"Yeah, let's sleep now," Bird said. "In the morning, we can decide where to go."

° ° °

When the sun rose, the night chill had seeped into every muscle and bone in Bird's body. He was one solid ache, and he was sure Hijohn felt worse. But the cool wind that blew in over the water tasted of unfettered tides. Bird offered up gratitude to the spirits, for the moist fog on his face, for the absence of walls between him and the elements. They ate apples and the last of the berries.

"You still determined to go north?" Hijohn asked.

"Yeah," Bird said. "And you? Still heading south?"

"Yeah."

"How are you going to get around the camp if you head back where we just came from?"

"Look." Hijohn bent down and scratched a rough map into the dirt with a stick. "I can guess roughly where we are. Here's the work camp, down in that flat area, and here's these hills to the north of it. But all of it's on this kind of bulge that juts out from the coast. I'm going to head east until I pick up the South Coastal Hills—the Motherrocks, we call them. They run all the way back down to Angel City."

"Can you make it that far? Alone?"

"I won't have to. I know where to find friends in these mountains. But north of here there isn't much. You'll run into the dunes, where there isn't too much cover, and then hills again. Farther up, when you get close to Slotown, there's one stretch where the old Coast Road runs right up next to the beach. The army still uses the road, and you can't bypass it to the east; they've got the area mined. If you get through, into the Irish Hills west of Slotown, you'll meet up with friends of ours who can help you."

"Thanks," Bird said. "What about you, Littlejohn?"

He shrugged. "There's nobody waiting for me down south. I guess I'll stick with you for a while."

"Well, then, this is goodbye," Hijohn said. "It doesn't seem enough somehow, just to say thanks, but there it is."

"*De nada,*" Bird said. He put his hands on Hijohn's shoulders, sending him one last flood of energy that eased his own muscles as he drew it up from the earth. "*Que te vaya bien, que vayas con Diosa. Que nunca tengas hambre. Que nunca tengas sed.*"

"What does that mean?" Littlejohn asked.

"May it go well for you, may you go with the Goddess. May you never hunger. May you never thirst."

"Never thirst," Hijohn said, as if he was considering the idea.

"Merry meet, and merry part," Bird said. "That's what Witches say."

"I remember my folks saying that," Littlejohn said. "And merry meet again."

"Take care," Hijohn said.

Bird filled Hijohn's pockets with apples and acorns. They watched as Hijohn made his slow and careful way up the streambed. He rounded a curve, and vanished.

"*Vamonos,*" Bird said. "Let's get going."

5

Above the sink in the small scrub room next to the epidemic ward some-one had posted a sign: WEAR YOUR MASKS; PREVENT THE SPREAD OF DISEASES. Underneath, in handwriting she recognized as Sam's, was a penciled note: *This means you, Madrone!* Madrone felt a strong temptation to scrawl some-thing nasty back, but she restrained herself. No matter how many times she explained, he couldn't seem to understand that she had other ways of protect-ing herself. And if they failed, gauze was useless.

She placed her hands on the sink and drew in a long breath, renewing her grounding, her connection with the earth. Silently, she checked her own aura and renewed her wards, the guardians she had created for herself in the *ch'i* worlds. She pictured them buzzing around her like a swarm of spirit bees. Then she waited, watching the mirror until broken patterns of light came together as an image, a reflection from some other realm. After a moment, she saw a face take form: female, old. The lines that crisscrossed the face became a net of light, like a spiderweb glinting under the moon above a dark pool. Madrone felt hands behind her hands, power she could lean on. She turned and entered the ward.

The big room was crowded with beds. Most of them were filled with children, who were especially vulnerable to the disease. Down the hall were wards for older people and pregnant women; she would visit them later. She stood for a moment, breathing in the air that carried the sweetish odor of death. Above it floated the pungent odor of moxa, the herb Lou was burning at the side of a young boy who lay still, his back full of acupuncture needles. She watched as Lou removed the needles, patting the boy on the shoulder and covering him with the blanket.

She couldn't look at Lou without thinking of Sandy. They had the same black silk hair, although Lou cropped his short and Sandy had let his grow down nearly to his waist. Usually he had worn it neatly wrapped and tucked at the nape of his neck, but when they were making love he would let it down to drape her like a tent. She had lain many times with her head nestled close to his, letting her fingers play with that hair, each separate shaft so thick and straight and spaced far from the others, a forest she could wander in.

Lou's eyes observed her quizzically over the white mask that concealed the rest of his face.

"You missed the meeting, love," he said. "Sam promised that if he caught you or anyone else without a mask, he'd give us all a demonstration of in vivo dissection."

"In other words, he'll skin you alive," Aviva said, coming up behind her. "He's serious, Madrone. This time he's really on a rampage." Her own bushy curls were covered with a cap, and her white gown was spotless.

Madrone shook her head. "He knows that's not how I work. Since when does he make the rules for us?"

"We all agreed to this one," Lou said.

"When? I never did."

"If you miss the meetings, you miss the decisions," Lou said.

"It was my day at Council. I can't be in two places at once."

"No?" Lou raised his eyebrows. "What kind of Witch are you?"

"The Wicked Witch of the West," Madrone said, but she went and got a mask from the scrub room and put it on. With it covering her mouth, she felt removed, isolated. "I hate this."

"So who likes it?" Aviva asked.

"You look tired," Lou said. "Had any sleep?"

"Have you?"

"You're working too hard," Aviva said.

"And you aren't? You're just lounging around here, the two of you, from six in the morning until midnight?"

"Languishing on our bloated healers' stipends," Lou said. "How was Council?"

"People are starting to get scared," Madrone told them, filling them in on the decisions that had been made.

"We're all scared," Aviva said. "What do you think about the disease? Do you think it's a weapon?"

"I for one don't care," Lou said. "I don't care if it's a Stewardship plot, a judgment by a vengeful God, or a misguided attempt at communication from space aliens. I just want to get rid of it. And I don't want to discuss it."

"What do you need from me here?" Madrone asked.

"A miracle cure," Lou replied.

"And while I'm working on it?"

They conferred for a few moments about the progress of their cases. Then Lou and Aviva moved on, while Madrone stood still for a moment and scanned the room, letting herself sink one level down into trance, so that the bodies disappeared into an interplay of lights. She was looking for an opening, someone or something that would call to her. There's got to be some way to *find* this thing, she thought. Goddess, show it to me and I will go wherever it leads, give whatever it takes.

Bright lights and dim lights, lines and shadows pulled and danced. At last she picked out the form of a young girl, lying on a bed in the corner. She went over, picked the child up, and sat down, propping her back against the wall. The child was semiconscious, and Madrone could smell the sweetness of decay on her breath. She let her own breath take her down, down. Down to where sounds and smells disappeared, down to the level where everything was energy, *ch'i,* and, below that, through the place where fear and pain and the light of spirits moving across the veil gave way to something even deeper. The level of *cause.*

Automatically Madrone's hands soothed the child, moved energy to reduce her fever. But behind Madrone's hands were other hands; behind her face hid the face of the Crone, the Old One, *La Vieja,* whose other name was the Reaper. Where Madrone was now, the upper world seemed dim. She was in the belly of Spider Woman, where the lines of probability were spun out into webs and nets. She could see them, some glowing and shining, some dim and broken, some filled with a sweet fragrance like fresh herbs, and some smelling of the sweet ketone stink of death.

In this place, patterns of probability were laid out like shifts in a landscape, hills and hollowed valleys and curving roads. But she had been here before, time after time, gone down road after shining road, hunting, finding neither cause nor cure for the fever. There had to be another way.

There was another way to heal, a dangerous way, a way everyone who had trained her had warned her against. Healers had died, trying it. But she was going to have to do something. She couldn't bear to go through '38 again. The city couldn't outlast another mass epidemic. Even now, their survival was precarious; there was too much work to be done and not enough hands to do it. But more—there were limits to how much people could stand to lose.

Am I strong enough? she wondered.

Silence reverberated through all the levels of possibility. No one would answer her. Goddesses and Gods, ancestors and orishas walked these roads, but none would appear and guide her through this choice. It was hers alone, her *geis,* maybe. In her mind she used the old Celtic word for the dare you have to take, the task you cannot refuse, the taboo that is doomed to be broken.

The child moaned in her lap. She was about six years old, her long brown braids tied with blue ribbons. Someone loved this child, carefully braided her hair, took pleasure in her prettiness.

Deliberately, Madrone dropped her protection, envisioning an opening in her own aura, dismissing her wards, taking off her mask. She bent her head down over the child's midriff to suck the disease from her solar plexus, feeling at the same time the ancient mouth of the Reaper draw the elusive *thing* she sought out of the child's body into hers. The girl's aura flared bright.

It was one of the oldest forms of healing known, and the most risky. Absorb the disease; then cure it inside yourself.

Almost instantly, Madrone began to fear she had made a mistake. The sickness moved so quickly. She could feel her ears ring and a feverish flush rise on her skin. She couldn't see but she sensed something racing inside her, racing toward her brain. If it got there before she did . . . but already she wasn't making sense. She felt dizzy and slumped back against the wall as sweat broke out on her forehead. She tried to call in power. Where was *La Vieja,* the Old One? Now Madrone herself felt old age creeping as an ache through her bones. Her blood was on fire, burning her youth away.

Diosa, this thing moved fast! Why couldn't she remember any Goddesses, any names of power? Or how to use her power? Things she'd known since she was a child. She wished she was a child; she wanted her mama, but Mama Rachel had died long ago in faraway Guadalupe. And Rio had come for her and brought her back to California to be safe, but now he was dead, and Johanna was dead, and only she was left with Maya: Yemaya, that was a name of power, that was the ocean, that was the true mother who could save her or drown her.

I'm drowning, Mama. Help me, send me something, someone to help me.

There was a sound in her ears like the roaring of the tide, and a light in her eyes like a moon over water, an old moon, Crone moon, crescent scythe of the Reaper. The tide surged at her feet; it was dark, alive, and as it receded it left behind a form that glided and spiraled and reared up with two heads— red-mouthed, gaping, fanged serpent's heads—that turned to stare at her with their narrow eyes.

The serpent's scales gleamed in the moonlight, pearly, iridescent. Madrone approached, hands extended.

"Coatlicue, Serpent Skirt," she whispered. "Tiamat, Mother of all the Gods. Let me come into you, hide me, save me."

The snake hissed like the tide receding over a gravel shore. The heads arched, turned to regard each other, and fused into one, with one great open mouth, that bent down toward Madrone. She smelled blood and ocean water. She saw the live, darting tongue, as it reached for her, wrapped around her waist. Then darkness closed over her, and she was burning and drowning all at once, until she could open her eyes again and look out over the snake's broad scaled snout.

She writhed, she crawled, she glided over a network of shining threads, her nostrils overwhelmed by the sharp smell of death. Something was still chasing her and she had no legs to run, but the muscles in her long belly rippled and she moved on them like waves.

She had lost her sense of time. She moved through a world of energies and causes that appeared like a forest of many kinds of trees, bordering on the ocean where the moon still rode the waves. She could smell her pursuer somewhere in the woods, getting closer, closing in.

It came out of the trees on her right. Suddenly it had her by the throat, in the soft place at the base of her triangular chin, and she was strangling and gasping for breath, struggling to free herself from the jaws of something much bigger than she was. She tried to bite, but her mouth clamped down on metal. She writhed and twisted, choking and gasping for breath. Her serpent's tail whipped back and forth, catching her attacker from behind and knocking it loose for just an instant. She sucked in a quick breath as claws gripped her back. Sharp teeth sank into the skin above her spine; in a moment they would sever the cord and she would die. Gathering her waning strength, she thrashed violently back and forth, but the claws held. Then something ripped loose from her back and she slid free, leaving her discarded skin behind.

The thing she was facing was like nothing she had ever seen before. She saw it as a giant insect but constructed, bolted together out of gray metal forms. Clamped to its back with an old-fashioned bicycle lock was a huge piece of thistledown, which reminded her of the way the common cold virus appeared on this plane. As she watched, the down rose into the air, lifted the metal thing, and dropped it on top of her. Then she was battling it again, but the more she bit and twisted, the more she hurt herself. The thing grabbed her by the tail and swung her around. She could see the ground spinning, and the trees. In a moment, it would dash out her brains. She was going to die, as Sandy had died, and the others. This thing was bigger than she was and would kill her on a tree. A madrone.

Madrone. As she said her own name, she shed again, sliding out of her skin and sailing through the air. The snake is kin to the bird, she thought, and shapeshifted, molding the *ch'i* of her body into scaly legs, wings. As a bird, she soared to the treetops, leaving the thing holding a clawful of snakeskin and colored scales.

She had no time to find out what kind of bird she was, only that her wings swept low in iridescent blues and greens and her tail was splendidly long. The bird trembled, as in some other realm of reality Madrone's body shuddered with fever.

Then the thing attacked again, uprooting the tree where Madrone-the-bird perched. She flew high up, but the higher she flew, the more the thing expanded. As a bird, she could barely escape it. She could not destroy it.

She was losing energy, too weak to match the thing's strength or try to grow to its size. She needed to rest. And the power of the serpent, she knew, lies in shedding and changing, one skin for another, letting go and letting go. Giving her own wings one long shake, Madrone squirmed free, out of the bird skin, which fluttered empty to the ground as she shifted again, becoming very, very small, a fly hiding in the thistledown as the thing stumbled blindly about, searching.

Cautiously, she crawled down to the lock that clamped the thistle to the monster. Finding the keyhole, she made herself smaller and smaller, until she could crawl inside. One by one, she tripped the hasps of the lock. The clasp opened, and the thistledown flew off.

She could hear the monster roaring in rage. The sound reverberated through her; her body ached and screamed with it, but she slowly crawled out of the keyhole and down the body of the thing, down plates of metal bolted together. It wheeled and turned, hunting for her. The surface was slick but her fly feet clung tight and her wings helped her keep her balance. She moved along its shiny surface until she came to what looked like a large lag bolt in the center of the thing's back.

She needed a tool. She thought of the ocean again, the bright crescent moon shining just beyond her grasp. She needed hands to reach with, a form like her own human body that lay somewhere, sweating and gasping, containing this battle. *Mujer Serpiente,* mother of changes, let me be myself within myself. She shifted again, taking human form, clinging to the thing's back like a monkey.

Again, it screamed and twisted, spinning around and around, bucking and leaping, trying to dislodge her. She held on but she could do nothing else. She couldn't reach the moonbow, couldn't change anything. The monster moved with terrifying force; all around them trees were crashing; the fabric of cause was torn. It leaped up and slammed itself down on its back. Pain shot through her; she was crushed, unable to breathe, head and eyes throbbing. The forest was shattered, the beach pitted with chasms. Some part of her dimly knew what she was seeing: the *ch'i*-world reflection of her own physical body's deterioration. Now holes were torn in the ocean, the water was sucked down into whirlpools, carrying the wind down with it, sucking the moon down out of the sky. Soon the light would go out. The ocean floor emerged, dry. But she reached again for the moon as it sank and this time she caught it, gripped it hard in her fist.

In her hand, the moonbow became a crescent wrench. The thing rose up and began bucking and twisting. Holding on tight to its back with her left hand, she fit the wrench to the bolt with her right hand and began to turn.

The bolt was frozen in place, and she began to feel despair. She didn't have the strength to turn it. Her legs were cramping and her grip getting weaker. Sweat poured down her face.

"Mama, Yemaya, Johanna, somebody, anybody," she whispered. "*Te suplico,* I beg you, help me."

She called up her last reserves of strength and poured them all into her arm, her grip. The monster threw itself from side to side; her head was shaken back and forth until her neck ached with whiplash. But she kept pressure on the wrench. It seemed to move ever so slightly. The thing smashed down again, flinging itself on top of her. Once again pain shot through her. Her left hand cramped into paralysis, as frozen as the thing's metallic claw.

The wrench slipped off the bolt, and with enormous effort she slowly brought it back as the thing rose again, twisting and turning. The wrench kept sliding off the bolt. She wanted to scream with frustration, but when she managed to grasp the bolt again, and turn, she felt definite movement. She pushed harder, and the bolt moved a quarter turn.

Now suddenly she had hope, and hope gave her energy. She turned the bolt again and again. The thing's pace began to slacken. It bellowed and thrashed, but its movements lacked something of their force. She hurt all over, but centimeter by centimeter, turn by turn, the bolt came undone.

The end came suddenly. The bolt turned, the monster's head fell off and clattered to the ground. She was left sitting in a pile of metallic rubble that smelled of acetone.

Madrone sat still. She felt cool. In the physical world, her fever must have broken. She had passed the crisis, but she was exhausted on every level of her being, as if her life force had been drained from her. She had won, but she wondered if she were going to be able to come back.

Slowly she became aware that the landscape had changed. The forest and the ocean were both gone. Instead, she was in a place where all the lines of probability were gathered together, like many threads bundled into rope, like infinite paths converging into roads. Three roads. The crossroads. She was in the place where three roads meet. Facing her, sitting on a three-legged stool in the dust of the crossroads, was an old, old woman. She was dressed in a black cloak that seemed to shift and dissolve around her. She looked like *La Vieja* but, as Madrone watched, her face began to change, becoming scaly, its bones extending outward and the eyes narrowing into a serpent's head. Her dress was red and black, like the flag of Guadalupe, Madrone thought. Hearing a soft sound, she looked down. The ground beneath her feet was alive with snakes, their iridescent scales gleaming and flashing as they glided along, their bodies making a soft sound on the dirt, *shhh, shhh.* And then she could hear them singing, their narrow tongues flicking in and out of gaping mouths.

Mujer Serpiente, cambia su piel,
Snake Woman, shedding her skin . . .

The sound of the chant wove in and out of a soft hissing that surrounded her, and the serpent's face that regarded her split down the middle. Beneath, she could see *La Vieja,* Tiamat, Dragon Lady, Snake Woman—the form of Coatlicue, Mother of the Gods they called Cihuacoatl—the midwives' patron, her face chalk white as if covered with powdered bone, on her back a cradleboard tied with rainbow straps. Madrone dipped her head in respect. When she raised her eyes, Snake Woman had taken the cradleboard from her back. She held it out to Madrone.

Madrone reached inside the mouth of the cradleboard, which was suddenly alive, a snake's mouth, a birth canal pulsing and pushing forth something her skillful hands could guide to light.

But what she brought forth was not a live child but a bundle wrapped in red and black cloth. Slowly, she unwrapped it. Within was a black obsidian knife.

Suddenly Madrone felt cold, as if bone dust already were falling on her skin, leaching away blood and life. Is this what it means, then? she thought. Death?

She reached for the knife, and it changed in her hand to something familiar, a surgical knife, like the one she used after a birth, to cut the cord. To cut the cord was to complete the birth, and to give birth was *dar a luz,* which meant to give to light, and death itself was a cutting of the cord, too, and a giving to light. Perhaps a greater light.

She longed for that light, to fall into it, swirling down into depth beyond depth, into a deep, deep stillness where there was nothing but peace.

From her own navel a cord twined, a pulsing twined spiral of red and a blue so dark it was almost black, a chain that held her. And the knife could free her. In a moment, she would cut the cord and be free. In just a moment. As soon as she remembered something. What?

She had been in the middle of something; there was something she needed to think about, but what? Somewhere back where she had a body she felt, as from a great distance, a touch. She heard a whisper. Her name. Madrone.

Why?

She wanted to be with Sandy. And all the rest of them: Rachel, Johanna, Rio. With Bird. She hadn't wanted to die at the hands of the monster, but really, she didn't mind dying at all when *La Serpiente* offered her peace. Death would be so restful.

The monster. The thing—that was what she had to think about.

No, it wasn't the thing, it was . . . what? Someone?

The child in her lap. And the child on the next bed, the woman in the next room, the old man in pain. What did she owe them? Their very existence seemed suddenly to weigh her down.

The cord twisted in her hands. It had become a snake, a pair of snakes, whose heads facing each other fused into the face of *La Vieja*/Snake Woman/Tiamat/Hecate/Coatlicue, all with the same challenging pair of eyes: not cold but implacable. The eyes were strands of gray appearing in her hair, wrinkles on the back of her hands. The eyes were a destination.

Her own hands held the cord and the knife. Choice.

The crossroads.

Madrone's mind moved slowly, like a diver underwater, pushing against all the weight of the ocean. She understood, suddenly, that she was not ready to die. And that it wasn't death that was implacable but the long arm of life, reaching, always reaching, with the offer of choice.

She would choose the burden of her vision.

"Lend me your knife," Madrone said, "and I will be your instrument."

∘ ∘ ∘

Her eyes were open and someone was looking into them, chafing her hands and calling her name. She blinked and took a breath.

"Madrone," the voice said. "It's Aviva. Madrone, can you hear me? Do you know who I am?"

Madrone nodded. The motion made her nauseated. "I'm okay."

"Thank God!"

The child on Madrone's lap was sleeping peacefully. She shifted her gently onto the floor. Every movement made her stomach churn.

"Up!" she gasped to Aviva, who helped her rise. Then she dashed to the bathroom and vomited.

She crouched in the bathroom, shaken, shaking. Slowly, she grounded herself, called up earth fire to heal the wounds that didn't show because they were not in her physical body. Wounds of the spirit.

She was so tired. But in her palms a fire burned, a power demanding to be used. Gripping the edge of the sink, she pulled herself up to her feet. Her legs were shaking. She had to steady herself with one hand while she splashed water on her face with the other. Breathe. Ground. She was alive, and that was the first victory. She had won through to this power, and that was another, even while her body screamed out at her for rest. Another breath, and she could balance on her feet. Another, and another, and yes, she could walk, unaided, back out to the ward.

"What happened?" Aviva was waiting, sponging a sick child. "I thought we'd lost you too, for a moment."

"It's okay," Madrone said, but it was hard to talk, because she was still mostly in the spiderweb world of the shifting lines of destiny. Her hands were on fire. She could see the child Aviva tended, and when the fire of her hands touched the child's throat, something shifted. Something fled. Yes, that was the way—and it was so easy now, except that she wanted so much to sleep, but they would die, then, while she slept, and if she could just breathe, and take another step to another bedside, and lay serpent fire on another destiny, and another, and another. . . .

If she could just forget sleep, and rest, and food, and time, easy to do here in the timeless center, and let this moment of healing become her dwelling place. . .

Five hours later, she collapsed.

6

A black crow became Bird's guide. He would see it fly up before them, to reveal a way across a ravine, or hear it call, beckoning them down a certain path at a crossroads. He and Littlejohn followed trails and overgrown dirt roads and fire roads, sometimes emerging onto a stretch of broken pavement buckled by tree roots, sometimes losing any semblance of trail and crawling on their hands and knees through the underbrush. The crow led them through the dunes that bordered the hill country and flapped down in an abandoned garden by a flat marshy lake where they were able to gather grapes and self-seeded tomatoes. They were still hungry, but they would survive.

Walking on the sand of the dunes strained Bird's sore muscles, but he pushed on. At times, they could follow a trail over bluffs that looked out on the water. Bird had tried, in the hills, to steer away from the sprawling vines of poison oak, but by the third day he was itching and miserable.

"It never affected me before," Bird complained. "I used to be able to roll in the stuff, and it never bothered me."

"Piss on it," Littlejohn said. "That'll take away the itching."

"Are you sure?"

"Anyway, it'll help. Can't you heal it?"

"I'm doing my best. But I'm not really a healer. When there's a life-and-death situation, sometimes something comes over me, but it seems to have deserted me now. If Sandy were here, he'd have an herb for the itch, and Madrone—she can make you feel better with a wave of her hand."

"Who are they?"

"My family. My lovers. If they're still alive."

They were silent. The long rush and hiss of the waves reached them where they sat, concealed under the sheltering branches of a live oak.

"What's going to happen when we get to your home?" Littlejohn asked suddenly.

"You'll be welcome there."

"Yeah? We'll see."

"I mean it."

"Sure. Your family's going to be real happy to see you come home dragging some faggot you picked up in the Pit."

"Littlejohn, when I say my family, I mean all my lovers and all their lovers
and kids and ex-lovers and everyone—and half of them are faggots, at least
half the time. We consider it a word to be proud of."

"They're going to welcome competition?"

"We don't think like that."

"Sure you don't."

"I'm not saying nobody ever gets jealous. But we work it out."

"Yeah, sure. Look, Charlie, what we done in the Pit don't necessarily
carry over outside. I understand that."

"I don't."

"We come from different worlds. You're a real Witch. You've got powers.
Me, the only thing I really know about magic is it makes you fair game for
every demonfucker who takes it into his head to kill you. When you get back
with your own kind, you won't want to hang around with me."

"I'll teach you," Bird said. "We'll all teach you." But he was trying to
convince himself, because he suspected maybe Littlejohn was right. Their
bodies joined, but barriers remained that Bird couldn't cross and maybe
feared to. Littlejohn was opaque to him.

"Hell, Charlie. When you get to know me outside the joint, you won't
even like me."

"Don't say that."

"It's the truth."

Some part of Littlejohn had already passed judgment on himself, or had
accepted the judgment of a world that never really wanted him anything but
dead or as something to use and throw away, a rag to wipe a dripping cock
with. Bird wanted to do battle with that thing, Littlejohn's demon, but he
couldn't say the words of challenge or reassurance because he did not know if
they were true. He didn't know Littlejohn, not really, not down in the soul
where it counted, and he ached for people he did know, who opened at his
touch and shared the same ground.

"Well, there's not much point in worrying about it," Bird said finally.
"We may never get to my home. And there may be nobody still alive there if
we do."

"Yeah, there's always that possibility," Littlejohn said. "But somehow I
think you'll find your people."

"Thanks."

"If they're anything like you, they'll be damn hard to kill."

o o o

They slept curled up together against the cold, burrowed into the roots of
trees. Bird cast a circle of protection around them and set wards, going

through the forms of the ritual although he didn't feel much power. But power follows practice, Maya always said. The more he used his magic, the stronger it would become.

In his dreams that night, he became a hawk, soaring over the hills to the north. The hills were green, as if it were early spring after a wet winter. In a blue cove squatted a domed structure, the old nuclear power plant that had been refurbished in the early twenties. Bird could see its energy field, like a living thing, and the small sparks within it that were the spirits of the men who operated it. One by one, the sparks winked out. The dome began to glow, and the grass and trees began to die.

He awoke shivering and sweating. He had had that dream before. When?

"What's wrong?" Littlejohn asked.

"Just a dream. An old dream. Nothing."

"You're shaking."

"I think it's part of what I still can't remember. How I got down here in the first place. What I did."

"Don't worry about it," Littlejohn said. "We're getting out. That's enough to occupy your mind."

As they made their way farther north, Bird got more and more nervous. They would soon reach the place where the coastline curved eastward to meet the convergence of the old Coast Road with the Inland Highway. The road ran right along the beach for nearly ten miles, Hijohn had warned them, with no cover. He could *feel* the road closing in on them, trapping them in a narrow cul-de-sac. If they were being hunted, they were approaching the perfect spot for an ambush. But the crow urged them on.

As dusk fell, Bird could make out a silver line of fencing. He felt the aura of an electronic barrier.

"Let's stop," he said. They waited for nightfall. The fenced-in land ahead of them was posted with military signs. Where the road curved to the edge of the coast and the fence began was a gate and checkpoint where armed guards patrolled.

Maybe he could kill the electricity long enough for them to get over the fence, but that might alert the guards to their presence, and they would still have miles to go on a road with little cover, where more vehicles than he ever remembered seeing at one time sped up and down, headlights glaring.

Bird looked thoughtfully at the water, where searchlights played at regular intervals. He grimaced. It could be contaminated with anything from sewage to radiation. But what choice did they have?

"Can you swim?" he asked Littlejohn.

"No, sorry."

Bird considered. The fence ran down to the water, but he didn't know how far into the water it ran. He stripped off his clothes.

"Wait here," he said. A searchlight played on the front of the fence, but he timed it and ran out during its shadow, hitting the ground and rolling when the light returned. He crawled along the edge of the fence and lowered himself into the water. It was bone-numbing cold. The waves sucked at his legs, trying to pull him under. But the fence ended before he got out of his depth. They could do it—barely.

Cautiously, he made his way back to Littlejohn, had him take off his clothes and follow. Bird rolled their clothes into a tight bundle and balanced it on his head as he led Littlejohn into the waves. For one awful moment, the searchlight caught them. They froze, kneeling down in the frigid water, listening for shouts. But the light passed, and no one came after them.

They crawled out on the other side. The barrier at the highway's edge formed a line of shadow just deep enough for them to lie in, side by side, huddling together to restore some warmth to their cold bodies. Bird's plan was to move in that shadow, crawling if necessary, running when the searchlights let them. A thick bank of fog covered the sky, offering some concealment even though the moon was nearly full, shedding a diffused, pearly light. They couldn't wait for moonset, which wouldn't come until nearly dawn. They needed to hurry; they had to be off the base or well hidden by daylight, so he urged Littlejohn to put on his pants and ragged shirt, and they set off.

If they stayed on their hands and knees, the searchlights and headlights passed over them. During the dark periods, they could run for it, throwing themselves down on the rough ground when the light returned. It was a hard way to travel. Bird thought about pilgrims, crawling to sacred places for penitence. His knees were soon bleeding and his hands scraped, but they had no choice except to go on.

After several hours, Bird began to wonder how long he could continue to force his body to move. He had no idea how much ground they had covered. Eight miles? Nine? The eastern sky began to glow with a dim gray light, and the stars were disappearing. He urged Littlejohn on. He thought he could see another line of fence ahead of them, maybe a mile away, where the road curved inland and the coastal hills bulged out to the west. They would find cover there, if they were over the fence before daylight came.

Gray turned to pink, and the black faded to blue. They were making good time, but not good enough. "Let's run for it," he said to Littlejohn, who nodded. They abandoned their cautious crawl and ran, flat out. Bird felt his body obeyed him only because he refused to consider the possibility that it wouldn't. There was no real strength or speed left in him, but somehow they made it to the fence. It was marked with a skull and crossbones and a sign WARNING: TOXIC TERRITORY.

Whatever lay on the other side couldn't be nearly as toxic as that road would be to them in a few minutes. Bird laid his hand on the fence and sent an energy spark to cut the electricity. It no longer mattered if they alerted the guards; as long as they got over the fence they could hide in the thick brush across the way. Littlejohn climbed quickly to the top and Bird moved to follow. He made it up a few feet and then his bad leg froze. His muscles refused to work.

Bird was stuck halfway up, sweating. Littlejohn looked back and saw him. "Come on," he whispered.

"Go on," Bird said. "I can't make it over."

Littlejohn turned, climbed back over the fence, grabbed Bird, and hoisted him over the top. They fell down together on the other side, landing heavily with the breath knocked out of them. After a moment, Bird felt himself. He was bruised, but nothing was broken.

"You okay?" he asked Littlejohn.

"Yeah."

"Thanks. Let's get out of here."

Only a small side road separated them from a new range of hills. They were soon across it and into the underbrush. They made it another mile from the gate before Bird's body finally gave out. He had just enough strength to crawl into the shelter of a grove of oaks and draw a magic circle around them. Then he collapsed. The sun shone down through the leaves, dried their clothes, and warmed their bodies, but they were unaware. They slept.

o   o   o

The day passed and the sun passed, drawing a line of shadow in its wake. Bird felt the chill in his sleep, stirred, and opened his eyes. Littlejohn was still asleep. Bird wanted to get up but his muscles were so stiff that he found he could only roll over very slowly and push himself up with his arms into a kneeling position. As he raised his head, he found himself staring into the barrel of an ancient shotgun.

For one moment, everything he could see seemed sharply outlined in light. A leaf, a branch, a patch of ground were imprinted on his retinas, last images to take with him into the spirit world. He knew he couldn't run; he must have pulled every muscle in his back and hips, and his neck was so sore he could only continue to raise his head very slowly. If he couldn't run, he would have to die; it was as simple as that. He would never go back to imprisonment.

But as his eyes traveled up the gun barrel, he became aware that he was not facing a guard. The hands on the gun were brown, cracked and dirty, with broken nails, but undeniably female. The arms connected to a body that had breasts under a ragged cotton shift. And the face—but when he reached the face, he froze again. The face was like nothing he had ever seen before. At first it seemed to be one gaping hole; then he discerned a lower lip, capped by an upper lip split in two around an open gash where a nose should have been. The face was framed in wild, uncombed dreadlocks. And the eyes . . .

But the eyes caught him. They were brown, wide-set under well-shaped brows, and as he looked at them he fell into their depths. He hadn't looked into eyes like that for years, but now he could stare, lingeringly, at eyes that opened to him and entered into him, that read exactly what he was thinking and feeling, that remained steady under his first shock. He wondered what it was like to live behind that face with those knowing eyes. They would never misread revulsion or rejection. But what he felt, in their depths, was compassion.

"Who's our mother?" a man's voice said behind him.

He pushed himself up to his feet and turned. No one was there. Am I hearing things now? he wondered, but then he looked down at a pistol trained on him, held by a man who ended at the hips. He was muscularly built and handsome, with round blue eyes and a thick, curling black beard covering most of his oak-brown face, but where his legs should be, Bird saw nothing, as if his trunk had sprung up out of the ground.

"Who's our mother?" the man said again.

Maybe this was an aftereffect of the drugs they'd been given. Littlejohn began to stir and Bird remembered, suddenly, his first meeting with Hijohn.

"The earth is our mother," Bird said.

"We must take care of her," came a voice from off to his left.

Littlejohn looked up. They were surrounded by a ring of armed figures, some with faces oddly distorted, others missing a hand or an arm or with some withered limb dangling. Bird counted seven of them.

"Who are you?" The first woman spoke. Her voice was thick and somewhat distorted, but it rang with a tone of confidence and authority. Bird turned to her again. He realized, looking again into those eyes, that he couldn't lie to her. She was reading him as well as any Witch might.

"My name is Bird," he said. "Bird Lavender Black Dragon." His own name tasted sweet on his tongue, and unfamiliar. It had been so many years since he had spoken it aloud. He felt something from Littlejohn, a small spark of hurt, and he realized he had never told him his real name. There was no help for that now. "This is Littlejohn."

"From?"

"We've escaped from the South, from a work crew. But I come from the North—from the City."

There was an excited murmur around them.

The woman said something that Bird couldn't quite understand. The legless man repeated it more clearly.

"You are Witches."

"Right."

"From the North?"

"He is," Littlejohn said.

"Are you being tracked?"

"No," Bird said.

"Hell," Littlejohn added, "if we were being tracked, we wouldn't be here; we'd be dead. Say, don't you think you could put those guns down?"

"We're fairly harmless, really," Bird said.

The woman's eyes held his, searching. She reminded him of Maya; he felt known to the core and, after a moment, accepted.

"Not harmless," she said, "but I will trust you."

Another murmur, and the guns were lowered. The woman stepped forward and held out her hands to Bird. He reached out, and she clasped his hands between hers warmly.

"Welcome," she said, and pointed to her own breast. "I am Rhea."

Bird felt her touch go through him like an electric shock. Suddenly he wanted to be taken into those arms, enfolded in that touch, to fall into the wells of those eyes. He felt the possibility in her of contact, and the need for it possessed him more strongly than hunger.

The man with no legs tucked the gun into his belt. He came forward, moving gracefully by balancing on his palms and swinging his torso between his arms.

"I'm Morton," he said. "Welcome to the dancing ground of the Monsters."

"Monsters?" Littlejohn asked.

Morton grinned. "That's us. Fits, don't you think?"

"They can't possibly answer that and be both honest and polite," a slender young woman said. Her long black hair was arranged in a mass of tiny braids that framed a catlike triangular face. Her left hand was shaped like a claw. "I'm Dana. Welcome."

"But who are you?" Bird asked. "And what are you doing here?"

"We live here," Rhea said.

"Isn't the land poisoned?"

"Look us over closely," Morton said. "We're all natives of Slotown and the Irish Hills, all born back when the old reactor was still running, probably leaking like crazy but what the hell did they care? Of course, you don't see the ones who died of cancer."

"And you still live here?" Littlejohn asked.

"We got to live somewhere," Dana said.

"It's livable," Morton said. "For us. Yeah, there's probably still radiation. It doesn't go away. But it's better now than it was. Ten years ago, in the big

epidemic, the Witches from the North sent down a raiding party. Shut the
thing down, smashed the controls. Died doing it too."

"Goddess give them peace," Dana murmured.

Above their heads, a crow called. A shell broke open somewhere in Bird's
spine, sending shivers of energy climbing to the top of his head. A jumble of
images flashed through his mind: long white corridors, and a round pit of a
room lined with dials and switches, and most of all a presence like a living
thing with its own strange beauty: matter liberating itself into pure power. A
presence that did not want to die.

But he had killed it.

"It's been better since then," Morton went on. "The Millennialists had
purged so many techchies that the Stewards didn't have the know-how left to
repair the reactor or start it up again. The land feels better now, and there've
been some kids born that are okay. Not to us—but there's some others in the
town, deserters from the army."

"We work to heal the land," Rhea said. "On the moons and the festivals."

Bird barely heard what she said. He remembered the cold feel of a gun in
his hand, an old-fashioned revolver Tom had brought them from the Forest
Communities. And if he followed the aim of the gun he saw a dough-white
face slimed with fear and a pasty hand pulling switch after switch to move
control rods in between fuel rods in patterned sequence, shutting the reactor
down. It had taken a long, long time. They had spelled each other, he and
Cleis and Zorah and Tom, holding the guns, forcing the man to do their will,
standing guard.

"We like to maintain the idea that this place is too toxic to deal with,"
Morton said. "Keeps away unwanted interference."

"When necessary, we make enough of an appearance to keep the rumors
current," Dana said.

Someone had come at him, another man, freckled and sandy-haired and
shouting something. Bird's hand had jerked, and the bullet caught the man
between the eyes, sending his spirit shrieking off in shock and outrage and his
body crashing at Bird's feet as the nuclear hum grew faint as a whining dog.
Yes, he remembered feeling the man die, looking down at his face as he had
looked down at his father's face after the Uprising.

Maybe all the dead look the same.

"How long have you lived here?" Littlejohn was asking, glancing curiously at Bird's remote eyes.

"Since the Hunger came," Dana said. "Most of us were kids, then. We
lived with our families in Slotown or at the state school. When food got short,
they threw us out."

When the last switch was pulled and the hum silenced, they'd emptied

their guns into the control panel. Which had left them unarmed and helpless
when the door exploded and the guards came in firing. Zorah had screamed,
Cleis moaned and fell as Tom cried out, and then they became the birds,
soaring away on an updraft. Something had hit Bird in the thigh. He remembered falling, falling in a blaze of pain. And then nothing.

"You okay?" Littlejohn asked. Bird nodded and tried to focus on Morton,
who was going on with his story.

"There was a woman, lived at Avila Beach. We call it Avalon Beach now,"
Morton said. "She took us in. Taught us some things—about growing food,
herbs. She had certain herbs she said would cure cancer, so she wasn't afraid
of the land. She was a good woman."

"The Millennialists took her away in '35," Dana said.

"Goddess give her peace," the others murmured around the circle. They
came forward and introduced themselves: Gardner, a small dwarflike man;
Anna, a woman with no left arm; and Holly and Heather, twin sisters with
humped backs.

Bird's head spun with names and memories. Ground, he told himself.
Stay in the present. Now. A secret seed of pride stirred in his gut. These were
his people, although they didn't know it. He had given them their lives. He
had committed one act that changed the world.

Are you here? he called silently to Cleis and Zorah and Tom. Do you
know that your lives bought something after all? Why can't I feel you? The air
had grown cold as the sky darkened, and he shivered.

"This is our ritual circle," Rhea said. "We were just about to set up for the
Full Moon Ritual when we stumbled on you two. Will you join us? We don't
often get to celebrate with Witches from other places."

"We'd be honored," Bird said.

The Monsters began busily building a fire in the pit at the center of the
clearing. Behind the trees, the sun was setting in a red glow. The air grew cool
as the sky turned from blue to indigo. Someone threw a blanket over Bird's
shoulders, and he clutched it gratefully. Light winked behind the branches of
the oaks in the east, and slowly a full moon rose to paint the dry grasses silver.

They crowded around the fire. Bird felt the warmth on his hands and
drew it into his body. He hadn't eaten in so long that he was almost beyond
hunger, light-headed, beginning to lose sight of the forms of things and recognize only the energies. His leg ached. Yes, he'd been shot there and it had
never healed right, and that was just one of the reasons he hurt. The fire felt
good, but he wondered how long he could continue to stand erect.

The Monsters set up an altar on a flat rock in the north. Dana lit a candle
in a glass jar, and the others brought out food from their baskets and placed it
around the altar, setting out loaves of bread, slabs of cheese, bowls of apples
and grapes, and steaming pots of stew.

Bird swallowed. His throat was dry, and now hunger stabbed at him. Littlejohn was staring at the food. Rhea came over and placed a hunk of bread in Bird's hands.

"Eat," she said. "You're hungry."

Bird didn't deny it. His hands trembled as he tore off a small corner of bread and threw it into the fire as an offering. Reverently, he bit into the bread and began to chew. Saliva sprang painfully into his cheeks, and he forced himself to chew slowly, not to tear at the bread like a ravenous animal.

Littlejohn was sitting on the ground, making whimpering sounds as he gulped down his portion. When Rhea saw how hungry the two men were, she and Dana brought them bowls of stew and more bread and sweet apple juice to wash the food down.

Before long, Bird realized he needed to control himself or he would be sick. "Take it easy," he said to Littlejohn. "If we eat too much now, we'll regret it."

"You can feast more later," Rhea said. Bird found himself more and more able to understand her speech as his sense of contact deepened. "Now it's time to begin the ritual."

They stood in a circle around the fire. Morton turned to Littlejohn. "Will you ground us?" he asked.

Littlejohn looked alarmed. "I don't know anything," he said. "You ask him." He jerked his head in Bird's direction. "He's a real Witch, from the North. And he's got real powers."

"We don't have too much in the way of powers," Morton said. "They killed our teacher when we were just getting started. But we've got books."

"Will you ground us?" Rhea asked Bird.

"I don't feel very grounded," he said. "Someone else ground us, and I'll —I'll cast the circle."

The small woman who lacked an arm stepped forward. Bird had forgotten her name. She picked up a book from behind the altar, opened it, and began reading.

The words sounded oddly familiar to Bird, but it took him a while to place them. With a shock, he realized what they were—an exercise out of one of Maya's early books, the one they used to amuse themselves with as children, giggling over what they considered to be simpleminded instructions, teasing Maya until she would finally turn on them and chase them out.

"You brats don't know how lucky you are," she'd yell at them. "Do you know what it's like to be raised your whole life not to feel, not to trust your intuition, not to notice if you see an aura or feel the energy move? And then try to turn around as an adult and try to learn it all? You put that book down!"

Now he realized that the woman was simply reading the directions for grounding, somewhat expressionlessly. With a breath, he grounded himself, sending roots of energy down through his feet into the earth, making contact with the earth's core fire and drawing in the moon's light. The reading ended. Everyone in the circle looked serious, even solemn, but he didn't see that their energy had significantly changed.

"Will you cast the circle now?" Rhea said.

He walked to the altar, still moving slowly and painfully, and considered the tools. They lay in their proper positions: in the east, the knife, the *athame,* tool of air, symbol of the mind's power to make divisions and separations; in the south, the wand, tool of fire, symbol of energy and the power to channel and direct it; in the west, a clay cup holding the water that represented emotion, fertility, love; and in the north, a five-pointed pentacle carved on a stone slab, symbol of earth, of the body, the five senses, five fingers and toes, the four elements, the Four Sacred Things, linked with the fifth, spirit.

"Can I use this *athame*?" he asked.

"It's mine," Morton said. "Go ahead."

Bird picked it up and held it for a moment, feeling its power and something of Morton in it. Stubborn strength. Determination to survive. He walked out to the center and stood by the fire. Taking a deep breath, he let his own energy extend out to include the whole circle, to link with their willingness and intention to come together. When he felt the energy of the circle become one whole, he grounded it, sending it down through his own body into the earth, then drawing it back up again. He looked around. Good. The patterns had changed, as he'd hoped, and they were all connected to the earth.

Starting in the north, he walked around the circle, using the knife to draw around them in the air a ring of protection that sprang up as a flickering blue flame. At each of the four quarters, he drew a pentacle. Behind him, he heard a murmur of surprise, as if they'd never before seen the circle manifest. Maybe they hadn't, he reflected, as he returned the knife to the altar.

"By the earth that is her body, and by the air that is her breath, and by the fire of her bright spirit, and by the living waters of her womb, the circle is cast," he said.

They called the four directions, the elements of the quarters, again by reading out of a book. People kept casting little glances toward him as if to say, Is this right? Are we really doing it right? He controlled his expression, but invoked secretly himself, sending his own energy out into the elemental realms to contact earth, air, fire, water. It had been a long, long time since he had stood in circle with others, and there was something touching about these halting, awkward attempts to keep the rites without really understanding how to raise and channel power.

Then several people picked up drums and began to beat a simple rhythm and sing an old chant that he recognized.

Silver shining wheel
Of radiance, radiance,
Mother, come to us.

They were calling the moon, the Goddess in her aspect as Abundant One, the Mother, she who sustains life, and Bird threw up his arms and thanked her, remembering his prayer in the prison and feeling the tears flow down his face as he felt her light shine. They had survived, and they were free.

Someone handed him a drum, a carved wooden cylinder with a skin head. He held it to the fire until the head tightened from the warmth and then began to play. His hands were stiff and they hurt, but as the rhythm built he grew numb to the pain. Only some of the other drummers were in time to the rhythm of the chant; the others wandered vaguely in and out, hitting the rhythm sometimes and missing it more often. He began with a strong, solid beat to bring them all into alignment and then let himself play with it, adding syncopation and counter-rhythms. The guitar had been his instrument, not the drum, but like every child of the City, he'd learned to drum before he learned to count, adding and subtracting and dividing by changing beats before he was ever introduced to numbers. Now he made the beat come alive, even as his battered hands kept him to simpler patterns and prevented him from trying fast runs and rolls.

Rhythm was old, old as the rhythm of the moon, swelling to full and waning to dark. His hands told him he would never make music again the way he had before, on guitar or piano; what he heard in his heart would remain locked there because his fingers were no longer capable of evoking its power. He was broken, like the strange, wounded company that surrounded him with their broken beat. Maybe this was all that was left, this maimed circle on the edge of a poisoned world; maybe he had no more home, no family; maybe there were no more circles of powerful Witches who knew how to tell energy from form; maybe there were no rings of sweet lovers waiting to welcome him back, no ancient crones who could talk with the spirits, no one still willing to fight for the survival of the earth, no one left even to remember the dead.

The chant peaked and died.

"The Goddess is here," Rhea said. "What chant shall we sing for the God?"

"I've got one," Bird said.

He began a new beat on the drum and sang a calling chant, hearing the rough voices around him pick it up as he visualized the stag he'd seen on the hill, with the sun between its antlers, the sun that in this season was declining so the long nights could come, wounding itself to allow the rain to return. He sang until he could almost feel antlers sprout on his own head.

Life to life gives itself away,
Day to night, and night to day.

"He is here," Rhea said.

They danced around the fire, making offerings, singing chants of healing and change. Bird pulled healing power down from the moon and spun it into a cone that could rise like a fountain and spill itself out over the land.

After the energy had been grounded, they sat silent, looking into the fire, listening to its messages. Couples began to steal away together, out of the circle, cutting through its fire and sealing it behind them. Bird lay on the earth, beside the fire, letting its warmth ease his sore muscles, drawing in energy to heal the breaks in his cells. He felt a hand on his shoulder. Turning, he looked into Rhea's eyes.

"Will you make the Great Rite with me?" she asked.

He felt it again—the desire, the pull of energy to energy—but he hesitated, casting a glance around the circle for Littlejohn. He didn't want to hurt him. But Littlejohn seemed to have disappeared. Maybe he too had found somebody.

Rhea's eyes were on him, waiting. Her hand on his shoulder was warm, smoldering. This isn't safe, he thought, even if his exhausted body still had strength left to rise. But it felt right. The power of the God still burned in him; his veins carried liquid fire. He could withhold nothing from these people, his people. Rhea led him outside the circle, into a small sheltered spot under the branches of a live oak, where she spread a blanket for them.

Bird looked into Rhea's eyes. They were old and dark and luminous. Her face changed, no longer seeming grotesque but absolutely right, a mirror for the damaged land that like the face survived to harbor the possibility of growth and change.

Her body against his hands felt like soft loam as she lowered herself onto him, and he was the sun come down to earth at last. He opened to her fully and gave himself over to the power she harbored within her, and she opened to him, revealing pain and beauty that answered his own pain. She was broken as he was broken, as this land was broken but, thanks to him and to the others who had suffered and died for it, not destroyed. She was the bitter brew that nonetheless healed, like one of Sandy's mixtures, the homeopathic drop of poison that cured, the tainted land that still fed life. He brought the sun to her, the dying, weakening, wounded sun that consumes itself as it gives light, as he had brought to the land his own life-sustaining willingness to give himself away. And so he received back the bittersweet gift of the land, and rained.

o o o

The sound of distant waves woke Bird in the morning. His bed was a pallet on a wood floor, covered with old blankets. Sun poured through a window. When he turned his head, he could glimpse the ocean. He yawned and stretched, feeling surprisingly good, or maybe not surprisingly. He had much to feel good about. His body had been fed, in every way, and he could reasonably look forward to being fed again. And they had done it—they had really and truly escaped. This was the first morning in nearly a decade when he could wake up without anticipating the likelihood of his own death before nightfall.

The door opened and Rhea entered, bearing a tray and two steaming cups of tea. Bird turned and smiled up at her. In the daylight, he could see her more clearly. She was no monster, only a woman with a cleft palate and a hesitant look in her eye, as if she expected him to turn away at the sight of her.

"Good morning," he said. "I feel good this morning. It's good to be here."

She sat down next to him in a graceful motion, balancing the tray so as not to spill the drinks. He took his cup and cradled it in his hands.

"Thanks," he said.

She gave him a long searching look, as if questioning what he was really feeling. He looked steadily into her eyes.

"Well," she said at last. "You're an unusual man. You still like me in the morning."

"I like you," Bird said. "You're very powerful and very beautiful."

"Now you tell lies."

"I wouldn't insult you by thinking I *could* lie to you. You'd see right through me. I've been so hungry for that. I wanted you the moment I saw you."

"The *first* moment?"

"Well, maybe not the first moment," Bird admitted. He waited, then grinned at her. "But after you put the gun down."

She looked slightly confused.

"That's a joke," Bird said.

"Oh."

"Never mind."

"Will you stay here, then? And be our teacher?"

"I can't, Rhea. I've got to go home. I've got to find my family—if they're still alive. I've been away from them for ten years."

"But you will stay for a while? Until you are stronger?"

"Sure."

"We need a teacher here. We need a healer. You could help us."

"I wish I could help you. I'll do what I can. But I've got to go home. You can understand that, can't you?"

"I understand. But I lay a *geis* on you—to come back. Or send us someone who can teach us."

She put her hands on his shoulders. He felt something settle on him, like a weight. I don't want it! he wanted to cry, but he held himself silent, and opened, and took it in. To carry a burden was to be alive.

"I accept," he said. "If I make it home, I'll be back. Or someone will."

"We must work together," Rhea said. "All of us, North and South and Center. We will work together, and we will survive."

He stayed, luxuriating in rest and food and a sense of refuge. Their food was simple but to Bird it seemed wonderful just to eat when he was hungry, to chew real vegetables and real bread instead of the slimy pastes of the prison. He and Littlejohn spent days lying out on the beach, shaded under a muslin tarp from the harsh sun but able to drink in its healing warmth. They were warned not to go into the water; people who did emerged with strange rashes and sometimes lost their hair. But they could watch the waves, and the light dancing on its surface, and be soothed by its rhythmic sounds. Bird was tired, more tired than he wanted to admit. His mind was pushing him on toward home, but his body nestled into the sand and refused to move. After the first morning, he gave up trying to fight it.

Littlejohn had moved in with Morton. Bird remained at Rhea's house. They lay next to each other in the long afternoons, in a silence edged with tension.

By the third day, Bird began to feel his energy returning. He sat up as the sun dipped into the water, laying a track of liquid gold at his feet. He wished he could walk that track to go home. And someday he would.

"Another day or two, and I think I'll be ready to push on," he said to Littlejohn. "How about you?"

Littlejohn shook his head. "I'm not going with you. I'm staying here."

"Why?" Bird asked, although he was not, in his heart, surprised.

"You never told me your name."

Bird had no answer. He couldn't even honestly say he was sorry. "Littlejohn, no matter what they say, this place can't be healthy to live in. I'm telling you, you'd be welcome at my home."

"I'm welcome here. And I am here."

"I can't argue with that."

"It's okay, Bird. You don't owe me anything."

"My life."

Littlejohn shrugged. "I owe you mine about five times over. Call it even, and quit while we're ahead, okay?"

"I'll miss you," Bird said.

"You'll know where I am. Maybe you'll be back."

o o o

That night Bird was eating a late dinner with Rhea when they heard a knock on the door. When Rhea opened it, two men walked in. One had brown skin and sandy blond hair, and the other was lighter of skin but with dark coiled African hair like Bird's. They both had the wiry look of those who survived on short rations, and although they seemed young, maybe in their mid-twenties, their faces were deeply wrinkled, like those of old men. Rhea let them in, and they came and sat at the table with Bird, nodding hello. Rhea offered them food, but they declined.

"Water will do us fine, if you've got it," the light-haired man said.

They sat and looked Bird over, closely. He looked back at them, wondering what was strange about them. Finally he realized: nothing. Aside from their wizened faces, they seemed completely sound. What were they doing with the Monsters? They reminded him of Hijohn. Bird wondered how he was getting along, if he'd found his friends and the way back to the precarious safety of his hills.

"You're the Witch from the North," the light-haired one said, finally.

Bird nodded.

The man stuck out his hand. "My name's John. Johnny Appleseed, you can call me. Apple, for short. This here's my friend John."

"Johnnycake," he said.

Bird suppressed a smile and told them who he was.

"I think maybe I know a friend of yours," he said. "A man named Hijohn."

They glanced sharply at each other.

"Where'd you meet him?"

"In prison." Bird told them the story.

"So you left him in the hills south of the dunes?"

"Five, maybe six days ago."

They exchanged glances. "That's good to know."

They fell silent while Bird finished his dinner. Rhea came back in with four glasses of water. The two men held theirs reverently for a moment, as if speaking a silent prayer.

They drank slowly and then stood up. "What kind of shape are you in?" Apple asked. "You up for a walk?"

"Sure," Bird said. "Why?"

"We've got some things to show you," Apple said. "Over the mountain."

o o o

They hiked up into the hills, following snaky trails and overgrown dirt roads. Bird's leg hurt, but he told himself it didn't and almost believed it. They seemed to climb up and up endlessly. Twilight had faded to dark, but the two men found their way by scent and touch and starlight, with Bird stumbling behind.

At last they halted below the crest of a hill. Sliding on their bellies for cover, they inched their way over to the edge of the ridge and peered out. Below them, they could see the whole valley that divided the Irish Hills from the Santa Lucias in the north. As they watched, the waning moon rose, spilling silver over a gridlike pattern of lights. Vehicles moved on the roadways, and searchlights rotated to train their glare on the hills.

"There it is," Johnnycake said. "Slo Valley."

"All of that's military," Apple said. "Troops, weapons, transport. Take a good look."

Bird looked. He didn't know how to make sense of what he saw, unless they were planning some major assault. Otherwise why mass so many troops and so much equipment together? And what was there to assault but the North?

After a few moments, he felt Johnnycake's hand on his shoulder, urging him back. They crept down into a ravine and sheltered under a scrub oak. Probably in a stand of poison oak, Bird thought. Maybe he could learn to change his body chemistry to resist the stuff.

"So now you see what we're up against," Apple said. "You see why we need someone like you."

"Who's us?" Bird asked. "Who are you?"

"We're the Web," Apple said.

"Like—the Resistance?" Bird asked.

"You're a Witch from the North. You see much of Angel City when you were down there in the Pit?"

"Just the inside of a cellblock," Bird said.

"It's dry down there, man. Dry. Rains maybe two, three weeks out of the year. And the Corporation owns all the water."

"Which corporation?" Bird asked.

"Does it matter? They've merged and remerged and taken each other over so many times they're really all the same thing. They own Angel City, pretty much. Own all the farmlands, all the seeds, all the farm equipment."

"They own the Millennialist preachers and the vid networks," Johnnycake said. "They own the Stewards and the government—what's left of it."

"And like I said, they own the water," Apple added.

"Charge heavy for it, too," Johnnycake said.

"You can tell the rich parts of town from twenty miles away. They're green. Everywhere else is brown, dead, thirsty."

"We've got Circles there," Johnnycake said. "We've got Circles everywhere. Down in the valley and hidden away in the hills. And they're thirsty. And sick."

"The Stewards control the antidotes. And the immunobooster drugs."

"Antidotes?"

"You had epidemics up north?" Apple asked.

"Yeah."

"Some are natural. Some ain't."

"There's plenty people don't like the Stewards, don't believe the Millennialists' bullshit," Johnnycake said. "There's plenty that would come to us, that *do* come to us."

"But they die," Apple said. "Without the boosters, they mostly die. That's why we need you. We need a healer."

"I'm not a healer," Bird said. "I'm a musician. Or I was, once."

"If you're not a healer, you're the closest thing to it we've seen," Apple said. "Littlejohn's told us about you. And you need us. We know you want to get back to your people; we can understand that. But think about what you seen tonight. Where do you think that army is planning to march to?"

"You need us," Johnnycake repeated. "You need us to be taking care of business down here. We need to work together."

"But why?" Bird asked. "Why invade us now, when they've left us alone for twenty years?"

"How much do you know about the history of the Southlands in those twenty years?" Apple asked.

"Not much," Bird admitted.

"You know that after the Hunger that began in the drought of '25, and the Collapse in '28, the Stewards' party declared martial law and suspended elections."

"That was when we threw them out, up north," Bird said.

"Well, down here it wasn't so easy. The Millennialists had a huge following, and they backed the Stewards. Anyway, they took power, and one of the first things they did was the Expulsion of Foreign Interests Act, in '29. See, one of the main Millennialist campaigns was against the Euros and Arabs and Asians and other foreign investors who they thought owned too much of the country. So they passed a law confiscating the property of all those who weren't born citizens and deported a lot of them.

"You can imagine that didn't go down too well. In Panasia, particularly. They nearly declared war, but they settled on a trade embargo, thinking that would bring us to our knees. It nearly did. Our economy is a wreck. We survive by scavenging parts of old machines and patching them back together."

"We do a lot of that too," Bird said. "But we've created some new technologies in the last twenty years. We do things with crystals that are hard to believe, and we've made some great advances in wind and solar power."

"We haven't done shit, except carry on so the rich can still believe they're rich and powerful. But even that is slowly crumbling away. We can't make new parts, for computers or vidsets or anything, only cannibalize old ones. Now we're running out. It used to be any poor asshole could afford a vidset to plug into; then it got to cost more and more: a month's pay, two months', six months'. This year, you can't buy one at any price. Things are desperate."

"So Waggoner, he's the head of the Stewards' party, he sent a diplomat to talk to the Panasians. And it seems they're willing to trade with us again, if we acknowledge our debt for the confiscations. But the thing is, what do we have that they want? Like I said, we don't manufacture much. We used to export a lot of vidfilms and widescreens and audiodiscs, but since the Millennialists 'cleaned up' the industry, there's nothing much anyone would want to watch. We sell some drugs, and there's a good trade in porn, but strictly black market. But there is something Panasia wants bad, always has."

"What?"

"Wood. That's where you come in, with the northern forests and the Golden Gate as a harbor to ship from."

"Never," Bird said. "We give years of our lives to those trees, planting them with our own hands. We'll die before we let them be cut down and shipped away."

"You may do that very thing," Apple said. "Think about what you saw down there. The Southlands may not be an economic power, but the Stewards can still mobilize the biggest military machine left on this end of the planet. All they lack is aircraft."

"So you don't think they'll bomb us?"

"They would if they could, but nobody has that level of technology anymore. And they won't need to. Easier to let a few bugs loose, pump up their army with the antidotes, move in, and mop up. Who's gonna stop them?"

"We might stop them," Johnnycake said. "An uprising down in the Southlands could stop them. That's why we need someone like you."

"I need to go home," Bird said. He repeated it to himself, like a mantra. Home, take me home. If what they said was true, and he believed it was, then more than ever he had to go back and warn the North. "I need to go home. But I will come back. Maybe with someone better than me at healing. I will come back. And we will work together."

"You'll need our help to get home," Johnnycake said. "There's no other way around Morro Bay. And we'll help you."

"But don't be too long coming back," Apple said. "You wait too long, and it'll be too late."

o o o

Rhea gave him a small pack stuffed with dried meat, cheese, and fruit, with a rolled blanket tied on. He said goodbye to her and to Littlejohn, and then Apple and Johnnycake put him aboard a smuggler's boat to take him up past Morro Bay. The captain was a woman who called herself Isis. Her skin was the color of blackstrap molasses, her nails were painted silver and red, her hair was plaited with hundreds of gold beads, and every single muscle on her body was sculpted and separately defined. Bird found her awesomely beautiful but Rhea had warned him that she didn't like men much, and this seemed to be true; she ignored him completely once he was safely stowed aboard. The ship was a strange pastiche of sails and a jerry-rigged engine powered by solar panels that leaned at crazy angles off the deck and masts. But Isis guided it skillfully past the old navy radar, which worked only sporadically, and left him at the old San Simeon pier.

He walked on through the rest of the night, following the old Coast Road north. As daylight approached, he hid and slept. The next day, he headed up into the mountainous country of Big Sur. After a few hours, the Coast Road disappeared, long ago crumbled into the sea. He picked his way north, following old trails or streams, eating berries and the dried meat and fruit from his pack.

o o o

Until his imprisonment, Bird had never thought much about his body except to appreciate its strength, its swift grace, its unending capacities for pleasure. He had never imagined that his body might be unequal to any challenge he gave it.

Now pain became the constant factor that permeated every move, every moment of time, the sharp counterpoint that in some odd way intensified the beauty of the rugged country. The shape of the ridges etched themselves in his aching ligaments and strained muscles. One sort of pain arose from the effort of pulling his body groaning and sweating up the long climbs, and another sort of pain was evoked by the stresses on his thighs and knees as he tried to brake his momentum on the long downhill stretches.

He kept heading north. Sometimes he toiled over the outflung arms of the mountains, catching glimpses of the ocean far over the green peaks. Much of the time he followed streams and rivers, making his way from rock to rock, crossing and crisscrossing, steadying himself with his walking stick or sliding and falling, wetting his ankles and banging his knees. Walking was harder by the rivers, but often he could find no trails and at least the streams offered him water. When the sun was hot on the ridges he sweated water as fast as he could drink it, and the small bottle he had brought from Avalon didn't hold enough to keep him from thirst.

His progress was slow, a matter of carrying on until he reached the end of endurance, then pushing on some more, ten more steps, twenty. Or pausing, finally, giving himself the space of ten breaths to rest, then pushing on before he was ready because if he waited to feel ready he might never move again. He tried every magical trick he knew to heal, to bind the pain, to distract himself, to focus on the iridescent green of the sycamore leaves, or the slightly tipsy flight of the soaring vultures. In the end, he just had to keep on, putting one foot in front of the other, pumping breath in and out of his lungs.

The mountains were thickly forested; only rarely did the trees thin out and reveal a long vista or a far-off view. Stands of giant redwoods gave way to groves of live oak, bay laurel, and madrone. In the underbrush, thickets of blackberries were interlaced with poison oak. His hands and arms bubbled and blistered and itched, but he ate the blackberries after the food in his pack gave out and carried on, stumbling on river stones that etched bruises onto his feet, missing leaps he once could have taken easily, falling and pulling himself back up again, bruised and sore. He slept wrapped up in his blanket, taking shelter under the trees from the searching winds that came up from the ocean.

He had lost track of how many days he had been traveling: maybe a week, maybe more. He made his way down a river so deep that he had to wade in up to his waist to cross. The cold numbed the ache in his muscles.

From the left bank, an odor rose that was somehow familiar, that reminded him of something. He sniffed again. What was it? Then he looked toward the bank and saw a series of crescent-shaped pools marked off from the stream with stones. He went over and touched the water. It was warm. Hot. Hot springs, he thought, and recognized the smell as sulfur. Suddenly he knew where he was. There was only one place in the interior of the mountains where the water seeped naturally hot up from the earth. He had been there, in the good years, backpacking with Madrone and the others.

Stripping off his clothes, he climbed into a pool where water trickled into a hollow bowl of rock. The bottom of the pool was slippery with green and black algae, and he slid down, resting his head on the edge, letting the heat soothe his legs. He closed his eyes and let the pain in his bones drain away.

He rested for a long while, his body melting into the rocks and the water, until finally he opened his eyes and became aware of his surroundings. First he noticed that the springs were well maintained; the rock walls that contained the pools were freshly repaired and patched with cement. In the branches of the madrone that overlooked the pool hung offerings: bright ribbons, cloth dolls, feathers, clay images of the Goddess with big hips and breasts and bellies and round eyes, images of the God, the stag with the sun between his horns, locks of hair tied with colored threads, stumps of wax from candles, dead flowers. He felt protected, welcomed, and he drifted into a healing trance.

When he awoke, the skin on his fingertips had shriveled and he knew it was time to get out. He climbed down and waded into the river, letting the icy shock of the cold water wake him and run through him. His body felt almost good.

It occurred to him that since this place was obviously visited and used, the trail must be maintained. As he remembered it, the Coast Road was twelve miles away, an easy day's walk for him once and still a distance he could cover in two days, if not one. And where there was a well-used trail, there would be people, friendly from the look of things, who might feed him and shelter him and help him out.

Maybe he was near the end of his road.

7

Really, Maya thought between breaths, when you came right down to it Madrone was as bad as the rest of them. Maya placed her left foot on the next step, paused for a moment, and then pulled herself up. She was old, but she refused to feel decrepit. I'm not in bad shape, she thought, it's just on the steps. Of course, it would be her luck to live out the end of her days in a house that rose up three stories above the basement, and where they had placed the kitchen on the second floor to catch the light. She shifted the basket of greens to her opposite arm. We should have put in an elevator when we were younger and rich. But no, that would have been indulgent. Wasteful of energy. Politically incorrect.

Laboriously, she hauled herself up another few steps. Thank Goddess we at least had sense enough to put in a dishwasher. And the compost toilets. Well, they were correct enough—and years ahead of everyone else.

But it was Madrone she was thinking about. Stop, rest, breathe, continue. Just like backpacking. Climbing the flanks of some mountain, looking for visions. Or trouble. Three long breaths, then renewed effort. That was the way to do it.

The girl was just plain worn out. And that wasn't a figure of speech, she feared. Worn out like a pair of blue jeans rubbed so thin between the thighs and patched so much on the knees that there was no way to fix them anymore. Used up. Ready to be discarded. Lying in bed for nearly a month now and still insisting, every time anyone asked, that she was fine, just fine, only needing sleep. . . .

Gratefully, Maya reached the door that led into the upstairs kitchen. She opened it and emptied her basket into the vegetable sink. After all these years, she was still pleased by the fact that her kitchen had two separate sinks, one for cooking, one for cleanup. She looked around the room with satisfaction. She could almost see the ghosts at the big round table in the center, Johanna expounding some educational theory, Rio stuffing cereal into a baby's mouth, Alix rolling out a pastry, and Ben cooking some elaborate Szechwan concoction. Which was the baby who would only stop crying when they all sang rounds in three-part harmony? And wasn't it Brigid who always wanted the silly one—how did it go?

My mama makes counterfeit whiskey,
My daddy makes counterfeit gin,
My sister makes love for ten dollars,
My God how the money rolls in!

That was an old song even then, because certainly back in the nineties, when Brigid was a child, ten dollars wouldn't have bought even the most down-and-out hooker. Why, she remembered walking down Haight Street when she was—what? Seventeen? Back in the sixties, and men would cruise by in cars and offer her twenty, even back then. She had been righteously insulted, of course. She did it for free or not at all.

Rolls in, rolls in,
My God how the money rolls in, rolls in . . .

She was humming aloud as she washed the vegetables, chopped up an onion, and set it to simmer in a soup pot full of water. What was the tune from originally? Some of that tomato sauce would go good in the soup, and she would make Madrone eat. "My Bonnie Lies Over the Ocean." That was it.

Bring back, bring back,
Oh, bring back my bonnie to me. . . .

My bonnie. My Johanna. My Rio. My Brigid. My Bird.

Stop it, she told herself. The truth is—then she laughed, remembering how Johanna used to tease her about that verbal habit.

"And just what is the truth?" Johanna used to say. "Tell us, O wise woman, what the truth is." That was because, after Maya's books became known, Johanna used to worry that she'd get above herself.

But the truth was—and shut up, Johanna, she said to the air—she was worried sick. *There* was an expression for you. That was all they needed, for her to get sick.

She chopped carrots and zucchini and celery and squash. The zucchini were overproducing as they always did, practically shouting at you as you walked by, "Here, eat. Please. No, take, there's plenty more. It's good for you."

Take, eat. This is my body, this is my blood. Jesus as Jewish mother—why had she never thought of that connection before? She would have to discuss it with Sister Marie.

Generations of her own Jewish mothers hung around the room as she cooked, perched precariously on light fixtures and window frames. Maya could hear them, scolding her. "Look how skinny the girl is. No wonder she collapsed." "Why didn't you feed her?" "Didn't you ever tell her to slow down, get some rest?"

"But she wouldn't listen to me," Maya said to them. "Now go away, you old bats."

But the truth is, she thought, I do feel responsible. I let her take care of me; I should have taken care of her. I'm a spoiled old woman, and she's too good for her own good. How does a child of Rio's line turn out to be practically a saint? Although come to think of it, maybe she simply inherited his taste for martyrdom.

I'm not responsible for her, she said, partly to herself, partly to the ghosts at the table, Rio and Johanna, who gazed at her with eyes that neither blamed nor absolved. She saw them, not as the old woman and man they had grown to be, but more like they were in their early forties, mature but still vigorous: Johanna dressed in that blue suit she always wore when she needed to address some board or committee and look respectable, Rio in his work clothes with dirt on his hands. Madrone's a grown woman. But I feel responsible, Maya admitted. Somehow she had failed, failed Johanna and Rio, failed herself. Madrone was the last—what was the word? Scion. Or did that only mean boys? The last scion of their triad—barring Bird, who could scarcely be counted on. And Maya should have looked after her better.

"Don't be a fool, old woman," Johanna said, but Maya brushed her away and persisted. Because if Madrone died, who was left? If Madrone herself could not survive, how could they expect that anyone would? Let alone the city, a green island in a toxic sea.

Maya put the kettle on. She would make tea, take some to Madrone, and leave some to placate the spirits. They preferred coffee, but that was just too bad. No one'd had coffee since the Uprising twenty years ago.

"It's not a failure of nurture I'm talking about," she said, sitting down at the table with the spirits of the dead. "It's a failure of inheritance. We've passed on a world that's impossible for the best of them to live in."

"Was it any better for us?" Rio asked.

"We made a life," Maya answered. "We used to sit in comfortable living rooms, talking about the end of the world. How the dolphins were dying in the South Atlantic or how the incidence of birth defects was rising near toxic waste dumps. Oh, I'm not saying we didn't try. All those years of organizing and marching and getting arrested for causes. We did our best. But it wasn't enough."

"There's no child in this city who goes to bed hungry," Johanna said.

"There's no living soul who doesn't have a home. That's one thing we worked for."

"And we had a few other minor victories," Rio added. "To name one, no one blew the world up in a nuclear war."

"Yet," Maya said.

"Maybe it's something connected with her having a body," Johanna said to Rio. "This sudden onset of cynicism. You know—hormones. Digestion. Shit like that."

"I'm not a cynic," Maya protested. "I admit the beauty of this city. It has a beautiful beating heart. It cares for its own, and for the stranger. Its streams run with clear water, and the trees that line its pathways bow under the weight of fruit anyone is free to pick. And yes, we had a hand in shaping it. But what does that mean if it can't survive?"

"It means it existed once," Rio said, "and so it is possible. Undeniably possible."

"But that's not enough for them, the young ones," Maya said. "They're different from us. They don't see this city as some precarious achievement, like attaining the summit of Kanchenjunga. To them, this is base camp. Just a starting point toward heights they have yet to reach. And it's home, all they know. They can't philosophize about its destruction; they just hurl themselves in front of the avalanche. What do you think Madrone is doing? How else do you account for Bird?"

"They're preservationists," Johanna said. "They have something to save. We were more arrogant. We wanted to remake the world according to our vision of what should be."

"And we did it," Rio said. "Partly."

"That's like a partly successful pregnancy," Maya said.

The kettle whistled. "Stop wallowing, girlfriend," Johanna said. "Bring us some tea and quit feeling sorry for yourself."

Maya put dried mint leaves into the Chinese pot she had bought fifty years ago on Grant Avenue. It was yellow, with a curving dragon wrapped around its side. She set cups in front of her shadowy friends.

"This is an early visitation," Maya said. "It's not even Rainreturn yet. *El Día de los Muertos* is weeks away."

"Madrone's got a wedge stuck in the gates between the worlds," Rio said. "So we took advantage. You seemed so lonely."

"I am lonely. Why shouldn't I be? You're dead. Madrone's semiconscious. Everybody else is gone."

"Strike up the sad violins," Johanna said. "Why don't you feed my granddaughter, pull her back from the edge?"

"How do I do that?"

"Surely you must have learned something in your overlong life that can help her choose."

"Choose what?"

"Whether to live or die."

∘ ∘ ∘

Maya fixed a tray for Madrone. She spooned soup into a porcelain Japanese bowl and set out toast and butter and napkins and a rose from the garden in the little Limoges vase she had bought many years ago on a trip to France. Maybe the little luxuries of life could seduce Madrone back. Or maybe Prince Charles and Lady Di could do it, their faces staring solemnly out from the surface of the bed tray.

Madrone lay in Nita's big four-poster bed. They had moved her down to the same floor as the kitchen, so Maya wouldn't have to climb so many stairs. Maya set down her carefully balanced tray. Madrone's eyes were closed; she was either asleep or determined to appear so. Where is she wandering? Maya wondered. What strange dimension between the worlds? She looks so small, like an ant carrying a burden too heavy for her. And I ache to share it, Maya thought, but I can't. For one thing, she won't let me, and for another, she's grown beyond the stage where she can hand her burdens over to the older ones. I'm part of her burden now. And Maya suddenly wished she were light, a husk of herself, easier to carry.

Or maybe I'm too much husk already, all shell, no meat. Maybe that's why I'm not reaching her. I hold out a cartoon of myself, old and crotchety and faintly amusing, mothering her and badgering her. But that role, too, is just another of the disguises we all cling to, posturing and scrabbling and marshaling our achievements so as not to have to look into reality's raw heart and see the wheels of the universe grinding down into dust. I know that, even if I can't seem to stop doing it. I knew it at seventeen, on one too many hits of that pure 1960's Owsley LSD. Far too young. I would have gone crazy for sure if Johanna hadn't come to me in the locker room and cupped her hand around my naked breast and saved me with the one thing that could cross the abyss. Touch. The touch of the heart. How can I bring that to Madrone?

∘ ∘ ∘

Madrone opened her eyes and looked up at the canopy embroidered with moons and stars. They made dancing patterns, networks of light in colors impossible to translate, that merged with the crystal webs behind her eyes. She wanted to stay where pain and weariness and emotion were only twists in the kaleidoscope of light. Her work was here, on this plane, now. The spirit knife in her hand allowed her to change the patterns, stirring them up to fall in new designs. Changing lives, changing fate. Easy.

She felt Maya's presence intrude on her peacefulness. The older woman's worry and fear burst around her like fireworks, exploding from a center to rain colored stars. Madrone watched the lights dance with detached fascination. It was so unnecessary, if Maya could only understand.

"Sit up," Maya said. "It's time you ate something."

Madrone didn't really want to eat; food took her away from the patterns. But the force of Maya's determination gripped her and propped her up. Arguing would be even more of a distraction, and while she was distracted, people would die. Maybe that didn't matter, really, but then that was why she had the knife, to fight off death. She couldn't put it down. Bright sun was streaming in through the big bay windows. Nita had hung crystals on the glass, and the sunlight made rainbows dance around the room. Rainbows of light, like in the web world, and when Madrone closed her eyes she could still see them, feed on them. They were better than bread.

Maya opened a window and hung out a card on a string.

"What's that?" Speaking was a great effort. Madrone could see the words as she could see her own breath on a cold day. They wove a pattern of color and then dissolved.

"A sign announcing your unchanged condition. Just as if you were the Queen of England. Saves me running up and down stairs five times a day."

"I'm sorry," Madrone whispered. She was sorry that Maya couldn't understand the lack of need for her fear. She was sorry that the colors around Maya's body were so disturbing she couldn't help but will the old woman away.

"Hmph." Maya snorted. "You're not sorry. If you were, you'd pull out of this half-astral state, get some food in you, and stop doing whatever it is you're doing." You would let me in, you would return to human form.

"I'm not doing anything."

"You lie. I can't see exactly what it is, but I see you doing something. Half the city has nominated you for sainthood. They leave offerings on the front steps, burn candles. Sick women claim they dream of you and wake up healed. Mothers about to give birth see your face and their wombs open. Meanwhile, you lie here, going into a decline in the worst Victorian manner."

"I'm just having . . . conversations. Really, I'm fine."

"If you say that to me one more time, I will personally slit your throat."

Madrone closed her eyes again. She wished Maya would just go away and leave her alone. Maybe if she drifted back to sleep. . . .

"Don't go back to sleep on me now, young lady. I'm talking to you. And besides, you need to eat something."

"I'm not hungry."

"The hell you're not. Eat your soup." But this isn't how I want to be with her, Maya thought. She is fading away, dying, and I can't break through. I can't reach her with my anger or my love.

Madrone obeyed, sipping the soup in grim and determined silence. Food was an anchor, chaining her back to the world. Lightly, and only for a short time. The energy the soup brought her was a pattern as hunger was a pattern as each disease was a pattern as life was one and death was another and they were all, each of them, so beautiful and complete in themselves that it took enormous will to choose one over another.

She had that will, but it was flagging. And maybe that was okay.

"It's okay to die," she said to Maya, setting down her spoon. She said it to make the fireworks stop, but it had the opposite effect, setting them whirling and bursting around her.

This is my karma, my *suerte,* Maya thought. I should have been nicer to my own mother, should have understood why she didn't want me taking drugs and sleeping with strange men.

"No," Maya said, and burst into tears. They were great spheres of light dropping from her eyes, opening into fields of white on white, like snow falling on a glacier. "Please eat. Eat something. One more bite."

"But the snow is so beautiful," Madrone said.

"But the snow is cold, baby." Maya had no idea what she was talking about, but she reached forward anyway to clasp Madrone's hand. Her hand was cold; it felt like one of the flexible ice packs they used to keep in the freezer for Alix to lie on when her back gave out. "Where you are is so cold."

The touch of the heart, Maya thought. If Madrone could feel that, it could save her. And if not, there was truly nothing Maya could do except to let her go. Losing and finding and losing again. Loosing her.

Cold was a pattern too, like a pinwheel of lace spinning in her back. And suddenly, Madrone wanted to reach for the warmth of Maya's hand. Maya's touch was a glow of fire that shattered the ice crystals around her. It was a living pattern of its own that throbbed with a red-blood beauty, beating like a heart. She could feel Maya's pulse. Her own blood sang weakly in her body as it moved and traveled the web of her veins.

"I'm cold," Madrone said. "I'm so cold." She wanted to be warm again, and human, wanted to taste hot soup and walk on two feet over the dry autumn grass. But that isn't for me anymore, she thought. In letting it go she could save it for others and stay here, in the cold place between the worlds. Yet even here, Maya's terrible pain pierced her.

"Eat," Maya said. "The soup is hot. It'll warm you." She sat on the bed beside Madrone and slid her arm behind her shoulders, cradling her.

But soup was not what she wanted. Maya's arms held her like chains, dragging her back to the heaviness of form. And what she wanted was the warmth of light, the burning, flesh-dissolving white heat, the center of the flame.

Maya's arms clasped her like twined serpents. "How dare you?" Maya said. "How dare you believe there is nothing more for you in life?"

But that's not what I believe, Madrone thought weakly. The serpents tightened their grip. She only wanted to shed her skin, to break free.

"I don't want soup," Madrone said. "I want—"

"I know," Maya said. "You want what we all want, the breakthrough, the total dissolution of boundaries and separations, enlightenment by the great straight upward path. And I am so angry at you!"

"I took the knife of Cihuacoatl," Madrone said, so softly that Maya had to lean close to hear her. "But I can't cut the cord. I can only make designs."

Maya had no doubt that Madrone made perfect sense to herself. "You had a vision?" she asked.

Madrone nodded her head, slowly, and then squeezed her eyes tight, as if the motion had pained her.

"And now," Maya said, "you're trying to refuse it."

"No," Madrone whispered, "I'm trying to carry it. But it's heavy."

"You would prefer, maybe, a lightweight vision?"

"This is how I'm carrying it."

"Bullshit! This is how you are trying to drop it like a hot potato. You're running so hard from it you're running straight out of life. I'm so disappointed in you! I thought Rio's granddaughter would have more guts, and Johanna's granddaughter would have more sense."

"I have guts."

"Then turn around. Oh, I see exactly where you are, Madrone. You're a long, long way down a long, long road, and at the end is that beautiful beckoning light. And it seems so easy—no, not just easy but right, and dramatically perfect, to leap right through the center of it. I know. I've been there. And behind you is nothing but the shit that's heavy to carry."

"What are you talking about?" Madrone whispered, because now Maya had her confused, and the lights were spinning and swirling in a way that hurt her eyes.

"I'm talking about that sweet seductive white light. We all face it, sooner or later, in some form. For Bird, it was a bad dream urging him south. For Rio it was alcohol and revolution. For me it was—oh, I don't know—I think more like it is for you. The seduction of my own great importance. You are so much like me, *ahijada*. But what good does it do? I can't give you my life. I can't give you your life."

Madrone could feel Maya crying behind her, draped across her back. Her tears fell like stones, as her words were stones, each one weighing Madrone down, making her heavier, more solid. "And is that what you want from me?" She addressed Snake Woman, who stood beside her. "To turn back?" Because now it seemed to her that she was indeed on a road, and the way forward into the light was clear and smooth, and behind her everything was dense and loud and heavy "What does it mean to be your instrument?"

"Turn and see," something whispered.

For the first time since she had opened her hand to take the knife of the Goddess, she felt fear. Because, yes, she wanted to turn, turn toward the warmth and the heat and the solid opacity of flesh. But she was so far down the road, and the way back was strewn with so many burdens to bear. Maybe she didn't have the strength. She was so tired. Maybe it was already too late.

Slowly, pushing through air dense as stone, she turned. Gravity gripped her arms, pulling her down. She thought her knees would buckle under the strain, but she steadied herself, as she used to on the first day of a long trek into the mountains, tightening the belt on a heavy pack.

The first of her burdens confronted her: a weeping old woman. Okay, Cihuacoatl, you sharp-toothed Snake Hag, Madrone said silently. If this is what you want from me, I'll see what I can do.

She turned in the bed to embrace Maya, letting her own arms clutch the old woman's bony shoulders and cradle her head. "Don't cry, *abuelita,* don't cry. It's okay. I won't die on you."

Maya continued to cry, but now with relief at hearing Madrone sound like herself again.

So now I have Maya to carry, Madrone thought, and all the ones still sick in the city, the hospital where I haven't been now for how long? Burdens, expectations: they sat heavy on her shoulders, pressing her back into her body. Just for a moment she longed to go somewhere where nobody knew her, where no one would expect miracles or be disappointed by her limitations. But she was here now, with her arms full and candles burning in front of her door.

"It's okay," she said again, to Maya. "It's really going to be all right."

Now I have become the child, Maya thought. This is what it means to grow old. I play at nagging, nurturing, feeding. But in the end, the young must comfort me.

8

Bird had so often reconstructed the city in his mind that to move along its pathways in the flesh left him feeling translucent, as if he were actually walking around inside his head. He had prayed for this moment, but now that he was here he felt a cold sense of dread. The city looked relatively unchanged. Somewhat emptier. The rows of old Victorians still stood ankle deep in beds of squash and soybeans and cherry tomatoes. Brooks and streamlets still meandered by, feeding the verdant gardens. Fruit trees he remembered as saplings now arched and stretched, fully mature and heavily laden. As he rounded the corner to his own block, he could see children, real children, weeding the garden and playing on the path. He found himself shaking. He had wondered, sometimes, if there would be any children left.

His leg had started acting up in the last hike to the coast. He'd had to stop and wait when it went into spasm and wouldn't hold him. He stopped for a moment now, balancing precariously, breathing deeply, letting go. He would know, soon enough, who had lived and who had died.

The doorway of Black Dragon House looked like an altar to the dead, or perhaps the shrine of a saint. From a second-story window hung a placard that read STILL IMPROVING. He stared at it for a long moment, wondering what it meant. Was it an affirmation, a political stance? He shook his head, confused. The stairs that led up to the front door were covered with votive candles, bunches of flowers in glass jars, plates of fruit, and baskets of bread. Only a narrow path was left for walking, and he looked at it in dismay, not sure if his unsteady legs could carry him up. Clearly somebody had died, and he willed himself not to ask who but to turn to the narrow side door that led through the passage beside the basement to the back yard. It was unlocked, and he let himself in, closing it behind him.

In a pool of shade on the patch of grass next to the herb garden, someone lay sleeping. Yes, Bird thought, as he set down his knapsack and knelt beside the still form, yes, it was Madrone. He could hardly bear to breathe. She was alive.

She was beautiful in her sleep, her hair sprawling on the grass, her skin ruddy as true madrone bark, her eyelids fluttering in dream. He wanted to touch her but he didn't want to wake her. She looked so tired. He could see, even in her sleep, lines of strain and weariness. She looked thinner than he remembered, and when he looked closely he could see a pallor under the bronze of her cheeks. But she was real, she lived. He would have to learn to believe it, to believe that he lived too.

Madrone woke, feeling chilled. Someone was sitting next to her. For a sleepy, automatic moment, she thought it was Sandy; then memory came back to her, aching. She opened her eyes. She had been a long way down and was slow coming back. Maybe she was getting to be like Maya, seeing ghosts—a Bird ghost, older, grayer, grimmer than the boy she remembered.

"It's really me," he said.

"Bird?"

"*El mismo*. The same."

"You're alive?"

He laughed. He was alive and he was glad, glad. "Feel me."

He held out his hand and she took it, but what she felt was not the slender, supple fingers she expected but an old man's hand, knotted with old pain. Still, it was no ghost but warm flesh.

"You broke your hand," she said.

"They broke it for me. I can't play guitar for you anymore."

She reached for him and held him close, and then she began to cry. He wanted to cry too, but he had learned not to; what he had frozen in himself wasn't ready yet to thaw. He would wait until he knew whom he was crying for.

After a while she pulled back, to look at him. His face was thinner, the skin pitted and leathery, his dark eyes staring out at her from deep, shadowed hollows. Etched in his skin, she could read lines of hunger and pain. He was no longer the beautiful boy she remembered. Tenderly, wonderingly, she reached up and touched his temple. Yes, he was real, a hauntingly familiar stranger.

"I can't believe it," she said. "*¡Estás vivo!* You're really alive. You're really here."

With her eyes open, she was still more beautiful. He wanted not to move, not to speak, just to hold this shattering happiness forever in the stillness of the moment. And yet he suspected he could let it go and still new happiness would unfold. She would continue to look at him. She would continue to exist.

"I can hardly believe it myself," he said at last. "I was afraid I'd come back and find you all were dead."

"Enough are," she said.

Now it comes, he thought, the pain, but I can bear it now.

"I saw the front steps," he said. "The candles and the *ofrendas*."

Madrone laughed. "Oh, those are for me. People seem to have developed an inflated sense of my capabilities lately. And I've been sick. But not dead."

"Who is?"

She reached out and took his hand. "Your brother."

That hurt. He let it sink down and turn itself into pain. "And?"

"Sandy is the latest."

"No."

"Yes." Her eyes were brimming with tears, and a current of comfort passed between their hands. How different it feels to mourn him together, Madrone thought. Relentlessly, she continued. "And most of the old ones. Rio."

"Maya?"

She smiled at him, grateful to offer good news. "Napping up in her bedroom."

"*¿Es verdad?*"

"No shit! *She* always said you were too mean to kill. I should have believed her. But I couldn't stand wondering what was happening to you, if you were alive. It was easier to believe you were dead. Was it bad, Bird?"

"It wasn't good."

"Will you tell me about it?"

"Yeah, in time. Not now. Tell me who else?"

She told him, then, the whole litany of the dead. They were silent. He felt a terrible mixture of loss and relief. He wanted to mourn and he wanted to laugh. He'd grieved so much already; what was left was more like a wicked sense of triumph that somebody survived.

"*Madre Tierra,*" he said. "I'm sorry about Sandy. So very sorry. And Marley, and all of them. *Lo siento, lo siento mucho.* And where are the others?"

"Sage and Nita and Holybear are up on the Delta, at their experimental ponds. They'll be back after Rainreturn."

"How are you? Are you well? You look tired."

"I'm fine. I was sick, like I said, but I'm getting better."

Something closed off in her as she spoke, and Bird suspected she was lying. She didn't look fine, she looked faded, as if she might suddenly wink out and enter some other dimension. He wanted to grab her, wrap his body around her, and shelter her.

"Are you hungry?" she asked. "There'll be soup in a little while. We should feast you. Tomatoes are ripe, and of course there's zucchini. Tofu. We could harvest some catfish from the tanks in the greenhouse. Something went wrong with one of them, but the rest are okay. I wish we had eggs, but the hens aren't laying well."

"It sounds like a feast," he said. "What happened to the chickens?"

"I don't know. The neighbors have been looking after them. It's probably something with their feed. I guess I've let a lot of things go since Sandy died."

"How's the water?"

"Holding out real well this year. You can take a bath or a long hot shower if you want." She could sit with him forever, talking about food, about water. There was so much more they would need to say, but they didn't need to say it now.

"I need a long one." He smiled. "I came the last eighty miles in the back of a chicken truck."

"I don't care." Madrone stood up and put her arms around him, reaching for his mouth with hers. She wanted to suck him in and hold him and keep him safe and alive forever.

He wanted her with an ache that was like a note vibrating all through his body, crying, Now! Here! In the dirt! To wait a quarter of an hour might mean to wait forever; the world could shift, she could suddenly disappear.

"*Te quiero,*" Bird said. "I want you."

"I know. Here and now? With the Sisters likely to look out the window?"

"Yeah. Does it seem like a bad idea?" They smiled at each other.

"We have the whole night. We have tomorrow and the night after that and the night after that. As long as we can stay alive."

"It doesn't seem possible."

"It is. It's true."

"Okay. I'll try to believe it."

"You go see your grandmother," she told him.

"Right. I should see her first. I want to see her."

"I'll round us up some food."

"Okay."

He turned to walk up the back steps, and she watched him go. He moved slowly as he climbed the stairs, as if his body hurt him. She still thought of him as a boy who ran so fast and leaped so far that he almost did fly. Suddenly she ran after him, grabbing at his ankle through the stair rails.

"Bird!"

"What is it?"

She took a long breath and laughed, then, letting go. "I just had to touch you. I was afraid I made you up in my mind. That if I didn't see you for a moment, you'd disappear."

"I know. I feel the same way. But I'm home now, and I have no intention of disappearing."

○　○　○

He knew the house was real and that he was really there, in the body, because his body hurt. His bad leg ached as he clumped awkwardly up the stairs and entered the kitchen through the back door. Odd to walk into that room and find no one there. In his memory it was always crowded with people, tea brewing, dinner cooking, arguments and laughter around the table. He continued down the hall and stood in the doorway of Maya's room.

She was nestling under her afghan, and she looked frail and old, transformed into the Crone herself. Her hair glowed white in the sunlight, and her face was a luminescent map of wrinkles. Her skin seemed transparent, as if she were already halfway to the Shining Isles. And she was speaking in a low voice to someone who wasn't there.

"It's me, *abuelita*. It's Bird."

She recognized him, without surprise but with relief, because it had been so long since he'd come to her that she had begun to fear he was irretrievably lost.

"Bird. Come in. Where have you been? Where are you now? You look remarkably substantial. I believe you actually cast a shadow. Doesn't that drain you?"

"I'm really here this time, *abuela*. Body and all."

She sat up, then, and opened her eyes wide.

"Bird!"

He came to her and she clung to him, weeping into his cropped hair. He was warm and solid and real in her arms. She could feel the beating of his heart against her heart and the pulse of his blood, blood of her blood. "Bird!" she crooned over and over again. "Bird. Bird. Bird. My baby!"

He was bent over the bed in an awkward position and finally she became aware that she was hurting him, so she let him go.

"Sit there where I can look at you," she directed him.

Maya shivered with happiness. She held herself still, as if the joy might dissolve away if she moved. He is not lost, she thought. My line, Brigid's line, is restored. For a moment, she thought she felt the presence of her daughter, brushing soft spirit lips against the nape of her neck.

Bird perched on the edge of the bed, facing her. She took his hand, rubbing and stroking and patting it. The knuckles were swollen and misshapen, clotted with old pain. She looked into his eyes, searching for traces of everything he'd thought and felt and suffered.

"When you look at me like that," he said, "I feel like you know everything. And it's okay."

"It's not okay. It's unforgivable, going off and leaving us like that. But I forgive you anyway. You're alive, and you're here, and that's what's important. Tell me about it. You were hurt."

"I recovered, more or less."

"Where were you? In prison down there?"

"Yeah."

"My poor baby. How'd you get out?"

"I escaped."

"Well, you certainly took your own sweet time about it."

"Maya! How can you say that? It's a miracle I got out at all!"

"Nonsense. What do you think we raised you for? To be a jailbird?"

"That pun is what's unforgivable."

"I'm an old lady," she said. "I can make all the puns I want. Now come here and hug me again. You smell like a barn, but I don't care."

Her arms ached to enclose him. She could see the stiff and awkward way he held his body, could feel the intimations of pain behind his eyes.

Her arms felt frail around him. Some little-boy part of him nestled down to be held. But he was the strong one now, the one who should catch her up in a tight embrace and keep her from slipping away into the whispering world of the disembodied.

Finally she let him go again. "Well, now, have you seen Madrone?"

He smiled. "She seems to want to feed me."

"She would. How are you? Do you need anything? Want anything?"

"Oh, I want to eat and sleep and fuck and wash all at the same time, and I want to tell you everything that's happened to me in the last ten years, and hear everything that's gone on here. And I just want to sit here in the sun and look at you. I can't believe I'm really home."

"It's a miracle." Maya raised her eyebrows and solemnly nodded her head. "The Old Bitch has finally come through with a genuine miracle!"

o   o   o

The upstairs bathroom had a skylight over the shower, and the light made rainbows in the water as it splashed over Bird's skin. He sang a cleansing chant as he washed himself, letting the colors and the light and the water carry away more than the physical stink, letting the despair he'd carried on his back like a dead thing dissolve and run down the drain too.

When he stepped out, finally, Madrone was waiting. She handed him a towel and he rubbed himself dry, turning away from her, feeling suddenly a little shy. The moment in the garden had passed. In this moment, he was afraid. So much time had gone by, so much had changed. He had, and she had. They were, in reality, strangers to each other. And yet so close. She was like a lost part of his history, sprung up to smile at him and look him over with eyes that saw too much. He wrapped the towel around himself, hiding.

But he couldn't hide from Madrone. She was a healer, after all, and she knew bodies. In his stance, by the way he shifted his weight or the slight awkwardness of his movements as he lifted his arm, she could trace the flow of pain, the twisted muscles and the sore ligaments, the breaks that hadn't healed right and the old wounds. The Bird she remembered had worn his body as lightly as an animal did and moved with a predator's grace. She reached for his hand.

"Come into my room," she said. "Let me give you a massage."

∘ ∘ ∘

The sun poured down onto the bed through another skylight. He lay in a pool of warmth while she worked on the knotted muscles in his lower back and the nodes of pain in his hip. Her fingers read his history.

She was afraid too. He understood that, suddenly. She was afraid, and she was keeping him at a distance by healing and feeding. Giving out, giving out, generating a power that in the very force of its giving kept him away. He rolled over on his back, looked up at her, and grabbed her hands.

"I want to look at you," he said. "I want to look into your eyes and talk to you."

She let out her breath slowly. "Yes."

"I want to say I'm sorry. *Lo siento.* Sorry I didn't make love to you one last time before I went."

She could see just a suspicion of dampness around his eyes, and she bent forward and kissed them lightly. "It would have been unbearable, knowing it was the last time. Anyway, if you recall, I was being rather a bitch, yelling at you. I'm sorry for that."

"I was so scared. I didn't want to die. I couldn't bear hearing you tell me why I shouldn't go."

"I kept trying and trying to reach you after. Did you ever feel me?"

"*Sí,* I felt you. I feel you now."

"But you were right," Madrone said. "I guess I believe now that you were right to go."

"I don't know. Right and wrong somehow don't seem to apply. I only know I had to do it."

"Do you regret it now?"

"It was so different from what I imagined. I was afraid of dying. But dying would have been over quick, and this just went on and on and on. The other three all died, you know. Sometimes I regretted surviving. But not now."

"No, not now."

He took her face in his hands and kissed her, and then the spark was back between them, the aching and the wanting. He pulled back.

"Madrone, I've been with all sorts of people, done things I can't even remember. I don't know if this is safe for you."

Her eyes seemed to lose focus as she observed the spirit colors that played around his body. "You're safe," she said.

"How can you be sure? Shouldn't I have a blood test or something?"

"A blood test only works if you know what you're looking for. I trust my psychic vision more. My wards would warn me if you were carrying a disease. I'd smell it."

She slid out of her shirt and her pants and held him. She wanted him with an intensity she had forgotten existed. He was the elusive stranger from an unfamiliar world and at the same time the most familiar, the most loved and safe and innocent part of her own past. When he touched her it was like the tracings of fire on her skin, and she wrapped her arms around him and twined her legs around his, wanting to encompass him, to take him into the dark core where everything melted and he could be made new again.

He was hard. He had been dying of thirst and she was a sweet well of water. He held himself back, taking time to touch her and stroke her, but she pushed his hand away. She wanted to be filled with him; later there would be time for all the intricacies of orgasm.

"Come into me," she whispered. "I want you there."

She guided him into her. He felt her open to him, body and mind, and he could hold nothing back.

After a while, they pulled apart. *"Lo siento,"* he whispered. "I came too fast. It wasn't very good for you."

"Don't be an asshole," she said gently. "It was wonderful. Being with you again is wonderful. And we have plenty of time." She began kissing him, starting from his forehead and his soft hair, working gently and thoroughly down, to his eyes, the bridge of his nose, lingering a long time on his lips. By the time she reached his throat, he was hard again.

This time she could feel him holding back, taking his time, remembering his practiced skill at the art of touch. She remembered his fingers as feather-light, almost fluid. Now, through the faint tremor in their tips she could feel the underlying stiffness and the pain, the pain he carried in his body and the rage at the core, so like her own. And she could feel his power, pressing against the edges of her mind, a deeper and broader stream than she had known in him before, with hard stones in the center she could sense but not feel, and deep currents that ran into chambers underground. As her own power was deeper now, forged out of sadness and pain and anger. They were not elf children anymore, and that had to be, but something delicate and sweet was gone. Pleasure and pain swirled through her, bittersweet, pooled in her hollow places, swelled, and burst forth in a flight of birds released from some tight cage into the open air. She slid down onto him, and his hard thrust inside her kept the great wings beating until, after a long time, he began to throb and moan and spill. And then she just wanted to hold him, as if he were a great bird, slowly shivering to stillness in her arms.

∘ ∘ ∘

Bird brought the rain with him. Or so it seemed. The sky began to cloud over while Maya cooked dinner. She had lit every candle in the house so that the common room blazed with fire, and set the table with her best lace cloth and the old china that had belonged to her grandmother. She prepared ratatouille and salad, soup and bread—a real feast. Sudden unexpected happiness had made her feel light. It had been a long time since they'd had a reason for celebration, and she wanted to make the most of it.

They ate slowly, savoring the food, the candlelight, their mutual presence. As they finished dinner, they heard the first drops, an unmistakable drumbeat on the roof. Madrone opened a window, and the blessed smell of damp earth rose up. It was the odor of returning life, the earth's yearly promise of renewal.

"It's an omen," Madrone said. "The rains have come."

They rushed out the front door, Madrone clearing the steps of candles and offerings so Bird wouldn't stumble. Up and down the pathways, doors were opening and people were running out to dance deliriously. Children dashed about with bowls and pots to catch the first rainwater. Next door, the Sisters knelt in the mud to give the prayer of thanksgiving. Even Maya danced, skipping, albeit somewhat stiffly, down the path to join the crowd of people streaming into the park around the corner. They caught hands and were whirled into the snake dance, the spiral, the long chain turning on itself and winding back out, like the renewal of generations, Maya always thought, passing face after face of neighbors and friends in the mad dance. It seemed to her that she could feel Rio's hand clasping hers on the left, Johanna's on the right.

Fireworks exploded and rained down in colors that mingled bright fire with the drops. Soon everyone's hair and clothes were damp and streaming, but they only laughed. The rain had come, even a bit early this year, and they welcomed it in the hope that it would return again and again through the winter, turning the brown hills green, filling the cisterns and replenishing the aquifers, feeding the life in the gardens and fields that fed the people.

They danced until they were too exhausted to dance anymore. When they left, the spiral was still winding, and the high, carrying voice of the main singer sent the words of the litany after them:

Rain is our sister, our mother,
our father, our brother,
our sweetest, most missed,
and longed-for lover.
So if you've ever loved anyone,
If you've ever missed someone
and longed to see that face

and cried for the touch of those hands,
lift your hands to the rain, now,
turn your face to the rain, now,
and feel your beloved come
in rain. . . .

9

Bird slept for three days, waking only to eat or piss. Then he got up from the bed and went to work. He needed to feel tools in his hands, to look back at a row of freshly turned earth or a new patch on a rotted piece of siding and know that his hands could still make food and shelter, if not music.

The first thing he fixed was the roof, where Sandy had been working when the virus struck him down. Bird found a pile of shingles and a hammer, right where Sandy had dropped them when the seizure hit. For a moment, he had an eerie sense that if he turned his head he'd find Sandy sitting beside him, ready to complete the task. A wave of sadness passed over him. They had been close friends and, occasionally, lovers, usually in odd moments and adventurous places. Like this one. He could imagine Sandy turning to him, a glint in his eye, and saying, "You ever tried it on the roof? No? Want to?" And then after a steamy interval, they would go back to work. And later, someone would be sure to make some remark about odd sounds coming from the roof in the middle of the day and were there tomcats prowling up there, or what?

They would have shared secrets. Or maybe not. The Sandy in his mind was still eighteen years old, as the Bird in his mind was nineteen. He'd never celebrated his twentieth birthday, on the Day of the Reaper. He'd never celebrated his twenty-ninth, or any of the ones in between. Sometimes it seemed only a few months had passed since he went away, because the intervening years were gone from his memory, a glitch in the fabric of reality. Yet so much had happened, so much had changed, that at other times he felt he had been gone for centuries.

A lot had been neglected since Sandy died. Bird fixed the wind generator and weeded the garden, planted the winter beds of greens and broccoli. The fish had died in one of the big aquaculture tanks that warmed the greenhouse with the heat stored in their water. Bird drained the tank and shoveled the stinking mass of dead fish and foliage into the compost pile.

"Thanks," Madrone said. "That tank was weighing on my mind; I just couldn't face it. But really, Bird, you don't have to do every single one of the dirtiest and nastiest jobs. I'll take care of some of that—in a few days. I just need a little more time to rest up."

They were lying in her bed, basking in the early morning sun streaming in through the skylight. He raised himself up on one elbow and let his finger trace the pattern light made on her skin. She didn't look almost well to him; she looked thin, delicate, exhausted. He wanted to hold her in his arms and shelter her, pour strength into her even though he wasn't sure where it would come from, maybe from the sheer effort he put into barricading his own body's pain.

"*No te preocupes,*" he said. "Not to worry. Even the shit in the compost toilets here smells sweet to me, now."

"At least you should go to Neighborhood Council, get back on the Boards," Madrone said. "You might as well get your work credits for all this."

"I went yesterday," Bird said.

Madrone could feel some part of him shrink back inside, withdrawing from her. She rolled over on her side, to look into his eyes.

"*¿Qué pasó?*" she asked.

"Nothing. At first they were surprised that I was still alive. Then they offered to give me back my Musician's stipend. I turned it down."

"Why?"

For an answer, he showed her his hand. She took it, kissed it tenderly and placed it against her cheek. Under the skin she could feel the stiffness, and against her closed lids she saw lines of fiery energy around the scarred joints.

"You don't know what you can do with practice yet, Bird. And acupuncture can help those joints."

"Well, when I've practiced they can give me a stipend. In the meantime I'd rather be useful than subsidized."

"Maya kept all your guitars. They're in the storeroom."

"How sentimental," Bird said. Madrone could feel his emotions close up like a sow bug rolling away from a probing finger. She sighed and didn't press him further.

There was a lot he didn't speak about. At times Madrone felt the two of them in a common glow; at other moments the glow clouded over: she heard silent rolls of thunder and waited for lightning to flash.

She sighed again, wondering why she still felt so tired, why she wasn't happier. She should be happy. True, Sandy was dead but she couldn't mourn for him forever. She had encouraged Bird to take his room and given Bird his clothes, since his own had disappeared long ago. Maybe that was a mistake. She was always catching sight of a familiar sweater on a distant figure, feeling her heart leap and then crash when the figure turned and was Bird. Well, not crash, exactly, because she couldn't look at Bird and not feel lifted, lifted like a kite dodging and dipping through joy and pain. Bird was his own miracle but he was still not-Sandy, as in a way everything in the world had become not-Sandy at his death, flat, dull, joyless.

But that wasn't fair to Bird. She loved Bird. And yet Bird in his own way was also not-Bird, not the Bird she remembered, who was clear and open as the blue spring-fed pool of her power place high in the mountains. Making love had been like falling into clear water, opening under opening, sinking to depth after glassy depth. They had had nothing to hide. But this Bird was half a stranger, who dragged around an aching body and concealed his pain, who covered secrets he wouldn't talk about under stone silence. And she held her own secrets too, and her worries.

"I'm going to go back to work tomorrow," Madrone said.

"Are you sure you're well enough?"

"I'll take it easy."

Bird snorted.

"I will. But there's still so much to be done right now, even with the epidemic on the wane. I can't lie around forever."

o o o

Madrone knew something was wrong by the quality of silence that descended on the meeting room at the hospital as she entered. The group was small that morning, just Sam and Lou and Aviva, along with Lourdes, the young midwife, and Rick, the herbalist who had taken Sandy's place. They all turned to look at her as she sank gratefully into one of the big old armchairs that furnished the healers' lounge. The short walk to the hospital had tired her more than she wanted to admit.

"What are you doing here?" Sam asked bluntly.

"I feel ready to come back to work," Madrone said.

"If I thought you meant that," Sam said, "I'd have serious questions about your professional judgment."

"Light work," Madrone said. "I thought I could ease back into it."

"Ease?" Lou said. "Madrone, love, you don't know how to ease into a lawn chair on a sunny day. Your throttle has only one setting that I've ever observed, and that's full speed ahead."

"I know you're anxious to come back to work, but you need more convalescent time." Aviva smiled at her kindly.

"We're not so shorthanded," Sam said. "The epidemic's pretty much over, never really got going. Luck was with us, on this one. So we're back to our normal level of chaos."

"But I miss work," Madrone said. "I even miss all of you."

"Good. Then when you do come back, maybe you'll appreciate us at our true value," Lou said.

"Seriously, Madrone," Sam said. "If you sent a patient in your condition back to work, I'd call it criminal neglect."

They were right. Madrone knew it, but still she fought back tears. She was so tired of being sick, tired of being tired. She wanted to be her old self again.

"Since she's here, why shouldn't she at least stay for the meeting?" Rick suggested. He was a handsome man, with warm black eyes and a curling black beard, and Madrone suspected she would like working with him.

"Sure, let her stay," Lourdes added, smiling at Madrone shyly.

She looks up to me too much, Madrone thought. It will hold her back from developing the confidence she should have. I'll have to work on that, when I'm better.

"Actually, I'd like to have your input on this discussion," Sam said. "We're back on the same old question again."

"What same old question?"

"The question of whether this last epidemic amounts to germ warfare and, if so, what we should do about it."

"Defense Council has been riding our asses," Lou said. "They think it's an attack, but they want some definitive answer from us."

"That was what it looked like to me," Madrone said. "When I *saw* it, it was like something constructed from metal and bolts and bicycle locks."

"Can you diagram it?" Aviva asked. "That might help Flore work up a computer model, figure out the morphic field equations. Because if new attacks come, they're likely to be constructed along similar lines."

"I can't diagram the molecular structure," Madrone said. "I wish I could. But that isn't how it works. The mind translates patterns of energy and *ch'i* and molecular structure into symbols, things. I could draw them, but it'd look pretty silly."

"You should sit down and talk to Flore anyway," Sam said. "What seems silly to you might make some kind of sense to her, once she runs it by the crystals in the big computer."

"I could do that," Madrone said.

"If only one of us could go down there, take a look for ourselves," Sam said. "It galls me, you know. I remember when there used to be two, three flights an hour to LA, right out of San Francisco International Airport. International, they called it, because you could hop on a plane and go anywhere: Paris, Bali, Honolulu, Detroit. Or I could have picked up the telephone and made a call to a colleague. . . ."

"It must have been wonderful to fly," Aviva said dreamily, "back when you didn't have to worry about ozone sinkholes or a freak Haravatski wind knocking the plane out of the sky. I'd love to be able to take off for anywhere in the world I wanted to go."

"We're losing our focus," Lou said. "It's not 1998 anymore, it's 2048. Unless you and Sam sprout wings, we can't fly. We can't even walk into the

Southlands and hope to come back alive. I don't think anyone's visited there in twenty years and lived to tell the tale."

"That's not true," Madrone said. "Bird was down there for almost ten years. And now he's back."

"Bird?" Lou asked.

"Maya's grandson. My *compa* from long ago. He came back two weeks ago."

"Madrone, that's wonderful news!" Aviva said.

"Does he have any information about the diseases?" Sam asked. "Have you talked to him about them?"

Madrone shook her head. "He drops hints, but he won't say much about it."

"Would he come talk to us?" Sam asked.

"I'm sure he would. In fact, that would be one way to get him to come see you. He had some injuries that weren't treated and didn't heal right. But every time I suggest a consultation, he blows up at me."

"Well, it's bound to be a hard transition for him," Sam said. "Give him time. Maybe I should just wander by your house some evening, call on Maya."

"You're a dirty old man, Sam," Lou said.

Sam waved the comment aside. "There's another matter I want to take up with you, Madrone."

"What's that?"

"I want to know what the hell happened to you."

Madrone sighed and shifted in her chair, wondering where to begin. Yes, they were right, she wasn't well yet. The very thought of explaining made her tired.

"I think I can say something about that," Lou said. "Am I wrong, or did you drop your shields and absorb the virus from the González girl?"

Madrone nodded. "Yeah, I did."

"Now, psychic healing is not my forte," Sam said, "but I do know that that is not one of the approved techniques."

"For a reason," Aviva said. "It's extremely dangerous."

"I noticed," Madrone said.

"Why didn't you discuss what you were going to do?" Lou said. "We could have given you some backup."

"You didn't even cast a circle," Aviva said.

"I didn't plan it," Madrone said. "I just saw the possibility and grabbed it. I was afraid to wait and talk about it—afraid the probabilities might shift again if I waited even a second."

"The probabilities nearly shifted you out," Rick said.

"I know."

"If you had done the same work with a circle behind you, maybe you wouldn't have gone nearly over the edge," Aviva said.

"Maybe," Madrone said. "But maybe there's just a price that has to be paid for certain kinds of work."

"Well, don't pay it again," Sam said. "Once is enough."

"It was worth it," Madrone said. "I changed the *aumakua,* or, if you prefer, the morphic field that generated the disease. As you pointed out, Sam, the epidemic is over."

"I'm glad of that," Sam said. "But I for one would like to keep you alive and around until you get to be an old crock like me. In my judgment, that's what we need from you: not martyrdom, survival."

"That's high on my list of priorities," Madrone said. She was angry now, which was better than feeling humiliated. "Believe it or not, I've never wanted to be a martyr."

"Then stop acting as if it were your personal, unique, and lone responsibility to save the life of every dying person in this watershed," Sam said. "Your first responsibility is to heal yourself. You aren't worth a pot of piss to anyone else if you can't do that."

Madrone looked away from him. He was right, they were all right, but she hated, *hated,* to be fussed at. "Are you done with the lecture, Sam?"

"Take it to heart."

"I will, Sam. I'll be good. I'll go home and rest up and lie in the sun. And I won't do anything dramatic."

"Not without consulting the rest of us first," Lou said. "We care about you, Madrone."

o o o

Madrone slipped through the side passage into the back garden. Bird was digging in the herb bed, wearing Sandy's jeans and his favorite blue shirt. If she stood where she was, and squinted her eyes, she could make believe for a moment that it was Sandy. Bird's arms were darker and his hair tightly curled, not long and straight and black. But if he held still, if he didn't move . . . she shook her head and cleared her eyes, feeling for a moment as if she had been caught in what the Sisters would call a sin.

To atone for her thoughts, she went over to Bird, touched his shoulder, and kissed him lightly on the ear. She felt sore inside from the Council meeting. Couldn't anyone say, "Nice work, Madrone. Thanks for saving our asses"? But of course people did say that, all day long, burning candles on her doorstep, leaving baskets of fruit and tiresome bunches of flowers. Maybe she did want to be a martyr after all, or a saint, like the Three Martyred Sisters of Guadalupe, tortured to death by the Cartel back in the nineties. She remembered their shrine, on the main road where she played near the clinic where her mother always seemed to be busy, too busy, healing. Until the soldiers came. But that was so long ago that now she could hardly remember her mother's face separate from the picture she kept on her ancestor altar. Suddenly Madrone wanted to cry, for her mother, for Sandy; she wanted Bird to notice her distress and hold her against his shoulder, like Sandy would have done. But he was absorbed in his own work, and it wasn't really fair to bitch and scream and work out her own bad mood on him.

Instead she asked, in a carefully neutral voice, what he was doing.

"Moving the comfrey," he said. "It's taking over the whole bed here. I thought I'd move it back into the shade."

Madrone stiffened. "That's Sandy's comfrey. He planted it there. He wanted it there."

"I'm sure he did," Bird said. "Now I want it somewhere else."

They had planted it there together, making love on the bare earth, singing healing chants under a crescent moon. She had spread his ashes under it. Now its roots were dangling, its leaves drooping like a desecration.

"You should ask me before you go messing around with the garden," Madrone said.

They were going to fight, Bird realized. He had felt it building for days, and he had hoped it wouldn't happen, but the tension was there, like a cold current under the hot storms of their passion. Funny, how when they could open to each other they were so good together; they rang like a pure-forged bell, and the sweet overtones would stay with him for days. But now the sound clanged harshly. He didn't want to fight with her, but he also didn't want to, couldn't, open, couldn't let her in to walk through his patchwork memories. They were too raw; he hadn't yet been able to sort them out for himself. She was waiting for his answer, with the look on her face that he hated, because it made him feel like an interloper, someone who had no right to be in this place. And it was his home too, damn it!

"Well, pardon me," he said. "I wasn't aware that I needed your personal permission."

"It's Sandy's garden. He took care of it."

"Yeah. Well, now I'm taking care of it. Sandy is dead."

"That's no reason to—to rub him out. Like he never existed."

"Madrone. ¡Por Diosa! What the fuck is wrong with you?"

She was aware that she had left reason behind, that she was pushing him away when what she really wanted and needed was to draw him close. But she couldn't seem to stop herself.

"I want you to have some respect for him, that's all. For what he wanted. You can't just come back and make all these changes. It's too soon."

Bird took a long, deep breath. He felt she was shoving him back into shadows where he had no face and no memory. "I'm trying to be useful," he said quietly. "I can't stand feeling like a ghost. I just want to put my hands in the earth."

Madrone's eyes were filled with tears. "You're always wearing his clothes," she said, knowing she was being unfair. I gave him those clothes myself, and now I want to rip them off his back. But I love him too. What's wrong with me?

They stared at each other. Calmly, deliberately, Bird stripped off Sandy's shirt. He unzipped his pants and stepped out of them, leaving them in a heap on the ground. He could think of a hundred things to say to her, but he bit down on all of them. Naked and silent, he turned and walked away.

Madrone put the comfrey back into its hole and patted the dirt down around it. Its leaves still hung down like dead things. Burying her face in the discarded shirt, she lay on the ground and wept.

o   o   o

Maya was sitting reading in the common room when Bird clumped his heavy way naked up the back stairs and came in, covered with sweat, looking grim. "You want to talk about it?" she asked.

He shook his head. He didn't want to talk. He could hear Madrone crying in the garden and he almost wanted to go back, make it up, comfort her, but his leg hurt and the stairs seemed a barrier that stretched for miles. Maybe his leg was getting worse. He could walk on it all right, but going upstairs was hard and going downstairs more painful yet. He didn't want to think about it.

At that moment, they heard a commotion below. The front door opened and slammed, and footsteps came up the stairs.

"We're here! We're home!"

They were back from the Delta, Manzanita and Sage and Holybear. Nita ran in first, her wild hair swarming around her, and grabbed Maya in a big hug. Sage and Holybear followed, carrying big baskets of vegetables and fruits, which they set down on the table.

"Where's Bird?" Sage called. "Is he really real?"

Then they were hugging him and Maya and somehow they were all wrapped up together, just holding each other in a sweet stillness.

In the silence, they could hear Madrone sobbing outside. Bird was crying too, and Maya felt tears in her own eyes. Sandy should have been here for this reunion. There were so many who should have been here. The room felt thick with ghosts.

At last they pulled apart, to look at one another. Nita, who could never remain sad for long, was grinning. She was short, and Bird looked down at her, seeing mostly hair, an electrified brown cloud curling and crackling out to its tips. There were a few more lines surrounding her round brown eyes. Otherwise she hadn't changed at all.

Holybear was swathed in some gauzy pink fabric. His skin was far too pale to withstand the sun in these days of diminished ozone, and he had to cover up carefully. He removed the large straw hat that shaded his face, revealing a mass of fuzzy red hair that added another several inches to his already considerable height. Peering out over a pair of heart-shaped sunglasses, he observed Bird.

"It is you," he said. "*¡Qué milagro!* We thought for sure you were dead!"

"No such luck, man," Bird said, smiling and pounding him on the back.

"Madrone sent us word on the Net, so we wrapped up our experiments as soon as we could," Sage said. "*Diosa,* it's good to see you!"

"You too," Bird said. "You look as good as ever." With her hazel-brown eyes and the afternoon light glinting in hints of gold in her hair, she reminded Bird of wheat standing in a field. Her skin was tanned almost darker than her hair, and Maya frowned.

"You're too dark," she said. "Don't you know better than to go in the sun uncovered? You'll get skin cancer."

Sage just grinned. "I bathe in aloe vera every night."

Bird's leg was hurting badly. With no clothing to screen him, they could clearly see the clench of muscles that kept his awkward balance.

"You're hurt," Nita said.

He shook his head. "I'm fine."

"I've got an herb for you," Sage said, moving to the stove to take the kettle and fill it with water. "It'll help relax those muscles."

"I said I'm fine."

For a moment, an awkward tension hung in the air. Holybear broke it by removing his sunglasses altogether, to gaze at Bird with frank appreciation, and some envy.

"You dark, dark men," he said. "Would that I could run around naked and virile."

"Are you worried about your virility?" Sage asked. "Would you like a candid assessment?"

"Are you asking for a demonstration?" Holybear countered.

"Forget it. Where's Madrone?" Nita asked.

"Did we interrupt something?" Holybear asked.

"Just a fight," Bird said.

"Ah," said Holybear. "Madrone?"

"It's been two weeks," Bird said. "The honeymoon's over."

"You want to talk about it?" Sage asked.

He shrugged. "I think I want to put some clothes on. I'm getting cold." He turned to Holybear. "Got anything I can borrow?"

"Come, brother." Holybear rose to his feet and took Bird by the arm. "We go play dress-up."

As soon as they were gone, Nita turned to Maya. "What happened to him?"

"He hasn't talked about it."

"He needs to talk. It's all stewing around inside, like something fermenting into vinegar."

"I know that. You know that. Any four-year-old child that'd grown up in this house you'd think would know that. Ah, well, maybe he'll get around to it now that you're all here."

Nita frowned. "I think I'll go down and see Madrone." She left out the back door, running lightly down the back stairs.

Sage breathed an exaggerated sigh of relief and sank down on the couch. "Praise the Goddess," she said. "Nita's got a new set of problems to manage. Now maybe I'll get some peace."

                                    ◦ ◦ ◦

Madrone's crying had given way to quiet misery. She lay still, her face buried in the earth. Then she felt a hand on her shoulder.

"It's me," Nita said. *"¿Qué pasó?"*

Madrone took her hand and pressed it against her cheek. It felt cool, soft, comforting.

"Nada," she said.

"Bullshit." Nita slid her arm around Madrone's shoulders. She recognized Sandy's shirt and touched it softly. "I miss him too," she said. "It hurts. It hurts a lot."

They sat together for a while, not needing to talk. The sun had left the garden, and Madrone shivered suddenly.

"Well," she said, "I've been a real bitch to Bird."

"I don't doubt it."

"I just needed somebody to hold me and tell me I'm really wonderful."

"You're wonderful," Nita said, squeezing her tighter and kissing the tear that dripped down her cheek.

"So instead I picked a fight."

"You do tend to do that, you know."

"Why couldn't he see what I needed? Isn't he supposed to be as psychic as the rest of us?"

"Since when have psychic abilities ever been the least help in anyone's love life?"

"You would have known. Sandy would have." She began to cry again.

Nita rocked her and kissed her again, on the forehead. "Ah, but Sandy and I had years to get used to you."

"I'm tired of loving people who die."

Madrone shivered again and Nita hugged her. They kissed, long and lingering.

"I'm glad you're back," Madrone said.

"Me too."

° ° °

Clustered around the old round table, they passed bowls of salad and steamed squash and rice. The room was once again filled with light and noise and voices. Madrone had made peace with Bird before they ate, intercepting him as he carried a stack of plates to set the table.

"I'm sorry," she said. "You couldn't know that plant was where I scattered his ashes."

"Oh." He set down the plates and turned to her. "You could have told me."

"I know." She put her arms around him and they hugged. "I was an asshole. I'm sorry."

"It's okay. I'm sorry too. I could have seen that you were just missing him."

"I was just hurting," Madrone said. "And it always makes me mean. I don't really want you to be Sandy."

"That's a good thing."

"But I want to know you. You've shut me out, Bird."

He stiffened, then let out a long breath. "All right. That's true."

"So?"

"So I'll try."

° ° °

They spent dinner talking over the latest gossip and catching up on news, carefully avoiding the serious questions that hovered like latent images just below the surface. When the meal was done and the kitchen cleaned up, they settled back into the chairs and couches that filled the other half of the big common room. Sage brewed tea from fresh herbs from the garden. Maya moved to her chair under the lamp and picked up the afghan she was knitting. Her eyes were no longer good enough for embroidery, but she could still observe every nuance of each interaction in the room.

Bird and Madrone sat close together, settled on the couch in the bay window. Madrone couldn't seem to keep her hand from traveling over to touch Bird, to rest on his thigh or stroke the hairs on his arm. Her fingers reassured her that he was still there, still alive.

He welcomed her touch because it seemed to sink through the veil that kept settling over him, separating him from the scene as if it were happening to someone else, as if he were still trapped in his own prison of what was unsaid. Why was it so hard to talk? He had come back to warn them, here in the North. Yet now that he was home he felt reluctant to speak, as if by naming the danger he would cause it to manifest.

"So tell us about it," Holybear said to Bird. "*¿Qué pasó?*"

Bird was drinking out of one of the delicate Chinese teacups, and he turned it around, feeling the fragility of the porcelain between his thick, clumsy fingers. How easily it could be broken, crushed. He was balanced precariously between two worlds, like alternate realities, positive and negative space, trying hard to keep them apart, because if they came together, one would be destroyed.

"What's worrying you?" Manzanita asked.

Finally he spoke. "War."

There was a stillness in the room, like the glassy surface of a lake before someone plunges in.

"We are at war," Madrone said at last. "We have been at war for a long time. Maybe our whole lives."

Bird looked at her sharply. Her face was expressionless, but somewhere under its surface he sensed movement, like a boiling under the earth's crust. If she let that out, he thought, she would be awesome, but then of course she did, every day, in her healing. No wonder offerings still cluttered the front steps.

"What do you mean?" he asked.

"I mean that every day since *Las Cuatro Viejas* took their picks to the streets, we've been living in a state of siege. We're not free. We're not even safe. In the last ten years, we have lost a third of the city. One out of three. We're just fighting diseases instead of guns."

"Is that what you think about the epidemics?" Holybear said. "That they're some kind of biological warfare?"

"That seems to be the growing consensus on the Healers' Council. Also, Defense thinks so. But it's beyond even that."

"What do you mean?" Sage asked.

"I mean that's where the battle is coming down right now—around survival. Basic biological survival. And we're losing. I'm telling you, this last one scared me. Things aren't right. They seem all right on the surface, but they aren't right."

"No, they aren't," Manzanita said. "We went up the Delta and over to the North Bay, did some sampling. It's not good. And there was another mass of sea lion deaths up past Mendocino. I'm scared to eat fish anymore."

"But this has been happening for fifty years or more," Maya said.

"And what if it's reaching the critical point?" Madrone said. "When did they ban chlorofluorocarbons? Back in the mid-nineties? How many more years before we can hope to restore the ozone?"

"Twenty, maybe thirty," Holybear said.

"And who knows how much of the forests are left, or what the Stewardships are dumping into the sea?"

"When I was young," Maya said, "each spring brought back songbirds that nested in the rain forests of the Amazon."

"You should have made videos," Nita said.

Holybear turned to Bird. "But what you're talking about is something else, right? Something undeniably warlike—guns and bombs and soldiers?"

"I came back up the coast," Bird said. "The whole valley, down past the ruins of Slotown, is one big militarized zone. Troops everywhere. They're being trained to march on the North. On us."

"How do you know that?" Holybear asked.

"I met some deserters, back in the hills. With the Monsters."

"Monsters?"

"That's what they call themselves. They helped us."

"Who's us?" Nita asked.

"Me and my—friend. It's a long story."

"We've got all night," Maya said.

"You won't like it."

"Nobody's forcing you to tell it," she said. "If you want to keep it bottled up and stay shielded, shut down, and miserable, like you've been the last two weeks, you've got a right to do that. Just don't expect us not to notice."

"And comment on it," Holybear added.

"And bitch about it," Sage said.

Bird almost started to smile, but his mouth fell back into its set line. "I don't know why this is so hard for me to talk about. I haven't wanted to shut people out. I guess I've gotten used to keeping secrets."

"Keep all the secrets you want," Maya said.

"As long as you don't mind her divining what they are," Sage said.

"You mean you don't know it all already?" Bird said. "I'm disappointed in you."

"I don't know everything. I write stories, but that doesn't make me the Omniscient Narrator of life."

"What happened?" Sage asked softly.

He told them, beginning with the dreams that had led him and the others down to the Southlands.

"It started with Cleis, really, or with my infatuation with her. I was obsessed—even though I knew I was hurting you." He turned to Madrone and pressed her hand. "Even though I knew she really wanted Zorah more than me, and Zorah wanted Tom—so naturally we all four started to sleep together. And we kept on having the same dreams—all of them about the South. It was the height of the big epidemic, everyone was dying all around us, and we weren't the only ones that had the idea that it might be a good time for a scouting trip. You know their nuclear capacity had always given Defense

Council nightmares. If the Stewards were as weak as we were, maybe we could do something about it. And we did, although this part is where the details start to get a bit fuzzy in my mind."

He described the attack on the nuclear reactor, as clearly as he could remember. The others interrupted often with questions, so it took a long time to tell.

Madrone cradled his hands between her hands, as if she could heal them, make them new. His face was turned away from hers, but when he described the deaths of Cleis and Zorah and Tom, he looked up and met her eyes, letting a barrier between them drop.

"I'm sorry," she said.

He shrugged, reluctant to go on, to take himself back into the pain and share it here. For a moment, the others, with their straight limbs and strong bodies, seemed like plants grown under glass, sheltered. For just a moment, he hated their unbroken hands.

"Well," he said finally in a flat voice, looking down at the rug, "a lot of the next part I don't remember too clearly. Pain, but I survived that. They worked me over pretty good, a couple of times. Asked a lot of questions, about magic. How did we get into the plant? Was I a Witch? Where from? I got scared that I wouldn't be able to hold out much longer, especially if they used drugs. So I did something. I kind of . . . rolled my mind up into a ball and hid it away."

"How'd you do that?" Nita asked.

"I don't know, exactly. The next thing I knew, ten years had gone by. I don't remember any of it."

Well, that was out now, Maya thought, as they sat in silence, and maybe that was the worst of it.

"That must have been hard," Holybear said.

"It's just . . . gone," Bird said. "Sometimes a piece will come back, a scene or a phrase or a feeling in my body, but disconnected. Out of context. It makes me kind of crazy to think about it. I don't know where I was or what I did."

"Then what happened?" Nita asked.

"I woke up. It was like—like going to sleep at night and waking up the next day and finding out it was ten years later. Only it was night when I woke up, and I was in bed with this kid and it seemed like we'd been lovers for a long time, but I couldn't remember who he was, and I wasn't too sure who I was either. I was locked up in this horrible place, and I thought I was going to be trapped there for the rest of my life. That was pretty bad."

"You have a gift for understatement," Sage said.

"It was worse, in a way, than being beat up, because it just seemed so normal, like it could go on forever. Like it *had* gone on forever. There didn't seem to be any reason why it should change. And—it was strange. When I first woke up, I did a healing." He told them about Hijohn. "But after that, I couldn't seem to get hold of any power. Couldn't trance much, couldn't *shift* anything. I finally did a real simple spell. Actually, I didn't think it would work, but I guess it did."

He described the escape and the journey north, the meeting with the Monsters, the troops he had seen massing in Slo Valley, what the deserters had told him about the diseases.

"So they are weapons," Madrone said. "I thought so, but I still find it hard to believe."

"Some of them are, at least," Bird said.

"And they have antidotes?" Sage asked.

"Antidotes for some things, and general immunoboosters," Bird said. "You get them if you're in the army, or if you're in good with the Millennialists. Otherwise, you take your chances. A lot of people die. That's why they need a healer."

"What they need is mass rebellion," Holybear said.

"They're working on it," Bird said. "In the meantime, staying alive is a pretty big challenge."

"Healers' Council will want to hear this," Madrone said. "Will you come talk to us?"

Bird nodded.

"I want to hear the rest of your story," Maya said. "How'd you get back here from—where'd you say? Slotown? Is that what they're calling San Luis Obispo these days?"

"Right, like Los Angeles," Bird gave the word its Spanish pronunciation, "turned into Angel City." He told them the rest of it, then, about the long hike back up the coast. What he didn't say was how hard that walk had been, how his body had screamed its protest at every step, how very close he had come to lying down and giving up. But they could hear what he edited out echoing in the pauses and hesitations between his words. Madrone worked pain from the knots in his fingers. She knew.

"And?" Maya said when he finished.

"And what?"

"And whatever it is that's still sticking in the back of your throat."

Bird swallowed. Yes, she was right, it was sitting there, the thing he was reluctant to admit, even to himself.

"Well, it's this," he said finally. "What I told you is what I remember. But how do I know for sure that it's really what happened? Maybe it wasn't *me* that did something to my mind; maybe they did. Maybe I really broke and told them everything."

"No one would blame you," Maya said.

"I know," Bird said. "I wouldn't even blame myself. But I feel responsible. Did I let them know that the city has nothing they would call defenses? Is that why they're invading now?"

"But whatever you might have told them," Holybear said, "you would have told them ten years ago. They would have invaded then, not now."

"I guess you're right. I keep getting time mixed up in my mind. It all seems compressed and scrambled."

"You did good, Bird," Sage said. "As good as you could. As good as anyone could."

"It's just not knowing. Not trusting my own memory."

Oddly, once it was out he felt relieved. The others regarded him steadily. What had he feared? Their judgment, their condemnation? But that made no sense. Madrone pressed his hand. No one spoke, because there was nothing to say, and yet slowly Bird felt comforted.

"So what are you going to do?" Manzanita asked at last.

"Go back. I said I would."

"How?" Sage asked.

"The way I came, I guess. Walk."

They were silent again. He looked out at five pairs of eyes that stripped away his outer coverings and saw the energy lines in his body. Pain stood out on him like a tracery of red veins.

"I can walk," Bird said. His voice sounded defensive. "I walked here, didn't I?"

Maya looked intently at her embroidery. Madrone closed her eyes. On the inside of her lids, she saw herself walking in the canyons of the coastal hills, alone. From her belt hung a sheathed knife. She blinked to make the vision go away.

"They want a healer," she said. "You're not a healer."

"I'll do in a pinch."

"Somebody should go. Sam's already making noises to that effect, in the Healers' Council. But not you, Bird. You've been through enough."

"Who can say what's enough? Who can say what it's going to take to survive, if they really bring war here?"

"Let the Healers' Council decide who goes," Madrone said.

"Why should I? You yourself just said I'm not a healer."

"She's right, Bird," Holybear said. "You're back home now, where we do things collectively, remember? This isn't your battle alone."

His words echoed Sam's. Madrone shifted her weight and looked up to find Nita staring at her.

"Don't you get funny ideas, either," Nita said. "You don't look fit enough to fry rice, let alone invade the Southlands. What the hell happened to you, girl?"

"You work too hard, epidemic or no epidemic," Sage said.

Maya snorted. "She did more than that. Go ahead, tell them."

"Explain, please," Holybear said.

"All right." Madrone withdrew her hand from Bird's and faced the others. I have nothing to be ashamed of, she told herself. "We weren't having any luck getting at the virus, either with magic or with lab work. So I went after the *aumakua*."

"The what?" Bird asked.

"The oversoul, or the morphogenetic field, if you want to get technical. You studied morphic field theory, didn't you?"

"Mostly as it relates to music," Bird said.

"In the *ch'i* worlds, something like a virus is a collective entity. What we *see* of it is a symbolic representation of actual form-generating forces," Holybear explained. "So what happens to its *ch'i* image reverberates in the physical world."

"And?" Sage asked Madrone.

"I absorbed it," Madrone admitted.

"Are you kidding?" Holybear looked at her, shocked. "Madrone, are you sane? Don't you realize how dangerous that is? *Diosa,* if that's true I'm surprised the Healers' Council left you running loose."

"I knew it was dangerous," Madrone said. "But it felt right. And it worked."

"You nearly died," Maya said. "You're still not well."

"But I don't understand," Nita said. "Who was in your circle? Wasn't your backup strong enough?"

"I didn't call a circle together," Madrone admitted. "I just . . . it just came to me to do it, one morning—there was a possibility I could grasp if I acted that moment. So I did."

"That goes beyond stupid," Sage said. "That's suicidal."

"It worked," Madrone repeated.

"Luck doesn't justify recklessness," Holybear said.

"You understand, don't you?" Madrone turned to Bird. "It was like a *geis.* It was laid on me."

"I understand, *cariño,* what it is to do what you have to do and wonder afterward if you were brave or dumb." He slid his arm around her shoulder. "And to pay for it. And frankly, to me it seems you've paid a pretty heavy price. You need a good long rest."

"Healers' Council agrees. They wouldn't let me start back to work yet."

"I'm glad *they* have some sense, at least," Maya said.

"I have sense. I'm sure a nice long rest would be good for me, in some other world. But we live in this one, and who among us gets what's good for us? Did Sandy? Did you? And will any of us, if what Bird says is true?"

In the quiet, Maya's knitting needles clicked together in a rhythm like a slow drumroll.

"So what do we do here, when the troops come marching up the highway?" Holybear broke the silence.

"I don't know," Bird said.

"We've never known," Maya said. She stabbed at the yarn with her needle. "We've been afraid of an invasion ever since Lily and Alice had their great moment of drama with the pickaxes and the pavement, but we've never known what to do if it happened."

"We'll fight it," Bird said. "Like we did before." He slid his arm around Madrone's shoulder and held her close.

"Of course we'll fight it," Holybear said. "I'd just feel a whole hell of a lot better if I thought we could win it."

"We were damn lucky before," Maya said. "We can't count on the same constellation of circumstances again. We could just as easily all have ended up dead."

"We were still right to resist," Bird said. "Smartly or stupidly or even suicidally. Believe me, I've seen it down there. Even if we'd all died, it would have been a thousand thousand times better."

"We did okay," Nita said. "I have faith that we'll do okay again."

"But I'm not looking forward to it," Sage said. "I'm afraid."

Maya was suddenly very, very tired. "We have to think about this," she said. "We have to take it to the full Council. We won't figure it out tonight."

"Have you taken it to Defense Council?" Nita asked Bird.

"Not yet."

"Maybe it should go directly to the City Council," Sage suggested.

Nita considered for a moment. "No. If he does that, Defense will get their backs up. Go to them first, and then go talk to Cress on the Water Council, just sort of off the record. Call him *hermano,* buddy up to him, and get him behind you. *Then* go to City Council, preferably on a day when Sal's facilitating."

"Listen to Nita," Holybear said. "She's Toxics' prime strategist."

Maya stood up. She wanted to be alone with her fears and her memories and her own rage. "I'm an old lady. I'm going to bed. You're all very brave and I can't say I'm not proud of you, even if I'd like to fold you up safe and keep you in my dresser drawers. It's Rio coming out in you, Madrone. You can't help it. And you, Bird. I should never, never, never have let your grandfather knock me up just because I thought he was the bravest man I'd ever met. I knew at the time I'd regret it, and I do. I do." She was standing there, crying down onto her knitting, and Bird stood up and hugged her.

"Don't lie, *abuelita,*" he said, kissing the top of her head. "You know you don't mean a word of that."

"I do," Maya said.

"Well, you're doomed to pay for your sins, then, I guess," Bird said. "Because here we are, the curse of your old age."

"¡Qué suerte!" Sage murmured. The word meant luck tinged with fate, and Maya didn't argue.

o o o

When Maya was gone, they sat in silence for a moment, Bird with his head sunk down on his chest and his eyes closed, as if he had not yet fully emerged from his story. Nita yawned.

"It's time for bed," Sage said.

"The operative question here," Holybear said, "is, who's going to bed with whom?"

The question brought Bird out of his reverie. He looked up, slowly. There was a speculative light in Holybear's eyes, but Bird wasn't sure of his meaning. The others had all been lovers for a long time, but he hadn't been part of their circle. He had been lovers with Sandy and with Madrone, but separately, and he had never tasted the others, or the whole they made together. Maybe they preferred to keep it that way.

"Don't worry about me," Bird said.

"Asshole," Madrone whispered softly.

"Actually, he meant that as an invitation," Sage said.

Bird looked from her to Holybear and around the room. What he saw sent a faint smile to his face. "Is there consensus on that?"

"I'm greedy. I want us all," Nita said.

"We need to be together," Sage said, and Madrone nodded her agreement.

o o o

They unrolled the soft rug in the ritual room and lit candles in the four directions. In three breaths, they grounded and quickly cast a circle.

"Madrone first," Nita said.

She slid off her clothes and stood in the center of the circle. The others surrounded her and began to chant her name softly. She closed her eyes and let herself be stroked, by the sound of their voices, by the soft touch of their hands, until her skin became electric, charged with fire. She opened to them, feeling them catch and hold the pain that seemed to her bottomless: the sorrow that rose up because Sandy, who should have been there, was missing from the circle; the sorrow and the rage that went deeper, into the very core where her power to heal arose. Their hands seemed to move through her body, deep into her, down to that core, as they teased and roused her, sliding lightly over the nipples of her breasts, brushing gently the tips of her pubic hair. Lips lightly touched her breasts.

"Thou art Goddess," they chorused softly.

Madrone opened her eyes and stepped out into the circle, as Manzanita entered to have the Goddess stroked into her. Then it was Sage's turn, and then, one by one, they called the God into the men, with delicate touches that left them rampant. They all stood for a moment in a circular embrace. Madrone and Sage were next to each other, their breasts touching. Bird had one arm around Nita's shoulders, clasping Madrone's hand behind Nita's back. His other arm circled Holybear's waist and brushed Sage's hip. They were linked, each in contact with the rest, and as they matched their breathing, they began to sink into the deeper link, into the point where each was part of the whole that was them all, until the energy opened, each of them a velvet petal unfolding from a bud with a common heart, and they began to move together, in a dance of hands, lips, breasts, cocks, vulvas, an interweaving of energies that sounded high notes and deep notes and syncopated rhythms of pleasure.

The circle knew her, Madrone realized. There was a mouth on each of her breasts and they sucked to the surface her unspilled tears like milk. Tears were streaming down her cheeks and Nita was holding her head, crooning to her until beneath the flood she could feel the solid ground of the body, each cell gripping life in its fist, squeezing and caressing and exulting in life. There was a mouth on her vulva and a tongue that played against her like a dare, until her tears turned to laughter and awe at the body's capacity for pleasure. Pleasure shook her until she could no longer contain it; she began to arch her back and shake, and as the pulse inside her began to beat the mouth changed to a warm thrust that carried pleasure deep inside her and sustained it while she fell. The core of pleasure shone like an apple, like a place she could glimpse between the pulses of orgasm, and Sandy was there somehow, not lost to her but smiling, juice dripping from his mouth.

She lay still, letting the shine settle within her, and then she laid her hands on Bird's back, and suddenly three of them were massaging him from behind, digging their skilled fingers into the sore muscles, pouring heat into the hurting places and spreading warmth through him, down to the root where Holybear was sucking the pain out of him, sucking and spitting and sucking again, until Bird could feel in his body again the promise of power and release, and the promise rose up in him, and the hands were all over him, carrying that promise into every nerve ending and cell so they vibrated together, so his body became one sounding chord that spilled hope out over the flesh that pressed against him and shuddered in response to his pleasure.

The dance went on until each had been healed and renewed. The skylight in the ritual room was beginning to glow blue with dawn light when they pulled blankets from the corner, curled up in a pile, and fell asleep.

o o o

Down below, alone in her room, Maya dreamed of Johanna and Rio. They were on the coast, where a still lagoon of water pooled behind a sandstone rock shaped like a whale. On the other side of the rock the waves foamed and sucked and pounded, but here the water was still, and they were sheltered from the wind. They lay naked on dunes of white sand, sliding down from time to time to dip into water so cold it turned Maya's belly fish white, gave a blue cast to Johanna's dark skin. The rock seemed full of faces, stone brows and deep-set eyes and straight chiseled lips, spirits stern but benevolent.

All day they watched the sun make a track across the sky. At night they lit a fire at their campsite and ate beans and rice, which Maya had left to soak in the morning. They watched the sparks flare and die into gray ash. The fire was alive, as the rock was alive, and Maya could feel the great life beating and breathing and pulsing through all of them and everything around them. She wanted to embrace it. She wanted the touch of rock and fire and tree roots on her naked skin, to peel herself open and be touched deeper. No one spoke, but she thought they all felt the same. They did not need to speak to one another about these things. She loved them; she wanted them to touch her like the night air did. The moon rose out of the river and turned their skin silver.

10

"On a hilltop reached by a spiral path, on an island in the middle of a lake, in the middle of a woods, nine old women guard the city with their magic," Maya said, panting a bit as they climbed the hill. "Sounds like a story, doesn't it?"

"Why did they pick this place?" Madrone asked.

"They wanted to be in the center of the city but somehow removed from it. They wanted seclusion for *listening* and *dreaming,* but without isolation."

"You'd think they'd also have wanted a gondola, or even an elevator," Madrone said. She was breathing heavily herself, and that worried her. Really, by now she should be recovered enough to keep pace easily with Maya. Maybe she needed to start doing some more regular exercise. Running. Dancing, maybe. Bird trailed behind, trying to hide his struggle to keep up.

"Ah, well, they're purists," Maya said. "And it makes for a better story. 'Early one morning, up the hill'—let's see, what verb best describes it— 'crept? climbed? staggered? three pilgrims. . . .'"

"The lame, the halt, and the blind." Madrone completed the phrase.

"I'm not lame," Bird said. At the tension in his voice, the two women stopped and watched him come toward them. His face was grim with suppressed pain.

"All right," Madrone said. "You can be the halt, whatever that is."

"Whatever it is," Maya said, "it's a good idea. Let's rest for a minute."

They paused, looking down at the blue glint of water through treetops. Bird caught up to them, and Madrone moved behind him to dig practiced fingers into the sore muscles at the small of his back, where his uneven gait put stress on the spine.

"Ow, *mierda,* you're hurting me," he complained.

"Hush up, child. This is good for you."

"I'm fine, Madrone. Leave me alone."

"You're not fine, Bird."

"I am. I'm a lot better than I was."

"You're worse," Madrone said. "What did Sam say?"

Bird simply compressed his lips.

"Well?"

"He wants to cut me up and put me back together again his way. Break the bones in my leg and hip and reset them."

"Sam can be a bit overbearing, but he's very conservative about surgery. If he says you need it, you probably do," Madrone said.

"I'll think about it," he said, in a tone that indicated he wouldn't.

Madrone exchanged a glance with Maya. "Let me work on your hip," she said, patting his ass gently. "Bend over, boy."

"Fuck you!" He whirled on her, such rage in his voice that she and Maya both stepped away. Madrone blinked back tears.

Something was struggling to the surface of his memory, as hard as he struggled to push it back. There were the gray walls again, and the steel bars—but he couldn't, didn't want to remember the rest of it, not here on this hill with Maya and Madrone both looking at him in that way. He was already sweating, and Madrone was about to cry.

"Shit, *cariño,* I'm sorry," he said, coming over and putting his arms around her. "It was just those particular words. . . ."

"Another bad memory?" Madrone murmured.

He nodded.

"I'm sorry I keep hurting you," she whispered.

"Not your fault," he said, kissing her eyes. "And no, I don't need to talk about it. I really don't."

"Okay, Bird."

He held her tightly for a moment. She was a shield against the pain that flooded him suddenly, not with memories but with physical sensation. He wanted to vomit, but he fought the urge.

She could feel him shaking.

"You're okay," she murmured. *"Estás bien. Estás aquí, conmigo y con Maya. Estás seguro."*

She continued saying soothing things in Spanish until his breathing steadied. Spanish always comforted him; maybe they'd do better if she stopped speaking English to him altogether, but her Spanish voice was only one of her voices, and anyway, she couldn't shelter him from the memories forever, only help to steady him through.

"It's hard to believe," Maya said, "that this is the very place where I first met Rio. Look—see that spot on the bank over there, where the lawn comes down to the water? It was my first day in San Francisco, after I ran away from home, at the beginning of what we called the Summer of Love. Over eighty years ago. I'd hitchhiked up from LA and spent the night in some crash pad overrun with roaches, and by that I mean bugs." She grimaced. "Just thinking about it makes my skin crawl. First thing in the morning, I headed for the park, where whole tribes of flower children were dancing and drumming and generating clouds of marijuana smoke on Hippie Hill. They intimidated me. I was afraid they'd find out I wasn't as cool as I looked. So I made my way to the edge of the lake, where I sat trying to convince myself that I was on a spiritual quest, not just scared and lonely. Rio rowed up to me in a stolen boat and carried me off. Within ten minutes we were fucking, possibly under this very tree."

"He was a fast mover, old *Tío* Rio," Bird said, smiling.

"In those days, we got right down to business. When it was over, he looked at me and said, 'Let's spend the rest of our lives together. What's your name?' "

"How romantic," Madrone said.

"Are you being sarcastic?"

"Half and half."

"The odd thing was that we did," Maya said. "Spend the rest of our lives together, that is—except for a couple of decades here and there. Funny how long those years seemed then, and how short they seem now. Are you rested? Because we still have quite a climb."

At the top, the path broadened out into a small meadow. A clear pool stood on one side, and to the north a series of low domes rose above the ground. They were shingled with wood, and the sun glinted on the glass skylights on their tops. Near the entrance of the largest dome was a small circular depression, lined with a bank of turf that curved around three sides like a green bench. A low stone table stood in the center.

The door opened and a woman stepped out. Her face was as lined as Maya's, her silver hair pulled neatly back into a knot at the nape of her neck, her eyes narrow and curved as eucalyptus leaves. She wore a flowing silk tunic, peacock blue trimmed with lavender, over a pair of black sweat pants.

"Lily," Maya said. "Lily Fong. How many years has it been?"

"Not as long as that," Lily said, clasping Maya's hand. "I saw you, Maya, just a month or two ago, on the Day of the Reaper. That was a powerful story you told."

"Why didn't you come forward?" Maya asked. "You would have been honored if we'd known you were there."

"That's why I took care that you didn't know. It's a dreary business, being a living legend."

"Tell me about it," Maya said.

Lily smiled. "Why don't you come and join Defense Council, Maya? You qualify."

"I can't stand going to meetings anymore," Maya said. "It destroys my concentration. But this is Madrone, whom you know. And my grandson, Bird. We've come to confer with the Council."

"Sit down," Lily said, waving them over to the sunken table. "So you are Bird. Yes, we have been waiting for you. The Council has sent me to talk with you."

"Can't we talk to the whole group at once?" Maya asked.

Lily shook her head. "Today I am the ears and mouth of the Nine. The others have their own work to do, and they too find that meetings disturb their concentration. Sit down. I'll bring some tea."

She reentered the dome and emerged a few moments later with a laden tray. They sat on the green bank around the stone table, and Lily handed them cups and served them tea from a porcelain pot carved with birds and leopards.

"This is beautiful," Maya said. "It's a museum piece."

"Yes, the museum is kind to us with their treasures. And they enjoy being used." She turned to Bird. "So you are the one who has returned from the Southlands, of whom the Voices have spoken. What news do you bring us?"

"Not good news, I'm afraid."

"Don't be afraid. Just take your time and tell your story."

She listened attentively as he spoke, interrupting from time to time with questions.

"So that's where it stands," he said. "As far as I know, the preparations for an invasion are well under way."

"You've answered a number of questions," Lily said, "and raised others. The epidemics, for example."

"Apparently, down south they're either still cooking the damn bugs up or they've got so many running loose it's hard to survive without the antidotes. I suspect that last one was an attempt to weaken us, soften us up before they try to come in. But I don't know for sure. I know it's one way they control people in the Southlands. You work for the Stewards, or you don't get access to the medicines. Or water."

"We've suspected an attack was brewing for some time," Lily said. "We've *dreamed* it. But we don't know when it will come."

"I don't know either," Bird said.

"How much do they know about us?"

Bird stared for a moment at the embossed design on his cup, tracing the outline of a glazed leopard. It was beautiful and fierce and fragile, like a lot of things. "They think the North is a hotbed of powerful Witches, each of us at Satan's beck and call. They're afraid of our magic, which is probably what's kept them away all this time. Aside from that, they don't seem to know much, from what I could tell. Which, bear in mind, was sort of from a limited perspective. If I can believe what I remember, I didn't tell them anything. But to be honest, *Doña* Lily, I don't know if I can believe what I remember, or if what I remember is all of what I did."

"And that troubles you greatly," she said.

"Of course."

"If you had told them the truth, if you had said to them, 'Our city is defended by nine old women who *listen* and *dream*,' would they have believed you?"

Bird laughed. "No."

"So don't torment yourself. Perhaps what you told them does not matter."

"You mean it was all for nothing?" Bird said quietly. "All that pain? That I could just as well have cooperated for all the good it did?"

"No, I don't mean that. Resistance to violence is never useless. You did well, if only for the example you provided, of choice. But not just for that. Certainly, information is important. Information is power. I just mean that no information is useful unless the mind is prepared to receive it. And now you understand our strategy."

"What do you mean?"

Lily was silent as she poured out another round of tea. She looked at each of them closely, as if judging what she should say. Then she spoke.

"After the Uprising, we found ourselves caught in a dilemma. We knew that war was responsible for shaping the world into all the forms we wanted to change—and yet there we were, surrounded by hostile enemies who might, at any moment, attack and destroy us. This was the dilemma that every peaceful culture has faced for the last five thousand years, at least. And this was our one advantage—that we had history behind us. We had seen all possible solutions played out, from resistance to retreat to acquiescence, and we knew none of them worked. That saved us a great deal of time. We didn't have to waste our energies stockpiling weapons or drilling troops; we could jump right to the heart of the matter, which was magic."

"In what sense?" Madrone asked.

Lily nodded at Maya. "You remember that Dion Fortune quote you've always been so fond of? That magic is the art of changing consciousness at will? You can look at a war as a massing of arms and matériel and troops, but you can also see it as something else—as a delicate web of interwoven choices made by human beings, made out of a certain consciousness. The decision to order an attack, the choice to obey or disobey an order, to fire or not to fire a weapon. Armies and, indeed, any culture that supports them must convince the people that all the decisions are made already, and they have no choice. But that is never true. So, mad as it may seem, this is the terrain upon which we base our defense of this city—the landscape of consciousness."

"I don't understand," Bird said. He set his cup down and looked at the woman, wondering suddenly if she were wise or simply crazy.

"Look at it this way. You went to the power plant, and I'm sure you used your magic to get in. Am I right? Spells of invisibility and protection, charms to neutralize the electronic security systems, rituals for power. And all so you could stand before the men who controlled it, with guns, and force them to take actions they didn't want to take."

"That about describes it," Bird said.

"And you probably thought you were great magicians."

"Not for long."

"But consider this—how much greater would have been the magic if those men you fought could have themselves simply chosen to close the plant?"

"It would have taken more magic than I've got to have reached those particular men," Bird said. "I don't know. Sure, we would have been better off. Maybe Cleis and Tom and Zorah would still be alive. But I don't know whether manipulating their minds is really an ethical improvement over simple force."

"I'm not talking about manipulation. I'm speaking about vision. Expanding the parameters of possibility."

"I would have had to expand my own parameters pretty damn far to believe for a moment that the consciousness of those guys could change that much."

"Consciousness is the most stubborn substance in the cosmos, and the most fluid. It can be rigid as concrete, and it can change in an instant. A song can change it, or a story, or a fragrance wafting by on the wind."

"You mean if I'd sung the right song to those guys, or said the magic words, they would have changed just like that?"

"Who is to say? I have heard that you are a fine musician."

"I was once. Not anymore."

"Then you have denied the gift that perhaps was meant to be your true weapon. I'm sorry to hear it."

"I haven't denied it. It was taken from me."

"No. A gift like that cannot be taken."

"It can be destroyed."

"No. If you think so, it is because you have not yet truly learned to use it. And when you do, who knows? It may prove to be a weapon more powerful than all their bombs and rifles."

"It doesn't sound very practical to me, Lily," Bird said. "I'm sorry to say so. But I've seen it, down there. You haven't."

"Bird, child, like your grandmother we Nine are of another era. We have stood, eye to gun barrel, with the greatest military machine the world has ever produced. The forces of the Stewards are nothing but the last vestiges of its power. We are not naïve about armies and military power. On the contrary.

"But I ask you, what is practical? Would it have been practical for us to devote our scarce resources and human energies to building weapons and recruiting a standing army, when we needed every scrap of earth and drop of water and the power of every human hand for survival, for healing the earth's wounds? War is the great waster, as much in the preparations for it as in the waging of it. We learned that, at least, from the last century, as that same military drained the country and destroyed our true wealth. But we have nothing left to waste. We would have traded an uncertain future for sure misery and still not have been able to withstand the armed might of the Stewards."

"And where does that leave us, when armies come marching up the peninsula?" Maya asked.

"It leaves us with what we have built of this city and this watershed, which is in itself a possibility not counted on by those who would attack us. That is where our hope lies. We are what we wanted to become," Lily said.

"But can we preserve what we are?" Maya asked.

"To wage war, one must believe in an enemy. If we refuse to be enemies, how can they fight us?" Lily said.

"Easily," Bird said. "They can walk right over us."

"I don't deny it's a gamble. None of us, even the strongest Dreamers, knows what will happen. Only that there is hope but no certainty. We must continue to *listen*," Lily said. "And heal. You must heal, Bird. You've been to war. You've spilled blood, and you've suffered. You need cleansing."

"I'm sure I do."

"Do you have a power place you can go to?"

"I did ten years ago," Bird said. "This time of year, you'd need skis to get anywhere near it. And I have to admit I'm not quite up to skis."

"I'm glad you admit there's something you're not up to," Madrone murmured.

"Go somewhere," Lily said.

"Where I need to go, where I'm promised to go, is back. Back to the South."

Lily closed her eyes, *listening* deeply to an inner voice. Golden motes of dust swarmed in the late-afternoon sun.

"Yes, someone must go there. But not you. That road is not for you now."

"That remains to be seen," Bird said.

"It has been foreseen."

"They asked for a healer," Madrone said. "Maybe we can find somebody from the Healers' Council. There's a lot we'd like to know about their biotechnology."

"Ah, Madrone." Lily turned and gave her a searching look, then smiled. "What do you dream these days?"

Madrone sat silent, reluctant to answer the question. "In my dreams, I do what I should be doing awake," she said finally. "I take care of people."

"And do they get better? In waking life?"

"Apparently so."

"Cheater," Maya said. "You're supposed to be resting."

"I can't control my dreams."

"The hell you can't."

"Leave the girl alone, Maya," Lily said. "As Bird has said, these diseases are attacks. Well, how do you think we work? She's already a healer; now she's becoming a Dreamer."

"She shouldn't be working at all," Maya said. "She should be regaining her health."

"But she is deeply entwined with the city's group soul. To regain her health, she must help us all regain our health."

"She needs to learn to take care of herself," Maya said.

"Would you please stop discussing me in the third person?" Madrone interrupted. "I'm right here, lucid and fully functional."

"Notice what you dream, Madrone," Lily said. "The road to the South may be for you."

"The hell it will," Bird said. "If you think I'm not strong enough to go, look at her. She can barely climb a hill without gasping."

Madrone gave him what he called her "fuck you" look, but respect for Lily's presence kept her silent. I'll end up going out of stubbornness, she thought, because I resent Bird's attempts to protect me, even though the thought of going terrifies me. I'll end up going to prove I'm not afraid, when I am. But no, it's not even thinkable. I'm needed here.

"This all should be discussed in full Council," Maya said, rising to her feet.

"Of course," Lily agreed.

"But we wanted to consult you first," Bird said.

"Naturally." Lily smiled. "What else is Defense Council for? And if you're smart, you'll have a private word with the Water Council first. Cress would be good. Don't tell him I suggested it."

"Thank you, Lily," Bird said. "Please give our respects to the others of the Nine."

"Given and received," Lily said.

11

In late October, or Ancestor Moon as some liked to call it, Black Dragon House became a shrine to the dead. Over the years Halloween, now called by its original Celtic name of Samhain, had merged with the Mexican Day of the Dead, *El Día de los Muertos,* celebrated on November 2. Now the holiday season extended for weeks. Families set up *altares* in memory of loved ones. Children sucked on sugar skulls and played with toy skeletons. Dancers, musicians, and artists prepared the most elaborate Pagan rituals of the year, while the Sisters next door celebrated masses for All Souls and All Saints. On the final night, half the city turned out in skeleton masks to parade through the streets.

Bird flatly refused to attend any public gatherings. "You all go ahead," he said. "I'm just not ready. I'll be fine by myself."

"Don't be stupid," Madrone said. "We can celebrate at home this year."

"You don't have to for my sake."

"Maybe we want to," Holybear said. "Maybe we're grateful you're back among the living, not ranked with the Beloved Dead."

They prepared the house for their private celebration. Up in the ritual room, votive candles burned continuously before old photos. Sage and Nita cut banners out of thin colored paper and tacked them along ceiling beams and table edges. Holybear raided the garden for marigolds, the flower traditionally used for offerings to the ancestors.

Maya made an *altar* for Johanna and Rio that commandeered one corner of the living room. In Johanna's favorite chair, she placed a stack of needlepoint pillows and a rainbow-colored knitted afghan. On Rio's she folded the stained sleeping bag he'd carried on so many trips. On the table between them she placed books, along with the brightly painted skeletons she had bought in Mexico long ago—a female skeleton addressing a group of children for Johanna, a male skeleton carrying a basket of food for Rio. And candles, votive candles in glass jars with inscriptions to High John the Conqueror and the Seven African Powers, the orishas. And shells, small cowrie shells on a basketry plate for reading oracles, large cowries for abundance, conch shells with their openings carved for blowing, beach shells and rocks from the coast. Along the table's edge, redwood boughs and pine cones surrounded big mugs that would once have held coffee but now held the substitute brewed from grains.

"One more epidemic, one more round of deaths," Maya sighed, "and the living are going to be crowded out of the house between Samhain and Yule. As it is, there's no free horizontal surface to set down so much as a teacup."

Madrone set up a small *altar* for Sandy next to the door of the room that was now Bird's. She covered a low table with red cloth, and beside his picture she placed a collection of herbs and tinctures, his flute, a bowl of rice, his poetry books, and his stained gardening gloves. She stood a vase of chrysanthemums between a carved statue of the Irish Goddess Brigid, for his Celtic great-grandmother, and a small statue of the Goddess of Compassion, Kuan Yin, to honor his ancestors from China. Then she sat in the hallway and cried. After a while she heard Bird's heavy footsteps clumping up the stairs. He came and sat down beside her and put his arm around her shoulder, not saying anything, just sharing her grief. She felt comforted to have him there. These were the good moments, when they could just be together, without arguing, without worrying about what was going to come. Finally she stopped crying, and he kissed her.

"Did you set up an *altar* for me when I was gone?" he asked.

"I tried. Maya would never let me. She said it was bad magic; it was wishing you dead. We had terrible fights about it."

"What would you have put on it?"

She hesitated for a moment, then said, "Your guitar, of course. I tried to set it up on top of the piano. I had a miniature windsurfing board and a pair of skis and candles and flowers."

His silence intensified so deeply that if she hadn't been touching him she would have believed he had disappeared.

"Where did you go?" she asked. "What are you thinking?"

"I was thinking you might just as well have set the *altar* up. That Bird is dead."

Best not to respond to that remark, Madrone told herself. Instead she asked him what *altares* he was planning.

"Maya and I did a small one for my mother in Maya's room," he said. "You should come see it—it's beautiful. Maya saved all of Mom's rock collections, from the time she was a girl, and her notebooks where she worked out the original theorems for intelligent crystal technology."

"Maya is the world's worst pack rat. She can't get rid of anything."

"The whole time we worked on the *altar,* Maya kept grumbling, 'I named her Brigid, for the Goddess of Poetry, and what did she like? Rocks, nothing but rocks. Other girls played with dolls; she played with rocks, talking to them, dressing them up, giving them little rock tea parties, counting them over and over again. How did I produce a child like that?' "

Madrone laughed. "She ought to be grateful. If it wasn't for your mother's way with crystals, we wouldn't have the Net, and Maya would be writing longhand instead of tapping away on her keyboard. What are you going to do for your dad and Marley?"

"Just play their music. I fixed the speakers on the sound system, and Maya has a whole collection of discs, every saxophone solo my dad ever blew and all of Marley's percussion recordings."

"I should do an *altar* for my mother," Madrone said. "But somehow when it comes to the point I never can. I don't know why. Holybear did a nice one for his mom, dripping in lace. And with a nice picture of her—I don't remember her ever looking so beautiful in life. But then she already had cancer when I first knew her. We're lucky we come of African and *Indio* stock; that milk-white skin is a real liability."

She's chattering, Bird thought, dodging something.

"Do you remember your mother clearly?"

Madrone looked up at him. "Why do you want to know?"

"Memories are precious. Even bad ones. They make us who we are."

She sighed, nestling deeper into the shelter of his arm. "Sometimes I remember her rocking me and singing to me. And the way she smelled after a day in the clinic, of medicines and disinfectant and just a little tang of the sour smell of the poor. And once, I remember, she took me into the jungle with her to gather plants. She told me not to be afraid of snakes, to sit quietly and listen to the animals and plants and try to understand what they were telling us. Mostly I just remember a feeling, a sense of safety and warmth and everything being okay. And then . . ."

She stopped speaking. She could never remember what had happened, only a sickness in her stomach, a pressure in the back of her eyes. Bird tightened his arm around her. It's there in your touch too, Madrone wanted to say. The same warmth, the same peace, the little crawling worm of fear. . . .

"Then what, *querida*?"

Why was he probing this wound? Did she ask him how he felt about Brigid coughing her lungs out in the big epidemic? Or seeing his father shot down in the street during the Uprising? Did Nita talk about the day she went home from the university to find both her parents gasping for breath and dying almost in unison? No, they were all a bunch of orphans, except for Sage, whose father was still hale and hearty up in the mountains. They had all been bereaved. Better not to whine about it.

He patted her gently. "What happened?"

"Then I remember this bare little room in a bare little house, where there wasn't much to eat but I couldn't complain, because everybody was so afraid there. I never saw her again, but somehow I knew she was dead."

He held her closer, for a moment, but she pulled away.

"Then Rio came," she went on quickly. "I'd never seen a man who looked like him before, with such white bushy hair and eyebrows and a big white beard. Like the pictures of Santa Claus in one of my books. Although not as fat. So I trusted him. I thought he was going to take me to the North Pole."

Bird laughed. "Was it a disappointment to land here instead?"

"A bit," Madrone admitted. "I wanted to see the reindeer."

"I remember when you arrived, that first night when we all came over here for dinner to meet you, my mom and dad and Marley and me. How old were you? Six? Seven? You were so little and pretty and sad."

"You were nice to me," Madrone said. "You and Marley went outside to play ball, and you asked me to come along. And you spoke Spanish to me, because I wasn't used to so much English. Your accent sounded pretty funny, though."

"I fell madly in love with you," Bird said. "You awakened some instinctive male protective urge in me."

Madrone stiffened abruptly. "Well, you can curb it now," she snapped. "We're not seven years old anymore."

He pulled back from her. Where did that come from? he wondered. We were so close just a minute ago, but she's like a cat with a wound, who lashes out when you stroke too close to the sore place. And aren't you the same? a voice asked him. We could fight now, he thought, but instead he grinned at her.

"But I'm still madly in love with you."

She stuck her tongue out at him, and he caught it between his lips and wrapped his arms around her and kissed her tenderly.

Here is the peace, the safety, that was shattered long ago, Madrone thought. In his arms. I should let him shelter me a bit, stop jabbing at him, leave my own fear behind.

But the fear remained.

° ° °

Samhain night was Madrone's twenty-ninth birthday, and they spent it cooking. By family tradition, the birthday celebrant was allowed to request a favorite meal. Because Halloween was the night the ancestors returned to visit, they combined her birthday feast with an ancestor feast, each making a dish that would be pleasing to their own ancestors. Madrone's favorite food was the *mole* Maya had learned to cook long ago in Mexico that took twenty-four spices and seven different kinds of chiles and three days to prepare.

"That's bound to please somebody dead," Madrone said.

"Rio always liked it," Maya admitted, "even if all his ancestors were Irish and Cockney. I'll mash up some potatoes on the side."

Madrone insisted on cooking too, even though it was her birthday. She made *pupusas* in the style of Guadalupe, to placate the ghost of the father she never knew. Holybear baked challah, Nita made rice and beans, and Sage made an English trifle with pound cake, strawberry jam, and real cream.

"What should I cook?" Bird asked, feeling a little superfluous in the flurry of activity that filled the kitchen.

"A salad?" Nita suggested.

"Yeah, I could do that." He didn't sound excited.

"What did your dad like?"

"Greens, black-eyed peas, corn bread, sushi, Thai shrimp soup, and that cream of carrot soup that Johanna taught my mom to make."

"Well," Maya said, "you cook up a mess of greens in vinegar, and Johanna may well materialize."

When dinner was ready, they placed small portions of each dish on plates and set them out on all the altars to the dead.

"Another feast of staggering variety, if questionable digestibility," Holybear said. "Here's to Madrone! May she live, if not forever, at least for a good long time yet!"

Over dessert, they told stories about the dead. Madrone told the one story she knew about her father: how he had been a student in the University of Guadalupe until one morning he stepped out of his front door and tripped over the body of a child who had died in the night from hunger. Instead of going to class that day, he had gone to the mountains to join the revolution.

Bird talked of his brother, Marley, how in the drought of '33 he had gone up on Twin Peaks and drummed for four days without stopping, until the rain came. Nita spoke of her great-grandmother, who had come over from the Philippines after World War II and raised eight children alone after their father disappeared with another woman. Sage told about the night her great-uncle Seth, an itinerant Louisiana preacher, stopped a lynching by talking in tongues until he went into convulsions, giving the intended victim a chance to escape. Maya was unusually quiet, concentrating on her knitting even when Holybear told the story of his grandfather Ben's most famous political trial, an event she had witnessed personally.

"You're awfully quiet, *abuelita*," Bird said. He was sitting between Madrone and Holybear on the big couch, with Nita perched on the arm, and they all faced Maya, smiling. "What are you thinking?"

"I'm thinking that we are all descended from survivors here. Like Bermuda grass or the cockroach, we should be hard to stamp out."

"Not a very flattering comparison," Nita complained. "Why not like mint, or blackberries, or even ivy? They also spread all over the place and are hard to kill."

"Tell us a story," Bird said to Maya. "It's your turn. Something instructive and inspirational."

"I've written my stories," Maya said. "There they are in that pile of books on the table."

"Read us one, then," Sage suggested, glancing up from the bright green-and-gold afghan she was crocheting.

"Is there something wrong with your eyes?"

"No, but you can't get off so easy," Nita said. "Tell us a story!"

"Tell us a story! Tell us a story!" they clamored.

"Which of the dead should I tell about?"

"To hell with the dead. Tell us about you. You'll be dead all too soon, and then *we'll* have to tell your story," Bird said.

Maya sighed, laying her knitting in her lap. "What I keep thinking about is the discussion we had with Lily."

"About how to resist the Stewards?" Madrone asked.

"Sometimes it seems to me that I've been having the same arguments, over and over, for eighty years. Violence or nonviolence, how to struggle, where to draw the lines? Debate after debate, while all around us violence continued to rage unchecked. If I tell you a story tonight, it will be a war story."

"Go ahead," Bird said quietly. "Maybe a war story is what we need to hear."

"The first war I remember was Vietnam." Maya settled back in her chair, closing her eyes as if resting before a long climb. "We used to watch the evening news, Rio and I, on an old black-and-white TV. We were living in one big room, converted from an old garage, in Berkeley. He'd gone back to school, which I took as a personal betrayal. Nevertheless, I stuck with him."

"Why was it a betrayal?" Nita asked.

Maya opened her eyes and looked at her. "Because when I first met him he'd seemed like someone from another star. Unbound by the mundane. An outlaw, a pirate, a savior in a black leather jacket with hair halfway down to his ass—which in those days marked a man as a radical. He'd seemed so free. We'd lived on air, traveling up and down the coast in his van, stoned out of our minds with rock music blaring out of the eight-track. We'd made love on the beach in a rainstorm with the waves breaking over our naked bodies. How could a man like that take midterms and worry about a grade point average?

"Besides, my mother was constantly nagging *me* to go back to school. I couldn't forgive him for doing what I was so strongly resisting."

"Why didn't you want to go back to school?" Nita asked.

"I'd dropped out and run away after Johanna and I got busted. Caught, that is, making love on the locker room floor of our high school gymnasium, after taking a little too much LSD. After that I couldn't stand structures, hierarchies. They all seemed false to me, arenas where people preened and postured and attempted to impress themselves. I didn't want that. I didn't want a degree, I wanted an absolute: enlightenment by the great straight upward path, something real." She sighed. "I thought I had it with Rio, but what I had was another form of fantasy. We weren't living on air, we were living on the money he made selling dope. I had sand up my crotch from fucking on the beach, and he was proclaiming 'free love' and getting my best friend pregnant, although I didn't find out about that until years later. Pregnant with your mother." She nodded at Madrone. "So I suppose we should thank him."

"I'll set a little more of that cream trifle on his *altar*," Madrone said.

"Actually, going back to school was one of the most sensible things he'd ever done. If he'd only stuck with it." She picked up her knitting and stared at it. "But I was talking about the war. One of those news images is still seared into my brain: a woman on fire, burned with napalm, running and screaming and clutching her burning baby. She haunted me. Whenever I felt bad, when Rio and I were fighting or when I caught cold or wanted to crawl in bed with menstrual cramps, I'd think of her. How could I feel sorry for myself in the face of her suffering? And whenever I felt good, when the wisteria bloomed or sometimes in the middle of making love, I would think of her and feel ashamed. How could I dare be happy, when some other woman, just like me, was burning down to the bone?"

She jabbed her needle into the yarn and swore softly as she dropped a stitch.

"Go on, *abuelita*," Bird said.

"We tried everything we could think of to stop the war. Marching in demonstrations, blockading the draft board, badgering shoppers outside the supermarket. Nothing worked. The war went on and on. Rio's brother was killed in it. That's when he started drinking, coming home late and passing out on the couch, breaking up the furniture. He dropped out of school, but I was not happy about it. He'd begun to frighten me."

"But you stayed with him?" Sage said.

"I continued to persuade myself that each binge would be his last. What can I say? I loved him, and I wasn't clear on my alternatives. Anyway, the longer the war went on, the more frustrated we got. We went from singing 'Ain't Gonna Study War No More' to shouting 'Off the Pigs,' from shouting to smashing windows and setting bonfires in the streets. Most people never went any further, but the atmosphere was changed. A few of us, like the group

Rio and I joined, we started parading around the woods with guns and talking about bombs. It seemed justified. Compared to the violence being done in our name to the Vietnamese, compared to the violence of the police against us, what did it matter if a cop car got torched now and then or the Bank of America burned? BRING THE WAR HOME! That was our slogan."

"That's understandable," Bird said.

"Perfectly," Maya admitted. "Still, it was a failure of imagination. That's what I regret—what we might have done if we hadn't let our vision be constricted. And I knew it at the time, but I didn't know how to talk about it. I knew it from one of the big riots in Berkeley; I don't even remember exactly which issue it was now, Cambodia or People's Park or whatever. But they'd brought in the National Guard, and there were troops up and down Telegraph Avenue, and barricades, and helicopters overhead. They'd set off tear gas, and the whole crowd was running and yelling in rage and panic. I'd lost Rio in the confusion. My eyes were burning and I was running with a cop behind me, when I heard this loud sharp sound. They were firing into the crowd. Just birdshot, but I had no way to know that then. I thought I was going to die.

"Suddenly I got very calm. I didn't want to run anymore, so I slowed down and the cop ran right by me and started chasing somebody else. If I was going to die, I wanted to do it with dignity, consciously, so I started walking very slowly up the street toward the shots. Everyone else was running away. Around me was all this motion and commotion, but I was a stillness at the center. I walked straight up to one of the Guardsmen who were firing at us and just looked at him, looked into his eyes. I wanted to see who it was that was going to kill me.

"He was young, about my age. His eyes were brown, like mine, and I could see he was scared, like I was scared. We were just the same. All of a sudden I knew that, and he knew it too. I could see it in his face. His hands were shaking, and he lowered his rifle. I knew, then, what could really end the war."

She closed her eyes. For a moment, she felt Rio sitting beside her, his big hand on her shoulder.

"I wish I had been able to tell you," she said to Rio. "To cut through all the rhetoric we spouted and make you understand. But instead I just went along with you, until it got too weird and I had to leave. Do you forgive me?"

"*Madrina,*" Madrone said softly. "Speak to the living, not the dead. We're here with you."

Maya opened her eyes, but they were gauzy, distant. She spoke softly, half entranced. "I ran away from Rio, to the mountains, where I stayed alone until autumn. It was a dry year; the snow was late in coming. Other backpackers

left me food, and I learned to survive on very little. Every night I dreamed that
Rio had somehow managed to find me, that he was lying next to me cradling
my body in his arms. Every morning I woke alone. The rocks are very beautiful up there, a clean granite, gray-white with dark flecks and little sparkles of
quartz. After I had been alone for a while, they began to speak to me. Everything came alive and had its own voice, and I could hear it. The Goddess
claimed me, although I didn't yet know any of her names. Without knowing
the word for it, I became a Witch."

Her voice had sunk to a dreamy murmur, and they sat in silence for a
moment, lulled by its spell.

"What did Rio do when you left him?" Bird asked finally.

Maya sat up. Her eyes snapped back into focus. "He threw himself into
acts of political bravado. His group planted a bomb in the offices of a chemical factory, another at the local draft board. Their third action went wrong.
The bomb went off too soon, before they could phone in a warning, and the
night guard at the Federal Building died. She happened to be a woman, a
black woman at that. Before I left, we'd moved into a flat in the City we shared
with our friends. The police came after them, shot the place up, burned it
down and our friends with it."

"How horrible," Nita said.

"Rio wasn't in the flat. He was in his van, dead drunk. The police found
him the next morning. They arrested him and took him off to prison, where he
spent the next thirteen years."

Rio's arm weighed on her shoulder; he was almost palpable. Well, it *is*
Halloween, Maya thought.

"That was the price he paid. I changed my name and ran away, to New
York and then to Mexico. I didn't see him again until late in the eighties, when
everything had changed. Not least both of us. But that's another story."

"And the moral?" Holybear asked.

"The ends don't justify the means," Maya said. "That was what I learned
from Vietnam, from the war and the protests against it. The means shape the
ends. You become what you do."

"It's almost midnight," Sage said. "Shall we go upstairs?"

They lit candles in the ritual room at the top of the house, cast a circle,
invoked the Reaper and her counterpart, the Guide. Maya led them down the
trance roads, to the shores of a dark ocean. A ship lay waiting to carry them
away to the Island, the place in the spirit worlds where the dead and the
unborn walked in the orchards of the Goddess beneath ever-fruiting trees.

o o o

Maya was staring down into the center of a dark cauldron. Inside, spiral
galaxies swirled in a dark night sky. The turning stars were the souls of the
dead, of the unborn. They were all fates, all possibilities.

One star flew toward her, growing huge and white hot until it burst and Johanna stood beside her.

"She's gonna go," Johanna said. "The girl's gonna go."

"Go where?" Maya asked.

"To the Southlands. Where else?"

"No."

"How can you say no? She's needed there."

"No," Maya said. "I can't stand it. I've lost enough."

Johanna snorted. "It's her road to walk. You can't block it, and you can't smooth it for her."

"I can complain, anyway," Maya said.

"You be good, girlfriend. You owe me one."

"Owe you one what?"

"A favor."

"In return for what?"

"All the many years I put up with you."

"You were lucky. What do you want?"

"Let her go. Let go easy."

"You know I'll do that, in the end."

"Do it in the beginning. She needs your help, not your fear."

◦ ◦ ◦

Bird waited. He thought he was sitting on a log, under a flowering tree that was lit by a mother-of-pearl glow from within. He wondered who would come to him. His mother? His father or brother? Cleis, or Zorah, or Tom? Or himself, maybe, that Bird who skied and ran and whose supple fingers were the instrument of the great music. What would that Bird have to say to him now?

In the stillness, an old man approached. It was Rio. He looked old but vigorous, his white hair shaggy and his beard full. But not like Santa Claus, Bird thought. There was nothing jolly about him.

"What was it like for you, all those years in prison?" Bird asked.

Rio seated himself on a mound and fixed his eyes on a high branch. "I was terribly lonely. Maya never wrote to me. My family disowned me. And I despised myself."

"Why?" Bird asked. "Because of the woman who died?"

"Because I traced all my mistakes back to my own weakness. The drinking and the drugs were a part of it, but at the core was a kind of cowardice, a sliding away from pain. I had to face that in myself, and it was the worst time in my life. But I got lucky."

"How?"

"I was in the punishment cell, one time. For a long time. Too long. All the windows were blocked and the door was solid steel. There was no light.

Eventually I couldn't bear it any longer. I wanted out so bad I was shaking, and there was no way out. In a little while, I thought, I'd begin to scream and never stop again.

"I tried to calm myself by remembering things. Maya's touch, and the wet smells of sex, but that was intolerable; it just made me ache and rage. Then I started to remember the wind on the coast and the fresh rain on my face and the clean, cold air roaring in over the ocean. I concentrated on it, that clean, clean wind, until I began to dream about it. When things are really bad, you know, you begin to think you could pledge your life to anything that touches you with kindness. There was one ray of sunlight that leaked through the window cover. It was the most beautiful thing I'd ever seen, that narrow beam of light, and I began to feel like I could talk to it, could ask it to speak for me to the wind and the rocks and ask them to forgive me. But then I realized that the sunlight and the wind and the rain and the rocks didn't care what I'd done or left undone. It had nothing to do with them. The grace they offer can't be earned or lost. It's just their nature to cleanse and scour and heal.

"I had always been afraid to face myself. Somehow the memory of the wind gave me courage. I felt stained and heavy, like tar that clings to your feet after a walk on a spoiled beach. But when I made up my mind to turn toward my own pain, everything changed. I found myself face to face with a beauty that offered itself in every dust mote dancing in a crack of light, in me no less. So I healed, slowly. There seemed to be a kind of compassion inherent in the very nature of things. I pledged myself to that. I swore my hands would never kill again."

Rio changed as he spoke, beginning to glow like the trees but with a golden light. I don't shine like that, Bird thought; I'm still heavy, opaque with bitterness and hope.

"When I was in their prison, all I thought about was getting out," Bird said.

"You were never really in despair. Maybe you never will be. You had nothing to reproach yourself with."

"But I did kill a man."

"When?"

"In our action. One of the operators of the plant. A big, freckled, white-skinned guy. He came at me roaring and called me 'nigger' and—I don't know, my hands just seemed to pull the trigger of the rifle I was holding. Then his eyes were staring out, surprised, glassy as marbles, and there was blood leaking out of his mouth."

Then his face turned into my father's face, lying dead on the ground before me, Bird thought. But he didn't admit that even to the dead.

"How should I feel about that?" Bird asked.

"I can't tell you how to feel."

"But I don't know. Was I right or wrong? Did I have the right to do it? What do I owe, now, to his ghost? Or to his unborn children? But if I hadn't shot him, he would have killed me. The plant might still be up and running, leaking its poisons. And how many would die then?"

"Maybe we can't answer these questions," Rio said. "But here's one for you. Would you kill again?"

Bird sat very still for a moment. "No," he said finally. "Oh, maybe I would if there was no other choice, but I would rather try Lily's way. Even if I'm not convinced it will work."

"There is always a choice," Rio said. "Sometimes the choice is to die instead."

"It's not death that scares me. It's losing—losing this city, seeing it turn into what the Southlands have become. I'd happily die to prevent that, but I'd hate to die and have it happen anyway."

"But would you kill to prevent it?" Rio asked.

"I don't know. I really don't know."

o o o

Madrone was riding on a wave of undulating space, carrying her down and down. Then she was at the crossroads, the still point where all possibilities extended out like the spines of a sea urchin, herself in the hollow center. One road glowed like a path lined with *luminarias* at Yule. As she looked down that road she saw herself, walking south. It was a dry road; her mouth ached for water, and she couldn't see the end of it, except that it seemed to lead on into her shapeless fears.

She shook her head, trying to make the road fade, hoping some other path would open up. But it remained: shining, implacable.

"I don't want it," Madrone protested, but without heart. She knew in the end she would not refuse. "Why me?"

In the road was a snake, iridescent, pearly skinned, who fixed her with an eye in which light played among subtle colors.

"Because of your gifts," the snake said and rustled off, leaving her sitting on the Island of the Dead.

Sandy came to her. He held out his hands. They were rough, with the dirt of the garden still in their pores. She remembered how he used to wash at the end of the day, and duck his head under the faucet to splash water on his face, and the tuneless songs he would hum. They had been the ordinary background noise of her life. She hadn't realized then how the sounds contained the essence of her love for him.

"We all come here, eventually," Sandy said. "But don't rush it, Madrone. You just have to bear the time of being alive. Enjoy it, even. I want you to enjoy it."

"I do," Madrone said. "I will."

"It's a hard road, the road to the Southlands. You can survive it, but not if you take it because you're trying to die. Your death won't change anything. Your life might."

"I don't want to die," she said. "I only wanted to stay in the cold place because the light was so beautiful there. But no more. I don't want that anymore."

"Bird has grounded you."

"That sounds funny."

"I'm glad for you. I bless you," Sandy said. "I'm only just the slightest hair jealous."

"Sandy, I'm scared shitless. I don't want to go to the Southlands. I'm a healer, not a hera."

"If it's really your road, if you are really meant to take it, you'll find the courage."

"Where?" Madrone asked.

He bent over her, draping her with his waterfall of black hair, and kissed her. Then he was gone.

                        ○   ○   ○

When they opened the circle, they shared pomegranates from the Delta.

"What did you see?" Maya asked them.

"I saw myself going to the South," Madrone said. "I don't want to go. I'm afraid. But that was my vision."

Bird took her hand and gripped it tightly. They sat silently together, staring into the heart of a candle flame in the dark.

12

The Healers' Council met in a small conference room at the hospital. The walls were decorated with colorful murals, herbs grew in pots under the window, but the room still looked like what it was, a square box, product of the sterile architecture of the past century. Madrone sighed and helped herself to a muffin from the plate on the low table in the center of the room. Bird had been speaking, telling the story of his journeys in the Southlands. Sam and the others had quizzed him thoroughly on everything he knew about the epidemics and their origins, which wasn't much. Today's meeting was unusually crowded, fifteen or twenty people crammed onto couches or sprawled on the floor. Now they were all silent, considering.

"The Web asked for a healer," Bird said. "They need help. The Stewards control the antidotes and the boosters, and without them people die."

"I wish I could get a look at one of their boosters in my lab," said a slim woman wearing a dragon-embossed robe of a style popular on the north side of the city.

"We all wish that," Sam said. "The question is, is it worth risking somebody's life to go down there and try to bring some back?"

"They need a healer," Bird said again. "I'm willing to go, but I'm not one."

Sam looked at him, frowned, and turned away in silent dismissal. Fuck you, Bird wanted to say. I'm no cripple. I can do whatever I need to do. But he held his tongue.

"Do we owe them anything?" Lou asked.

"I do," Bird said firmly.

"I think we do," Sam said slowly. "First, out of simple humanity. And strategically, there's no better deterrent to foreign wars than rebellion at home. If the Stewards are tied up fighting in the Southlands, that might keep them from invading us, or lessen their forces if they do come."

"But who could we send?" Aviva asked.

"Someone who could work with the supplies and the resources the hill people have," Sam said.

"Which are?" Lou asked.

"Pretty much nothing, as far as I could tell," Bird said reluctantly. "They don't need a doctor so much as a miracle worker, a shaman who can cure with her or his hands alone."

Nobody looked at Madrone. They all stared down at the rug or picked apart the remains of their muffins.

"I don't want to go," Madrone said. "I'm not crazy. I want to stay here, where I'm useful and needed."

"You have every right to that choice," Sam said.

"But I will go," she went on, "if you all think I should. I'm willing to go. It comes into my visions and my dreams at night. Maybe I'm meant to go."

"No!" Lourdes and Aviva exclaimed together. Sam turned to look at her, the lines in his face deepening.

"It seems a waste," he said.

"Are you well enough?" Lou asked.

"Not today," Madrone admitted. "But in another couple of weeks— before Yule, anyway. Honestly, Lou, I'm not overestimating my strength. I could come back to work now. But for hiking down the coast and facing what comes after, I'd need a bit of time to get in shape and prepare."

Sam turned to the woman in the dragon robe. "Do you have anyone on the north side who might be willing to go?"

She shook her head. "We have many specialists, and our research on *ch'i* mapping is very advanced. But we must have equipment to heal; herbs and pharmaceuticals and facilities to sterilize our acupuncture needles. True psychic healers are scarce, and of those on our team, three are in their sixties and one is blind. I can't see any of them making that journey."

"Same on the west side," a man said.

"I don't like this," Sam said.

"I don't like it either," Madrone said. "But even less do I like the thought of weathering more and more epidemics until we're so weak the Stewardship troops can just march in and pick us off. If there's a chance of preventing that, it seems worth taking."

"I especially don't like you going alone," Sam went on. "Maybe Defense has someone they could send with you."

"I'll go with her," Bird said. "I know the way."

Sam expelled a long breath through his teeth. "Bird, I've already told you this once. You've sustained severe damage. Much of it is correctable, with some surgery and a lot of physical therapy, if you start on it soon. If you don't, if you continue to stress the tendons and ligaments, you're going to get worse. There is no question of your going back to the Southlands at this time."

Bird's mouth was set in a grim line, but he didn't answer. Madrone spoke up quickly.

"I might only go as far as the Monsters, down by Slotown. That should be relatively safe. I can help them out, train some of their people, and maybe they can get me some samples of the boosters. With luck, I'll be back in a month or two."

"Goddess go with you," Aviva murmured.

"I don't like it," Sam repeated.

o o o

"What does it mean to become a Dreamer?" Madrone asked. She was sitting with Lily at the little table in the clearing outside the house of the Nine. They were drinking some strange astringent tea out of a round black pot. The tea left her tongue feeling stripped and dry, but the colors of the day seemed brighter, more clear.

"There is the world of physical form," Lily said. "What we know and can touch. And there are the realms of the *ch'i* world, realms of energies and spirits that infuse and underlie the physical. The division between the worlds is never absolute. Always there is bleed-through. So a Dreamer stands on the boundary. Did you know the German word for Witch, *Hexe,* comes from *haggibutzu,* she who sits on the hedge?"

"Actually I did know that," Madrone said. "I read it in one of Maya's books." She drummed her fingers restlessly on the table edge. Maybe Lily could not tell her what she needed to know. Will I live or die?

"In an ordinary dream, the spirit world speaks to us. But a Dreamer can speak back, can make shapes and patterns in that world that later take form in this."

"So is that what my dreams are doing? Is that what I did when I was so sick?"

"There are many different ways to *dream.* Some do it at night, with their eyes closed, some open-eyed in the light of day. Some, like Maya, tell stories that become the dreams of many."

"I have two sets of dreams," Madrone said. "Often I still dream that I am seeing patients and healing people. I wake up tired, from those. But I have other dreams, now, dreams of a dry landscape, and clouds of dust, and thirst, terrible thirst. In those dreams I am always trying to find water, or to bring water to someone. And then I wake."

Lily examined her tea, favoring Madrone with only the briefest of glances.

"The journey to the South is not an easy one. But you have come to the point where you need to gather power, and that is never easy. So this is your challenge—to bring healing to the sick, to bring water to the dry lands."

"Is it? Lily, I don't know what to do. I want to go and I'm afraid to go. I'm afraid to be hurt like Bird's been hurt. And I'm afraid of other things—things I can't name or see clearly. Can learning to be a Dreamer help me overcome those fears?"

Lily rose. "Come, child. I cannot answer those questions for you. I can only give you a few tools to work with."

Madrone followed her through the doorway of the round house and down a spiral staircase that seemed to lead straight underground. The air was cool and dark. After a while Lily led her through a low archway into a vaulted hall, lined with doors on either side. She opened one and Madrone followed her into a round dark room. A candle cast a warm glow over the whitewashed walls. Underfoot was soft carpeting.

"Lie down," Lily said. Madrone obeyed, letting her body sink into the rug, closing her eyes.

"Now," Lily said, "here is the breathing pattern for lucid *dreaming*." She led Madrone through a series of meditations, monitoring her breath, moving her hands through Madrone's aura, weaving new patterns with the energy. Madrone was asleep but not asleep, flying. I am free now, she thought, I can go anywhere, anywhere I want. I want to go home, a child's voice within her cried. She was rushing on the wind, south, always south, far past the dry Southlands of California, over the deserts and high plateaus of Mexico, south toward the tiny country of Guadalupe, sandwiched between Nicaragua and El Salvador, where a small whitewashed house stood beside a dusty road, its door ripped from its hinges—

"No!" Madrone sat bolt upright, sweating and shouting. Lily looked at her in alarm.

"What's wrong?"

Madrone shivered. "Lily, I don't think I can do this."

"Where did you go?"

"I started to go home, the home I was born in, down in Guadalupe, the home where my mother died. I don't want to see that, Lily. Is that what I have to do, to be a Dreamer?"

"What you have to do first is learn control," Lily said in a calm voice. "Although it's true that a strong Dreamer must not fear to face anything the mind can hold."

"But I do fear. I can't help it."

"Where there's fear, there is power," Lily said.

"I'm not sure I want power," Madrone said. "Sometimes it seems like I already have too much. It weighs me down."

"But what you want is not the issue here. Power has chosen you to be its instrument. Would you refuse it? Refuse your own vision?"

Madrone fought for a moment to slow her own breathing. Her heartbeat steadied.

"You know the answer to that," she said. "All right. Better put me down into trance so I can try again, now, before I lose my nerve."

° ° °

Madrone prepared to go. She sorted through Black Dragon's sixty-year accumulation of camping gear, picking out what she might need and assembling her pack. She harvested the herb gardens, replenished medicines, and made herself a compact kit to take away. She distilled a six-month supply of violet-leaf tincture for Sister Marie's cancer. Almost daily she went to the island in the lake to meet with Lily and practice her *dreaming.* She went with Maya to Council to sit beside Bird as he told the city what he had seen in the Southlands and alerted them to the possibility of war. In the ensuing debate, she kept silent about her plan to go south. Lily had advised her not to broadcast her intentions.

Every day, Madrone took long walks to strengthen herself. She studied old maps until she nearly had them memorized. But each attempt she made to go over routes and plans with Bird ended in a fight.

Bird was a haunted man. He was haunted by the anticipated silence of the house without Madrone's presence, and by visions of things happening to her so horrible he could not allow them to reach more than the edges of his mind. As a result, he went around staring into corners, fearing what waited to pounce from the periphery of his vision.

He knew that he had to go with her. Over and over again she told him no, but she found no one else to take his place. The Council could not spare a second healer. Sage and Nita and Holybear were engaged in work vital to Toxics that could not be abandoned, and there was nobody else she knew and trusted well enough to take into mortal danger. So Bird continued in his stubborn determination to accompany her himself.

The alternative was unbearable: far easier to bear the physical pain of the journey than the fear and helplessness of staying behind. He practiced by ignoring the considerable pain he was in continuously, as overstressed muscles and ligaments rebelled and went into spasm. He never complained, and he tried hard to hide it, especially from himself. Nevertheless, every time he pulled himself upstairs or clumped downstairs, the very air ached. He insisted on digging in the garden and turning the compost pile even though Holybear yelled at him for half an hour afterward, warning that he was going to do himself serious injury. He went out of his way to bring Maya things she'd left upstairs or downstairs, until she became terrified of ever putting anything down for fear of forgetting it and causing him another trip.

Madrone finally lost patience with him. They were all in the common room after dinner and she was going over an old geological survey map of Big Sur, asking him if he knew which trails were still good and where they had disappeared.

"Don't worry about it," he said. "I'll show you when we get there."

"Bird," she said tensely, "I don't know how to say this to you, because I've said it fifty times already and you haven't seemed to understand, so let me say it again in words of one syllable: You are not going. You no go. *No vas a ir.* You stay here. *Aquí.* Home. *¿Comprendes?*"

"You don't have to be insulting, Madrone. It's my decision, and I've made it. I'm going. I have to go."

"Hey, you're not alone here," Holybear said.

"That's right," Sage agreed. "This is something that affects all of us. It's not a decision you get to make on your own."

"I've made it," Bird said.

"I block that decision," Madrone said.

"You can't block me from doing something I need to do."

"I can block me from having anything to do with it. Bird, what is the matter with you? Are you out of your mind? Haven't you noticed that you can barely make it down to the garden, let alone hike back down the coast range? It's not that I don't want you to come. *Diosa,* I'd give anything to have you along on this, if I thought you could do it. But you can't."

"I *did* it. How the fuck do you think I got back here? Don't tell me I can't do it, because I did do it—and I feel a hell of a lot stronger now than I did then."

"You don't look stronger," Nita said.

"I am stronger. Every day. You don't know what my body feels like to me."

"We know," all four of them said at once.

"Bird, we are Witches. We know things. It's our business, you know that. You can't hide pain around here, any more than you could hide a decomposing rat from the dogs. We smell it," Holybear said.

"Pain doesn't bother me."

The silence that followed this statement seemed to crackle with the comments everybody held back. Madrone walked out of the room.

"Well, it doesn't," Bird said.

The silence only deepened. Maya focused carefully on her knitting. Bird looked around for someone to give him reassurance, but they all had their eyes turned down and inward. The atmosphere was heavy; they all sensed that someone was about to get hurt. Madrone came back in, carrying her pack. Her cheeks were flushed and her lips were set.

"Okay," she said. "You win. You can come. You can do anything. Mind over matter. I give up. Just one thing, though. I'd like you to show me how you're going to carry your pack."

She held it out toward Bird, with the straps and frame facing him. He looked at her and saw her eyes, hard as little black stones. Then he looked at the rest of them. But they held nothing out to him.

"Sure," he said, shrugging his shoulders. Then he slipped his arms into the straps of the pack. Madrone let it go, and as the weight fell on him, his face turned ashy gray. He cinched the waist belt. Beads of sweat stood out on his forehead.

"It'll be all right in a minute," he said, and shifted his weight as if he were trying to walk. Then his leg crumpled under him and he collapsed on the floor with a soft, strangled cry.

Instantly they were all around him, pulling the pack off and holding and stroking him and each other.

"Are you hurt?" Sage asked.

Bird was biting back tears. Maya wondered why he couldn't just let go and cry. Who taught him to be stoic? she asked, but no one answered. You, Rio? His father? Not me. Not Brigid.

"You bastards," he said. Madrone ran her hands over his hip, Sage rubbed his shoulders, Nita ran for an ice pack, and Holybear put his arms around Bird.

"Just cry," he said. "Cry it out. You'll feel better."

"I don't want to cry it out. I don't want you to comfort me. I just want not to be broken anymore."

He did cry then. They were all crying, Maya in her corner and the others in their circle. "You're healers, damn it—heal me! Give me my body back. Give me my hands!"

But all they could give him was the touch of their hands, their bodies. It wasn't enough, but it was something. Quietly Maya got up and left the room.

° ° °

Maya lay on her bed, her arms outstretched, holding her breath. "Come and get me, death," she whispered. "I want to go now."

"Fold your wings, you old bat," Johanna said, looking down on her with her own arms crossed over her chest. "Who do you think you are, Jesus Christ?"

"I was on a talk show with him once," Maya said. "Remember? Back in 1999. He said he'd returned for the New Millennium, but he was disgusted with the world. So he went away again. Tell me, you should know now. Was he the real Jesus?"

"I'm not here to debate theology with you. Sit up, girl. You're not dead yet."

"I want to be. I can't bear to stick around and watch the sufferings of the young."

"Why not? Are they more fragile than we were? Hell no, these kids are tougher than those biscuits you used to make, the ones we called bullets. Anyway, this is no time to turn wimpy on me. You're still needed."

"I'm going on strike. Besides, I can't *do* anything! What can I do for Madrone, except worry? What can I do for Bird?"

"Leave him his own pain. Don't try to bear it for him. Come on, Maya, sit up and let me put my arms around you."

Maya sat up. Her arms caressed her own shoulders as she rocked, cradled in the arms of the dead.

"We had our challenges and our suffering," Johanna said. "Leave the young their turn."

"But their turn is so much harder than ours was! It is, Johanna, don't pretend it's not! And that's not right. That's not what we worked for!"

"What we worked for was to give them a turn at all. Given the way things were going when we were young, we should claim it as a victory that they're alive and still have a world to suffer in."

o o o

Bird sat in the garden. The moon had caressed his sore back, but it was dipping down below the neighbor's roofline, and the air was chilly. Still he couldn't bring himself to move, to get up and go in and face Madrone again, with her camping gear spread out all over her room and a look of determined kindness in her eyes.

The cold creeping along his shoulder blades felt almost like a hand. If he closed his eyes, he saw Rio's face, his hair and beard blue-white in the starlight.

"I'm disappointed in you," Rio said. "I thought you had more guts."

"Lay off me, will you?" Bird said. "Or try another tactic. That one won't fly. Believe me, Rio, nobody in the world can accuse me of not having guts. I have nothing more to prove on that score."

"It's not your machismo I'm talking about, it's another kind of courage. And I'm not criticizing. Who am I to judge you? I just wish you had the courage to let yourself really feel your wounds."

"I am doing that right now. Right now! I'm just sitting here feeling how my leg hurts and my back hurts and my fingers are stiff and heavy and nothing works right, okay? I can't go south with Madrone, I know that now; I can't play my music; I'm altogether fucked up and fairly useless, and I admit it to you."

"But those aren't the wounds I'm talking about," Rio said. "Listen, Bird. There's something that happens to you when you've been through things that other people haven't. When you've encountered possibilities of ugliness that they don't know about. We both know this, you and I. How it feels like you have to hold the pain for them, to contain it somehow and keep from spilling it out."

"That's why there's so much I can't talk about," Bird said.

Rio shook his head. "It doesn't work that way, Bird. It just eats away at you from the inside. It's hurting you."

"What can I do?"

"You know what you've got to do. The instinct is to close. But you've got to open."

"I don't know how."

"You know. First open your mouth. Then you'll be able to open your heart again."

○ ○ ○

Bird approached Madrone the next day, as she was carrying an armload of herbs from the garden.

"Can I talk to you?"

"Sure. Let me put these down." She placed them in the sink and followed him into his room, sitting beside him on the bed.

He took a deep breath and began. "I know I've been an asshole, Madrone. I'm sorry. You're the one who needs help right now, and I'm going to try to give you all the help I can."

She took his hands and held them in hers. He was suddenly so dear to her. She would have given anything for the power to heal all his wounds instantly. Maybe Lily was right, maybe she was not content with her limitations.

"Bird, you can get better, you know. I mean, you can at least improve. But you've got to take care of yourself. Give your body a chance to heal. There's exercises I can show you for your back, and Lou could do acupuncture for you. Maybe you should talk to Sam again too, let him go ahead and reset that hip."

She could feel him starting to close, but then he took a deep breath, exhaled, and smiled at her.

"Okay, I'll think about it. I'd just hate to be immobilized in a cast when the Stewards' army marches in."

"Maybe you'll be out of the cast by then. You'd be surprised how soon Sam can get you walking—at least on crutches." Madrone heard the urging in her own voice, and it sounded like whining, pleading. Wrong. She was not meeting him in what he had come to offer. But she couldn't stop herself. "And then whatever comes down, you'd be better prepared to deal with it."

"We're talking about my shit again," Bird said. "I want to know what you need that I can give you."

"Information."

"I'll give you all I have." He wrapped his arms around her and held her. "Is that all?"

He had opened to her, and she could do no less for him. "I'm scared. I'm terrified. How do I do something I'm so scared to do?"

He held her tight, wondering what words of reassurance to say when he feared for her so much himself.

"I'm scared to do the things you've done, and go where you've been," Madrone said. "I'm scared to come back broken."

There it was, he thought. The unspeakable thing that I felt hiding behind her kindness. She pities me, and she is afraid of becoming like me. No wonder I couldn't open up to her. But it's all out now, we've just got to let it go.

"I can't tell you everything's going to be all right, because that would be a lie," Bird said. "I don't know how it will be."

"I don't want you to tell me that. I want you to tell me something about fear. Everybody in this family is always so fucking brave. I feel like a misfit."

Bird laughed and held her tighter. "No, love, you're not a misfit. And I, for one, am not that brave. If I had known what was going to happen, I can't say I would have gone. I was young and dumb and thought I was just going to die, which seemed romantic and inevitable if you remember the times. Everyone was dying. *Todo el mundo.*"

"It seemed that way."

"All I can say is, it's not that the fear goes away but that it changes. When something really bad is happening, it's just what's happening. So you face it, because in that moment you don't really have any choice."

"I guess I know that," Madrone said. "It's like going through a difficult birth. You can't stop it, so you just do it. But it's now, thinking about it beforehand, that's so hard. Weren't you scared before you went away?"

"I was terrified."

"I don't want to die," Madrone said. "I wish you were going with me. I'm scared of being alone."

"I will be with you, in spirit as we like to say." Bird tightened his arms around her and bent his head low. "Not a moment of any day will go by when some part of me won't be with you."

"I know." They clung together, and his body felt so sweet against hers that she didn't know how she could ever bring herself to let go.

Finally he pulled back, kissing her lightly on the forehead. "I want to give you something to take with you," he said. "And I've thought and thought about it. Something you couldn't lose, something nobody can take from you. So, I've made you a little song."

"Bird!"

"I can't really play it for you, but—come here." He took her hand and led her over to the bench beside the upright piano, which took up one wall. "Sit here and let me sing it."

She sat beside him on the bench, knowing what this gift had cost him. Awkwardly, his hands picked out a few key chords, a halting melody. He sang, his voice husky but still the true, resonant voice that she remembered.

The song he had made for her was a little piece of his own music, the music that came to him when he was almost dead and brought him back to life, the music that every now and then had given his own hands the power to heal. He could never do it justice; even when his hands had been whole and in the prime of their skill, at most he could have played an echo of what he heard in his mind. And now all he could do was hint at the melody with stumbling notes and sing a little of it without words. He felt embarrassed, but when he stopped she shook her head.

"Don't stop, Bird. That's beautiful."

He could see in her face that she was moved, he hoped not just with pity.

"And now," he said, making himself smile, "you have to learn it. And then it'll be yours, and you can sing it as you hike down the coast, and when you're afraid, and if . . . and if . . . *Diosa,* Madrone. . . ." He couldn't speak anymore; all he could do was look at her and hold her. She was warm and alive and whole in his arms, and when they were together like this he could feel himself flowing out to her, feeding her and being fed in turn. How could he bear to believe that in a little while she'd be gone?

"This is going to be a good week," he said. "We're just going to love each other, and be good to each other, and build up our memories. Memories are important. They're something you can hold on to."

He was as good as his word. He dredged his mind for every scrap of information she might find useful—descriptions of places, names of people, stories, rumors, gossip, customs. Things came back to him that he'd forgotten: scraps of conversation overheard in the prison, the taste of moldy bread, thirst. During the day while the others were working they rode gondolas around the city, laughing together, walking on the sea dikes and climbing the green hills. They went to the ceremonies of the Ohlone and Miwok and Pomo tribes who came down to the city in the autumn to offer their ancient dances as gifts. He let her massage him, digging her strong fingers into his sore ligaments; he let her questions dig into the sore places in his soul.

At night, because he knew it would please her, he opened the piano and struggled to play, although it hurt him more than he could express. In his mind, his hands were the fluid expression of what he heard inside himself; now they were clumsy, like bundles of rags tied to sticks, thumping and crashing out a few broken chords. Nevertheless he kept on, he sang, because he understood that what she really needed from him was to know how to face the unfaceable. And he could only give her that knowledge by example.

And she sat, watching him, hearing the power in his awkward, banging music, loving him so much she could hardly bear to breathe.

Much to his surprise, Bird began to notice his playing improve. It was still rough, but not quite as rough. There were movements he could make that he couldn't before. When no one was around, he tried scales, simple runs.

He would never be the musician he once was, but still there existed the possibility that he could improve enough to let music be his vehicle. With the thought came a new dimension of fear. He had no surety that with all the work in the world he could become even that good, yet he had no excuse not to try.

○ ○ ○

They made love most of the night, but when the blue light of morning came, the others slipped out, leaving Bird and Madrone alone. She clung to him, not intending to arouse him, but just to look into his eyes, feel the precise curve of his cheeks over their bones and the soft wiry curls of his new-grown beard, and then he was hard against her and she drew him into her, wanting only to lie still and be filled with him and remember him, but there was so much love in his eyes that she shuddered under him, drinking him in.

"What are you going to do when I'm gone?" she asked when they were through.

"I'll be a good boy," Bird said. "I'm going to let Sam knock me apart and put me back together again. I'll play my scales. I'll tell cheerful lies to Maya."

"We might never see each other again. We might never be in each other like this again," Madrone whispered.

"We'll see each other, alive or dead. If I die first, I'll haunt you."

"It's not the same," Madrone said.

"I'm giving you six months," Bird said. "After that, I don't care if I'm in six different pieces and the whole Stewards' army is encamped in our greenhouse. I'm coming down to get you if I have to crawl."

○ ○ ○

She left in the morning, on the back of a wagon heading back south from the weekly market. Maya had said her goodbyes in the house, too upset to speak much. She cupped Madrone's head between her hands, looked long and deep into her eyes, memorizing them, and then let her go. Bird and Sage and Nita and Holybear walked down with her to the market and watched as the wagon lumbered down the old freeway, until it disappeared in the distance. Then they accompanied Bird to the hospital.

"Okay, Sam," he said. "Do your dirty work. I'm yours, now."

13

Madrone laid another stick on her fire, watching the warm light of the sunset color the ocean waves gold and violet. If her count was correct, it was the night of the Winter Solstice. She'd been traveling for two weeks now, making her slow way down through the coastal mountains, through canyons thick with redwoods and the peeling madrones, their gray outer bark pulled back to reveal the reds and bronzes and purples of the papery inner bark and, beneath it, smooth green-gold skin. They were her talismans; she too was stripping and peeling. It had been so long since she had spent days in silence. It had been so long since she'd had no one to answer to, no one to be responsible for except herself.

Now she waited in a place Bird had described, the strip of sand with the rotting pier at the southern end of the mountains, where the land leveled off into rolling dunes. It might be days, he had said, maybe longer, before the Web sent a boat to cruise the pickup site. They traded, he'd been told, with some of the groups inland from here, but the pickups came irregularly. Certainly she had seen no one else here. While she had conserved her food, gathering nuts from the woods and living off the land as much as possible, she couldn't wait forever. She had a sudden picture of herself, old as Maya, still waiting, never knowing when to give up and turn back and go home.

Suddenly she wished, more than anything, that she were home. In the city now the gondolas would be filled with people laughing and singing, on their way to the beaches, where they would plunge into the cold, cold waters of winter to cleanse themselves of the faults of the year, ignoring for this one night the threat of toxins. The sea dikes would be alight with fires, and as dark fell the gondolas would come alive with the flames of candles, carrying the Yule fire back to the hearths. Then later there would be food: roast wild pig brought down to the City by the Wild Boar People, exiles banished for antisocial behavior who were allowed back at this time of year to sell their wares at market. For the vegetarians, plates would be piled high with tofu and sweet potatoes and bowls would brim with red chile.

In Black Dragon House, the *altares* for the dead had been taken down before Madrone left. The family *altar* was rearranged to feature a nativity scene, in which a statue of the Venus of Willendorf, ample and fertile, stood next to a golden ball that represented the sun, reborn on the Solstice out of the womb of Mother Night. Madrone had helped Sage collect figurines and small stuffed animals to witness the central scene: plastic dinosaurs, carved wooden dogs playing instruments, small painted angels from Germany, a wind-up Godzilla devouring Dorothy from *The Wizard of Oz,* a set of clay snakes made long ago by a child.

Tonight at home they were all together, keeping vigil all night long, baking the Solstice bread that filled the house with its fragrance, singing and drumming and telling stories. At dawn they would climb the hills, ringing bells and beating drums, to chant and dance as the sun rose. They were not lonely.

Maybe she should have waited until after the holidays. But once she had made up her mind, delay had become unbearable. No, she couldn't have gone through the celebrations, knowing all along that each thing she did might be for the last time.

She shivered. Her fire was going well, and she placed a fat log on top and waited as it caught. The sun was almost down. Really, there ought to be a battery of ritual drummers here to raise power. Alone in the silence, with only the power she could raise with an act of will, she stripped quickly and walked into the waves. The water burned cold on her legs and thighs. She waded in gingerly up to her breast and, bracing herself against the pull of the tide, splashed her face and the crown of her head and the nape of her neck. Let it go, sickness and despair and hurt and loss, anger and humiliation and all the pain of the year. Wash it away, take it with the turning of the tide, the turning of the wheel.

Light played around her, silver and gold and purple. She sang the old Yoruba chant to Yemaya, the Sea Goddess:

Yemaya Asesu, Asesu Yemaya,
Yemaya olodo, olodo Yemaya. . . .

∘ ∘ ∘

Three more days went by before the boat came. It appeared on the horizon, its patched sails looking like a collection of rags on sticks. Windspinners and solar panels dangled at odd angles, but it moved at a fast pace through the water, swooping into the bay and pulling up by the dock. The slender boat was about thirty feet long, trailing a small dinghy which a dark figure hauled to the side. With a graceful leap, the sailor swung into it and began rowing toward shore.

Madrone stood up and waved her arms in a wide circle above her head. She felt a rush of anticipation, mixed with fear. At last it was really beginning, this work—after the next few moments there would be no backing out, no last chance to change her mind and go home.

The hull scraped on the sand. Madrone ran to grab the painter and haul it up. Before she could touch the rope, a laser rifle stared into her eyes.

"You move, and I fry your eyes like eggs on a griddle."

The voice was deep and resonant but clearly a woman's. Madrone took a step back. She was shocked but not really frightened; it seemed too strange to her, unreal to be actually facing a real weapon in hostile hands. She stifled an impulse to laugh.

"Now, who the Jesus are you?" the woman asked. Her skin shone dark like the waves at night, her hair was braided close to her head and studded with gold beads, her eyes were hidden behind dark glasses. Blue pants and a shirt of some soft material hugged the contours of her body. Each slight motion set muscles rippling beneath the cloth.

"My name is Madrone. I'm a healer from the North. Bird sent me."

The woman regarded her for a long moment, without lowering the gun.

"If that's true," she said at last, "then you can tell me my name."

Gracias a la Diosa, Bird had prepared her well.

"Isis," Madrone said.

"Haul me in," Isis said, sitting back as Madrone grabbed the rope and began to pull the heavy load. But in an instant the woman leaped out and dragged the boat up on the beach as if it were weightless.

She must be incredibly strong, Madrone thought, as the woman stuck out her hand in greeting. Madrone clasped it. She felt a sudden surge of raw attraction, like an electrical charge, exciting and disconcerting.

How do I act? she asked herself suddenly. What rules apply here? Everyone she knew in her ordinary life was part of too-familiar context, a history. They knew her already, or at least her reputation. They knew her family and her Council and her patients and her history. She was accountable to them all. Here she could be anyone, do anything. There were no expectations; there was no one to disappoint. For just a moment, she savored the possibilities.

"You alone here?"

Madrone nodded.

"No traders been by?"

"Not in the last few days."

"Well, all right then. I'll try again next week. Climb aboard."

o o o

Isis rowed them out to the ship. Madrone climbed the rope ladder and hoisted herself over the rail.

"You do any sailing?" Isis asked.

"I grew up sailing the Bay."

"You know what I mean if I say, 'Ease the jib halyard'?"

"Yeah."

" 'Make fast the sheet'?"

"You'll have to show me how she's rigged, but I really do know how to sail."

"Okay, then, sailor, let's make sail."

o o o

By nightfall, they were far out to sea. Isis brewed sage tea on a small stove in her compact but complete cabin. A bed nestled under the curving bow, and padded benches along the walls appeared to fold out into other beds. A table folded down, and a sink and cooler completed the galley. They dined on the last of Madrone's rice and Isis' fresh-caught sea bass, which Madrone ate with some uneasiness. It tasted delicious, but she couldn't help but think of Nita's repeated warnings about toxins in ocean fish. When they were finished, Isis carefully cleared away the dishes, washing them and setting them on shelves behind rails. She pulled out a bottle of wine.

"You like wine?" she asked. "This is an excellent Cabernet. I raided it myself from the storehouse of the Chief Steward of Long Beach."

"We don't get much wine in the City," Madrone said. "We're still rehabil-itating most of the old vineyard land—it got so toxed out from pesticides—but I've always enjoyed it when I could get it."

"You'll like this," Isis assured her, pouring out two ruby glasses full.

They sat facing each other, a little awkwardly. There were a thousand things Madrone wanted to ask, but she didn't know how to begin.

"So you're a healer," Isis said. "What does that mean? What exactly do you do?"

"A lot of things," Madrone said. "I deliver babies and teach women how to stay healthy and eat right when they're pregnant. I treat diseases, either with medicines, if we have them, or with herbs, or with *ch'i,* with energy."

"And people have to pay you for help?"

Madrone shook her head. "No. Nobody in the North pays for medical care. It's free to all. The City pays me a stipend, as it does for most healers. Some of us put in for hours worked instead, but frankly, if I charged for my hours, the City couldn't afford me." It was the standard joke in the Council, but Isis looked blank. "I mean, keeping track of the hours is too much trouble."

"What about drugs?" Isis asked. "Who pays for the boosters?"

"Immunoboosters? We don't have them. The Stewards took all that with them when we rebelled. We've had to develop alternatives."

"And they work? You really get along without the Stewards' drugs?"

"Yes and no," Madrone said. "We've had bad epidemics. We get through each one, but we keep losing people. I'd like to examine some boosters, find out how they work. If we could come up with something similar, it might save a lot of lives."

"I can get you some," Isis said.

"Really?"

"No problem. Honey, I am one hot pirate. You want something, I can get it for you."

"How did you become a pirate?" Madrone asked.

"I was a runner. Bred, raised, and trained for it. So the first chance I got, I ran—off." She laughed. "Stole my sweetstick's boat. He fell overboard." She winked.

I didn't hear that, Madrone thought, or she didn't mean what she seemed to mean by it. "What's a runner?"

"A racer. See?" Isis extended her leg and hiked her loose trousers up to the top of her thigh. The leg was like a sculpture, each separate muscle delineated, hard, perfectly formed. Madrone had a sudden urge to run her fingers over the dark velvet of Isis' skin and feel the steel strength ripple under her hands. "I was the pride of the Valley, once."

The pirate swiveled in her chair, propping her legs against the opposite wall so that her pants slid down and left them bare to view.

"More wine?"

Madrone felt a slight glow, but she nodded. The wine tasted astringent on her tongue but rich in the back of her throat.

"How much of a healer are you?" Isis asked.

"What do you mean?"

"Can you free me from the drugs?"

"What drugs? I don't understand?"

"Those of us who are bred for runners, we're raised on certain hormones and steroids. That's how we develop strength and speed. But you got to keep on them, otherwise you kind of fall apart. That's why most of us are afraid to leave."

"But you did."

"I did. But I spend half my godforsaken life raiding pharmacies. I'm not free."

Something else was teasing at Madrone.

"You keep saying 'bred for it.' What do you mean?"

"I mean, bred. You know, engineered. They give our mamas a contract. All the Stewardships have their own teams of racers, their own training farms and breeding contracts. It's an industry. So is the gambling."

"You mean they breed people like you might breed animals? For certain traits?"

"We're not exactly people to them."

"That's horrible."

"It's not the worst way to live," Isis said, admiring her own legs as she crossed the left over the right. "You get treated well. The best quality food, and you never lack for water. Of course you train hard, but I didn't mind that. And I used to love the racing. It was just servicing the big bettors that I couldn't get behind."

Madrone felt stupid, constantly having to ask things to be explained that Isis assumed were understood.

"You mean?"

"I mean fucking them. Sucking them off. And, of course, the older you get, the less running you do and the more fucking. Until you get too old even for that. I could see the trend, if you follow me. So I split."

"I thought fornication was the biggest Millennialist sin," Madrone said.

"Oh, it is. They complain all the time about immorality in the Stewardships, but how immoral can it be if there's money in it? And technically it's not fornication if one party has no immortal soul."

"What?"

"Fornication is what you do with another person. We're not people. Our mamas did something to lose their immortal souls, like getting raped, maybe, or selling their bodies to put some food on the table. And our holy sacred genes have been tampered with. That makes us a sort of higher animal."

"That's insane."

"Nobody ever rated the Millennialists high in sanity."

"To us," Madrone said, "everything has a soul. Or a spirit, at least. Consciousness. Animals, plants. Air and fire and water and earth. Like it says in the Declaration of the Four Sacred Things, 'We are part of the earth life, and so sacred. No one of us stands higher or lower than any other.' "

"But you breed animals, don't you?" Isis said. "You eat them?"

"That's one of the most long-standing debates we have in the City, throughout the watershed, really. It comes up over and over again in Council. A lot of people think we all should be strict vegetarians, not eat any animals, not eat eggs or cheese or drink milk, because you can't really raise animals for dairy without killing the males. But a lot of us believe we can't do without the animals—not just for meat but for the part they play in the whole system. We need their wastes for fertilizer; we use every part of the ones we do kill."

"So how do you decide?"

"At this point, every household and every farm pretty much decides for itself. We all believe the animals have to be treated well when they're alive and killed with the least possible suffering, with rituals to honor their spirits. I don't know. My household keeps chickens for eggs, and we eat the hens when they get old. We raise fish in tanks for food and for the nutrients in their waste, and the heat that stays trapped in their water keeps our greenhouses warm. We've had goats, and on our country land they raise a cow or two."

"And what do you believe, personally?"

"That there's a qualitative difference between your mind and that of a chicken."

"Maybe. But they're breeding runners stupider every year. And there's new drugs for that. Really, as far as they're concerned, intelligence only gets in the way. They get too many like us, the ones who can't take it. Who get out. Who fight back."

"Well, there you have it," Madrone said. "I have yet to meet a revolutionary chicken."

"I eat what I can get," Isis said. "I often don't have one whole hell of a lot of choice, if you follow me. But when I do have a choice, I never eat anything raised or bred in captivity."

"If you ever come north," Madrone said, "you'll have company."

There was a long pause. Isis' eyes seemed to bore into Madrone's own, and she could neither meet them comfortably nor look away.

"So, if you're really a healer," Isis said slowly, "then get me free of the drugs."

"I don't know," Madrone said.

"Try."

"Of course I'll try. That's what I'm here for."

"Try now."

There was something unnerving about Isis' eyes, a steeliness. If I fail, Madrone wondered, do I go overboard? Is this a test? At the same time, she had to clench her fists in her lap to keep her hands from wandering over to Isis' thigh.

"Lie down for a minute," Madrone said, although she couldn't help but feel the suggestion was—well, suggestive.

Isis smiled. "Would you like me to take off my clothes?"

"Uh, that would help," Madrone admitted.

Stretching and still smiling, Isis dropped her trousers and slipped out of her shirt, revealing possibilities of the human form Madrone had never imagined. She moved over to the bed and lay down, face up, with a languid grace that seemed to Madrone like an invitation.

"Just relax. Breathe deep." Madrone sat next to Isis and laid a hand on her thigh, feeling the firm muscle underneath, and desire like an electric skin. And something more, a sense of the body as a fantastic pet to be cared for and tended and groomed. Great power and great pain.

"Deeper. Breathe a little deeper. And relax." Madrone let her own senses sink deeper, down to where she could feel the balance, the chemistry, the hormones that flowed from glands and swam in the blood. She sensed strange things, the drugs maybe, associations she had never encountered before, as if parts of the woman's biochemistry were heated up, moving at a faster rate than all the rest—and, perhaps, aging just as fast. Burning, burning up, burning out.

Madrone's hands traveled to the pirate's throat and the center of her forehead. An image came, a river in an artificial channel, so wide and deep that without the rushing force of the waters the bed would collapse. Could she change the riverbed? No, but an adjustment to the glands, the pituitary, the ovaries, and, yes, flow could be sustained without the drugs, not at quite the same level, perhaps, but enough to prevent collapse of the system. Probably.

"I can do something for you," Madrone said. "Not a complete change— you will have slightly less strength and somewhat less energy. And it won't lengthen your life. But you won't be dependent on outside drugs, although there are herbs I'd recommend. And it could be dangerous. I could be wrong about what will happen; there is the possibility that this could bring on a systemic collapse. It's not likely, but it is possible."

"Hell, raiding pharmacies is dangerous," Isis said, "and unlikely to prolong my life. Make sail."

It had been a long time since she'd worked, Madrone realized, as she moved from sensing to sending power. Like pouring a river through a river, light through light. She saw the changes as subtle shifts in color, patterns. Her hands danced through the other woman's *ch'i*. It was done. Enough.

"I'll check you tomorrow again," Madrone said, suddenly exhausted. Leaning back on the pillows, she closed her eyes. Was there any food left, she wondered? She needed to be fed, restored.

Suddenly she felt hands traveling along her body, moving up from her waist, over her breasts. They left a trail of sharp desire, which I should resist, she thought. I don't know this woman.

"Now let me do something for you," Isis whispered.

Madrone stiffened. "You don't have to. It's not fee for service."

"I want to."

Have I ever made love with a stranger? Madrone thought. All her lovers were old friends, the kids she'd grown up with, the co-workers she'd grown to know over time. The idea frightened and yet excited her. It went with this unexpected gift of freedom, the release from expectations. No, she didn't know this woman, who was stranger than anyone she had ever encountered before. And Isis didn't know her, could anticipate nothing of what she might feel. They could do or be anything together.

"Don't you want to?" Isis asked. And just for a moment Madrone could feel the other woman's vulnerability. I could hurt her, Madrone thought, and the realization made her tender.

"I want to," Madrone said. She let her own hands slide over Isis's body, which she knew already so intimately, down to its cellular structure. Isis pulled Madrone's shirt off and slid her hands down her pants. Madrone felt

Isis' hard belly, her grooved thighs, letting her hands and tongue and the warmth of her own flesh awaken fire from the sculpted form. Under the body lay the mind, the heart, and she searched for it, until she found it, fierce pride and rage that matched her own. Like two lava flows, they converged, erupting, igniting all they touched.

When they were done and she lay back against the pillows, Madrone half expected the bedclothes to be smoldering.

     ○ ○ ○

They sailed down the coast, past the empty beaches and the hills just blushed silver-green from the early winter rains. They went slowly, by night, moving only in the hours of darkness until exhaustion claimed them, anchoring in hidden coves by day. Each afternoon Madrone was awakened by Isis' practiced hands on her body, arousing, caressing, lingering in her most sensitive spots. Sex with Isis was pure art; there was nothing in it of the sweet playfulness she had with Nita or the depths she'd shared with Bird or just the simple everyday happiness of partnership she'd felt with Sandy. Isis made love like she sailed her boat, with great concentration and awareness of every current and shift in the wind. Her fingers maneuvered Madrone through tides of pleasure that rose and receded like the great ocean swells. Again and again she brought Madrone to the hovering weightless place just before the crest; then she liked to ease off, building the tension and pleasure both until, with just a slight change in rhythm or pressure, she'd make Madrone tumble over the edge and come and come and come. Rarely would Isis allow Madrone to reciprocate. She was comfortable giving pleasure, ill at ease receiving it.

They dodged beacons and searchlights, steering clear of the increasing traffic of boats as they neared Morro Bay. On shore, they could make out gray barracks and roads and machinery. That night they passed the ghostly, weathered domes of a dead nuclear reactor and sailed into the haven of Avalon Bay.

     ○ ○ ○

Bird had prepared her for the Monsters, and so Madrone was not surprised by the appearance of the people who came out to greet them. Everyone seemed to know Isis, and while the men kept a respectful distance, a circle of women and young girls crowded around her, chatting eagerly. An older woman, who bore herself with an air of authority and confidence, came toward Madrone. The woman's eyes were clear and steady over the gash that ran from her nostrils to her chin. Madrone recognized a badly cleft palate. She felt rage stir in the bottom of her belly, because this could have been corrected when the woman was small. As so much could have been corrected, and wasn't.

"I'm Rhea," the woman said, in a voice resonant although somewhat blurred.

"Bird spoke of you," Madrone said. "He sent me here. I'm Madrone. I'm a healer."

"Welcome."

She was given quarters in Rhea's house—a mat on the floor, low but comfortable, perhaps the very one Bird himself had slept on. Madrone felt close to him suddenly, as she traced his route in reverse. Where was he now? Had he healed yet from Sam's ministrations? Was he walking better, with less pain? If she could close her eyes, and reach out to him . . . but Rhea was calling her to dinner.

A table was laden with pots of soup and vegetables and plates of fried fish, and people were helping themselves, buffet style. Isis came up and handed Madrone a filled plate.

"Eat hearty," she said. "This is the last decent food outside the warehouses of the Stewards that we're likely to see."

There was a friendly crowd gathered in Rhea's front room and spilling outside to the porch that overlooked the bay. Some Madrone identified as Monsters, but many seemed to be perfectly well-shaped young men, often in the rags of a uniform.

"We've been flooded with deserters lately," Rhea said, standing at Madrone's elbow. "Nobody wants to fight this new war they're gearing up for."

"War on the North?" Madrone asked quietly.

"That seems to be the plan. We've got a lot of sickness among the boys, though. Seems once they're off the boosters for a week or two they start to cough and puke, and everything that goes in one end leaks right out the other."

"Maybe I can help."

"Sure hope so."

"That's why I'm here," Madrone said. "To help any way I can."

"What about us?" Rhea said, touching Madrone's elbow and looking into her eyes. "Can you help us?"

It cost her to ask that, Madrone thought. She is a woman of great pride. She answered, pitching her voice low and gentle.

"I'm sorry, Rhea. I can keep you alive, but I can't regrow lost limbs or change your face. I'm a healer, not a miracle worker."

"Your friend worked a few, from what I hear."

"Bird?" Madrone smiled, patting Rhea's hand. "Ah, but you see, he's a miracle worker but not a healer."

"What do you mean?"

"I mean sometimes in a life-or-death situation gifts come to us that are beyond what we can usually handle. Miracles happen. But to be a healer is to try to learn to make lesser miracles happen regularly and predictably."

"If you can do anything near what Bird did, and do it regularly, we'll be set," said a young man coming up to them. He was slightly built, hardly more than a boy, with dark hair that he tossed back from his forehead as he regarded Madrone with bright blue eyes. "So you're the one Bird sent. I guess he found his people, then."

"Yes, he did." Madrone smiled. "He wanted to come back here himself, but his legs were in pretty bad shape."

"I know. I was with him in the Pit. Name's Littlejohn." He stuck out his hand, and Madrone took it.

"He's spoken of you."

"I bet he has."

"He said if I met you to give you his love."

"He said that, did he?"

"Yes, that was what he said."

Littlejohn just stood, thoughtful but expressionless. Yet somehow Madrone felt they would be friends. They were linked through Bird, who had made it back from this place to his home, in spite of everything. That was one miracle. Surely others would follow.

The room was filled with sick young men, tossing on makeshift pallets of old blankets, their breath wheezing and whistling through fluid-filled lungs. Madrone picked one at random and laid her hand on his forehead. He was flushed, feverish, murmuring to himself in his sleep. *Diosa,* there were so many of them, how could she heal them all? And really the place needed a thorough cleaning; she was starting to cough herself, from the dust. She would take the matter up with Rhea. They needed more organization, more basic nursing care. But now she needed concentration.

Slowing her own breath, she *searched* her patient's aura. Well, there was plenty to see here, no difficulty finding causes for his condition. She moved through clouds of dandelion fluff, taking care not to breathe it in. But this was nothing unusual, just the signature of a common rhinovirus in the *ch'i* worlds. Fetid swamps of bacteria pooled in the moist crevices of his lungs. Could that really be all? A common cold run riot into pneumonia?

She shifted her perception, looking for the red glow of the bloodstream. There it was. She dove in, allowed her consciousness to swim down the arteries, taste the iron and rust of the hemoglobin. But where were the white cells? *Diosa,* this would be so much easier with a lab and a microscope. She hated having to depend completely on her own psychic vision. Still, this is why I came, she told herself, and continued on, looking now for the lymph system. Then she was wandering through a dry riverbed, littered with stones. She dug her hands into the soft soil at the bottom. Yes, there was still some moisture deep under the surface, but she could not tell if it would ever rise again.

"There's good news and bad news," Madrone told Isis and Rhea over supper. Rhea had made a pot of beans, and Madrone dipped chunks of bread into the

broth, eating hungrily. She felt drained but at the same time happy. Healing
was exhausting, demanding, but it was what she was born to do, and she was
glad to be working again. "We don't seem to be up against anything too odd
or nasty, and that's good. Mostly common colds, flu, some intestinal parasites.
But the problem is that all these guys have immune systems that are basically
nonfunctional. I don't know exactly how the boosters work, but it seems they
create a dependency. Once they're withdrawn, the system has lost the ability
to stimulate itself. Maybe in time it'll come back. Maybe it won't."

"What can we do?" Rhea asked.

"Steal us a boatload of antivirals?" Madrone said to Isis.

Isis shook her head. "They don't stock them up here. Just boosters, highs,
and lows. Maybe the hillboys farther south can get some, but the problem of
transporting large quantities . . . you'll see for yourself what it's like when
you go down there."

Madrone shifted uneasily. Everyone seemed to expect that when she had
brought the situation under control here, she would move on to join the
groups in the southern mountains. Should I? she wondered. Here there is
relative safety, but further on? I don't want to go, but then again, I didn't
want to come here, and I am desperately needed. Do I have the right to back
away from the struggle?

But that was not the question at hand. Right now she had to deal with the
situation here. "Look, this is what I'd like to try," she said. "First, any new
deserters that haven't gotten sick yet, I want isolated for a week or two. Keep
them away from crowds, from the sickrooms. I'll show you how to make
masks that can protect them from bacteria. And there're some questions of
basic hygiene we can go into. Then maybe I can look at their immune systems,
see if there's a way to kickstart them again, or if they may revive naturally,
given time.

"Next I want to see your herb gardens and take a walk out into the
woods. The more we can do with herbs, the more we can save my energy,
which has its limits. I can heal some of these guys, but I can't heal thirty
desperately sick men tomorrow and then heal them again the next day, and
the next. And Isis, if you can get me some boosters . . . I don't know how
I'll analyze them without any equipment, but I'll think of something."

                                    ◦ ◦ ◦

Given direction, the Monsters made good workers, Madrone noted. Within a
week, they had thoroughly cleaned the sickroom, harvested and dried the
herbs Madrone pointed out, and brewed and served vats of tea. She taught
them to apply compresses for fever and gave them seeds of echinacea to plant
for the future. The latest group of deserters, masked and gloved and housed
apart, remained relatively healthy. The days passed. New moon gave way to
full moon. In the North, the streets of Old Chinatown would be filled with

people carrying home blossoming cherry branches, and in the moonlit night the silk-and-brocade dragon would wind through the streets in a great procession of drummers and dancers. What year was this in Chinese astrology, the Year of the Rat, or the Horse, or the Snake? She should know; she had lost count. But that was another world, *otro mundo.* In this world, some of the sick progressed. Some died.

○ ○ ○

Madrone walked out into the forest, where the morning sun shone down on a spreading live oak. Under it the grass was a rich green from the winter rains, and she spread a blanket and lay down where the leaves let mottled sunlight warm her in patches. The warmth would help. In her hand she held a blue pill, one of the boosters Isis had obtained for her. She was debating what to do with it.

I know what I have to do, she told herself, but she hesitated. Without a lab, without equipment, she had no way to analyze the pill. She could attempt to read its *ch'i,* to divine its molecular structure, but no psychic vision was that acute.

But if she took it herself, she could observe its effects on her own body, watch her own immune system respond to the drug.

You've been down this road before, girl, she told herself. How many lectures did you get on the theme that a healer should never experiment on her own body? But what else can I do?

I'm not as arrogant as I once was. I don't believe I can necessarily overcome every assault, and my own immune system is presently working just fine, thank you. If it ain't broke, don't mess with it, as Johanna would say. Nevertheless, I'm going to do this, aren't I?

She opened her water bottle, spilled a few drops as an offering, and held it up to the sun.

"¡*Salud!*" she said out loud. Since the toast meant "to your health," it seemed appropriate. Popping the pill into her mouth, she swallowed the water and lay on the ground to wait.

She dozed for about half an hour. Really, she was exhausted, so tired that since she'd begun her healing work she had declined all of Isis' offers to spend a night aboard the boat. Finally some subtle shift in her body's chemistry woke her. She called in her spirit helpers, shifted her breathing to the pattern that put her deep into trance, and began to observe her own bloodstream.

She swam in clear serum, salty like the ocean, and her own cells looked like fish, lively darting red fish, and white fish of various shapes and sizes, some large and stately, exuding colors and tastes that clarified the waters where they passed, some active, sharp-toothed, moving in to devour intruders.

The stream felt healthy, full of life. But something was off, abnormal; she couldn't quite identify how or what. She turned, to make her way upstream against the pressure of her own blood, the closed door of her own valves. This is silly, she told herself, you're forgetting what you know about magic. Just visualize where you want to be.

The bone marrow, where white cells are born. She was there, suddenly, amid the good brown earth of a garden, a nursery. And the white cells were no longer fish but a kind of flower, which grew up from the soil on long stems, turning themselves into balloons and floating off. And now, yes, there was a difference here, a new taste, a new scent, as if someone had poured a chemical fertilizer on honest ground, and the plants were rooting and blossoming at a hurried pace.

This one dose won't hurt me, Madrone thought, but if I were to take this drug day after day, year after year, like any chemical it would eventually exhaust the soil. And then, to remove it suddenly . . .

I still don't know what it is, only vaguely what it does, and I had already guessed that much. I'm tiring now and cannot track this any further alone, without backup. I've learned that much, at least.

Breathing slowly, she let the sunlight playing on her face call her back.

o o o

"So that's it," Madrone said. She was sitting with Rhea and Isis on the porch of Rhea's house, watching the waves lick the golden tail of the sunset. Littlejohn had wandered up to join them, and Isis had moved pointedly away from him. Madrone, embarrassed by her rudeness, gave him a warm smile. "I still don't know exactly what the boosters are, but I can make an educated guess. I suspect they're synthetic cytokines."

"What?" Littlejohn asked.

"Cytokines are like hormones for the immune system. They stimulate white blood-cell production."

"If you say so, baby," Isis said. "What does that all mean to us?"

"It means you're lucky if you're off them, luckier still if you never were on them. I can't believe it's safe in the long run, to overstimulate the bone marrow like that. I would think you'd see a lot of leukemia after a few years."

"I got off them a few years ago," Isis said. "It was too much hassle, raiding for them and the steroids both. So I loaded up the boat with food and water, sailed off to a nice secluded cove I know"—she winked at Madrone—"and hung out for a month. Sure, I got sick, but I got over it. Since then, I've taken my chances."

"That's good to know," Madrone said. "It shows that the system can restore its own functioning naturally. If you were alone on the boat, you were isolated from contact with the worst infections during your most vulnerable period."

"So what do we do now?" Rhea asked.

"Continue doing what we've been doing. Unfortunately, I can't just make a metabolic adjustment for these men. Their bone marrow is like an overfarmed field; it needs building up. But herbs are very good for that, and I can teach you all the points on the body to stimulate. We don't have acupuncture needles, but massage and pressure can do a lot."

Isis slid close to her and murmured in her ear. "I got some points I'd like you to stimulate for me. How about tonight?"

Before Madrone could answer, Littlejohn spoke up.

"I got word from Hijohn today, from the camps above Angel City. Wants to know how soon you think you can head down that way. I volunteered to guide you when you go."

"Not for a few weeks," Madrone said quickly. "At least. I want to monitor these men, see if their white cells kick in." And then I want to go home, she thought, but already she suspected that she wouldn't. Her dreams were still full of dry, dusty roads and thirst.

Now there was nothing left of the sun but a pink glow in the sky and a few splashes of color playing on the dark troughs of the waves. I need to get this information back home, Madrone thought. But does it justify my returning? It's still only a guess, at best, not so different from the speculations we kick around over muffins at morning meetings. I still haven't learned what causes our epidemics or examined any of the antidotes. I still haven't done much to help the Web divert significant numbers of soldiers from the invasion. Maybe I should go further into the South.

"I'll send him that message. Can I tell him you'll come in three, four weeks?"

"Let me sleep on it."

Littlejohn left, and Rhea went into the house, leaving Madrone and Isis alone together.

"Come back with me to the boat tonight," Isis said, sliding her hand around Madrone's waist. "I'll be good to you. You won't be sorry."

Madrone wriggled, to shift Isis' hand away from her own breast. What's wrong with me? she wondered. Is it just fatigue? But that's never kept me from wanting sex before. Yet with Bird or Nita or Sandy, who understood her, lovemaking would have filled her empty places, replenished her like a drink of cool water after a long run. With Isis, sex was a physical performance, demanding endurance she didn't have.

"I know you're tired," Isis said. "I won't bother you if you don't want. But I could feed you and rub your back, and you sleep so nice on the water."

"Maybe tomorrow," Madrone said. "I'll come early. I should check you anyway to see how you're adjusting without the steroids. They should be pretty much out of your system by now."

"Come tonight."

"I've got work to do."

"What kind of work you got to do at night?"

"Dreaming." As she said it, she realized it was true.

o o o

In her dream, she was swimming, not flying, but swimming through the air, which was viscous and thick. The air tugged at her like a riptide, pulling her south. Yes, that is how I feel, she thought: caught in a current too strong for me, taking me away. But I have to learn to resist; otherwise the tide will carry me south to thirst in the City of Angels. Maybe I will go there, but it must be my choice; I can't just drift into it. Yet her real fear seemed to lie beyond the hill camps and the dry streets below. She was not afraid to join the fight in the South, only afraid to go closer once again to the empty place in her own memory.

Lily. I am dreaming to Lily, she told herself firmly. Lily, Lily, Lily: she said the name until a face appeared, eyes like two inverted smiles blinking at her in the night.

"Madrone. Are you all right?"

"I have some information for the Healers' Council."

"Give it to me."

Madrone explained to her what she suspected about the boosters. Then she had to wait and explain it again, while Lily wrote down the terms she was unfamiliar with.

"And the invasion?" Lily asked.

"I don't know. Rumor here is they're gearing up for sometime in the spring."

"And you, child? Are you well?"

"They want me to go further south, into Angel City itself. I'm afraid. But that doesn't matter. I mean, it doesn't seem a reason not to do it."

"Where there's fear, there is power."

"You've said that to me before. Lily, how do I know this is real, that you're actually hearing me, that Sam will really get this message? What if it's all just in my mind?"

"I can't prove it to you," Lily said. "I can tell you that Maya is well, that Bird has had surgery and is mending nicely, that the rains have been good this winter. I can tell you to trust."

"I don't have much choice, do I?"

"And I give you one piece of advice. Train your replacements before you go. Don't let these people get dependent on you. Ultimately that's no healthier for them than depending on the boosters."

"I've begun that, Lily. I'm going to train teams to work with herbs and pressure points and massage. I've given lectures on germ theory and *ch'i* and basic cleanliness."

"And try to have a little fun."

The image of Isis rose up in the dreamspace even though Madrone attempted to fix her concentration somewhere else and banish it. Lily's thin eyebrows made two perfect arcs.

"Have a lot of fun," she said. Then Madrone slipped out of the lucid place and into other dreams, where she and Isis lay next to each other, bronze against blue-black skin. But no one is steering the boat, Madrone wanted to cry. Isis placed a hand on Madrone's lips, covered them with her own. She couldn't speak, and then she no longer wanted to speak. The ocean rocked them gently as the boat drifted south.

14

A dry wind blew down the canyon. Madrone and Littlejohn climbed a trail that wound up the flanks of the hills above the bed of a dry stream. Madrone shifted the load on her back. Besides her own pack, she had slung a five-gallon water container, filled from the solar still at the coast. She wasn't too sure about the safety of sea water, but Littlejohn claimed the distillation process removed heavy metals and toxins. And anyway, his look had seemed to say, when you've been here a bit longer you won't care.

She was in the South, at last. For almost three months, she'd stayed with the Monsters, healing and teaching and training. By the end of her second month, the survival rate among deserters was close to ninety percent. The work there would never be done, but it had passed the point of greatest urgency.

Isis had sailed them down the coast, insisting that Littlejohn sleep on the deck. She was full of dire warnings and gloomy forebodings.

"You watch your ass," she said to Madrone. "Don't do anything brave and stupid."

"I'm not stupid, and I'm not very brave, so I should be okay." In fact Madrone was still afraid, but nobody else knew that, unless her fear leaked through her dreams and alerted Bird, back home. At times she felt him close to her and heard his song playing in her mind.

The dry air sucked moisture from her cheeks and seared her lips. The straps of her heavy pack dug into her shoulders; she hooked her thumbs underneath to redistribute the weight. They climbed swiftly, hugging the cover of the feathery chamise and the broad-leafed toyon. Here and there the path ducked under the thin shade of a stand of live oaks, their curled, leathery leaves blue-green in the dusty air. Stands of sage anointed them with pungent odors as they brushed by. Overhead, a pair of vultures wheeled in slightly tipsy circles, waiting. She heard no sounds but their own muffled footsteps and the rattling wind.

After a couple of hours, the streambed branched. They walked on the canyon floor, over the cracked mud of dry pools and the stones deposited by currents long ago.

"Is there ever water here?" Madrone asked.

"It flows for a few weeks, in the middle of winter. If the rains are good."

The trees were taller, sycamores with their mottled bark and great valley oaks. They were shaded by the walls of the canyon itself, and Madrone blessed the cooler air, which eased, slightly, the painful dryness inside her nostrils. She wanted to stop and drink, but Littlejohn didn't suggest it, and she felt sensitive about depleting their precious water supplies.

They were sheltered from view under the trees, and she could see Littlejohn relax, his walk becoming looser, more rhythmic. The canyon narrowed and the streambed wound on and on.

They rounded a curve at a narrow point, and suddenly Madrone found herself staring down into the barrel of an old rifle. Its bearer looked to be about fourteen years old, a slight brown boy with long greasy hair falling over his eyes. She was impressed. She hadn't seen him or heard him move.

"Who is our mother?" the boy asked.

"The earth is our mother," Littlejohn replied. "How ya doin', Begood?"

"Oldjohn died last night," the boy said. "We took his body up to the rock. Who's that you got with you?"

"The healer."

The nose of the rifle dropped abruptly. The boy's eyes stared at Madrone with a mixture of awe and skepticism that made her uneasy.

"Drink deep on the day of victory," he said.

Madrone was confused, but then she recognized that the phrase was a ritual greeting, like "May you never thirst."

"*Que nunca tengas hambre. Que nunca tengas sed,*" she replied.

Littlejohn blanched. Begood's eyes darted quickly around as if searching for someone who might overhear them.

"That's Spanish, isn't it?" Littlejohn said. "I haven't heard it since I was a kid, except from Bird when he'd get excited."

"Watch out," Begood warned. "Anyone in Angel City hears you talk like that, you be in the pens before you can turn around, with no more claim to a soul to call your own. They don't hold with foreign devil tongues, the Stewards."

He led them on through a barrier of brush, behind another outcropping of rock. There, on a flat stretch of ground where the valley floor widened, about twenty people lay sprawled under the trees. In the center, a ring of stones surrounded cold ashes. Two figures moved among the bodies, and they stepped forward to greet the new arrivals.

"It's the healer," Begood announced.

A man with a wild gray beard and staring blue eyes introduced himself as

Baptist. The second figure was slight and thin, almost genderless in a ragged pair of jeans and a gray length of cotton wrapped round her head and upper body. Her name, she said, was Arachne, but people called her Rocky.

"Drink deep," everyone said, but nobody offered any water, and Madrone still felt hesitant to ask, even though her throat was raw and burning. She felt almost obscenely wet, as if every cell in her body was comparatively bloated. These people seemed to be covered with a fine layer of dust. Their skin had a leathery look to it, like the leaves of the live oak or the feather-dry foliage of white sage.

She chewed her dry tongue and swallowed, which made her thirst seem worse. Looking around, Madrone felt dismayed. Was this the Web, the heart of the resistance, this collection of gasping bodies and old rags? Was this what she had come to serve?

"Have you had much experience with flu?" Rocky asked.

Madrone simply nodded.

"Would you come look at Hijohn? He's dying."

Rocky drew her over to one of the prone bodies. He was naked under the grimy blanket that Madrone drew back. A smell assaulted her, of old shit and dried urine and sweat. Rocky, kneeling beside her, looked up, a faintly defensive note in her voice.

"We try to keep them clean," she said. "But there isn't enough water to wash them very often."

"That's okay." The man was emaciated, unconscious; his wizened head on his skinny body reminded her of a dried apple on a stick. Hijohn. Was this Bird's friend? When she felt down the energy lines of the body, she could read traces of old breaks and healed fractures, a history of pain. For a moment, she thought she could almost hear a long sustained note, sung in Bird's voice. She went deeper, feeling for the cause of his labored breath and weak pulse. Exhaustion. Fever and malnutrition. And, underneath, a virus she recognized as one of the simple ones that in the well-nourished produce a three-day illness, hardly worse than a bad cold.

"Is he in withdrawal from the boosters?" she asked.

Rocky shook her head no. "He was never on them."

Madrone felt a slight sense of relief, then a deepening of fear as she began to understand the implications. For she could heal, but if what they really needed was food, and rest, and water . . . ?

An old joke raced through her mind, something about instant water . . . just add water. She put it aside and began breathing and focusing to draw her spirit helpers, laying her hands on Hijohn. After a moment she stood up, went over to the streambed, and searched until she found a smooth, round stone. She held it to each of the four directions in turn, gathering energy. Then, returning to Hijohn, she passed it over his body, drawing out the sickness and shaking it off onto the ground.

"His fever's gone down," Rocky said, touching his forehead.

Madrone nodded. "He'll be okay. Can we give him some water?"

Rocky nodded and returned with a small cup. "Hijohn," she said, "can you sit up?"

The man groaned and opened his eyes. Rocky supported his head while Madrone held the cup to his lips. She noticed how carefully he drank, first taking a small sip and holding it on his tongue for a long moment, then rolling it in his mouth, and then, after another long moment, swallowing. He repeated the process again. Three of his swallows drained the cup.

"Can he have more?" Madrone asked. "By rights, he should drink and drink to flush his system."

Rocky looked alarmed. "I'll bring him another cup," she said. "But it's been a bad year for water."

"We just brought ten gallons up with us."

"Yeah, but those are for the cisterns. For summer, when even the wells run dry."

"At least one more cup," Madrone said. She worked on him again with the stone, trying to use energy for the cleansing that should have come from water, trying to still the clamoring panic in her body, which had begun to whisper insidiously, "If this is all *he* gets, how much will *you* get?"

I can survive, she told herself. If they can survive, surely I can survive. But suddenly she was filled with the image of the stream that ran outside Black Dragon House. She could smell the moist earth of the gardens it fed, she could hear its musical voice and feel the slippery coolness on her fingers. What am I doing here? she asked, and then thrust the thought aside. For certainly there was no lack of work here for her.

She worked on other men with fever and flu. As she looked around the clearing, she realized that she and Rocky were the only women.

"Aren't there any other women here?" she asked.

"There are some. You'll meet them, when it's time," Rocky said. Madrone sensed something concealed in her voice, but she couldn't read the emotion behind it.

"Are there any more to look at?" she asked, when she had finished tending all the men.

Rocky hesitated. "There's one. But he's being cared for—differently."

"I'd like to see him."

Rocky looked at Baptist, who was walking toward them with an armful of firewood. A conversation took place between them in a few gestures, the raising of an eyebrow, the slight shrug of a shoulder. It made Madrone homesick. There was nobody here she could talk to like that, with the change of the set of her head on her shoulders or the soft escape of breath from her lips.

"This way," Rocky said. She led Madrone farther down the path, away from camp, to an isolated patch of shade under a sycamore. She pointed down, and Madrone looked at a piece of ground that seemed alive. As they drew closer and she made out the figure that lay there, she drew in a breath in shock. It was a human figure, entirely covered with swarming bees. They were crawling and moving over every inch of the body's surface, setting up a loud and angry hum, forming in a small cloud of arrivals and departures. She couldn't tell if the figure was female or male, awake or unconscious, whole or half devoured. She felt sick. It was like an image out of an old horror video brought to life.

She moved to go to the aid of the figure on the ground, but Rocky grabbed her arm and held her back. "No," she said, "he's fine. They're helping him. But he's enchanted. Don't touch him or you'll make the little sisters angry."

Madrone stopped. Ground, she told herself. Listen. When she listened, she heard the hum of bees, businesslike, purposeful. When she *felt* for the man on the ground, she felt rest after weariness, healing after wounding. There was no horror there and no fear. Only in her own mind.

"I don't understand," Madrone said.

"The little sisters are our friends. They're how we live up here. They feed us, and they tend the wounded."

Honey was antiseptic, Madrone knew that. There were worse things to put on wounds. And if they smeared wounds with honey, bees would come. But something deeper was happening here.

"Can I go closer?"

Rocky shook her head. "It's not safe, because the sisters don't know you yet. But soon the Melissa will come to give him water. Then, maybe."

They squatted down to wait. The hot sun beat on the back of Madrone's neck. She could smell the blooming wild lilac; its scent made the air sweet and she could almost feed on it. It could almost ease her thirst.

It was not long before they saw something appear from behind the trees, a woman wearing a cloud of bees like a cloak. Their buzzing was a sustained hum, like a chant. The air seemed to vibrate in harmony, and Madrone felt it move through her body like a sudden rush of intoxication. She smelled something on the wind, like the distilled essence of wild blossoms: honey. The woman seemed to be wearing no other covering but the bees; they crawled over her body like a second skin.

"The Melissa," Rocky whispered.

The Melissa's eyes, the only part of her not cloaked by the bodies of insects, gleamed darkly. A single bee broke loose from the mass and flew toward them, circling them a number of times as if sniffing them out.

"Hold still," Rocky warned.

Madrone grounded herself. She had always liked bees, had even worked the hives herself from time to time, and she tried to beam toward this emissary her admiration and good intentions. The bee flew back to the swarm, disappearing among the others. After a moment, a hole seemed to open in the cloud, to reveal the woman's face. She smiled.

"Drink deep," she said. "You are the healer from the North."

Madrone nodded. "Never thirst," she said in English, since Spanish seemed to produce such shock and alarm.

The Melissa gestured toward the wounded man, inviting Madrone to come closer. "Don't fear the sisters," she said. "With me, you are safe."

Together they knelt beside the body on the ground. Madrone at first had difficulty seeing an aura around him. The energies and colors were obscured by the flying bees. As she watched for another moment, she realized that the bees were not separate from the man. They had become his aura, his vitality, and their movements were shifting and sustaining his energy field much as she would have used her hands and her own spirit power to strengthen his link to life. As she watched more closely, she saw that the movements of the insects corresponded precisely to the treelike pattern of a healthy energy flow. The inner layer, of those who actually crawled on his skin, was like the etheric body, the most dense layer of the energy field. The others, swarming about a foot away, moved in a circular route from his feet up the center line of his body, branching out along his arms and continuing up over his head, to fan out and touch the ground before returning.

When she looked closer, she could see his wounds. They looked like laser burns, and she winced in sympathy. There were raw patches over his face and down his left side, and his left arm had apparently suffered a long gash. But that was closed, the edges of the wound bound together with a brown, sticky substance in weblike lines. All the wounded places were covered with honey, and the torn flesh looked clean, pink, and healthy. She could sense no signs of infection.

"Propylis," the Melissa said, pointing at the binding on his arm. "And in here." She indicated the water jug she carried, which she held to the man's lips, giving him a few careful drops. "Taste?"

Madrone nodded and opened her own mouth to receive a drop of something wet and sweet and strong. It lay on her tongue, burning like fire but tasting like all the compacted fertilizing power of the spring blossoms. For one moment, before it dissolved, she was no longer hungry or thirsty.

"That's wonderful," Madrone said.

"It is our way of healing. We don't have much, here in the hills, but we have learned to use what we have."

"I would like to learn your way of healing," Madrone said. "It's very strange and wonderful. And maybe I can teach you ours."

"Maybe," said the Melissa. "The sisters work with us to heal wounds, but we who are bonded to them cannot come near the sick. They have a horror of illness. In the hive, they kill the sick bees. The wounded, too—but over the years we have been able to teach them to work with us on injuries, as long as they don't get infected. It was difficult to train them. We have had to enter into the hive mind and become part of it. But it has also become part of us. I don't know if we can learn your magic. And if you learn ours—well, once you come into the hive, maybe you won't want to leave. It's very sweet."

                         ∘ ∘ ∘

Madrone spent the rest of the afternoon rechecking her patients in the grove and scouting the hillside and streambed for herbs. She was allotted a small amount of water for her patients, but fuel was in short supply. They lit fires only at night, Littlejohn said, so she couldn't brew medicinal teas. She found a few water jugs of clear glass and filled them with bruised leaves and blossoms for sun tea. She would have liked to bathe her patients, but that was out of the question. The bees cleaned wounds; as for the rest, when the rains came, everyone would wash.

But the rains were not expected for the next half year.

"It's not so bad," Rocky told her. "This time of year, you can always hike up to the waterfall."

As dusk fell, Littlejohn lit a small fire in the ring of stones and cooked up a broth of stewed acorns. They sat together in a circle, after the sick were fed. Madrone felt her body crying out for something to drink. Baptist handed out cups, and Madrone restrained herself from snatching one from his slow hands. As Rocky poured water, Madrone stared at the clear stream, wondering how she could bear the dryness of her tongue for even another minute.

When all the cups were filled, they lifted them high.

"Drink deep on our day of victory," they said in unison, and sat, gazing at the water for a moment. Madrone had been raised to treat water as sacred, but she sensed in that circle a reverence greater than she had ever imagined, a reverence she was rapidly coming to share. She swirled the water gently in her cup. She had never really appreciated the stuff before, how crystalline and transparent it was, how eager to take the form of its container, how it shaped and molded everything it touched. These hills, this flat bed of land, the course of the stream, the physical properties of the trunks of trees, the rounded shape of the stone in her pocket, her own body's form and the texture of her skin— everything on earth was some revelation of water. Blessed water.

Carefully, she took a small sip on her tongue, as she had seen Hijohn do.

Oh, this wasn't a drink, it was a sacrament. Every gland in her body seemed to leap for joy; her heart was racing. Let it sit for a moment, feel the coolness, swirl it in your mouth to wet every cranny, then let it sit again, until it takes on the temperature of blood. She could flick her tongue and set up miniature currents and waves; in her mouth was an ocean, a whitewater river like the wild streams of the high mountains she and Bird had rafted together. Finally, finally, when she could hold out no longer, she swallowed, dividing that small pool into five or six or ten sections, taking just a little each time to let the dry throat bathe again and again in that blessed sensation of wetness. And then she began all over again.

When the cup was empty, she could have drunk another five. But nobody asked for more. They served her a bowl full of a food that was strange to her: a nut-flour paste mixed with honey. She would have preferred an honest plate of rice and beans, but she ate thankfully and, when her bowl was empty, could have eaten twice as much again. But nobody asked for or offered seconds.

When dinner was over, they sat around the fire, talking as it burned to embers and died to ash. Baptist and Rocky were shelling acorns and grinding them between flat stones, their hands working automatically. Madrone offered to help, but Rocky told her to wait and learn during daylight. Hijohn sat propped up against a boulder, wrapped in his blanket.

"This may sound like a stupid question," Madrone said, "but what do you do up here? I mean, what's the purpose of these camps?"

"Different purposes," Hijohn said. He spoke slowly, wearily, but his face had good color. "First, we're a refuge for the ones who just can't take it anymore down below. We give them somewhere to go, mostly west and north of here, where we have larger camps above the beach. Maybe you'll get up to them one of these days. There's more women there, and kids even, and more water. But the camps down here, close to the city, they're for raids. We let the Stewards know that everything ain't under control. Maybe we blow up a water line one place or cut their communication lines somewhere else. John Brown, that the bees are tending, he got shot bustin' people out of the pens. Sometimes we raid a food distribution depot, give the stuff away. Steal from the rich, give to the poor, you know."

"And are you having much success?" Madrone asked. She was trying to keep her voice neutral, but some of her doubts leaked into it.

"Maybe this doesn't look like much to you, but it's growing all the time. We're like fleas on the back of the beast, you know. Or like bees. One sting won't do you much harm—but enough of them all together can kill you."

Madrone stared into the firepit, where the last embers were turning from glowing red to gray.

"What do you really want from me?" she asked.

"Three things. It's true, we need a healer. As you can see. I would probably be dead today myself if not for you, and I'm thankful. But more than that, the people here, we got to learn our own powers. We can't depend on Witches from the North, we've got to have magic of our own. We got some, you've seen the bees. But we need more." Hijohn's voice sounded weak to her, and she wondered if, as a healer, she was remiss in not insisting he go back to sleep. But he continued.

"And there's a third thing. The Web is strong, but it's also divided. We got the camps up here in the hills, but we got houses in the city too. Lots of groups, different groups, and they don't all know each other or trust each other. They don't have a sense of being one thing all together."

"And you think maybe I can provide that?"

"Maybe. You can provide a focus, maybe, that can bring some of them together. That's why I'm hoping, after you've been up here in the hills for a bit and helped us out, that we can send you down to the city."

The idea made Madrone shudder secretly, but she said simply, "I'm here to help. I'll go wherever I can be useful."

"I hate the city, myself," Hijohn said. "Up here, whatever else is happening, you got earth under your feet, and trees, and air you can actually breathe. Down there, it's nothing but poison. There's grown men down there that have never seen a tree. But some like it."

"What's your city like?" Rocky asked a little shyly.

"We have lots of trees," Madrone said. "Trees everywhere, and gardens. Fruit trees and walnut trees and avocados, wherever there's a sheltered spot. We grow a lot of our own food, right in the city. And there's water everywhere —not that we have a lot of it, but we conserve it carefully, in cisterns and graywater tanks so we can reuse it, and in the irrigation channels. But as much as possible we let it flow freely, in open streams that crisscross the pathways, so you can always hear it and smell it and sit beside it, watching it play with the light."

"And people don't steal it?" Baptist asked.

"Nobody owns it, so nobody can steal it. And everybody has as much as they need, because we all take care of it together."

"But the poor people, what do they do?"

"There are no poor people. In our city, nobody is thirsty. Nobody goes hungry."

She knew she was telling the truth, and yet her words began to sound unlikely, a fantasy tale of some mythical place she had invented herself, a dream too good to be true.

"Keep telling us that," Hijohn said abruptly. "People won't believe you, but that won't matter. It don't even matter if it's true or not. Just keep telling us it is."

"It is true," Madrone said. "It could be like that here. We know a lot about reclaiming dry lands. Rivers could run through the valleys, like they did a long time ago. People could have enough to eat and drink."

"Just let it be possible," Hijohn said. "True is great, but possible is enough."

"A lot of things are possible," Rocky said, and Madrone agreed. One of the names of the Goddess was All Possibility, and Madrone wished, for one moment, for a more comforting deity, one who would at least claim that only the good possibilities would come to pass.

"All means all," she heard a voice in her mind whisper. "I proliferate, I don't discriminate. But you have the knife. I spin a billion billion threads, now, cut some and weave with the rest."

"I'm a healer, not a weaver," Madrone answered back.

"Same difference."

15

It had been too long since Maya had walked out in the City. The hills were still green from the winter rains, the trees growing bushy with the new leaves of spring. The slanting rays of the late-afternoon sun lit leaves and flowers with an inner glow. Rose moon, she liked to call it, when everything was budding, burgeoning, bursting forth with color and scent and the promise of fruit. She felt giddy, attractive—not young, exactly, merely immortal.

She walked slowly, supported by Bird on her left and Holybear on her right. Not bad for an old lady, to be flanked by two such handsome men, she thought. Although Bird still worried her. Sam claimed the operation was a success; the casts had been off for several weeks now and Bird had quickly weaned himself off crutches. He walked with more ease and she seldom saw the pain lines crease his face. But she didn't trust him. If her weight became a burden, he would never let her know.

Bird caught Maya's anxious glances and smiled at her. "I'm fine, *abuelita*," he said. "You can quit worrying about me."

"I'll never quit worrying about you. Especially not on a night when we venture forth to reconnect with our Jewish roots. Worry is an integral part of our heritage, you know."

"Then worry about fending off Sam's attentions," Bird said.

They were invited to celebrate the first night of Passover at Levanah House, a Jewish collective out in the fog belt where Madrone's friend Aviva lived. Sam would be there too; he had especially requested Maya's company. She wasn't sure how she felt about him. Over the last few weeks he had been a frequent visitor at Black Dragon House. Ostensibly, he was checking on Bird's progress, but he spent much of his time sipping herb tea in the kitchen with Maya.

"What if I don't want to?"

"Then worry about fending off Rio's ghost. And Johanna's too, for that matter."

"We were always very advanced about such things."

Bird smiled, hoping she wouldn't notice that his smile had a forced quality. Yes, he was better, but he still felt like a clumsy approximation of himself, not quite able to walk, or work, or play his music, never able to silence his own worries about what was to come.

The weather is all wrong, he thought. Instead of this ridiculous sunshine, we should have storm clouds, gray skies, gloom. Madrone had been gone for months, with no word but the occasional dreams Lily reported. Defense had sent other scouts south. They brought back word of armies gathering, massing, moving slowly up the old freeways, repairing them as they came.

And yet the rosebushes were still heavy with buds and the city was busy with its usual spring planting and mending and cleaning. That morning he had gone to the central market. Farmers were in from the Delta with bushels of rice and black beans and soybeans, the last winter broccoli and artichokes, the first ripe strawberries. He had maneuvered carefully through the crowds to buy dried apples and raisins and bags of walnuts to make the *charoset,* the ritual food that would be their contribution to tonight's meal.

It was a good year, Bird reflected, as he browsed the stalls rich with surpluses. Sam had been encouraging him to walk, but only in the last few days had he felt strong enough to venture very far. He was profoundly relieved to see something besides the familiar walls of the rooms at Black Dragon House.

He hadn't realized what a toll enforced immobility would take on him. Not the pain, but the nightmares, in which he woke again and again, alone in the dark, abandoned by the living and the dead. He hadn't wanted to speak of it to the others, but they had sensed something, and after the first few nights Holybear moved a pad into his room and slept at the foot of his bed.

"You don't have to do that," Bird said.

"Maybe I want to," Holybear said, removing the blue silk robe he wore over green silk pajamas and hanging it neatly on the back of the door.

"You want to get woken up five times a night by my stupid dreams?"

"Yeah." Holybear settled down on the mat, folding his hands behind his head. "When your dreams wake you up, I want to be there. In case you need anything. And so you know you're not alone."

The nights passed somewhat better after that, and when Bird's body had healed enough so that a chance touch no longer jarred and pained him, Holybear moved into his bed. His even breath kept the nightmares at bay.

But Bird was still disturbed by this morning's encounter in the market. He had walked out of his way to avoid the area where musical instruments were sold. But as he'd turned to skirt the covered section where crafts and hitech products were peddled, he'd heard his name and someone had grabbed him suddenly in a hug so vigorous it nearly upset his precarious balance. He'd wobbled dangerously until hands steadied him from behind.

The small dynamic woman who had grabbed him pulled back with a grin.

Her dark eyes were wet crescents under a sheet of black hair that she shook back from her face. "I heard that you'd risen up from the dead, like—who was that dude?"

"Lazarus," said a deep voice behind him. Its owner moved around into his sight. "Good to see you again, man. *¿Cómo estás?*"

"Sachiko, Walker—good to see you too."

"How come you don't come around the Guild, *hombre*? We could use you."

Bird jerked his chin down toward his hand. "I'm not exactly playing much music these days," he said.

He had thought he was over the hurt of that but he realized, watching Sachiko's face register shock, then horror, then pity, and then carefully close to conceal all emotion, that he would never be over it.

"You don't need to play to have ideas," Walker said. "Besides, we're your friends, aren't we?"

"A long time ago," Bird said. "I don't even know who's in the Guild now."

Walker proceeded to fill him in on all the woes and triumphs of the Musicians' Guild over the last decade. Bird tried to smile, but as he listened to accounts of death he felt mostly pain. He was remembering what Madrone had said, that they had lost a third of the city. Yes, it was true, and it hurt.

"Come around," Sachiko had urged him again. "You can still sing, can't you, Bird? And write? Any fool can play guitar, but nobody else writes songs like you did."

Maybe he was needed, after all. Maybe half a musician was better than nothing.

But he couldn't accept that. Maybe he would never again be more than half himself in every other area of life, but music was too important. Better to let it go than to bring a shoddy offering to the Goddess.

"You used to have a beautiful voice," Sachiko went on.

"My voice is shot," Bird said. "Just forget it. There's no music left in me." He had thought maybe there would be, when Madrone was still there, and he had tried, for her. But she was gone, and he couldn't seem to try for himself. Abruptly he turned away from Sachiko and Walker and walked off without saying goodbye.

"You're awfully quiet," Maya said to him. "Are you okay?"

"I told you to stop worrying about me. Let me worry myself in peace, all right?"

"So now you're the one who's worrying!"

"You bet."

"Madrone?" Holybear asked softly.

"Of course I'm worried about her. Worried sick. And I'm worried about this city. Council heard our warning, but nobody seems to know what to do. We have no arms worth speaking of, even if we could reach consensus on how to use them. I tell you, I wish I'd gone south again, just because I don't think I can bear to be here when the armies come north."

Maya was silent. Although she tried, she could think of nothing to say.

"Everything's so beautiful," Bird continued. "The streams are full of water, and the markets are spilling over with food and flowers and crafts. And it all seems unreal to me. What good is it all if we can't defend it? And how do we defend it without becoming what we're defending against?"

"I can't answer that," Maya said. "But look, tonight is the Seder, when we remember how the Jews were freed from slavery in Egypt. The great liberation holiday. If it happened once, who's to say it can't happen again? We have to believe it can, Bird, even if it goes against our common sense. We have to believe in miracles, just as we have to believe that the days will get longer in the springtime, that the rains will return in the fall. What could be more of a miracle than that?"

"I wish the future looked that dependable," Holybear said.

"It never has been, certainly not in my life," Maya said. "I remember Johanna and I, when we were about twelve years old, walking home from school during the Cuban missile crisis, wondering if we were going to hear the whistle and see the flash. And yet, against all odds, here I am in a beautiful white dress, walking out in a city where streams run clear through fertile gardens and nobody goes hungry or lacks shelter or companionship or beauty. Worried, mind you, by a possible romantic entanglement in the tenth decade of my life."

Bird smiled. "You want me to cheer up?"

"Immediately, before I'm forced to reinvent the profession of psychotherapy. Oh, I know you need your depression and despair, certainly you've earned your right to wallow in misery, but I'm selfish. This could be my last Seder, and I want to enjoy it."

Maya, Bird, and Holybear turned a corner and headed for the base of the tower supporting the bright-painted gondolas that would carry them high over the city's twining paths and gardens. The tower was newly repainted by the Transport Collective so that iridescent colors played in subtle patterns across its struts. The windspinner at its crown was marked with a spiral. As the blades revolved, the spiral turned inward, a vortex sucking the eye in and beyond.

"I don't like that spinner," Maya said. "It seems ominous, somehow."

"That's because you're a writer," Holybear said. "You think in symbols. In my case, it's just a constant reminder of a math class I had to drop my third year at the university. Shall we take the elevator?"

"I can walk," both Bird and Maya protested in unison, and then laughed.

"I'll meet you on top," Holybear said. "Since I'm the one carrying half a ton of *charoset,* I'm going to take the elevator."

○ ○ ○

Levanah House was built for formal entertaining, with high-ceilinged drawing rooms whose French doors opened onto a back patio. Now long plank tables covered with white cloths flanked by an odd assortment of folding chairs filled the gracious rooms. Aviva was bustling about with carafes of wine, a rare treat these days, and plates of matzoh, the flat ritual bread. Sam came forward to greet them. He smiled at Maya, a speculative light in the dark eyes that nestled under his bushy brows, and gripped her in a firm hug that lasted just a beat or two longer than was necessary. All right, Maya admitted to herself, there is an attraction here, if I wanted to get myself mixed up with such an old coot—not that he isn't two decades younger than myself. But who's counting? she asked herself as he looked at her with frank appreciation.

Sam greeted them. "Any news of Madrone?"

She shook her head.

"I'm sorry. I hope she's okay. She's a rare one, you know. A rare spirit."

"I know."

He gave Bird's legs a professional glance. "How's the hip?" he asked.

"Better, you old butcher. A lot better."

"And the hands?"

"Slow," Bird said, in the voice that warned off further questions. And slow was the word for them, he thought, creaking up and down the piano in labored scales as he attempted to demonstrate some simple exercise for Rosa. Sometimes he regretted agreeing to Sister Marie's request that he give the girl piano lessons, but she had been so persuasive. "Rosa's lost her whole family," Marie had said. "Even the baby died last week. Oh, Bird, it would mean so much to her. She's very musical, and it would give her back something of her own. And besides, she's at that age . . . you know."

"Know what?"

"She has a terrible crush on you."

Rosa did look up at him with adoring brown eyes as he banged the keys and swore and sweated, and she was a nice girl, who worked hard and undoubtedly had some talent. If she would only stop asking so damned many questions.

"How did you hurt your hands, Bird?"

"A guard smashed them when I was in prison, down in the Southlands." He answered curtly, looking at the music, away from the shock in her eyes, which somehow intensified his own hurt.

"Why, Bird? Why did they do that?"

"They wanted me to tell them something I didn't want to tell them."

"What?"

"*Diosa,* I don't remember what, exactly. I didn't want to tell them anything they could use against us."

"Did it hurt?" she asked quietly.

"Of course it hurt. Look, don't think about it, *querida.* It happened a long time ago. Think about getting the timing right on those triplets."

She did think about it. He could tell by the way she gazed at him with a mixture of pity and worship that made him want to slam the lid down on the piano keys and tell Marie to find her another teacher. But he couldn't do that, not to a little girl. And the lessons forced him to play a bit, so he could answer with an honest "yes" when Sam asked if he was keeping up with his exercises.

"I'm not noticing anything I could call improvement," Bird said.

"Give it time."

"I'm not sure we have time."

Sam made no answer.

"Let's begin," Aviva called out. "Outside, everybody."

o o o

The ritual itself, Maya reflected, had added a bit of Pagan seasoning to its Jewish essence. She could almost hear the voices of her grandparents, sniffing in mild disapproval as Aviva led them into the garden to bless the elements and acknowledge the Four Sacred Things. Then the participants washed one another's hands as a rite of purification and filed back indoors.

When they were all seated at the table, Aviva held aloft the plate of sacred foods.

"Here is the egg of life and the greens of spring," Aviva said. "The bitter herbs, that stand for the bitterness of slavery, and the shankbone—in this case, a roasted chicken neck—to symbolize the burnt offerings brought to the Temple in Jerusalem."

"Perfectly Orthodox," Maya whispered to her ghosts.

Aviva continued. "And here is the *charoset,* this mixture of apples and nuts and wine and spices, which they always told us stood for the mortar in the bricks the Hebrews laid for their masters. But we know these are the sacred fruits of the ancient Goddess, apples of life, wine of intoxication, the tree fruits that honor Asherah, who stood reduced to the form of a pillar in the Temple of Solomon and who later was expelled from worship. Yet her memory was never truly erased, and down through the centuries her gifts have sweetened for us the harshness of life, even as this food sweetens the bitter herbs we dip into it. Let us taste it tonight as a token that no true power can ever wholly be lost, and as a promise that, whatever bitterness lies ahead, we will also find sweetness."

Maya could feel her ancestors bristle at the mention of the Goddess. Everything changes with time, or it dies, she told them silently. Be glad this ritual is still so alive. Now shut up or go away.

Ari, a black-bearded bear of a man seated at Aviva's side, stood up.

"I dedicate the first cup of wine to the ancestors," he said. "I honor the ancestors who were slaves under the Pharaohs."

One by one, going around the table, they spoke.

"I honor my ancestors who were stolen from Africa to slave on this continent."

"I honor the ancestors of this land, enslaved by the Spanish."

"I honor my ancestors who died in the concentration camps of the Nazis."

"I honor my ancestors who died in the Palestinian relocation camps."

"I honor my ancestors who died at the hands of the Stewards in our struggle for freedom."

"I honor those who will die in the struggles to come."

A silence fell on the table, broken by the sweet soprano voice of a young woman who sang a blessing in Hebrew. They drank the first cup of wine.

As the wine took hold, the arguments began. And that was quite traditional, Maya thought. She remembered the Seders of her childhood as nuggets of ritual embedded in a matrix of lively discussion, her uncles disputing fine points of ritual, her father, when he attended, challenging every reference to external divine aid, her grandmother popping up periodically to complain loudly to her grandfather, "Oy, Jake, hurry up. People have to eat."

As Aviva and Holybear argued amiably, Bird sat wrapped in silence. Maya reached over and touched his hand. He patted her hand abstractedly and gave her the little false smile she hated to see.

Sam was reading from the Haggadah, the book of prayers and songs and stories. " 'And the Source of All brought us out of Egypt, with a strong arm and an outstretched hand.' " He paused, looking up at them over his thick reading glasses. "What does that mean to us? Personally, after the Millennialists, I'm wary of any sort of divine intervention. I come from the fine old leftist Jewish secularist tradition, where we were taught to use the strength of our own arms and hands. If there's a God or Goddess offering deliverance, it had better be us."

"I read it as hope," Aviva said. "Hope is the source of strength. We can depend on our own arms and hands, but we can't do anything without hope."

"But it's not just individual hope," a woman Maya didn't recognize said. "The strong arm is what we can lean on when all of our arms are working together."

"God is our united support," Ari said.

"But what about when you're all alone?" asked the woman with the sweet voice.

"You still have the strength of the group to draw on."

"And what if you don't? What if you go against the group?" Holybear asked. "Are you then removed from the reach of the Goddess?"

In the pause that followed, Bird spoke. He was looking down at his wineglass and his voice seemed far away, as if he had to come back from a great distance to meet them.

"I have been in Egypt," he said. They all turned to look at him. "And yeah, my own hands and arms and mind and magic got me out. But it wasn't just me. And it wasn't just the collective strength, because that seemed pretty damn far away at the time, and the people I was with—even together, we didn't have much in the way of strength. So I can't tell you what it was. It wasn't an old guy with a beard, and it wasn't a big lady in the sky. But when I was trapped there, something did reach for me."

"How do we invoke that?" Holybear asked quietly. "Where do we put in our order for divine intervention? Because without it, if it's only our own arms and hands, however united, frankly I don't think we're going to win this one."

"I'm not talking about winning or losing," Bird said. "I'm not even talking about getting free or getting caught or living or dying, really. I'm trying to say that *this,* this livingness we're all in and of, has something in it that reaches for freedom. Maybe that quality isn't first or most central. It could be just like a single thin thread buried in a whole carpet. But it's there. The outstretched hand is there. If you reach for it, it'll grab you back."

Aviva broke the silence that followed Bird's statement by pouring out a new round of wine, and the ritual went on. They drank, they ate matzoh and dipped bitter herbs into *charoset,* they consumed an enormous meal of all the old foods Maya remembered: matzoh balls in chicken soup or vegetable broth for the vegetarians, gefilte fish that Ari had made from his grandmother's recipe, roast chicken and potatoes and steamed vegetables. Aviva's young niece stole the *afikomen,* the piece of matzoh set aside to end the meal, and Ari had to ransom it back by promising to let her off weeding the garden for a week.

Finally they settled back for the closing. A full cup of wine, traditionally reserved for the prophet Elijah, stood in the center of the table.

"Let's open the door for Elijah," Aviva said, "and sing his song."

Maya had remained relatively quiet throughout the evening, but at this she had to speak up. "Oh, no!" she said. "You're not really going to invoke that old religious fanatic, are you? I protest!"

"Why?" Ari asked. "What's wrong with Elijah?"

"He slaughtered the priests of Baal, the consorts of the Goddess," Maya said, "for no other reason than that they held to the traditions of their own land. He's the Junipero Serra of the Bible, your typical racist imperialist bigot. Why the hell should we feed him? Better we should invoke the spirit of Jezebel!"

"I just want to sing the song," Sam said. "I'm not proposing we raise his ghost."

"You're talking about singing an invocation, opening a door to a spirit and feeding him," Maya said. "I'm sorry, to me that's an act of magic."

"Do you know what the song means?" somebody asked.

"It means Elijah the Prophet, Elijah the Tishbite, Elijah the Giladite. Place names. It's talking about where he's from," said a young boy.

"But what about the second verse?" His older sister spoke up. "I'll translate it for you; it says, 'Swiftly, in our days, will come our Lord, the Messiah, son of David.'"

"Yeah, what about that, Sam?" Maya said. "You, the secularist, calling for the Messiah to deliver us."

"I just like the song," Sam protested. "Is that a crime? It brings back happy memories of my childhood. The whole family sitting around the Seder table, fighting like we are now."

"Can I suggest a compromise?" Aviva said. "We'll sing the song, to keep Sam happy, but with the door closed. Then we'll open the door and call in the spirits of all those who have been murdered throughout history because of religious intolerance, and we'll feed them."

"There isn't food enough in all the granaries of the world to feed all those ghosts!" Maya said.

"Symbolically, we'll feed them. And ask them to help us withstand the coming times."

"I can live with that," Maya agreed.

"I just want to sing the song," Sam said. "I don't care if we invoke Elijah, Jezebel, Santa Claus, or the Easter Bunny. Once a year, I like to hear this song."

With the door closed, they sang.

Eliyahu HaNavi, Eliyahu HaTishbi,
Eliyahu, Eliyahu, Eliyahu HaGiladi. . . .

The minor strains filled the room, seeped out over the threshold into the night. Then Aviva opened the door, and the spirits of the dead rushed in. Maya thought she could see them, still faintly aglow with the light of the full moon, and hungry. For a moment the air was thick with their presence; then as the door swung shut they slipped out, back into the moonlit night where the tattered rags of old roads glinted like threads of a web. Far to the south, armies gathered. In the hills and dry canyons, the moon made mirrors out of shallow traces of water.

o   o   o

That night Maya dreamed of the prophet Elijah. He came and sat at the foot of her bed. Much to her surprise, she realized he was a redheaded man.

"What do you want, you old bigot?" she asked him. "I know you and I know your story. You're nothing but a murderer with an inflated reputation."

"I want you," he said.

"Forget it."

"I want to help you."

"And what help have you ever been? Did you help the four hundred priests of Baal that you slaughtered in Jezebel's time? Did you help the hundreds of generations who starved and sweated and suffered and, instead of raising a hand to better their own lot, waited on you to herald the Messiah? And what about women? Have you ever raised a finger of your hallowed and prophetic hand to help a single Jewish woman escape from an unhappy marriage, or learn to read the sacred books, or express her own thoughts and have them heard by the congregation? For hundreds of generations, Jewish women have invited you in each year to eat the sacred foods prepared by their own hands, the egg and the greens, the salt water of tears and the sweet *charoset,* the unleavened matzoh—bread of affliction, we call it—yet when have you ever lightened so much as a crumb of our affliction? And I'll tell you something else—those foods are the real carriers of the tradition, the sacred mysteries. Not what comes out of your men's mouths, the words and the stories and the endless arguments and explanations, but what we women provide to put into your mouth, the taste of pain, the taste of spring, the taste of hope and new beginnings." Maya was sitting up in bed now. The room was filled with a faint light that seemed to emanate from the prophet's body, and this made her angrier still. "What in hell are you doing here in my bedroom, you old fraud? Get out! I'm not opening any doors for you or leaving you any offerings. In my book, you are the enemy."

Elijah shifted his white robe, hitching it up on his left shoulder, and settled himself more comfortably on the bed.

"Are you finished? Can I get a word in?"

"I say to you what my grandmother would say—feh!"

"Maya, since that's what you choose to call yourself, let me just ask you this. What happens to the enemy who is invited to share the feast? Does the enemy not transform?"

"What are you trying to tell me? That you've gone over to the side of the Goddess?"

"You'll never know if you don't stop yelling at me."

"I'm not yelling! But you barge into my bedroom uninvited, refuse to leave, invade my space, as we used to say, so don't be surprised if I get a little testy."

"I'm only here to do my job."

"Which is what?"

"You know what. I'm the herald of the Messiah. I am the forerunner of deliverance, the harbinger of redemption."

"Did I send out for a Messiah? I'm sorry, I don't remember. Look, Elijah, this one's been done already, and not done well. The last Messiah gave us two thousand years of grief. Crusades, pogroms, missionaries, holy wars. Now the Millennialists. Do we really need another round?"

"Maya, you're an old woman, but I'm even older than you. Hasn't it occurred to you that redemption might have changed its form in the last few millennia? How could it not? Is not God change?"

"Jehovah? Doesn't sound like him."

"Goddess, then. Does the name matter so much, or the form of the mythical divine genitalia? Maya, for year after year, generation after generation, I have been fed each spring by women. I have tasted the spring and the tears and the blood until something in me wanted to rise up and dance, to roll in the mud. I'm a changed man, Maya. Can't you see? The Messiah I herald has become the redemption of the earth."

He was gazing at her with eyes that glowed softly, like water mirroring clouds. Oh, this is my problem, Maya thought, I always fall for them, the wounded men. Wouldn't you think that at my age I would have outgrown it? Nevertheless, she could feel his appeal.

"How can I trust you?" she asked, finally.

"Touch me."

She reached a tentative finger forward, and he clasped her hand in his big freckled hand, the red hairs on its back glinting in the lamplight. Something moved through her, like a great unfolding tear wringing itself loose and flooding her, washing her clean, clean, so that all her empty, hurting spaces shone with light. The room filled with light, golden and silver and palest green, like tender new leaves budding off an old shoot, and a fragrance like the morning of flowers.

"Listen to me, Maya," Elijah said. "Tell your enemies this: 'There is a place set for you at our table, if you will choose to join us.'"

Then he was gone. She sank into a dreamless, silver sleep. In the morning, when Bird brought in her tea, he sniffed the air curiously.

"Why does your room smell like roses?" he asked.

16

In her mind, Madrone often carried on conversations with Maya or Bird. She had been in the hill camp for over a week; its discomforts had become familiar. You can get used to anything, she imagined herself explaining, as she stirred honey into acorn meal to make a meager breakfast, no different from her meager supper the night before. You can get used to hunger and thirst. The trick is not to think about it, or not to admit you were thinking about it. Goddess knows, there's no lack of distractions.

Her days were full of tasks, tending the sick and aiding the Melissa with the wounded, shelling the narrow acorns of the live oaks and the fat corns from the valley oaks, grinding meal, leaching its bitter tannic acid in such running water as they could find. She felt herself getting tougher, drier, more self-enclosed, like a leathery-leafed bush of the chapparal, which turns only the edges of its leaves toward the sun.

Night after night she tried to *dream* back to Lily and the Council, but all she dreamed of was water, rain pouring down on the roof of Black Dragon House, the sound of the little stream outside their front door, the roaring of a river in a gorge high up in the Sierras, bowls of water left on altars as offerings, hot water pouring over her body in the shower.

There is one thing I can't get used to, Maya, she imagined herself saying. I can adjust to the meager diet, I can even put up with thirst, chewing on a raw acorn to let its astringent taste distract my mouth from its need for water. But I cannot get used to the dirt, the smell of my own unwashed body, the greasy strings of my hair. And what's worse, the condition of my patients, which hardly bears thinking about.

When her moon blood came, Rocky showed her the piles of soft mosses she had gathered to use as pads, but there were still smears on her legs and hands and everything began to smell and taste of iron.

"I have got to have a bath," she said finally to Rocky one morning. "I don't care if I have to hike back down to the coast or I have to commandeer a water truck single-handed. I just can't live like this!"

Rocky laughed. "Maybe somebody can take you to the waterfall. It's a two-, three-hour hike to get there, so it doesn't often seem worth it to me. But if you want to go, I'll ask Hijohn to take you. He needs to exercise, build his strength back up before he goes off on a raid again."

"That sounds like a long way," Madrone said doubtfully. "Maybe I shouldn't."

"I guess they can all survive without you for an afternoon. I'll pack you some acorns."

Hijohn came for her a little while later. He had a sack of acorns slung across his back and a rifle over his shoulder.

"Ready?" he asked.

Madrone nodded. The rifle made her nervous. Arms were not generally in evidence around camp; she hadn't seen any since her arrival.

"Do we really need that?" she asked.

"I wouldn't bother to carry it if we didn't need it. We'll be going outside the area our scouts keep guard on. We could run into patrols, anything."

"And if we did, you'd shoot them?"

"If they saw us, and we couldn't get away from them, I might have to. Does that bother you?"

"Of course it bothers me. It makes me sick to think about it. Doesn't it bother you?"

"I try to avoid it," Hijohn said. "But this is a war, Madrone. And that's what war is about. Killing or dying."

"I know about war," Madrone snapped. "I was born in Guadalupe, down in Central America. My mother was killed by a death squad. During the Uprising, I saw people shot. I know it happens. But that doesn't mean I have to accept it or like it."

"You don't have to like it," Hijohn said. "But you do have to accept it. Unless you know of an alternative, up in your miracle city?"

Madrone was silent. What was happening in the City? she wondered. Were they carrying offerings of spring flowers down to the Bay and chanting ancient stories of Persephone's return? What would they do when war came to them?

"No?" Hijohn asked.

"We're not a miracle," Madrone told him. "We've just learned how to live in peace with each other. That's not so hard to do. But what will happen when war comes to us—I don't know."

"In the meantime," Hijohn said, "let's go have our bath. Any trouble, lie flat, let me handle it."

Hijohn led Madrone to a path almost invisible in the thick brush. They followed a stream that at first was nothing but a suggestion of damp, a trickle of mud, a string of small puddles covered with the green slime of algae. Farther up, they came upon a slightly deeper pool, maybe the depth of a finger joint, still scummy and stagnant. As they hiked on, they saw the almost imperceptible beginnings of movement in the water, a mere suggestion of ripples. They followed the streambed past rock pools and hollows until the slow trickle became a flow. At last they heard the sweet and musical sound, note upon note, of falling water.

They scrambled over a ledge of rock and climbed on. Madrone felt she could drink through her ears, she was so thirsty for even the sound of water. At last they reached the pool, knee-deep at most, and the falls only a thin stream sliding down a sheer rock. At home, Madrone thought, we wouldn't have called this a puddle, let alone a waterfall, but she wasn't complaining. It was enough of a fall to have a voice, and to have hollowed out a rounded space in the sandstone cliff where reflections danced.

They knelt and drank. The water tasted slightly of algae but Madrone didn't care. *Diosa,* it was good, so good, to drink her fill, all that she wanted. She dipped her hands in the water and splashed it over her face, letting the drops fall back down, laughing. When they finished drinking, they filled their water containers.

"I'll wander off, if you like, and let you bathe in peace," Hijohn said.

"You don't really have to," Madrone said. "I mean, where I come from we're not shy about nakedness."

"You sure?"

She nodded and slipped out of her shirt and pants. His eyes followed her as she stepped into the pool, squatted, and splashed herself. Maybe this isn't wise, she thought suddenly. It's too suggestive. The pool was so small they couldn't both fit in without rubbing against each other. Hijohn turned away, perching on a rock and turning his back to the pool and looking out over the canyon they'd hiked through. Madrone found herself mildly disappointed. You're incorrigible, she told herself. Just because you haven't had any sex for a while. Shame on you. He's not even really what you'd call attractive, except that clearly in these parts, he's the alpha male.

She rubbed sand over her skin to wear away the ingrained dirt, scrubbing hard as if to clean away her thoughts. Water was better than a lover anyway, she thought, it reached more of her intimate places, penetrated her pores more thoroughly, left her clean. She scrubbed her scalp with sand and rinsed her hair, then climbed up on a rock to dry.

"Your turn," she said to Hijohn. "I'm afraid it's a bit muddy, now, though."

"I don't mind." He smiled at her. Yes, he has a really nice smile, she thought. "Keep watch down the canyon, will you? If you see anything suspicious, give a yell." He placed the rifle on the ground beside the pool, carefully within his reach.

Dutifully she turned and looked down canyon. Which will keep my eyes from straying where they ought not to go, she told herself, aware of Hijohn undressing behind her. The bright green of new oak leaves, the blue-green of white sage, and the yellow-green of the budding tops of white-barked sycamore made moving patterns in the gray chaparral. Wild lilacs bloomed in white-blue clusters of tiny star-shaped flowers that sweated perfume, sending the bees into frenzied bouts of work. Orange butterflies darted over black-eyed Susans that bloomed beside vines of the wild white morning glory and other flowers she couldn't name, silver, purple, blue.

"I hope you meant what you said about nakedness," Hijohn said, suddenly appearing behind her on the rock, "because I've just washed our clothes."

She helped him spread them out to dry. They sat sunning themselves, the rifle lying at Hijohn's side. A foot of space separated them, and the air between them seemed to press against her bare flesh.

Madrone's hair was nearly dry. She sat up and began twisting it into braids.

"Why don't you leave it loose?" Hijohn asked. "It looks pretty that way."

"It collects things if I don't braid it. Wraps its little tendrils around leaves and twigs and tries to hang me from branches. Really, I should cut it but I can't bring myself to, yet. Sandy always liked it long."

"Who's Sandy?"

"My *compañero,* partner, lover. He was. He died last summer."

"I'm sorry."

They sat in a silence that eventually began to feel awkward.

"Have you always lived like this?" Madrone asked Hijohn. "How did you come to the hills?"

"You wouldn't think it to look at me," Hijohn said, "but my father and mother were both actors in the widescreens. Real good-looking people. When the Stewards took over, they let the Millennialists clean up the industry. They wanted everybody to sign the Millennialist Creed. My dad wouldn't do it. Neither would my mother. A lot of folks in the industry resisted and wouldn't sign. One day they rounded them all up, sent the women to the pens. That was the last I saw of my mom. My dad had been out on location with a crew, wrapping up the last shoot he'd been hired for before the crackdown. Some of the guys got word of what was happening, hid out in the desert, armed themselves. My dad snuck into town and grabbed me out of the school where they'd stuck me, and we joined them. I was nine years old. We began raiding the pens, but we never did find my mother."

So he's my age, exactly, Madrone thought. To look at him, he could be forty.

"What are the pens, exactly?"

"Some of them are like whorehouses, where they service the soldiers. Some are like farms, where they breed soldiers and runners and other things."

"Oh." It seemed inadequate, but she could think of nothing else to say. *These are things too horrible to comprehend, like the African slave trade or the Nazi death camps. They left her numb in response. But they were real, and happening now. They could even happen to her.*

"I'm sorry about your mother," she said, her words sounding flat and stupid.

"That was a long time ago. I'm sure she's dead now. Women don't survive in the pens for twenty years."

He's gone numb too. How else do you bear the unbearable memory, the image that burns the back of your eyes? Like me, he is a motherless child.

"So you see why I carry a rifle," Hijohn went on. "If it was a choice between killing a guy or letting them take you to the pens, which would you rather I did?"

The pens are real, and they could happen to me. It was a cold thought. *Not a new thought—I know what happened to Bird, to Hijohn himself—but it seems so much closer here, so much more real.*

"I can't answer that." Madrone turned to meet his eyes, but they were fixed on the trail that led back downstream below them. "I understand why you carry a gun. It's just that I was always taught that the ends don't justify the means, that the means determine the ends you can reach. That peace can't grow out of violence."

"No, but violence can clear away some of the underbrush," Hijohn said. "Make a little space and light."

"I'm not from here," Madrone said, touching his arm lightly and then drawing her hand back. "I can't presume to tell you how to fight. But I believe there's got to be another sort of power, somewhere, somehow, different from violence and maybe in its own way stronger, if we can learn how to find it and wield it." *Is that the type of power I'm meant to gather? Can I find it in these dry harsh hills?*

"Get down!" Hijohn said suddenly, shoving her so hard that she rolled off the rock into the brush. In an instant he had the rifle and was lying, prone, gazing into the scope.

"What's wrong?" Madrone whispered. She fought to steady her own breath. Her pulse throbbed in her throat. *Diosa, we were talking theory and now it is happening. What if he kills someone to protect me? What if he doesn't? Goddess, Maya, why did I come here?*

"Someone's coming up the path," Hijohn whispered. "Back off slowly, behind the rock, so it covers you. I'll follow."

She crawled backward, the stony ground hard on her knees. Hijohn slid gracefully down the rock, his eyes never leaving the path. Madrone could hear no footsteps, only the hum of bees in the bright sunlight.

A bee circled her face, broke away to nose Hijohn. Oh, Goddess, that's all we need, to get stung right now, she thought. But Hijohn slowly lowered his gun.

"I think it's okay," he said. "It's the sisters."

Then the sound of bees filled the canyon. Thousands of them seemed to be buzzing and humming and darting out to taste the nectar of her sweat.

"Come out, Madrone," the Melissa called. "The sisters have sent for you."

Madrone slowly stood and came out from behind the rock, next to Hijohn. The Melissa's eyes were dark hollows behind the living skin of moving bees that covered her face and body. She looked alien, no longer quite human.

"What do they want with me?" Madrone asked.

"It's time you learned to be one of us."

Maybe it was the rush of adrenaline still in her bloodstream, but Madrone's heart was still thumping, her breath still shallow and tight.

"What do I have to do?"

"You must be initiated. Now is the time, while the wild lilac is still in bloom."

"What does that involve?"

"For the next nine days, you will belong to us."

"Nine days! I don't know if I can be away for nine days." She looked at Hijohn, half begging for an excuse, a way out. Hijohn only shrugged.

"When the bees call, we don't argue," he said.

"But people will die," Madrone said, "if I'm not there to tend them and heal them."

"Others will live, if you gather power," the Melissa said. "Come!"

Madrone could not refuse. Quickly she put on her still-damp clothes and followed the Melissa back down the canyon.

                                    o   o   o

The Melissa led her on a side trail over a ridge and down to another streambed, this one nearly dry. They hiked up to a rocky outcropping where long ago a river had scoured a small hole in a bank, a dome-shaped cave just large enough for one person to lie curled up inside. Outside the cave sat a group of women, each cloaked in bees like the Melissa. Together, they appeared less like human forms than vortexes of whirling energies, a dance of beating wings that fanned the air around them and threw the brown dust into whirlwinds. They greeted Madrone with a bobbing gesture that set the bees humming even louder. The noise filled Madrone's head, canceling thought and memory, leaving nothing but a kind of primal fear.

"What's going to happen?" Madrone whispered.

The Melissa did not answer.

There is nothing to be afraid of, Madrone told herself. Where there's fear, there's power. Strangeness, it's just strangeness, mammal fear of the insect world, breathe it away. But they closed in around her, and for one long moment she fought stark panic.

She was surrounded by bees, humming and buzzing so that she could no longer think or feel or fear. Hands pulled her shirt over her head, slid her pants down and off her feet, unbraided her long hair. They poured honey over her body and rubbed it all through her hair. When the Melissa brought a shell to her lips, she had one last urge to resist, to hold on to herself unchanged. But the Melissa jerked her head back and poured the liquid down her throat so she had to swallow or choke. She gulped it down, swallow after swallow, tasting fermented honey and something else, feeling her throat and belly catch fire, and the fire shoot through her and change her. Everything around her disappeared and there was nothing left but sweet fire inside her, and outside, the buzzing, fragrant air.

Sweetness. She was immersed in sweetness. Her sense of smell was augmented. The scent of wild lilacs on the air now became the overriding quality of the universe. Each breath filled her with the promise of food and love and abundant life. Sweetness carried her, launched her on wings. She was suspended in the scented air, following her nose to bury herself deep in the heart of blossoms. Her body felt the magnetic pull of the North Pole just as it felt the pull of gravity. Petals brushed her with their moist velvet touch, and she plunged into their depths, filling her nostrils with scent until her whole body quivered, extending her tongue to sip delicate nectar so that she was all sweetness, inside and out.

Some human part of her mind cried out, fighting to contain the aromas that moved through her and around her, to name them, describe them, limit them. Sage. Lilac. Those were names she could hold to, and names kept her anchored to herself. Oak. Madrone.

"Don't fight the change." She heard the Melissa's voice, coming to her not in words but in a rasping vibration, a tone in the air, a scent. "Let go. Let go."

She was falling; then she was flying. Lilac was not a name but a realm of the air that called her into places where her whole body throbbed with delight. Sage was a universe, pungent, bracing. Hold on! her human mind cried. "Let go," the Melissa buzzed and hummed and murmured. Madrone's own fear was a stench she could hardly bear. The meat of her body stank of blood. "Rise," the Melissa said. Madrone wanted to clutch her human form but she no longer had hands to grip with, only wings that beat incessantly, gossamer propellers to carry her away from something lying dead below her that she did not want to remember. No, Mama, not now. What are you doing here? You are long ago and far away and I want, and I don't want, to be pulled down to drown in the warm red milk of your body. The air was filled with a sound that might have been her own voice screaming.

"Let go," the Melissa whispered. "Let yourself rise. Follow the sweetness."

"Rise," mumured the voices of the sisters, whether human or bee Madrone could no longer tell. "Rise and fly. Fly away."

Yes, and why not? Why not fly, when it was so easy, and her wings were pulling her into the air, pulling her apart the more she tried to hold on. But if she just let go they would lift her. She could let them lift her away from all the horrors locked in her own human memory, and dissolve, transform, take wing.

Madrone was lying in the cave, with no awareness of how she'd gotten there. It was warm and felt safe, like a womb, like a hive. She was covered in honey and there were bees with her constantly, a blanket of them, feeding from her body. The tickling of their thread feet, the almost imperceptible rasp of their tongues brought every nerve alive in her body. Then something stung her in the center of her forehead. It pulsed and throbbed, she couldn't even call it pain; in this state the word had no meaning.

She was moving in the dark safe hive, where body brushed against scented body, learning from movement and smell what the hive knew, the paths through the air to the nectar flow, the health of the brood, the golden warmth of the sun. And under it all, the queen's smell, something that crept into her and soothed her with a deep sense of rightness, the way the milky smell of the breast soothes a baby. I remember this, she would have cried out if she had had words; oh, Mama, I have missed you so—but before she could sink into the brood smell, her bee body swelled and elongated. She was the queen, nurtured on royal jelly, emerging with strong wings out of the womb-dark hive to soar for the first and only time up into the light, up and up, her strong wings beating the sweet air, chased by a cloud of drones. Only the strongest could catch her, could plunge himself into her in one ecstatic midair moment and fill her with the brood to come. She longed for that moment; she ached for it, but before it came she shifted again.

Now she was not the queen, but the drone, spiraling higher and higher in the air, quickened to life for the one mad moment of flight that was life's purpose, wings whipping the air in pursuit of the golden flying body that was the aim of all desire. Drone entered queen, shaft buried itself in bee flesh, and she was both at once, singing in union, letting go and spilling all and receiving all. Until the moment ended. The drone pulled away, ripping out his own guts, relinquishing his honey drop of the hive's life so that life itself might pass from drone to queen to egg. She felt a tearing in her belly; something gave way. The hive was a vessel, sweetness pouring itself through form, in and out, so that queen and drone and worker were only flashing, sparkling, momentary configurations of the morphic kaleidoscope, each individual an impermanent convergence of golden liquid and lacy wing, dissolving and forming, dying and being born.

Within her own body flowed rivers of scent and taste, and suddenly she knew them in a way even she, a healer, never had before—knew the scents her sweat could produce and what each signified and how they could be messages and conversations and offerings. The bees rasped at her sweat with probing tongues. Was it human hands or gauze wings that stroked her until honey dripped from her breasts and streams of nectar poured from between her thighs? Something was tasting her, tasting what she offered, and all was sweet.

The Melissa touched the center of Madrone's forehead, where the stung place still throbbed. With a tiny knife, she opened a flowerlike wound. A drop of blood appeared, and the bees swarmed, curious, to taste.

"We share nectar with the sisters," the Melissa said. Then she packed the wound with propylis. Madrone would have a small blossomlike scar. The sweat that beaded on that scar would be sweet, her own nectar to feed the sisters.

o o o

Slowly Madrone became aware that she was no longer in the cave. Time had passed; she had no idea how long she had been lying in the shade of an arching, pale sycamore. Bees hummed lazily around her; their sound was now like music to her, operas and symphonies and oratorios, and at the same time like a crowd of gossiping friends, telling her everything she needed to know. A piece of acorn bread lay under her hand, and as she ate it she felt her mind beginning to return. She felt a sense of vertigo, almost a double vision. She could see through multifaceted insect eyes more easily than she could look at things straight on in her old human way.

The humming grew louder, and her vision shifted as the energy changed again. The Melissa was sitting beside her.

"How do you feel?" the Melissa asked.

Madrone was surprised to hear the question in words. They seemed awkward, clumsy, unnecessary when a molecule of scent could convey the same thing. She gave her answer as she had learned to do, in a bead of sweat on her eye spot that carried in its chemistry the taste of wonder and confusion.

"No, answer in words," the Melissa said. "It is time for you to take back your words. You will need them."

Madrone closed her eyes. She knew there was an answer to the question, but words seemed primitive and inadequate compared to the delicate subtleties of taste and smell.

"You must speak," the Melissa said.

"Why?"

"Because you must return to the human world and be the healer needed there. The hive is not for you."

The buried nugget of her human self stirred and shifted. I know that, Madrone thought. It smells right. But the hive is sweetness and rest and peace and soft bodies endlessly brushing and touching and pleasuring one another. Remembering, she let the odor of her body plead to stay.

"You would not want it forever. You would resist and beg for your name back."

And that also smelled right. Madrone sighed and opened her eyes.

"How do you feel?" the Melissa asked again.

"All right," Madrone managed to say, and laughed at the imprecision of words. "A little—disoriented."

"It will pass as you eat more. Rest today, and practice your new powers, and tomorrow perhaps we will take you back to camp."

"How—what—"

"You must anchor the bee vision, so you can call it back or shut it off at will. Here, touch your forehead, on the bee spot. And remember your old self, and call her back. Say your human name."

"Madrone." She shook her head slightly, as her vision cleared and the world resolved itself back into separate objects.

"And now touch the spot again, remember the hive smell, and let the bee sense return."

Again, vision shifted, letting scent replace sight and knowing replace thinking.

"And now call yourself back again."

Madrone hesitated, the words not making sense, until the Melissa picked up Madrone's hand and placed it on her forehead again. "Your name," she reminded her.

"Madrone."

"Practice that change, until you can remember it when you're in your bee mind and do it at will. Can you do that?"

"Yes. I've been doing stuff like that since I was a baby. I just need to work at it a bit—and to want to come back."

"That is always the challenge. The hive is very sweet."

"But you—you stay in the bee mind, and yet you walk and talk and interact with other humans."

"As little as possible. But I have many many years behind me of this shapeshifting, and the other Melissas also. You are very new, and we have given you only the small initiation."

"If that was the small one, Goddess save me from the big one!"

"It may come to you in time, but I think that dance is not yours. The big initiation takes everything, and when you emerge you are yourself no longer but part of us, as every bee is part of the hive. But we have taken nothing from you—not your name, not your power. All will be as it was before. You are not of the hive, as we are, but you will be able to draw upon the sisters for help and nourishment and protection."

"How? How do I do that?"

"Through your bee spot. Come into your bee mind now, and I will teach you how to call the sisters when you need them."

Madrone touched the spot and let her breath and memory take her back into the sweetness. The bees cloaking the Melissa's face shifted, like the parting of a veil, and from the blossomlike scar in the center of her forehead a crystal bead of sweat emerged. Madrone leaned forward and touched the tip of her tongue to the drop. Her whole body came alive with longing. She was called, she had to come, she wanted to come. The taste changed. She sensed danger; she was filled with rage, it shook her body and she was ready to rip herself apart and die in defense of the source of sweetness. And then the taste changed again, and she knew hunger, an emptiness demanding to be filled, and then again it changed and she knew she was meant to carry a complex scent back to the hive and dance. Then her hand was being slapped against her own forehead again, and once more she returned to her human self.

"Today we will work on just these four things; the call to the bees, the call for protection, the call for food, and the message call. If you can learn these four, you will do well."

"And the healing that you do with the bees—can I learn that?"

The Melissa shook her head. "That comes after the big initiation, and even then it is tricky and dangerous. It goes against the nature of the little sisters, which is to kill the sick and wounded for the sake of the whole, not to cherish the individual parts."

"And what you've taught me, does that go against their nature?"

"What I have taught you works with their nature. It is how they communicate. Even so, never make the mistake of thinking you control them. They are wild. They will aid you if they wish to, but they will not always understand you, and with all you have learned in these days, you still only barely begin to understand them."

"How did you learn all this? Who taught you?"

"The old woman taught me, as she taught us all."

"And who is the old woman?"

"In the time of the great sickness and the hunger, when the Stewards came to power, she fled to these canyons to live quietly and secretly, for she was a Witch. She grew a garden and kept bees, and when her friends and family died in the epidemic, and she was lonely, she spoke to the bees and grew more and more like them, until she shared some of their secrets and learned to brew the nectar that opens the bee mind. She trained us all."

"Is she still alive? Can I meet her?"

The Melissa was silent. Madrone lay back, suddenly exhausted. Through the dappled shade, spots of sunlight shone red behind her lids.

"Rest a bit," the Melissa said. "I will bring more bread, and then we will practice again."

She dozed. In her dream, she saw Lily's face. The old woman cupped her hands and lifted them to the center of her brow, where there was a waterfall. She held them out to Madrone, offering her a drink. Madrone dipped her face into the cool water, lapped with her tongue like an animal. She tasted urgency, and fear.

17

It seemed to Maya that the whole City had come to Council. She recognized many people, some she hadn't seen in years, since she stopped going to meetings of the Writers' Guild, but they were surrounded by ranks of strangers crowded into every spare corner of space, practically sitting in the laps of the masked Voices. The crowd provided visual relief from the tension in the room. San Franciscans had always loved costume, Maya reflected. Now fashion had become tribal; one's garb announced one's loyalties and identity. The contingent from northside favored high-collared jackets in soft brocades, chrysanthemum-patterned silks, sarongs, or plain denim trousers vaguely reminiscent of the China of the 1970s. The neighbors of Black Dragon House sported ponchos and brightly embroidered cotton shirts. The tecchies wore unadorned jumpsuits in solid colors, the delegations from the Tribal Lands upriver wore their full traditional regalia complete with feather cloaks and basketry hats, while the Fairy men from center city were bedecked with scarves and costume jewelry. Within those broader categories were hundreds of variations: a woman with five dangling earrings in each lobe, a slim man in a rhinestone-studded vest, a tall person of indeterminate sex in a leotard and tutu. Hair was shaved, sculpted, braided, twined, cornrowed, dreadlocked, colored, beaded, and freely hanging loose. Maya herself wore crone's black. Simple, she thought, and well suited to her age and purported dignity.

In one corner sat groups from the Forest Communities to the east and north, sporting rough work clothes and heavy boots. Around the room sat clusters of representatives from the other cities that hugged the Bay and the habitable spots of the river valleys. Against the far wall sat the representatives of the Wild Boar People, their matted hair caked with dirt. Council had sent them a special invitation for this meeting. People left a moat of empty space around them, and windows were opened in their vicinity.

The crowd settled down after a great deal of jostling, shuffling, and adjusting of feet and arms and legs. Bird sat squashed against Maya's right side, with Sage crammed between his legs. On her left, Nita perched on Holybear's lap. When everyone was settled, a man and a woman rose in the center.

"I'm Joseph."

"I'm Salal. We're the Crows, the facilitators, for this morning."

On the signers' platform a young woman began translating the words of those who preferred not to speak and sign simultaneously. The meeting had begun.

Joseph lit a candle, and Salal formally invited in the spirits of the Four Sacred Things. Maya felt the atmosphere of the room deepen, as the Voices went into trance. A woman in a white headcloth and flowing skirts stood up and called Elegba the Trickster, God of the Crossroads. Sage rose and called Hecate. A very young man stood up and invoked the ancestors. Sister Marie, who was seated not far from them, asked for the blessing of the Virgin. A man Maya recognized from the Seder recited the Shema. The calling went on and on, until finally Sam stood up.

"Look, I don't want to step on anybody's religion. But we can call all the spirits in the universe, and in the end we're still going to have to decide what to do. Maybe we'd better get on with it, before the Stewards' troops get over San Bruno Hill."

There was a slight ripple of laughter, as Joseph asked, "Are we ready to begin the discussion?"

"Yes," the room thundered.

"All right, then." He peered around the room with his dark, narrow eyes, running his hands over the brush of his clipped black hair. "There's only one main question on the agenda today, and that is: What the hell are we going to do?"

"Can we hear a report from Defense first?" Salal suggested. "What exactly is the situation?"

The woman who rose to speak looked to be in her eighties. She had clear gray eyes and short-cropped white hair, and Maya recognized her, suddenly, as Greta Jeanne, one of *Las Cuatro*. Beside her, Lily was seated, dressed in a simple black shift. She and Maya exchanged nods of greeting.

"There's an army of approximately five thousand marching up the old Highway 101," Greta said. "They're repairing the road as they go, and we assume that when they reach the good stretch on the peninsula, which should be in about a week, they'll bring up trucks from the South. Along the same route they're also laying rail, which the Santa Cruz and peninsula councils have been sabotaging rather systematically. They're well armed with laser rifles, handguns, and, we assume, other weapons."

"Five thousand—that's not so bad," someone murmured.

"That's only the advance guard. Their main purpose seems to be to protect the road-building operations. There's more on the way."

"How many more?" Salal asked.

Bird stood. All eyes in the room turned to look at him. He felt almost ashamed, as if by bringing news of the invasion he were somehow responsible for it. "From what I saw last summer," he said, "there could easily be at least ten times that many."

"How the hell do they feed all those people?" someone murmured.

"They feed on people like us," Bird said. "They'll eat up our gardens, our fields, and our optimism pretty quick." He sat down.

"And what do we have in the way of defensive resources?" Joseph asked.

Lily stood up and carefully enumerated the numbers of available weapons in the City's defenses. The discussion left Maya somewhat lost, but she could see Bird's face looking more and more grim. Holybear wore a glum mask, and even Manzanita wasn't smiling.

"Why didn't we start weapons production three months ago?" a young woman asked.

"We have no factories to make guns and bombs and laser rifles," said a large man whom Maya had seen before, speaking for the Technicians' Guild. "We have no consensus to build them. And if we had, it would have been at the expense of something else, food production or communications or transport. Especially if you remember that we were recovering from another epidemic, and it's been hard enough to keep basic services going."

"That's exactly what they wanted. We could have tightened our belts," said a young man who was, in Maya's opinion, already far too thin.

"Maybe," the big man said. "But if we start choosing guns over food and water, we become what we're fighting against."

"But if we lose to the Stewards, we won't have the luxury of choosing food or water or anything else."

"That's the dilemma patriarchy has posed for the last five thousand years," Greta said.

"I don't find that grounds for optimism," Sam said. "In all those five thousand years, has the peaceful side ever won out?"

Why is it so hard to believe in war? Bird thought. I've been to the Southlands, I've faced their power, and yet I still can't grasp that they'll succeed in imposing it here. He wanted to ask Maya if every war she'd lived through had seemed unreal.

"Isn't that our collective challenge, then?" Lily said. "If we don't have guns, we have vision and imagination."

"A vision ain't much protection against a laser rifle," a voice called from the back of the crowd.

The talk went on interminably, as strategy after strategy was proposed, examined, and eventually abandoned as unpromising, if not hopeless.

"Don't give up," Lily addressed the room as discussion lagged. "We are simply challenged now to extend our imaginations beyond solutions that have been tried before."

"Well, we seem to have exhausted all practical, rational, and reasonable approaches to this situation," Salal said. "What it comes down to is, nobody can see a way out. Am I wrong? So either we need a miracle, an evacuation plan, or a proposal for how to go down with dignity."

She doesn't believe it either, Bird noted. Not really. Otherwise how could she sound so cheerful, tossing her flame-red hair and smiling as she talks of despair?

The Speaker stirred and made her careful way to the west, bending her ear to Salmon.

"Friend Salmon says, 'You have placed spawn in Los Lobos Creek, and we will return. Don't give up. Listen to the storyteller.' "

The masked figure inclined its head toward Maya. She found herself staring into its eyes.

She had hoped to avoid speaking today, had prayed that Defense had some secret plan that would absolve her from sharing her vision. And it's partly embarrassment, she admitted to herself, that for over half a century I've been spokeswoman for the Goddess, and here at the crucial moment I turn up with a visitation from an Old Testament prophet. Am I merely getting senile? More than that, the implications of her vision scared her. It seemed to call for qualities of courage and vision she was not sure that anyone possessed.

Reluctantly, she stood up. "I'm a storyteller," she said, "and I had a vision. I don't much like it, and I'm not sure what good it might do us. But for what it's worth, here it is." She told them about her visit with the prophet Elijah, and they listened respectfully. She finished with the words Elijah had spoken to her: "What happens to the enemy who is invited to share the feast? Does the enemy not transform? Tell your enemies this: There is a place set for you at our table, if you will choose to join us."

Silence intensified throughout the room.

"So what you're proposing is?" Joseph asked.

"Nonviolent resistance."

"Something like that seems indicated," Salal said. "Given that success in violent resistance seems beyond our means."

"How does it work?" a young woman from the Forest Communities asked.

"Like the king of Denmark," Maya said. The faces around her looked puzzled. "Don't they teach you history? In World War Two, when the Nazis took over most of Europe, they issued a proclamation that all Jews had to wear a yellow star on their clothing. It was the first step toward rounding them up and sending them to the ovens. And most countries collaborated. But in Denmark, the day after the law was proclaimed, the king rode out wearing a yellow star, and so did everybody else. Their Jews survived."

"But how would it work here?" someone else asked.

Maya answered. "Suppose that nobody in the city obeys the invaders, or helps them, or gives them information? Suppose all we say to the soldiers when they come, is: 'There is a place set for you at our table, if you will choose to join us'?"

"Complete noncooperation?" Greta asked.

"I'm not a Gandhian," Maya said. "I've worked in nonviolent movements all my life, but I've never believed in the spiritual benefits of self-immolation. To be honest, I don't know if this will work. In part it depends on the enemy we're facing, and how ruthless they're willing to be."

Bird stood again. He had been arguing this with Maya all week, and he was still unsure whether he would come around to agreeing with her. "They are ruthless." He spoke slowly, signing his own words as he went, as if deliberately to display his broken hands. "I've been up against some of them, and frankly I can't envision them transforming, even under the influence of our sweet characters. But there is this. Of those first five thousand, at least forty-five hundred are going to be black, brown, yellow, red, or some combination, mixed with just plain poor. And they're in the army because they come out of a world you can't even imagine—I can hardly imagine it myself, even though I was locked up in it for ten years—where the color of your skin determines everything about you; where if you don't have money, not only don't you eat, you don't drink. These guys, they may never have seen free-running water. They're going to come marching in here, and it's going to look like paradise on earth to them.

"So it just might work. Some of them might welcome an invitation to come over. But not all. If we do this, some of us are going to die. Some of us are going to be hurt, imprisoned, beaten, tortured."

"And if we fight?" Lily asked.

"We would be fighting—just in a different way," Nita said.

"If we fight them with guns?" Lily went on. She spoke from her seat, quietly, yet her voice carried across the room and rang with authority. "Aren't some of us going to die, be imprisoned, tortured, then? Aren't we just forgoing the satisfaction of taking a few of them along with us?"

"Don't knock that satisfaction," Bird said. "It's real."

"Real it may be," Lily said, "but it is an indulgence we cannot afford. Because what is on trial here is not just us. We stand on the ridgeline of the future, the great divide determining whether or not what we have built can survive."

"It will survive if we have the guts to defend it," said Cress of the Water Council, rising and pushing back the red bandanna that bound his dark hair. He glared defiantly at Lily, taking in Bird also with a hostile glance and looking, Maya thought, like an old poster of Che Guevara that had hung in the grease-spattered kitchen she'd shared with Rio in the sixties.

Mierda, Bird thought, not Cress. Lily was right, we should have talked to him privately first. But Bird had resisted the idea. He remembered Cress from a decade back, when his name had been Carlos and he had shown such talent on the guitar that the Musicians' Guild had offered him membership. He'd declined and joined the Water Council.

"Why?" Bird had asked, meeting him in the market a few days later. "You're good, *hombre.*"

"Because music is a luxury. Water is a necessity."

"Music is more than a luxury. We all know what happens to a society that doesn't value music and art and dance."

"We all know what happens to a society that doesn't protect its own survival!" Carlos/Cress had turned to stare coldly into Bird's eyes. "Or maybe you don't. I do. I was born in Fresno. I know what it's like when the temperature climbs up above a hundred and ten degrees, day after day, and the crops bake and die, and there's less and less every week to eat. My folks didn't want to leave, like most did, so they hung on until the quake of '27. By then we'd pumped so much water out of the aquifers that the land fell in on the empty water table when the tremblor hit. Every standing structure fell. My baby sister and I were buried under our house, pinned by the roof beams. I can still hear her voice, calling for water, getting weaker and weaker until she died."

Bird had opened his mouth to say something, but Carlos went on without giving him a chance to speak.

"Three days later my dad dug us out. My brothers were dead, my mother was dead, but the two of us survived. We headed out for the Bay, unlike most of the misled fuckers who believed the Millennialists about the hotbed of Satan worship here. They headed for the Oregon border, or south to the labor camps of LA, where I'm sure the Stewards picked their bones if they didn't die on the road. But we walked here. It took us three weeks, in the heat, rationing every damn drop of water. Believe me, we weren't singing any songs. We weren't worrying about music."

Bird had laid a sympathetic hand on Carlos's shoulder, but he shrugged it off and pulled away abruptly, walking off with only a curt goodbye.

He told me more than he intended, Bird thought now, opened more than he meant to, and so he hated me, because I couldn't truly meet him then, when I was what? Eighteen? How could I have matched the authority of his suffering? Not then.

But now? Now he hates me because in the arena of competitive suffering, I have an edge.

"Our guts are not in question here," Lily said. "If courage were all we needed, we would not be worried. But wars are not fought just with guts, or even with weapons. They are struggles of consciousness."

A TRUE REVOLUTIONARY IS MOTIVATED BY GREAT FEELINGS OF LOVE. That was what the poster of Che had said, Maya remembered.

"Consciousness moves to a rhythm," Lily went on. "It follows a beat, you could say. When disparate consciousnesses meet, they become more alike, just as two clocks beating to different rhythms set down next to each other will entrain."

"What does that mean to us?" Cress asked.

"It means the invaders, coming into proximity with us, will become more like us in spite of themselves."

"But doesn't it also mean that we will become more like them?" Bird asked, although he hated to appear to be on Cress's side. And hasn't it already happened to me, ten years in that place, so that I no longer really fit here?

"That is the question we must face and the art that we must develop," Lily answered. "The art of remaining who we truly are. If we can hold on to what we are, then even our enemies must change."

"You're asking for miracles," Cress complained.

"Only a miracle can save us. And who will make miracles for us if not ourselves?"

"We need tools to make miracles with. We need weapons, and we still have some time. What if we were to start production immediately, round the clock, gift work from everyone?" the woman sitting next to Cress suggested.

"We don't have the metal, our factories aren't tooled for weapons production, and there is no possible way that in a few weeks, or even a few years, we can equal the destructive capacities of a society that has made weapons their top priority for generations," said a woman in the plain garb of the techies.

"And if we defend ourselves in the old ways, with force," Lily said, "we will revert to the old ways of thinking and doing things, and lose what we've built."

"I'm not willing to lie back and let the Stewards run all over me," Cress said. "I'm not willing to let them destroy what we have here. Water Council is in consensus about this. We will fight and die, if need be, to protect the waters."

"Fighting is all very well," Lily said, "but winning is more to the point."

"We will win, or die trying."

"More likely," someone called from the back of the room.

"That's it," Lily said. "What good does it do to die trying, if you lose in the end? The result—for the waters, for the salmon, for the trees, for the people—will be just the same."

"What good does it do to give up and not try at all?" Cress countered. "At least we would have a chance, however slim."

"We're not talking about giving up," Greta said. "We're talking about a different way of fighting."

"Fight fire with fire!" yelled one of the Wild Boar People.

"And burn down the whole watershed!" another voice called out.

"Quiet, please!" Salal shouted. "We have a process here, let's stick to it. Lily, you have the floor."

"Cress, I sympathize with the strength of your commitment," Lily said. "But you don't understand what is at stake here."

"The hell I don't. Don't patronize me!"

"Forgive me, I should have put it differently. We of Defense Council see this struggle as more than a question of whether or not the Stewards can take over here. Crucial as that question is, something even broader is at stake. Greta put it well when she said that this dilemma has faced every peaceful culture for the last five millennia, at least. Once this drive for power-over and domination appeared on the planet, it became a force that no one could escape for more than a breathing space. For either we submit, and it triumphs, or we mobilize to fight against it, diverting our energies and resources and transforming ourselves into what we do not want to be. It's like a virus, mindlessly destructive, yet we cannot eradicate it without changing our own internal balance.

"We must develop an immunity to that virus. Not just for ourselves, but for the planet. We've had a little space of time in isolation, where we could pretend that life could carry on here without too much regard for what went on elsewhere, if only because we had no means to affect it. We have used that time well. We have shown in this City—in this watershed—that even on this ruined and ravaged and poisoned earth, people can live well together, can care for one another, can heal and build in harmony with what is around us. We have demonstrated hope. Now it is up to us to sustain that hope, not to abandon it to the despair of violence."

Maya rose. This is my vision, she thought; if I believe it, if even a kernel of me believes it and trusts it, I must speak for it. "I support what Lily is saying. Many years ago, the poet Diane di Prima wrote a line that comes back to me now: 'The only war that counts is the war against the imagination.' I often wondered what she meant by it, but now I think I understand. All war is first waged in the imagination, first conducted to limit our dreams and visions, to make us accept within ourselves its terms, to believe that our only choices are those that it lays before us. If we let the terms of force describe the terrain of our battle, we will lose. But if we hold to the power of our visions, our heartbeats, our imagination, we can fight on our own turf, which is the landscape of consciousness. There, the enemy cannot help but transform."

She paused for breath. I'm orating, she thought, but that's okay, the subject calls for it.

"We old women have learned from our history and its mistakes. Many of you are too young to remember the wealth of the old society, the incredible resources, the power of its technology, the firepower of its weaponry, the sheer abundance of things, so many that they could be shamelessly squandered and wasted. Precious water was fouled by sewage and toxins; whole industries were built to manufacture things to be used once and then discarded.

"But the greatest waste was war. I remember how we watched in frustration as all of that wealth, so many lives of blooming young men and women, all of our ingenuity and resources were poured down the hole of war after war. The Cold War, the Vietnam War, the Middle East, Latin America, riots in our own burning ghettos, big wars and small wars and endless preparation for nuclear war. We waged war on ourselves with nuclear testing, gave our own citizens cancer and then denied responsibility, poisoned the sacred lands of the Indians and turned great rivers into radioactive sewers, and every time there was a glimpse of peace, we scurried to find a new enemy so we could continue this mindless wasting. Blowing up our wealth, burning it off, turning it into poisons and toxins, shooting it in the belly, shipping it home in body bags, murdering our own children and everybody else's.

"And meanwhile we decayed. When I was born, when I grew up in the fifties, we believed our country was the land of opportunity, where nobody was doomed to remain poor, where every person of goodwill had a chance to rise. By the time my child was born in the nineties, beggars were crowding the streets of every city, accosting shoppers in the malls. There were camps of homeless in the parks and empty lots, young people going to war with each other for drugs and booze and a few bucks. Our compassion eroded faster than the topsoil, and when we began to notice the earth changes, the droughts and the warming and the die-offs of the animals, the hole in the ozone layer and the epidemics of strange diseases that showed our own immune systems faltering, when we still had a chance to save so much and avert the worst of what followed, we continued to distract ourselves with war.

"What I say, what I have always said, is there has got to be an end to it. Now is the time to make an end. There will never be a better time, because there is always a reason to fight and kill and build more guns and weapons. Twenty years ago when we founded this Council we said, 'Make an end to it— we will not waste what hope is left to us by building weapons of war.' We knew this day would come; we hoped only that when it did we would have other kinds of weapons to fight with. Now it's here. Now we had better be ready to take up the challenge, as Lily said. Or we will die, and perhaps the earth will rethink this whole experiment in consciousness and start afresh to grow some other form, less aggressive maybe, less extreme, less surprising."

There was a long moment of silence when she finished, and then applause echoed through the hall.

Good one, Maya, Bird thought. You've convinced me.

When the room grew quiet again, Joseph spoke. "Who else has something to say?"

Sachiko from the Musicians' Guild rose. "It seems to me that this decision is both strategic and spiritual. We have a lot of differences in this city. We come from different ancestors, different cultural traditions, different values, different religions—"

"Water is my religion!" Cress shouted, interrupting her. "Water is my politics, and water is my strategy!"

Several people applauded, but Salal glared at him. "Interrupting is a form of bullying, Cress. Wait your turn."

The Speaker raised her hand, calling for silence, and bent her ear to the Salmon mask.

"Friend Salmon says, 'Learn from water. Water is malleable, water is gentle, but drops of water wear away stone, and everything it touches is shaped by its passing.'" She sat down again.

"I was trying to say something," Sachiko said.

"Please continue." Joseph nodded at her.

"What I wanted to say is this. Spiritually, we come from many different traditions, but what we hold in common, what unites us all, is the Declaration of the Four Sacred Things. It tells us that air, fire, water, and earth are sacred because nothing can live without them. It says that they have a value that goes beyond human ends. And it says that all living beings are part of the earth life, and so sacred.

"Some of us interpret this to mean that killing is wrong, that we cannot engage in war. Some of us won't even kill a chicken or a catfish. But others among us believe that it tells us to fight and, if need be, sacrifice ourselves to protect the sacred things.

"If this question were only spiritual, we could debate it all day and never come to consensus, because we don't agree and maybe we shouldn't agree. Maybe we need both views in this city. But our dilemma is also practical. And we've already acknowledged that we don't have the weapons to win a war against the Stewards.

"So what I want to know is, why are we still arguing about *whether* or not we should use nonviolence? We don't have another option, so let's stop wasting time. What we need to be discussing is *how* to use nonviolence and noncooperation, and make them effective, and win."

She sat down to a storm of applause. But Cress jumped to his feet.

"Why do we assume we can't win a war? Guerrilla tactics have worked before, in situations just like this, when an invading power tries to conquer a people with strong morale. Why are we limiting ourselves? Sure, try non-violent resistance, but why rule out sabotage or judicious assassination? We could pick off their leaders and capture more weapons if we can't produce them."

Bird rose.

"We haven't ruled out sabotage," he said. "Already down the peninsula our friends are blowing up their rail lines. That's different from killing people. Guerrilla wars can be won, but not quickly or easily. Assassinations bring reprisals. We can kill some of them, but they can afford to lose hundreds, thousands, for every one of us, because every single person in this city is precious to us."

"You're afraid," Cress said. "They've intimidated you. You're scared to take them on."

I'll take you on, asshole, Bird thought, but before he could speak he felt Holybear's restraining hand on his arm, heard him whisper, *"Cálmate."* And why am I letting him get to me? Bird asked himself. Am I secretly afraid that he's right?

A low murmur ran through the crowd. He's lost their sympathy, Bird realized. He's gone too far.

"I am afraid," Bird admitted. "We're all afraid. We have reason to be. For five thousand years, Cress, men have been goading one another into acts of brutality and stupidity by calling each other cowards. Well, it doesn't matter what you call me. This threat is real. We can't just use it as an arena to prove our courage or our machismo or our dedication or anything else, or we'll all be destroyed. We've got to think this out clearly. Don't interrupt me; I have the floor."

Cress had half risen to speak, but he sat down again. Submission, Bird thought, like a dog dropping his tail. And already I feel calmer. Will we ever evolve beyond this?

"Let me speak to the issue of strategy," Bird went on. "I don't know if nonviolent resistance will work, but if it does it will be because the ordinary soldiers come to realize that fighting us is not truly in their own best interests. We know that; we don't know if they can be brought to see it. But we can't convince them of it by shooting them. We've got to commit ourselves one way or the other—to try to destroy them or to win them over.

"From a purely strategic point of view, I think the second course of action is a better bet. But as Sachiko said, this decision is not just one of strategy." He paused. Rio's ghost hand rested on his shoulder. They are all listening to me so intently, Bird thought, as if they think I know what I'm talking about. And do I? Maybe not, but Rio, I've thought about what you asked me at Samhain. I've thought long and deep.

"There's another question here that we need to face clearly," Bird went on. "Not whether we're ready to die, because many of us will die whether we're ready or not. The question we each have to answer is whether we're willing to kill. This war doesn't start when the troops arrive, it's been going on most of my lifetime. I have almost died already in it, and I have killed. It's very easy to kill once you take up a weapon in your hand. Nothing is easier or more natural. My hands aren't worth much anymore, but still I don't want to put them to work making weapons or holding weapons. I do not want to kill again."

Now the room was absolutely still. They trust me, Bird thought. My words carry weight with them. Except for Cress and his faction, who hate me a little. *Diosa,* I hope I'm right.

Nobody spoke. Cress's head was sunk into his shoulders, and the other members of Water Council were nodding thoughtfully.

"Do we have an agreement in principle that this is the direction we want to take?" Joseph asked.

"How can we agree to something in principle if we don't know what the plan is?" someone called.

"We're agreeing to the principle of a strategy of resistance based on nonviolence and noncooperation."

"Then let's work out the strategy before we agree to it," someone shouted.

"Okay." Joseph gave in. "Who has practical suggestions or concerns to raise?"

"This is the proposal from Defense," Greta said. "That we do not aid them or cooperate with them in any way. That we don't insult or antagonize individuals, but refuse to obey any order or command. If they attempt to destroy something of ours, we physically but nonviolently block them. And yes, we like Maya's suggestion, that we offer them a place at our table. And mean it. Certainly there is room here for more people, should some of them wish to settle."

"Are there questions on that proposal?" Salal asked. "Or concerns to raise?"

"I have one," Cress said. He faced Bird. "You said we have to commit ourselves one way or the other. Okay. Water Council isn't too happy with this proposal but we won't block it. We won't oppose the will of the city. But if we adopt it, we have to be prepared to go all the way. No collaboration. No cooperation, in the big things or the small things. No giving way to their attempts to intimidate us."

"Agreed," Bird said, although a little squirrel of uneasiness ran down his back. It's so easy to be absolute in theory, he thought, but when they come?

Cress stood for a moment, surveying the room, commanding it. Heads nodded at him in every direction. Satisfied, he sat down.

"Other concerns?" Salal asked.

"I have one," Bird said. For days he'd been trying to picture in his imagination what might happen, what might work. "They'll look for our leaders. We ought to let them find a few."

"We don't have leaders," one of Cress's circle objected.

"That could be argued," Holybear said.

"Defense will volunteer," Greta offered.

"No offense, Greta," Bird said, "but you don't understand the way they think. They're never in a millennium going to believe that the city is led by a bunch of old women. They're going to look for the biggest, strongest men they can find. Pick a few, to throw to them."

"Human sacrifices?"

"Volunteers," Bird said.

"What are you suggesting?" Salal asked.

"We set up a pseudo-council," said an older man. "It wouldn't have to be big."

"Hell, no," Bird said. "It's more believable to them if it's small, and one guy is the head of it. You could have a woman or two—actually, that'd be better. There's a whole thing they have about women and this city; they'd be disappointed if they didn't find *any* women in power."

"It should represent all the races," Greta said. "Not just because of reprisals. Because we'll also be sending a message to all of them, the ones we hope to turn."

They talked on about the composition of the group, until Salal called for volunteers.

"I'll volunteer," Sister Marie said, rising to her feet.

"But you're not well," Sage objected.

"I have very little to lose."

There was another long moment of silence; then, slowly, Bird rose to his feet. Now it comes, he thought. Let me open my mouth and there's no going back, once again. His jaw felt heavy, reluctant to move, but he forced it open.

"I'll volunteer," he said. "It was my suggestion—it's only right that I should volunteer for it."

Maya had reached out her hand as if to pull him back down, but she let it drop in midair. Pain, almost physical in its intensity, shrieked through her body. Oh, Goddess. Not him. Not again. It's not fair.

"Besides," he said, "maybe more than anybody else here, I do know what we're getting into. I know how their system works. I think this is the way I can be most useful."

"You can be most useful if you use your true gift," Lily said.

"Maybe I know better than you what that is." Maybe it's a talent for endurance, not for music, Lily. Fuck you anyway.

"Haven't you suffered enough, Bird?" Sam asked.

"When the Stewards come, Sam, we're all going to suffer."

"Are you sure you can take it?" Cress asked.

Lily intervened before Bird could speak. "Nobody is ever sure what they can or cannot withstand. Are you so sure of your own endurance, Cress?"

"I'm not leaping forward eagerly to be our leader," Cress said.

"I don't want to be anybody's leader," Bird said. "If there are questions about my motivations, believe me, I'll happily withdraw."

"No, no, we want you," voices chorused from around the hall, and he was acclaimed by consensus. Cress remained silent.

The discussion went on, but Maya heard no more of it. Bird sat back down, and Sage laid her hand on his knee in sympathy. But why give me sympathy more than others? Bird thought. What I said is true. Who can predict who will suffer and who escape, when the war comes?

Lou stood up to volunteer but was rejected. The city couldn't spare its healers. Finally they chose graceful, dark-eyed Lan, a teacher of Indonesian dance who had lost his wife and child to the last disease, and white-haired Roberto, Salal's grandfather, a robust man in his early seventies.

"Other concerns or additions to the proposal?" Joseph asked.

"The East Bay towns have a suggestion," said a tall woman in a green cape, "and I believe the North Bay is with us on this."

"What's that?" Salal asked.

"Blow up the bridges."

There was dead silence in the room.

"If war is like a virus, shouldn't we try as much as possible to isolate it? We've already demolished the stretch of old roadbed leading up the east side of the Bay from the San Jose contaminated area. We think they'll head straight on up the peninsula, not try to go our way. Once they're here, the bridges are their main routes east and north. If they have to repair them, or cross by water, it could delay them considerably. Especially if we remove water transport from this side."

"It won't stop them, it'll only delay them," came an objection.

"But who knows what will happen in that time? Maybe they will transform. Maybe we'll have time to come up with some other plan."

"But then if we win?" a young man in the tunic favored by the techchies asked. "Do we have the resources to repair the bridges?"

"Considering that they were built in the 1930s, we ought to be able to muster up the technological expertise," the woman said.

"It's not the technology, but the iron and steel and the industrial infrastructure," protested an older man. "We are in most ways a backward, primitive country compared to the United States of the 1930s."

"Engineering Council has considered this. We can do it if we have to do it."

"It's a waste," Maya protested.

"But perhaps a worthwhile one," Lily said. "We cannot hope to come out of this completely pure. Bridges can be rebuilt, lives cannot."

Maya winced. She loved the bridges, the graceful arch of the Golden Gate, the long sweep of the Bay Bridge. They were human-made, yet they had the grace and beauty and rightness of natural objects. But she kept silent. Let this be the worst sacrifice they made, and she would not complain.

There was more discussion, but the group generally seemed to feel that sacrificing the bridges made sense.

"Okay, here's the full proposal," Salal said. "We mount a campaign of nonviolent noncooperation, refusing all aid to the enemy, offering the soldiers a place at our table if they will join us. We have chosen a Liaison Council to interface with them and pose as the leadership of the city. And before the soldiers arrive, we blow the bridges and attempt to make transportation a major problem. Anything I've forgotten?"

"Training," Greta said. "We need to train ourselves for this encounter just as if we were going into battle with weapons."

"I can help with that," Bird said.

"Do we have consensus?"

"The Wild Boar People will spear the ass of anybody who messes with us," said a dreadlocked figure from the corner. "That has always been our position, and we hold to it."

"Of course," Salal said.

One of the booted figures in the corner rose. "The Forest Communities stand aside. We won't interfere with you here in the City, but we're not ready to commit ourselves to a nonviolent stance at this time. We need to go back home and talk this over. To tell you the truth, I don't know what the answer will be. We have a good stockpile of rifles, the roads and rail lines into our lands are easily cut and guarded, and the trees are our families. I tend to think we'll fight if the fight comes to us. But if you have folks you want to protect, or things you need to preserve, we can offer a refuge if you come soon. There's places in the mountains where armies will never go. And whatever happens down below here, whatever becomes of the City, some of us will survive. Remember that."

"The East Bay towns will have to consider our own strategies," said their representative. "We have listened to the debate; we will report our decision at another Council."

A woman Maya recognized from the Pomo Dances in the autumn stood. "The Tribes cannot say yet what we will do. We have listened to the words of the Elders, and we listen with respect. Now we will go back to talk among ourselves."

"Well then, do we have consensus?" Salal asked again.

Around the room, people raised their clasped hands in the sign of agreement.

"That's a victory right there," Holybear murmured.

Maya put her face in her hands and wept.

18

I am changed, Madrone thought. The bees have marked me, as surely as their scar sits on my forehead. She moved through a world that came to her now as much through instinct and smell as through sight. Even when she stayed out of the bee mind, she knew what was blossoming and who was about to become ill. She walked through zones of smells, pungent sage, new-leafed oak or sycamore, human sweat. She knew where the birds nested and where scurrying mice piled their droppings. People had their own unique fragrances; her nose told her more than her hands or eyes about the energies moving in their bodies, about their needs and lacks and imbalances, about states of arousal, anger, or fear. She often felt mildly nauseated, without appetite in spite of the meager diet. The honey that infused all they ate nourished her more fully than she would have believed possible.

The sun was hotter in spring, and no one moved much by day. Even the able-bodied spent much of their time sleeping in the shade. The flu had abated, but Baptist had woken one night crying out in agony. Madrone had gone to him to try to soothe the pain. The ammonia tinge of the air around him told her he had a blocked kidney. Her hands did the rest, shifting his energies, feeling out the obstruction, easing and stretching the tubes of the ureter so the stone could pass. By morning, he was sleeping peacefully, and she was exhausted.

"How's Baptist?" Hijohn asked her, coming over to squat companionably beside her as she perched on a log to drink her morning's ration of water.

I'm getting to be like a dog, Madrone thought, smelling her own adrenaline rush of irritation. Don't interrupt me when I'm eating or drinking. But she answered him courteously.

"He's better. I was able to strengthen his kidney *ch'i,* and he passed the stone. But it could happen to him again—or to any of us. We all need more water."

"We need a lot of things."

"Hijohn, what about some sort of rotation, between the camps with more water and this one? Like, three months on and off, even—just to get everyone good and hydrated periodically. Otherwise, over the years you're going to get out-and-out renal failure."

"What's that?"

"The shutdown of the kidneys."

"Is that so?"

"It's so."

"The good camps are too far away."

"Far away from what?"

Hijohn looked up at her and smiled, his lips stretching into a challenging line. "Maybe it's time we sent you on a raid."

He smelled a lot like the trees, like acorns and honey, and she had a sudden urge to reach out and touch his wizened cheeks. *Diosa,* Madrone thought, I do find him attractive. She'd been too long without a lover, except for the bee women, and what they had done had only amplified her need for touch, skin on her skin.

"What kind of raid?"

"Pharmacy. The boys down in Hollywood thought if you went with them, you could help them identify some of the drugs."

"Is it dangerous?" Madrone couldn't help but ask.

"Everything's dangerous. But they'll take good care of you. Littlejohn and Begood'll be your guides."

○　○　○

They hiked along the ridge, the mountains folding away below them in the darkness, stars glittering overhead. A belt of lights gleamed below them, jewels studding the night on the sloping edges of the hills. Beyond, in the flat basin, factories glowed eerily. Here and there a steady flame from a chimney pot illumined a cloud of smoke.

They crouched in the shadow of a clump of bushes and looked down on the freeway, which stretched like a concrete river cleaving the hills below them.

"You've got a good head for heights, I hope," Littlejohn said.

"Good enough," Madrone said, swallowing nervously. The motion only irritated her already dry throat. Actually, she hated heights. The summer they had done their rock-climbing course, when she was fourteen, had been one of near torture for her. But, she reflected, it had taught her what it was intended to teach—that she could face a fear and move on through.

Below them on the roadbed, lights raced back and forth: cars, supply trucks, troops moving to and from the military camps that filled what Begood called Saint Ferd's Valley. Madrone stared at the lights, almost hypnotized. She hadn't seen so many motor vehicles moving at once since her early childhood. It was a strange sight, like a time warp. Gas-powered cars. The smell of the chemicals the cars released in their passing burned the inside of her nose.

They moved so smoothly and confidently, as if nothing were wrong, as if tankers still plied the oceans filled with oil from faraway lands and planes still spanned the continents and the Central Valley were still rich, populated farmland, not uninhabitable desert.

"Where do they get the gas and metal and rubber for the tires?" she asked.

"They still drill a bit, offshore, down by Long Beach. They brew some gasohol. And they cannibalize. There's huge factories down in the flats where they take apart old cars and make new ones for the military and the rich. You got to be rich to afford the driving permit. Don't you use cars in the North?"

"Very little. We have a few electric vehicles, mostly for emergencies—fire pumps and ambulances. We can't support a private motor vehicle for every person. We can't spare the land to drive and park on, let alone the resources to build and maintain them."

"What do you do, then?"

"We use bicycles and horses, some, and trains to move heavy goods. A few electrotrucks, that go where there aren't any rail lines. And we have good public transport networks all around the Bay." She could have happily gone on for hours, describing the Transport Collective and the gondolas in intricate detail, but she could not avoid the ascent ahead forever. "Is that what we have to cross?"

To their right, a concrete overpass spanned the road. It was partially supported by a skeleton of steel, protection against earthquakes, that provided a crisscrossing grid of interlocking beams.

"That's it," Littlejohn said.

"It's the jungle gym from hell," Madrone said brightly.

"The beams are the best way to go," Begood said. "If you can do it. Otherwise we have to shoot the guard."

The guard paced back and forth on the roadway above them. Yes, it would be unfortunate to shoot him just to save herself the trip across the beams, but it was tempting.

"The lower support beam's your best bet," Littlejohn said. "It's broad enough—about a foot wide. The only problem's getting on and off it. Or if you freeze up in the middle."

"If you think you might panic in the middle," Begood said, "it'd be better to just shoot the guard and get it over with, than to have to peel you off and end up shooting all sorts of guards later, not to mention risking getting our asses fried. Remember the time Oldjohn froze up midway? Shit, we practically had to carry him out to the middle supports, and then he couldn't get back on the beam and dawn was coming. We ended up stuck out there all day, hiding out behind the overhang until it got dark again. Hijohn had to hike back, steal some rope, shoot the guard after all, and then we had to haul Oldjohn up the side, in broad daylight. There we were, out on the middle of the bridge, with no cover, and a whole platoon of Stewardship troops bearing down on us—"

"I can do it," Madrone said, "if we just go ahead and don't think about it. Can we go now?"

Quietly, they crept down the side of the hill to the base of the overpass. Littlejohn climbed the struts that led to the main beam, pulling himself gracefully up from one to the next. Madrone followed, wishing her arms were stronger. Begood came behind, occasionally giving her a welcome push.

The concrete surface of the overpass stretched above them, curving in two gentle arches supported in the center by thick piers anchored in the middle divider of the freeway. A scaffolding of steel framing followed the contours. Littlejohn swung himself onto the central support beam and stood up. Confidently, he walked out, balanced a hundred feet above the roadway.

"Just one thing," Begood said cheerfully. "If you fall, try not to scream."

"Sure," Madrone said, taking a deep breath that choked her with the fumes from below. Don't think about it, just do it, she told herself, and stepped out.

If she thought of the beam as a line on the ground, she could walk it easily, fearlessly. If there were nowhere to fall, she couldn't fear falling and wouldn't fall. And if her heart would just stop that silly pounding, and her stomach stop that twisting sensation . . .

Every twenty feet or so, a steel pier stretched vertically up from the beam to connect with the support struts that ran beneath the concrete. Littlejohn grabbed them with both hands and swung his body around them. When she reached the first one, she did the same. Not bad, she thought, although her hands were sweaty and slippery and the moment when she had to release her weight from one foot before she could solidly place the other was terrible. She remembered, suddenly, one of those afternoons on the rocks. She was halfway up a cliff, and she stuck fast, couldn't move up or down. Nita had been her partner, and she was getting excited, yelling down instructions and exhortations. Then Bird had come by and had suggested, very calmly, that she open her eyes and look at where she wanted to go and think how to get there. She did. Remembering that, she was around the second pier. She thought of Bird sitting down at the piano, his hands so clumsy at the keys, and the song he had made for her came back to her as she wiggled onto the concrete supports of the central piers.

"Halfway," Littlejohn said. "You want to rest?"

"No, let's get it over with," Madrone said. The second half, with Bird's song ringing inside her, was a little easier. But by the time they reached the opposite side, her shirt was soaked through with sweat, and as they touched the ground she noticed her knees were trembling. Begood landed beside her.

"Good girl," Littlejohn said.

"Let's go," Madrone said.

○ ○ ○

The hills on the east side of the freeway were far more populated than those on the west. They made their way along a roadway lined by enormous estates. From time to time, cars approached, and the three flung themselves into bushes or hid behind trees until the headlights swept past them. All Madrone's senses were alert. She could smell unseen roses that clambered up walls, she could scent dogs far enough away to skirt the edges of their territory and prevent them from barking.

They walked for what seemed like hours. Madrone was thirsty, but she popped a raw acorn into her mouth and let its astringent bite distract her. The moon sailed over them, a thin, waning crescent. She was tired, so tired she felt she was walking in her sleep. No more cars passed; it was almost dawn.

They were still high on the ridge as the light from the soon-to-rise sun made a pink smear on the basin's eastern rim. High bushes of feathery chamise gave them some cover, and Madrone could look through their concealing spires and see the panorama spread out below.

The vast flat plain of the basin was dust dry. A haze hovered over the jumbled forms of cracked buildings and crumbling structures. No discernible lines of roads or streets and no spots of green relieved the patchwork of gray and brown. Only here and there, towering black stumps of dead palm trees marched in uneven lines, the ragged sentinels of ancient avenues.

A narrow band of green hugged the base of the hills and sent tendrils up into some of the eastern canyons. Compared to the drab of the plain, the green looked almost obscene, too bright, somehow, almost artificial. She could see, on the nearer slopes, rich houses surrounded by terraced and landscaped gardens. Far to the east, the towers of downtown rose in vertical spires of metal and glass.

"Hurry," Littlejohn said, motioning them down a side road that soon dead-ended at a wire fence. Beyond, a dirt road led into a canyon. They climbed the fence and scrambled down the road, reaching the cover of brush around the dry streambed just as the sun rose full in the sky.

The word "camp," Madrone thought, was a gross exaggeration for what they found, which consisted of two men and one woman huddled in the hollow under a bush.

"Drink deep," they murmured, a greeting which more and more sounded to Madrone like pure sarcasm. Littlejohn uncorked a water bottle and passed it around for a carefully measured swallow.

"Go easy," he warned Madrone. "You guys have any water?"

"A cup or two's all we got left," said the man closer to Madrone. He was short and slight, hardly more than a boy, but his brown, leathery skin made him look ancient. "They call me Big John," he said, winking. "This here's Joan Dark and Johnny Come Lately."

Lately was dry and dark as a bean that's lain too long in the sun, but he had a wide friendly grin and green eyes that looked speculatively into Madrone's. Joan Dark was silent, and Madrone smelled sickness on her, and pain.

"You the healer?" Lately asked.

"Yes, I'm Madrone."

"Can you look at Joan? She took a bullet graze a couple of nights ago, and now it's infected."

Joan was thin to the point of emaciation, and her half-moon eyes were shrouded, wary. Madrone unwrapped a bandage of rough, dirty cloth from the woman's stringy thigh. The stench assaulted her. The wound was shallow, but the flesh around it was inflamed and an ominous red streak went up her thigh into her groin.

"Can we spare any water for washing?"

The others exchanged glances.

"We don't have much," Littlejohn said.

"She can have mine," Lately said.

"We'll all share a bit," Littlejohn said. "But go easy on it."

Madrone nodded, pulled out one of the clean rags she had stashed in her pack, and wet it gingerly. Carefully, she swabbed out what she could of the dirt that clogged the wound. What did they want from her? Wave a magic wand and make everything better, when there was nothing, nothing to work with, not even the most basic necessities? Oh, she was angry, not at these men, not even at the lawn-enveloped mansions that clung to the hill above them, but at the sheer greed and waste of it all.

"I'll be all right by tonight," Joan murmured.

"No, you won't," Madrone said. "You have a very serious infection, and you need to lie still and quiet and rest."

"Can't you heal it?"

Madrone sighed. "I can give you some energy and relieve some pain. But without being able to wash it properly—even if I could magically kill off this batch of microbes, the dirt in the wound would reinfect it."

"What can we do?" Lately whispered.

"Look for anti-infectins when we raid the pharmacy. Isn't there anywhere we can take her where she could be cared for?"

"There's Katy's place, down in the city," Littlejohn said.

"How far is that?"

"Ten, fifteen miles."

"That's too far."

Littlejohn shrugged. Madrone bit her lips again. It wasn't their fault that all these warm and comfortable houses perched so blithely on the ridge were closed to them.

"She frets," Begood explained to Big John. "Where she comes from, this doesn't happen."

"No? Wounds don't get infected?"

"People are cared for," Madrone said, "whatever happens. And nobody lacks water for something as basic as washing." And then she had to tell them again about the running streams, and the streets planted with fruit trees, and the gardens. My fairy tale, she thought. The sun rose higher, and she was overwhelmed by exhaustion after doing what she could for Joan. They curled into the shadow of the brush and slept.

o o o

They woke at sunset, ate some acorns dipped in honey, drank. When darkness fell, Madrone washed Joan's wound again. She was weak and feverish and didn't even argue when they left her alone, wrapped in a blanket and provided with all the food and water they could spare. They headed up the path, stopping as Big John and Lately removed a pair of shotguns from a cache in the side of the canyon. Littlejohn and Begood were carrying their laser rifles. Lately handed Madrone a pistol but she just stood, looking at it, feeling its cold weight in her hand.

"I can't take it," she said.

"I'll show you how to fire it," Littlejohn said. "It's the simplest thing we've got."

She shook her head. "I know how to shoot a pistol. We learned in school. Our teachers said we had to be familiar with guns to understand history. I just don't want to kill anyone."

"Nobody wants to kill anyone," Littlejohn said patiently. "If all goes well, we won't. This is just a precaution."

She remembered the feel of the guns they'd practiced with, the recoil as bullets exploded out, the challenge of hitting a target and the horror at the thought of what that force could do to living flesh. Could she pull the trigger, end some unknown person's life? If it were a choice, between that and the pens? Or losing her own life? Her hand was shaking.

"I can't take it."

"Then you're an added danger to all of us," Big John said. "If you won't defend yourself, and you won't defend us—"

"I just don't think I could do it."

"You don't know until you try," Begood said.

"I can't."

"Don't push her," Littlejohn said. "She'll be a worse danger to us all if she gets jumpy with a gun in her hand. Leave her be. This is gonna be cake, right? Nobody's gonna shoot nobody tonight."

She was grateful to Littlejohn but she still felt shaken, oddly ashamed. Because this is not so much a stand I take from conviction, she admitted, but from some instinctive revulsion. If I'm really such a pacifist, I shouldn't be here. I shouldn't be working with them and supporting their fight. But I don't know that I am, that I would go to the pens rather than let these men kill another man to protect me. And if I feel that way I should defend myself.

But I can't.

"Come on, then," Big John said.

o o o

The pharmacy was on the edge of the valley on the north side of the mountains. Two hours of fast hiking brought them to a sheltered hollow on the lower slopes of the last hill, where they could look down on a huge metal warehouse, surrounded by chain-link fence with barbed wire strung on top. Armed guards patrolled the gate. Madrone and her companions sat in the dark, reeking of wariness and excitement.

"What are we waiting for?" Madrone whispered.

"Guard change," Littlejohn said. "Ah, there it comes."

Below them, two new men approached the gate guards, talked for a moment, and then took their places.

"Who's our friend?" Littlejohn whispered.

"The tall one," Lately said.

The taller of the two guards left his post and began making the rounds of the perimeter inside the chain-link fence.

"What's happening?" Madrone asked.

"He's supposed to unlock the back gate for us and deactivate the alarm," Big John said. "He's part of the Web."

They waited. Madrone tried to calm herself. She suspected the others were enjoying themselves. But I'm not made for this sort of thing, she thought. I'm not like Cleis, who craved danger and died for it. I don't want to die or kill.

After a wait that seemed endless, the tall guard returned to the front gate.

"Okay," Lately whispered. "Littlejohn, you stay here, cover the front entrance. Don't shoot anyone unless you have to, and don't shoot our friend whatever you do. If there's trouble, give the call. Begood, you come down with us, cover the side gate. Any trouble coming, try to get in, give us a warning. Okay, let's go."

They ran silently, crouching in the shadows, around the line of the fence to the southeast corner, out of sight of the gate on the west side. A small door opened into the chain-link fence, and cautiously, Lately pushed on it. It opened.

"Come on."

Madrone followed Lately and Big John, running quickly across the twenty feet of open space that separated the gate from a small side entrance into the warehouse.

"Pray that our friend really turned off the alarm," Lately said, flashing a grin at Madrone as he pressed against the blank metal door. It opened inward.

"Home free," he said.

Inside, the smells of a thousand chemicals assaulted her. She felt dizzy, almost numb with overload. Forests of high metal racks surrounded them, stacked high with boxes and bottles and containers.

"Where do they get all this? Where does it come from?" she whispered, astounded at the sheer abundance. There were more pills here, in this one warehouse, than in all the storehouses of the Bay Area combined.

"They have factories all over the Valley, strictly under military control," Lately told her. "And farms, up and down the coast, where they grow some of the materials. A few of them are free farms, but a lot of them are labor camps. You can sign on if you're unemployed, work seven days a week in the hot sun for three years, and live like a dog, but you get all the highs and lows you can swallow. Those houses with their green lawns that you passed up in the hills, this is where a lot of them get their money. And the black market in highs and lows is especially profitable."

"Nothing is labeled!" Madrone said. "How do we know what anything is?"

"Big John's gone to get the scanner," Lately said. "You just sit tight here, let us bring you things. We're looking for boosters, for highs and lows, and you tell us what else."

"Why highs and lows?"

"To sell. And give to our friends, keep them happy. We got to finance this somehow."

She wasn't at all happy with the answer, but there was nothing she could do about it. Big John returned with the scanner, which looked like a square magnifying glass on a stick.

"Here's how it works," Lately said, taking down a box of pills from a shelf. "The labels are all in dot code on the front, see?" He pointed out a pattern of black dots, and she nodded. "Hold the scanner up and look through."

When she looked into the lens, a name and a price appeared.

"Well, this would be very helpful if I knew what any of these things were," Madrone said.

"Don't you? I thought you knew about medications."

"Some. We use drugs back home that we can culture or distill from what we grow, antibiotics and antivirals and anti-infectins. They're more effective for some conditions than herbs or acupuncture or our other methods. But the Stewards have things I only know about in theory, and then by their Latin names or their chemical structure, not their brand names. Maybe I can make some guesses."

"A lot of stuff, we can recognize," Lately said.

"Can you find me some boosters? I'd like to examine them."

"Sure. But if you want something for Joan, you'll have to tell us what to look for."

"I have no idea what it would look like," Madrone said, dismayed. "Capsules, probably, not tablets—if that's any help." Her head was beginning to ache with the smells around her. If she could focus her bee sense, put it to use somehow. . . .

"Wait a minute, I've thought of something I could try. Bring me some things, and I'll see if I can find out what they are."

She sat down in a corner, with a pen Big John found for her. Touching her bee spot, she let herself go into the trance, but not all the way. I need to keep my human mind intact, to think and name and write, while I open the other senses. Melissa, can I do this?

"Here's some capsules," Lately said, placing a box on her knees. She broke one open, sniffed a few grains of powder, touched her tongue to them delicately.

Taste and smell exploded in her brain, she was flying through orange groves, lemons blossomed, fruited, sweated through their pungent skin.

She touched her bee spot again, wrote Vitamin C on the box of capsules, and held out her hand for Lately's next offering.

By the time she had sorted through fifteen or twenty different drugs, her head was throbbing and the gray metal shelves and boxes swam in kaleidoscopic patterns in front of her eyes. There was so much here, she found herself infected with a kind of greed. Drugs to ease pain and drugs to stimulate tissue growth and drugs to reduce tumors. Drugs to undo the effects of other drugs. If she could only study them, analyze them, know exactly how they worked. Her bee sense could help her recognize drugs that she knew, but there were tantalizing hints of other things here, antidotes to the epidemics maybe, advances as yet unfamiliar in the North. But without more time, more equipment, more backup, she couldn't know.

"*Diosa,* I don't know if I can handle any more," she said as Big John brought another box to her.

"We've got a full load of the pleasure drugs," he said. "Do you have what you want?"

"I found some antibacterials and antivirals," Madrone said. "These, and these. And here are some painkillers; they're always useful. You can take the scanner, load up more of these."

They brought her boxes and bottles and she sorted frantically. What to take, what to leave?

"Hurry," Lately said. "We've got to be out of here before four o'clock check. That's ten minutes from now, and we've got to clean up first."

"Put these boxes back," Madrone said, indicating a pile of her rejects. "If I can just find a good general anti-infectin. . . ."

Big John returned boxes to shelves; Lately packed their backpacks with Madrone's selections. She felt her own fear growing, but it was hard to tear herself away, not to try tasting just one more, and one more.

"Here," she said. "Take this, and—"

"That's all," Lately said. "We don't have room or time for more. Big John, run the scanner back. Take your pack, Madrone. Don't forget to wipe for fingerprints."

Her hands were shaking as she picked up the pack. The ground seemed to be moving under her feet, and her head weighed enough to drag her down. Big John grabbed the scanner and ran swiftly through the corridors, returning quickly. "Out," Lately hissed, and now she could smell real fear in him. Cautiously, he pushed the door open a crack, scanned the pavement outside, and motioned to them to come on. "Fast," he said.

They ran out, Madrone's heart pounding. The pavement seemed elastic under her feet, and she could hardly tell which way was up or down. Big John grabbed her hand and pulled her along, but the twenty feet between the door and the gate seemed to stretch for miles. They heard a long whistle, like a mournful bird, as Begood waved them through, shutting the gate behind them and clicking the lock shut. "Down," he whispered, and they threw themselves flat into the shadows outside the fence and lay there scarcely breathing as footsteps passed behind them, just on the other side of the fence. He'll smell us, Madrone thought. Her own fear was so strong she was sure it tainted the air for miles. But the footsteps passed by, and when they turned the corner Lately motioned them on again. They climbed silently up the dry hillside to the sheltered hollow where Littlejohn waited. Madrone's legs felt weak; she was surprised they could bear her weight, but they did.

"No trouble?" Lately whispered to Littlejohn.

"All okay. You?"

"Close, but not too close," Lately whispered. "If our friend gets that door locked again, and the alarm on, they'll never know they were raided until they take inventory."

And now they were enjoying themselves, Madrone thought, like boys playing an exciting game. Would I? If I did this regularly, if I do this regularly, will I get to like it, the adrenaline rush, the fear and relief?

"How'd you like your first raid?" Lately asked, grinning at her.

"I like it now," she said. "Now that it's over."

"It's not over yet," Littlejohn said. "Let's get out of here."

19

Crossing the freeway, like so many other things in life, was easier the second time, Madrone reflected. She and Littlejohn and Begood had spent another two days in the raiders' camp, while she fed Joan Dark anti-infectins and sent Littlejohn scouring the canyons for water. When they left, the woman's injured leg no longer smelled of death. The red streak was gone, and the wound was beginning to heal.

They had hiked through the night. Madrone was feeling light-headed, still half in the bee world, still not quite grounded after the intensity of the night spent testing drugs. The food in the last few days was even scantier than usual, but what she felt was not hunger but lightness, as if she could launch herself on gauze wings and fly. Maybe the boundaries between the bee mind and her ordinary mind were permanently blurred. The route was a succession of plant smells, fragrance after fragrance, wafting down from the well-watered gardens above. She was intoxicated by carob and night-blooming jasmine and other sweet traces she could not name. Lights whirled in kaleidoscope patterns, as if prisms were fixed before her eyes.

The bee mind carried her lightly across the narrow scaffolding under the freeway. Suddenly heights were no threat; she could balance, surefooted, on a narrow stamen or velvet flower petal.

Once past the freeway, they decided to risk hiking during the day. True, they were visible there on the unsheltered crown of the hills, but anyone coming after them would also be visible from far away. The canyons would offer quick cover if they needed it. Begood set the pace, and they made good time. Madrone was grateful for the long walk, a chance to sink into her body's rhythms and her own thoughts. She felt depleted; walking the hills always restored her vital energy.

Her eyes darted around with the insect alertness that had become second nature. As always, she was thirsty, but she had learned not to think about it, as she didn't think about hunger or the dry, gritty texture of her skin. But she allowed herself to take pleasure in the smooth movements of her muscles, the strength of her body and its capacity to endure. Below them the hills rippled away, cloaked in shreds of early-morning fog. Behind them the sun slowly rose, painting the land with a glowing, golden edge. To the south, the city lay at their feet. To the north, they could see, spread out across the flat valley, the straight lines of roads and barracks and the supply depots of the military lands. Already, there was activity, lights moving purposefully back and forth along the roads. A convoy of trucks crept north along the freeway.

They walked on. The sun got hotter and no shade protected them. After another hour or so, Madrone began to feel nauseated. She could hardly focus her eyes; everything changed and shifted and split into multiple images of itself. Her head was pounding, and her light pack weighed her down. She realized that she had reached the delicate edge where thirst triggered dehydration. There was still one swallow of water left in her bottle. She drained it, savoring each drop.

"How much farther?" she asked Littlejohn.

"About ten miles. We should be there by evening."

"Is there water on the way?"

"Not unless we steal it."

The cold realization crept over Madrone that she wasn't going to make it. Strange, because she didn't feel that badly, but she knew what the headache and the swimming black spots in her eyes portended. She couldn't do it. Not with all the Witch's will in the world; she couldn't walk another ten miles in that sun without more to drink.

"I can't make it," she said. "I need to drink."

Littlejohn looked at her sharply. I've never said that to them before, Madrone thought. I've never complained. So he must believe me.

"I've got a little bit of water," Begood said. "You can have it."

A wave of love washed over her. Her knees felt weak and she sat down abruptly. If her eyes had not been too dry for tears, she would have cried.

"Give her a swallow," Littlejohn said. "I'm about out. But there's no way around it, we're going to have to raid."

"I'm sorry," Madrone said.

"It's my fault. I haven't done this route in a while—I forgot how long it was, and how hot during the day. Maybe we should have carried more water, but I wanted to leave them enough at the camp."

"There's just no way around it," Begood said. "It's a route that calls for a water stop."

"There's houses down in the canyon, not too far from here. We can hit one of them, Madrone, can you walk on at all?"

"Sure," she said, struggling to rise from the dust. Littlejohn offered his hand, and she stood up, balancing herself precariously. Her head felt heavy, throbbing. She would try not to think about it.

They continued for another quarter mile, until the path snaked around the head of a canyon. Below them, strung out along the road on the valley floor, were the last outposts of rich houses with high chain-link fences surrounding their lush green lawns. The most secluded house was white, a collection of sculpted stucco boxes and soaring glass domes that enclosed greenery, gleaming like a sugar cube in the center of grass so green it seemed unreal. In the midst of dense stands of foliage, ferns and hibiscus and flowering vines, something pulled Madrone's eyes like a magnet.

"What's that?" she asked, pointing.

It was blue, bluer than the cloudless sky above their heads, and gleaming with reflected light and bands of light crossing and crisscrossing below its surface in moiré patterns.

"A big pool of water," Begood said. "The rich people like to go in it with their whole bodies."

"That's what I thought it was," Madrone said, "but I couldn't believe it." She could smell the water, though, and it filled her whole body with longing.

"Me neither," Begood said. "You'd think it'd kill you, to get that wet."

Madrone laughed. "No, Begood. It doesn't kill you, unless you try to breathe it. Where I come from, people swim all the time."

He looked at her and shrugged. It was just one more incomprehensible thing about her.

She clearly remembered swimming, in rivers and streams and mountain lakes, in the city pool down the street, but the memory was distant, like that of some unbelievable luxury.

"The fence is not too far from the pool," Littlejohn said. "And there's pretty good cover most of the way down. Could be electrified, but it doesn't look it."

"It's not," Madrone said. "I would smell it."

Littlejohn looked at her a little oddly, but he continued. "This is how we do it. Begood, you stay up here, take the rifle, and cover our backs while Madrone and I go down."

"Why don't you let me go down with you?" Begood asked. "She's already shaky."

"I want her to drink her fill. And she's no good with the gun. You are. I'll cut us through the fence. Fill the water containers first, then drink. Any trouble, everybody scatters. Madrone, you know the way home? Could you find it on your own?"

"I think so." Hijohn had given her a thorough geography lesson before she left on the raid. She thought back to what he had told her. "I'd just follow the ridge, right? The fire road runs along it all the way to the oak grove, and from there I know how to go."

"Right. Go at night," Littlejohn said.

Madrone nodded. Please, Goddess, don't let it come to that. She followed Littlejohn down the hillside, keeping low under cover of the brush, sliding carefully down the steep places. They waited, hearts pounding, for the sound of a shout or an electronic alarm. All was quiet. About twenty feet up from the pool, a high chain-link fence topped with barbed wire enclosed the last sloping section of ground. Littlejohn pointed. Between one section of posts, the dirt had eroded away so they could slide under the bottom of the fence. He wouldn't have to cut it.

Madrone nodded, slid down close to the fence, undid her pack, and pushed it through. No sound, no motion. Quickly, she followed, pressing herself flat into the dust to slide past the prongs of wire. Littlejohn followed her.

When they reached the bottom, she removed her two water bottles from her pack. They peered out at the yard. All seemed quiet. The curtains were closed at the back of the house; not even a breath of air moved.

"Now," Littlejohn said.

They ran to the edge of the pool, dipped their water bottles in, and filled them. The water felt cool on Madrone's dry hands. The smell surrounded her, cool and sweet, like the odor of love. She filled a second bottle, and Littlejohn went to work on their gallon jug. It had been so long since she'd felt water on her hands. Her skin ached for moisture.

The bottles were full, and danger or no, she had to drink. She bent down and scooped water into her mouth from her hands. Funny, she'd gotten so used to the slow, prolonged savoring of each mouthful that it was hard to make herself drink quickly, but that was what was called for here: take in as much as she could of this unbelievable abundance of clear, cool water. There was so much of it. It had a slight chemical tang, chlorine, maybe, but not enough to disturb her ecstasy. She could feel each mouthful, restoring her life, and she lay at the edge and plunged her whole head in. *Diosa,* it was so cool, it eased her throbbing temples and the grainy dust behind her eyes. Oh Goddess. She wanted to plunge her whole body in, just for a moment, to be cool and wet and clean. It was crazy. It was dangerous. Littlejohn was still drinking beside her, and suddenly she gave in, pulling off her shirt and pants and slipping over the side into the welcoming water.

"Have you lost your fucking mind?" She heard Littlejohn behind her, but she was weightless, careless, caressed by water, drinking it in through her pores and her shrunken cells, feeling the pressure of it sliding past her limbs and streaming through her fingers, feeling it press against her with its weight as she plunged down, down. Her ears rang with muffled sounds. She touched the bottom, twisted, and struck out for the surface again.

When her head broke the surface of the water, Littlejohn was gone. So were her water bottles. Above her head, she heard an owl call in the daylight —the signal for danger. Up on the fire road, she heard shouts, the sound of an engine. A shot rang out.

Oh shit, she thought. Shit, shit, shit. I've done it now.

She needed to run, but she didn't know where to go. The sounds were directly above her, in line with the hole under the fence. If she took that route, she'd land right in their arms. But was there another way out? She couldn't make herself leave the pool; she was paralyzed, trapped.

The voices were coming closer. Now she could hear crashing in the bushes above her. But she couldn't decide what to do; she couldn't move. The coldness of the water seemed to drain away her life. She could duck under the surface, shut her eyes—but there was nowhere there to hide. She pictured a bullet sinking into her flesh, and the red seeping through to stain the clarity of the blue.

"Girl!"

A woman's voice hit her like a slap. She turned her head toward the house.

"Get your ass in here, girl!"

For a moment, she thought Johanna was calling her, the woman in the doorway looked so much like her. Automatically, she did what the voice said, vaulting out of the pool, grabbing her clothes and pack, and running over the grass so as not to leave wet footprints on the patio coping. The shouts and noises above were getting closer, but she ducked in the door and it closed behind her.

"Give me those things," the woman said, grabbing Madrone's clothes and directing her into a small anteroom off the kitchen. She looked to be in her fifties, and while her stance and voice and her dark molasses skin were like Johanna's, her features were different, her nose sharper and her wide lips tightly compressed. She wore a white uniform.

"You put those things on." She jerked her chin toward a uniform and apron hanging on a hook. "Wrap that head scarf so it covers your wet hair. Then you join me in the kitchen, through that door, and keep your mouth shut."

Madrone did as she was told, slipping a starched white dress over her head, pulling black slippers onto her feet, and wrapping the white headcloth low to cover the scar on her forehead, tucking in her hair so no damp strands showed. She emerged from the anteroom and entered the kitchen, a square white room gleaming with marble and white tile. It smelled of scouring powder and green things and her own fear.

Beside a white porcelain sink stood a cutting board laden with vegetables. The woman pushed her over there, stuck a knife in her hands, and said one word.

"Chop."

Madrone began slicing carrots. She moved automatically, slowly. The fragrance of the vegetables almost overpowered her. Each cut released more and more of the sweet fresh smell.

I've got to stay out of the bee mind, she thought, fighting for control. Surreptitiously, she touched her bee spot, murmuring her own human name under her breath.

Behind her she heard the woman's steps as she moved, and her voice as she hummed to herself. Outside, she heard yells, a loud crash, and a man's deep voice.

"Open the gate! We're security!"

There was more noise, footsteps running from the house to the yard and back, more angry shouting. Madrone concentrated on the carrots. If she just carefully sliced each round, without letting herself be distracted, she would survive. She would become what she appeared to be, innocent, authorized to exist. *Chop.*

Unhurriedly, the woman moved to the door. Don't smell, look. Use your eyes, focus, one thing at a time. Each round of carrot was like a mandala, paler orange patterns embedded in a matrix of deep orange. She wanted to taste it. She wanted to feel its sweet crisp flesh crunching under her teeth, feel it yielding up its store of nourishment to her famished body. She wanted the glowing jewel-like tomatoes and the pale fresh heart of the cucumbers with their translucent store of seeds. Her jaws ached as saliva spurted into her mouth; her stomach twisted. She could not, could not, steal this food, with the unknown woman somewhere behind her who had saved her for reasons still not clear. She could not, could not, risk popping a few rounds of carrots into her mouth. No.

The door opened behind her, and she heard them come in. Carefully, she stole one glance around. The woman was flanked by five burly young men in khaki uniforms. They wore sunglasses that concealed their eyes.

"We're just going to check the house. You sure you didn't see any suspicious persons around the pool area?"

"I been in here all morning fixing this luncheon for Miss Sara. I ain't seen a thing. Becky, you peel those cucumbers before you slice them, you hear?"

Madrone found a peeler in the drawer below the cutting board and went to work over the sink.

"You, girl—you seen anything?" one of the men asked her. She looked up, widened her eyes, and shook her head no. The less she spoke and revealed the accent of the North, the better, she thought. They continued to search through the kitchen and adjoining rooms, stomping and shouting to one another. Madrone kept her eyes glued to the cucumber, which emerged white and gleaming from under its green peel. How long had it been since she'd eaten fresh vegetables like these? *Diosa,* at home I used to go into the garden and pick them. She remembered Johanna standing in the kitchen of their country place, chopping vegetables for stew. She remembered Maya in the City kitchen, making soup, and the bushels of tomatoes they would blend for salsa, and the zucchinis, so overabundant that people groaned at the sight of them. Goddess, they had been so rich!

The cucumbers were peeled, and she began slicing them. Were they watching her? Were their sharp eyes boring beneath her scarf to discover her wet hair? Why, oh why had she succumbed to temptation and taken that swim? She would never survive like this. She would never get back home.

A door in the opposite wall opened, and suddenly the men became quiet.

"What is all this?" said a woman's voice. It was a young voice, but it rang with a tone of authority and an inbred assurance.

Madrone peeked up quickly. The woman was tall, slender, with blond hair that swept up and back from her head in wings, defying gravity. She wore a white dress, modestly cut but of such fine material that as it shifted and billowed around her it revealed every dimension of her sculpted figure. Her skin was calla-lily white and her blue eyes delicately outlined with color. Madrone wanted to stare at her, but she forced her eyes back down, sneaking little glances with her head bent. She was like something crafted, each movement, each tone in her voice, the precise shading of her cheekbones and the carefully drawn outline of her lips, calculated to suggest seduction. Madrone had never seen anyone quite like her. Some of Holybear's Fairy friends, maybe, who might spend days dressing up for a ritual, putting henna in their hair and drawing spirals around their eyes. But the effect was quite different.

Maybe it was the nearness of death, these soldiers behind her with their nervous weapons, searching. Suddenly all the cravings of her body were awake and clamoring. She wanted life. She wanted the sweet caressing water and the cool, wet center of the cucumber and she wanted the woman who stood in the doorway and flicked her eyes over Madrone, registering surprise so subtly that Madrone saw no change in her features, only a tremor in her aura.

"Security, ma'am," one of the men said. "Command post up the hill spotted suspicious activity around your pool. Water thieves, probably."

"Nonsense."

"There seems to be some evidence of disturbance, ma'am. The guard in our command post up the hill saw somebody actually in the pool."

Command post up the hill, Madrone thought. A good piece of information to know.

"In it? Bodily?"

"That's right, ma'am."

"Mary Ellen, have the gardener drain it and disinfect it."

"Yes, ma'am."

"Pardon me, ma'am, but what we're trying to say is, this looks like more than just water theft. Could be Witchcraft."

"Oh, be serious. There're no Witches around here."

"What else could it be, ma'am? These hillboys don't swim. They're afraid of the water."

"But why would a Witch go in our pool?"

Madrone, slicing tomatoes with the knife, wondered seriously if she should plunge it into her own heart. What chance did she have of walking out of here alive and free? How much pain could she withstand if they took her? She wasn't like Hijohn; she didn't have his stolid endurance. Or like Bird. And she knew so many routes and plans and faces.

"It's a way of cursing, ma'am. They leave their Devil spirits in the water, and when you go in, they get you. Anyway, we'd like to check the house."

There would be blood all over these clean white walls, and it would be a hell of a way to repay the woman who had sheltered her. No, to kill herself would be a betrayal. And she didn't want to die. She wanted the sweet taste of juice on her tongue, she wanted to run her fingers over the contours of the body under the floating dress and feel limbs shudder under hers and feel a heart rise to embrace her loneliness.

"I can't believe anyone got into the house."

"You never know, ma'am. Anyway, where else could the Witch have gone? We had the yard surrounded."

Did Littlejohn get away? And Begood? Had she killed them with her indulgence? *Diosa*, what had gotten into her? She must have been possessed, for real.

"Well, check the house, by all means. I'll be in the atrium. But hurry, please. I've got half a dozen women coming for lunch in an hour."

Madrone heard the door close. After a moment, the guards left the kitchen.

"If you're done with those vegetables, you can start on the potatoes," Mary Ellen said, gesturing to a basket that stood beside the sink. "Don't talk until they're out of the house." Madrone obeyed, scrubbing and peeling, while from the rooms beyond they heard muffled sounds of searching.

After a long time, the outer door slammed closed. Madrone could feel tension drain from the kitchen. Mary Ellen let out a long soft sigh, which again reminded Madrone of her grandmother. Johanna's skin had been just that shade of dark, dark brown, and her hair had also had the texture of silver wire.

"Thank you," Madrone said. "You saved my life."

Mary Ellen snorted, but before she could reply the blond woman walked back in. She moved with the assurance of ownership, sitting herself down on a kitchen stool.

"Pour me a drink," she said to Mary Ellen, who moved to a cupboard with a slight disapproving glance and poured out a dark liquor into a small shot glass. "Pour yourself a drink."

"No, thank you, Miss Sara."

"And you?"

"Just water, thanks," Madrone said.

Mary Ellen directed her with a glance to a second kitchen stool and brought her a glass and a small bottle of spring water from the refrigerator. She settled herself with the same.

"Well," Sara said, "who the hell are you?"

Madrone was distracted by the water on her tongue, which she drank slowly, blessing her good fortune. Whatever might be about to happen seemed less important than the undeniable truth that for this moment, at least, she was no longer thirsty.

"Well?"

Madrone looked up and met her eyes, blue, like the pool. "I guess I'm your resident Witch."

"What were you doing in my swimming pool?"

Madrone was still staring at the blond woman's face. Clearly, she was used to being stared at, admired. Her face was calm under Madrone's gaze, patient like a cat receiving homage.

"I was overcome by temptation, by the chance to get clean. I'm sorry. It was a stupid thing to do."

"That it was," Mary Ellen agreed.

Sara shot her a quick glance of disapproval and resumed her questions.

"You're with the hillboys, right?"

"Right."

"Well, you're not what I would have expected. I didn't think they cared about being clean."

"When you don't have water, after a while you stop caring."

"But you didn't stop."

"Unfortunately, no."

"But where did you learn to swim?"

"Where I come from, it's a normal thing to do."

"And where is that?"

"The North," Madrone said. They waited, Mary Ellen letting out another soft sigh. They wanted her story, and maybe she owed it to them in exchange for her life. "I came down here to help the Web; they'd asked us for someone. Because I'm a healer."

A spark jumped between the other two women.

"What kind of healer?" Sara asked.

Madrone felt herself stiffen at the woman's tone. If I were a cat, she thought, the hairs on my back would be bristling. She wasn't used to be talked to like a servant, and maybe it was time to assert some dignity.

"Back home, I did primarily midwifery and gynecology. Here, given what there is to work with, what I do is what you might call laying on of hands. We've done away with the old hierarchies in the North, but I was educated at the university through what they used to call an M.D. Plus training in herbs and Chinese medicine. Do you have a problem I can help you with?"

Sara looked at her, perplexed. "I didn't know they still let women be doctors in the North. And I didn't realize they let your people into universities."

"What people?" Madrone asked, confused.

"You know, colored people," Sara said, looking for the first time as if she were not in control. "You *are* black, aren't you?"

"Some of my ancestors came from Africa, if that's what you mean. Some came from Ireland, Spain, Scotland, France, and the tribes that inhabited the Central American coastal rain forests. What does that make me?"

"Touched with the tarbrush," Mary Ellen said, but softly.

"If they kept all people of African ancestry out of the universities, they'd be pretty empty," Madrone said, "since the entire human race originated there."

"Many would rather forget that fact," Mary Ellen said.

"My mother was a doctor," Madrone went on. "My grandmother was a psychologist, and *her* mother was a registered nurse, so I guess you could say that being a healer runs in our family."

Sara stared at her, trying to take in something she couldn't quite comprehend, and then suddenly she smiled, not the seductive arc with which she had favored them earlier but a broad tomboy grin that made her whole face come alive.

"Well, I can't match that," she said. "In my case, my mother was a whore."

Madrone looked at her, shocked in turn.

"A high-class whore, of course," Sara said. "She married her best client. So I guess I too follow the family profession."

"Don't be giving bad names to yourself," Mary Ellen said. She turned to Madrone. "And don't be all day staring at that cucumber. If you want it so bad, eat it."

She tossed some vegetables into a bowl and set it in front of Madrone. Madrone placed a slice of cucumber in her mouth. She almost wished the other two women would go away, so she could simply savor its coolness on her tongue. She could hardly concentrate on what they were saying.

Mary Ellen was placing vegetables in a bowl, making a salad. Madrone ate with Sara's eyes fixed on her, slightly uncomfortable under that gaze.

"Maybe she can help the child," Sara said.

"Your ladies be here in half an hour."

"Yes. I'm thinking of that."

"And Mr. Hall, what if he be coming home?"

"He's gone for the week again, thank Jesus. What is your name?" she asked Madrone.

Madrone resisted the temptation to stuff all the remaining vegetables in her mouth at once. She debated making up a name for them, but it seemed unnecessary. Her own name was in nobody's files. "Madrone. If I can help you, I will."

"I'll finish the lunch," Mary Ellen said. "You take her."

At the bottom of the house, dug into the hillside, were two dimly lit rooms, servants' quarters. By the standards of the hills, of course, they were luxurious, with real beds and blankets and chests for clothes. On one bed lay a small child, a girl who looked about five years old, and Madrone could see by the wavering, dull light that played over her skin that she was very ill. There was a grayish tone to her nut-brown skin, and a bluish cast to her lips.

"Her name is Angela," Sara said. "She's my niece. Can you help her?"

"I don't know." Madrone knelt beside the child and laid a hand over her chest. Slowing her breath, she let herself *feel* the patterns of the girl's energy. Yes, what she had suspected from her first glance at her aura was true.

"She has blood cancer," Madrone said. "Leukemia."

"Yes, that's what we've suspected."

"But there are drugs for that. Gene therapy and antivirals and white-cell boosters. Any regular doctor can treat her."

"But no doctor *will* treat her. Officially she's Mary Ellen's child."

"I don't understand."

"My sister, who was never very wise, had a little dalliance with Mary Ellen's son. They were discreet but not careful, and she got pregnant. Oh, we tried to get her an abortion but it was too dangerous—the Millennialists were on a campaign and nobody would do it. So we sent her off to our country house, and when the child came, Mary Ellen passed it off as hers. They might have gotten away with it if they'd had sense enough to break off the affair, but they didn't. And so eventually, of course, one of the other servants denounced them. Charles ran off to the hills, and Lisa—well, we no longer speak of her."

That's an odd turn of phrase, Madrone thought, but she said simply, "I'm sorry."

"I loved my sister, headstrong little idiot that she was. I'd like to save her child."

"I could tell you what drugs to get, and how to administer them."

"It's too dangerous. Don't you see—we can't afford to call any attention to her existence. What if my husband found out? Mary Ellen could go to the pens for having an illegitimate child. They don't usually enforce it with the blacks, but if we rub their noses in it, trying to doctor her, they'd have to."

"Your husband doesn't know?"

"My husband is an odious man. I never tell him anything." The words were spoken without emotion, but Madrone heard the whiplash of pain behind them. She didn't know what to say.

"I suppose this all looks pretty good to you," Sara said. "This house, the money, the water—"

"No, it doesn't look good to me." Madrone turned and faced her. The blue eyes were cold, but like something flash-frozen in the first cold of winter, something pleading, aching to melt. "To me it looks like a form of hell."

Sara flashed her wry grin. "You know an alternative?"

"Yes," Madrone said seriously. "As a matter of fact, I do." The child moaned and opened her eyes. Madrone read pain in them, and Sara stooped and laid a hand on the girl's forehead.

"Angela, this nice lady is here to help you. She knows a lot of special magic, but it only will work if you keep it a secret. Never, never tell anybody about her. Promise?"

The girl nodded. Her eyes were huge and round and dark, and suddenly Madrone couldn't stand the look in them. She wasn't ready to take on a healing of this magnitude; she needed food and rest. How long had it been since she'd slept? But she couldn't ignore the child's pain. Closing her own eyes and calling in her power, she soothed the inflammation and poured vitality through the girl's bloodstream, released pressure on swollen joints, and rewove the patterns of her *ch'i*. Her own energy was running low and she still hadn't tackled the cause of the disease, but she knew suddenly that she didn't have the strength to go deeper. Reluctantly, she withdrew. The child would have a remission, at least, and maybe Madrone could come back later and finish, when she was fed and rested, if she ever again were fed and rested. She had been here too long already, and yet she didn't see how she could leave unobserved before dark. Suddenly Madrone was so tired that all she could do was slump down against the wall and close her own eyes. Just for a moment.

She awoke to find Sara still standing above her, looking down, her face unreadable.

"The child looks better," she said.

"She's improved but not cured," Madrone said. "I don't know—I might be able to cure her, but I can't do it today. I just don't have the strength."

"I can see that." Sara smiled again, the urchin grin that cut through the polished surface. "You need more than ten minutes of sleep."

"A lot more."

"We don't expect miracles from you."

Why not? Madrone thought. Everybody else does. And I produce them just often enough to keep them hoping.

"I'm not talking about miracles," she said, shaking her head. "I'm talking about just a little more juice than I've got today. Or a few lousy credits' worth of drugs." It was back, suddenly, her rage, burning away her tiredness, making her feel invincible. Maybe she should tackle the child again now—but she had learned to distrust this state, knowing how the energy could suddenly drain away, leaving her spent. And she still had miles of trail to cover tonight, and the security forces to dodge. And she desperately needed to eat some more. "I don't know, maybe I can come back another time. Or maybe next time we raid a pharmacy I can bring you some pills for her."

"It's ironic," Sara said. "My husband manages a drug company. They send truckloads out to the labor camps. If I could think of a plausible story— but no. It's just too dangerous. Anyway, how can I thank you?"

"You already saved my life once today. If I could eat something and drink something, you'd save it again."

"Would you care to join me and the other ladies for lunch? Perhaps you could talk to us about where you come from."

"Are you out of your mind?"

"No. You can trust us. These friends—they're more than friends, really. We're a group—well, you'll see. The hillboys aren't the only ones trying to make changes."

"I've got to get out of here somehow," Madrone said.

"Stay here until after dark. Then I'll drive you somewhere if you want."

Madrone feared that she was trusting Sara only because she was too tired to think for herself. But I *am* too tired to think for myself, she admitted, so why not go along with her? I could learn something.

"Okay," she said. With a great effort, she pulled herself up and once more leaned down to touch the forehead of the sleeping child. "She should be all right for a while, now. Let her rest."

         o   o   o

Six women were grouped around a long table in the atrium, a glass-covered enclosure crowded with tropical plants. The air felt soft and moist. An artificial stream flowed over stones set into the back wall and splashed into a tiled pool where water lilies bloomed. Philodendrons twined along the rafters, and banks of orchids bloomed in the corners. Ferns hung over the table, and potted palms rose gracefully from wicker baskets. Madrone stood still for a moment, inhaling the scents of damp earth and dripping leaves. She had hungered so for the sound of running water. For a moment, she felt that she would give anything, betray anyone, to stay in that cool green room and never be thirsty again.

Mary Ellen had exchanged Madrone's uniform for clothes she called more suitable. They seemed to Madrone to reflect somebody's fantasy of a revolutionary, or perhaps more of a colonial explorer: designer jungle fatigues. The women at the table were slender and elegant in pale-colored dresses that set off the rose and lilac undertones of their light skin. It was strange to see so many very pale women all gathered together, like a bed artificially devoted to one variety of flower. Madrone felt like a sagebrush in a garden of lilies.

Gold-edged china and cut-glass crystal goblets were set at each place, and vases overflowed with scented flowers. And the food! Not acorn mush and honey but crisp salad and vegetables, chicken in delicate sauce, fresh-baked bread, and, for dessert, sweet little cakes with sugar icing. The smells alone nearly knocked Madrone over.

Throughout the meal, the other women chatted among themselves, occasionally stealing a curious glance at Madrone but not drawing her into the conversation. She was grateful to be left alone; it took all her concentration to eat slowly and remember her manners.

When the cakes were finished and the women sat sipping tea from rose-patterned cups, Sara motioned them to silence.

"We have a very special guest today, ladies," she said. "As you may know, twenty years ago when the Stewards' Party consolidated its power, isolated areas broke away. Our guest is from one of those areas, from the North. She is down here at great personal risk and sacrifice, and I have asked her to speak to us about the social conditions of her area."

All eyes focused on Madrone. Slowly, she set down her teacup and looked around the room. When she focused on their faces, they became distinct individuals. Now she noticed differences of dress and age and expression.

"My name is Madrone," she began. By habit, she was starting to sign her words as she spoke them, as she would in a Council meeting. But the ripple of discomfort that passed over the women's faces reminded her that they were not accustomed to the signs, so she placed her hands in her lap. The women were nervous enough already, the scent of fear was an acrid tinge under the sweet smells of perfume and flowers and cake and tea. "I come from San Francisco, which we sometimes call *Hierba Buena,* or *Gum Sahn,* or simply the City. I work there as a healer—a doctor, you would say—and I'm down here to offer service to those who are opposing the rule of the Stewards."

"They have women doctors in the North?" one woman exclaimed.

"In the North, a woman can do any kind of work she wants to do and is trained for."

An excited buzz went around the room, which was ended by an older woman, whose gray cap of hair crowned a thin, pinched face.

"I was a doctor," she said. "No, I *am* a doctor. The Stewards can take away a license, but they can't remove my knowledge and skill. So don't act like a woman doctor is a zebra, for Jesus' sake. It's not such an exotic thing to be."

"Thank you, Beth," Sara interrupted smoothly. "Madrone, please go on."

"Where I come from, we believe there are Four Sacred Things," Madrone began.

"Like the Four Purities of the Millennialists?" queried a small woman with delicate bones.

"What are they?" Madrone asked.

"Moral Purity, Family Purity, Racial Purity, and Spiritual Purity."

"Not exactly," Madrone said. "The Four Sacred Things are earth, air, fire, and water. Nobody can own them or profit from them, and it's our responsibility to heal them and take care of them. That's the basis of our politics and our economy."

This sparked a new round of questions, and once again Madrone found herself telling what she had come to think of as her fairy tale.

"Everybody has enough food and water. Everybody has a place to live and care when they're sick. It's hard, sometimes, because we've had so many die from the epidemics. There's still so much to heal, in the earth and the waters. But we share, and we have enough. Because everybody works, and works hard. No one is supported just for being . . ." She hesitated, aware she was about to say something that might offend these women, but Sara chimed in.

"Being ornamental?"

"Or of a certain race or class or parentage," Madrone added.

"But how do you force people to work when they don't want to?"

"We don't. People want to work, just as naturally as a child wants to walk and talk. Everybody wants to make some contribution."

"And if someone doesn't?"

Madrone shrugged. "Someone who really didn't want to work could survive on a basic stipend, but it wouldn't allow for many luxuries. Sometimes people are sick and can't work, or they have a *ch'i* deficiency and don't have much energy. Then we try to heal them. Sometimes people don't like a particular kind of work, but there's always something else to be done. I can't imagine healthy people not wanting to do anything. They'd be terribly bored, and isolated, and shamed. We'd probably send them to the mind healers."

"That's different," said the woman next to Madrone. "Here we have to corral them into farm camps and bribe them with increased water rations to get them into the factories. And still most of them would rather beg than work."

"Spare us your prejudices, Judith," Beth said. "Don't you know that for every open job there's fifty who want one and can't get one?"

"I know you like to believe that, but I've been advertising for a new gardener's boy for the last month and only had one applicant, who couldn't read and didn't know shit from a shovel, if you'll pardon my language."

"I won't," Beth said. "Although it's not your profanity I object to but the ignorance behind it. How can we expect the lower classes to learn to read when the schools we provide for the poor are nothing but Millennialist indoctrination camps? And what are you offering to pay your gardener? A pittance and a few swallows of water? Have you tried offering a living wage?"

"Please, ladies!" Sara said. "Our guest has limited time with us. We have the rest of our lives to argue with each other."

"And that's about the most we're capable of doing," Beth grumbled, but she sat quietly as a woman at the end of the table addressed Madrone.

"What about the dirty, nasty jobs? Who picks up the garbage?"

"Every household has its own compost. And collecting the papers and bottles and recyclable things—a lot of people think that's a really fun job. You get to circulate around the neighborhood, catch up on all the gossip. But the unpopular and dangerous things, like toxic cleanups—first we put out on the computer nets that we need volunteers. If we don't get them, we choose them by lottery, from those who owe gift work to the region. You see, we each are obligated for a certain number of hours of gift work each year. Mostly, you can choose what you want to do. Or if you have a very vital skill, like being a healer, you can do it in your own specialty. Personally, in good years, when there's no epidemics, I like to do something different, for a change. Tree planting or fruit picking, something outdoors and physical."

"So what you have," Beth said, "is the perfect communist society. I thought those theories were discredited back in the nineties."

"No, we don't," Madrone said. "For one thing, we could debate whether Marxist theory was discredited or simply its particular twentieth-century implementations; it's a discussion some people like to go on about endlessly. Are you familiar with Moraga's Theory of the Limitations of Complexity, for example?"

"No," Beth admitted.

"She's an economist who's also well versed in the principles of chaos theory. To put it simply, she says the old giant state socialist countries like the Soviet Union failed because they attempted too much control over too much complexity. She makes the same criticism of much twentieth-century technology. And she traces it back to the mechanistic philosophy of the Enlightenment, which saw nature as a great machine, something we could ultimately know and completely control." You're laying it on a bit thick, Madrone told herself, but she was enjoying herself, watching the expressions change from a slight air of condescension to outright astonishment. More than that, she thought, as she caught a spark in the eyes of Beth and one or two others, I've been as hungry for this as for vegetables: talk, discussion, something to stretch the mind more than the question of which ridge to cross next.

"I would love to talk with you more about that," Beth said, "but I suspect what these ladies most want to know is how your system functions."

"We don't have centralized control of the economy, although we do have as much coordination as possible. We don't have production quotas, for example. Work groups set their own goals and run their own affairs and barter in the markets for credits. But we've come to understand wealth and account for it in different ways. Marx said that wealth came from labor, but we say there are three different sources, and labor is only one, the most variable. There is also the stored labor of the past: for example, a house that was built a generation ago, or my grandmother's English bone china. That sort of wealth should also be shared fairly, not hoarded up in a few families. And finally there's wealth that is based on the resources of the earth, on the Four Sacred Things, and that wealth no one can profit from individually."

"Do you use money?" the woman next to her asked.

"Our credits function like money, but they're not backed by gold or silver. They're backed by energy, human and other sorts, and our basic unit of value is the calorie. So a product is valued by how much energy goes into its production, in terms of labor and fuel and materials that themselves require energy to produce. And part of that accounting is how much energy it takes to replace a resource that is used. Something that works with solar or wind power becomes very cheap. Anything requiring irreplaceable fossil fuels is generally too expensive to think about."

"But do you have rich and poor?" the same woman asked.

"We're each guaranteed a share of the wealth of the past and of the resources, which translates into a basic stipend of credits. As I said before, you could live on that, frugally, if you really didn't want to work. But if you do work, you earn work credits, and the more you work the more you earn, so there's incentive for those who want personal advancement. And if you do something really spectacular, achieve something fabulous, people bring you gifts."

"Don't people cheat?" asked a woman at the end of the table.

"All the accounts are public. Your whole work group sees the bill you put in each week, and believe me, they know if it's accurate. If not, you'll hear about it, and if necessary they'll bring it up before your Guild or Council. Of course, some jobs don't lend themselves to counting hours, like mine, or like being an artist or a musician. We get a fixed stipend."

"But how do you keep track of these credits? Do you have a computer system?" Beth asked.

"A very sophisticated one," Madrone said. "It's based on silicon crystals we grow from sea water. The tecchies direct their formation by visualization. It's a very specialized skill, and not everyone can learn to do it."

"So you have an advanced technology. You're not a primitive utopia," Sara said.

"We're not a utopia at all, and our technology is as advanced as it can be, given our limitations and the general depletion of resources. But we've had to make some hard choices. After the Uprising, every tool and device and process was reevaluated according to the Five Criteria of True Wealth that Latasha Burton developed."

"Which are?" Beth asked.

"Usefulness. Sustainability—meaning that it must generate or save as much energy as it consumes and doesn't depend on nonrenewable resources. Beauty. Healing for the earth, or at least not being destructive. Nurturing for the spirit. Private automobiles failed, for example. They're certainly useful and many people maintained that they can be beautiful, but they weren't sustainable. Computers based on our new crystals passed, and the Net we created also provides communication, news, accounting, lots of things. We've also made advances in solar and wind power and small-scale agriculture. Some industries disappeared—there are no vidsets or widescreens because we couldn't support the infrastructure they needed. Others had to change. We print a lot of books, but we make paper from hemp, not from trees."

"What about women's work? Do you have servants who clean your houses and mind the children?" Judith asked.

"We all do that sort of work, not just women but men too. And it's all paid for. Every household gets credits for a certain number of working hours per person, for home maintenance and for child care, or care of anyone who might need it. You can trade those credits around any way you like—keep them if you do your own work or assign them to somebody else if you'd rather get someone else to do it for you. And there are usually some people around, like students, who want to pick up a few credits without having to commit to a work group."

"And marriage?" Sara asked.

"That's a personal arrangement between the people involved. Sometimes it's based on their religion, if they belong to one that has rules about those things. But it's no longer an economic arrangement. If a woman—or a man— wants to stay home and take care of the house and the kids, they'd collect all those work credits and they'd be valued just as much as for work done outside the home, because all work is valued the same."

"What do you mean?"

"I mean a healer's work isn't worth more per hour than a farmer's or a teacher's. Oh, we kick it around in Council all the time, there're endless debates about it, but it always comes down to the fact that our system cannot work if we start to say one person's work or skill is worth more than somebody else's. An economic system is like an organism, and to function all its parts are necessary."

"So divorce is legal?" Sara asked.

"Isn't it legal here?"

"It's a sin," Sara said, and Madrone thought her voice sounded somewhat wistful. "You lose your immortal soul. Unless you have money for an offering to secure a dispensation."

"Which women never have on their own," Beth said. "Only the men."

"Some men," Judith said. "Not most men. Even well-off men are rarely that rich."

"It's not legal or illegal back home," Madrone said. "We don't have a whole lot of laws about those things. It's just up to the people involved. Unless there's some sort of problem they can't agree about—say, if they have kids and they can't agree who will take them. Then they have to bring in a Mediator or take it to their Neighborhood Council."

"So a man can just leave his wife for someone younger or better looking?"

"If that's what he wants to do. Or she can leave him, for a better-looking man. Or woman. But she doesn't depend on him for her living, so she's never left without support."

"The argument here," another woman said, "is that the Moral Purity laws protect women. Without them, men would just run wild, raping women on the streets."

"Whereas *with* the laws," Beth said, "men have women in their own privately stocked reserves, one for the wife, one for the mistress, one for anything or anyone they care to order from the catalogs."

"Don't you have a lot of rape and perversion?" a woman asked, ignoring Beth's comment.

"We don't have any perversion."

"Oh, come," Beth said. "Every human society on the face of this earth has had homosexuality."

Madrone laughed. "We have plenty of that. Is that what's considered perversion?"

"Among other things. What about incest and child molesting?"

"We don't have the kind of social isolation that breeds it. We have a lot of different kinds of families. Some of us grow up in big collectives, like I did. Some are in extended families, with aunts and uncles and cousins and grandparents; some in small nuclear families. But we make sure that no family is isolated. The Neighborhood Councils form support groups of people from different kinds of households and backgrounds—to give different perspectives. So every kid has half a dozen aunties and uncles from the time they're tiny. They're encouraged to talk about things, to ask for help, to protect themselves. And we train all our children, early on, in self-defense, both girls and boys. Oh, I've read a lot about incest and child abuse, but we don't have the climate of secrecy and shame that lets it go on for any length of time. I'm not saying it never happens, but nothing supports it. The same with rape. Our men aren't raised to believe they have the right to rape. In fact, we consider it the most shameful, degraded thing a man could do."

"What if it does happen?" the small woman asked.

"If it does? First, everybody in his family would talk to the person and tell him how shocked and horrible they feel. So would his *compas,* his friends and lovers, his Guild or Council, his Neighborhood Council, maybe the whole City Council. He wouldn't be welcome in anybody's house, or work group, or to eat with anybody. The mind healers might take him in if he wanted to get better—but it would take him years to regain people's trust. Maybe he'd have to go off to the hills to live with the Wild Boar People, the ones who can't fit into society."

"And if he won't go? How do you make him? Do you have police?"

"We find it's better not to assign that role to any one group of people. For one thing, they generally aren't around when you really need them, and for another, they tend to abuse their power. Instead, like I said, we're all trained in self-defense, and as we get older we get more advanced Peacekeeper training—how to intervene in a heated conflict, how to restrain somebody. If there's a fight, let's say, which happens from time to time although it's fairly rare, whoever happens to be around will take care of it. I did once see a man banished to go live with the Wild Boar People. He was yelling and fighting, but there were ten people around him and they got his arms into restraints. It was very upsetting to watch, although they didn't hurt him. They put him on a fire truck, and I guess someone drove him up to the Sonoma Hills, where the Wild Boar People live by hunting feral pigs. Once you're banished, your name and picture go out on the Net. Everybody knows who you are, and you can't come back unless the City Council approves. For ten days in midwinter, though, we let some of the Wild Boar People come in to market to sell their pigs. But that's all."

"But if you're unarmed, couldn't one maniac with a laser rifle take over your whole city?" Judith said.

"No," Madrone said. "Somebody would stop him. People would stop him together, even if some of them got killed doing it."

"A few men, then," Judith said. "An organized group with modern weaponry."

"Well, I guess we'll soon find out, won't we?" Beth said. "If the rumors from the army prove true."

"What rumors?" Madrone asked. "Have they attacked us?"

"Not yet," Beth said. "But they seem to be gearing up for it."

Oh, Goddess, no, Madrone thought. I want to go home. I don't want to be here with these strange women asking me endless questions. Maybe I shouldn't be telling them any of this. How do I know they aren't spies? Didn't Bird suffer and nearly die to avoid revealing what I've just blurted out over lunch—that we have no real defenses?

"That takes care of Moral Purity and Family Purity," the small woman went on. "Do you have laws about Racial Purity?"

Maybe I should just shut up. But Hijohn told me to talk to people. Of course, he wasn't thinking of these women, but how are they supposed to have any hope of change down here if they don't know what is possible?

"Don't you want to answer?" the woman asked.

"She's tired," Sara said.

"No, I'm okay," Madrone said. I've told them enough already, there's no point in stopping now. She smiled. "Racial Purity would be hard to enforce, when we're such a bunch of mongrels."

"That didn't stop them here," Beth said. "They just classified people one race or the other, sometimes rather arbitrarily. I've seen some blacks as light as me, and a few whites darker than you who knew the right officials to bribe when the classifications were made."

"Actually, we honor our ancestors, but we don't think a lot about race, exactly," Madrone said. "We consider it a concept designed to separate people. We try to honor all our different heritages and histories. Diversity is part of our strength. It enriches us."

"So is it unusual for people of—uh, your race to be doctors?" asked a woman who wore her dark hair in a towering construction piled precariously on her head. "Did you go to the university?"

"Anyone who wants to can go to the university, if there's something you want to study. It has nothing to do with what color you are or what genitals you're born with."

"In theory that's true here," Beth said. The women looked at her, amazed. "I'm serious. There's no law on the books preventing women from studying to be doctors or engineers or heads of corporations. Blacks or Latins, either. They just rig the admissions tests so the wrong ones don't get in."

"We don't have admissions tests to the university," Madrone said. "If you aren't prepared for the work, you find out pretty quickly and get help, or go do something else."

"But not everyone is intelligent enough for academic work," Beth said. "Surely you aren't trying to tell us that."

"Not everyone is, or is interested," Madrone admitted. "But if you're not good at intellectual work, if it's frustrating, why would you stay there when you can go find some work to do where you *can* make your contribution?"

They talked on, asking Madrone about the Uprising, about the Councils and the work groups and the history of the last twenty years, until Madrone's head began to ache.

"Tell me about this group," she said at last. "What is it you are trying to do together?"

The women fell silent, looking at each other, reluctant to speak. Finally Sara answered.

"We want to improve life for women. But we don't know how. The Millennialists are very powerful. So we meet, to learn and discuss and think."

"Which is an improvement in and of itself," Beth said. "Despite all our disagreements, before this group began I was perishing for lack of stimulating conversation."

"Do you have any contact with the Web?" Madrone asked.

A shocked silence filled the room. Beth's face closed, as if she were protecting something.

"They're not exactly our sort of people," Judith explained. She giggled, a little nervously. "Can you see us running around with rifles, covered with dirt?"

Madrone caught Beth's eye. The older woman's lips curved in the barest suggestion of a sarcastic smile.

"You could learn from them," Madrone said. "They could learn from you. Maybe I could help get you together."

Sara looked at her watch and stood up.

"I'm sorry to say this, ladies, but we need to end. It's after three, and I know many of you have to go."

They thanked Madrone profusely, some with tears in their eyes. The woman with the piled hair came over and kissed her cheek, but Madrone could feel the effort she made not to shrink back from contact with her flesh.

This is racism! Madrone realized, with a slight sense of triumph, as if she had run across a rare herb she had heard of but never seen before. They are actually afraid to touch me! And she made a point of shaking hands with each of them. Only Beth clasped her hand with real warmth.

"I would so love to talk with you, for days and days and days," she said. "You remind me of a better time. I live right near the university—I run a sorority house of nursing students. It's on Gayley Avenue, right near the old main gate. A big pink building, you can't miss it. Come and see me if you ever can, or if you need a refuge, or just a few days of rest. . . ."

"Thanks," Madrone said. She reached out and hugged the older woman, wishing suddenly that she could go with her and sate herself with conversation as much as with food and water.

∘ ∘ ∘

The women were gone. Madrone sat, refreshed by an hour's nap, nestled into the couch in Sara's room, facing a broad expanse of glass that looked out over the city. The sky turned from a cold pale blue to indigo. Lights began to appear, defining the contours of the hills. Sara pulled the filmy white curtains open a little wider, then curled up on the couch next to Madrone. The room was very white around them: walls painted in a soft white-on-white glaze, the giant four-poster bed behind them, draped in antique white linens, heavy as an accusation.

Madrone had wanted to talk about the idea of a meeting between the Web and Sara's group of women. But each time she broached the subject, Sara shifted it away. Now she was telling Madrone the full story of her wayward younger sister. They were drinking wine, something white and fruity that pleased Madrone's bee mind even as it deepened the languor in her limbs.

"Sometimes I almost envy Lisa," Sara said, with a sigh and a long look at Madrone. She dropped her lashes. "At least she knew what it was to love, or believed she did."

There's a cue here, Madrone thought. What am I supposed to say? "Haven't you ever known love?"

"Lust is as close as I've come. And you? Who do you love?"

Sandy of the gull-wing eyes and black waterfall hair, sweet Nita who understands me so well, Sage, Holybear, Bird, poor broken Bird with his brave song. "Many," Madrone replied. "Love is easy for me."

"Then love me," Sara whispered, setting down her wineglass and catching Madrone's hand and pressing it first to her heart, then to her breast, then down across her belly to the mound between her legs. "I've never met anyone like you. Teach me what love is."

Madrone wasn't sure if she were being seduced, cajoled, or commanded. Before she could either move closer or pull away, Sara slid into her arms and pressed against her body. Their breasts touched, rubbed. The dregs of Madrone's wine spilled behind her; she let the empty glass slide out of her hands. A heartbeat thrummed in the center of her vulva. Sara's slender forefinger traced the line of Madrone's lips, as if outlining a target. Then Sara kissed her. All Madrone's suppressed hungers awoke at once. She is playing with me, Madrone thought. I am her dark and dangerous toy. But the thought could not reach her body or deter its response.

When she opened to Sara, she felt all the woman's attention and skill and intelligence bent on pleasing her, on sensing each response to the most subtle movement of hand or hips or tongue, and intensifying until Madrone felt weak, unable to resist. Madrone felt handled and yet she could not complain, in fact she almost wanted to beg for more, more pleasure, more water, more soft silken sheets and delicate, calculated caresses. *Diosa,* it had been too long since she had been touched, fed.

"Did I please you?" Sara whispered.

"Yes, of course. And you?"

"It gives me pleasure to give pleasure. It's what I'm good at."

Madrone felt she should protest, respond, but her lids were closing, her arms heavy as lead. Forget about introducing her to Hijohn, Madrone thought sleepily. Those women aren't willing to face real danger. No, it's Isis that Sara should meet. They are very much alike. Then she was asleep, a shadow in the all-white room.

○ ○ ○

Madrone had Sara drive her to a canyon farther west where she could pick up a fire road and return to the ridge trail. It was the middle of the night; a late moon was rising. She shouldered a pack replenished with water and food.

"Will you come back?" Sara whispered.

"I'll try," Madrone said. "If I don't, it's not because I don't want to."

"I'll worry about you."

"Que te vaya bien," Madrone whispered.

"What does that mean?"

"May it go well with you."

○ ○ ○

By the time she staggered into camp, dawn was breaking and the old moon was moving down toward the western horizon. Baptist challenged her and, when she answered, threw down his gun and hugged her.

"Madrone! We were afraid they'd got you this time."

"No, I got away. What about Begood and Littlejohn?"

"Begood came in earlier, told us what happened. Littlejohn just made it back about an hour ago."

"Thank the Goddess."

"Hijohn wants to hear what happened. But he's asleep."

"Let him rest. I'll tell him in the morning. I napped today but I could use some more rest myself."

She found a flat patch underneath a chamise bush, pulled her blanket around her, and closed her eyes. Everything's all right, she told herself. Nobody was killed, nobody was captured, and here I am, clean and well fed and otherwise satisfied too. But in her uneasy dreams, flowers were trampled under heavy-booted marching feet.

20

Maya was always feeding Bird, presenting bowls of washed fruit to him as midnight snacks, waking him with omelets and home-baked bread. She squandered eggs recklessly and sacrificed the older chickens for soup. She depleted their honey stores for cookies and cakes.

"Thanks, Maya, but I'm full," Bird would say gently.

She'd shake her head insistently. "Eat. You need to build up your strength."

"Maya, even to placate the long line of Jewish mothers from which you and I are descended, I cannot eat another bite."

Maya could see the strain he was under, but she couldn't talk to him about it because she knew she would break down crying and lamenting. That wouldn't be fair to him, to burden him with her grief when she wanted to support him with her love.

More and more, he spent his time out of the house. There were meetings to attend, trainings to organize, strategies to decide.

"On the left, you are soldiers of the Stewardship," Sister Marie said, addressing two long lines of people gathered for training. "You're armed, and you've been told to go into people's homes and cut off their water. The line on the right, you are City people, and it is your homes the soldiers are entering. Go!"

Chaos ensued, as fifty people approached their partners and began talking, gesturing, and shouting all at once. Bird and Marie watched, as did small clumps of bystanders enjoying the sun in the park. The grass was green and the ancient cedars stood watch unconcerned. It was hard to believe, Bird thought, that anything bad could really happen.

"Do you think we've given them enough time?" Marie asked.

"Let them run a few minutes more," Bird said. "Remind me, what role play are we doing next?"

"The holding pen," Marie said. "For the people caught stealing water."

"Good. That's a good one."

"You don't think we're overstressing water in the training?"

"We can't stress it too much. Water is life. It's the first thing they'll try to gain control over."

"I think it's time," Marie said. Suddenly her face contorted with pain. Bird took her arm and supported her. With a few deep breaths, she steadied herself. "I'm sorry. I think the cancer's gone into my back."

"You're working too hard. You should be resting, trying to heal."

"I want to be useful, as long as I can. It's going to take all of us pushing ourselves pretty hard to get everyone in the city through one of these trainings in the next two weeks."

"We've got to train other trainers," Bird said.

"We start tonight," Marie said, "now that we've worked out some material and have a little experience ourselves. Hey, this group has gone way over time." She blew a clay whistle that hung from a thong around her neck. "Time! Stop! Now, think for a moment, everybody, about how you feel, what worked and what didn't work. Soldiers, how did it feel to be in your position?"

"I was surprised at how nervous I felt, going into a strange home. I was afraid, even though I had a gun," a woman said.

"I felt very powerful, like everybody should be scared of me and obey me. But the woman who confronted me—she was so calm and seemed so sure of herself, I didn't know what to do," said the man next to her, and they continued responding, down the line.

"And on the other side?" Marie asked. "How did it feel to be invaded?"

"I was terrified. I had to stop and ground and listen for my heartbeat. And then somehow I became very calm, and I could face this person and speak calmly and not lose myself," said Sachiko from the Musicians' Guild.

"I lost it! I just couldn't believe that some guy thought he could come into my house and push me around! I started screaming!" said the woman next to her.

"And how did that feel to you, soldier?"

"I was comfortable with it. It was what I expected. I knew how to handle it," her partner said.

"Let's go on," Marie suggested.

A group of children led by Rosa crossed the grass and came over to them.

"Can we join the training?" Rosa asked.

Marie and Bird exchanged glances.

"I hate to think of children involved in these things," Marie said.

"But if war really comes, they will be," Bird said.

"I know. Yes, Rosa, certainly you can join."

They marked out an area of the grass for the pen, and the trainees waited while Bird and Marie conferred. Then, wearing soldiers' caps and carrying clubs made from bundled papers, Bird and Marie entered through imaginary gates, grabbed hold of one of the larger and more vocal men, and began to drag him out. The group, well prepared, surrounded them, singing and chanting and placing their bodies between the guards and the gates.

Bird and Marie pulled on their victim and were on the verge of dragging him free when Rosa and her friends hurled themselves onto his chest and clung like monkeys, singing all the while. Bird beat on them with his paper club, cursing and swearing, while the group broke into shouts and yells. When Marie finally blew her whistle to call time, everyone was wet with sweat and quite a few bruises were distributed around.

"Rosa!" Bird said. "When somebody beats on you like that, let go, for Goddess' sake! If this had been a real club, you'd have a broken arm, a broken head, a broken back."

"But I thought the idea was not to let go, no matter what they do to you," Rosa said.

"The idea is survival, not martyrdom," Marie said.

"But why, Bird?" Rosa asked. Her eyes were lifted up to his face, but they slid down involuntarily to glance at his hands. "That wasn't what you did. You didn't give in to them, even though they hurt you."

"They just didn't hurt me enough," Bird said. "In time, I would have. Anybody would have. Besides, that was different."

"What was different about it?"

"For one thing, I was grown up. You're still a kid."

"You told me you were nineteen. That's not so grown up. And I'm thirteen already."

"Let's not argue about this," Marie said. "The point is, for everybody, that we're not in an endurance contest. You may be called upon to make great sacrifices, we all may be. But part of successful struggle is also knowing when to retreat."

By the time they finished the role plays and the discussions afterward, the sun had traveled a long arc over the grass and Bird now shivered in the shadow cast by the buildings across the street.

"That's enough for today," he said. "Marie and I have work tonight, but we'll be back in the park tomorrow. Tell your friends."

Marie sat on a bench as the group broke up, stopping in little knots to chat. Rosa stood, looking somewhat shyly at Bird, but before she could approach him Sachiko came over.

"I don't suppose, in your busy schedule, you'd have time to come by and lend us your ear for an hour or two. We're working on the music for May Day, and it's not coming right."

"That's optimistic," Bird said. "You think we'll have a May Day?"

"The day will certainly come, whatever else does. And we want to be ready for it."

Bird sighed. Marie was sitting, exhausted, on a bench, her lips gray. He really ought to make her rest tonight, train the new trainers himself.

"I just can't think about it now," he said to Sachiko. "When this is all over, maybe."

"Are you sure?"

"Don't push me, Sacha. I said no!" Bird's voice came out more harshly than he had intended, and he turned away from the hurt he saw in Sachiko's dark eyes. I'm being an asshole, he told himself. I should turn back, apologize. But his rudeness had the desired effect. She went away.

∘ ∘ ∘

"Is it nonviolence or psychological warfare?" Bird asked Lily, who had left the seclusion of the island and spent most of her time now in the central city, watching the training, talking to people, wandering through the orchards and the gardens.

She and Bird were sitting in the back yard of Black Dragon House. He was sweaty from his day in the park, and sore from being tackled by an overly enthusiastic soldier in one of the role plays. Marie was lying down, and he was glad in his hour or two of free time to sit. Lately he found himself so restless that he could only relax when his body had been worked to exhaustion.

"It's a question that's come up in the training. Is our goal to convert the enemy, turn them loving and peaceful and kind, or just to keep them continuously off balance?"

"Our strategy," Lily said, "is to refuse to participate in the patterns that perpetuate violence. If we succeed, it is likely that we will do both—knock our opponents off balance and convert some of them."

Bird looked at her. She seemed so calm, so sure of her beliefs, so cool and clean in a white silk shirt. While he had dirt under his nails from pulling a few weeds, and his mind was equally encrusted with doubts.

"Lily, I want to believe we can win this way, but it takes an act of faith on my part, I have to tell you. Even though I spoke for it in Council, and what I said is true: I don't want to kill. But I've been down there, I know what we'll be facing. Every day I wake up tempted to go beg the Council to reconsider fortifying the San Bruno mountains and mining Highway 101."

"That temptation will always be with us. Force seems so clear, so simple and direct. When I was young, one of my brother's friends had a van with a bumper sticker on it that said, FORCE, IT WORKS! And nobody can deny that it does. But meeting force with force produces nothing but what is already known and planned for and expected. It's what has already been done, over and over, for thousands of years."

"Because it *does* work," Bird said.

Lily brushed a fly off the sleeve of her jacket. "There used to be a saying, 'Insanity is repeating the same acts and expecting different results.'"

"Yeah, but insanity is also hoping for results that are extremely unlikely from the particular acts you take."

Lily stood, smoothed her skirt, and looked down at Bird where he sprawled on the grass.

"Bird, you are absolutely entitled to your doubts and fears. We all have them. But if we proceed with our plans, not to repeat the same acts but to do something different, a different outcome will happen."

"We don't know what that will be."

"Suffering, undoubtedly. Miracles, maybe. Change."

                              o   o   o

While Bird had little appetite for food, he craved sex. The big bed in the ritual room was in use every night. He lay nestled among Sage and Nita and Holybear, soaking up touch. Although he never spoke about fear, they could feel it leak from his skin. He wanted things he had never allowed before: hands on his scars, fingers kneading the strained muscles around his old wounds.

Downstairs, Maya slept with Doctor Sam. He had appeared late one night and asked to come in. A fresh batch of cookies was in the oven that she had made for Bird, knowing full well he might eat, at most, one of them. Sam devoured a plateful while they sat looking at each other for a long time. His face drooped like a man burdened with too many years, and the lines around his gray eyes were deep and thick. His eyebrows, bushy white sprouts that shot up and furrowed deep when he concentrated, still reminded her of her father. Not a handsome man, but not unattractive.

He sighed.

"Hard day?" she inquired.

"A hell of a day. We're getting refugees from down the peninsula. Casualties. I'd give a lot to have Madrone back right now."

"We all would. Sam, if you don't mind me asking, why are you here?"

"You need me, Maya. I'm a grandfather, I know how you feel in a way the young ones can't. And I need you."

"I'm nearly old enough to be your mother," she said, nibbling delicately at the edge of a cookie.

He smiled at her. "At our age, that hardly matters."

"Sam, I'm practically moribund! Are you some sort of necrophiliac?"

He reached across the table, took the cookie out of her hand, and held it. "Maya, you are a beautiful, powerful, attractive woman. The lines on your face are the calligraphy of your history." His thumbs caressed her palms and she began to feel the old pulse in her vulva waken, her breasts as hungry for petting as cats. "Of course, maybe you don't want an ugly old geezer like me."

"You're not ugly, Sam. I would call you—distinguished."

"Ruggedly handsome?"

She pursed her lips thoughtfully. "Well, rugged, anyway. And I've always admired your eyebrows." She felt an urge to touch them, actually, to pet the wiry and unruly hairs that adorned his eyes, and, having nothing to lose, she removed one hand from his grip and stroked his face. He closed his eyes, basking in her touch.

"I like that. You're a very sensual woman."

"You don't know the half of it yet."

"I'm eager to learn." He smiled, opening his eyes and looking into hers with such warmth and friendliness that her better judgment began to melt away.

"I thought all that was over for me," Maya said. "Anyway, I'm not sure I remember how."

"I remember. I'll remind you of any salient points you forget."

"But I don't love you, Sam."

"You will. Before this is over, Maya, we will need each other so desperately that we will fall in love by default." He reached out and touched her cheek. His hand was rough, but his moves delicate, sure: a surgeon's hand, she thought. In some ways he reminded her of Rio in his old age, grizzled but still cocky. How sweet it had been, just to wake in the morning curled up next to him, his back nestled against hers, to turn and hold him and smell his skin and feel his warmth. Yes, it might be nice to have that comfort again.

"Your skin is soft as flour," he said.

"What kind of flower?"

"No, flour, like baking flour."

"What kind of simile is that?"

"Can you think of anything softer or more sensual than dipping your hands into a mound of fresh white flour?"

"Maybe one or two things." She ran her hands over the fringe of hair on the sides of his head and over his bald scalp.

"Why do you sigh?" he asked her.

"After such a long wild life, to think I'd end up with a Jewish doctor."

"You've had worse," he said. "May I kiss you?"

"Give it a try."

He walked around the table, and she rose to meet him as he slid his hands over her back, pressing his lips to hers. Yes, her body was humming and singing in a way she thought was over long ago.

"I've had worse," she admitted.

"Come on, let's go to bed."

Bird didn't talk about fear, but he could smell it in his own sweat. He had to shit, it seemed, ten times a day. When he met with Defense Council, or with

Marie and Lan and Roberto, he spoke reassuringly, in a low, calm voice. When he tended Sister Marie during one of her bad nights, his presence was comforting, grounded, soothing.

"I understand pain," she'd said through gritted teeth. "That doesn't scare me—heaven knows I've lived through enough of it. But in spite of all the role plays we've led, I still can't really imagine what it's like, Bird, to face torturers."

"Don't think about it," he said. "It may never come to that. Maybe we're making a mistake with all this training and anticipating. Maybe it would be better just to wait until it happens and trust that we'll have the strength to face it when it comes."

"And if I don't?"

"Well, chances are by that time you won't have a whole hell of a lot of choice in the matter."

There were things he couldn't talk about to anyone. Not to Maya, whose own fear and grief was barely contained. Sam was spending his free time with her now, and Bird was glad, because it lessened the intensity of her focus on him. Not to Marie or Roberto or Lan, certainly. Not to Sage and Nita and Holybear. They were worried enough for him and a touch guilty besides, because they were preparing to move to the relative safety of the high mountains.

"I hate to leave you," Nita said, as the four of them jostled for position on the big bed in the ritual room. Her head rested under his chin, and he could look over the thatch of her wild hair to meet Holybear's blue eyes peering anxiously into his own. "But we've got six years of work invested in these cultures. The cell lines are irreplaceable."

"We argued with Toxics Council," Sage said, curling her long body against Bird's back, "but they convinced us not to risk the experiments. If we can really breed a microbe that can break down toxic residues in salt water, we could reclaim the bay."

"If the bay is still ours to reclaim," Holybear said glumly.

"We have to believe it will be," Bird said. "We have to act as if we will win, or we've already lost. Toxics is right. You've got to protect your work, because that's what we're fighting for." He could sound so sure, so strong, as if he believed in the possibility of victory, as if he weren't afraid. Better than crying "Don't leave me!" or, worse, begging them to take him along.

"It doesn't feel right," Nita said. "It feels like deserting you."

"You're doing me a favor," Bird said. "If you're gone, I won't have to worry about you. And no one can use you against me."

"You really feel okay about us going?" Sage asked.

"I feel okay about all of us going to sleep. I've got a training early tomorrow morning."

At three in the morning, Bird woke up moaning from a nightmare. He was trembling, drenched with sweat. Where was he? In the ritual room, with Sage and Nita and Holybear still asleep. He couldn't remember the dream, but he felt it, like a chill in the air, and quietly he disentangled a blanket, wrapped himself in it, and sat by the window watching the moon. Under the blanket he was shaking. He hoped the rest of them stayed asleep, but then Holybear's hand was on his shoulder.

"You've got to talk to us about it," he said. "Even if it hurts us."

Bird shook his head. They were around him now, all three of them, holding him in a multi-armed embrace. "There's nothing to talk about. I'm just scared, is what it comes down to."

"What did you dream?" Sage asked.

It came back to him when she spoke, and he shivered. "I keep dreaming that I wake up someplace dark and cold. I can't feel the earth, and the air is old and stale and smells of shit. And then I hear footsteps, in the corridor outside, and the rattle of keys. And I know that they're coming for me—and it's going to begin again."

There was nothing they could say, but they held him tighter.

"I'm waiting for it now. That's what's so hard. When it's actually happening, it'll be okay. I mean, it'll just be what's happening. But I hate the waiting."

"Is it a fear or a memory?" Holybear asked.

"I don't know. Both, maybe."

"I'm sorry."

"I wish there were something we could do for you," Sage said.

"Talk to Maya for me. I should do it myself, but I just can't look her in the face around this."

"Sure."

"Tell her, if something bad comes down, if it looks like something is going to happen to me, to stay home. I don't want her to come out and watch."

"She'll want to."

"I can stand a lot, but I can't stand that. Having her watch."

"Okay," Holybear said. "I'll tell her."

                              o o o

In the morning, they said goodbye. Bird walked them down to the docks, where they boarded a small sailboat. They would head upriver and, from there, somewhere. He wouldn't let them tell him; already he knew far too much. He watched the white dot of their sail until it disappeared on the other side of the bridge. And then, for a long time, he watched the emptiness where the boat had been.

                              o o o

His days were taken up with training and meetings, planning strategies, telling over and over again everything he knew about the ways of the South. The telling brought back memories he had tried to repress. Even the lost years began to yield up incidents and bits of knowledge.

He came home at night stuffed with pain that he couldn't bring himself to unload on Maya. Everybody else was gone. Only Rosa still came for her piano lessons, in the late afternoons when training was over for the day. Sometimes he actually forgot his fear, watching her concentrate as she struggled with a new piece of music.

One night, after she had gone, he found himself absently fingering the keys on the piano. His fingers were stiff, and they ached, but he banged out a few chords, a trickle of melody. Then he grabbed paper and pen and began to write the notes as he heard them pouring through his mind. No, he couldn't play, except awkwardly and painfully, but he could write the music out and leave it, and maybe, someday, somebody else would play it. Writing out the music was like talking to someone who could understand without guilt or judgment. He forgot time and fear. Afterward he could sleep through the night even though he slept alone.

He came to depend on the hour each night he spent by himself, picking out on the piano the bones of tunes he heard fully fleshed in his mind. The struggle to capture his music kept him sane, calm, steady. He guarded that time jealously, shutting the door on Maya and Sam, refusing to be distracted. Music had become vital to him, necessary as water.

21

The ruined roadbeds of the City of Angels still ran laser straight across the basin, mile after mile, but each route was studded with obstacles, piles of rubble from buildings collapsed in old quakes and never rebuilt. Around their bases clustered shacks thrown together from the reclaimed ruins. Corpses of trees reared their heads at the edges of old crossroads, now swallowed under dead hulks of metal and cardboard shelters.

Madrone and Hijohn maneuvered their way through the refuse-clogged paths. Children picked through the rubble, fiercely guarding their collections of old cans and broken bottles, glancing up with hungry eyes as they passed. The spring heat had been fierce in the shaded, waterless canyons; here on the asphalt it was brutal. Madrone began to wonder if she had made the right decision. Hijohn had suggested she spend some time teaching healing in the city's center, where he claimed there was ample water. The plan had seemed good, but now she was not so sure. The canyon had its own beauty, even in austerity; these streets were an assault. Her bee mind buzzed alarm at the stench, and her instincts scented danger everywhere.

They skirted a solid concrete building where a long line of people waited in the glare of the sun. They looked hungry, and the air around them reeked of hopelessness.

"Water line," Hijohn said. "If you got a ration card, you can line up every day and collect your water. Half a gallon."

"That's not enough. You can barely survive on that in this heat."

"Yeah, but you can survive, that's what makes the difference. The hard-liners want to kill the program. Say it's supporting idleness in the lower classes."

A windowless concrete monolith stretched for most of the next block, and they detoured carefully around it.

"Factory," Hijohn said. "We're getting into the industrial area."

"It looks like a prison," Madrone said.

"Feels like it too. I did a stint in one, one summer. The Web thought we could organize the workers."

"What was it like?"

"Like hell. Punch in, punch out, dock your pay if you're five minutes late. Then ten hours under white-hot lights, bent over a table monkeying with things so small you could hardly see them. We put together electronic stuff out of scavenged parts. My job was to take apart old radios, tape players. Never did learn how to put anything together."

"Did you organize a union?"

"What they call unions run the factories. They provide the management."

"There's no counter-union? No movement to strike for better conditions?"

"We tried to get something together, but people are scared. Their pay is shit, but it's better than being out on the streets with no job at all—and no water. No, we got some recruits for the hills, but that was all. This system can't be reformed. We got to tear it all down, root it out, and start fresh. . . . Here's where we turn. We don't want to go too deep into the factory zone, because the Corporate Guard checks there for passes."

They turned down a street and soon were winding their way through a neighborhood of twisted lanes and shacks. The faces Madrone passed were as withered and dry as her own had become, and on them she saw the look of haggard endurance she felt in her own eyes. I've begun to feel at home here, she realized.

After a while, the crowded paths gave way to broad stretches of open, dusty ground. Hijohn's eyes darted around uneasily. The long walk was beginning to tell on Madrone, but she forced herself to keep up. In the distance, she could hear shouting, and what sounded like shots, and Hijohn increased the pace until they were almost running.

"Gang territory," he said. "Mostly they don't bother the Web, but they could just as easily shoot us by accident."

Madrone tried to create an energy web of protection around them, visualizing it as light and color, but the image did little to quell her nervousness. Finally they ducked into the protection of buildings.

"Now we're in territory the Web controls," Hijohn said. "The liberated zone." Madrone thought to herself that "discarded zone" might be a more accurate term. She couldn't imagine why the Stewards would want this place. If anything the people looked dirtier, thinner, and shabbier. The streets were a confusion of pathways among buildings that seemed to be standing more out of inertia than any structural integrity. Most likely the Stewards were quite happy to have this area occupied by the Web. Falling plaster probably kept mortality high and saved bullets.

On and on they walked, until the soles of Madrone's feet began to burn in her shoes from the heat of the pavement. She was too dehydrated to sweat. As they went deeper into the zone, she began to hear a sound on the air, a pulsing beat like a muffled drum. At last they pushed through a narrow opening between two leaning stucco buildings.

Madrone stopped, amazed. They had come to an open square where the ground was shaded from the sun's harsh rays by stretched, filmy cloths. The buildings that formed the boundaries of the plaza seemed well cared for, solid, gleaming with whitewash. And around their bases actual plants grew, each one swaddled in moisture-conserving plastic, fenced off and protected but alive and green. She smelled moisture, and everywhere she looked she saw evidence of care and attention. Bright murals were painted on the walls, and the wooden posts that supported the canopies were intricately carved.

In the diffused light under the canopies, a small crowd was gathered. In the center, three men and two women were drumming. Others were gathered around them singing. One woman's voice soared above the others, dipping and flashing in harmony.

> Open your eyes, there's a new day dawning,
> Freedom will rise like the morning sun. . . .

It was an old song Madrone had heard Johanna sing, and a little shiver of energy rippled up her spine and made the roots of her hair rise. This was where Johanna came from. Maybe she had walked these same streets; maybe one of these houses had stood in the ghetto where she liked to claim she'd grown up, even though Maya did claim that ghetto was purely mythical. In that case, maybe this had once been the nice middle-class neighborhood where Maya and Johanna lived next door to each other. It didn't matter. What mattered was that something in Madrone sank down through her feet and claimed the land. This was her land too. This was her fight. A spark of hope within her caught fire and blazed. When she looked around at the singers in the square, they became incandescent, as she herself began to shine. Action fever, Maya used to call it. A type of madness, like falling in love.

When the song ended, the crowd turned to welcome them. The woman who had been singing harmony came over to them. She had brown eyes, a round pregnant belly, and skin the color of dark honey. Her long black hair was pinned up, like the queen of Spain, Madrone thought. She should have combs of tortoiseshell and silver and blood-red roses as adornments instead of hairpins bent out of old wires. But here there were no flowers. The woman smiled at Madrone even as her eyes searched out Hijohn, brightening as she looked at him. A flush crept up her cheeks.

"Welcome," she said. "My name is Katy. Short for Hecate. Although really it's short for Katherine, but don't tell."

"I'm Madrone."

"You're the healer. I'm so glad you're here. We've been waiting and hoping." Katy started to reach out her hand, then shook her head, laughing, and grabbed Madrone in a hug. Madrone felt her body stiffen and then relax.

Diosa, she thought, how long has it been since anyone has so spontaneously hugged me? She was as thirsty for that contact as she was for water.

"My turn," Hijohn said, and embraced Katy. His arms tightened around her, and Madrone saw a look of such tenderness come over his wizened face that she was almost embarrassed. It was an aspect of him she would never have suspected existed, a sweet, moist kernel hidden beneath the dry shell. They kissed for a long moment, and Madrone was suddenly filled with homesickness. Sandy and she had kissed like that, and Bird—she had just begun to feel it with him, that sense of being home and complete. Whatever had possessed her to leave?

Finally they pulled away from each other. Katy smiled at Madrone, a little apologetically. "You must be tired, with all that walking. Come inside."

They ducked through a doorway into a dark room that smelled of earth and oil and cornmeal. Katy kept one hand lingering on Hijohn's arm or just grazing his body, as if she needed physical reassurance that he was really there. Madrone shivered, suddenly feeling her hunger and thirst.

"Sit," Katy said, pointing to a bench by an old plastic table, relic of some earlier world. Madrone sat gratefully, leaning back and closing her eyes. When she opened them, Katy had set a large glass of water before her. Madrone held it in her hands for a moment, their slight tremor her prayer of thanks, and then slowly, gratefully, she drank.

"We've got plenty of water here," Katy said. "We run an illegal tap into a city pipe. So drink all you want."

Those were words Madrone had given up thinking about together: *plenty* and *water.* She savored every sip, making it last, unable to believe she could truly have more until Katy set a pitcher down in front of her.

"You drink like someone from the hills," she said.

"She *is* from the hills," Hijohn said. He had joined her at the table and was savoring his water as she did hers. But his eyes rested on Katy's belly. "How are you? You doin' okay?"

"Fine," Katy said.

"Is that true?"

"Yes."

Hijohn turned to Madrone. "Maybe you'll check her out? Just to be sure?"

Madrone smiled. He looked such an unlikely nervous daddy, but why shouldn't he be? Why shouldn't he have a sweet side too?

"Of course. Don't worry, Katy, I'll take good care of you. And if you need someone for the birth, that's my area of specialty. I love catching babies."

A glance passed between Katy and Hijohn, relief and something deeper than relief. They're both young, Madrone realized. No older than I am, and even though I feel ancient that's not really very old. They carry so much. Who do either of them have to lean on? No wonder Hijohn brought me here.

"This life must be hard for you," Katy said. "Not what you're used to."

"It's not an easy life for anyone," Madrone said.

"No." Katy's hand rested a moment on her round belly, a protective gesture that Madrone envied, suddenly, in a physical way. Would she ever be pregnant, feel life moving inside her, smell the milky odor of her own child? Or had she given that up, too, by coming down here? The sense of loss was a hollow, aching emptiness in the air in front of her. Then, as if she had conjured a child, one appeared in her lap and another two were hanging on Katy's arms and the room was filled with them. She looked down. The child in her lap was small, about five years old and blond, her hair corn-silk yellow, her skin like new kernels of white corn, translucent and smooth, her features delicately carved. Large blue eyes gazed into hers, wide-open and yet at the same time somehow shielded, as if they concealed invisible wounds.

"What's your name, honey?" she asked.

The child did not answer.

"She doesn't speak," Katy said. "She doesn't have a name, either. The Angels just brought her in yesterday. You can name her if you want."

"She should have a pretty name," Madrone said. "Something delicate but strong. Like a wildflower that looks fragile but spreads all over the place. Poppy, maybe."

"That's a cute name. Is that a flower?"

"It's a flower, like a little golden cup, that grows wild on the hills in spring. Used to be the official state flower, before the Stewards took over."

"I think I remember it," Katy said. "When I was little, my dad sometimes took us to the ocean, and there were flowers growing by the road. Yellow, and they tasted hot when you bit them."

"That's wild mustard. Poppies are more orangey-gold, and they grow low to the ground."

"It's a pretty name."

The room filled with people who crowded around the table and squatted in corners on the floor, and Katy was dishing up beans and tortillas, which they called corn crackers, and saying in a voice that was soft and clear yet somehow penetrated the din, "Tell us about where you come from, Madrone. We need to know. Is it true that water runs through the streets there?"

"It's true," Madrone said, and told her tale again, even though with each telling it sounded less likely, even to her. "There are streams everywhere, and gardens, and everybody has enough to eat and drink. Every child goes to school."

"Every child?" a young girl asked. "Even the poor ones?"

"There are no poor ones," Madrone said. "Oh, some people have a little more than others, but everyone has enough."

"Who does the work if there aren't any poor ones?" the girl asked.

"We all do. Everybody works, and works hard. But we enjoy it, because we're working for ourselves, not the Stewards and the Managers. We grow a lot of our own food, we use all our land carefully, and our water, and we share what we have so that everybody has enough."

"What kind of food do you grow?" a woman asked.

The question sparked a long discussion of organic gardening and aquaculture and the principles of permaculture.

"We don't just plant a garden, we create an ecosystem that can sustain itself as much as possible with a minimum of outside energy—including our own. Everything serves more than one function. For example, we used to keep a couple of geese, who ate weeds and insects and scared away stray cats. Their wastes fertilized the soil, and we ate their eggs and used their feathers in quilts and jackets. Or take the streams. We brought back the natural streambeds, brought the water up out of drainage pipes and let it flow free. Over time, we hope to restore the salmon runs. But the streams provide habitat for all kinds of insects and birds and small animals. We stock them with fish and freshwater crawdads, and we divert some of the water for irrigation. Kids like to play in them and swim in the ponds."

As she spoke, she noticed four tall figures standing aloof on the outskirts of the group. They had the same blond, ethereal, almost androgynous beauty as Poppy, and they appeared young, maybe fourteen or fifteen. She couldn't tell if they were girls or boys. They could have all been brothers and sisters, cousins, twins; not just their coloring and delicate form but something in their stance linked them to each other. An animal wariness. Like cats, they stood aloof from the crowd in the room, observing. They made Madrone nervous. They did not take part in the conversation but simply watched, their blue eyes glittering like carefully polished stones.

She continued talking as dinner was consumed, answering questions, explaining everything from trade agreements in the watershed to the preferred methods of mulch. The children listened in rapt fascination and the adults with skepticism.

"What I want to know," Hijohn said, "is how you got out from under the Stewards."

"They never took hold," Madrone said. "When they grabbed for power in '28, we didn't go along with them."

"That easy, eh?" one of the men said. "You just say, 'No, thank you,' and they say, 'Oh, fine, goodbye'?"

Everybody laughed.

"It wasn't easy," Madrone said. "I was just a child, but I remember how hungry we were that winter. People starved—because the Stewards controlled our supply lines for food and seeds and oil. And not everybody agreed with the Uprising. Quite a lot would have been happy to join the Stewards."

"Did you kill them?" Hijohn asked.

"No. That was one thing we'd learned from history. Any revolution that starts murdering its opposition becomes just as bad as the thing it fights against."

"What did you do?"

"We talked, we persuaded, or we encouraged them to leave. A lot fled purely out of their own fear. We gathered seeds and shared them and tore up the streets for gardens and we survived without bloodshed. Or without much. They shot a few of us during the changes."

"I would like it to happen that way here," Katy said. "Peacefully. Without violence."

"Well, it won't," Hijohn said. "Not here. It's too entrenched, and those who have power aren't willing to give any of it up. Not the smallest fragment. Not until we blow it up in their faces or burn it out from under them."

A silence fell over the room. Poppy pushed away her own plate but snatched food from Madrone's. Katy ladled her up a second helping of beans, for which Madrone was grateful. In spite of the abundance of water, food seemed to be in meager supply.

"And what happened here?" Madrone asked. "How did the Stewards take over so completely?"

"The Collapse of '27 began it," Katy said. "I don't know what it was like up north, but down here it was grim. I was just a kid, but I remember the quake, how frightened I was when the ground began shaking. It was the worst I've ever felt. The epicenter was only a few miles north of here."

"We felt some tremors all the way up in the City," Madrone said.

"But the quake wasn't the real problem," Hijohn said. "It destroyed a lot, water lines and gas pumps and roads, so it was hard to get food and water into the city. But a lot of the city was already in ruins from decades of riots and fires and bombings. And the Central Valley was almost dead from years of abuse and from climate change. Food was already scarce. What the whiteflies and the redflies hadn't ruined, the dust storms buried, and the land was salty from irrigation. Still, the worst problem was the fuckers who ran the Corporation. They'd been stockpiling grain and seed and medical supplies, waiting for their opportunity. The quake gave it to them."

"The Stewards were their political front," Katy said. "They declared martial law, and the Corporation backed them. People who supported the Stewards got fed and cared for; those who opposed them were considered traitors and left to starve."

"And people just gave in to them?" Madrone said. "They didn't try to fight back?"

"Plenty did," Hijohn said. "Some of us are fighting still."

"There were food riots and water riots and armed bands that attacked Corporation warehouses," Katy said. "In some ways, that made it worse. People got scared. And frankly, a lot of people were happy to see somebody take over and establish order, no matter what kind. We had refugees streaming in from the Central Valley, shootouts night after night in the streets, whole sections of the city burned down. The Stewards were well organized and efficient, and they seemed to stand for the kind of security people longed for."

"But we were holding our own," Hijohn said. "We weren't as well organized as the Stewards, I'll grant you that, but we were building a strong network among a lot of different groups, even some of the refugees."

"Until the epidemic," Katy said. "The refugees brought disease with them, people said."

"Not all the people," Hijohn countered. "A lot of us thought the Corporation cooked up some bug in its lab and let it loose to rid the region of undesirables."

"Well, the Millennialists said it was the wages of sin and immorality," Katy countered. "And more people believed them than believed our side. There were mass conversions, even though the Corporation developed a drug to treat the disease with suspicious speed. But of course the drugs and the vaccines and the immunoboosters weren't offered to the undesirables."

"The Millennialists cut a deal with the Stewards," Hijohn said. "They gave religious backing to the new order, and in return, once things had calmed down, the Stewards passed laws enforcing the Four Purities."

"There were the Moral Purity laws first, which outlawed all sorts of fornication, rape, incest, and child abuse. People went along with them—they didn't seem so bad. Until we found out that if you violated them, you officially lost your immortal soul, which made you fair game for rape and enforced prostitution, if you were a woman, and your children prey for all sorts of abuse."

"And the Corporation makes a profit from it all," Hijohn said.

"Then there were the Family Purity laws, which threw women out of most professions. The Spiritual Purity laws outlawed proselytizing for any religion that advocated or didn't strongly oppose the worship of Satan, which was defined roughly as anything the Millennialists didn't like, even other Christian denominations. Especially other Christians—they were close competition, and anyone who preached God's love and mercy and compassion was practically an agent of Old Nick himself. My father was minister of a big Methodist church, and he hung on, barely, for a while. But then came the Racial Purity laws. Everybody had to register as one race or another. That was when my father lost his congregation. My mother was Mexican, raised Catholic, but she'd converted. She died in the epidemic. My dad refused to register himself as white, or me as Latin. He preached a sermon against the whole program in his church, told the congregation not to register either. That night the Millennialists burned his church down."

Poppy shifted restlessly in Madrone's arms and wriggled down to the floor. She crawled under the table and emerged at Katy's feet. Around the room, people were stacking their plates, clearing the tables, and scraping leftovers into bowls.

"Almost time to put you to work." Hijohn smiled at Madrone. "And time for me to go." He nodded a goodbye and slipped out the door. Katy's eyes followed his back until it disappeared. Then she turned her attention to the child who had crawled into her lap.

"You want some more food, Poppy?" she asked.

One of the blonds at the door spoke.

"You gave her a name?"

"Yeah."

"It's not an Angel name. It don't come from the book."

"What book?" Madrone asked.

"They take their names from the list of Fallen Angels in the Book of Repudiation," Katy explained.

"She ought to have an Angel name."

"She's got a flower name," Katy said. "It's a beautiful name. You didn't keep her with the Angels; you brought her here. So leave her be, now."

"What kind of name is Madrone?" a small boy asked.

"I'm named for a tree," Madrone said, "a very beautiful tree that grows in the hills and canyons by the coast."

"Do trees grow where you come from?" a small boy asked Madrone.

"Lots of trees," Madrone said. "We go up to the mountains every year and plant thousands of them. We plant fruit trees along all the walkways in our city, so in the spring when they blossom it's beautiful with pink and white flowers, and in the summer, when they ripen, you can reach out your hand anywhere and taste something sweet. And no, we don't worry about people stealing the fruit, because it belongs to everybody, and there's so much of it that everyone has more than enough."

Her words fell into an aching silence.

"Will we have trees someday?" the same young boy asked.

"Yes," Katy said with certainty. "We will have trees everywhere, and so much fruit we'll have to bottle it for jam. That's sweet stuff you put on bread; we used to have it when I was a kid."

Really, Madrone thought, it wasn't good to remember fruit, sweet juicy plums and crisp apples and velvet, dripping apricots. And strawberries nestled among the green leaves at the foot of the rosebushes. Better to savor the beans and water. And she wondered, suddenly, about Katy, suffering the fierce hunger of pregnancy. What nourishment was that child receiving in the womb? Was there any way to get her some fruit and vegetables?

When the remains of dinner were completely cleared away, they all gathered in an inner room. Madrone faced a roomful of hopeful eyes, dark eyes, light eyes, in faces of every shade from porcelain to ebony. The weight of their expectations felt suddenly almost too heavy to bear. She was supposed to transform them all into healers? How?

At the back of the room, the blonds stood poised for flight, the lines of their bodies suggesting a detached cynicism. They refused to sit, but they listened.

Where to start? She had often trained healers, but they had started from the same assumptions and understandings of the world. She had no idea what these people believed. She was only barely beginning to understand the world they lived in. But they were waiting for her, and she would have to begin somewhere. At the beginning, Johanna would say. She took a deep breath and spoke.

"There are many ways to be a healer, but this is what we believe about it and what I was taught when I began. We say that there are Four Sacred Things, and the fifth is spirit. And when you live in right relation to the four, you gain the power to contact the fifth. The four are earth, air, fire, and water. They live in the four directions, north, east, south, and west. No one can own them or put a price on them. To live in right relation is to preserve them and protect them, never to waste them, always to share what we have of them and to return all we take from them to the cycles of regeneration. Together they form the magic circle, which is the circle of life. And the understanding of that circle is the beginning of all healing.

"So let's begin by putting that circle inside ourselves. We call it grounding, touching the four within us and around us. Close your eyes and feel your breath. That's the first sacred thing inside us, the breath, which opens the roads of the mind and the imagination. Let it come in and out of our lungs, bring it down deep. We can't live without it, but when it's there, there's always as much as we need. You know, you may not have enough to eat or drink. But they haven't figured out yet how to charge you for the air."

"Give them time," someone murmured, and everybody laughed.

"That's good," Madrone said. "Spirits like laughter. And they like you to breathe deep. Your breath is the beginning of power. And when it's strong in you, let it awaken the second sacred thing, your fire, your energy. You can feel it first by noticing how you *do* feel. Strong or weak, awake or tired? Imagine your energy like a force flowing through you, as if you were a tree and you had roots going down into the earth. Can everyone picture a tree?"

"No," several of them called out. Madrone stopped for a moment, shaken.

"Come on up to the hills, man," someone else called out, and again there was laughter.

"Imagine yourself as a rat," another voice called. "Sneaking around in the city streets, living off garbage."

"Imagine yourself as a buzzard, looking down on the hills looking for something to eat, and you see these little hulks of people and you pass right on by, because they're so dried up and bloodless you can't even smell them."

"Oh, shut up!" someone else called. "Let her go on. If you want to argue rats and hillboys, take it outside."

"A plant, then," Madrone said quickly. "Any kind of plant—with roots that go down into the earth. And those roots are your energy, your life force, and they go down through the dirt and the dust and the soil, and down through the rock, and down through the third sacred thing, the water that is hidden under the earth, and let them flow down to the fire in the earth's heart. And the earth is the fourth sacred thing, and the fire that is her blood becomes the source of your energy. That's the power you draw on, and it's always there. You can use your breath to draw it up, and it flows through you, like water. . . ."

She went on, leading them through the visualization of the treelike energy flow in the body, teaching them to fill the branches and leaves of their auras with earth fire, to draw down the power of the stars and become whole.

Afterward, they talked about what each of them had felt. She set them to work in pairs, feeling each other's auras, and wandered among them to answer questions. This project she had undertaken seemed daunting now. There was so much for them to learn—for anyone to learn, really. About energies, and then all the simple, physical, practical things: first aid, the dressing of wounds, herbs. Maybe that would be a good way to end for tonight, a balance to the esoteric stuff. She would teach them artificial respiration and, tomorrow, how to stanch a flow of blood. Mix the spiritual and the practical, so that everybody would learn something, no matter what their talents or deficiencies. And the hillboys, at least, could learn the uses of white sage and black sage, mugwort and bay laurel and manzanita bark.

But the great powers, the spirit powers—how were they to be invoked here? She thought about her own vision quest, that journey up into the rugged mountains when she was sixteen, three days and three nights without food or water. Now it seemed the height of luxury to her, to be surrounded by the beauty of the high mountains, to refrain from drinking because water was all around you when you wanted it, springs of it, streams and pools and lakes and bogs. All the things she had taken for granted as the birthright of every person now seemed marks of incredible privilege. What vision quest could they do here, in these streets? Some of them could go to the hills, maybe, but the others, the rats who had never been five miles north to the green belts or ten miles west to the ocean, who had never seen a living tree or a meadow all green with grass or any wild growing things except a few stray cactus and creosote bushes, what about them? And those strange blonds with impenetrable auras, like ice?

She ended the session, finally, and then she had to fend off thanks for another half an hour, until she could crawl exhausted into her sleeping bag in the corner of the main room.

She grounded herself, shutting out the sounds of others bedding down for the night, and mentally cleansed herself, imagining clear warm water cascading over her body and washing away the frustrations and pain of the day. Let it go, this feeling of an impossible weight on her shoulders. Let it go, this disbelief in hope. Let it go, the impulse to yell at her own students, insult them, call them stupid only because the depth of their ignorance hurt her so much. Let go, let go, into sleep. Healing sleep.

She was on the edge of sleep when she felt a small body nestle against her. It was the child, Poppy, and Madrone pulled her close and let her nestle into the warmth of the bag. The child turned and began to fondle Madrone's breast with her tiny hand. Instantly Madrone jolted awake. Where was she? What was happening?

Poppy's hand slid down Madrone's belly with a practiced, unchildlike gesture. The girl's limbs trembled.

Gently, Madrone pulled the child's hand away from her own body. She felt sick. How do I handle this? she wondered. What do I say? This was not a thing a child would do on her own. Someone had done something terrible to this girl.

"No, honey, I don't want you to do that. That's a grown-up thing to do, not for children."

The girl wrenched her hand out of Madrone's grip and reached for her again, a little mewling sound of fear coming from her lips. Madrone took her hand again and smelled the child's fear, an acrid perfume pouring over her. She was engulfed in the girl's terror, like every fear she had ever felt amplified, fear of pain, fear of abandonment and hunger and death, a craving that could never be assuaged, and, in all of it, no center, nothing to hold on to. She wanted to hold the child but she felt blocked—would Poppy feel it only as yet another violation, a demand? *Diosa,* what had happened to her?

The girl began screaming out loud and pulled away from Madrone, to run through the crowded room and bang against the wall. Madrone looked on, stunned, but Katy was instantly alert and on her feet. She tossed the child into a blanket and wrapped her in it, tightly, like a swaddling cloth, so tight she couldn't move, and then she held her and rocked her, crooning softly, "It's all right. It's all right. You're safe here, baby. You're safe."

Poppy had woken the whole room, and Madrone heard the groans and rustlings and sighs as everyone shifted back toward sleep. She was too shaken to relax. Katy stood up and carried the child outside, to the courtyard, and Madrone rose and followed her.

Outside, the canopies diffused the light of a bright moon, so that the air seemed to glow silver. Katy sat on the bench, a shadowed madonna, and Madrone joined her. The child had stopped screaming, and as Katy rocked and soothed her, her breathing became even and finally took on the slow rhythms of sleep.

"She'll be okay," Katy said. "These ones get the nightmares."

"It wasn't that," Madrone said. "She—she started to—to feel me. Sexually. And when I stopped her, she panicked."

"Ah, well, of course she would, wouldn't she now?" Katy said.

"What do you mean?"

"Her life has taught her only one way to secure affection or care. To survive. You blocked that for her."

"Damn right. And I would again."

"Well, she'll learn, maybe, that there's other roads to love. And then again, maybe she won't. Maybe none of us has the time or the energy or the optimism left to teach her that. She's so very young, it seems like there should be some hope for her still. Some choice. But maybe she's already marked for the Angels."

"Who or what are the Angels?"

"You know—the blond ones who hover around the edge of things. Raphael, Ariel, Gabriel, and Uriel. Their gang is called the Avenging Angels. Sometimes the Angels of Death."

"They're separate from your group?"

"We're uneasy allies. They're killers," Katy said. "Make no mistake about it. Oh, I understand why. Still, they scare me. They're so cold. It's like no human warmth can touch them. Maybe it never has. Beautiful monsters, but they're on our side. It's dangerous to breed such hate. I can understand why they don't let many of them grow up. Aside from the turn-on of killing them, of course."

"What are you talking about?"

"The blonds. They were toys for rich men. Bred for it. Raised and trained from birth. For sex and pain."

"Children?"

"They say if you're into it, the younger the better."

"But what . . . why?"

"They're little and delicate and beautiful, and you can do anything you want to them. Anything. And when you use one up, well, there's another, just as little and cute and pretty coming up behind. I'm telling you, Madrone, they breed them. It's an industry. With catalogs and videos and accessories. Instruments of torture."

"I can't believe that."

"It's true. And in revenge, the Angels steal kids, bust up houses, burn them down. Kill people. They probably take quite a bit of pleasure in doing it, too. I don't like it, but I can't blame them. You see, they're ones who somehow got out. Grew up. God—or Goddess—only knows what happened to them. They don't tell. They just stare at you with those blue marble eyes."

Madrone sat silent for a moment, too shocked to speak. In Katy's arms, Poppy murmured and wriggled.

"I wasn't raised to believe in evil, Katy. But I can't think of another word for this," she said finally.

"There isn't any other word for it. Where you come from—they don't have sex shops and torture clubs?"

"No. Goddess, no! We have a fair amount of sex, privately. I certainly never lacked for it before I came down here. But it's not—marketed. And that's what I don't understand: how can the Millennialists let this go on? They're so anti-sex."

"The Millennialists are the backbone of the industry. All that repression has to find its outlet somewhere. And remember, it's not fornication if it's done with the soulless—conveniently defined as anyone who isn't a good enough Millennialist. Also, it helps if it turns a profit."

The moon peaked over the edge of the canopy. Madrone gazed up. Here as at home, *la luna* was round and white, marked by the same shadows, changing in the same waxing and waning rhythms. Madrone somehow found that hard to believe. How could the same moon shine on such different worlds?

"There's so much here I just don't know about," she said finally.

"You can ask me anything, Madrone. I want to help you all I can, because of what you're bringing to us."

"I don't even know what to ask, because it's so foreign to everything I expect. And I'm not really bringing that much, I'm afraid. Katy, I don't really know what I can do here. Can I really teach these people anything that's worth the effort and the danger of gathering here? Learning to be a healer takes years, and that's with advantages you can't even conceive of."

"You've already achieved more than you realize."

"What? If you've noticed anything, please tell me."

"First of all, you've got the hillboys and the rats and the Angels all working together on something. That's never happened before. Yeah, there's some tension, but nobody's pulling knives on each other. Generally, they're as territorial as the other gangs. In fact, they're not so different from the other gangs as they'd like to think. That's really how this all started, you know— street gangs and hill gangs and a few key people with enough vision to mold it into something more.

"And that's the other thing you've brought—the vision. Talk about the North, Madrone. Tell us about the streams and the fruit trees and how you organize your tree-planting brigades. Because we've got to know that things can be different, that they *are* different somewhere. That's the only thing that really sets us apart from the street gangs—the vision. Well, the gangs are probably better armed. But you're living, walking proof that this isn't the only way things can ever be. All you have to do is walk into a room, and we can see by the set of your head on your shoulders and the way you move in your body that you come from somewhere else."

"Is it that obvious?"

"You move like someone who's never questioned her right to have a body. To exist, to breathe, to take up space. I've been watching you all night. It's not arrogance, like the rich people. It's not the hard, elegant gesture, like the Angels. It's just—solid. Sure. As if you'd never learned to look down on anyone or bend to someone who looks down on you. Oh, I'm jealous. When I look at you, I feel so jealous I could cry, or hate you. But I don't. I would like, just once in my life, to be in a place where everybody stood and moved and walked like you."

"I don't want to make people feel bad. It's funny, I almost hate to talk about the North, even though I do, incessantly. It feels like bragging. Flaunting something people can't have."

"Brag about it. Flaunt it, tantalize us with it. Make us eat our hearts out. It's so much better to be envious than hopeless."

"And it makes me homesick," Madrone said.

"You've made a great sacrifice to come here. Most of us in this fight simply had nothing to lose, but you did. And don't think we don't appreciate it, even if some smart-mouths act like assholes."

"But I didn't do it to be appreciated. I don't want gratitude. I mean, that has nothing to do with why I came or what I'm doing here. It only gets in the way."

"Why did you come down here? If I lived in a place where water flowed through the streets, I wouldn't leave."

Madrone laughed. "Maybe I just didn't know what I was getting myself into. Maybe it's our family curse. The Goddess picks on us, lays these visions on us. Sends us off to do her dirty work. But what can you do? If you want to be true to your own power, you have to answer the call when it comes."

"Are you sorry?"

"At every meal—or non-meal. But seriously, no, I'm not. What's going on here is real. There's no place to escape from it. Even back home, the battle's on its way. So I don't mind being on the front lines. But what about you? You seem different from a lot of the others. How did you get into this?"

"My dad and I moved down here after the Millennialists burned his church. He used to say that the poor were the ones who really needed him, anyway. That was back in '32, when I was eleven, old enough to be a help to him. We started the gardens here, back before water got quite so hard to get. And he organized people. Actually, my dad stopped talking about God much after we came here. Mostly he talked about food and water. When I asked him about it, he'd just say that food and water were God to the poor."

"Amen," Madrone said.

"He died five years later, but I kept on. I couldn't see joining the boys in the hills, running around with two rusty guns and calling yourself a revolution. I thought we had to begin to build something, to show people how things could be different. So here I am. And you? What is it about you we don't know?"

"I'm tired," Madrone said. "I'm tired and cranky and inside myself I whine all day long. I want to go home. I want to take a long hot bath and pick ripe tomatoes from the garden and sleep in my own bed with sheets. But I won't go home now. I'm too angry and heartsick and stubborn to go home until we win something. Anything. And sometimes I wish I could kill and get pleasure out of it too. It seems such a simple solution."

"I know."

"Maybe Hijohn is right. Maybe it's better just to burn it all down, even if we all burn with it."

"That's the temptation," Katy said. "But is that how you won your revolution?"

"No. We did it the long, slow way. It took lifetimes to lay the groundwork for it. Some of the old ones spent their whole lives talking, organizing, trying one thing after another, never expecting to see real change. Some of them didn't. The Uprising seemed to happen in an instant, but it was half a century in the making."

"Well, there it is," Katy said.

They sat for a moment, watching the silvery moonlight play on the gauze above their heads. She's a remarkable woman, Madrone thought. In her presence I feel comforted.

"I'm glad I found you, Katy. I needed a friend here so bad. Just someone I can really talk to."

"Me too." Poppy was asleep, and Katy gently set her down. "Are you still hungry? I saved back a couple of corn crackers."

"I could kill or die for one, Katy, if you'd only call it what it is: a *tortilla*, not a corn cracker. *¡Diosa!* It makes my mouth pucker."

"Torteeya," Katy said. "I know that. My mother spoke Spanish, but I didn't learn much. And what I did know I had beat out of me when I was a kid, after the Millennialists got the Stewards to pass the Language Laws. It's still hard to get the words off my tongue."

"Well," Madrone said, "if you want to make *una revolución,* you're gonna have to remember how to roll your *r*'s."

They shared tortillas and the scrapings from the pot of beans. Katy took the child and went back inside to sleep, but Madrone no longer felt her fatigue. She sat outside, on the doorstep, where the canopies did not quite reach and she could look up to a narrow patch of open sky. Stars glittered up there, out of reach. She wanted someone to hold her and rock her and tell her that everything was going to be okay, but no one was there. Mama? Johanna? Why do you haunt Maya and never come to me?

And then suddenly she was there, just a presence, like a vapor on the wind, something warm and dark and comforting and, at the same time, challenging.

Johanna, we are not going to win here, Madrone found herself whispering. We're facing an enemy too ruthless. And if we can't defeat them here, how can we defeat them at home?

Silence.

Johanna, I'm going to die down here. I'll never lie in the mint in the Black Dragon garden or make love in the ritual room or bring Maya her morning tea and sit in the sun and talk again. I'll never have a baby. And what's worse, maybe, I'll never see these streets transformed into the fields and gardens they could be, never see the streams running free from the hills down across these plains. Johanna, are you with me? Did you ever feel this hopelessness? Do you feel it now?

More silence. The dark intensified, congealed into an almost solid presence that yet remained black and silent. What do the dead have to say to those who grab with both hands at precarious life? Hold on. Let go.

22

Maya had cooked Bird his favorite lunch, nachos and hot sauce and refried beans. He sat staring at them for a long time, while she hovered anxiously.

"You've got to eat," she said.

"I know I should eat. The tension's just getting to me, that's all. The waiting. I almost wish they'd come, just to get it over with." Dutifully, he scooped up a big wad of beans in a cheese-draped chip and raised it to his mouth.

They heard the door open below and a clattering of feet on the stairs. Rosa burst into the room.

"They're here!" she cried. "They're coming up the old freeway, over San Bruno Hill!"

Bird set the chip down, rose, and without a word walked out of the room. Maya heard him grab his jacket, heard the uneven cadence of his steps on the stairs. The door slammed.

He is terribly afraid, she told herself. That's why he didn't turn and say goodbye. Not because he doesn't love me.

She sat there alone, staring at his empty chair and the plate of food he had barely touched. That was what hurt her, somehow, that he hadn't had a chance to finish his food. Just a few short minutes ago, when she had been heating the beans and putting chips and cheese in the oven, he had been there, alive, free. She could have said anything she wanted to him. She could have touched his warm skin or stroked his hair.

I always tried to be so careful, she thought. I gave up caffeine when I was pregnant with his mother. I didn't touch a drop of alcohol. And Brigid, when she was carrying him—she wouldn't eat a thing they hadn't grown themselves. Oh, she had spent years picking up rubber bands and thumbtacks and things that could choke a baby. They had installed catches in all the bottom cupboards to keep children out, and still to this day it was awkward to open the doors.

But you can't keep them safe, she thought. Sooner or later they find a way to get themselves broken.

She turned and grabbed the handle of the cupboard and yanked it so hard that the safety catch snapped and broke. She banged it shut again and kicked it. Now I'm starting to cry, she thought. Well, good, that's okay. Goddamn it, I have something to cry about.

Hours later, when Sam came in, she was sitting on the floor, sobbing, with the plastic safety catches she had ripped off the cupboard doors strewn all around her.

o   o   o

Most of the old freeways had been torn down as earthquakes weakened them, or later, after the Uprising, when trucking was replaced by the solar trains. But one stretch remained, an old segment of Highway 101 coming up from the south, carrying electric or alcohol-fueled trucks and horse-drawn wagons from the peninsula farms. Now it spilled down an off ramp into Market Street, not far from the open plaza that fronted Old City Hall. Bird met Marie, Roberto, and Lan there. Together they waited. It was market day, and the plaza was crowded with stalls and bright awnings, bins of vegetables and grains and ripe fruit.

"We present quite a picture of abundance," Roberto remarked.

"Not for long," Lan said.

Even as they spoke, it became clear that word had gone out. Vendors began packing their wares with quiet efficiency. Slowly, a crowd was growing, subdued and silent. Marie reached for Bird's hand and drew him into a circle with Lan and Roberto. "Let's breathe together," she said. "And pray, to whatever gods you believe in."

They stood in silence for a moment. I still can't really believe this is happening, Bird thought. The following night was May Eve, Beltane. There would be no bonfires on the hill, no dawn dances the following morning to Sachiko's sweet music, no maypole. *Madre Tierra,* help us. Help me. Let me find the strength I will need.

Then they heard a loud rumble, followed by a boom that shook the ground. Marie clenched Bird's hand.

"The bridges," she whispered. "We've blown the bridges."

Another explosion followed, louder than the first. Tears hung in Lan's eyes and Bird blinked back his own. Even now all the boats left in the City were casting off, setting sail for the east or north side of the Bay. Even now they were being cut off, isolated.

"Let's go down by Market Street," Bird said, breaking the silence. "I want to see what's coming at us."

The four moved down to where the plaza joined the street and stood beside the fountain, an affair of tumbling concrete blocks dating back to the

1970s. There they had a clear view of the off ramp constructed to lead directly to the central market. The asphalt surface seemed to be alive, swarming with a movement that resolved itself into line after line of men in dull gray uniforms, marching in perfect step, like a many-legged machine, orderly, regular, disciplined.

Bird felt oddly calm, as if his fear had compressed into a diamond-hard stone somewhere far below the surface of his mind. The waiting was over. They were here. They were real.

The vanguard of the marching lines reached the curb near the fountain. Out of the ranked masses of men, one stepped forward. His eyes were invisible behind a mirrored visor, and his hands were taut on the stock of the laser rifle held clenched before him. The men, Bird noticed, were sorted by color like a box of crayons, the molasses and mahogany in one platoon, ocher and umber in another, beige and tan and shades of pink together.

"I am Commander Pershing Nelson, Acting Commander of the Fourth Army of the Stewardship," he barked. "Who is in charge here?"

Now it comes, Bird thought. The four of them stepped forward together.

"We are here to repossess this land in the name of the Corporate Stewardship, from which it was stolen," the Commander said. "If you cooperate, we are prepared to be lenient. Resist, and we can be merciless."

He waited. There was silence throughout the crowd. He looked at the four of them and finally fixed on Roberto, the oldest male.

"You. I'm waiting for an answer. We're offering you a chance to surrender without bloodshed. You're outnumbered and outarmed. All we ask in return is a little cooperation in bringing this city under proper management. Answer me!"

Roberto's face was calm and composed. He looked into the Commander's eyes and said mildly, "There is a place set for you at our table, if you will choose to join us."

"What?"

"There is a place set for you at our table, if you will choose to join us."

"What is that supposed to mean?"

Marie stepped forward. "I am Sister Marie Seraphim, of the Order of Our Blessed Lady of the Waters, and one of the freely elected representatives of this city. What we mean is that we will never cooperate with violence, neither by submitting to it nor by using it."

"You got to do one or the other, lady," the Commander said. "I suggest you submit and save us all a lot of trouble."

"We propose an alternative," Marie said, pitching her voice to carry to the ranked troops. "Your armies are swollen with the poor and the dispossessed from your own land. We are a small population now, decimated by famine and epidemics, in an area that once housed and fed hundreds of thousands more.

We can find room for those who wish to join us, to live the way we do, with respect for the Four Sacred Things, air, fire, water, and earth. We are not a wealthy people; everything we have depends on our mutual cooperation. But for those who wish to join us we can make a place."

"Joining you is not the issue in question," Nelson said. "We are here to impose the power and authority of the Stewardship."

"We do not recognize that authority," Marie said.

"I'm not offering you a choice in the matter."

"Nevertheless we have made our choice, which is to make this offering to each one of you. There is a place set for you at our table, if you will choose to join us." Her voice rang out over the assembled troops, and she arched her neck to meet the eyes of the darker soldiers far down in the ranks.

"I'm not accustomed to arguing with women," Nelson said to Roberto.

Marie smiled pleasantly. "Then you have some new experiences in store."

Nelson ignored her, speaking directly to Roberto again. "Get this. We're moving in here, and we're taking over. This is not a game. Now, I need your cooperation in billeting my men. As I said, if you show the right spirit, this can go pretty easy on you. If not, I'll put my men where I decide to put them, and you may be sorry about that."

"There is a place set for you at our table," Roberto said.

"The next person who says that's gonna be sorry they did."

Lan, Roberto, Bird, Marie, and all the massed crowd chorused together, "There is a place set for you at our table, if you will choose to join us."

The Commander slapped Roberto across the face with his hand.

"Say it again, boy. Go ahead, just say it again."

That wasn't smart, Bird thought. We've only provoked him into losing control. And if he hooks Roberto into this duel, we'll have a murder here. Now comes my turn.

He stepped forward.

"We don't accept your authority," Bird said. "We will do nothing to aid you in any way. We will not cooperate, we will resist you in every way short of violence. But we will never stop offering you the choice to join with what is here instead of attempting to conquer and control it."

Nelson's face twisted contemptuously. "I am really not accustomed to taking advice from niggers."

Bird had not heard that term since his escape from the Southlands prison. It struck him as strangely archaic, a weapon out of some bizarre past, as if the officer had suddenly rushed at him with a bronze spear or a stone ax. A ripple of disturbance went through the troops. It was hardly audible, just a low murmur in the darker divisions, like the growl of a dog disturbed from sleep.

There is tension here, Bird thought, a crack, something we can exploit. The hold on this army is tenuous. I must remember this.

Marie opened her mouth to speak, but Bird motioned her back. He needed to handle this himself.

"We are not accustomed to hear that word used in this city," Bird said, pitching his singer's voice so that it carried far back through the ranks of men. "There are no barriers of color here. I say this to you, brothers, black and Latin and Chino and white too, that we set an equal place at our table for all who choose to join us."

Nelson swung his rifle and smashed Bird in the side of the head. The impact hit him with a shock that chased away pain. He stood still, unflinching.

Well, it's better than being dead, he thought. Blood trickled down his cheeks and wet the collar of his shirt.

"You do not understand," Marie said to the Commander. She was angry, Bird knew, because of the bright red spots that appeared on her cheeks, but her voice was still low and calm. "You do not understand the power that we have in this city. It is a power you can never destroy or conquer, that will not bend to your will."

The officer turned his back to her. "Prepare to make camp!" he barked at his men. "Johnson, cordon off the area. Bring up the tents." He turned back and addressed the crowd. "I want everybody out of here before I count ten!"

Lan sat down.

I'm ready to go, Bird thought. His head was starting to hurt. I could give a little, here, but he sat down too. Roberto, Marie, and the crowd followed.

Nelson turned to his second-in-command. "Clear this area, Jones. I don't care how you do it—drag them away, run trucks over them, shoot them, but get it clear!" He stomped off, going down the lines, his chest thrust forward and his ribbons bobbing.

"You heard the Commander," Jones barked, trying to look sure of himself. Nobody moved. "Men, get rid of them!"

The men remained standing.

"Well, what the holy hell are you waiting for?"

"Sir," one of the men asked quietly, "what exactly do you want us to do?"

"Drag them off. That's an order! And don't be too gentle about it!"

The soldiers moved forward, looking scared. If we had guns, Bird thought, concealed under our clothing or in our boots, this would be a highly effective trap. But we don't. The crowd began chanting, "Hold our ground! Hold our ground!" His head hurt badly, now, with a throbbing that changed to a flare of pain as two officers grabbed his ankles and pulled him along the ground. He tried to become as limp and heavy as possible, but his neck tensed in spite of himself to keep his head from banging on the pavement. His shirt rode up his back and his bare skin scraped against the pavement. Around him he could hear blows being struck and occasional screams of panic as the chant got ragged.

Sing, he thought, we should be singing. As loudly as he could, he began to sing.

"We are the power in everyone, we are the dance of the moon and sun. . . ."

Around him, voices took up the chant, and it flowed over the crowd and the soldiers both, until they were all of them linked in the same harmonies, the same rhythm, coming not through the ears but direct through the body, or something deeper than the body, sustaining them with the beat.

"We are the hope that will not hide, we are the turning of the tide. . . ."

o o o

The streets filled with soldiers that night. They seemed to be everywhere, marching up and down beside the streams, tramping through the open gardens, kicking at turf in the park, pulling ripe fruit off the boughs. Bird maneuvered his way around them, ducking into the doorways of friends, hiding in the shadows of trees. Sam had bandaged his head; Maya had cooed and fussed and nursed him and tried to make him stay inside, but he had to talk to Lan and Marie and Roberto.

A wooden footbridge crossed the stream that ran south from the hill. He decided to avoid it, heading instead for the stepping stones, where he had always preferred to cross as a boy. They'd played endless games there, pretending the river was full of piranhas, crocodiles, dangers, as they tottered from stone to stone. Now the dangers were real and he took the stones at a run. His bad leg still bothered him a bit, but it was better than it had been; he could compensate for his awkward gait at only a moderate cost to his balance, and some pain. But he slipped on the last stone, twisted awkwardly in the air, and crashed heavily onto the opposite bank, nearly coming down on a still figure who crouched in the shadows.

"*Discúlpame,*" Bird said. "Forgive me."

The figure did not move. Bird caught his breath and looked at the man. A soldier knelt by the river, his hands in the water, tears on his face. Something about him reminded Bird of Littlejohn, the same slight, undernourished build, the stringy hair.

"You okay?" Bird asked. The man had a laser rifle at his feet, but somehow Bird didn't feel afraid.

"Where does it come from, all this water?" the man asked. There was a dreamy tone to his voice, as if he'd been smoking lows.

"From the hill, from the rains, from the reservoir above, from runoff from watering the gardens," Bird said.

"But the water just runs through the street here. Anyone can steal it."

"It's free," Bird said. "Nobody has to steal water here. Nobody has to pay for it. Nobody profits from it. Water is sacred to us."

"My brother got shot for stealing water. I got put in the army."

"Take what you need here," Bird said. "Bathe in it, swim in it, it's clean. You can even drink it, although generally we filter it first."

"But we're here to take your water away from you."

I've been going along with Maya and Lily. I've put my life on the line for their vision, Bird thought, but this is the first moment I feel an actual glimmer of hope that we might win. He squatted beside the soldier and pitched his voice low, almost crooning as he spoke.

"You can't take away what's freely given. We'll never stand by and see our waters harmed or wasted or polluted. But what you need, you're welcome to."

"I don't understand."

"There is a place set for you at our table. We invite you to join us. You don't have to stay in the army."

"You mean I could join your side, fight with you?"

"Fight in our way, yes."

"But what about the boosters?"

"Immunoboosters?"

"Once you're on them, they say you'll die if you don't get them."

"Not always," Bird said. "I've known deserters who lived. But it's a risk. We have healers, though, and doctors. They can help you."

Just then they heard a loud cry from the cross street behind them.

"My unit," the soldier explained. "Got to go!"

"Think about it," Bird said. "The offer stands."

Grabbing his gun, the soldier ran off.

○   ○   ○

A strange calm settled over the city. Life resumed a veneer of normality. People worked in their gardens, cooked food and ate it, changed the diapers on the babies. But they stayed near their own homes. The markets were deserted, the cafés empty at night, the streets nearly unused except for companies of soldiers making their way through the labyrinthine net of walkways and pathways and vehicle corridors that twined through the city. They seemed lost, most of the time, stunned into silence by the abundance of hanging fruit and the colorful banks of flowers.

For three days Sam went to the hospital at his usual time, but on the third day he returned in midmorning. The soldiers had commandeered the hospital, turning the civilian patients out into the streets. The Healers' Council had anticipated this eventuality; each patient was assigned to a house or family, and Lou and Aviva made sure they all got there. Sam had returned to Black Dragon House to pace the kitchen, fuming.

"It's war, all right," he said. "I didn't think I'd react this way, but when that punk walked in and ordered me out of my own hospital, where I've worked since before he was regretfully conceived, I wanted to kill him. I wanted to shove a fist in his gut and rip his limbs off. How's your head, by the way, Bird?"

"Fine," he said, although it still ached. He was pouring himself a cup of herb tea, wondering how long they would continue to be allowed these simple comforts.

"You always say you're fine, even when you're half dead," Maya complained.

"My head is okay," Bird said. "In an odd way, I almost feel better, now that something's happened. We're not waiting anymore. Of course I'm worried, like everybody else. What can we do about the boosters, Sam? Half this army would come over to us tomorrow if they weren't afraid of withdrawal. We'd still have the other half to deal with, but the odds would be a bit more even."

"I had hoped Madrone would be back by now," Sam said. "Although maybe she's better off where she is. But without knowing exactly what they're using, it's tough."

"Maybe we can find out," Bird said thoughtfully. "Raid them, or catch a soldier and drain his blood."

"Is that nonviolent?" Sam asked.

"We'll drain it gently."

Sam grabbed his jacket up from the couch where he'd flung it.

"Where are you going, old man?" Maya asked.

"Out to check on my patients."

"You be careful."

"I'm extremely careful. I have every intention of living to see our victory."

"We might have one," Bird said. "We might not."

"We need more than just a victory," Maya said. "We need to win in such a way that everything changes, that we're not threatened again. Because I don't want to go through this one more time, or have others go through it after us."

"I'll see what I can arrange," Sam said. The door closed behind him.

"Will you be okay alone?" Bird asked Maya.

"Where are *you* going?"

"Another meeting." He leaned over and kissed her. "I know all the thousand things you want to say to me. You don't have to say any of them. I will be careful."

Maya reached up and touched his cheek. She'd bloodied her nails ripping the catches off the cabinet doors, and the dried blood matched what seeped through his bandages.

"But I want to go with you," she said. "Inside this withered husk lives a nineteen-year-old street-fighting woman who doesn't understand why she should stay behind."

Bird laughed. "To keep her out of trouble, that's why. And preserve your reputation. How would it look after that great speech on nonviolence if you up and chucked a few rocks at the soldiers?"

He was teasing her, but instead of laughing her eyes filled with tears, and her lips trembled. She is old, Bird realized. If I die, she won't survive long. The knowledge settled onto his shoulders as one more weight.

"But I can't do anything!" she cried. Bird reached over and hugged her, thinking all the while, I can't stay to comfort her, I've got to go.

"Do some magic," he said. "That's what you're good at."

She nodded as he slipped out the door. Later, when she cast the ritual circle and lit a candle in the center, no spirits came to her. Wax sputtered and dripped. In the empty air, nothing spoke.

23

"This looks like the place," Madrone said. She was standing with Hijohn on one of the side streets that wound uphill beside the grounds of the great university that sprawled over the rising foothills at the edge of the mountains. The streets around were thronged with students and professors, servants on errands, and beggars with outstretched hands in stained and ragged clothes like those she and Hijohn wore. Madrone was observing a large pink house, one of the many comfortable old houses that lined the street.

"Third house from the corner," Hijohn agreed. "This is it."

A flight of steps went up to the main entrance, but he led them around the side to a back door and knocked quietly. The door opened, and a young woman in a blue headcloth ushered them into a large institutional kitchen, where an older woman in a voluminous apron was chopping vegetables. She looked up at them, assessed them carefully, and then resumed work.

"We're here to see Beth," Madrone said.

"I'll get her. Sit down."

Madrone and Hijohn took seats at a small table nestled under a high window. The woman in the headcloth brought them each a glass of water, and Madrone thanked her. After their hot, dusty trek from Katy's enclave through the scorched streets of early May, the water was welcome as love.

"What is this house?" Hijohn asked. "Who lives here?"

"Nursing students," the woman answered. "Miss Beth is their house-mother." She turned away, back to her vegetables, and they sat in silence. Madrone was grateful for a moment of rest. Walking through the city always wore her out, much more than a trek through the hills. I should be used to it by now, she thought, but even with her bee senses tightly shut down, the air itself was an assault, carrying the odors of filth and the stench of hunger into her unwilling nostrils.

She wondered what Beth wanted. The message had come through the network, passed on by one of their contacts at the hospital. Beth was the gray-haired woman at Sara's luncheon, the woman who herself had once been a doctor. What was it like for her, Madrone wondered, to have that work taken away? What would I do if it happened to me? Exactly what I'm doing now, I guess.

Hijohn had volunteered to be her guide. He was down from the mountains, on one of the missions he invented partly, Madrone suspected, to visit Katy. He came often, and for three or four days he and Katy would linger close together, gazing at each other's faces with yearning, tender eyes. Then they would fight about something, strategy or politics or where to put their meager resources, and Hijohn would go.

They had been on one of their downhill slides, and he was eager for escape. "I'll take you, and on the way back we can cruise by the hill camps, see how they're fixed." Madrone had agreed, although "cruise" meant a twenty-mile hike over rugged terrain in the waterless heat of late spring.

"You came!" Beth hurried into the room, shutting the door behind her, and embraced Madrone. "Thank you for coming! Let's go into the other room, where it's more private."

They followed her through a door and down a stairway that led to the basement, furnished with rugs and old couches. It was comfortable, unpretentious, like the living room of the house Madrone had shared when she was at school in Berkeley.

"Now," Beth said, "no one can interrupt us. Gloria and Marta will watch the door."

She looked at Hijohn, smiling inquisitively, as they settled into chairs.

"My friend Hijohn," Madrone said. "This is Beth, one of the women I told you about, that I met the day I took the swim."

"I wasn't sure the message would reach you," Beth said. "But I do a little doctoring, sometimes, for people who need help, and some of them have connections to the Web. It was good of you to come, with no explanation."

"I've wanted you two to meet," Madrone said. "All the groups working for change should have some contact with each other."

"I'm not sure the women you met are working for anything," Beth said. "Talking is more their line—and mine too, I'm afraid. Real change might terrify us."

"And it might not," Hijohn said. "Every revolution starts with talk. Sometimes talk breeds action."

Beth peered at him for a moment, as if she were considering how to think about him.

"Sometimes it does," she admitted. "Do you have the magic formula to make that happen?"

She was half teasing, but he answered her seriously. "There's no magic about it, just patience. You take it one step at a time. Start with something safe, but something you can do. Collecting clothes for the poor. Raising money"—he winked and grinned at her—"for us."

"We'd like that," Beth said. "A low-cost revolutionary thrill."

"It wouldn't have to be low-cost. We'll take as much as we can get. And put it to good use, where it's needed most."

"I'm sure you would." She shifted her attention to Madrone. "You're probably wondering what this is about."

Madrone waited expectantly. Beth was dressed in a simple blue shift covered with a white apron, her neat gray cap of hair brushed smooth. She looked softer than she had seemed at Sara's, more matronly, but submerged tension lurked beneath the surface of her eyes.

"I need to ask for your help."

"What's the problem?"

Beth hesitated. She looked around nervously, as if checking to be absolutely sure no one could overhear them. Her voice dropped so low that Madrone could hardly make out the last word.

"How do you feel about . . . abortion?"

Madrone shrugged. "I've done quite a few, although it isn't a very common procedure back home. We're all trained to monitor our cycles pretty closely, from the time we first begin to bleed. And we know how to block conception. But there are times when abortion is necessary. Although I always feel a little sad, especially nowadays when so many women who try can't seem to get pregnant." Was that what Beth wanted her to do? But it was a simple enough procedure; surely she could handle that herself.

Beth looked at her long and thoughtfully and then sighed, as if she'd made up her mind. "Come."

She shifted a pile of empty boxes on a back wall, revealing a low doorway. Leaving Hijohn in the main room, Madrone followed her into a tiny, almost airless room, lit by a single candle. On a mattress on the floor, a young woman lay, moaning and tossing, her face flushed and feverish, her long chestnut hair damp and tangled.

Madrone stooped down and touched the woman's distended belly. She opened her bee sense and smelled putrefaction, death.

"How do you feel?" she murmured to the woman. "I'm Madrone. I'm going to try to help you."

"Not so good," the woman whispered.

"What happened?"

The woman closed her eyes. She opened her lips to answer, then closed them again.

"Something went wrong," Beth said. "I didn't do it—I don't know who did. She came to us, hemorrhaging and feverish, three nights ago. Of course she couldn't go to the hospital. Perhaps you don't know how they treat abortants."

"I can guess," Madrone said grimly.

"If she survived with her womb intact, she'd go to be a breeder for the Angels. If she lost her womb, she'd be sent off as entertainment for the troops."

"Have you examined her?"

"Her womb seems to be intact."

"Gracias a la Diosa."

Beth drew in her breath, shocked, then let it out with a sigh.

Madrone smiled. "A few words of Spanish scare you more than blood?"

"Reflex. I'm sorry. Anyway, I think the abortion was incomplete. There's tissue still in there, causing the bleeding and the infection."

Madrone rocked back on her heels, considering.

"She'll probably expel it. Or we could go in and scrape her out, if we had the instruments and a sterile room."

"I have instruments. I saved mine. They've been boiled, and they're ready if we want them. But this is the only room we can work in safely. Upstairs it's too public; the women come in and out all day from their classes and their work shifts. Some of them would sympathize, but not all."

"This room worries me," Madrone said.

"It's impossible to get it really clean, let alone sterile," Beth agreed.

"I can work with her *ch'i,* lower her fever, but I can't cure her if there's an ongoing source of infection. She'll relapse as soon as I'm gone. What herbs do you have in the house? A good uterine stimulant might help. Do you have pennyroyal or golden seal?"

"Nothing," Beth admitted. "It's too dangerous."

"And I don't suppose we can get our hands on any antibacterials or antivirals or boosters?"

"Not unless you have some from the black market. All those things are so strictly regulated."

Madrone considered what she had in her bag. The drugs from the raid on the pharmacy were long gone, and while she had a standing order in with the hillboys for anti-infectins, they got used up as fast as they could be supplied. *Diosa,* if she ever got back home to her well-stocked shelves of drugs and herbs, black and blue cohosh, shepherd's purse, rue. . . . Well, she had some dried mugwort in her bag; maybe that would help.

"I've got something for tea. Do you have any parsley? That's common enough. And garlic—garlic might help her immune system."

"We can get those."

"Here." Madrone rummaged through her bag and gave Beth the packet of mugwort. "Make some tea from that, and another tea of fresh parsley steeped in boiling water, and then crush in a few cloves of garlic. Maybe add a little honey to sweeten it and give her some strength. And if you bring down a cloth and some cool water, I'll sponge her off, try to lower her fever a bit. Meanwhile, I'll see what I can do with her *ch'i.*"

"Her what?"

"Her vital energy."

"I'd like to watch."

"There won't be much to see."

Beth left the room, and Madrone settled into her healing trance, matching her breath to the woman's shallow respiration, opening her bee senses and her inner sight. With the back of her nail she lifted a bead of sweat from the woman's brow, brought it to her lips, and tasted it. Her bee mind learned what was fermenting in the woman's belly and brewing in her veins; her human mind had names for these things and slowly, slowly, she was bringing them together, matching tastes and smells and names and the play of colors and energies and forms, not yet shifting anything, just watching.

Beth returned. Madrone could smell the steeped herbs, the sweet honey. They filled the room with the scent of life. She murmured names to put against tastes and smells and the chemical tang on her awakened tongue. Suddenly she knew what she could do for the woman.

"Honey," she said to Beth. "Bring me honey."

When Beth returned with a bowl of honey and a spoon, Madrone took it in her hands, cradling it like a ritual vessel. Contractions, she thought, and visualized a womb rippling and opening and cleansing itself. She strengthened the image until she could feel it begin in her own body. Breathing deep, she concentrated. Time stopped; nothing existed but the image she created, which was also a feeling, a smell, a taste in the back of her throat. She held it until her own blood changed, until the image became a taste in her saliva, a tang in her own sweat that welled up from the scar in the center of her forehead. A drop of that sweat fell into the honey, a catalyst that altered its energy patterns. Madrone breathed *ch'i* into the golden liquid, feeding the change, waiting until it was complete, until the honey itself became the brew she needed.

She fed the woman a spoonful, placed her hand again on the swollen belly, and waited. Moaning, the woman closed her eyes. Madrone focused on the honey again, strengthening its power to contract the womb. A wave shuddered through the woman's belly and she began to gush blood, introducing an iron taste to the air. Madrone was ready with the right elixir to bring the womb clamping down and stanch the flow.

She called for more honey, honey with garlic steeping in it, and visualized blood cleansing itself, white cells surrounding the alien organisms, as she called up the taste of healing drugs. Once again she turned her own sweat into the homeopathic drop that changed and cured.

"Keep feeding her this," Madrone said. "A spoonful every hour. I think she'll be okay."

"What did you do?"

"I wish I could explain it to you. I'm not sure I even know myself. And I'm too tired, now."

"You've been sitting here for hours, no wonder. Come out, let her sleep, and eat something."

They emerged again, into the room where Hijohn was waiting.

"I'll bring you some food," Beth said.

"How'd it go?" Hijohn asked.

"Okay. I learned I could do something I didn't know I could do. A bee thing," Madrone said. "But I'm drained."

"Can you travel? We could cover a lot of ground before dawn."

"Do we have to?"

"Or stay the day here. Not too safe."

"If I can eat first. . . ."

Beth brought soup and potatoes and bread, and Madrone ate ravenously. Hijohn had had one dinner, but he did not decline a second.

"Must you go?" Beth said. "You could sleep the day here—you need some rest after that."

"Not safe," Hijohn said. "Not for us, not for you."

Beth looked distressed. "Isn't there anything else I can offer you?"

"A bath," Madrone said. "Just a quick one." They had plenty of water to drink at Katy's, and she kept herself clean with sponge baths, but full immersion was an undreamed-of luxury.

Beth hesitated. "That's a little awkward."

"That's okay," Madrone said politely, concealing her disappointment. "Don't worry about it." Had she ever really lived in a place where she had taken for granted her right to shower daily?

"We're not rich, like Sara and her friends," Beth explained. "The students here come from the rapidly vanishing middle class. Nursing is one of the few jobs still open to women, and the girls I take in expect to work rather than marry. Oftentimes their fathers won't support them, or they begrudge them every penny. So we try to keep costs down. That means we're very sparing with water."

"It's really okay," Madrone said again, sorry now that she'd asked. "You don't have to apologize."

"It's just that we keep a strict water log, and if I drew a bath for you I'd have to explain it. Baths are for special occasions, like birthdays or graduation. A shower, now . . . you could take a quick shower."

"I'd love that."

Beth looked questioningly at Hijohn, who shook his head.

"I washed in the sink. That's wet enough for me."

"I'll set the meter for you, and get you a towel," Beth said to Madrone. "It's late, so the women should be in their beds, but let me scout the hallway for you in case someone's coming back from a late shift."

"The noise of the shower won't wake them?"

"They're used to it. They all work night hours from time to time."

The bathroom was white and clean, with old-fashioned fixtures, including a toilet that flushed with water. It appeared, however, to be flushed as seldom as possible. Beth closed the lid and showed Madrone how to work the shower.

"You press this button here, and it holds back the water. So you can wet down, and then stop the water while you soap up, and then you should have enough time to rinse clean. The water shuts off after five minutes."

"I'm an expert at short showers," Madrone assured her. "My grandmother considered a long shower to be a sin akin to leaving food on your plate."

"Leave the stopper in, if you don't mind," Beth said. "We catch the waste water, use it to scrub the floors. But be careful, it makes for slippery footing."

"I'll be fine."

The water was hot, and Madrone let her fatigue wash away with the spray that played over her body as she counted sixty seconds. Then she turned off the water and soaped herself, scrubbing at the ingrained dirt on her elbows and knees, and rinsed. At home they showered carefully and conserved water voluntarily because it was sacred. Here they did the same, because it was expensive, and the meter cut you off if you transgressed. Perhaps it was just as well. If she'd had unlimited access to water, she might stay in the shower all the remaining night, ruining their chance to escape before dawn.

She dried and dressed, wishing she could wash her ragged shirt and threadbare pants. They had a tear in one knee. Maybe Beth would lend her thread and a needle and something to wear while she mended them.

She opened the door a crack and checked the hallway. All clear. Quickly, she ran back to the basement room. Beth and Hijohn were deep in conversation.

"It's the children," Beth said. "So many of them aren't on the Lists and can't get so much as a painkiller if they need it. I try to help as many as I can. Some of the students here work with me. Sometimes they can get pills, prescriptions left over when somebody dies, supplies that a clerk gets careless with. But the danger to them is great. If they were caught, they'd go to the pens."

"We can get you boosters, anti-infectins, anything you want if we know how to recognize it," Hijohn said. "No problem. We pull raids all the time."

"What would you want in return?" Beth asked.

"Some doctoring, from time to time. A place to hide out once in a while.

And you could let people know who's helping you. Carefully. We want them to thank the Web for their kid's life and support us."

"I think we have a deal," Beth said. She turned to Madrone and smiled. "You were right about wanting us to meet. We *can* help each other. Do you feel refreshed now?"

"Much better. If I could just have some sewing things, to mend these pants?"

"I'll get them for you."

She went up the stairs and returned with a needle and thread and a skirt for Madrone to wear while Beth herself repaired the rips. Madrone leaned back, closed her eyes. Soon, soon they should go; she shouldn't fall asleep. Better to wake, talk, ask questions.

"Beth, while you were still in practice, you must have used the boosters. What are they? How do they work?"

Beth sighed. "My specialty was gynecology. Some of our patients were on boosters, but twenty years ago, that wasn't yet the norm. Even then, the Corporation was very cagey about their precise chemical composition. Oh, we knew they worked by stimulating the immune system, possibly by encouraging the T-cells to reproduce more rapidly. They were a by-product of research on the immunodeficiency diseases, after all. And many of us suspected they might have adverse side effects or, at the very least, would produce dependency."

"They do," Madrone said.

"The Corporation was extremely reticent to divulge any of that information, except to its own doctors. Those of us who worked independently were left out in the cold."

"What was it like for you to lose your license?" Madrone asked.

"Like a nightmare. Oh, we saw the reports of the law on the vidscreens, my partner and I, but we really couldn't believe they could kick women out of medicine, that they could get away with it. I had a small practice with Mary, who was also my lover for fifteen years. Does that shock you?"

"Does what shock me?"

"That I had a woman lover."

"Should that shock me? It's quite normal back home. My grandmother had a woman lover for most of her life. And I've had a few myself."

Beth threw a glance at Hijohn, but his face remained neutral. "The Web has no position on homosexuality," he said.

"High time it got one, then," Beth said. "You can't tear this system down without destroying all forms of repression. But I was telling you about my license. We had a meeting of the Women's Gynecology Association, and we all decided unanimously to ignore the new Family Purity laws and continue to practice. We figured they couldn't prosecute us all. We were wrong.

"Things went along okay for about a month. And then one day, in the middle of clinic, there came a loud knocking on the door. I was examining a young woman and I told her to dress quickly. By the time we got out into the waiting room, it was filled with a dozen police and an equal number of wailing women. Mary and I didn't resist arrest; we let them handcuff us and march us out to their car and take us down to the station, where we expected to be booked and released. You see, we were still thinking like physicians, members of a powerful class, used to being treated with respect."

Beth's eyes were focused on her mending and her words followed the jerks of her needle as she pushed it roughly through the cloth.

"Instead, they stripped us naked and had us bend over so they could peer up the cracks in our asses. They dressed us in prison clothes and locked us up in separate cells, where we remained for a week. When our lawyer finally reached us, he advised us to sign a confession, take the Oath of Repudiation, recant. I took his advice. To this day I can't say if I'm sorry or glad. They staged a huge public ceremony, a thousand women professionals paraded before the vidcams to parrot their oath and display their humiliation. They lit a huge bonfire, downtown it was, just outside the entrance to the Central Mall, and we each walked up and placed our licenses and diplomas in the fire. So we survived. Mary refused, and I never saw her again. I try not to speculate on her end."

I don't want to hear any more stories, Madrone thought. I don't want to take on the burden of Mary's ghost, like my mother's ghost, like the spirits of how many women healers, burned Witches, priestesses defiled? Suddenly Madrone wanted desperately to get out of Beth's house, out of the dark basement room that in her mind reeked of women's blood and the faint sweet smell of tropical flowers.

They left two hours before dawn. The woman Madrone had healed, whose name she never learned, was resting quietly, her fever down, her pulse stronger.

"Just keep giving her that honey 'til it's all gone. And after, just regular garlic honey. She'll make it. I'll be back, if I can, but that's a big if."

"Come back when you can," Beth said. "If there's ever help I can give you, I will."

o o o

Already in May, night was the only sane time to travel in the sun-scorched hills. Their route lay across the freeway, and Hijohn hurried them along, making the most out of each dark minute until Madrone wanted to scream with weariness. He showed no sympathy for her.

"You been across that bridge. Want to try it in full daylight, get yourself shot?"

She couldn't argue with his logic, even though she wondered to herself whether falling off the bridge from fatigue would be much better. But they made it over. The narrow scaffolding had by now become so familiar it no longer scared her.

Hijohn led her down a side canyon and up again on the fire road to the crest of the hills, racing against the dawn. Just as the sun's first searchlight rays reached over the hill's rim, they slipped down a twisting, hidden trail that wound like a tunnel beneath overarching stands of dry brush. Madrone slid in the dust or scraped along on her bottom, but Hijohn moved surely, as if each foot had a separate contract with the earth to support his moving weight. Full light found them at the bottom of a canyon, concealed by trees from the houses that loomed above. The air was fragrant with sage, and the nearly dry streambed was occasionally puddled with mud. They rounded a bend where a stand of pale, mottled sycamores threw heavy branches up in an open-armed embrace of the sky.

Madrone stooped down to bury her hands in the cool mud. Where the water pooled, only an inch or so deep, a clump of giant cattails raised their proud stalks eight feet high. Their presence stunned her. What were they doing here, these giant plants of the wetlands, making do on so little, just memories and promises of water?

"Here," Hijohn said, indicating with a toss of his head the dense shade under an arching live oak, whose blue-green leathery leaves concealed the green buds of acorns to come. She followed him under to nestle in a clear patch he made among the leaves.

"Hungry?" he asked.

"Always," Madrone replied.

Hijohn smiled. "Try this." He indicated a wild grass, running its feathery fronds between his finger and thumbnail to produce a light sprinkling of minute seeds. Madrone imitated him and found that they crunched under her teeth in a tantalizing way.

"Good?" he asked.

"It's sort of like eating," Madrone admitted. "A few hours of this and I might collect a mouthful."

"You can get a lot of good protein this way," Hijohn said. "And we've got all day."

"*Que nunca tengas hambre.*"

"What does that mean?"

" 'May you never hunger.' It's what we say back home."

"Nice," Hijohn said. "It's a nice sentiment. May it come true some day."

"That's a nice sentiment too."

Madrone stretched out on the ground. It felt almost soft under her, embracing, welcoming. She could sleep now, and rest, and then, when she woke again, think about what she'd done and what it might mean.

"Madrone?"

"Yeah?"

"I've got to tell you something."

"What? What is it?"

"News. Beth told me; she said it came on the vidnets while you were doing your healing."

"Tell me, Hijohn."

"The army in the North—they say they've entered your city, taken over. They're declaring a great victory."

No, Madrone thought. It isn't true. It can't be true. They had known all along the invasion must come, and yet she still could not wholly believe it. The City must still remain, green and watered, her refuge, her safe home.

"Do you trust the vidnet reports? Do you think it's true?"

Hijohn shrugged. "Could be. Could be true, could be lies. But it's likely to be true. I'm sorry."

She buried her face in her arms for a moment. Her disbelief dissolved away, leaving her suddenly sick with worry. Maya, Lily, Bird—where are you? Why can't I reach you? How do I go on, weak with fear for you? And for me? But the spirit world was silent.

"I'm afraid," Madrone said softly, lifting her head. "I'm so afraid for them all. I want to go home."

He reached over and placed his hand on hers. It was warm and woke forgotten hungers. She was aware of his battered, stubborn body, breathing and sweating so near to hers, walking proof of life's implacable tenacity.

"You're fighting for them here," Hijohn said. "Helping us, working with us—it's the best thing you could do for them."

"But I can't see them, touch them, know what's happening to them. Oh, Goddess, what am I going to do?"

"There's nothing much you can do, except what you're doing already. So we'll just keep on."

"Aren't you ever afraid?" she asked.

"Of course. Often. It's normal to be scared. Nobody wants to die. I don't even want to get beat up one more time, if I have a choice about it."

"But you never act afraid. You never show it."

"What good would it do to act afraid?" he asked. "It wouldn't change anything."

"I'd feel like I had company. I'm afraid all the time."

"That's because you're smart. Nobody sane is brave."

"You are."

"No, I'm not. I just do things. Being afraid or not afraid—it's not impor tant. You just do things."

What she wanted to do, suddenly, was to let her healer's fingers trace his scars. *Diosa*, she thought, I need comfort. It's been too long since I've been touched and held and loved. I need somebody else's arms around me to stop me picturing Bird's face twisted in pain, Maya's body lying broken on the pavement. Oh, stop, stop it! Better to think about Hijohn, alive beside her. Was his hand on hers just for comfort, or was he asking, promising more?

"How do you do things?" she asked. "How do you survive what they do to you? And then keep on living in this world?"

He turned and looked at her. His eyes were a dark brown, and as they met hers she felt a rush of excitement through her body, ringing down through all her hollow places like the sound of bronze bells.

"There've been times I've wanted to die," he admitted. "From pain, or hopelessness, or fear. Fear of pain. But that passes. In the end, pain is not important. Living is."

"Living in a world full of murderers and torturers?"

Hijohn shrugged. "They're not so different from you and me. They just don't have the same vision to hold on to. Without a vision, human beings are nasty creatures."

He was not like Sandy or Bird or even Holybear, whose energies were always sparking and flying and playing around them in colors. His were contained, a cool frosted indigo like the clumps of tantalizing, inedible berries in the scrub. She couldn't read him, couldn't divine his intentions or desires.

He leaned over and brushed her lips with his. "That's why you are so important to us," he murmured. There was a suggestion of heat in the millimeter of air between their lips. What about Katy? Madrone wondered, imperceptibly pulling back from Hijohn. But how could she begrudge me this brief moment of comfort? Then they were pressed together, their bodies clinging, nursing, drinking each other as their lips fused. They broke apart to wriggle out of their clothes. Madrone slid her hands down his back, over his buttocks, over the traces of healed wounds and the hardened ridges of old scars, and then up to touch his small, proud cock. He moaned, as his fingers found the lips of her vulva, and then in one motion he guided himself into her. She was surprised, wet but not really ready yet, still expecting more touch, a longer ascension. But he was pumping furiously, and then moaning, and in a moment it was over. He groaned aloud, and she felt him gush and shrink.

Hijohn rolled off her and looked anxiously into her face.

"Okay for you?" he asked.

She lay on her back, stunned into silence. Didn't he know? Couldn't he feel? Was it possible to be both such a hero and so ignorant?

Evidently so. It was the gap again, the chasm that opened continuously before her feet each time she thought she was getting close to someone down here. Different worlds, different lives.

Who would have taught him how to please a woman, answered his questions, as Maya and Johanna and Rio had answered hers? When would he have had the luxury of the forest year she'd shared with Bird and the others, the time to experiment and taste and play? And while they had learned young to open up, he had survived by closing down.

"Wasn't too good for you, was it?" he asked.

She sighed. "Hijohn, there's some things I need to teach you."

"You like it better with women, maybe?"

"Not necessarily. It's the person I care about, not the form of their genitals. But it helps to have a little bit of—well, technique."

"Show me."

She instructed him slowly, gently. They had all day, and a little water, and the lesson kept her mind from imagining horrors she was helpless to prevent, wounds she was too far away to heal. She showed him the secret pleasure points of her body, and how to build the intensity from light and delicate touch to wild animal release. He learned eagerly, if a bit awkwardly. Bird's fingers had once had a musician's assured touch, Sandy's hands held the heat of a healer, Nita's moved with the delicate grace of a scientist. Hijohn was merely direct but willing. Still, the day passed rapidly.

"Would Katy like this?" he asked, when they lay, satiated at last, stewing in their mingled sweat.

"Try it with her and see."

"I don't know. She's bound to wonder why I've suddenly changed my style."

"Tell her it's my gift to her."

He pulled away suddenly and looked down at her in alarm. "You don't think I mean to tell her about this, do you?"

The gap was there again. Suddenly he was miles away, in some other world.

"You mean you wouldn't tell her?" Madrone asked. "You'd keep it a secret?"

"Why would I tell her? It would only hurt her."

"Would it really?"

"Sure it would."

"But why?"

"What do you mean, why?"

"Why should it hurt her that we took pleasure together, here where there's so much hardship and so little comfort to take?"

"It would, believe me."

"Then why did you do it if you knew it would hurt her?"

"Won't hurt her if she don't know about it."

"But how can you keep it from her? Won't she know when she looks at you, or me, or sees how the energy has changed between us? Won't she feel it?"

"We aren't all Witches like you, sweet. She won't know unless you tell her."

"But how can I lie to her and be her friend? We talk about you—women do talk about these things, you know. How can you lie to her and be her lover?"

"You mean you don't ever lie to your lovers?"

"What would be the point? They'd know I was lying."

"You'd just go home from here and say, 'Hey, Charlie, I got lonesome for you but I fucked Hijohn, and here's a few tricks he taught me'?"

"Yes."

"And he'd say, 'Next time you see him, tell him thanks'?"

"Yes, more or less."

"Now I know you're lying. You must get jealous."

"Of course we do. I've been jealous myself, like once when Bird was infatuated with this other woman and stopped paying attention to me. But it doesn't hurt me to think of him taking pleasure with other people now, when I'm not even there. I assume he is. Unless he's deathly ill, or locked up, or severely injured, I know he is."

"Well, that's the way I believe, myself. But Katy sees it differently. So you won't tell her, will you? Promise?"

"Hijohn, I can't promise that. I don't know what I'll do."

"You've got to promise."

"I've got to do what feels right to me at the time."

"Shit."

He turned away from her, staring up at the sky behind the cupped, prickly leaves.

"Then I'll have to tell her," he said. The energy between them was gone. They lay next to each other, but separated by a void as sullen as oak's blue shade.

"That might be a good idea."

"Oh, shit."

"Are you mad?"

"I never get mad. It's a waste of food."

"I'm sorry if it makes trouble between you and Katy. I wouldn't want to do that."

He patted her hand absently, his face closed, his touch heavy as wet clay.

"Let's get some sleep now, okay?" he said. "We've got a lot of ground to cover tonight."

He rolled over, his back to her, and dozed, but Madrone lay awake a long time, watching the blistering sun move across a white, empty sky.

24

An unaccustomed silence woke Maya in the middle of the night. At first she couldn't identify what was wrong, only that, as she emerged out of a disturbed dream, she felt disoriented, not sure where she was.

"Sam," she said, poking him gently. "Wake up, Sam. Something's wrong."

He woke instantly, a legacy of his years of training on emergency wards. "Are you okay? Where does it hurt?"

"Nothing hurts. But something's wrong—something doesn't feel right. Listen."

He listened. "I don't hear anything."

"That's right. The stream—it's silent." For twenty years she had slept lulled by that music, since they had first blocked the street and liberated the water from its underground pipeways back to its restored bed. The sound of water was her security, her healing. No one, they said in the City, could be wholly ill or sad near the sound of running water, and so they had created nets of streams and pools and little waterfalls that sang almost as sweetly as falling rain. And now the song was gone.

"Sam, what's happened? Where is the stream?"

"Soldiers must have dammed it," Sam said.

Maya threw off the covers. "Let's go see."

o o o

The walkways that ran in front of the house gleamed under the moonlight. The moon was waning, Crone's moon, time of ending and dissolving, Maya thought. The soldiers had imposed a curfew after dusk. For a week, people had obeyed. But tonight Maya and Sam were not the only ones out: others had apparently been woken by the stilling of the accustomed sound or by networks sounding the alarm. Door after door opened and people thronged the walkways, heading silently, grimly, up toward the slopes of the hill where the reservoir lay.

Maya walked slowly, leaning on Sam's arm. She was afraid. This was the confrontation; this was war at last. Bird, she thought, will he survive this? He had not been sleeping in his room. Often he stayed all night after a meeting with the Council to avoid the risk of running the curfew. But he would come for this battle, she was sure of it.

The crowd climbing the hill grew, a dark tide rising to the level shelf of land where a deep pool held the spring water that fed the streams. A group of soldiers was closing the floodgates with sandbags and cement. A much larger platoon stood guard, laser rifles trained on the crowd. Old Salvia Westin from the Water Council was addressing the guards, her silver-wire hair flashing under the moon as she tossed her head.

"You don't understand," she said. "I've worked fifteen years perfecting that stream. It's not just water, it's a living community of incredible complexity and beauty. Fish and insects and plants and birds depend on it. To dam it is to destroy it, to take its life! You are murderers. Murderers!" Her voice was rising in pitch and a young man stepped forward, put a hand on her arm, and whispered something in her ear. She shook free of his arm, but he spoke to her again, and reluctantly she moved away. The soldiers stood expressionless.

"There is still a place for you at our table, if you will choose to join us," the young man said.

"Yes," people chorused, "even now, there is a place for you."

But Maya could hear other mutterings, and even a few shouts and threats. Tension rippled through the line of soldiers.

"We will never let you take our water!" someone shouted, too far back for Maya to see.

"Try and stop us," one of the soldiers taunted, and there was a surge in the crowd that might have pushed them all forward onto the rifles of the soldiers when suddenly Maya heard the beat of a drum. The sound was soft, hardly audible to the ears but more of a pulse in the body, a heartbeat, at once insistent and utterly calm. Two women and one man walked up to the edge of the floodgates and sat down, their bodies just in the spot where the next load of cement was due to be dumped.

The commander of the guards walked over to them. He was a young man who strutted with his shoulders thrust back and his chest ballooned out.

"Move," he said. "Or we'll make you move."

They sat, impassive, silent.

"We've been easy on you people so far, but we're cracking down now. Game time is over."

"You will have to take our lives to take our water," one of the women said. The silence in the crowd was absolute.

"There is a place set for you at our table, if you will choose to join us," the man said.

The officer gestured to his men. "Carry on building. If they don't get out of the way, cement them in."

The men moved hesitantly forward with a hose attached to a mixing machine. The machine began to roar. The crowd surged forward, and suddenly twenty or thirty people were crowded around the floodgates, between the soldiers and their objective. Instead of sitting like the first three, they kept moving in a writhing mass. Plastocement spewed out of the hose, and they tromped through it, keeping it from setting.

"I give you ten seconds, and then we shoot," the officer yelled. "This is no game! Ten. Nine. Eight. . . ."

There was a sudden flare of lights and the screech of a phalanx of motorcycles coming to a halt behind him.

"Attention!" a voice thundered.

A large man dismounted from the sidecar of the lead cycle. Instantly the soldiers formed an honor guard on either side of him. He wore an elaborate uniform decorated with stripes and gold braid and medals hanging from colored ribbons. The gray of his clothing leached color from his bone-pale skin, but mottled red and blue veins tinted his cheeks and nose and forehead. His body was solid, robust, although he carried a paunch that protruded over his gunbelt, and his gray eyes gleamed like bullets.

"What goes on here, Jones?" he asked.

"General Alexander, sir, these people are obstructing the work. Request permission to execute, sir."

"Request permission? What the hell do you think we issue you rifles for? Is this how you carry out your command?"

"Sir—"

Behind Maya the crowd stirred and parted. Through the opening came Bird and Lan and Roberto, led by Marie. Bird looked grim, remote. His eyes never turned to greet Maya.

"General," Marie said, her musical voice pitched to carry, "as the elected representatives of this city, we are here to lodge a formal protest."

"Lodge your ass!" came a voice from the back of the crowd. Somebody hushed him, and the drumbeat intensified.

"Water runs free in this city," Marie went on, "and belongs to everybody. Indeed, water is one of the Four Sacred Things that nobody can own or desecrate. No one in this city goes thirsty. No one begs for water or has ever had to steal it." She was speaking, Maya realized, not to the General but to the lines of ordinary soldiers behind him. "We are pledged to see that this does not change. Because we preserve our waters, there is plenty for everyone, even for you. Living in our way, none of you need ever thirst again. And there is a place already set for you at our table, if you will choose to join us."

Bird stood behind Marie, to back her up. They had agreed that she would speak first. Everything seemed etched in glass, translucent, already fading. This is exactly like one of the role plays we set up in the training, he thought.

Maybe when it's over we'll all sit down and process together, ask the General how he feels? He almost wanted to laugh, but he bit his lips. Somewhere behind him was the drumbeat, and the sound steadied him.

General Alexander looked at the four of them. He seemed unsure as to which one of them he should address. Marie was white, but a woman; Roberto was the oldest and largest male, but brown. In the space of time his quandary bought, more people joined those massed by the floodgates.

Finally he seized on Roberto, looking him in the eye.

"Understand this," he said. "All water belongs to the Corporation by executive order. Water is a scarce and precious natural resource, made more scarce by the wasteful squanderings of the greedy and ignorant. For this reason, the Stewards have assumed control of all water resources, for their better preservation and distribution. Now either you order your followers to cease obstructing our lawful work here or, I'm warning you, there will be bloodshed. And you will be responsible."

Roberto's face was calm and composed. He looked into the General's eyes and said mildly, "You misunderstand. We cannot order anyone to do anything. We are the ears and voice of the people; we express their will. We cannot command them to do ours, even if we wanted to cooperate with you. But we of this city will never cooperate in the theft of our own waters. Water is sacred, one of the things we will risk our lives for. And still there is a place set for you at our table, if you will choose to join us."

The General drew his pistol and shot Roberto through the temple.

Roberto made no sound. His eyes opened wide; then blood burst from his nostrils, a dark stain in the dark night, as he fell. The crowd gasped.

General Alexander turned to Lan.

"Do you understand me now when I say we are not playing games here? I'm not asking you for cooperation, I'm telling you you don't have a choice. If you want to die for your right to waste water, we can provide the opportunity. Now, boy, what do you say?"

Now it comes, Bird thought, and oddly enough he wasn't afraid any longer. There was nothing more he had to do, except stand there and, when his turn came, say one phrase. Easy, and then it would be over quickly. No long-drawn-out waiting, no agony. He would die out here, in the moonlight, in this perfect clarity that settled over him. Suddenly it seemed he could see every face in the crowd, gleaming silver under the moon, could feel the green gardens still alive below them, and hear the singing of the wind in the spinners above and the drumbeat like the city's phantom heart. To die in this moment was not so bad. Maya was nearby; he wished he could meet her eyes and smile, but he was not that brave.

"There is a place set for you at our table, if you will choose to join us," Lan said, and died.

My turn now, Bird thought, as the General turned to him. He was barely aware of what the man was saying, as he thought, one by one, of the people he loved. *Adiosa,* Madrone. I wish I could have seen you one more time. Goodbye, Maya. I'm sorry I can't kiss you goodbye. *Adiosa,* Sage and Manzanita and you, too, Holybear.

Alexander was waiting. Bird opened his mouth to speak.

Suddenly there was a stir in the crowd. A flock of children, led by Rosa, dodged through the masses of stunned people. Before anyone could move, they had surrounded Bird and Marie and the two bodies on the ground. The officers stepped back in surprise, while Bird was barricaded by a ring of children five deep.

"There is a place for you at our table," Rosa said to the General, smiling her brightest and most engaging smile, "if you will choose to join us." She favored the whole line of men with a broad and friendly grin. Some of them were sweating visibly.

Bird felt sick with the sudden descent of terror. Damn those kids! Damn their emulation and their hero worship and those stupid trainings that made them think they were prepared for this. If something happened to Rosa . . .

The General looked amused.

"Okay, Jones, this is about your speed. Let's see you handle this."

Jones stepped forward. "You kids get out of here," he said. "I don't want to hurt no kids, but I will if I have to."

They remained, silent and smiling. How could they smile? Bird wondered. He couldn't, even if it would have saved their lives.

"I'm counting to three. One, two . . ."

A young boy Bird didn't know stepped up next to Rosa.

"Three."

Nobody moved. Jones looked at the kids, back to his men, back to the kids again.

"I warned you. I don't want to do this, but I will if you don't move. Now I'm giving you one more chance. One, two, three."

"There's a place set for you at our table, if you will choose to join us," the boy said.

The soldier slowly drew his gun, pointed it at Rosa.

"Move."

The line of children held firm.

He took a step forward, thrust the nose of the pistol under her chin, and said, again, "Move."

Bird felt cold. He could see the muscles tense in the man's arm, see his eye narrow, and his finger begin to squeeze. If I could only grab the gun, he thought, but if I make a move toward him, she'll be dead.

Then there was a loud noise and the officer crumpled, a dark bleeding hole through the back of his neck. Somewhere down the line, a soldier threw down his gun and began running wildly away from the open space around the reservoir. Others ran after him, while the crowd surged between the fleeing man and his pursuers. People were running and screaming, but the crowd around Bird was packed too tight to move. His body wanted to run but his mind said, No, wait. This was what he'd volunteered for. Then there were shots into the crowd, and more screams, and as the people scattered a soldier stuck a gun into Bird's back, grabbed his arm, and pinned it behind him.

"Got the little bitch!" someone yelled behind him. Bird twisted his head to catch a glimpse of a struggling Rosa being roughly searched and hand-cuffed. Then his own hands were cuffed together, and he and Sister Marie were led away.

◦ ◦ ◦

"What happened?" Maya prodded Sam. "Bird? Is Bird okay?" She had heard the shots, but the crowd around her blocked her view.

"I think we've got a deserter," Sam said. "Evidently one of the soldiers shot the guy who had the gun on Rosa."

The crowd shifted again. A line of soldiers marched by. Maya glimpsed Bird in their midst and Marie, walking. Rosa, kicking and screaming, was being carried by two big men.

"Go home," Sam said to Maya, pressing her hand tightly. "We can't do anything for them right now. I'm going to stay and see to the wounded."

Maya's body took her home, while her mind ranged the city like a dog, trying to follow Bird. But he was gone. Not dead, she thought, but nowhere she could reach him. It was Rio's voice she finally heard in her ear.

"Leave it," he said. "You can't help him through this. His ordeal will be that much worse if he feels you present."

"Can you help him?"

"Maybe. I'll be there, at any rate, for whatever good a ghost can do. But you leave him alone. Leave him his dignity."

◦ ◦ ◦

Sam brought the deserter home with him. The oldest Cooper boy found him crouched behind their compost bin, shaking in fear and shock. The Coopers had exchanged his uniform for a shirt and jeans and brought him to Sam, who had set up an impromptu emergency ward in a nearby house. Several people had been grazed by bullets, and one man had been shot in the shoulder, but Lan and Roberto were the only fatalities. Just before dawn, Sam brought the deserter back through the empty streets to Black Dragon House.

Maya had not slept. She'd brewed up the roasted grains that Sam claimed resembled coffee, and she served the two men, moving automatically, trying not to think about Bird, trying not to think about bodies falling and waiting for one of them to be his. The young man's hands were trembling, his dark eyes darted nervously about the kitchen, and his brown skin had an undertone of gray.

Maya shook herself free of her own worries and smiled at him reassuringly. "It'll be okay," she said. "You did a good thing. What's your name?"

"Larry, ma'am."

"You don't have to ma'am me. Just call me Maya. What can I fix you to eat? We don't have the widest variety, but I could fry up some potatoes, and I believe I can offer you an egg."

"Anything, anything would be fine, ma'am."

"We appreciate what you did."

"I had to do it. Couldn't stand by and watch him kill no little girl. I ain't from the pens like some of them. I come from a family. Had a mother, sisters."

"What are the pens?" Maya asked as she heated oil in a pan. She would minister to this young man, who had saved Bird's life, out of gratitude and as a little bargain with the fates. I'll be good to him, Goddess; you be good to Bird.

"Where they breed soldiers, ma'am."

"Breed them?"

"That's how they get so many. Half these guys come out of the pens."

"You mean, breed them like . . . cattle?" Sam asked, settling himself next to Larry with a cup of brew.

"They got no souls, like regular people, so it's no sin to breed them."

"Perhaps you'd better explain a little more."

"Say a woman loses her immortal soul—"

"How would she do that?" Sam asked.

"Could be anything. Stealing water. Violating the Purities."

"I'm afraid we're quite ignorant," Maya said. "You'll have to explain everything to us. What are the Purities?"

"You know, Moral Purity, Racial Purity, Family Purity, Spiritual Purity. Like say she goes to bed with some guy who isn't Authorized for her. Or someone overhears her questioning the Incarnation. If she's young and good-looking, they send her off to entertain the troops. If she's a bit older, she goes straight to the pens and they breed her for soldiers."

"I can't believe that. How do they justify it?" Maya said.

"It's your choice, ma'am, to preserve your immortal soul or throw it away. Unless, of course, you come out of the pens and don't got one to begin with. But if you destroy your immortal soul with wickedness, then all that's left of value in you is your body, and your only redemption is to let the state use your body as it sees fit, for the greater good."

"Do you believe that?" Sam asked.

Larry shrugged. "I threw my soul away stealing water for my family. The soul may be immortal, but the body ain't. It's got to drink. That's how I landed in the army. You get caught in peacetime, they throw you in jail or put you on one of the work levees. Get caught in wartime, you join the army. I don't know if I got an immortal soul or not—I guess if you're poor, your soul is pretty thin to begin with."

"I believe you have a soul," Maya said, stirring the eggs with a wooden spoon and lifting them off the burner as they congealed. "You've proved that tonight."

"I got something in me that won't stand to see a little girl killed," Larry said. "Don't know if that's a soul. Don't know if there's a Purity that speaks to that. Don't much care, to tell the truth." He flashed a shy grin. Then his face clouded.

"They say you don't got the boosters, true?"

"Immunoboosters? I'm afraid we don't," Sam said. "Not for the last twenty years. You've been taking them?"

"We all do. They're in our rations. They keep us alive, keep us in their power. Afraid to run off, come over to you people. They say we'll die without them. Is that true?"

"I hope not," Sam said. "I'm a doctor, and I will certainly do everything within my power to see that you don't. But we don't have much experience with them here in this city. I've read all the literature we have, but it's all more than twenty years old. The current generation of drugs could work quite differently. I'll want to take a look at your blood chemistry, run some tests. I suspect you'll be sick for a while, maybe severely. But I have hopes that you can weather the transition period and survive."

"They'll search your houses."

"We have a place to hide you," Maya said. "When we remodeled the house, years ago, we threw in a few hidey-holes, up under the eaves. Not luxurious, but adequate. When you're ready to sleep, I'll take you up there."

The eggs were done, and Maya set the food in front of the men. Larry ate heartily and fast, like a wary dog, glancing up at them from time to time as if he were afraid they might suddenly turn on him and snatch the food away.

"This is sure good," he said. "Real good. This is real food, don't get it often in the army. We eat the powdered stuff."

"Enjoy," Maya said. "And relax. Take your time. You can have more when that's done."

"Why are you white folks taking all this trouble with me?"

Maya and Sam exchanged glances. We *are* both white, she thought, and I never really thought about it, which is shocking, really. All those years with Johanna, race didn't exactly divide us but was always present, somehow, an awareness we could never lose because it was necessary for survival. But for twenty years, now, it hasn't been. Until the Stewards came.

"In this city," Maya said, "we don't judge a person by their race or color or who your ancestors were. That's not important to us. It's interesting to know, and to learn the history of your roots, but it doesn't determine what you can be or how well you're treated. Besides, you saved the lives of some people whom we love very much. You risked your life for theirs. That makes you one of us."

Larry looked up at her thoughtfully. She could see he was trying to understand her words, but she wasn't sure if they really made sense to him.

"The day we marched in here, we saw you had all different colors that spoke for you," he said finally. "We talked about it back at base. Where we come from, you don't see that. It's a violation of the Purities."

"We have no purities here," Maya said. "Only the Four Sacred Things, air, fire, water, and earth. And the fifth, the spirit, which is at least sometimes human and cannot be lost."

They installed him in the low space behind the cabinets in the big room upstairs. Maya gave him blankets, water from their reserves in the cistern, and a jar to piss in. Downstairs, Sam carefully cleared away all traces of their meal, washing the dishes, drying them, and putting them away.

"He's tucked in," Maya said. "Put the kettle on, will you? I need some tea."

"You should try to get some sleep."

"In a bit. Is there anything else we need to get rid of?"

"I think we're okay. Let them search if they want to."

Maya sat down on the sofa. "I'm still in shock, I think. Did we win or lose? Roberto and Lan and Goddess knows how many others are dead. . . ."

"Bird is alive."

"Maybe that's worse for him. We are in open war now. Our lines broke, we ran from their guns. . . ."

"One of them broke too, and so Rosa is alive, and they know that they cannot necessarily control their own men."

"Oh, Sam, I feel responsible, with that dream of mine. I can't help it. If we were facing an army of Larrys I have no doubt we would win in the end. But troops of bred killers? How are we going to reach them? I wish that vision had come to someone else. I wish I were dead instead of the others."

"You don't really." Sam sat down next to her, put his arm around her, and kissed the top of her head. "This is hard, Maya, very hard, but there is some sweetness left at the end of life for us. Don't despair. If we believe in what we say we do, in the essential humanity of every person, then we have to believe that even the born-and-bred psychopaths are somehow reachable."

"I'm not despairing, I'm just worried sick."

She tipped her face toward his, and he kissed her. They sat together, waiting in silence for a knock on the door.

o   o   o

When the soldiers came, they searched everywhere. It's a form of violation, Maya thought, watching them poke through Madrone's underwear drawer. A rape of one's possessions. They left papers strewn and scattered over the floor, food spilled from jars, books knocked off shelves, furniture overturned. They searched the cupboards that fronted Larry's hiding space, pulled boxes out and opened them, ripped doors off their hinges. Maya held her breath, willing them to move on, praying they wouldn't push too hard at the panels in back, or slide them forward. Not a sound came from behind the wall.

The soldiers left, finally, and she breathed a sigh of relief. It was okay. They had not found Larry. If only Bird were home, safe, under the wing of her care. How was she going to sleep tonight, and the next night, and the night after that? What were they doing to him?

"You're a Witch," Johanna murmured in her ear. "Don't revert to that Jewish culture thing, trying to ward off the worst by torturing yourself with worry. Think like a Witch now. Surround him with protection, with your love."

Maya tried. She lay in bed, sleepless, visualizing Bird's face with light around him. But the light wavered and flickered. Her love and protection no longer seemed very powerful.

o   o   o

The dry streambed gaped like a yellow scar on the city's green face. Silver trout gasped, flopped, and died, to be gathered by children. A few were rescued, flung into deep pools that had not yet evaporated. The corpses of the others were distributed among the people, consumed for that night's dinner. Maya and Sam fed trout to their deserter. At midnight they were awakened by a deep rumble and the blast of an explosion. Shortly afterward, the stream began to flow again.

"Those hotheads on the Water Council," Sam said. "I bet they've blown up the dam. I knew they'd be up to something."

"What do you think will happen?" Maya whispered, her throat dry with fear for Bird.

The next morning, soldiers shot five people taken at random from the streets in the Central Plaza. The army rebuilt the dam and began work to enclose the other streams in the city. Two nights later, another explosion rocked the silence, and again the water flowed. That morning, ten people were shot.

"How long can this go on?" Maya asked.

"Till they give up, or we do," Sam said.

"Water Council doesn't have consensus from the full Council to keep blowing the dams."

"No, but they won't get much opposition, either."

"What about the dead?"

"The dead don't have a voice on the Council."

"That's an oversight," Maya said.

25

Bird closed his eyes. Mostly he preferred to see what was coming at him, to preserve at least that much control. But he could not bear to look in the eyes of his torturers, to see on their faces that serious, intent, and probing look. It was too much like the look on a lover's face or, he imagined, in his own eyes, making love to Madrone, when she gaped in ecstasy. Maybe we men need to do this, he thought, one way or another, in order to know we exist. We need to leave our mark on another body, to make it feel our power. He closed his eyes against the mingling of cruelty and sex he saw in the faces above him, so as not to be forever tainted. And yet he could feel himself being changed.

He had lost count of the days, of how many times they had gone to work on him, of how many hours he had suffered. Certainly weeks had passed since he was arrested—but how many? He had no idea. At first, he'd felt confident. I can get used to this, he thought, I can endure. The neural probes they used on him left no marks. They did no physical damage; they simply stimulated the pain neurons in the body directly. I could even come out of this with no more of me broken, maybe. A dangerous hope, a hope that could be used against him, and Bird tried to put it out of his mind. Hope would make him vulnerable, manipulable. Like fear. Better to resign himself to death.

But death was far away. That was the catch. As hours lengthened into what seemed like days or eternities, Bird began to understand. If they'd simply been beating him, he would have gone into shock by now, maybe bled to death from internal wounds, at least gone numb. Instead, his body seemed capable of perpetual fresh responses to pain, and he was awed at the intensity and variety of pain the body could produce. What they could do to a finger, or the sensitive skin inside his arm. An eyelid, a toe, a nipple, the ridge of skin that rimmed his cock. This is what being raped is like, he thought. He was exposed, violated, and he couldn't seem to lift himself out of his body, to escape, even for a moment, from wide-open consciousness of the pain. When he began to weaken, from thirst and hunger, they jammed a tube down his throat and poured in gruel. When he threw it back up, trying but failing to inhale the vomit and choke and die, they stuck a tube in his arm and fed him intravenously.

They are taking good care of me, he realized, and that thought made him afraid in a new way. Why? What do they want to use me for? He could feel himself approaching the limits of his ability to resist. He could hold out a long time, but even he could not hold out forever. Let me die, let me die, let me die, he prayed. They called the Reaper the Implacable One, but that was wrong. She was mercy, grace, the release that would not come to him. No, what was implacable was life, his life, that kept his lungs breathing and his heart pumping against his will. His body betrayed him, responding with such a full orchestra of agonies to what? To nothing, a beam of photons, the tickling of a laser a few atoms wide. He would never trust it again.

The moment came when he could not tolerate one more descent and emergence into the extremities of pain. Something shifted in him, some ground of himself that he thought was solid dissolved and melted away. I am going to break, he realized. Behind his closed eyes he saw a face, like an old woman with serpent skin. *La Serpiente, La Segadora,* the Reaper. Mama, this is as far as I can go. In one more breath, I will give way, and open my mouth, and be gone.

"Talk to us. Answer our questions."

He couldn't stand it. Whatever will of his own was left was contradicted by every impulse of his body. He was going to talk, to make some sound, say something, anything to stave off pain. And once he began, how would he be able to stop, to force his lips to say certain words, not others? He couldn't seem to die, and even if he did they would only drag someone new into this dilemma. Anything he did to escape the pain would only visit it on someone else. No, they had to break somebody. Let it be him, he was already half ruined. Or was he just making excuses? Maya, *abuela,* Lily, Madrone, I'm sorry.

He talked. Once he began, he told them whatever they wanted to know. What was the point of suffering over one question or another, when he knew he would tell them all in the end? Only to buy a little more time—for what? For nothing. He told them that the real Defense Council was nine old women hidden somewhere. He did not know where, and all the pain they applied could not make him know, for which he was glad because if he had known he would surely have told them. He explained to them the city's strategy of noncooperation. He told them how the city was organized, how work was divided and credits were assigned, how the power grids were operated, how fish were bred in the aquaculture tanks. Anything, everything. What he knew about healing. How the city had thrown off the last epidemic. Name names, he was told. He named Madrone—after all, she was gone and they would never find her.

The questions went on and on, and the exhaustion, after how long without sleeping? He no longer knew or cared. What mattered was pleasing them, getting them to believe him. Sometimes they did; sometimes, even when he told the truth, they did not.

"You have destroyed your data bases."

"No, we haven't done that."

"You lie. Nothing will function for us. None of the hardware responds to our commands."

"No, no, they won't function under stress. They don't work that way."

"What do you mean?"

"Look, I'm not a tecchie, I can't really explain this very well. Maybe if I had some water. . . ." Earlier, when he still had his soul, he had refused food and water, but now he begged like a child for it.

"Just answer the questions."

"A little water . . ."

They placed a cup in his hand. He couldn't see anything, or maybe his eyes were still closed, he wasn't sure anymore, and the water tasted like blood. It was cool on his tongue and it bought a respite; maybe that was a bad idea because it gave him something they could take away, something more for him to fear.

"The data bases?"

"They're all based on crystals," he said, barely audibly, "and the crystals have a consciousness of their own. They cooperate with us, as long as they want to. We don't command them."

"You cooperate with rocks?"

"That's how it works. The tecchies spend a long time in meditation before they try to work out a program. It's tough, believe me. I had to do it in school."

"You lie."

"It's the truth. I swear to you!"

He was beyond what he could endure, but he endured more, until they tired of the question.

"What is the secret weapon?"

"What weapon?"

"The secret weapon that gives you all such confidence."

"We don't have a secret weapon."

"Don't lie. We know you do. The old woman told us so herself."

"What old woman?"

"Your cancerous friend who was arrested with you. 'There is a power here you will never defeat or understand,' she said, on the first morning of the invasion. What is the power we do not understand?"

"That power is not a weapon. It's a metaphor."

"Liar. Armies are not defeated by metaphors."

"I mean she didn't mean that literally. She meant—spirit."

"The power is a spirit?"

"Right, our spirit."

"How do you harness and command this demonic spirit?"

His head hurt so badly he wished they would put a bullet into it.

"Not that kind of spirit. A feeling spirit."

"Armies are not defeated by feelings. Tell us what the weapon is."

"I can't!"

"You will find that you can."

"I mean I can't because it isn't what you think."

A nice quick bullet that would stop everything, as his father had been stopped, as he himself had stopped a man once. But he had to think, to think what to say. It's not the truth that matters, some exhausted part of his brain acknowledged. I can't satisfy them with truth, I have to tell them what they expect to hear. What they're capable of believing. There was something hopeful about that, but he couldn't focus on it. He existed only to make sounds that would bring some short relief from pain.

"Perhaps he needs a reminder of what we can do to him if he continues in this stubbornness?"

It was almost funny, Bird thought, a hilarious comedy of miscommunication, but he was beyond laughing, and after a while he was crying and pleading and begging them to let him die.

But he didn't die. They stopped, just before he lost consciousness.

"Tell us about the weapon."

Dear Goddess, *Diosa mía,* Mama, Rio, somebody, anybody, I can't stand this and there is no way even to break. I would tell them anything if I could only think of something to tell them. My tongue won't work; I will never be whole again.

"We are losing patience. You will see that up until now we have been restrained."

The voices that came to him were the voices of the dead. "You think you cannot bear this, but we have borne worse: the rack, the stake, the Middle Passage, the torture of children, the forced labor, stone upon stone, while the people died of disease. We have already borne every unbearable thing human beings can do to each other, and why should you escape, or expect the rescue that never came to us? Are you so much better than we?"

No, no, but help me, please, Goddess, please, please. He was no longer sure whom he was talking to, whether he was begging aloud or in his mind; the dead were thick and swirling in the room.

"What is the weapon?"

He screamed, or thought he screamed; he was no longer quite sure of what was inside him and what was outside. Something hurt his ears and he thought it was his own voice. I don't want to die of fear, he thought. I just want to die, to join the ghosts who are safe and winged and out of their pain.

"Again? Do you need more persuading?"

"The dead!" he cried out. "I swear on the Four Sacred Things, on the Goddess, ow—on Jesus, on anyone you want, name it and I'll swear on it, our weapon is the dead."

"What do you mean by that?"

"Ghosts, hauntings," he said wildly, desperately, "poltergeists. Things moving through the air on their own. You don't have to believe it—the Goddess does it. The power of Hecate is in us. Every one of us you kill becomes a ghost. We'll haunt you. Kill a Witch, and you'll never be free again."

Even as he spoke his words grew dark wings. There was a cold wind in the chamber, and the dead swarmed through as if he had indeed opened a gate for them.

"You don't see them yet," Bird said, "but soon, soon. And you will never be free. Don't you see? It's a trap. The whole thing is a trap we set for you, to deliver you into the hands of the dead, who will take you to Hecate, the Reaper, the Goddess of Death."

He could talk on and on to them, forever, as long as his words bought a moment free from the pain. This is what I have become, a traitor, a liar, living from moment to moment, breath to breath.

But they believed him.

"Tell us more."

"Water—I need water."

They gave him another drink. He savored it on his parched tongue; it was cool on his throat, almost like forgiveness. He drank slowly; while he drank nothing was real to him but the cup, and the water, and his own body swallowing.

"Enough. Tell us more, and you can have more to drink."

He nodded dully. What more was there to tell? But he was not the grandson of the city's foremost storyteller for nothing. Great Mother, Dark Mother, Mother of Rebirth, forgive me for what I am about to do. I have seen your face, and in your eyes I see reflected the limits of my strength. He took a deep breath and began to tell them what they wanted to hear.

"Every child in the city is dedicated to Hecate at birth. And what she offers us is this—anyone who hurts us, anyone who kills us, belongs to her. She will take your soul and ride it and drag it into hell for eternal torments that will make this stuff look like a birthday party. And the ghosts will haunt you. That's why there's no violence in this city—everybody knows better. The Goddess of Death keeps the peace for us."

o o o

They put him in a dark room to recover. For a long time his own mistreated neurons fired and misfired at random, carrying on the work of the torturers. The relief when the storms of pain finally quieted was almost worse than the pain itself, for with every moment his fear grew that they would begin again. There was one small blanket and he huddled under it, shaking. I'm in shock, he thought, I've got to keep warm, I've got to not think about what happened or what will happen. They were subtle experts, this bunch; nothing was broken, there were no outward wounds. Yet. But I've got to think what to do. This is only the beginning. They'll want more from me.

His eyes were assaulted with a brief flash of light, as a door opened and someone was tossed into the closet where he was locked up. The door slammed again. Bird reached out and touched a naked shoulder. A young girl's voice screamed in panic.

"It's okay," he said hoarsely. "I won't hurt you."

"Bird?"

"Rosa?"

She began to weep silently. He wrapped her in the blanket and hugged her through its coarse cloth.

"Marie is dead."

He didn't know what to say, so he just hugged her tighter. Marie is lucky, he thought.

"Did they hurt you?"

She nodded, her head moving up and down under his chin.

"Did they rape you?" He had to ask it.

"I fought them. But there were too many."

"I'm sorry, baby. I'm so sorry."

"I told them things," Rosa said.

"Of course you did, honey, I know."

"I couldn't help it."

"No, you couldn't. I told them things too."

"You, Bird?"

Somehow that question hurt him more than anything.

The next morning they came for them both. The General himself interrogated Bird.

"Her fate is in your hands," the General said. "Cooperate with us, and she will be left alone. Disobey, and we send her to the breaking pens for new whores. Which, since she wasn't bred to it, will be hard for her. And you will watch."

"How can I believe you'll do what you say?"

"You can see her every day. Talk with her. Have her yourself, if you like."

"She's thirteen years old!"

"For some, a little past the prime. Never mind."

"What do you want me to do?"

"There are ways we can use you. We need a liaison to your own people, someone who can command their respect and cooperation."

"They are not used to being commanded in any way."

"Then it's time they got used to it."

o   o   o

He put on their uniform and walked out in the city, flanked by two guards who stayed with him everywhere. They wanted him to wear their uniform as a sign of his defeat, to shatter the morale of the city and say to the people. See, here is one of yours who has turned. He wore it as a warning to them all, a way of saying, Watch out, I am no longer your friend, no longer the one you trusted. Put no faith in me.

Bird walked through the Central Plaza. The market stalls were shuttered, the streambed dry. The city looked like he felt, shattered. Two soldiers walked with him, one on either side. His dog chain, his tether.

They flanked him as he settled himself at the far end of the plaza, near Market Street, beside the old sculpture fountain of upended concrete forms that was dry now.

A woman he recognized was coming toward them: Sachiko, from the Musicians' Guild. Strange, that she could still walk these pathways, the rainbow reflections on her black hair dancing in the sunlight, while he was ruined and Rosa . . . Better not to pursue those thoughts. Better just to do what he needed to do.

She averted her face from the soldiers as she passed them, but he called out to her. "Sachiko!"

She turned, saw his uniform, and poised to run. He called to her again. "Don't be afraid, it's me, Bird."

"Bird!"

The first spontaneous joy that leaped to her eyes froze rapidly into shock as she took in the significance of his uniform. Bird wanted to turn away but he forced himself to meet her eyes, even though the effort sent a tattoo of pain playing over his skin. They've done something to me, Bird thought. My emotions are dead; what's left is this random burst of neurons, my inner firing squad.

"Why are you wearing their uniform?"

He didn't answer her question. "Will you do something for me?"

"Sure, Bird."

"I need to speak with somebody on the Council." The guards would be recording everything he said, and they might get suspicious if he used Sign too overtly. But he turned slightly, to hide his right hand from their view, and quickly his fingers spelled "Lily." "Could you find someone from the Council, bring them here?"

Sachiko's eyes flicked down to his hand, back to his face.

"I'll try. Bird, are you okay?"

"Thanks," he said, and closed his eyes, a dismissal. Sachiko's footsteps clattered on the pavement as she hurried off. Bird leaned back on the bench and sank into the well of darkness that closed over him, an exhaustion so deep that sleep could not touch it, a sensation of falling and falling, endlessly falling, with no bottom to hit, no ground to stand on.

He had no idea how much time had passed when he looked up to see Lily standing in front of him. He hadn't noticed her arrival. She was dressed in a simple green tunic, her hair pulled austerely back, her eyes kind. He wanted to look away.

"Bird!"

He spoke quickly, to get it out and said before he lost his nerve. "I'm not a very good hero, Lily. I talked to them. I told them everything."

The kindness in Lily's eyes did not waver. "No one expects you to be superhuman."

He wanted desperately to look away from her eyes, but he couldn't seem to move.

"Maybe I do. Maybe we all need to be, or we'll lose. Lily, I don't see how we can win here."

"You don't have to see."

He glanced at his guards, who remained beside him, impassive as the cement seat beneath them. Nevertheless they had eyes and ears and wore recording devices.

"I told them about the weapon," he said.

"What weapon?"

"They kept asking about the secret weapon. Really, it was Marie who told them, that first day, when she said there was a power here they could never conquer. They—they kept on me until I told them what the power was."

There was a subtle shift in Lily's face, a glint of something almost like humor.

"What did you tell them?"

"I told them how we're pledged to Hecate and can call up the dead, and how the dead will haunt anyone who kills one of us."

He thought he felt something ripple through his guards, a shiver, stifled before it became perceptible.

"You told them that?" Lily said, her expression unreadable.

"I told them all about it. All the details. I couldn't help myself."

"I see."

"They finally believed me," Bird said. "I'm sorry."

"But they want more from you," Lily said. "What?"

"They want me to be their liaison, to try to get more cooperation out of people. Starting tomorrow, they're going to issue water ration cards. Everyone has to have one, if they want to get any water."

Her eyes were dark half moons above a grim horizon. "And what do they have to do to get one?"

"Sign a pledge not to oppose the Stewards, and say the Millennialist Creed." He paused. Better say it all. "I'll be handing them out, here in the plaza, starting tomorrow morning."

"No one will come. Surely you know that, Bird."

Of course I do, he wanted to yell at her, why do you think I agreed to do it? But the guards were listening, and besides, it wasn't true. He would have agreed to almost anything, to protect Rosa. No, to save himself more pain. She was staring at him so hard that maybe she could read his mind.

"Will you do something for me, Lily?" he said at last.

"If I can."

"Put a flower on my grandmother's grave for me. Tell her I'm sorry. I'm sorry I wasn't stronger." He hoped to Goddess she would understand what he meant. He'd told the Stewards that his family was dead, that that had been a prerequisite for all members of the Council, so there would be no hostages to hold against them. Please, Goddess, let Maya stay away. If they found her, found out who she was . . .

"No one's strength is endless," Lily said, her voice soft. "I am sure you endured much, and will endure more. I wish you could be spared and healed."

She was offering him a forgiveness he didn't deserve and could not accept. Not because he had failed; anyone could fail, but because he was going to go on failing, betraying.

"I should have died with Roberto and Lan. Marie is dead, now, too."

"Leave the inflicting of pain to the conquerors, Bird. Don't do it to yourself."

Bird wished he could read something in her eyes, pity or judgment or compassion. But they were blank as stones.

"There is a place set for you at our table, Bird, waiting for you to come home." She turned to his guards and smiled. "And for you, and you also."

She turned and walked away. Her words reverberated in him, like the ripples of pain from a kick in the gut. They made him what he had made himself, an enemy, a stranger.

∘ ∘ ∘

The next morning, when he arrived at the plaza, a small circle waited beside the fountain: Lily, Sam, Cress from the Water Council, and a woman he did not recognize. They opened the circle as he approached, making a space for him.

Bird stopped. He was flanked by his two guards. Motioning to them to keep a few paces back, he approached the circle, feeling a great reluctance to enter. How could he sit with them while he wore the uniform of the enemy? But there were certain things you had to do, he knew, that you only could do by closing off, shutting down. Don't think, don't imagine what they will think of you, just step in and sit, and do not look into the eyes that turn to you, do not notice too closely how the energy shifts, as they observe you, bought and broken.

"Bird!" Sam said.

"You're still alive!" Cress said. It sounded almost like an accusation. Cress looked thinner than Bird remembered; gray streaked his dark hair and blue shadows pooled under his black eyes.

"I'm here representing the Fourth Stewardship Expeditionary Force. They've asked me to be their liaison." His voice was still hoarse, he wasn't sure why. Probably from screaming, maybe just dry from the meager rations of water they gave in the barracks where he had been moved two nights before.

"You're cooperating with them?" Cress asked. "You've betrayed our strategy!"

"I know." Don't apologize, don't explain. Apologies could not help.

"You were the one who made the glorious speeches about nonviolence in Council! You didn't want to kill, you said, and everybody got so damn offended when I raised questions. And now you're wearing their uniform!"

"I told you," Bird said, his voice toneless, "I'm working for them. I don't defend it, it's just what is."

There was a long silence in the circle. Bird's two guards watched warily from the bench behind them.

"Are you okay?" Sam asked. The lines on his face had deepened; he had aged in the last weeks.

Bird wasn't sure how to answer him. "They didn't break anything this time," he said finally. Except me.

"Did they hurt you?"

"That's what they do, Sam. They hurt people. They're good at what they do."

"You look okay," Cress said suspiciously.

"So do you," Bird replied. He was mad, and that was a relief from feeling simply wretched. But he understood now what had puzzled him at the time, why they had been so careful with him, leaving no marks. They didn't want another visible victim. No, they had cast him as a traitor.

"Lay off him, Cress," Sam said. "We trust you, Bird."

Bird shook his head, and let his eyes glance up to his guards. "I'm work-ing for *them* now." Don't trust me. That's why I'm wearing this damn outfit, so you remember not to trust me.

"You're on their side?" Cress said. "Is that what you're saying?"

"You heard what I said."

"They broke you down, and you gave in to them."

He had to say it out loud, Bird thought. He had to name it, rub my nose in the shit. But it didn't really matter.

"What do you want, Cress?" he asked.

"Tell your keepers—"

"Cress!" Lily broke in. "If we can practice nonviolence toward our en-emy, we can at least show a little common courtesy toward each other."

"I apologize, Lily. I just can't work up a whole lot of sympathy toward a collaborator, especially one who talked us into this whole miserable losing plan to begin with. How do we know when he first started working for them? How do we know he wasn't collaborating all along, talking us out of armed resistance?"

"Shut up, Cress," Sam said. "This is getting us nowhere."

"Half of Water Council was arrested last night at the dam. They shot them this morning," Lily said to Bird.

Bird said nothing. He could hear a stream flowing somewhere behind them, but he imagined that it would be stopped again, before long.

"Are you here to accept the ration cards?" he asked tonelessly, for the benefit of the guards' recorders.

"No," Lily said.

"Never," Cress said. Sam shook his head no.

"I'm Ming Pei from Toxics," the young woman said. Bird didn't recog-nize her, and surely he would have remembered that triangular cat's face if he'd seen her before. "We're very concerned about the filtration systems. They're not going to work properly with the streams only flowing intermit-tently. Can't you explain to them why we need to maintain the flow of water? It's to their own benefit."

"It won't do any good to explain," Bird said.

"Surely some of them, at least, must be reasonable human beings," Ming Pei said. "Try."

"You don't understand," Bird said. "The General isn't interested in filtra-tion systems or stream ecology, he's interested in taking control of the city. And he knows how to go about doing that. Believe me, he's an expert. A third of his troops are bred and raised purely for the army." Would they catch the information in that? "The Elite Corps. They don't know anything different, and they're not susceptible to nonviolent persuasion. The others, the ones they scrape up off the streets, they're way high on doomdust half the time, and anyway they're all hooked on the boosters. You can't reach any of them with reason. Or with anything I can think of."

"They're human beings," Lily said.

"That's debatable," Bird said.

"They are capable of transformation."

"Maybe."

There was a long silence. "You want the ration cards?" Bird asked again. "I'll be here every morning. Tell people."

"Shove them up your ass!" Cress said. The others remained silent.

Finally Sam spoke. "We're getting nowhere here. Perhaps it's time to end this conversation. If you like, Bird, I'll take a message to Maya for you."

Oh, shut up, shut up, shut up! *Diosa,* Sam, don't you know any better than that? Bird shook his head, glancing back at his guards.

"Sure, take Yemaya an offering for me," Bird said, deliberately mispronouncing the name, accenting the second syllable so that it sounded like "Maya." "Give the Goddess of the Ocean a shell. It won't do any good." Maybe that would cover it, maybe not.

"You can come home, you know," Lily said. "We know you are trying to do your best in a bad situation, Bird, but this hurts us. It hurts us all."

Bird shook his head. "I can't. If it wasn't me doing this, they'd just put someone else through it." And send Rosa to the pens, and probably kill all of you.

"That's accepting their terms and letting them define the situation," Cress blurted out. "Even if they kill us all, one by one, we should continue resisting. Anything else is just a rationalization for betrayal!"

"Then I'm a traitor, all right, Cress? Would you like to shoot me yourself, or call in the Wild Boar People to do it? Go ahead, go right the fuck ahead!"

"No, Bird. We won't shoot you," Lily said, laying a restraining hand on Cress's shoulder, as he opened his mouth to respond. "Hush, Cress. I believe this meeting is over. Bird, there is a place for you at our table when you join us again."

He couldn't hold back the tears that leaked down onto his face. Abruptly, he turned and walked away, his guards trailing like alert dogs. He could barely keep himself from dissolving into sobs, and Sam and Lily would have comforted him and taken him back in, and then his guards would have shot them all. Or worse. And then what would happen to Rosa? What would happen to her anyway? Was he just kidding himself to believe his actions had any impact at all on her fate? Oh, it was the oldest trap in the world, and he knew it, and yet he could not get himself out.

People passed him by; he didn't look at them or meet their eyes. His guards followed him but kept their distance, leaving him to walk alone in a bubble of inviolate air.

26

"Today," Madrone said, "we're going to work on anchoring." Her students looked up at her expectantly. They were spread out over the courtyard, the light gauze shading them from the midsummer heat that made the inner rooms unbearable. The child Poppy was curled up in one corner, napping with a few other young ones.

Summer Solstice had barely come and gone. She shuddered to think of what the heat would be like in August. Better not to anticipate, just to trust that she would endure as already she had endured more than she would have imagined possible. They had celebrated the holiday, although Madrone had stretched her imagination to create a ritual from their meager resources. Solstice was a time for offerings, for flower-decked spirit boats to be set ablaze as they drifted across the bay, for all-night bonfires and wreaths of roses and midnight outdoor feasts. Here they could not risk fire, and no flowers grew. Instead they had made a sun in the open court, with kernels of corn, and offered it to the marauding birds.

How had they celebrated at home, she wondered? The vidnets were reporting the invasion as a stunning success, but there were no reporters allowed to cover the war in person, only press dispatches from the military Madrone tried her best to disbelieve. Nevertheless she feared they were, in essence, true. Her dreams were cloudy and full of gunshots and sudden endings. Lily's face appeared preoccupied, when she appeared at all, and she wouldn't speak.

I should go home, she thought. What is happening to Maya and Bird and the others? I should be there to share their suffering, to take care of them. But I'm needed here. I cannot drop this work now, half done.

Over the weeks and months that Madrone had been training this gathering at Katy's, many had dropped away. But many remained, from a spectrum of groups: city gangs and Angels and hill gangs escaping the summer heat. Littlejohn was down from the hills, along with Begood, who showed a strong talent for healing. Rafe and Gabriel, cool Angel blonds, had sensitive, skillful hands.

Madrone was surprised with what she had accomplished. Her students understood basic sanitation and first aid, they knew acupressure points for relieving pain and strengthening *ch'i,* how to administer many of the drugs they acquired on raids and how to ease withdrawal from the boosters. Now she was guiding them deeper into the mysteries of healing, teaching them to feel and move the subtle energies that underlie the physical body.

"Anchoring is a way to get quickly in and out of particular levels of trance," she went on, "by keying each level to its own image and phrase and to a physical touch on a part of the body. So find yourself a partner now, and take a moment to acquaint yourself with your partner's basic energy pattern, their aura. You can use any of the methods we learned before—whatever works best for you—your eyes or your hands."

They worked well together now, seldom needing her help. She squatted against the wall of the building, her knees drawn up to her chest, and let her eyes close. Katy was working with Rafe at the far side of the courtyard, but Madrone could feel her pain and anger like waves pressing her own body into the concrete. She wished she had never touched Hijohn, or had let him lie to Katy, who walked around now with a stricken look in her large dark eyes.

Madrone had tried to talk to her about it, catching her outside in the courtyard after the others went to bed. "Katy, I'm sorry," she'd said. "I really, truly, honestly didn't know how hurt you'd be by this."

"Didn't you?" Katy's eyes were black sparks in the dark. "Or didn't you care?"

"Katy, I'm from a different place. A different world. Maybe I should have stopped to think it out—but it never occurred to me that what we did could hurt you."

"Don't lie to me, Madrone. That just makes it worse."

"I'm not lying!" Now don't get mad, Madrone told herself. If you get pulled into her anger, you'll cut the last cord that swings across this gap, and she'll be alone on the other side with the baby coming, and you'll be alone here with all your skills, unable to help. "Katy, please, I'm asking you to try to believe me—or, if not believe, at least imagine that I might be telling you the truth. I didn't know. I would never willingly have done something to hurt you."

She stopped, because there were corollaries she didn't wish to pursue. Hijohn had known how hurt Katy would be, and it hadn't stopped him. Which was, Madrone suspected, the real source of Katy's pain.

"Hijohn is a man," Katy said, as if she were following Madrone's thoughts. "And the best of them are all the same when it comes to sex. But women ought to stick together."

There's a lifetime of assumptions here, Madrone thought, assumptions I don't share and can't even identify. She felt tired, suddenly, too tired to argue.

I am alone now, she thought. Katy was as close as I had to a friend here, and now that's gone. Hijohn was as close as I've come to a lover in a long while, and he's cut off too.

"Now that I know how you feel, I would never do it again," Madrone said. "It's not like we're going to carry it on, or threaten what you and he have. It was just—one moment. An impulse. I was scared, Katy. I needed comfort, and he responded."

"That's the problem with you, Madrone. Everything you need, you think you have a right to reach for and take. Every impulse you have, you follow. You get an impulse to take a swim in broad daylight in some rich woman's pool, for Jesus' sake, and endanger everybody's life and everything we've built here. You get an impulse to have sex, you have sex. You're like some animal! Arrogant as the rich people!"

"That's not fair!"

"Anyway, it doesn't matter to me whether you carry on or not. I'm through with him. You've changed him, and now you've poisoned what we had. I'll always feel you in the midst of our lovemaking, if ever we do again."

Ah, Madrone thought, there's a slight contradiction here. She's through with him, yet still thinking about making love with him. Maybe there's hope. Because they need each other so much in this place where love is as scarce as water. I would really hate to think I've wrecked what they had together.

"Do you have to take it that way?" Madrone asked, her voice very low and neutral. "Can't you take it as a gift?"

"Don't be patronizing."

"I just mean that every new lover expands the range of our possibilities, we say."

"That's sick. Love is a feeling, a commitment, not a—a craft."

"A little skill doesn't hurt."

"Maybe I liked him the way he was."

"Katy, you couldn't have, honestly."

"How can you say that? What do you know about me or what I want?"

"I know anatomy."

"You're just being insulting."

I will try one more time, Madrone thought, and then let it go. "Katy, listen to the blessing we say to our lovers on Beltane Eve:

> 'My love, you are a river fed by many streams.
> I bless all who have shaped you,
> The lovers whose delights still dance patterns on your back,
> Those who carved your channels deeper, broader, wider,
> Whitewater and backwater lovers,

Swamp lovers, sun-warmed estuary lovers,
Lovers with surface tension,
Lovers like boulders,
Like ice forming and breaking,
Lovers that fill and spill with the tides.
I bless those who have taught you
    and those who have pleased you
    and those who have hurt you,
All those who have made you who you are.' "

"Now I know I'm glad to be a Christian," Katy said.

                    ◦ ◦ ◦

Madrone roused herself and led the group into the next phase of the exercise.

"Now find an anchor for this state, a place you can touch, as you breathe, to bring you back, a word you can say, an image to hold in your mind. Concentrate, make it strong." She gave them a moment and then began a soft whispered chant to guide them into trance, down toward the level where emotions translated to plays of color and sound and energy. Yes, she could see Katy's rage there, red lights flickering over a brown ball of pain. She could hear it, like a vibration, a thrumming that seemed to penetrate from outside her.

Rafe was out of trance, alert, worried. Something was wrong.

"Come back now," Madrone said. "Use your anchors. That's right. Bring yourselves up and out."

A shadow fell cold on the back of her neck. "Copter!" someone screamed. Everyone began to run frantically around the courtyard. A red stain blossomed on the heart of a child, she opened her mouth to scream and blood streamed out. Then Madrone heard the gunfire, ripping through the canopies, tearing into flesh and stucco and the tender bodies of spindly plants.

"Inside!" someone yelled.

"No! Don't get trapped!"

But they were already trapped. Madrone could see troops emerge from both passageways into the square. She tried to run, but there was no place to go. Where was Katy? And Poppy? The gunfire was loud in her ears. She expected that, at any moment, the red blossom would burst forth in her. A laser beam hit the canopies and they burst into flame, filling the air with smoke and drifting pieces of ash. She was beyond fear, only saddened, somehow, as she watched bullets rip through the brave, struggling plants along the wall. So much work, so much care. All gone.

Then someone grabbed her arm and jerked her roughly into motion. It was Rafe.

"Come on!" he yelled, grabbing her arm as he pulled her over to the far edge of the courtyard. He shoved her behind him. She could see armed soldiers in a passageway so narrow that only one could fit through at a time. As the first soldier emerged, Rafe let something fly from his hand with a subtle, almost casual motion. Madrone heard a thud, and the soldier fell, a knife through his heart. While she stood, shocked, Rafe grabbed the laser rifle that clattered to the ground, shot the next two soldiers who emerged, and tossed a second rifle into the hands of Littlejohn, who dropped to his knees and began firing at the fuselage of the helicopter.

"Let's go!" Rafe shouted at her. The soldiers had dropped back from the corridor.

"Katy!" she screamed, but he grabbed her arm and pulled.

"You can't help her. And it's you they really want."

Behind her, she heard a dull moan and a sharp crack. She turned, to see Littlejohn twist and fall, the side of his head shattered, flecks of bone and brain plastered to the wall.

"Come on!" Rafe grabbed her arm. They squeezed down the narrow passageway, emerging behind a spray of laser fire from Rafe's rifle. The soldiers were stationed behind a barrier directly outside the opening, waiting to pick them off. Rafe halted. Inside Madrone's gut, liquid fire churned. We're still trapped, she thought. We'll never get out of here.

Then behind them they heard a whine of metal in air and a thundering crash. The helicopter went down, bursting into flames in the courtyard. She could feel the heat behind her and hear screams.

"Outa here!" the lead soldier yelled to his men. "Take cover before the fuel tank explodes!" The soldiers turned and ran around the corner, to another entrance. Rafe held his fire, and when they were gone, Madrone followed him into the street.

He hugged the sides of the buildings, moving at a near run, his eyes searching all around. Behind them they heard a rumble and a loud explosion. Katy and Poppy, all the others—would any of them survive?

Before them stretched a jumble of broken concrete blocks where a freeway overpass had collapsed, and Rafe led Madrone from block to block, ducking behind them for cover. They were almost through to the other side when they heard a voice call "Halt!"

About thirty yards ahead, five guards stood, aiming laser rifles straight at the two of them. Rafe shoved her down behind a pile of stones, dove for a dirt mound nearby, and fired. Bullets ricocheted around them, and a laser beam raised a fountain of dust.

"Move!" he yelled. "Keep low."

She ran, crouched close to the ground, choosing a route by pure instinct. Around her she heard more shots, then silence.

"Come on!"

Rafe was running now and she followed, terror helping her match his speed. A building loomed up before them, its entrance blocked by nailed boards. Rafe grabbed at them, pulling hard, and they swung aside to reveal a concealed doorway. Quickly they ducked inside, replaced the boards behind them, and ran down an empty, dusty corridor.

At the end of the hallway, a narrow stair led down to a basement. They picked their way through the dark until they came to a trapdoor. Rafe pulled it up and motioned her down. She felt for the rungs of a metal ladder and began climbing downward. He followed close behind, shutting the door above them, cutting off the last of the dim light. Feeling her way rung by rung, she descended in the dark, wondering as she went how deep this hole was, how long she could control her shaky arms.

Finally her leading foot hit solid ground. Carefully she let go of the ladder, backing away just far enough to let Rafe descend. She took hold of his shirt as, sure as a bat, he found his way through the pitch-dark corridors.

After a long time, she began to see light ahead, a dim glow that glared alarmingly in her dilated pupils. They emerged through an archway into a broad expanse of concrete, supported by pillars of cement and steel, some long-forgotten structure of the old world. Madrone couldn't quite imagine what it had been built for. In some areas, curtains were hung between the pillars to mark off private spaces. In others, the curtains were raised and she could see little camps, with rugs and pillows and blankets. In the center, a small fire burned, and the concrete ceiling above was marked with soot. Around her were unimproved areas, vast expanses of gray flooring marked only by flecked, ancient paint in parallel diagonal lines.

"Welcome to Heaven," Rafe said.

He led her to the fire, where chairs and couches were arranged in a rough but comfortable circle. They joined the group that was sitting there, brewing a kettle on the flames.

Madrone couldn't tell by looking if the person tending the kettle was female or male, but her voice was high-pitched and melodious as she looked up at Rafe and spoke. "What's happening?"

"The rats got smoked out. Bad news."

"All of them?"

"Seemed like it. I saw some of the kids get hit, and Littlejohn, from the hills; they splashed his brains all over the pavement. We may have lost Gaby, too."

Littlejohn, Madrone thought. She couldn't yet feel his death. It seemed too sudden. How could he *be* one minute, and not be the next, not be alive, not be somewhere stalking the thirsty canyons? Maya, *madrina,* did I do something wrong? Was I not vigilant enough to stay out of the Bad Reality?

"I told Hijohn it was stupid to have all those people gather in the same place," Rafe went on. "The bigsticks brought in a copter."

"Where in hell did they get a copter?" someone asked from behind her.

"They got a warehouse full in the Valley. Can't fly unless the weather's real clear, though," said the woman with the kettle.

"That one won't fly again," Rafe said. "Neither will a lot of rats and hillboys, poor soulless fuckers. I saved the healer, though. This is her."

"Hello," they said.

Madrone's eyes were beginning to be accustomed to the darkness. She was surrounded by a group of the most physically striking people she had ever seen. They were all young—she doubted that any were older than twenty, especially in this climate, which aged people so rapidly. Almost all were as blond as Rafe, with the same long limbs and slender bodies, and nearly androgynous, the boys soft-skinned, the girls hard-muscled. They could have been cousins. Or, she thought, it was more like a breed of show dogs—greyhounds or Afghans. There were a few redheads, and several girls with flowing black hair and skin golden as the inside of ripe plums. Three or four of the group were dark as gleaming shadows, with sculpted muscles that reminded her of Isis.

"You want anything?" one of them asked. "Water? We got plenty, from an illegal line we run. Food? We got things down here you've maybe never tasted. Chocolate. Sex? Someone'll happily do you. What do you like? Men? Women? Kids? There's some great young ass running around this place."

Madrone wasn't sure she had heard what she just heard, so she pretended she hadn't. What she wanted was to cry, to lie down and not rise up again, to be able to feel Littlejohn's death and mourn him, to be home with Bird and Nita and Holybear and Sage, and Maya downstairs writing her memoirs. She wanted Katy and Poppy to suddenly, miraculously, appear in this place. Heaven. Maybe she, like so many others, was already dead?

"Water," she said. "Are you making tea? I'd love some tea."

They brought her tea on a silver tray, in a cup that, she noted, was real Wedgwood china, as fine as anything Johanna had collected in her affluent days. Somewhere in the back they had an actual refrigerator, from which they brought her cream, and someone produced a plate of delicate, buttery cookies. The tea was fragrant and, as she sipped it, she recognized a taste she had forgotten from her childhood, when Maya used to sneak her a sip of her afternoon Earl Grey. Imported black tea. What reality had she stumbled into?

As she looked up from her teacup, she noticed that a crowd of small children had gathered from the corners of the vast space and were staring at her curiously. Like the older ones, they had big eyes and fine bones, delicate, appealing, as if the best specimens of mostly the white race had been collected to match the china.

"Where do you get this stuff?" Madrone asked. "Like the tea and cookies?"

"Raids," said Michael, who could have been Rafe's twin. He had stopped coming to the training, but Madrone recognized him from the early weeks.

"But where does it come from? Are the Stewards still trading with Asia and Europe and Africa?"

"I don't know," Michael said. "We just steal it."

"I know," a young woman said. She had the darkest skin Madrone had ever seen, violet-tinged, velvety in the dim light, and she wore only a white silk skirt that barely covered her ass. Her features were perfectly sculpted, and her long hair was blond and silken. Is it real? Madrone wondered. Is it a wig, or is she the result of yet another breeding program?

The woman tossed her head back, making her hair shimmer in the dim light, and smiled suggestively at Madrone. "I used to belong to a man in the shipping trade. They still come in from overseas, the big boats, when the storms don't get them. But all this stuff is very rare and precious now. Couldn't buy it for a year's ration of water. Makes it more fun to steal."

Madrone listened to them chatter on, about prizes they had collected on raids and what they most liked to eat. It distracted her from the great, hollow, terrible feeling inside that threatened to well up and drown her. Was Katy dead? No, that was wrong, wrong. She should be ready to birth, to bring forth life, not death. And I've made her last days unhappy and separated her from Hijohn. Maybe if he'd been with us, he could have saved her. Maybe. . . .

The curtains parted, and Gabriel came in. She was breathing hard, sweat dripping down the perfect planes of her face, her calla-lily skin flushed with pink.

"You made it," Rafe said. "Celestial!"

"Lemme have some water," Gaby said.

"What happened after we got out?"

"Copter blew, man, burned the place. All charcoal, now. Lotta people got out, some didn't. Littlejohn got shot. Dead. They caught Katy and that Angel kid and took them somewhere. Caught me too, but I got away from them." She grinned.

Madrone sat, silent. She ached inside. Littlejohn had always been kind to her, always tried to help her. And he had known Bird, was a link to him. Now Bird seemed even further away, so remote he might never have existed. But grieving for Littlejohn seemed a pleasant indulgence, a luxury appropriate to a different world. In this world, *El Mundo Malo,* what was happening to Katy and Poppy?

"Can't we do anything for them?" Madrone asked. "You go on raids all the time—can't we steal them back?"

Rafe shrugged. "Where will they be, do you think?"

"They might send Katy to the breeder pens," Michael suggested.

"Nah, not ready to pop as she is. They don't want just anything coming out of those pens. They'll take her to the Research Center, do some experiment on her," Rafe said.

"Where is that?" Madrone asked.

"Up at the university. In the Medical Center."

"And Poppy?"

"She'll never make it back to the pens," Gaby said. "That Stewwie bigstick's bound to make a private deal somewhere."

"Who with?" Rafe speculated. "Who likes 'em fresh caught and has the cash to buy off a bigstick?"

"Marichal, up Spring Canyon. Stebner, down by the beach. Or any of the widescreen men."

"Nah, they're all buying on the up-and-up these days, strictly government issue. Too much spotlight for them."

"Could be anybody," Gaby admitted. "But let's send the scouts out to check the most likely. I'm just in the mood to do it to somebody after that."

"We got some new guns," Rafe said. "Might as well put them to use."

The scouts were small and brown and ordinary looking, fed on the bounty of the Angels for their usefulness. They were dispatched, and Madrone settled back with the others to wait.

"Tell us about the North," Gaby said. "I like to hear your stories."

"I'm not sure I can talk about it right now," Madrone said. "I'm too worried."

"Did you hear the army's issued a proclamation of victory?" Gaby said.

"Do you believe them?" Michael asked.

Gaby shrugged. "Stands to reason they'd win, if the North don't got no army."

"We don't—we didn't. We didn't want to starve people in order to support it," Madrone said.

"Never bothered anyone around these parts," Rafe said. "And a lot of good it done you now."

"Tell us your stories anyway," Gaby pleaded. "Even if it's all blown up and burned down, I like to hear how it used to be. It'll pass the time while we wait for the scouts to come back."

"So would sleep," Rafe said.

"Ah, come on."

I can't bear to tell my fairy tale now, Madrone thought. I don't believe it anymore. But Gaby looked so eager and so young, almost innocent for a moment, like any child wanting a story. Reluctantly, Madrone began.

"In the North, water runs freely through the City in open streams, where ducks can bathe and kids swim and catch fish. Nobody owns anybody else, and everybody has enough to eat and drink. . . ."

◦ ◦ ◦

The pink mansion was set among green lawns, surrounded by a high stone wall, electric fencing, and a security system worthy of an unpopular head of state. As raiders, Madrone considered, the Angels lacked the hillboys' caution and finesse, but they made up for it with sheer nerve and complete ruthlessness. After word came back that a new Angel child had been purchased at Stebner's, Rafe and Michael and Gaby and Madrone had hiked all night through the deserted streets, reaching the beach resorts just before dawn. They were out long after curfew, but Rafe simply shot any guard who challenged them. To disarm the alarm system, Michael tossed a live cat into the electric fence. As it screamed and spit and writhed in agony, one of the guards came out to turn off the system and remove it. As soon as it was disarmed, Rafe shot him.

"Wait here, till we call you," Michael said. "If we don't come out, get yourself back to the hills."

She was only too happy to wait. They frightened her, almost as much as the soldiers and the Stewards. They killed so calmly, so coldly. All right, Madrone thought, huddling between the wall and a large evergreen, it's true that I don't want to see it. I'm a hypocrite. I want to save Poppy and I won't challenge them on their violence, because how can I? Their violence saved my life. And look what's been done to them—not that it condones murder but it does explain their lack of empathy. Still, if killing has to happen I prefer it to happen out of my sight, so I can pretend I have no part in it.

She heard a few shots, but mostly silence, and then Gaby gave a short whistle and called her name.

"Over the wall. It's okay, now."

Madrone hoisted herself up, the rough stones providing purchase for her hands and feet. She pulled herself over the top and leaped down, landing in a crouch.

"Come on," Gaby said. Her face looked grim and Madrone began to be even more afraid.

The living room in the mansion was enormous, white-carpeted, lined with windows that overlooked the ocean, glinting pink and gold and rose as the early light glowed through the low fog. Rafe seemed almost lost in the expanse of luminous walls and low couches. He was bending over something, and looked up as Madrone entered.

"He's yours, Madrone," Rafe said.

At Rafe's feet lay a man, trussed, naked, a gag tied tightly over his mouth, only his eyes looking out at her, terrified. He had shit with fear, and the stench mingled with the other smells in the room: blood and urine and vomit. Poppy's broken body lay crumpled in a corner, like a discarded doll.

Madrone stood, shocked into silence, her eyes distracted by the changing panorama of light and water that played in the distance.

"He's yours," Rafe repeated.

"What do you mean, he's mine?" Madrone asked.

"To kill," Rafe said. "Take your time. Enjoy it." He smiled, and Madrone suddenly remembered a kitten she'd had as a small child, who used to bring home gifts of half-dead mice, cocking her head with that same eagerness to please.

She wanted to vomit.

"No," Madrone said. "Uh, thanks, but no. No, I don't want to kill him."

"Take a look at Poppy, what's left of her," Rafe said. "You'll change your mind."

I don't want to look at her, Madrone thought, or I will be haunted for the rest of my life. But the room was full of Angel eyes, cold and blue, watching her. This is our life, they seemed to say. How can you heal us if you cannot bear to look at it?

She made herself kneel down beside the small body, touch the cold flesh. Blood streamed from Poppy's nostrils and the torn flesh between her legs. There were other marks on her that Madrone's eyes observed but her mind refused to comprehend. She was going to be sick. Something opened in her mind, like a cover sliding off a well, and she was tumbling down the years to stand above another broken, bloodied female body. No, she thought, this is what I don't want to see, what I cannot remember and still go on living: my mother, after the men got through with her, and I crept out into the silence, and I saw. Kneeling, she gently touched Poppy's cold skin, as she had touched her mother's face, hopefully, but she didn't move. She didn't move.

She stuffed her fist into her mouth. Abruptly, she stood up.

"The nerves close to the surface of the skin are most sensitive," Gaby said. "But of course you know that."

No, Madrone wanted to scream, I know nothing about this. I know nothing about torture, nothing about death.

"We should get out of here within the hour, to be safe. That should be enough time to do it right."

"Maybe you want one of the boys to rape him first?" Gaby suggested.

Madrone found herself nearly saying yes, just to buy time. The man was mewling behind his gag and shit was still leaking out his behind and she couldn't look at his eyes without wondering if her mother had looked like that. She could almost grab the knife, to close those eyes, to stop the spreading of this pain and the staining of this carpet. Oh, she wasn't making sense and she had to think, think.

"You don't understand," she said. "I don't want to kill him. I've never killed anybody."

"It's fun," Rafe assured her. "You'll get to like it."

"No, I can't. I can't."

I can't shut it out, now. All these years I have held it down, because I didn't want to remember her like that. I wanted to remember her face, and I can't. I never could. Only now the blood, and the terrible cold stare of her eyes.

Rafe laughed.

"If you leave him alive, he'll make more Poppies," Gaby said. "He'll identify you."

Like Poppy's eyes. Like this man's burning, fearful eyes could be, in a moment. Glassy and blind, his skin that clammy cold. And it was only fair, because his eyes had seen, had watched as his hands . . . no, she couldn't think about that.

"If it has to be done, you do it," Madrone said. "But quick and clean. Don't drag it out."

"Why not?" Rafe asked. "That's the fun part."

"That's what he did to Poppy," Michael said. "Would you like me to describe exactly how she got those particular wounds?"

"No," Madrone said quickly.

"She'd rather not know," Rafe said, a note in his voice that scared her. "She'd rather keep her own hands clean. I know what you're thinking—it's what they all think. Leave it to the Angels; let them do the dirty work. They're born with blood under their nails."

But I know too much. It's what I can't unknow that is killing me. And I would like to hurt him. I would like him to pay for what he's done. I'd like them all to pay, all the torturers and rapists and the death squads. *Diosa*, Coatlicue, shall I become an instrument of your justice and clean the world for you?

"You wanted this raid," Gaby said.

I took the knife of the Reaper, but if I take up this knife and let the rage in me taste blood, what will I become? How will I ever come back?

Think, think, think! Use your mind, girl. Ground. Remember who you are, and who you want to be.

Madrone took a long, deep breath.

"Poppy's dead," she said. "Killing him won't bring her back."

"It'll remove scum from a dirty world," Michael said. "But if you don't want to do it, maybe you'd like to watch me. I'm told that I'm good with my hands. Better with a knife."

"I'm asking you not to," Madrone said. She was fighting for breath, and her words came in gasps. "Not to torture him, not to spin out his death. Maybe it might be fun for you—maybe it might even be just—but that doesn't make it right."

"Don't matter if it's right," Gaby said. "Don't you want revenge?"

"I do," Madrone admitted. "I could tear his heart out. Torture is too good for him. But that's not what I'm thinking of. We become what we do. If we do these things, how do we become something better than what he is? How can we build something all together?"

"Who says the Angels are interested in building anything with a pack of rats and dried-up hillboys?" Rafe asked.

She was very afraid, now, afraid of the way they looked at her, eyes almost as glassy as those of the dead. She had betrayed them, judged them. They would not forgive her.

Am I just too cowardly to kill him? Too squeamish, like those who eat meat but refuse to wield the knife?

In the distance, a siren wailed.

"That's it," Gaby said. "We're outa time."

"Outa here, too," Rafe said, plunging a knife into the man's heart. They left as he gurgled, spouted blood, and died.

"Scatter," Rafe called when they hit the street, and suddenly everyone around her was gone.

This is my punishment, Madrone thought, her heart pounding in panic. She knew none of their secret routes in and out of this district, no hiding holes, no places to disappear.

She had to get away, and fast. She had to get off this street, with its blank-walled estates where no one ever walked. Blindly, she turned and ran, away from the sound of sirens.

27

Madrone forced herself to walk steadily, as if she had a perfect right to be where she was. All her senses were alert, her eyes flicked nervously back and forth. She had made her way quickly out of the affluent sectors, heading south and east to the rubble-filled streets of the flats and the floodplains, where the rising waters of the ocean poured through a gap in the broken dikes to drown streets and submerge buildings.

The afternoon sun was a dull sheen behind a bank of gray fog that sat heavily on the horizon. Around her the wreckage of tall buildings thrust spires out of the water. A few desperately poor people had staked out precarious homes in the upper floors of the submerged high rises. Coming and going by boat or on the labyrinth of half-rotted boardwalks, they survived until high tides or storms shifted the buildings' foundations and they crumbled into burial mounds.

She had been on the run since morning, with nothing to eat, and she was beginning to tire. She needed a refuge. She needed food and sleep and somebody's warm arms to harbor her and lull her and help her forget, or she needed time and safety in which to probe and release her memories.

Did you feel like this, Mama? Hunted? Afraid? Or did it all happen too quickly? Why can't I ever feel a hint of your presence, as I feel Johanna, or Sandy sometimes? Where did you go?

Something shifted in the air around her, a subtle change as if for just a moment the pressure changed. A voice spoke to her, rough and male, in the slurred Spanish of Guadalupe. *"Cuida tus espaldas, hija."* Watch your back, child.

Madrone's bee-keen hearing picked up the scratchy, metallic sound of a com device behind her. Patrols. She was on a street leading straight to the main promenade along what passed for beachfront; ahead of her was nothing but water and the disintegrating piers that led out over the drowned lands. But she could not double back.

"Sigue tu rumbo." Keep walking. Don't hesitate.

Who was this ancestor speaking to her? She strode out onto the promenade, her footsteps echoing on the wooden boards. The water looked ominous to her. Johanna's warnings echoed in her mind: "Don't go in that water, you hear? You don't know what's in it."

"¡Cuidado!"

Footsteps drummed behind her, ahead of her, reverberating like a drum tattoo. Another patrol, coming toward her. Trapped.

Now what do I do, whoever you are? Am I going to die now? Is that why the veil between the worlds is suddenly thin?

Ahead of her, the skeleton of an old pier branched off, heading across the water. The central supports were gone, but the side supports made a narrow bridge, and she took it, balancing lightly on the narrow struts. It was no worse than crossing the freeway, she told herself, although the water frightened her. She shuddered at the thought of falling in, not just because of the cold and the possible toxins but because of what was submerged below, corpses of houses and bones of the drowned, secrets, death. A shout came from behind her. She walked faster, the water lapping at her heels, licking its lips. Another shout. And now the pier ended, the struts broken in midair.

So this is the end, Papa. It must be you, coming in the shadow of my mother's memory, speaking in the *acento* of Guadalupe. I never really believed in you, but you were a sort of hillboy, weren't you? What does a true revolutionary do at the end?

"Haz lo que hay que hacer." Do what there is to do.

Shivering, she kicked off her shoes and slipped out of her clothes. This is the dark place, the place I never wanted to go. But there is nowhere else. The shout came again, from close behind her. Too close. She dove.

Cold hit her like a shock wave. She held her breath and swam underwater as long as she could, until finally she had to surface for breath. The crumbling dikes made a breakwater; within their circuit the waves were calm but she was trapped. Already she could see patrols heading out on the narrow roadway that ran along the top of the dikes. A flare of laser fire split the air. She gulped a deep breath and submerged again, giving herself to the current, which carried her swiftly out through the gap. It pulled her down and took her racing between the rocks; she began to panic as she tried to struggle toward the surface through churning whirlpools that spun her around and down.

Stay calm, she told herself, trying to slow her pounding heart. Fear will kill you now if you let it. Yemaya, Ocean Mama, carry me now. I am yours—don't hurt me, Mama.

She was through the breakwater, and now the current relented and let her shoot up to the surface to gulp air. She was out in the open ocean where huge waves rolled up, rounded and glassy, foaming at the mouth. She remembered trips to the clean beaches of the Sonoma coast, when she was a child. Face the waves, Rio had said, don't try to dodge them, dive straight into them. Maya had made it a metaphor for life. And she could do it, gliding through each breaker as it struck, making herself sleek and lean as the waves pummeled her. Up for air and then head on into the next one, up when the force abated and gasp a breath before the next, again and again, until she thought she would cry from exhaustion.

And then suddenly she was through them, out beyond the impact zone, into the smooth swell. She was warm now, and the fog lifted to let a hint of sun transform the day from gray to blue. She felt strong, exhilarated. She had made it, and now she could swim forever, heading north with the current toward the mouths of the canyons that led to the hills. How far? Five miles? Ten? How far could she swim? If I go slow, if I take my time, as far as I have to.

The ocean was the mother of life. She remembered tales of medieval women of Italy who had held hands, in masses, and walked into the sea to drown, escaping the tortures of the Witch burners. At worst, she would join them. But maybe some of them, too, had escaped and swum off to safety?

The sun traveled in its low arc, moving west to meet her.

○ ○ ○

Not long before sunset, she realized she was in trouble. She had swum for hours, she thought, and she was tired and chilled. She had no idea how many miles she had covered, only that she had made it north, helped by the strong pull of the current, past the high cliffs of the palisades, to where the mountains rose steeply up from the lashing surf. Along that stretch of shore were only a few beaches, one or two openings to dry creek beds marking where water flowed during the brief rains. If only she could reach one, get ashore there, and make her way up into the mountains. . . .

Night was falling, and even if she got ashore the hike up to the camps would be long and cold; she'd be wet and naked in the dark. But now she must not, could not think about that; she would concentrate on landing, returning to earth. In the distance she could see an impression in the cliffs, a darker stain against the rocks that meant the crevice of a creek, and gathering her waning strength, she struck out.

For about ten minutes, she swam with a strong crawl, slow but steady, watching her breathing and instructing her weary feet to kick. She broke for a moment, treading water and shaking her hair clear of her eyes to see how far she'd come.

The creek was farther away. Even as she stopped for a moment, the strong current was pulling her away, north and west, always west, out to sea.

No, she thought. I'm tired, Mama Ocean. Let me go. Before she could panic, she struck out again, changed the angle of her direction slightly, swimming more vigorously. She made some progress this time, the shore came a tiny bit closer, even though she was still drifting north of the creek's mouth.

But if I try harder, she thought, even as her legs began to feel heavy as stones and her breath labored in and out of her chest. I can always try a little harder, can't I? Because it can't be ending like this. No. I'm not ready to have it end.

If the ocean would only pause for a moment, give her a chance to rest, to collect herself. She had a sudden understanding of all the mothers she had ever heard cry out in the middle of labor, "Stop! I can't go through with this!" But they were laboring into life, and she had always been confident that they could trust their women's bodies to withstand the coming of life. As she trusted her body, heavy and tired and cold as it was, to get her through this.

Yemaya, I am your child. You can't be meaning to kill me now. It doesn't make sense to go through so much and die in you.

"But I am relentless, implacable. I am not your body, but bigger than your body. I never stop." And even as she was hearing the words in her mind, the riptide was sucking her out, drinking in one smooth pull the distance she'd gained so laboriously. .

I'm just tired, she thought. But I'm strong. I can go on. I can always go on, as long as I have to. I can't give in.

Just then a wave caught her from behind, splashing its lip over her head so that she inhaled just a breath of water, like the fumes of a laugh. Suddenly she was gasping. Her lungs wanted to expel all their air but they wouldn't breathe in, and her stone feet and arms were too heavy to move.

I've got to keep trying, she thought. But underneath was another voice, whispering, "I can't do it. I need help. I can't make it back alone." Desperately she made one more attempt to swim. If I go with the current, don't try to fight it, maybe it'll take me somewhere else where I might find an easier way in.

But the current was only taking her out, and after three strokes her heart was pounding and her breath labored.

I've just got to stop and catch my breath, she thought, rolling over on her back. If I can just catch my breath, just rest. . . .

She lay on her back, the ocean carrying her, blue water around her, blue sky above her as the sun dipped ominously close to the waves. She was in the ocean and the ocean was in her, flowing in the salt water of her veins, gurgling through her lungs with each whistling breath. But I want to live, she thought. Here is the moment of my death, the gate we all pass through, the gate I've come so close to before, that I've seen so many slip across. And I'm not ready for it. I want to live.

I want to live. And there's not a damn thing I can do about it. I cannot save myself. There's nothing more for me to do now, except wait, and hope, and breathe. Try to slow it down, to steady the heart, to breathe in, through the water and the pain. Don't think about the sun, soon to hiss its steamy way down below the water. Don't think about cold, the body's heat running out into this icy bath. Just breathe and think about living. Drinking hot tea on Isis' boat. Being dirty and thirsty in the canyons, longing for water, praying for water. The sun bright and the bees humming, coming to extract that sweetness. Yes, I can feel it beading on my forehead; if there were any bees here, lost in the middle of this water, they could still be fed from me. I am your water flower, Mother, be gentle with me. I will live as long as I can, in you, because nothing in me truly wants to die.

She closed her eyes, feeling a tickle on her forehead like the threads of bee feet, but her ears heard only the sounds of water, and when she opened her eyes, she saw nothing but the blue of water and the paler blue of the sky.

And all the while, the sun, like her, rode the swells into the west.

∘ ∘ ∘

"Well, you are in a mess now, girl," Johanna said. "How many times did I tell you to stay out of the water? What is the point of giving you advice if you don't follow it?"

Madrone had closed her eyes so she wouldn't see the sun set, and she couldn't tell where Johanna was. Close, undoubtedly. I am halfway through the veil myself, she thought, maybe more.

"Didn't I tell you, always get someone to cover your back?"

Maybe I should open my eyes, Madrone thought. If this is the last sunset I'll ever see, maybe I shouldn't miss it.

"Answer me, girl."

"Help me, Johanna. Be nice to me. Please."

"Help you? I've tried, child, time and time again, but you insist on going up against forces too strong for you."

But my lids are too heavy. Still, I can see the sun through them, a red glow through my own blood.

"I don't want you, Johanna. Go away. I want my mama, my real mama. Why doesn't she come to me?"

Why can't I remember her face, her living voice, instead of the cold touch of her dead skin? Mama, where are you?

Madrone heard nothing but the wind and the ringing of her ears cradled by water.

Why do you leave me all alone here? Not a word, not a whisper of presence. Mama, am I going to find you now after all these years? And what will I find? I can't remember, I can't remember your smell or your touch or anything you ever said to me; it's as if you'd disintegrated, as if you'd never been.

But I remember now, I remember you told me to hide. And I hid. I heard you screaming and I didn't help you. I touched you, and you were all cold and bloody and I thought I'd hurt you.

I want to be cleansed of this. Look, Mama, there's water leaking out of my eyes, I never did cry for you before, and now the tears are hot on my cold skin and salty like this water that carries me. I believe you are there, somewhere, you must be, you can't not be anywhere. How do I cleanse this memory so I can come back to you? I'm reaching for you, but my arm is a cold weight on the water, too heavy to lift. You'll just have to believe me, that I'm reaching, I'm opening.

But she was only opening to water. It poured out of her eyes and lapped her face and soaked the tissues of her lungs, it was in her as she was in it, and she imagined it washing through her brain, soaking through her memories. Cleansing. She opened, imagining her whole self splitting wide so that there was no longer any separation between her and the waves. They washed through her as the breeze played through her sodden lungs and the radiant blazing sun, in its descent, lit up her bowels. If this is dying, she thought, it's not so bad. It's a clean death, no blood, no pain, just a ride on the tide, tides of life, tides of sickness and death, great currents of *ch'i* that ebb and flow, great life womb that births and swallows and reclaims even memories.

So this is what it means to become one with the Goddess. To turn into water, water of life, water of birth and death and all that passes between, joy and pain. Yes, the pain of my laboring lungs and spirit holding to life with both hands as death loosens my grip. My pain, my mother's pain, it's all the same, the terrible screaming pain of a child tortured to death, the wink-out pain of every plankton cell frying in the leached ozone, the lament of the long-gone whales.

Why are we like this? You, Yemaya, womb of all life, what have you given birth to, and why? Why, why, why?

"Well, I like to experiment."

The voice was like Johanna's or Maya's or Yemaya's, familiar, the most deeply familiar voice Madrone had ever heard, as if her cells had known it forever.

"And yes, I've always had a tendency to go to extremes," the voice said. "I'm a gambler, for high stakes. And no game is really exciting unless there's a possibility you might lose."

No, don't be the Goddess, don't give me philosophy, be my mother. My own mother.

"But, child, what else could I possibly be? Am I not the mother of all life? Didn't I give you my knife, make you my daughter?"

That was you? I thought it was *La Serpiente*.

"From where does the serpent arise? Who does the midwife serve if not the mother and the new life? What cord can be cut that has not first been spun into being?"

But I just want to be rocked and cradled and held. The sun was red fire lapping the waves.

"But I am rocking you in my great lap. The whole world's waters are your cradle."

I can't survive your love, Mama. It's too strong for me. I'm dissolving, losing my self in you. And I love you but I liked being me. But I can't save myself or anyone. Forgive me for failing you, Mama.

The sun was gone, the sky filled with an orange glow that began to fade.

"But you haven't failed me, child. All you promised to be was my instrument."

My instrument. Like a trumpet or a harp or the bray of a conch shell. Music roared through her. Madrone heard Bird's song and then music from some deeper source his songs only echoed, like the hum of a thousand bees and the royal scent on the air, like the moment just before coming when everything compresses down into a point of incipient pleasure, like the release of wave after wave after wave. . . .

So it wasn't a knife after all, Madrone thought, but another sort of instrument. She felt light, suddenly, a great weight she had been carrying dissolved, she was floating, weightless, and around her head were thousands upon thousands of golden bees, fanning the air with their wings so that it smelled sweet, sweet. . . .

° ° °

"Over there," the Melissa cried out.

"You be spotter, don't take your eyes off it," Isis directed. "Ready about! Cast off. Pull in that sheet. Here we go."

Under the swarm on the water was a human form. The bees were crawling up and down an inert body that floated like driftwood.

"It's alive," the Melissa said. "The sisters are singing distress but not death. Hurry."

Isis maneuvered the boat as close as she dared to the floating figure.

"I can't come in any farther," she said. "You swim?"

The Melissa gave her a shocked look.

"Ever row a boat?"

"Never."

Isis sighed. "All right. Look, you sit here and take the tiller. I'm going to let the sails flap in the wind, and we won't go nowhere. That's right, keep it just like that—if the boat starts moving that way, pull it in the opposite direction. Right. Now, can you call off the sisters? I don't want to get stung to death out there."

The Melissa closed her eyes.

o o o

Madrone felt something change. It was the humming, the humming was gone. She was sorry, she missed it already. Maybe I'm dead, she thought, and cautiously, she opened her eyes. If this was death, it was a lot like life, an expanse of blue water rapidly darkening to indigo in the twilight.

"Hey!"

She thought she heard a sound and tried to answer, but nothing much came out of her lips. Then there was a face near her face.

"You!" Isis said. "What the hell are you doing out here?"

"I'm drowning." Madrone managed a hoarse whisper.

"I can see that. Can you grab hold of this ring?" She pushed a white foam donut into Madrone's hand, which closed over it.

"Can you grip it tight?"

Madrone nodded. Her hand closed on the ring like a claw. Isis disappeared, and soon Madrone felt herself being towed through the water. For a moment, she felt a sense of loss. She had been ocean, Goddess, life itself. Now she was one small piece of life, moving through the water, another alien form.

At the side of the boat, Isis hoisted Madrone on her back, carried her up the ladder, and deposited her on deck. Madrone rolled over, tried to breathe, and expelled a gush of orange-red bloody water.

Like a birth, she thought, as she vomited again.

"We've got to get her warm," Isis said, taking the tiller from the Melissa and making fast the jib sheet. "Take her down below. Get her warm. Let her drink some honey water."

My birth. Born of water, out of the ocean, womb of life. Reborn.

I guess I'm going to live after all.

28

"I want to see him!" Maya stood, gripping the edge of the round kitchen table with her hands, her knuckles white. Sam sat across from her, his dark brows knitted together, his lips folded tight.

"He seemed to indicate that you should keep away. It's too dangerous, Maya. I was stupid to mention your name."

"I don't care, he's my grandson. I get to run some risks in this too!"

"You'll shame him, Maya. You'll put the final seal on his humiliation!"

"Bullshit!"

Sam blew out his breath in a long sigh and said in a more conciliatory tone, "He's got guards with him all the time. If they learn you're his grandmother, you'll be a prime candidate as a hostage."

"I don't care. I'm old, Sam, what do I care if I die? It's long overdue."

"What, I'm not reason enough to live? I thought you enjoyed our little anatomy lessons."

"Don't make jokes right now, Sam."

"Forgive me." He reached across the table and stroked her hand. "That's how I deal with pain."

"*It's* not how *I* deal with pain! I want to do something about it! I want my grandson!"

"Leave him alone, Maya. You can't do anything for him right now."

"Maybe I could help him."

"You can help him by staying away. Maya, you're an old woman, you've fought a lot of battles; can't you just sit this one out?"

"Sit it out! You're as old as I am!"

"I'm fifteen years younger than you!"

"Men age faster! They wear out sooner! Not soon enough, as far as I'm concerned!"

But she stayed away from the Plaza.

○ ○ ○

No one took the ration cards. After the first morning, no one spoke to Bird when he appeared in the Plaza every morning, flanked by his two guards, his shadows. They even looked sort of like him, the same dirt-brown skin, close-cropped wire-wool hair, and black eyes. All the men in this unit looked like that; it was days before he could tell one from another, except for the numbers emblazoned on their gray uniforms. Not that it mattered—they had no names; as far as he could tell they addressed each other by shortened versions of their ID numbers, Threetwo, Sixforty, as they spoke in the lingo that Bird remembered from prison, the staccato dialect of the pens, clipped and abbreviated as if those who spoke it were not entitled to use as many words as other people.

The barracks was a former office in an old government building, with desks removed and rows of pallets lying under windows that would not open. On his first night, Ohnine, the biggest guy in the unit, suddenly rushed at him, fists flailing, letting out a bloodcurdling scream. Bird sighed: he had been through this before; it was prison all over again. He grabbed Ohnine's right arm, twisted, and flipped him over on his back. Ohnine recovered quickly, rolled back onto his feet, and came at Bird with a knife. Bird's foot connected with Ohnine's solar plexus, and in a moment he had knocked the knife out of his hand, where it skittered across the floor.

"Don't even bother," Bird said, as Ohnine started to get up again. "I cut my teeth on tougher guys than you. Don't care if you come from the pens. I come from the street, man. I'm Satan's favorite child. I'm big brother to five thousand devils, and I eat demons for breakfast." He realized, suddenly, that he was enjoying himself. So much for nonviolence, he thought. Given the opportunity, he would like nothing better than to beat the shit out of every man in this place. And if he had a gun, if he could train it on the General's brow and pull the trigger and watch his brains splatter out on the ground. . . .

But he didn't really want to kill these guys. They were kind of pitiful, actually, and now that he'd beaten up their leader, they'd probably be his best friends, in time-honored male tradition.

In an odd way, Bird felt at home with them. He had walked out of the charmed circle of love and friendship and community; they had never been inside it. Their tales of their upbringing were harrowing. They liked to brag about whippings they'd received and beatings they'd endured as children. They'd grown up together. His unit had come from the pens and gone through training as one, providing for each other their only taste of affection and loyalty.

"Don't trust nobody, man, outside your unit," Ohnine told him. After Bird had passed Ohnine's initiation test, Ohnine adopted him, bunked beside him. Bird taught him some simple throws, and in return he told Bird things. "You better be tight with your unit, because that's all you can trust. Your unit can make you or break you. Save your life or take your life. We stand together, and nobody messes with that."

He thought a lot about the discussion in the Plaza. Was Lily right? Were they capable of transformation? Compassion seemed to have been bred out of them or knocked out. They would defend to the death any member of the unit challenged from outside, but among themselves, their greatest pleasure seemed to come from beating or hurting or humiliating one another in large or small ways.

"Hey, you soulless demonfucker, lick my ass!"

"Gonna break your head, fat boy!"

"Suck my dick!"

Nevertheless they were not completely removed from kindness. He sensed in Ohnine a kind of sympathy. On Bird's worst days, when the daily purgatory in the park had worn him out and he lay huddled on his bunk sick with vertigo and self-hatred, Ohnine would come and sit by him.

"Leave me alone," Bird would say, but Ohnine would stay.

"Don't beat yourself up," he told Bird once. "Guards are made through torture, man. We all been through it too. You got to go to that edge in yourself, past that point where you think you got control."

Bird looked up at him, amazed. Just for one moment, they were actually meeting, soul to soul. He was being offered comfort, absolution.

"I broke," Bird said.

"We all break. Sure, man, I know how you think, we all think that way, we think, Hey, I'm the one can beat it, they may break you but they won't break me. But we all break. And once you know that, it give you confidence when it come your turn to break somebody else down. Because you know he gonna do it, no matter what he say or what he think. You can have patience, you can stay calm."

Will that happen to me? Bird thought. Will I turn into a breaker, a torturer?

"Tell you how we do it, man. You got a client—that's what we call the stick we're working on—you got to get him to give you just a little bit. Don't break him on something big, to start, but you pick some little thing, something he can say, Hey, why not do it, why not say it? Ain't worth the pain to hold out. Get him used to giving way, 'cause once he start he gonna give and give and give. Then you make him do the next thing, small thing again, move him along gradual like. Step by step. Till by the end, you got him lickin' your hand like a dog. And that's a damn good feeling, to take a strong man down that road."

Is he warning me? Is that the route laid out for my feet to walk? How far along have I come? Don't I already feel it shifting under my feet? And Bird was falling, down and down again, but not quite in a vacuum now. Something else was there. The unit. Against his will, he was part of something.

The questions that haunted him at night kept him from sleeping well.

When would the General get tired of him and order him killed? How long could he protect Rosa? What worse things than he had already done could they make him do?

Then there were the night sounds from the room down the hall. The men pressed him to join them. "You in the unit, you got to taste the meat," they said, laughing at him when he declined. They could have Rosa in there. Whoever they had in there was someone's daughter, sister, friend—no, he wouldn't go in. But he didn't stop them, didn't throw his body in front of their path as Rosa had for him.

"Fresh meat tonight," Sixforty announced to the room where the men were hanging out. "Got us a city girl lined up to break in. Soon as the rec room opens."

"Give her to Birdie boy first," Ohnine said. "Time he tasted something raw."

"No," Bird said, before he could stop himself. It was dangerous to oppose them too bluntly, too honestly.

"Don't like pussy?" Ohnine taunted him, an ominous undertone in his voice.

"I like women," Bird said in a low, serious voice. Stay calm, don't get defensive. "I love women." And the thought of the woman who lay in the next room, trussed as his victim, made him want to vomit. He couldn't rape a woman. It would be a betrayal of every comforting touch he had ever felt, of every rising and spilling of pleasure, of something so deep in himself that it was still intact below all the levels of loss and betrayal. That surprised him, and made him afraid again. So he still had something to lose.

"One waiting for you in the next room."

What to say to them? "None of the women I love would have anything to do with me, ever again, if I raped another woman."

"Who's gonna tell them?"

"When you love somebody, when you really open to them, you can't keep a secret like that. They would know. It would change me."

"Guess it's a good thing I don't love nobody," Ohnine said. The others laughed. The tension eased slightly.

I should let it go, Bird thought, but maybe, just maybe, there could be an opening here.

"It's a sad thing," Bird said. "To love somebody is really beautiful. To make love to a woman who really wants you, or a man—"

"You do it with men?" Ohnine said.

"Sure, why not?"

There was silence around them.

"That's evil! That's the way demons get into you," Sixforty said.

"Come on, do you really believe that? All you guys here together all the time, don't tell me none of you ever do it to each other?"

The temperature of the room seemed to drop, suddenly. The silence intensified. Uh-oh, Bird thought. Should have kept your mouth shut, boy.

"You calling us faggots?" Ohnine asked.

What do I do now? Bird asked himself. Back down and grovel or bluff it out, barrel on ahead? How many of them can I take? They're all force, no finesse, but still there's fifteen or twenty of them, and one of me. . . .

"No," Bird said. "I'm not calling nobody nothing."

"You a faggot yourself, then?"

Shit. If he apologized and groveled, they would kill him. But that part of him that was broken cried out to do just that, to fall on the floor and whimper, anything, to avoid pain.

"We don't allow faggots in this unit. Got to be a real man to hang with this unit," Ohnine said, and the others chorused their agreement.

"Let's find out," Bird said wearily. "Let's find out how many of you real men I can take out before you kill me, twenty on one. That's real manly." But his heart wasn't in it, and they sensed it, like wild dogs sensing weakness in their prey.

But Ohnine doesn't really want to kill me, Bird thought. He's probably under orders not to kill me. No, more than that, he kind of likes me. What'll he do?

"I got a better idea," Ohnine said. "Take him to the rec room. You a man, prove it there."

Shit, Bird thought, as the men noisily agreed and shoved him down the hall, he thinks he's doing me a favor.

The rec room was a windowless office, refurbished with a low bed with a metal grid for a headboard. A young girl lay there, naked, her arms extended over her head and her wrists clamped to the grid. Not Rosa, Bird saw with relief, and then felt ashamed of himself, because whoever she was, her life was not worth less than Rosa's. Surely not less than his own. He could see blood on her mouth and bruises, and her eyes were both terrified and defiant.

She recognized him. Maybe she'd seen him at Council, maybe she'd been in one of his trainings. He didn't know her but she knew who he was. He could tell, by the way her eyes suddenly softened with relief and then darkened with a deeper terror.

"Take her, man." They were stripping off his shirt and pulling his pants down, revealing his old scars. "Or we take her for you, one by one. You can watch. Then we carve our numbers in her ass and your prick."

The girl was broadcasting terror so strongly that he could hardly focus. I am not going to do this, Bird thought, even if I were willing to, even if I

convinced myself that I could break her more gently than they would, my cock
will never rise for this. But how long will that hold true? If I stay with them
long enough, if I continue this falling and falling and falling, will I fall into
some place in me that finds this very fear erotic? Or will they lead me to it, the
way Ohnine said, gradual like, step by step?

Now the men were grabbing at her legs and she was kicking out viciously,
intelligently, karate kicks that drew blood.

"Watch out, she a live one!"

"My fucking nose, man! She broke my fucking nose!"

"Cut her, you sinlicker! She move again, cut her devil foot off!"

"No, just back off. Let Birdie take her, if he can."

There was, just for a moment, a breathing space. Room to maneuver. Not
much, not long. Now. Use your brain, boy. Think of some way out of this or
die ugly.

The room stank of fear. But fear can be a weapon. He remembered his
martial arts teacher saying that, over and over again. Your opponent's fear is
your leverage.

"Any of you sticks ever raped a Witch before?" Bird asked quietly.

They were silent, suddenly.

"Why you ask?" Ohnine said.

"I didn't think so."

"What you mean?"

"No, I'm not going to take her. I know better."

"What you know?"

"Go ahead, kill me. I'm sure you could do it, all of you together. Course it
might *take* all of you, together. But I'd welcome it, man. I'd prefer it."

Ohnine and the others backed off.

"Don't trust you. What you know?"

"Nothing."

"We your unit, man. You know something, you owe us."

"Don't owe you nothin'. Go ahead, take her. Kill me. I'm happy to die."

"You want to come back and haunt us, don't you, man? You turn our
souls over to the demons."

It was working, Bird thought. They were afraid to kill him. His lie had
made them afraid.

"What you know, man? You tell us what you know. We brothers."

"I know what happens when you rape a Witch."

"What?"

"I'd rather die," Bird said. "Any day."

"Shit."

o   o   o

They dressed the girl and sent her home. Bird never learned her name. It didn't matter. She had escaped; that was victory, he supposed, if not by nonviolence then at least by trickery. He was amazed that he had won. They miscalculated, he thought. If this was part of their plan, to bring me along, to break me down, further and further, step by step, they made a mistake. No wonder. In their world, rape would be a small thing, not worth the pain to resist. More than that—a pleasure, a reward. How could they know that for me it would be the worst thing, the step I will not come to until the last, the bitterest end? But he was still afraid, still falling. He would not escape.

29

Madrone sat shivering in the far bunk, wrapped in every blanket Isis' boat provided. Each breath she took hurt her lungs, but it felt good to breathe, good even to hurt, to feel her heart racing in her chest. Shock and hypothermia, some part of her noted. Her body felt completely drained; every last bit of energy had been spent. But she was alive.

"Drink," the Melissa said, bringing a cup of hot water laced with honey to Madrone's lips. She sipped, savoring the liquid on her tongue, the sweetness.

"She okay?" Isis said, poking her head down from the deck.

"She will be, with rest," the Melissa said.

"Hang on." Isis retreated above, and they heard the sound of the anchor chain being paid out over the bow.

"We're fixed for the night," she said, entering the cabin and closing the hatch behind her. "Now, want to tell us what happened?"

Madrone sipped again. It was hard to believe she was really here, on Isis' boat, not still floating, a cold corpse on a dark night occan.

"We heard about the raid," Isis said.

"Littlejohn's dead," Madrone said. "And they caught Katy."

"Shit."

"Drink," the Melissa said again.

"You escaped?" Isis said.

"The Angels helped me." Slowly, haltingly, Madrone told the story.

"So they saved their own tails when the heat came, and left you," Isis said. "Those slime! You can't trust them. I hate them like poison."

Madrone closed her eyes. She was too weary to hold the lids open.

"I'm due for a run up to see the Monsters tomorrow. Want to come along? Three days up, two days back."

Madrone shook her head. "I need to find Katy. Save Katy. That's too long to wait."

"The shape you're in, you gonna find nobody and nothing but your own grave."

"They think she's at the Research Center," Madrone said, her voice still barely audible. "At the university."

"Might just as well be on the moon."

Madrone shook her head. "Beth will help."

"Who's Beth?"

"A friend. A doctor—used to be. Years ago." Madrone paused, gathered her strength, and then explained. "I'll go stay with her, rest, figure out how to rescue Katy."

She wasn't sure where she got the conviction that she could rescue Katy, but it was growing in her moment by moment. She had been saved for something. Why, when so many others were dead, if not to save somebody else? *I couldn't help Poppy, I couldn't save my own mother from the men who killed her. I have to save Katy.* She had to do it, therefore she could.

"You are one crazy woman. You feel like a little fifteen-mile hike through the canyons right now?"

Madrone shook her head. "Need a ride." She paused, still panting. "Sara might do it."

"Who the hell is Sara?"

"Another friend. Rich white lady, lives in a big house in the canyon. Where I took the swim. She helped before."

"And how do we get to her?"

Madrone sighed and sank back into the blankets. She was too tired to think any further.

"Katy was a good woman," the Melissa said, "but she has gone beyond our help now."

"No," Madrone said. "I promised her."

"Promised her what?" Isis asked.

"Promised I'd be there when her baby comes."

"Circumstances have changed."

"I have to try. I have to!"

"All right," Isis said. "Don't get all in a froth about it. You tell me how to find your friend's house, and I'll take a run out there, see what she's willing to do."

o o o

When Madrone closed her eyes, she dreamed she was back in the water, floating, waiting, lifting out of her body to fly. She wanted to go home. Someone was calling her home. Bird—no, she was the bird, winging north along the sun-baked coast, over the mountains and the last stands of redwood and madrone. And then she was home, but the streams were dry and the gardens withering and Maya sat in the kitchen of Black Dragon House, all alone. "I'm home," Madrone said, but she was invisible, a ghost. Maya's eyes were ancient and full of old grief. Her face changed, shifted, and Madrone was looking into Lily's eyes.

"Everything's gone wrong," Madrone whispered. "Everything I tried to do down here has been destroyed."

"Come home," Lily said.

"I have to try to salvage something."

"Come home."

"Lily, I remembered. I remembered my mother's death."

"Come home."

"But they've defeated you. And I can't bear it."

"You belong here. Come home."

She woke, feverish, to sip more honey water and a bit of acorn broth. But when she slept, again she was back in the water, struggling with the last of her strength against an overwhelming tide.

o　o　o

Isis returned an hour after dawn.

"Sorry it took so long," she said. "Had to wait for her old man to clear out. You ready? She's gone up a few miles to the beach club, she'll be back for you in half an hour. Come on, I'll row you in, if you still want to go. You know your face is plastered on every vidcom from here to the border, along with some pretty bloody pictures of a couple dead bodies. Girl, those Angels screwed you."

"What do you mean?"

"Must have been a security camera in that house. Course they don't care about shit like that, they all look just like each other. But you're unique. And I'm afraid you're a marked woman now."

Madrone was too tired to react, too tired to think. She followed Isis into the boat, forcing herself to stare at the water as they made their way to shore.

"Listen," Isis said as she helped Madrone out of the boat onto the sand. "Your friend has a key to the Yacht Club gate. Six days from now, after dark, I'll wait for you at the end of Pier C. If you need to get away, I'll take you where you want to go."

"I want to go home," Madrone said, without thinking.

"Might be time," Isis said. "Be a lot tougher down here with your stats on vid."

"Why the Yacht Club? Isn't that dangerous?"

"Safest mooring on this stretch of beach. Last place they look for a pirate. Now, can you make it up that path?"

"If I have to."

The path wound up the shoulder of the hill, and Madrone made it, barely, by willing her exhausted body to go on. She waited, hidden by a clump of wild mustard, until a sleek black car pulled up and stopped. Sara opened the door, leaned on the rooftop for a moment as if admiring the view. Using the car to screen her from the roadway, Madrone ran, crouching, and slid into the back seat.

"Head down," Sara said, sliding behind the wheel and starting the engine. They were off.

o o o

They drove in silence, down the coast and then inland on the winding boulevard that ran by the feet of the canyons.

"Thanks for coming to get me," Madrone said after a long while.

"My pleasure," Sara said. "I've often thought about that day we spent together."

"Yes, me too," Madrone said.

"You never came back."

"It was too dangerous. I was afraid for you."

"You went to Beth's."

"Once. That was dangerous too. Twice would be much worse."

"It's okay, you don't have to lie or make excuses. I'm aware that you're not in love with me."

Santa Madre de todos los dioses, Madrone thought, what now?

"If you were," Sara said, "you would have risked anything to come back. As I would, for you," she added softly.

I am too tired for this, Madrone thought. I can barely think, much less answer her. But I have to say something. She was still crouched down in the back seat of the car, and she couldn't see Sara's face.

"I didn't know you felt like that."

"Wasn't it obvious?"

"It was . . . beautiful. Wonderful. But I didn't know you took it so seriously."

"You don't know me well."

"I don't," Madrone admitted. And you don't know me at all, she wanted to add, but she stopped herself. You are in love with your own fantasy. Why did sex get so complicated down here, when it had always been so simple before? How did she end up using people, hurting people? Because she was using Sara now, and she would use her more, if she needed to, to rescue Katy. Maybe that was wrong, but she was gaining a sharp, ruthless edge from using herself too hard. They were rounding a curve and she was suddenly nauseated, her bee senses outraged by the fumes and the speed.

"Did you really murder that little girl, like the vidnews said?" Sara asked abruptly.

"What little girl?"

"The little Angel girl. They showed pictures, in full detail. And the man. The vidnews love that sort of thing."

"No," Madrone said. "She was caught in the raid—they destroyed one of our bases. We went to the house to try to take her back, but we were too late. The man had killed her, and the Angels killed him. I couldn't stop them."

"I didn't think you would kill a little girl. The man I could understand. I could do that myself if only I could work up the nerve."

"Sara, I've never killed anybody. I hope I never have to. I was raised to believe in nonviolence."

"But you help the Web. And they kill people."

Madrone could not answer her. It's true, she thought, and I question it every day, every raid. But can I honestly imagine nonviolence transforming the Stebners of the world? Or the Angels practicing it? And yet we are not winning here with violence either. The car swerved again, and Madrone let out a soft moan.

"Are you okay?" Sara asked.

"Just motion sickness," Madrone said.

"We're almost there."

◦　◦　◦

Sara pulled the car up the drive and into the open garage at Beth's boarding-house.

"Wait here," she said to Madrone. "I'll find Beth."

"I'm not going anywhere," Madrone said. It was a relief to lie still, curled up on the back seat, with no movement to disturb her throbbing head. After a moment, Sara returned.

"Quick," she said.

Madrone slid out the car door and followed Sara. At the back of the garage, a door opened into the back hall, and from there a stairway led down to the basement room she remembered.

Madrone sank gratefully into one of the comfortable shabby couches scattered about the room. She began to cough.

"I've had Gloria put some tea on," Beth said, entering. The lines seemed scrolled a bit more deeply around her eyes, and her forehead furrowed as she felt Madrone's brow with the back of her hand. "You need some nursing and some feeding up. Sara tells me you almost drowned."

Madrone nodded. She was trying not to cough, but it was impossible to soothe her outraged lungs.

"That can have serious aftereffects, you know. Are you developing pneumonia?"

Madrone finally succeeded in taking a long, clear breath. "I don't think so."

"I'll get my stethoscope. You could have fluid in your lungs. The salt draws it in."

Madrone submitted to Beth's ministrations. Sara brought down tea and sandwiches, and they ate. It was nice, Madrone thought, to be fussed over and pampered a bit—by two white women, no less. *Diosa,* she had changed, to think of them that way. Yes, the Southlands had changed her.

She was tired. Too much had happened in the last few days, or maybe it was the fatigue of months settling on her at last. How good it would be to stay here, rest, not think about anything for a while. If it weren't for Katy. . . .

"I need help with something," Madrone said. "That's really what I came here for."

"What?"

"There's a woman, a friend of mine. She got caught in the raid. She's just about nine months pregnant, and we think she might be at the Research Center."

"Poor thing," Sara said.

"I want to get her out. Will you help me?"

"You don't ask for much, do you?" Beth said.

"It's important."

"It's impossible," Beth said. "The place is heavily guarded."

"I'll think of something."

"You'd better think about resting, recovering some strength."

"I can't rest, thinking about Katy in that place."

"You may have to."

Madrone bit down on her lower lip. I don't want to cry, I don't want to tell these women about my mother or Poppy and have them soothe me with their white hands. Goddess, what is wrong with me?

"Don't some of your girls have assignments there?" Sara asked. "Couldn't you at least find out if this girl is there?"

"We could do that," Beth admitted. "Marcia would do that for us. But how do you figure on getting in there and getting her out?"

"I'll think of something," Madrone repeated. "Maybe Marcia can tell me the routine, how they do their procedures. If I could get a uniform, I could go in as a nurse."

"You could never be a nurse. They don't let colored into the training programs."

"Fuck that!"

Beth stared at her in surprise. I'm losing it, Madrone thought. I'm very close to the edge of losing it.

"I'm sorry. I'm just not used to this racial bullshit. But they must let us darkies do something. Who the hell empties the bedpans?"

"Blacks do that," Beth said. "You could be an aide, maybe."

"That's what I'll be," Madrone said, smiling up at Beth. "I'll work something out. I have six days."

"Six days!"

"Before my pirate friend comes back. That's the only way I can figure to get out of here, after."

"You better rest quickly, then," Beth said. "Six days!"

"I'll help you," Sara said, pouring out a cup of tea and setting it on the low table in front of the couch where Madrone lay.

"Thanks, we'll need a driver."

"You'll need a hearse," Beth said.

"You're so encouraging," Sara said.

"Sara, are you out of your mind? You're no revolutionary. What if you get caught? What if your husband finds out?"

"He's already found out—about Angela. He thinks she's Mary Ellen's child, and he's given me a month to get rid of them both."

"Oh, no! How'd he find her?"

"He went down to the basement to look for his old golf clubs, Jesus knows why. It's not the sort of thing he does; usually he just bellows at me or the servants to find whatever it is. He was furious, not just that she was there but that I was lying to him."

"What are you going to do?" Beth asked.

"I want to come with you," Sara said to Madrone. "Mary Ellen and the baby too. When you go, we'll all go with you."

"Sara, this isn't a widescreen," Beth protested. "You have no idea what you're getting into."

"But I know what I'm getting out of. What else can I do? Can I throw my sister's child out into the street, and Mary Ellen, who's taken care of me all my life? And there's no life for Angela here, even if Lance hadn't found her. She may be black, but she's my flesh and blood too. I want to take her somewhere she can have a chance. I want to take her to the North."

"There's a war on in the North," Madrone said, closing her eyes.

"There's a war on here," Sara countered.

∘ ∘ ∘

If she ever got back home, Madrone vowed that she would never again complain about the blandness of General Hospital's architecture. She made her way down corridors so white and blank they could have been constructed for a sensory deprivation experiment. The overhead lighting cast no shadows. Nothing was differentiated; only the changing nameplates on doorways assured her that she was not merely on a treadmill, walking endlessly in the same place.

She was afraid. Dressed in white, clutching a handful of printouts on a clipboard, she tried to convince herself that she looked as if she belonged in these empty halls. Her white aide's cap covered the bee spot on her forehead, but her face, she thought, weathered and sun-dried and exposed on every vidscreen in the county, was too recognizable, too clearly out of place. Her very fear must have an odor that reeked of the streets and the hills. She walked on.

Third level down, Marcia had said. Fourth hallway over, second corridor to the left, five doors down, through the unmarked doorway that required a security access. Well, she would deal with that when she came to it, if she came to it.

Walk on, girl. Yes, Papa, I tried to get somebody to cover my back, but the best I could do was Sara's promise to be our driver. And Marcia's purloining of these whites and this ID card—Goddess grant that no one checks it. Papa, in spite of your blood in my veins, this is not what I was born for.

The stairway, now count, one flight—or, no, each turn and landing must be halfway there, yes, so here's the first doorway, down and down again, and the second level, on down and down—what was that noise? A door opening above. Do I stop? No, continue, that's right, steady, no break in the rhythm of footsteps and *gracias a diosa* those steps are going up, not down, getting fainter. And here is the doorway. Open into the corridor and walk left, step by step. So easy to get confused among these blank white walls. Don't they believe in signs? Or must anyone who ventures down here already know the way?

Down the hall a door opened. Steady, Madrone thought, just keep walking. She thought she heard a moan, but then the sound was cut off and a white-garbed figure hurried her way. She kept her eyes fixed on her destination and passed, not even noting whether the figure was female or male. Her heart was pounding, almost audible, and she slowed it, slowed her breathing, keeping the rhythm of her walk steady.

Through the first wing now, and, yes, here was the first set of double doors. They were secured with an electronic hand plate, and she paused for a moment. The corridor was empty. Think, girl, think back to those long afternoons of practice in the electronics lab. The mind is an electrical field, that was what their instructor had said. The skin carries electrical currents that can be modified by thought. Madrone had never had a real talent for it, not like Zorah, who undoubtedly would have ended as a crystal programmer if she had survived. But I did it, Madrone thought. I learned to make the lights go on and off, and it got to be easy, just a blip in the current the mind can make, like now, like that, and push, and let it go, yes, no alarms going off, just a glitch on any monitoring screen so slight and fleeting that no one would tag it as anything but random interference. She was sweating.

Now this won't do, she told herself. Deep breaths, calm. Cool. Close the pores. Walk on, step by step, another endless corridor. Stop the self-defeating thoughts, let the fear be—what was it Johanna used to say? Let the fear be a dandelion puff and blow it away. There. Wasn't she descended from a long line of warriors? This was nothing. Piece of cake. Keep telling yourself that, girl, and yes, palm on the next doorway and *blip,* and through.

See, it was getting easy. Nothing to it. Now, don't get overconfident, just steady. A doorway banged and white-coated men emerged wheeling a gurney where a shrouded figure moaned. They disappeared down the corridor. Madrone kept walking, only letting a slight tendril of her mind search the patterns of the prone figure. It was not Katy but someone else in torment, and Madrone withdrew with a sense of anguish and guilt. Somebody else I have failed and abandoned, who will be another bloody corpse to my credit someday. But I can't save everybody, she thought. Only if we win, if we have the victory. . . .

And then what? A voice whispered. Will the Angels run the research labs? How gentle will be the hillboys' revenge? She pushed that thought away. I can't afford it now, she thought, and anyway, there is such a thing as justice, isn't there? Besides, so far we don't show any signs of winning. Push that thought away too, and open the third door, and yes, just as Marcia said, a red warning light over the second corridor, deep breath now as she turned, count the doors, one, two, three, four. . . .

The fifth door opened just as she reached it. Without breaking stride, she walked on, steady, don't vary the pace, reabsorb that sweat before it shows. She heard voices behind her, and footsteps that followed hers. Walk on.

"We introduced X247 thirty-six hours ago and got a satisfactory fever developing, but so far that's all. I can't say we're getting cooperation from the subject, but then we never do with the ones caught wild."

"Yes, I prefer the bred strains myself, there's much more consistency in the data."

"But there's value in observations on diverse populations, and then the deterrent effect presumably counts for something."

"I don't know, that's a security matter. Anyway, she's about due to pop, and then we'll see some action."

"I was looking forward to some off-duty time tonight."

"Tough luck. I say we check her again in an hour. We want to observe every stage of progress."

The end of the corridor was approaching, barred with another door. *Diosa,* if you love me, get me out of here. Let me stay in the Good Reality, keep *El Mundo Malo* far away. There was another door on her right, and she turned aside, placing her palm on the lock and opening it, while praying fervently that no one would be there on the other side. She slipped in, letting the doctors pass by. The room was empty. Praise the earth!

I've made good time so far, Madrone assured herself. I haven't been stopped or caught or questioned. I'm almost there. I can afford to stop for five minutes, catch my breath, calm down. They said an hour. Maybe my *suerte* is running good today; five minutes earlier and I would have walked in on them. But there might be others. I just need to think for a moment. What am I prepared to do?

She was in a small room filled with shelves, binders, stacks of printouts, and humming computers. Some sort of record storage, she thought, and glanced down at the latest stack of printouts. At first they seemed to be simply strings of incomprehensible numbers and symbols and patterns, but as she looked harder, she began to recognize what they were—genetic patterns.

Santa Madre Tierra! she thought, could this be . . . ? She flipped through the printouts, looking at the titles. It could. It was. A worm of revulsion wriggled down her spine. These were the experimental records, the genotypes of viruses and retroviruses and bacteria and spirochetes.

She had come to the Southlands looking for the boosters, hoping for clues to the epidemics. And here it was, a treasure trove of information, more than she could handle or absorb or carry off.

What could she do? If only she had more time! She wasn't sure what system they were using and she didn't dare touch the computers—who knew what hidden security alarms she might trigger? The printouts were heavy and bulky, and how many could she carry away? The data slugs? Yes, she could take them, but if the theft was discovered before she found Katy . . . ?

What was more important, Katy's life or this information? Maybe she should just destroy it—but no, that was bound to be discovered and anyway, they must have backups in other locations. She couldn't stand here forever trying to make up her mind. At any moment, someone might return. Think, girl. Act.

Elegba, you trickster, God of the creative random act of chance, Mercury, God of thieves and communication, help me. Guide my hand to the right information. Protect me!

She grabbed a pocketful of metal slugs from the storage racks, replacing them with blanks she found in a box down below. From the bottom of the stack of printouts, she took half a hand's thickness of papers, affixed it to her clipboard, straightened her cap, and cautiously emerged. The corridor was clear. Counting carefully, she made her way back to the doorway from which the men had emerged. Placing her hand on the lock, she entered.

She was in a long hallway, lined with a grid of cages and barred doors. Each cell was just large enough to hold a prone figure and a small waste disposal unit. The light was blinding. On the front of each cell hung a chart, similar to the one she carried on her clipboard. At the end of the corridor sat an armed guard.

Everything was clean, white, sterile, and yet filled with a stench, not so much physical but atmospheric, of terror and pain and horror. Like her own. Dear Goddess, what was she going to do now?

"Who are you? What do you want?" The guard challenged her, laser gun pointing at her heart.

"Oh, I'm sorry, didn't Doctor inform you?" She attempted a sweet, ingratiating smile but suspected that what she achieved was more in the nature of a grimace. "I'm here to collect the primapara wilding female for transfer to surgical observation."

"That one?" The guard gestured with his chin toward a cell halfway down the row.

"Let me just check the chart and see if the ID number corresponds," she said, putting every ounce of glamour into her voice. Accept. Don't question. This is normal.

"No doctors didn't say nothin' to me about this."

"Are you sure?" she asked, in tones calculated to arouse subconscious resonances of doubt. Breathe. Walk. No sweat, no fear, voice warm with assurance. "Oh, I'm sure they must have told you. Maybe they forgot. Maybe you forgot."

A quick glance at the chart. The facts fit Katy, but she couldn't see well enough inside to identify who lay there. Damn, it was a lock needing a key—no electronics here. Damn and double damn.

"I'm sure they must have told you to unlock the door for me," she said. She had matched his body language and the rhythm of his breathing, she was swaying ever so slightly and pitched her voice with its most hypnotic ring. He reached for the keys, pulled one out of the ring, but in looking down at it the spell was broken.

"Wait a minute, let me see your orders," he said suspiciously.

Oh, shit, this was it. Live or die. "Here they are," she said softly, and as he came closer and bent to look at her clipboard, she raised her arms and slammed the board into the side of his neck with a sudden jerk, in the sensitive spot that brings unconsciousness. He fell. She hoped he wasn't dead, but she didn't have time to find out. She grabbed the key, opened the lock, and entered.

At first she didn't recognize the woman on the bed. Her hair was plastered back against her forehead, she was moaning and writhing, burning hot with fever and, yes, in early labor. But it was Katy. The same dark eyes, the same elegant cheeks now fine-drawn with pain. Her wrists were strapped down to the sides of the bed, and Madrone wondered how she would ever get her out. But looking closer, she realized the bed was actually a movable gurney. Praise the earth, for once this inhuman efficiency would serve some good end. She flung the cell door open and wheeled her out.

There were moans and cries coming from the other cells, but she couldn't stop. Quickly, she propped the guard's limp body back on his chair. He was alive and would be able to identify her when he came to, but if she wasn't long gone by then it wouldn't matter anyway. "I'm sorry," she called, to the souls she was abandoning, to the universe at random, propped her clipboard on the gurney near Katy's head, and wheeled her out.

Praise Hecate, praise Coatlicue, no one was in the corridor. When she thought of the whole long way back, she felt faint. Her heart was pounding now, she was still weak, and Goddess, I can't go on with this, I can't do it. But of course she would. Breathe. The slow, steady walk, step by step, back, and turn, forward to *blip* the door open, stick a foot in, and maneuver the gurney through. Out into the corridor.

Katy was thrashing and moaning. Madrone whispered to her, but she was delirious. This won't work, Madrone thought, we can't possibly get through all this without meeting anyone, and she was bound to attract attention. She pressed her fingers against Katy's neck, in the spot her self-defense teacher had called the oblivion point. Katy sighed and went limp, unconscious.

Johanna, Madrone said silently, if I never thanked you for my widely varied education, I thank you now. She pulled the sheet over Katy's head, and walked on, custodian of a corpse.

They were back to the first corridor when Katy began to come to. Madrone heard her moaning and pulled the sheet back. A writhing corpse would certainly attract attention. Maybe if she could just reduce the fever—right, you ninny, she told herself. You're a healer, so heal. Because how the hell are you going to get her up the stairway, anyway, on this thing? There was an elevator down the hall but Madrone couldn't bring herself to risk being trapped in a small box, with doctors and tecchies and who knows what able to observe them both closely. She pulled the gurney into the stairwell and placed her clammy hand on Katy's brow. Please, Great Mama, don't let anyone come in here just now. Cold, cold water: she visualized flowing streams, ice pools high in the mountains, currents from the melting glaciers, flooding Katy with so much *ch'i* that Madrone felt drained, dizzy. Once again she had almost gone too far. Another stubborn fucking *thing*, this disease, whatever it was, but the fever abated slightly and Katy opened eyes that blinked into lucidity.

"Hush," Madrone whispered. "I'm taking you out of here. Nod if you understand."

Katy nodded, then bit her lip as a cramp rippled over her belly.

"I hate to ask you at a time like this, but do you think you can walk if I help you?"

Katy's lips twisted but she didn't say no, and Madrone unbuckled the restraints that held her arms and legs and helped her off the gurney. She was naked under the sheet, so Madrone wrapped it around her and supported her as she staggered forward.

"Weak," she whispered.

"It's okay. Lean on me."

It was more than leaning, more like half carrying her, Madrone thought, as she maneuvered her up the stairs. *Diosa,* I'm never going to make it, I'm still weak myself from nearly drowning. But there's no choice, is there? Just go, step by step, up and up again, don't think about how many more are to come, and keep breathing. An old song sang itself in her head,

Step by step, we can climb the highest mountain,
Step by step. . . .

There were more words, but she couldn't remember them. No matter, just that phrase, repeating itself endlessly, idiotically, somehow helped her. She was sweating and panting. The blood was pounding in her ears. Pull in *ch'i,* pour it into Katy, keep her alive, keep herself alive, find it somewhere in these sterile halls. Johanna, help. Papa, help. Yemaya, you seem so far away now. Up, and up again. One flight gone and then half of another. Halfway there. Don't think about it, just the next step, or this one, or something else entirely. Rock climbing with Bird when they were teenagers, thinking she would cling forever to the side of that cliff, and somehow finding the strength to go up and up. Breathing. Here was air, there was nothing to stop her breathing. In, out. Up, lift. Another flight, only half a flight more to go now, and maybe she should stop and rest, her head pounding, but at any moment this grace of time could evaporate, and she still had to figure what to do when she reached the top. Five more steps. Four. Three. Two. One. Blessed be.

She tucked Katy into a corner. In the Good Reality, no one will come in here while I'm gone, and in the Next Best Reality, they won't notice her behind this doorway. "Rest a moment," she said. "Stay quiet, okay?"

Katy nodded again. Madrone wiped the sweat off her face, adjusted her cap down low on her forehead, steadied her breathing not to where she felt rested but to where she could control its pace, and went out.

How do I get her out of here? she thought. As a basket of laundry? Where do I find one, and why would I be taking it out-of-doors? In a wheelchair? Where do I get one? Down by the front entrance, somebody's bound to be released eventually and why shouldn't it be now? Yes, there was someone going out, now wait, and watch the procedure, oh, blessed holy mother of everything living—no guards, no forms, just wheeled straight out—and now, if my *suerte* holds, and no energetic types take the stairs instead of the elevators, and no one notices how I've slowed my pace down this corridor so as not to be lurking, and yes, here it comes, back in, now please, Mama, just help me pull this last one off.

"Oh, hey, thanks a heap," she said, smiling and approaching the tech wheeling the empty chair. "Just what I need! Can I take it?" She blinked at him through her lashes, hoping she looked flirtatious and not simply grotesque. He grinned and winked at her.

"All yours, pretty mama."

She winked back, hoping she didn't reek of sweat and fear, and headed back down the hall. There was one more bad moment, when she had to leave the chair to rouse Katy, and guide her out into the corridor, praying that no one was passing to wonder why an obviously sick woman was emerging from the stairwell. But their luck held. Katy collapsed into the chair, and Madrone covered her with a sheet and the hospital blanket from the gurney.

"Try to look happy," Madrone whispered, and wheeled on down the hall at a brisk but steady pace. Their time must be almost up. The trip up the stairwell had seemed to take an eternity, but even in objective time it had to be close to an hour or more since she had hidden from the doctors in the hallway. Had they returned to check on Katy? Oh, Goddess, let them linger over dinner, let them get drunk, let beautiful women seduce them for the night, let them choke on their food and die instantly of simultaneous heart failure. Yes, heart failure would be a poetically apt end. Breathe, now calm, now smile. Here is the entrance, with much coming and going, and with the last bit of *ch'i* you can muster up, wrap yourselves in the glamour that this is all entirely normal and expected, you are just wheeling a newly released patient to a waiting car, false labor, perhaps, nothing out of the ordinary, and, yes, there it was, the outside door, opening and closing, opening as in *El Mundo Bueno* it would open for them, automatically, normally, and yes, yes, with another breath, another step, they were going to make it, three more steps, two, one, pause, let the door open, and now, praise the earth, they were walking through.

As they passed through the doorway, the air was shattered with the shrieking of alarms.

∘ ∘ ∘

Bells clanged, sirens screeched; behind them Madrone heard shouted commands and running feet. She didn't stop to think but gripped the bars of Katy's wheelchair and ran, ignoring the winding ramp and bouncing down the flight of shallow steps. A voice shouted out, and a warning beam of laser fire split the air above her head. She continued on. The drive seemed a million miles away. She could see a black car there, waiting. Was it the right car? By the time they crossed the fifty feet of cement walkway between here and there, they might be crossing to the realm of the ancestors. She was so tired she no longer cared very much, as she willed her feet to keep moving, dodging, running, as she called out silently for help.

Another warning shout came from behind. A shot went wild, blasting the ground five yards beyond them. Another shot, and a bush burst into flame. And then they were surrounded by a swarm of bees. The sisters, Madrone thought, and she was part of the humming, buzzing, circling mass, her whole being filled with the scents of alarm and rage. Katy cried out, and Madrone placed a hand on her shoulder, gathered her last strength to protect her, send a mantle of *rightness* over her, even as part of her felt the swarm urge to kill the wrongness, the sickness, end the disease.

"Not her, not her," Madrone cried to them, but words were not the way to reach them, only smells and energies and images. They could smell the sickness in Katy, and it was stronger than the sense of danger from behind. She cried out again and covered her face with her hands.

"They're stinging me," she cried. "Make them stop!"

Madrone stopped running. Danger here, danger behind, but she needed a moment, no matter what it cost, just to stop, to breathe, to center. She threw herself over Katy, sheltering her with her body, trying to form the image, the scent, of the brood queen, she who must be protected at all cost, and behind them, back at the source of the stinging projectiles, danger, danger! She tried to remember the Melissa's training. Breathe, form the image, smell the scent, and let it well up as a bead of sweat in the center of her forehead. Yes, there was a change now; she heard screams from behind and could vaguely make out, through the cloud of bees around her, forms swinging and swatting and dashing back behind the safety of closed doors. Thank you, sisters. You have bought us a precious moment of time with your deaths.

She grasped the handles of the wheelchair again. A black car with smoked windows awaited them in the circular drive, a horn honked, and Madrone dashed toward it. She couldn't see who drove but a hand emerged that bore Sara's flashing diamond. *Diosa,* let it really be her!

Madrone flung open the back door. Katy tried to enter but her bulk stuck and Madrone pushed her roughly in and flung herself on top. The car careened out of the drive, its door still flying open, Katy crying out in pain. Somehow Madrone managed to get the door shut and to disentangle herself and Katy as Sara drove wildly out past the hospital grounds.

"What happened?" Sara asked.

"The alarms went wild as we went out the door."

"Check her for an ID bracelet, tattoo, anything they might have keyed to trigger an alarm."

"I should have thought of that," Madrone said.

"You can't think of everything."

There was a thin band of plastic around Katy's right arm. Madrone ripped it off with her teeth.

"Could it be thin white plastic?"

"Let's hope. It could be something implanted in her internal organs, to track her if she gets away."

Yes, the bracelet had a hum, when Madrone *felt* it. She should have noticed that. Rolling down the window, she tossed it out, letting it drift off behind them as Sara turned a sharp corner. What else? Breathing, she *felt* throughout Katy's body. But it seemed clear of other devices. Nevertheless, she was still in a serious condition. Labor had intensified, and her fever was rapidly returning. And Madrone herself was exhausted. But they had made it so far. Half a dozen bees were trapped in the car with them, and their sound was a comfort, but Madrone opened the window again and shooed them out. Sweet, sweet, she projected, beads of honey sweat, offerings, thanks. Without you, we would both be bloody rags on a pavement. You have given us back our lives.

30

"If I could just have five minutes of quiet and something to drink," Madrone said. Or sleep, she thought, even half an hour of sleep. *Diosa,* how was she going to carry on, exhausted to the point of dull fury now that the adrenaline wash of fear had left her beached, high and dry?

The cabin of Isis' boat was crammed with too many bodies. Katy was installed on the side bunk, her contractions coming faster now. Angela was crying, Mary Ellen was holding and soothing the child, and Isis was bustling around pulling life jackets out of cabinets and stowing supplies. They were all on edge, waiting for Sara's return.

"Or some food," Madrone went on. "Honey water, acorn grits, I don't care. . . ." If you would just all go away, for a moment, and leave me with no one else's weight to drag.

"Hmph." Mary Ellen snorted. "We can do better than that. Where's that bag of food I brought from Miss Sara's house? Angela baby, you hush now. Sit right here, you gonna be all right. I'll get some food for Miss Madrone."

"Just Madrone," Madrone said through gritted teeth. How could she be angry at the poor woman, but it grated on her, like an insult. "No miss, no mistress, no servants here. We're all equal now. Get used to it." That's right, be rude to the woman. She's trying to help you, and you're acting like a bitch. If only she could sleep for a night, a year, forever, before facing this next task. But Katy's moaning reminded her that she couldn't.

Mary Ellen smiled at her kindly, impervious to offense. "You want some fruit, maybe a little honey on it? Easy to digest. I'll slice you an apple, and I brought some juice for the baby."

"You're an—" Madrone stopped. She had started to say "angel" but the word made her gag. "A goddess."

Angela's cries continued to provide a descant to Katy's moans.

"I'm going up to make sail," Isis said.

"You need help?" Madrone asked.

"No. You rest up. As soon as Sara gets back, we're casting off. Mary

Ellen, there's life jackets in the closet by the head; better put one on the baby. And yourself, too, unless you swim. Madrone's already proved she's a Witch; toss her in the water and she floats like a cork."

"Eat," Mary Ellen said to Madrone. On the counter she had set sliced strawberries, a bowl of honey, toast and butter and cream. Madrone ate, as the teakettle boiled. She dipped a spoon into the honey and licked it, feeling a little energy return. Sara was taking a long time to get back from leaving the car.

"Leave it far away," Isis had told Sara, "so if they find it they won't right away come looking for a boat. Trash it a bit, take the hubcaps and radio, make it look like highflyers lifted it and dumped it later."

But that didn't mean you had to leave it halfway across the city, Madrone addressed the absent Sara. She hoped to Goddess nothing had happened to her.

Angela's crying was really going to drive her crazy. What was wrong with the child?

"Is she sick again?" Madrone asked. Mary Ellen nodded.

There was no end to it. Her strength was barely enough to hold out for Katy's and her own survival; there was the fever to deal with and whatever unknown disease it represented, and the birth itself didn't promise to be an easy one, after the trauma and horror of the past few days. But yes, Angela's cries were those of a child in pain. Did she have enough strength to spare to ease her?

She felt a sudden urge to throw the screaming girl over the side. A splash, and then blessed silence. Too bad, but she was just too loud.

I'm losing my compassion, she thought, and wished suddenly and sharply for Lou and Aviva and Sam and, yes, Sandy, who would have commiserated and said cynical things and then laughed. *Diosa,* she missed them, missed *compañeros* she could count on, who could speak with a wink of the eye and the slight inclination of a head. No one here really understood her, except maybe Katy, who lay there sweating and grunting and possibly going to die.

What am I going to do? I need somebody to heal me.

Angela was squalling louder and louder. All right, Madrone thought, at least I can shut her up. She laid her hands on the girl's head and went into that stillness of thought where her hands grew warm and seemed to cloud over and dissolve into the child's body. Goddess, she was tired. She couldn't think of anything to visualize, couldn't imagine moving any power through her stone-heavy hands. But her hands knew what to do, just resting on the child's head and heart, quieting her. The pain was mostly panic, Madrone decided.

"Sleep," she murmured to the girl. That was what she herself most needed and was unlikely to get. The child's breathing became deep and slow and even.

Madrone scrubbed her hands in the galley sink and then examined Katy. She was only a few centimeters dilated, not even a finger's width.

"Hang in there," Madrone murmured. "We've both got a long night ahead."

She heard voices overhead and the creaking of ropes. Sara must be back, thank the Goddess. Sails flapped, the rudder thumped into its seat. The boat listed to one side, and she felt them glide out of the mooring and get under way.

"You look spent," Mary Ellen said. "Let me do something for you."

"I need about six months of rest," Madrone said.

"Why don't you go lie down? I've seen babies born; I can sit with Katy for a while. Nothing be happening for a long time yet anyway."

"It's not just that. Katy's very sick, maybe dying. What she has is similar to something I have healed before, but I nearly died doing it, when I was stronger and a lot more rested than I am now. I'm afraid, Mary Ellen. How can I sit back and watch her die? But what if I don't have the strength to heal her?"

Mary Ellen sat down and put her arms around Madrone, who nestled into the woman's warm, lush body and began to cry. She felt like a child again, cuddled up to Johanna. Oh, if she could be held and rocked and nursed for a week!

"You're exhausted. You get some rest, and you may see an answer you don't see now."

"I wish I could believe there was one."

"You don't know."

Obediently, Madrone crawled into the forward bunk, in the triangular prow of the ship. I'll just rest for a few moments, she told herself. Body, let one hour of sleep serve for ten. But sleep seemed far away.

She lay watching her breath, trying to practice the relaxation techniques she had taught others so often. Muscle by muscle, limb by limb: tense and relax. Breathe deep. But instead of sleeping she was drifting, back onto a familiar road, the road outside their house in Guadalupe. Beside the door bloomed a bush with bright red flowers, *maravillosa* they used to call it, the marvelous flower. Madrone did not want to enter, but she did not resist. I know what is here now; there is nothing more to fear. But the room smelled sweet as she entered, fragrant with the incense her mother, Rachel, used to burn. As her eyes grew accustomed to the dim light, Madrone saw somebody in the old rocker that used to stand in the corner of the room. The chair moved back and forth, its runners making a rhythmic sound like a heartbeat.

Madrone moved closer. Her mother rose from the chair and held out her hands.

Madrone took a step back. For a moment, she wanted to run, afraid that if she touched those hands they would be cold corpse hands, afraid that if she looked into that face she would still see the wounds of death.

Her mother waited. Madrone took a deep breath and stood her ground.

"You cannot bring me back, you know," her mother said. "To heal is good. To rescue Katy was good too. But no matter how many lives you save or lose, mine is gone. You cannot bring me back."

Tears filled Madrone's eyes. "I know that. I'm not a baby, or a child, Mama. I only wanted your memory back, unstained."

Her mother reached out her hands. "You have that now."

Madrone reached for her. Her mother's hands were warm as she placed her own hands in them, healer's hands in healer's hands. Power flowed between them, fire and water and the sweet smell of honey from marvelous flowers.

"What do you want for yourself?" her mother asked.

"Nothing, Mama. Not for myself."

"Then you cannot heal. A healer must have a powerful desire for life and all that goes with it. Only then can you stand safely at the gates of death."

Suddenly Madrone was alone, back on another road, the ice road, where she had lingered so long in the *ch'i* worlds healing the virus; and, yes, the knife of *La Serpiente* was in her hand, and she was stirring again the patterns of fate like lines of a silver web. But something had changed, as if she were now in a different dimension from those energies, and her knife slid through them without disturbing them. She was too solid; they were like ghosts, insubstantial. She couldn't break loose from her body; bone and blood held her in a living web.

She did want to live. That was the difference; that was how she had changed. In these last months she had fought too hard for life. Never again would she rush open-armed into the embrace of death. She remembered the strength of her grip on the life preserver Isis had thrown her. From now on everything she did would proceed from that grip, whether she succeeded or failed. Someday she would die, but death would have to pry each separate finger loose. She might lose Katy or save her, but she could no longer use her own life as a bargaining chip.

So now what do I do? How do I heal? Must I let Katy die? Madrone wasn't sure whom she was asking, but suddenly her mother's face appeared to her inner sight. Or maybe it wasn't Rachel, maybe it was *La Serpiente, La Vieja,* the Old One, using Rachel's face as a mask, speaking in her familiar voice.

"In this situation, it's not enough to be a healer. You need to be a Witch."

Rachel was speaking in Spanish, and the word she used was *bruja,* sorceress.

"What do you mean?"

"You cannot cure this disease. So shift the reality the disease exists in."

"Just how do I do that? *Dígame, por favor.*"

"You've already begun. Attach your will to your own existence. Then you begin to gather your true power."

"Please, Mama, no philosophy; just tell me what to do."

"Create the Good Reality in your mind, clasp it with the same tenacity with which you hold to life, and leap into it."

"Oh, sure, that's perfectly clear."

But Rachel was gone and Madrone was wide awake suddenly, listening to the scraping of the anchor chain over the bow. They must be taking shelter for the night in one of Isis's secret coves. Madrone hoped they would be safely hidden.

She considered her mother's words. In *El Mundo Bueno,* what Katy had was not the old bad virus that had nearly killed Madrone herself, but—what? Some new experimental strain, not yet perfected. Still vulnerable, brittle, Madrone thought. Of course they would infect Katy with something new, not one they'd used already. Why hadn't she seen that? And yet in her mind she was still partly in the ice-crystal world of trance, and she was floating in cold, cold water, losing heat, losing life rapidly—no, she wouldn't accept this. The Good Reality was like the ice crust somewhere above her head, and she reached up with her knife, midwife's knife that cuts the cord, pierced a hole through the crystalline surface and hoisted herself up. Oh, Mama, let me now be in *El Mundo Bueno.* Let me be where Katy and I both can live, where what she has is curable. And as she shook her head and forced her body to sit straight up, she began to believe herself. How did she know what was causing Katy's fever? She'd let her own fear and despair trap her in an assumption she had never tested. Why, she hadn't even *looked* for this one yet. Why shouldn't it prove to be more susceptible than the last epidemic? And hadn't she gathered power in all these months? She had her bee mind to work with and something more. Her mother was right. From her own fierce hold on life came a solid strength she could draw on.

She rolled over and felt something sharp protrude into her hip. Reaching down into her pocket, she pulled out the handful of data slugs she had stolen from the lab. She had forgotten them, not that she could do anything with them here. At home maybe the tecchies could figure out how to read them. But the printouts? She had tossed the clipboard into the car, but had she remembered, in her exhaustion, to bring it on board the ship?

Laboriously she raised herself up and crawled out of the bunk. The rest had done her good but she was still tired. Her head felt heavy and her lungs still hurt.

"What you want?" Mary Ellen asked. She was seated on the edge of

Katy's bunk, holding her hand. "This child ain't coming for hours yet. I thought you were going to get some sleep."

"There was a clipboard with some papers on it. Did I bring it from the car?"

"Miss Sara found it when she left the car. It's over there on that shelf."

Madrone grabbed it and settled on the side bunk, next to the sleeping Angela, to look at it. But the long strings of numbers and figures were incomprehensible. They might be genetic records. These letters might represent strings of amino acids, and if she had days or weeks to devote to cryptography, and if she could remember those long-ago courses in genetic mapping, never a favorite subject . . . Better leave this for somebody else, if they ever made it back home.

Katy moaned. Mary Ellen was bathing her face and arms with a cool cloth, but she sighed.

"She's feverish. And it's rising."

"I'll look at her," Madrone said. She moved over to sit hunched at Katy's side, facing Mary Ellen. What reality am I holding to? she wondered, and for a moment felt a cold stone of fear in the bottom of her gut.

Mama, I doubt your premise. If will can make the world as we want it to be, why is the world as it is?

"Will can't always change the world," Rachel whispered in her mind, "but it can sure as hell try. Remember the strength of your grip on life."

Isis and Sara came down into the cabin. They were wind-blown, spray-drenched. Isis' muscles danced under her skin. The galley was a stage for her deft, sure, catlike movements. Sara's face glowed with spots of red, two warm suns in a pearly misted sky. Her corn-silk hair lay in ragged strands over her shoulders. She had lost her polish and sheen but not her beauty; it was just a little rougher, raw silk.

"Okay, Mama, I won't complain," Madrone whispered back to the voice in her mind. "Maybe we're skating on the edge of *El Mundo Malo,* maybe I'm exhausted, Katy nearly dying, Angela squalling, six of us jammed in this tiny space, days of undigested trauma behind me, but at least two of us are among the most ornamental women I've ever seen."

"Use them," Rachel told her.

"What do you mean?"

"Think about it."

But she had already thought about it; at least she had thought about how to back up her own flagging energies.

"Mary Ellen, you stay with Angie. Isis, Sara, I need your help."

"What do you want us to do?" Sara asked.

"Just stand and touch me—that's good, your hands on my back," Madrone said. "Yes, like that, behind my heart. Now breathe deeply together and imagine a flow, of water, maybe, or fire, or light, whatever image you like. A flow coming up from the earth and through your bodies and into me. Try to keep the picture in your minds—probably you'll lose your concentration from time to time, but that's okay, just pick it up again and keep breathing deep. All I need from you is raw energy."

They were locked together in silence, the three of them. Madrone's hands hovered over Katy's belly as she tried to fill herself with the energy of the other two. A wavering force filled her, not the steady flame of focused concentration she could have drawn on from Sandy or Aviva or Lou, but a flicker like a candle flame in a gusty wind. They weren't concentrating; they didn't know how. Madrone sighed. Okay, she would do the best she could.

Then suddenly the energy shifted. Between Isis and Sara, the air became viscous; subliminal thunder rumbled. Madrone could feel the tension shift to attraction. Slowly their hands migrated across her back until their fingers touched; an electric current poured through her.

"Use them," Rachel whispered again.

Madrone's tongue flicked on Katy's forehead, tasted her sweat. Her hands searched, they felt out the core of *wrongness* in Katy, pulled it forth for her inner eyes to see. Yes, there was something she recognized, a cousin of the earlier plague. The pulsing power behind her was like the swell of the ocean. She could ride on it—out, to rip loose connections, dissolve a link here, a protein there—and then in, to create something new, another bonding, so that the thing changed form and shape and function, melted and re-formed, until it became a harmless chunk of protein, just formed enough to mate with its own kind, transforming and undoing them. It was done.

"Honey," Madrone whispered, and Mary Ellen brought her a dishful. She let a drop of her sweat fall into the bowl, to charge the amber liquid with the energies of this change. They could feed it to Katy in small doses throughout the night. Maybe it wasn't necessary; the change felt complete. But it couldn't hurt.

Madrone shook out her hands and turned the power coming through her to a cool stream of water washing through Katy's body, easing the fever, cleansing, soothing, cooling. Her hands smoothed Katy's aura, and the power flowing through her was golden light. Katy was sleeping now, her breathing rhythmic and relaxed. Madrone felt drained, so tired she could hardly hold her head up.

"Take in something for yourself," Rachel whispered. Madrone nodded, breathing in the gold and the fire and the light.

"Thanks, Isis, Sara. Shake out your hands now, and you can relax. We've done good work here."

They pulled away, but as they faced each other Madrone could still sense the charge between them. *Maybe this will distract Sara from her infatuation with me, let me get some sleep. But, Diosa, when have I last felt that? Maybe when Bird came back. With Sandy it was just sweetness and steadiness, not this hovering electric tension. At any moment, lightning would zigzag through the narrow cabin, the downpour would begin.*

"We done?" Isis asked. "Now can we throw the rich white bitch overboard?"

Madrone heard Mary Ellen's indrawn breath. But Sara only smiled. It was an amazing smile, slow, knowing, inviting, confident.

"Just joking," Isis said. Slowly, with the slightest of winks, she returned Sara's smile.

It makes perfect sense, Madrone thought. *The black fringed iris, the white cupped lily, grown from the same soil, familiar with the parameters of the same beds. And me, I'm a little wild weed, not meant for this garden at all.* She was too tired to feel jealous, too tired to feel much of anything at all.

"Madrone, child, you go catch some sleep," Mary Ellen said.

"I can lie down right here on the floor and stay near Katy."

"No, you cannot. You go take the cabin, get some real rest. I'll stay with her and call you when you're needed. You two"—she pointed her chin at Isis and Sara—"it's a warm night. You can sleep up top."

o o o

Several hours later Mary Ellen roused Madrone. "It's time," she said. "Her water's broke. I cleaned up the bed, but I think you better come now."

Through the galley porthole, Madrone could see the waning crescent of the moon rising. She still felt tired, but some residue of energy had returned that she could draw on.

Katy's flesh was still cool, and Madrone breathed thanks to the Goddess. Waves of contractions rippled over her body. Her open eyes were lucid but filled with fear.

"Katy, it's okay. You're safe. You're safe, here."

"Madrone?"

"I'm here. I won't leave you."

Katy reached up her arms like a child reaching for comfort and buried her face in Madrone's shoulders.

"It's all right," Madrone murmured, patting and soothing her. "It's really all right now."

"I feel so shaky. Everything's rocking."

"We're on a boat, *querida.* We're sailing away, sailing home."

"Really?"

"Really."

Katy smiled, then grimaced as another contraction caught her.

"They're hurting me," she said. "They've done something to me. It still hurts, Madrone. It hurts bad."

"No, Katy, they're not hurting you now. You're having a baby, that's all. I know it feels like pain, but it's not a pain to fear."

"I can't help it, Madrone. I'm afraid. They've made me afraid."

"I know. But I'm here, and I've caught hundreds of babies, and I'm not afraid for you." And that, of course, is only partly true, because dear Goddess, here we are, with no midwife's bag, no herbs, no drugs, no clamps, no syringes, no backup, no help if anything goes wrong.

The night wore on. Katy labored but she wasn't making much progress, and Madrone sat, pushing down worry. Mary Ellen hovered, bathing Katy's face with soft cloths and giving her sips of water and teaspoonfuls of Madrone's honey. They had put Angela to sleep in the forward bunk. Sara and Isis were still asleep on deck.

"It won't come," Katy said. "Madrone, I want to stop. Please make it stop."

"I can't do that, *niña*. This is birth, it takes its own time. Here, hold my hand. Would you like a sip of water?"

"I just want it to be over."

"Just let go. Open."

"I can't. I'm afraid."

"I know, you've been in hell together, you and the kid. You don't want to let her out to face this world apart from you. But it's time. You can't keep her safe inside you any longer."

"I can't do it. I'm not strong enough, Madrone."

"Trust your body, Katy. Your woman's body has given birth for millions of years. It knows what to do."

"I don't. I don't know what to do. Oh, Madrone, I'm so glad you're here!"

"Me too."

"All that other stuff—it seems so far away now. It doesn't matter."

"Hush, don't even think about it. Just think about opening, like a flower opening to the sun."

"They killed our flowers. Madrone, they killed Littlejohn and—"

"No, *querida,* don't think about that now. I know what happened. There'll be time to talk about that tomorrow. Right now you need to imagine beautiful things, hopeful things. Think about light, the sun rising out of the earth. You know, in Spanish, Katy, there are two ways to say 'give birth.' There's *estar de parto,* which means to separate, to part, and *dar a luz,* which is to give to light. And that's what you've got to do: let go. Give your child to the light and give the light to her. Even in English, birth is something you give."

Katy let out a new cry, and Madrone checked her cervix once more. Praise the earth, she was open at last.

"Push, honey. Do you feel that urge to push? Mary Ellen, wake Sara and Isis, it won't be long now. And then support her back, will you? Go with it, Katy. Feel the contraction coming, take a deep breath, hold it, and push."

Madrone sang to her while the others gathered.

"Siente tu poder,
El poder de la mujer.
La madre primera,
Es la madre tierra."

"That means 'Feel your power, the power of the woman. The first mother is mother earth.' "

Katy sat up, leaning back on Mary Ellen's strong arms, dug her heels into the bunk, and began to push. Her fear was gone. On her face was a look of tremendous concentration; her skin glistened with sweat. Sara had come sleepily down the ladder from the deck, and Katy gripped her white arm so hard the veins stood out. Isis stood behind them, watching.

"Good work, Katy," Madrone said. "Isis, Sara—take her feet so she can get more leverage. Now, Katy, again—push!"

"I know," Katy said. "Don't tell me what to do."

"No, *querida,* I don't need to tell you. The wisdom is in your cells, in your womb, and they are here with us tonight, the mothers, all the mothers, every woman who has ever given birth, your mother, my mother too. Lean on them, let them support you, they will hold your back."

An hour passed, then another hour, almost unnoticed as they focused on Katy. At last, when Madrone checked Katy's vagina, she could feel the baby's head pushing against the lips.

"Good work!" Madrone said again, smiling up at Katy as she massaged and stretched her perineum. "I wish we had a mirror, so you could see your child's black curly hair. Bring us the head now."

Katy grunted, held her breath, and pushed hard as Mary Ellen wiped the sweat from her face. In a smooth motion, the baby's head emerged. A new person was coming forth into light, Madrone thought, who could at this moment be anyone or anything. Out of one being comes another, out of All Possibilities, one. Oh, most sacred mystery! Blessed be the Creative One, Mother of Surprises, fecund, more tenacious even than death.

But in the next contraction, the baby's head pulled back and its chin jammed against the perineum, its lips clenched and beginning to darken.

"Hands and knees," Madrone cried automatically. "Mary Ellen, help her flip. Support her, Isis."

"What's wrong?" Sara asked anxiously.

"Shoulder dystocia. There, get her over. Don't you worry, Katy, just relax."

"What in Jesus is that?" Isis asked.

"Stuck shoulders. I need to get in there and turn them."

She slid one hand up into the vagina, slipped two fingers of the other hand behind the baby's head. It called for a turning motion, like unscrewing a bolt; she had done it fifty times but never without tension. There was so much that could go wrong. If she dislocated the child's shoulder or broke its arm, or if this proved the one impossible to move. . . .

Stop those thoughts. Feel the timing, the contractions. Now.

"Push, Katy, push." She could feel the muscles bear down, as she pushed and pulled and twisted in that tight, narrow space, until suddenly everything gave way and the child slid free.

Her hands caught it, her eyes noted that it was a girl, and she placed the baby on Katy's belly. There was no suction bulb to clear its nostrils and throat, but the child opened her tiny mouth and began to breathe and cry.

Katy placed her hands on the child's back, stroking its skin wonderingly.

"It's so slimy," Isis whispered in alarm.

Madrone laughed. "That's the vernix that covers the skin in the womb to keep it healthy. In a moment we'll rub it in. Or rub some on your skin—there's nothing better for it."

But Isis' comments reminded her that a child should enter the world to blessings and praise. As she tied the string she had prepared around the umbilical cord, which still extended into Katy's vagina, she motioned to the others to gather around.

"We need to welcome her and give her blessings. Are your hands clean? Then one by one, stroke her gently, rub some of the vernix into her skin, and make a wish for her, something that comes from your own life. Then you will always have a link with her."

Madrone went first, rubbing a spiral pattern on the wet silk skin. "I wish that you may always find the healing you need."

"I wish that you will always have enough to eat and drink and share with others," Mary Ellen said.

"I wish that you will find true love," Sara said.

"I wish that you will escape every trap they set for you," Isis said.

Katy reached down and stroked the baby's arms and legs. "I wish you the strength to survive."

"Who will cut the cord and break the last link between the child and the womb?" Madrone asked.

"You do it," they all said, so she did, using the knife Mary Ellen had sterilized earlier.

"Be free, be strong, be yourself, be lucky, be proud to be a woman, be loved and loving; live among flowers, surrounded by free flowing waters; live in the sun's warmth, breathing clear air, nourished by moonlight and starlight; know that you are welcome, that you are a precious gift to us; be blessed," Madrone said.

The child cried and Katy lifted her to her breast to suck. With a last moan, she expelled the placenta, and Mary Ellen caught it in a basin while Madrone kneaded Katy's womb to help it contract. There was blood all over the bunk, but praise the Goddess she had hardly torn at all, and there was no hemorrhage.

"I'll clean up," Mary Ellen said. "You rest yourself, Madrone."

Madrone sat down at last. Her body was trembling; she was as exhausted as if she herself had given birth. Which she had, in a way. For she had rescued Katy from the lab, and if she hadn't, this child would already be dead, a specimen useful for data and products that didn't bear thinking of. Oh, she had saved this tiny life five times already, and *qué milagro* that it lived and breathed, that Katy's own hands could comfort and stroke it and hold it to her breast.

There were still dangers, still a hundred ways *El Mundo Malo* could reach up and grab them and suck them down. But now, just for now, she could savor her triumph. Something had turned. A new child had come to the world of light and dark, and I am still alive, Madrone thought, and the sun is rising over the swelling waves, and today, yes today, we are turning our faces toward home.

31

Maya's head ached. The meeting room was a dark basement garage, with people crowded and crammed into the space. It stank of sweat and fear, overlaid with a tinge of sage. The Voices in their masks were jammed together with everybody else. The discussion was heated, with nasty undertones, and in Maya's opinion had already gone on far too long.

"Bird has gone over to the enemy."

Cress from the Water Council addressed the room. His eyes were red and there was a three-day growth of beard over his narrow chin. He looks stretched too tight, Maya thought, like all of us. Still, I cannot help but dislike him.

"Don't say that!" protested Sachiko from the Musicians' Guild. "We don't know what they did to him."

"As far as that goes, we don't know that they did anything to him at all," Cress said. "No, don't shout me down! I have a right to raise this question. He disappears into the South for almost ten years, comes back a few months before the invading armies, just in time to talk us out of building any weapons or planning armed resistance. Now he's handing out their water ration cards. It's suspicious, that's all I'm saying."

Maya half rose to speak, but Sam laid a restraining arm on her. "You can't defend him," he whispered. "You're his grandmother."

For a moment Maya thought nobody else would speak. Then the big man sitting beside Sachiko rose. Maya recognized one of Bird's old friends, another guitarist. What was his name? Walker?

"I've known Bird many years," Walker said. "I can believe he might give way under torture. Any of us might. But I'll never believe he's a traitor. Even if he were, nobody should be tried in absentia by rumors and innuendo. Suspicions like yours, Cress, do more harm than ten collaborators. Especially if they keep us from supporting one of our own, who's been through Goddess only knows what."

"I'm not condemning him," Cress said. "Personally, I'm willing to believe he just overestimated his capacity to resist. But don't you all see, that proves my point. He's an example that when it comes down to the ultimate test, we can't withstand their force."

"Maybe he's still resisting, in his own way," Walker suggested.

"How? Running their rationing program?"

"Nobody's taken any of their cards yet," Walker said. "Why? Because almost every house in this city has a cistern, which is still pretty full from the winter rains. If Bird's a traitor, why hasn't he told them about the cisterns? Why haven't they done anything about them?"

An older woman wearing the handspun garments of the Silk Guild rose. "My daughter was captured by the soldiers. She is still too shocked and hurt to tell her story here in public, but I will tell it for her. They were going to rape her, a whole gang of them. She fought them but they tied her down to the bed. Then Bird came in." She paused. In the hush, Maya squeezed Sam's hand so hard that his fingers turned from red to white. "Somehow he talked them out of it," the woman went on. "He made them let her go. He is no traitor."

Maya let out a long sigh, and Sam patted her hand as she released his.

"That's not the question at hand here," Cress objected. "It's not Bird who's on trial, it's our whole strategy. We've been too naïve. What is it going to take to make us admit that noncooperation isn't working?"

"We expected casualties," Lily said. She was dressed in a simple gray shift, and she too looked tired and drawn. "We knew there would be suffering."

"Maybe it's time we inflicted some," Cress said.

In the silence that followed, Maya could feel the tensions in the room polarize. Yes, there were many who agreed with Cress, and there would be many more as the days wore on.

"Defense does not agree," Lily said.

"That goes without saying, but what do you suggest? We can't just go on lying down and eating their laser burns. We can't let them turn us all into Birds, one by one."

"I'm not proposing that we do." Lily's voice was calm. How does she do it? Maya thought. Does she practice in the mirror, or does it come from so many years of sitting meditation?

"Then propose something else," Cress challenged her. "The Forest people have held the railway right-of-way. The South Bay groups have blown the tracks and cut their supply lines."

"Is that true?" Salal, who was Crow of the meeting for the day, broke in. "Can anyone verify that piece of news?"

"It's true," said Lily. "Defense scouts brought us back the message two days ago."

"What have we done?" Cress continued on. "Besides serve as their victims?"

"Some of us, acting without consensus, have blown their dams." Lou from the Healers' Council stood and faced Cress. "Without that, perhaps there might not have been so many casualties."

"Without that," Cress countered, "we might already have used up the reserves in our cisterns."

"We're getting away from process," Salal said. She too looked weary and seemed to lack her usual sharp grasp on the meeting. Even her red hair had faded to a dull brown, its roots grown out. "If you want me to facilitate, you've got to wait and let me call on you. Does anybody have a proposal?"

"Defense does," Lily said.

"What is it?"

"Marie, before she died, told the army that there was a power in this city they would never be able to conquer. Apparently to them that meant we have some sort of secret weapon. So they tortured Bird until he told them what it was."

Maya grimaced. How can she say that so casually, so matter-of-factly? If it were *her* grandson . . .

"What did he tell them?" Salal asked.

"Why doesn't he tell *us* what it is?" someone muttered at the back of the room.

"Process, please!" Salal said sharply.

Lily went on. "He told them our weapon was the dead. That if they killed any one of us, they would be haunted. Our proposal is that we make his words come true."

"What do you mean?"

In the pause before Lily spoke, Maya thought she heard the beat of a drum.

"Defense proposes that we haunt the killers."

"Has Defense been recruiting among the dead?" Cress asked. "Are you suggesting we hold séances?"

Several people around the room snickered. Lily continued, unperturbed. "I'm not proposing that we raise the dead. I'm suggesting that we try to face the killers with the consequences of their actions, make their victims real to them. That we follow them, tell them stories about the ones they have shot down, never leaving them alone but continuing to offer them a place at our table."

"You're insane," Cress said.

"Won't more people get killed?" Sachiko asked.

"Yes," Lily said. "More people will die, in any case. But Cress is right about one thing—it is time now for us to become more active, more con-frontational."

"It might play on their fears," Salal said thoughtfully. "If they believe what Bird told them, it might unnerve them enough to destroy their morale."

"That may happen," Lily conceded, "but it is not our primary objective. We must continue to reach for their humanity, to believe that within the worst of the murderers lies some spark of the fifth sacred thing. If we can reach that, we will find victory even in death."

"You're completely insane," Cress said again. But after lengthy discussion, the Council adopted Lily's proposal. Cress and his faction stood aside.

o o o

The woman dressed in white approached the soldier stationed in the Central Plaza. Yes, he was the one. She would never forget him, the cold look on his face as his hand raised the gun to her brother's head. She approached him and looked him in the eye.

"My brother Jorge, that you killed yesterday, was a woodworker," the woman said. "When I was little he made me the most beautiful toys."

"Get out of my airspace," the soldier said.

"He made me a toy dog that rolled on wheels; you could pull it with a string, and her head bobbed up and down. He got in trouble, though, because when *Tía* Anna asked him, 'What are you making?' he looked her right in the eye and said, 'This is a bitch on wheels.' "

The woman's eyes held tears, and the soldier shuffled his feet uncomfortably. "I said get away from me!"

"Jorge could never resist a joke. I feel so sad that I will never hear his laugh again."

The soldier glanced behind him. "Look, lady, I didn't want to kill your brother, okay? Sorry I had to do it. Didn't have no choice about it."

"But you did choose; it was your hand on the gun. You ended his life without ever knowing him or seeing his smile."

"Him or me, lady. I don't shoot, next stick down the line shoot me."

"How do you know that? Is not that man, too, making his own choice? Maybe he too will choose to lay down his gun."

"He won't."

"We can never escape from choice. Every act we take or don't take. Every time we open our mouths or close our eyes."

"Fuck you! Get the Jesus away from me! I never had no choice, okay? Never had no brothers or no sisters! Nobody made no toys for me. I was bred for the army; I do what the army tell me."

"That is a terrible thing to do to a child. You have suffered. You are suffering now, in a new way. Because now you do have a choice to make. And I can see in your eyes that you understand this. It is the terrible gift you have come here to receive, and you will never be free of it again."

° ° °

The soldier patrolling the dam was a dark khaki-colored spot surrounded by moving figures in white. At first he pushed ruthlessly through the crowd, swinging his bayonet, but they followed him across the plaza.

"My son was a gardener," Mrs. Hernandez said, holding out a basket of ripe tomatoes. "Take, eat the fruit of the man you killed."

"Out of my way, lady." He shoved her aside and turned, to encounter a small girl.

"My *abuelo* told good stories," she said. "This is the story he told me about the woman in the mountain. . . ."

He turned abruptly away from her, only to encounter a tall man, who smiled and said, "My cousin liked baseball. Do you play sports? No one could touch him when it came to bat, even as old as he was—"

"I said get the fuck away from me!"

"Do you know how I felt, to see my son shot down, that bullet enter his head, that dear face I had washed so many times and watched as it grew and changed—"

"Shut up, lady!"

"Taste, taste these fruits so you will know what you destroyed!"

"Look, I was ordered to do it."

"Choice is always possible. You chose to obey. And now we are here to teach you the meaning of your choice."

"Clear the way!"

"Even now, there is choice. There is still a place set for you at our table, if you will join us."

"I said clear the fucking way!" He swung his rifle butt wildly, and it smashed the child in the head. She began to cry, and someone picked her up and soothed her, while a woman stepped forward.

"My daughter, who you have just injured, is six years old. She likes to sing. From the time she was an infant, she moved to music. From the time she could stand, she tried to dance."

"I'm warning you, get out of here or I'll kill a few more of you."

"Then others will come in our place, to show you the consequences of that choice. But still, let me tell you more about my brother—"

He turned and fled.

° ° °

Whether it was the superstition of the soldiers or whether the stubborn dead of the city continued to fight on in their own way, tales of other hauntings multiplied. Lan was seen wandering through the barracks, looking for his executioner. Phantom children were heard crying in the square. Lights were seen at night crossing the broken bridges, moving over the gaps where spans had fallen. The soldiers began to whisper among themselves that what Bird had said was true. To kill a Witch meant to be forever haunted.

One by one, a slow trickle of deserters began to take refuge in the City's houses.

o   o   o

"What's his T-cell count?" Sam asked.

"Nothing wrong with the count," Aviva said. "It's the activity level that seems to be compromised. Cytokine production's way down."

They were meeting in the kitchen of Black Dragon House, which Sam had turned into a makeshift hospital. The first few deserters had been sent out of the City, up to the Delta where the Stewards' army had not yet penetrated. But now that they were receiving a steady influx of soldiers, transportation had become a major problem. With the bridges down and no boats kept on the west side of the Bay, sneaking a soldier upriver required a major clandestine operation.

"Hmm," Sam said. "That confirms what we suspected about how the boosters work."

"By stimulating cell activity, rather than inducing replication," Lou said.

"Damn, I wish we had access to our own labs," Sam said.

"If we did, your friendly biochemists of the Toxics Council would brew you up something to compensate," Nita said. She had returned the previous night to try to replenish supplies of certain chemicals they needed in the lab they had established upriver. Her wild hair was pulled back into braids, and it left her thin face exposed, vulnerable. "As it is, I don't know how I'm going to get what we need. I guess the other approach would be to keep them in strict isolation until their immune systems recover and start to function normally."

"If they recover," Aviva said. She'd been chewing her lips, and they were red and chapped. "What if they don't?"

"The body is resilient," Lou said. "Already I've seen some improvement with acupuncture. The herbs help too. The problem is what they contract in the meantime. And we don't have any facilities to keep growing numbers of men in sterile isolation. It's hard enough to keep them hidden from the Patrols."

"We're starting to see flu, fungus, and thrush, and Goddess knows what all they're incubating," Aviva said.

Sam closed his eyes for a moment. His head felt too heavy, as if lead weights pulled at his jowls. "You know, I'm too old for this. I deserve a peaceful old age."

"You're worrying about Bird," Aviva said. "You're wearing yourself out."

"We're all worried," Nita said.

"I'm worried about holding Maya down," Sam said. "She wants to go haunt the General."

"Just let her try," Nita said grimly. "I'll kill her. Then she can haunt anyone she likes."

° ° °

"Are you okay?" Bird asked Rosa. His guards had brought him to her cell, a windowless conference room with a locked door, for his daily visit. My reward for treachery, he told himself.

Rosa nodded. She looked worn and thin and deeply depressed, but Bird could see no marks on her, no bruises. Not that that meant anything.

"You sure, *querida*? Are they feeding you enough? Are they giving you water?"

She nodded again. She hadn't spoken to him since the day he appeared in the uniform of the Stewards. Ah, well, at least *she* still had her integrity.

"They haven't hurt you?" She shook her head.

I'm the one who's hurt her, failed her.

"You could keep up with your piano practice, you know." He tried to sound cheerful, hearty. "Of course, you'd have to imagine the piano. But you could work on the timing for that Mozart piece I taught you. You don't want to have fallen way behind when this is over."

She looked up at him with such contempt that he fell silent. Right. Betrayal is bad enough; I don't have to compound it by being actively stupid. He nodded to his guards, but before he could leave the door opened and the General himself came in, followed by one of the guards Bird remembered from the torture sessions. A neural probe swung from his belt.

Shit. Oh, shit.

"We're not getting results." The General got straight to the point. "You've been sitting out in the Plaza for over a month now. Nobody's taken any ration cards. You've been holding out on us."

"No, no, I swear I haven't. I've done the best I could."

"Maybe you've forgotten the taste of the probe. Jordan, give him a shot."

The pain lashed through him as if every one of his nerve endings were a separate whip. He bit his tongue to keep from screaming. *Mierda,* the fucker must have it dialed up to maximum.

"Maybe the girl needs a taste," the General suggested.

"No," Bird said, before he could stop himself. "You promised you'd leave her alone."

"Give her a hit," the General ordered. "Just so we can hear her squeal."

Her scream rang through the room.

"You've got one more chance. Think about it. We listen to your tapes, boy. We know you haven't done shit for days except sit there on your nigger ass. Oh, and by the way, who is Maya?"

Fuck you, Sam. Oh, fuck you, fuck you, for ever mentioning that name. "Yemaya? She's the Goddess of the Ocean, the old African orisha." This time the pain started low, barely perceptible, and built and built until he was shaking and sweating and against his will began to scream.

"You've barely begun to experience the full possibilities of this thing," the General said, looking at the probe with admiration. "Jordan, go to work on the girl until this soulless little demonfucker stops trying to lie to us."

He was going to have to lie, but he was going to have to find a lie they would believe, the lie that would save him, because the truth would not set him free. No, Rosa's screams were unbearable but Maya's would be just as bad. They would hurt her, and she was old and frail. Maybe she, at least, could die. *Diosa,* thousands of Witches in this city, why couldn't anyone get them out of this? Shit.

Rosa, Rosa, I am sorry. I am going to have to talk, but I've got to wait a bit, they won't believe me if it comes too quick, too easy, so I'm going to have to numb myself to your cries. That is not a girl's voice I hear, it's a gull's shrill cry, it's a badly played violin. Goddess, if only it would stop. My teeth ache from it. How long must I spin this out?

"Okay, I'll tell you," he said at last. Jordan pulled away from Rosa's shivering body and brought the probe close to Bird again. "Maya is a demon, the chief demon of the City. If you send her a message, if you pay her with the blood of a living thing, a mouse or a rat, she'll help you."

Pain again, chords and harmonics and melodic runs.

"I am not your superstitious foot soldier," the General said. "Don't try to bullshit me. I want the truth. And I'm old enough to remember the days before the Stewardship came to power. There was a writer in these parts, one of the chief apologists for Satan. Name of Maya Greenwood, I believe. Is she the Maya in question?"

I could hold out longer, let them find out how much I could take again, let them torture Rosa into insanity, but for what? Because I know I'm going to tell them. He knows it too. Ohnine was right, it's the first break that's the hardest; after that it gets easier and easier to give in, more and more pointless to resist.

"Yeah," Bird admitted. And now I've betrayed someone new, committed one more unthinkable act, taken one more step down the road to places I still can't bear to imagine.

"What relation is she to you?"

"My grandmother."

"And where is she?"

"Upriver," he said in the same flat defeated tone in which he'd identified her. "We sent her off to the Forest Communities before this whole thing began."

"So you have ways to get messages across the bay?"

"Homing pigeons," Bird said. And there was an inspired idea, why hadn't they thought of it for real?

"If she's far away upriver, why were you so concerned to conceal her existence from me?"

"I was afraid. Afraid you'd seek her out and hurt her when you take the forests."

"Ah, so you anticipate our victory, then?" The General smiled.

"How can you lose?" Bird replied.

o o o

"My wife was the mother of five children," said the sad, stocky man in the Plaza. "I loved her dearly. Do you love someone? Can you imagine what it is like, to have her taken from you, to answer the cries of the children?"

The ghosts had come to the dry fountain where Bird kept his fruitless vigil, flanked by Ohnine and Threetwo and a squad of others. Bird could tell Ohnine was in his most dangerous mood, his eyes narrow, his voice on edge. None of them were sleeping well these days. Night after night the barracks were wakened by cries of fear, bad dreams.

The figures in white closed in. Bird felt afraid. They were his former friends, his neighbors, but now they were separate from him, as if he or they were already dead.

They ignored Bird and converged on Ohnine. Bird recognized Rob Johnson and his kids, distant cousins of his own father's kin. Nellie Johnson had been on the Water Council, and Ohnine, Bird knew, had been one of the executioners. Was it his own fault? Had he named her, caused her death? Wait, he wanted to call to the Johnsons, stop, don't bait this man, not today, not right now. But none of the ghosts would meet his eye.

"I'm not fucking around with you, man. You have until I count three to get out of here, or you can follow your Witch wife to hell," Ohnine said.

"Here are our children—"

The shot rang out as a red wound opened in Rob's temple. He fell. The oldest Johnson boy stepped forward. He looked about fifteen, rangy and tall, his voice wavering only slightly. "My father was a good man. He loved us, and he knew how to fix anything—"

Ohnine shot the boy in the forehead. His younger sister stepped over his falling body. I should do something, Bird thought, but he was frozen, immobilized with horror.

"My brother always tried to protect me," Iris Johnson said. "My mother and father loved us. Didn't anyone ever love you? Does your mother know that you kill mothers?"

He killed her too. Her eight-year-old sister stepped forward, and Ohnine, now wild-eyed and out of control, shot her before she could speak. There was another girl, younger still, who held the hand of a fat two-year-old. She broke down, flinging herself down on her father's body and crying, throwing only one reproachful look at the man who pointed his gun at her. Bird held his breath. Ohnine's hand was trembling.

"There is still a place for you at our table, brother, if you will choose to join us." An old man stepped forward. Ohnine swung his gun blindly, as a woman appeared behind him, and then another and another, on all sides, women and men and children, until Bird could hardly see Ohnine in their midst, all of them saying softly, "Now, even now there is a place for you."

I should be with them, Bird thought. I should have stopped him or died trying, stepped between him and his victims. But already I stand between other violence, other victims, and *Diosa,* I am not strong enough. I am breaking and falling, falling and breaking.

Ohnine dropped his gun and began to scream. The other soldiers watched impassively as Ohnine huddled in a tight knot around his own belly, puking on the paving stones and sobbing.

"Demons got him now," Threetwo said. The others nodded. Bird thought he heard a drum beating a funereal march. The little girl was crying and only the dead lay silent, as a phalanx of ghosts bore Ohnine away.

32

In the moonlight, the Golden Gate Bridge cast a jagged shadow as the boat passed below. Empty sky gaped through missing sections, and no festive lights decked the cables. A warning, Madrone thought. The city of her stories, her fabulous tales of abundance and freedom and magic, now brooded on dark and ominous hills. Was it already destroyed?

Steady, she told herself. You'll know soon enough. Isis had given her the tiller for the passage through the bay, and she steered them through the channels she knew so well, around the lee of Angel Island, past Alcatraz, around the curve of the peninsula into the open bay and south under the Bay Bridge, which gaped with twisted and jagged metal.

It's like returning to a lover whose arms have been broken, she thought. The bridges were more than structures, they were symbols of the City itself, as much a feature of the landscape as Twin Peaks or Mount Tamalpais to the north.

"Here's what I think we should do," Madrone said. "We anchor a little ways out in the bay. Isis and I'll take the dinghy in to shore, scout a bit, find out what's happening. The rest of you will wait for us on board."

The south waterfront had always been one of Madrone's favorite places, with its docks built out over half a mile of reclaimed wetlands. Usually the docks were thriving with activity, day or night. Boats would be putting out to fish the bay for those varieties of sea creatures that did not concentrate toxins in their bodies. Crews would be working on the giant filter banks that extracted heavy metals and neutralized other chemicals, cleaning the incoming waters as they rose with the tide to fill the marshlands. The markets were always lively, full of shrimp and crab and oysters cultivated in the filtered water, and little eating places noisy with conversation and the hum of the grinders turning shells to diatomaceous earth for the gardens. During the day, children learned to sail small boats or practiced kayaking and windsurfing. Overhead, great flocks of gulls wheeled and turned, while graceful white egrets and great blue herons stalked the shadows.

The docks always brought back the excitement of her first year at the university, before the epidemics, the thrill of living away from home and then coming home. She could have crossed the bay by train or bike but she always preferred, when possible, to sail. Arriving by water seemed like coming home from a long and mysterious voyage, another world. And now she *was* coming back from another world. Would anyone be left in her home to welcome her?

Madrone and Isis made fast the dinghy to a piling, climbed out onto the docks, and moved swiftly along them until they reached solid land. Cautiously, they headed out on the deserted walkways that wound their way west into the city. They were expert night stalkers, wary as cats, fading back into the shadows at any unanticipated noise. I am walking through my own city as if it were the abode of the enemy, Madrone thought, and so it is. The big collective houses and the small private cottages still stood surrounded by fruit trees and gardens held in a web of irrigation channels, but no water flowed in the streambeds. Madrone could see that the gardens were ragged, weeds growing unchecked, flowers and vines withered and dry.

They heard a far-off rumble, like thunder or an explosion. They walked on. With each step closer to her home, Madrone felt more and more afraid of what she would find.

Suddenly water came pouring down through the dry stream, foaming at the mouth. Like figures in a silent dance, people emerged from the houses and, without speaking, placed hoses in the flow, filled buckets and glass jars. Madrone hesitated for a moment.

"Water thieves," Isis remarked. "You got them here too."

"Never before," Madrone replied. "Water has always been free here." She was exhausted, near tears. Isis laid a hand on her shoulder.

"Steady," she said. "Maybe it will be again."

They walked on.

Black Dragon House still stood, its front garden as withered and shaggy as the others but otherwise looking the same. The windows were dark, and the front door did not open to Madrone's careful nudge.

"It's locked."

"What you want to do? Knock on it, and let them know you're here, or sneak in somehow?"

"It's not an easy house for that," Madrone said. The bottom story was the locked garage, and the door to the passageway beside it was locked, too. The front windows, above, were inaccessible. "Maybe around the back. Come on."

It was a street of old Victorian town houses that stood jammed up against one another, enclosing their common back gardens from four sides. Madrone led Isis around the block, where a narrow driveway separated two of the buildings, leading to a garage in back. It was blocked by a high fence, but Isis lifted Madrone to the top and then leaped up herself, catching the edge of the fence and pulling herself up and over. The back gardens, Madrone was glad to see, were in marginally better condition than the front—there were lettuces still moist and green, and a few dark globes hung from the tomato plants.

They made their way to the back of Black Dragon House. A low light burned in the back room, and the curtains were drawn. Madrone tried the handle on the back door; it was locked too. The potted aloe vera plant still stood on the back steps, and, yes, the key was still underneath it. She slipped the key into the lock and turned it cautiously. Silently, she took a step into the house.

"Who's there?" a voice demanded. A bright light was shining in her eyes. Isis was gone, out the door, but Madrone thought the voice sounded familiar.

"Sam? Is that you? What are you doing here?"

"Who are you? What are *you* doing here?"

"I live here, Sam. Don't you recognize me? It's Madrone."

"Madrone!"

"I've come home."

"Madrone!" He dropped the light and grabbed her in a fierce hug that nevertheless seemed frail, as if he were clinging to her strength. "I can't think of anyone on earth I'd rather have appear out of the night, just now."

"Where's Maya? Is she okay? And Bird and Nita and Sage and Holybear?"

"Maya's up in the ritual room, and Nita's catching some sleep upstairs. Sage and Holybear are upriver, should be getting back tomorrow or the next day. We've got a houseful of sick soldiers here, and none of us know quite what to do with them. Deserters. They're starting to come over to us, they really are, but we can't seem to keep them healthy."

"Bird?"

"Sit down, Madrone."

"Wait, let me call Isis back," she said, feeling sick inside because she was sure he was going to tell her he was dead. She leaned out the door and whistled, and Isis stepped into the small back porch where Sam had apparently been sleeping on the cot they kept for overflow guests.

"Isis—Sam."

"Pleased to meet you," Sam said, extending his hand, looking at her curiously.

Isis regarded him with caution, ignoring his proffered handshake. "Same to you," she said.

He closed the back door and shepherded them through the next room, which was lined with bodies, sleeping or moaning and turning. They went into the hallway and through into the front room, Maya's old office. Isis stared at the bookshelves, running her fingers along the bindings. Madrone settled down on the couch.

"Okay, Sam, tell me the bad news," Madrone said.

"He's alive," he said. "I don't know how to tell you this. He was arrested when they first marched in, along with Marie and Rosa. You remember her?"

"Little Rosa?"

"Right, the pretty one."

"Damn and hell!"

"Bird was locked away for a long while, and when he came out . . ."

"What, Sam? Just tell me."

"He was wearing their uniform and working for them."

"I don't believe it."

"Neither do a lot of people. Some say he must be working on some plan of his own. Others—well, tempers are short and suspicions running high. There've been accusations. But we can go into that later."

"What kind of accusations?"

"Bird was a strong voice in Council for nonviolent resistance. Some have speculated that he was in the pay of the enemy all along, that his job was to persuade us not to take up arms."

Oh, Bird, poor Bird, Madrone thought. No wonder I cannot reach you.

"What do you think, Sam?" Madrone asked.

"I've seen him and talked to him. He comes to the Plaza most mornings, to hand out water ration cards. Nobody takes them."

"And?"

"I think they did something terrible to him. No one is superhuman, Madrone. We all have a breaking point."

"That's the truth," Isis said.

When Madrone tried to reach for Bird all she could feel was a wall, barricading some pain she could not see. Bird, Bird, my love, secretly I imagined you here to greet me and love me; where are you now? What have they done to you?

"And how was it for you in the Southlands?" Sam asked.

"That's a long, long story. I learned a lot. Mostly about myself. I don't know if I accomplished much, but I tried."

"Did you learn anything about the boosters?"

"Quite a bit. I've got a good guess as to what they are, and with the Monsters I developed a protocol for withdrawal."

"Our best guess is that they function like synthetic cytokines," Sam said.

"You got it. We've got a few samples stashed away on the boat, and some other information you can look at. Do we still have access to the data banks?"

"No, but the Stewards don't either. The crystals went on strike—wouldn't function for them. Smart, those rocks. But, Madrone, how are you? Are you okay, I mean? Not hurt, are you?"

"I'm fine, Sam. Exhausted at the moment, but a night of rest should fix me up."

"Well, I'm glad to hear it, because as soon as you're up to it, we can put you to work."

Madrone glanced around the room. "How safe is it here, Sam? This house, I mean? I've got three other women who came up on the boat with us, and one of them gave birth a few nights ago. Plus the baby and a sick little girl."

"Nothing in this city is safe, love, but they could stay next door with the Sisters. And send your boat across the bay. We agreed in Council not to keep any water transport on this side, to help contain the invasion. So far that strategy has worked pretty well. We blew up the bridges before they arrived, they concentrated their troops here on the peninsula, and we've succeeded in isolating the infection."

"*You* blew the bridges? Not them?"

"So far there hasn't been any aerial bombardment. Frankly, I don't think they still have the functioning technology for it."

Madrone sighed. It was a great relief to learn that the people of the city had blown up the bridges themselves. If we destroyed them, we can rebuild them someday.

"But what are you doing here, Sam? What happened to the hospital?"

"The soldiers commandeered it. And we couldn't very well put deserters there. When all this started—well, to be truthful, Maya and I kind of shacked up together here, and I started bringing some of the sick ones home, and, well—"

"Sam, you old dog!"

"I love her, Madrone. Go up and see her, she's been worried sick about you."

o o o

The ritual room was another makeshift hospital ward. Madrone stepped cautiously over the sleeping bodies and made her way to the far end where Maya sat, looking out the window. The moon, just past its full, hung over Twin Peaks, and in its light Maya's hair was pure silver, her face narcissus white.

"I can't reach him," she said. "He's like a locked door. But I can feel his pain."

"It's me, *madrina*. Madrone. I'm home."

Madrone knelt beside Maya and took her hands. They felt frail, trembling in hers as Maya turned slowly to look at her.

"Madrone!" Her eyes filled with tears and Madrone leaned forward to embrace her. They hugged tightly, and then Maya pulled back and stroked Madrone's face. "What have they done to you? They've made an old woman of you, in those Southlands. You've got a scar!"

"The bees did that." Madrone smiled at her. "I'm okay, really I am. Just a little weatherbeaten. And you?"

Maya's head shook, so tightly it was barely more than a tremor. "I can't stand this, Madrone. They're hurting him, I know they're hurting him. Worse than before. And I can't do anything! I can't help him."

Madrone let out a long breath. "Can't anybody help him?"

"They won't try. They think he's betrayed us." Maya sounded almost like a child. She is really very old, Madrone thought. How long can she last? "I wanted to go haunt the General, but Sam won't let me." She sat up, then, and her voice recovered some of its usual tart humor. "Do you realize how long it's been since I've let a man tell me what to do?"

Madrone smiled. "I'm happy about you and Sam. You need someone. Someone to keep you in line. But what do you mean, 'haunt the General'?"

"It's part of our strategy. One of Lily's ideas. Whenever the soldiers kill somebody, the family dresses in white and follows him—the killer, I mean. They tell him stories about his victims, try to make them real. Mostly they just won't go away, won't leave the soldiers alone."

"And this is effective?" Madrone asked.

"You'd be surprised. We've got a house full of ones who've come over to our side. They say the dead haunt them, too."

"Trust the dead," Madrone said. She stood up. "I've got to take care of a few things, but I wanted to see you first. Oh, *madrina*, I'm glad you're alive."

"Enjoy it while it lasts," Maya said.

                                    o u o

Sam arranged for a neighbor boy to return to the boat with Isis. The plan was to ferry the others ashore, and then for Isis to take the boat across the bay. She would find a safe place to anchor, and someone would ferry her back the next night by dinghy.

"How badly do you need that sleep?" Sam asked Madrone.

"What are you asking?"

"There's a couple of cases I'd love for you to see if you're up to it."

"Sure, Sam. And I've got something for you to look at too."

"What's that?"

"Printouts of some computer records I stole. Data slugs too, if we can read them. I'm not sure, but they might have some information relevant to the epidemics."

"I'll take a look, after I show you around."

                                    o o o

"Bill, here, was one of the first—that was, what, about two weeks ago?" Sam said. "He's not doing too well, as you can see."

There were six patients in Sage's room, and Madrone knelt by the sickest of them.

"Two weeks? His immune system ought to be just beginning to recover."

"He's got the flu, though. We've kept him alive, but barely."

"Let me look at him."

She took a deep breath, let herself go into the bee mind. Would it work here, so far away from the hives? She bent her head and tasted a drop of his sweat.

"What's that? What's that you're doing?" Sam asked nervously.

Madrone grinned. "New technique. Instant chemical analysis." Then she closed herself to distractions and settled into the familiar work of healing.

She stopped when she began to feel the gray drag of exhaustion. Outside, the black night sky had taken on the azure luminosity of approaching day. Sam had already gone back to sleep, making Maya come to bed with him. Wearily, Madrone climbed the stairs to her own room and peeked in. The floor was covered with snoring bodies. She checked other rooms: every bed in the house seemed taken, but in one bed she recognized the dark froth of Nita's hair. Madrone kicked off her shoes, contemplated undressing but decided it was too much trouble, and climbed in beside Nita.

"Who'zat?" Nita murmured in her sleep.

"Madrone. I'm back."

"Mmm." Nita rolled over and then sat up, awake. "Madrone?"

"It's really me. You're not dreaming."

"Madrone!"

They hugged each other, laughing and crying.

"I can't believe it's really you," Nita said.

"I know. I can't believe I'm really here, in my own home. It seems so unlikely."

"Tell me all about it."

"Oh, Nita, I don't have the strength right now. It was hard. But I'd rather hear what's been happening to you."

"Not much. Sage and Holy and I missed out on the worst of it; we had to protect our cell lines. Otherwise even if we win we could be set back decades. So we took them upriver before the troops arrived. Now we've got a lab established there, and things are relatively under control, so I came back to replenish our supplies. You heard about Bird?"

"Sam told me."

"They torture prisoners, I've heard."

"I know."

They sat together, holding each other until Madrone began to shiver.

"You're cold, *querida*," Nita said. "Get under the blankets."

"Just tired," Madrone said. "So tired. I wish I could sleep for a week."

"I wish you could too, but I doubt you'll be allowed to. Anyway, I'll get up now and let you have the bed. *Diosa,* I'm glad you're back!"

。 。 。

"Fourth day no boosters, man."

"This is the shits."

"Shit's what we got to look forward to, 'less they get the trains through."

"You shit, man."

"Eat shit!"

They broke into loud laughter. Bird was lying on his bunk, listening to the voices around him, his eyes closed, falling through empty space. At times he thought he was chasing someone, Cleis who turned into Madrone who turned into Rosa.

"I loved you," he said, but she turned away and fled, and he was still falling.

"A unit ain't nothing without its commander. What we do now Ohnine's gone?"

"Pick a new commander."

"Who, you? Commander Asshole?"

"Fuck you!"

Bird rolled over and covered his head with the blanket. The dark was comforting. He wished he could crawl in deeper and disappear.

"You can't disappear, you got responsibilities."

It was Johanna's voice in his head. Although he couldn't see her face, he imagined it disapproving.

"I am failing them all," he told her. "I don't trust myself."

"Nonetheless, this is something you've got to see through, from beginning to end."

"Then let it end now. I want it to end," Bird cried out, but he was still falling and now he was past her.

"Maybe we shoulda followed Ohnine. He the commander."

"Followed him outa the army?"

"Man, you leave the army, you die."

"We dying here, without the boosters."

"They get the boosters, you wait. Don't you worry."

"The unit ought to stick together. We ought to stick behind the commander."

Rio was an old, bearded white man, like the Millennialists' God. Bird wanted to confess to him.

"I just stood there and let them be killed. I didn't try to stop them. I should have thrown my body in between them, saved them or died. Ohnine wouldn't have shot me."

"Don't bet on it."

"And if he had, that would've been better."

"Oh, stop it, Bird. Stop trying to make me into an agent of your punishment."

"What do you want me to do?"

"Stop pitying yourself and start thinking."

"I don't pity myself, I'm just afraid, Rio. Weren't you ever afraid?"

"I've been afraid," Rio said, and now Bird imagined a note of compassion into his voice. "Fear and shame and guilt and humiliation. Believe me, I've felt them all—worse than you, because I actually had something to feel guilty about. You've simply encountered a system of force that's stronger than you are. That's nothing to be ashamed of."

"I am ashamed."

"Of course you are, that's what force does to us all. But it's a useless emotion for you, right now. It's stopping you from thinking and noticing what's around you. Listen! Listen to what they're saying. They're on the verge of rebellion. You're possibly on the knife edge of victory, and you talk about wanting to die! Get out of that bed and do something useful."

"What happen to Ohnine, anyway?"

"Witches took him."

"What they do to him?"

Bird sat up.

"Hey, Bird, you tell us, what they gonna do to Ohnine?"

"They'll try to heal him," Bird said.

"What you mean?"

"They'll try to heal his mind, to keep him from killing like that again."

"But the dead gonna haunt him?"

"Right. But if he joins the Witches, they'll try to heal him."

"But he'll die without the boosters."

"Maybe not. I know of deserters who've survived. And the Witches will try to keep him alive."

"Why? He killed a whole family of them."

"Still, they'll try to keep him alive. We don't believe in revenge."

"Why not?"

"We let the dead take their own revenge."

"If they heal him, then what?"

"Then he'll live like the rest of them, if they win. Free and equal. Or die with the rest of them."

"What you mean, free and equal?"

"I mean nobody telling you what to do or wear or think. I mean your color doesn't matter and your ancestors get respect. I mean having enough to eat and drink, and a place to live you can call your own, and work to do that you feel good about."

"Ohnine gonna have all that?"

"Maybe."

"What do you mean, color don't matter?"

"Look at me," Bird said. "I'm as dark as the rest of you, and I was on the Council. I was a musician once—I went to the university. I could be anything I wanted to be."

"No shit, man?"

"That for real?"

"No shit."

"Man, we in the wrong fuckin' army, then," Threetwo said, and raucous laughter rang through the barracks. But there was an edge to it, an undertone of thought.

o o o

They moved him out of the barracks the next morning and locked him in a dark underground storage room where they let him wait for a very long time. He lay on a bare cold floor, shaking, trying to contain his fear. He had to fight to breathe, not to pant like a dog with his tongue lolling out. Slow. Take a long breath, in and out, count it: one, two, three, four, five. . . . His heart was racing. And they haven't even done anything to me yet. Stop, don't think about it. The fear is worse than the thing feared; Rio used to say that, and I wish I could believe it. Where there's fear, there is power. Maya said that, but you had it wrong, *abuelita*. Where there's power, there is fear.

What scared him most was Rio's suggestion that victory might be possible. The supply lines were down, soldiers were deserting every day—not many, but others were thinking about it. Maybe Lily's strategy was starting to work. If that were true, his resistance or compliance might still make a difference. The situation called for qualities he no longer possessed: courage, stamina, obstinacy. *Diosa,* he had no more left. How could he hold out against them when he knew that they could always hold out longer? It cost them nothing to inflict pain; it cost him everything to resist. And if they worked on Rosa? How long could he bear that?

But, Goddess help him, he would have to try again. Even if he were already on the road that would lead him to do abominations in the end, there was some honor left in prolonging the journey. Maybe even some dangerous, seductive hope.

But when they brought him to the General, it was not for questioning but for punishment.

"You've been lying to us," the General told him. "You've been holding out on us. That's not a wise thing to do, boy. You're not our only informant, you know. We have many ways of gathering information."

Bird said nothing. The guards that flanked the General were not from his own unit but from the Private Guard, and their white faces turned red and shiny under the hot lights they shone in Bird's eyes.

"Why didn't you tell us about the cisterns?" the General asked. "All that time you sat out in the Plaza, laughing at us, knowing damn well that nobody would sign on for rations as long as they had a full store of water sitting in the basement. Why did we have to discover this ourselves during a search?"

"You didn't ask," Bird said.

Then his punishment began.

33

"Lou!"

"Hey, Madrone!" They hugged fiercely, and Aviva, coming into the kitchen, threw her arms around them both.

"Madrone! Goddess, it's good to see you alive!"

"I never realized how much I'd miss you, till you were gone," Lou admitted.

"Me neither," Madrone said. "I wished for you both a thousand times down south, if only to have someone to bitch to."

"Well, it's just like old times around here," Aviva said. "Chaos, death, inadequate staff, business as usual. And you look exhausted, also as usual."

"Because I got my usual three hours of sleep," Madrone said. "We got back last night and Sam put me straight to work."

"War is hell," Lou said cheerfully.

∘ ∘ ∘

All morning Madrone moved in and out of trance, in and out of the bee mind that let her taste the chemistry at work in the feverish bodies she encountered. Around midday she looked up to see Sara observing her.

"Mary Ellen sent me to tell you lunch is ready and to make you come and eat it whether you want to or not."

"Make me, huh? Just how are you going to do that?"

"Force of personality. Come on."

Mary Ellen looked at home behind the stove, as if she had always lived at Black Dragon House, helping Maya dish up stew for platoons of sick soldiers. Sara, dressed in a simple shirt and jeans, her blond hair pulled plainly back from her face and braided, nevertheless looked out of place awkwardly balancing trays of food and returning with dirty dishes.

Lou, Aviva, and Madrone were settled around the big table, at work on their second round of stew when Sam came in.

"How goes it?" he asked. "Get any sleep, Madrone?"

"Not enough. So just to prove to you what a reformed character I am, after I eat I am going to take a nap."

"A nap!" Lou raised his eyebrows. "Don't you know there's a war on?"

"When can we get a readout on those data slugs?" Madrone asked Sam.

"I don't know. Flore is having to work completely undercover, and she had a hell of a time convincing the crystals on her palmtop to work, even for her. But she's running up the stats, and we're checking through the printouts. To put it very simply, it seems the boosters work not by upping the T-cell count but by subtly shifting the cytokine balance, so they produce more antibodies. Sudden withdrawal causes the T-cells to go on strike for a period that might last anywhere from a few days to a few weeks. After that, they seem to kick back in slowly if the patient hasn't already contracted something deadly."

"What does that mean in English?" Maya asked from the sink, where she was washing a stack of dishes in a frugal potful of water.

"If your immune system were an army," Sam explained, "it would be like feeding each of the soldiers a high that could keep him going day and night, without sleep. He'd be a much more efficient killer. But take the drug away, and he'd collapse. Maybe he'd die; maybe he'd just need a month or two of rest to recover."

"That's about what we figured empirically," Madrone said. "Down south, we kept them in isolation as much as possible and used herbs and pressure points to stimulate the immune system."

"Successfully?" Aviva asked.

"Not entirely. About sixty or seventy percent survived."

"That's a good rate, medically, but not quite a recruiting point," Lou said. "We can't bring in deserters with those odds."

"We can do better. We have resources here I didn't have down there."

"Then you must have been pretty bad off."

"In the hills, Lou, I didn't even have water to wash the shit off my patients' asses. And that's the literal truth."

There was silence around the table. Madrone broke it.

"Speaking of resources, Sam, do we have any available stocks of AL-431?"

"Yeah, I've got some down in the garage. Why?"

"Mary Ellen's granddaughter—who's Sara's niece—it's a long story. She's next door with the Sisters."

"I'll bring some up."

"Good. I'll stop by there this afternoon, after I have a little sleep."

Madrone had just closed her eyes when someone came in and perched on the end of her bed.

"Madrone? Are you asleep yet?"

She groaned, opening her eyes. "Not anymore." Sara was looking at her, her smile slight and hesitant.

"I just wanted to talk for a minute. I won't bother you long, I know you're tired."

"Sure," Madrone said, propping herself up on Maya's big pillows. "What is it?"

"I wanted to thank you—thank you for bringing me here."

"Uh, sure. Thank you for helping me rescue Katy. Sara, what is it you really want to talk about?"

"Us." Sara moved closer and took Madrone's hand. "Is there still an us to talk about?"

"Aren't you and Isis . . . ?"

"That's very powerful," Sara admitted. "But I thought you people weren't jealous."

"I'm not. But I'll bet Isis is. Look, Sara, I'm happy for you if you're happy. I'm frankly too exhausted right now to even think about sex or love."

"I didn't want you to feel—"

"Seduced and abandoned?" Madrone grinned.

"Something like that."

"Don't worry, Sara. Like I said, right now I barely have energy to keep on top of the work here without collapsing. If this war is ever over, who knows?"

"Can I help you in some way? Can I do anything for you?"

"You have been helping, you and Mary Ellen. Taking over the cooking and feeding and general nursing. It's far too much for Maya, but she'd never admit it. How is it for you, to be doing all this work? I know it's not what you're used to."

"I kind of like it," Sara admitted. "I've never been useful before."

"If the war ends—no, *when* the war ends, if you stay here, you can do any kind of work you want, you know. You could train for something, anything that interests you. Have you thought about that?"

"No," Sara admitted. "I never have."

"Well, think about it," Madrone said. "And now, I'm sorry, but I've really got to get some rest."

"I'll leave you," Sara said, bending over and kissing her lightly on the cheek. The imprint of her lips felt warm long after she had tiptoed out, closing the door behind her.

○ ○ ○

Katy was sitting in the sun in the back garden at the Sisters' house. The beds were ragged and weedy but still filled with flowers, pink and purple cosmos and red geraniums and scented herbs. With her dark hair hanging long and loose on her shoulders and her baby cradled in her arms, Katy mirrored the statue of Virgin and Child that nestled under the plum tree.

"How are you, Katy?" Madrone sat down on the dry grass next to her. "I like your hair down. I like it up, too, for that matter. Somewhere in my room I've got a pair of tortoiseshell combs I want to give you. My hair's too bushy for them, but they'll make you look like a true Spanish noblewoman from some other century."

Katy smiled. "I'm fine."

"I just checked Angela, started her on a new drug regimen. The pills and instructions are inside."

"Thanks so much, Madrone." Katy turned, shifting the sleeping baby. Her movement was unconsciously graceful, as if the child were still a part of her, and Madrone nodded approvingly. A sign of good bonding, that ease. Babies held like that would thrive.

"I'm so happy to be able to do something for her, finally. Something as simple as prescribing a few pills, which we didn't even have to raid a pharmacy for. Not yet, anyway, as long as our stores hold out."

Katy sighed. "It's so peaceful here in the sun. I can't think about raids or believe the war is really happening. I've never seen such a beautiful garden."

"You should see it in the spring, the way it was before the invasion, with all the fruit trees in bloom and plenty of water," Madrone said. "But you're really okay, everything right with the baby?"

"Fine, really fine."

"Any problems? Questions?"

"Madrone, I'm not unfamiliar with babies. I've tended dozens of them."

"I know. But your own can be different. And you had such an ordeal, those last days."

"You don't have to worry about me now. How about you, Madrone—are you okay?"

"I'm tired. I'm worried."

"Your family?"

"One of them's a prisoner."

"I'm sorry."

"They say Bird, my *compa*—my partner, I guess you'd say—they say he's gone over to the enemy. Wears their uniform and works for them. Some people think he's a traitor."

"Do you believe it?"

"I don't know."

"Your people here don't know much about coercion. Have a little tolerance."

"I do."

The baby stirred and cried, and Katy offered her breast, looking down at her lovingly while she sucked. "I'm beginning to enjoy her."

"Named her yet?"

"You should name her. Madrone, I'm sorry about that stupid fight we had. I know you didn't mean to hurt me. And I know that if it wasn't for you—"

"Don't even think about it, Katy, you'll curdle your milk. Do you miss Hijohn?"

"I do. I wish he could see his daughter."

"Someday he will."

"I wish he knew we were both still alive."

"Beth'll get word to him, somehow, that you escaped."

"The Southlands seem so far away, like another world. As if we really had died and gone to heaven."

"This is not heaven."

"It seems that way to me, if I close my eyes and don't think about what's happening."

"Anywhere can be heaven if you do that."

"No. Not anywhere." Katy's voice was sharp, pained, and Madrone fell silent.

"So what are you going to name my baby?" Katy asked.

Madrone thought for a moment. "Luz."

"Loose?"

"Not 'loose,' *luz,* for light and birth, as in *dar a luz.* Or Lucia, if you prefer."

"Lucia, I like that."

Madrone hesitated.

"What is it?" Katy asked.

"Would you name her Lucia Rachel? For my mother?"

"I'd be proud to."

"It's funny, Katy. She died such a long time ago, in Guadalupe, and all those years I could never remember her face or feel her close to me. Johanna, my grandmother, she was always hanging around with advice, living or dead. But not my own mother.

"But then, that day with the Angels, when we found Poppy and saw what they'd done to her, I remembered. My mother was a healer too, a doctor. She ran a clinic for poor children out in the back of beyond; we lived next door. The death squads liked to attack clinics; they thought free medical care was subversive, ungodly. Of course I didn't know that at the time. I just knew there was something my mother was worried about a lot. And then they came. She yelled at me to run away, and I hid in my own secret place, a little cubbyhole at the back of the closet. I think I heard her screaming. Then I waited and waited for her to come and get me and tell me it was safe. She didn't come."

Katy slid her arm around Madrone's shoulder. "How old were you?"

"I'd just turned seven."

"God! What happened then?"

"It was so silent. After a long time, I became more frightened of staying hidden in the dark than of coming out, so I crept out into the main room. My mother was lying very still. For a moment, I was mad and hurt. I thought she'd gone to sleep and forgotten me. So I went to her to wake her up and touched her hand. Her hand was so cold. Then I saw the blood."

Madrone was crying. At last I can cry, she told herself, safe here in the Sisters' garden, a few warm tears for you, Mama, my first love, my first loss.

Katy was stroking Madrone's shoulder and harboring the baby with her other arm. "I'm sorry. I'm so sorry."

"I knew about death. I just couldn't believe it had happened to my mother. She was always so confident; she knew so much. I just sat there with her until I fell asleep, hoping when I woke up everything would be all right again. In the morning, the neighbors came and got me. Then my grandfather flew down and brought me up here."

"She was a good woman, your mother. It will be a good name for the child."

"Thanks, Katy. I needed to tell that story to someone." Madrone squeezed Katy's hand and released it so Katy could shift the baby to her other breast.

"I'm glad you told me," Katy said, looking down into Lucia's murky blue eyes. "I feel a kinship with your mother. I've been sitting here wondering if I should go back to the Southlands. And if I do, what will happen to her?" She looked down at the baby, who was waving her small foot as she nursed.

"Give yourself some time before you try to answer that," Madrone said. "That's medical advice. It's too big a question to tackle now." She shifted the subject. "You like the name?"

"It's beautiful."

"Lucia Rachel she is, then. Maybe in a few days we'll have time for a naming ceremony."

"Is there something I could be doing to help you?" Katy asked. "You do look tired, and I know there's so much for you to do here."

"Just make sure Angela gets her medication on schedule. And rest."

"It seems so self-indulgent."

"Katy, you just gave birth less than a week ago, and it wasn't an easy birth. And you had a horrible time before that. You need to rest. Take this time to be with Lucia, to bond with her, give her a good start. She deserves it."

"I guess you're right. How're the others?"

Madrone smiled. "Poor Sara. The worm has turned. Mary Ellen orders her about, keeps her waiting on all of us, bringing us food and tea, tells her what to do continually, day and night. No more 'Miss Sara' now."

"I admire her. She gave up a lot. I'm not sure I would, if I'd ever had anything to lose."

"You would, if you felt it was right. You're that sort of person."

"I don't know. If I had a garden like this, a life where I felt it was my right beyond question to sit in the sun with my baby and watch these beautiful flowers grow, I'm not sure you could dislodge me."

"If you had it, you'd be used to it, like I was. And willing to leave it all for some dashing adventure."

"Regret it? Your trip into our world, I mean."

"I can't regret it, no. It's taught me to appreciate all this. But I regret what we all have to do to defend this, to try to create it out of that ugliness down there. I regret that we don't have peace. I'm tired, Katy, tired of fighting and struggling."

"You ought to sit out here with the flowers for a while yourself, you know."

"You're probably right." Madrone sighed and fell silent, looking at the bees in the borage plant. "There is something else you can do for me."

"What?"

"Come with me to see Bird. I'm afraid to go alone."

o   o   o

"Bird has disappeared," Nita said. "Nobody's seen him in the Plaza for two days."

Gone. Madrone stared bleakly at Nita. To think that she could have seen him, touched him, maybe, known for herself how he was. And now he was gone.

They were huddled around the kitchen table, drinking herb tea. It was late, and the patients were bedded down for the night. Sam lay on the couch, with his feet propped up. Mary Ellen sat in a corner, her head tipped back, snoring. Sara was washing the last load of dishes and cleaning the counters, while Maya rolled out a piecrust.

"Sara, sit down," Madrone said. Suddenly the cozy kitchen scene irritated her. What was Bird suffering while they were drinking tea? "You'll give yourself dishpan hands. We'll clean up when we're done."

"I don't mind. I'm trying to redeem my previously idle existence." Sara smiled. Tired as she was, her hair plastered by sweat to her forehead in strands, her hands reddened and chapped, when she favored the room with that long, seductive glance she still seemed mistress of treasures and secret pleasures. Nita's answering smile in return lasted just a beat or two longer than necessary, Madrone noted. Oh, well, she thought. Either I'll have to ship Sara back down south or let Isis fight off all my old girlfriends.

Isis, wandering in from the back door, intercepted the same look. She went over to Sara, slid her hand down her back and over her ass in a gesture of seduction and possession, leaned over, and kissed her on the mouth.

"How ya doin', honey?"

"Doin' dishes." Sara pulled her head away, slightly embarrassed.

"Leave off that, come sit with me."

"In a minute."

"Tell me how he was arrested," Madrone asked.

"It was a confrontation over water," Sam said from the couch. "When the army first dammed the streams, a couple of weeks after they invaded, people tried to block them. They shot two of the Liaison Council; then Rosa and a gang of kids got between them and Bird and Sister Marie. One of their own soldiers shot the guy who was about to kill Rosa, but they arrested her along with Bird and Marie."

"Poor Marie," Madrone said. "She was so sick. I can't imagine she's still alive. But what about Rosa? Has anyone seen her?"

"Not since they captured her," Aviva said.

"Do we know where she's being held?"

"No. My fear is she's been taken to what they so euphemistically call the Rec Center," Sam said.

"¡Mierda!"

"They're using her to pressure Bird," Maya said. "I'm sure of it." She turned her piecrust and thumped the rolling pin down on the board.

"No doubt," Isis said, as Sara put down her dishcloth and stood nestled against her chair. "They're ruthless slime, the bigsticks."

"The what?" Nita asked.

"You know. The highups in the army."

"Oh." She let out an involuntary sigh as Isis' hand slid down the outside of Sara's thigh.

"One of their favorite tactics is to find someone to turn traitor, to use as an example," Isis went on. "And they always succeed."

"I didn't think they would, with Bird," Madrone said.

"All it takes is the right leverage," Sara said. "For most people, physical pain is enough. For others, they find something else."

"Like Rosa," Maya said. "Goddess keep her."

"I'm tired, you know that?" Madrone said. "I'm just tired of this whole damn mess. Here and in the South and all over—it's not like we wouldn't have plenty of problems to solve just surviving even if we didn't have war and torture and incredible cruelty to deal with."

"Wait until you're as old as I am. Then you'll really be tired of it," Sam said.

Maya snorted, folded her crust, and lifted it into its tin. "I'm not tired. I'm just mad. If I hadn't made all those stirring speeches in Council about nonviolence, I'd go gunning for the General myself."

"You're not the only one who feels that way," Lou said. "I hear there's plenty of debate about our strategy. I'm not sure how much longer we can hold the shoot-'em-up faction at bay."

"But that would be a tragic mistake," Maya said in alarm. "To give up now!"

"You were the one who mentioned guns," Sam pointed out.

"I said *if* I hadn't made those speeches," Maya countered. "But I made them because I believe them. I'd like to shoot the General, just on a personal level. But that wouldn't end the violence. He'd only be replaced. We've got to go on struggling to find a different way, even if we lose."

"The problem is, losing in theory is a lot easier than losing in real life," Lou said.

"Who would know where Rosa's being kept?" Madrone changed the subject.

"One of Bird's guards came over awhile back. He might know. But there's a problem with him," Aviva said.

"What problem?"

"Well, to begin with he didn't just come over." Sam told Madrone the story of the Johnson family.

"You mean he shot them all?"

"All except the youngest two. Then he sort of fell apart. We brought him back to Lily's place, but he's still not eating or speaking."

"Great."

Isis looked up. "Those guards, they're the elite. Bred for it, not like your city rats and water thieves and roundups out of the unemployment lines. They're soldiers first and last. You got one of them to come over, you doin' good. Maybe the rest'll follow."

"Not so far," Nita said.

"Give them time."

"Can't anyone reach Bird, dream to him or to Rosa?" Madrone asked.

"People have tried," Sam said. "He's closed off."

"Lily hasn't reached him," Maya said. "Even I can't."

"I haven't tried," Madrone said. "But I will."

∘ ∘ ∘

In her dream, she was falling, nothing below her, nothing around her, falling through a gray space tinged with dread. Then Bird was there, falling with her, and she kept reaching out to him, wanting to touch him, wanting someone to hold to, but he fell away, tumbling down and down.

"There's no ground," he said. "There is nowhere to land."

"But what about your wings, Bird? Fly! Fly out of here!"

But he did not fly. He continued to fall.

34

Madrone was squeezed into a corner in the back of the basement that served as Council Hall. The carved wooden salmon mask of the Speaker for the west periodically grazed the top of her head, and she hoped the Speaker would not be moved to nod vigorously at some particularly persuasive speech. The room smelled of sweat and sage. Isis and Sara crouched intertwined beside her.

"How long do we keep on with this strategy?" Cress from Water Council was saying. "We're losing people every day; the crop situation is critical. When do we admit that we need some stronger action?"

"We keep on until the limitations of force become apparent to them," Lily said.

"They aren't apparent to me!" someone called from across the room, and several people laughed.

"Process!" reminded Joseph, who was facilitating.

"Force always thinks itself indomitable," Lily went on. "But in fact it is a very precarious sort of power, because to expend force requires the use of resources, energy, human lives. Force is extremely expensive to use."

"I don't know, Lily," said an older man. "With all due respect, it's also extremely costly to resist."

"Force works ninety percent through intimidation," Lily countered. "We obey not because of what they actually have done to us but because we fear what they will do and can do. But no system of domination can survive if it is actually required to use force every time it wants to be obeyed. If we refuse to obey, if we do no portion of their work for them, they must fall."

"But can we really do that, Lily?" Lou said. "Even Bird could only resist up to a point, and now he's working for them."

"He told them about the cisterns," said the yellow-haired woman sitting next to Cress. "They've been breaking up cisterns for the last three days, and five people have died so far trying to block them."

"They discovered the cisterns themselves, the day they searched the Chen place!" Walker jumped to his feet. "You can't blame everything that goes wrong on Bird!"

"Well, he hasn't been around the Plaza since they started in on the cisterns," Cress said. "Don't you think that means something?"

"What? What's it supposed to mean?" Walker countered.

"Bird is not the issue here," Lily insisted. "Why are we obsessed with Bird? Hero or traitor, he's only one person."

"He's a bellwether," Lou said, his low voice calm and contained. "Bearing in mind that I basically agree with your position, Lily, we still can't ignore Bird. He's a living example of what happens when force meets resistance, a microcosm of the struggle we're all facing. So we needed him to be a hero. Maybe that was naïve, unrealistic. Unfair, even. But it's true. His betrayal has disheartened us. I know damn well he's braver and tougher than I am. If he can't resist them, how can I? How can we?"

"Don't call it betrayal!" Nita protested.

"That's what everybody *is* calling it," Cress said.

"Then everybody is a fool," Lily said.

"Stick to the process, please!" Joseph cried. "Okay, Lou, your turn."

"Maybe we're fools, Lily," Lou said, "but that's what we have to work with, a population of fools and ordinary folks of limited reserves, not a city of saints. There's a limit to how much we can stand, and that limit is almost reached. So it's touch and go who is going to break first. And it may be us."

"What do you suggest?" Lily asked wearily.

"We need to escalate somehow. People need some way to express their rage. Not violence, just anger."

There was silence in the room. Isis nudged Madrone. "Am I allowed to speak here?"

Madrone nodded. "Just raise your hand. And pause occasionally so the Signer can follow you."

Joseph acknowledged Isis, and she stood.

"You people have a beautiful city here. I have walked all over it, looking for the poor sections, looking for the places where the houses are rotten and the gardens are dry, and at last I believe what Madrone here's been telling me all along, that you have built a place where everybody has enough. This is different, this is not what we're used to where I come from, and it's not what the soldiers are used to either. Doesn't surprise me that they're starting to desert. Because most of them are just poor sticks that get picked up off the street, get to choose between the army and jail. They're not your problem.

"Your problem is the Elite Corps, the ones that are born and bred and raised for the army, that don't know anything else. They're going to be the last to turn, if you can turn them at all. And if you can't turn them, you may have to kill them. I know that's not your way, but it's got to be faced. And they're not easy to kill."

"Do you have any ideas about how to reach them?" Sachiko asked.

"All I can say is this: they stick by their units. That's who they're loyal to, that's who they believe in. So if you can turn one of them from any unit, there's a good chance the others will follow. But getting that one—I don't know how to tell you to do that. Maybe work on the one you've got, the one that shot all those people. Maybe you can change him."

"Maybe pigs can fly," Cress called out. There was a ripple of laughter before the Speaker for the Voices motioned for silence.

"Friend Coyote has a message for us." The Speaker bent close to the muzzle of the Coyote mask in the south. "Coyote says, 'Remember your forgotten powers. Hold to the trickster, not the warrior. Do not despair.' "

"We won't answer this question tonight," Joseph said. "We've got to end now if we don't want the evening patrols to catch us on our way home. We will debate this again tomorrow night. Go safely. *Que les vaya bien.*"

o   o   o

Lily approached Madrone as the meeting broke up.

"Come home with me," she said. "I have healing work for you."

Madrone let out a long breath. "Lily, I haven't seen you in seven or eight months, I come back out of hell itself, and you can't even say hi before you put me to work?"

Lily's brows arched high. "What do you mean, I haven't seen you? I've *dreamed* you a dozen times." Then she pushed her hair back from her forehead, a gesture of weariness. "Forgive me, child. I'm becoming obsessed. But you're right, I should have greeted you. I greet you now. Welcome back."

She took hold of Madrone's shoulders and kissed her.

"And now I have work for you."

"Lily, Sam has a houseful of work for me. Is this really vital?"

"This is the most important work you can do."

o   o   o

"And how the hell do I heal this?" Madrone asked. They stood in the living room of the small flat where Lily had moved for the duration of the crisis. In one corner of the room Ohnine squatted, his head in his hands. His eyes, when he looked up, were vacant. Quietly, Lily drew Madrone out of the room and sat her down at a table in the tiny kitchen.

But Madrone stood up and paced the small room as she talked. She could not sit still. "Show me a virus, a nice wound, a broken leg, a kid stuck in the womb—but how the hell do I heal the mind of a man who shot down a whole family in cold blood?"

"He *did* stop."

"Sure, I give him credit for that. A five-year-old was too much for him. An eight-year old, he could waste, but—"

"Is there truly no part of you that can understand?"

"No."

"Absolutely no?"

"Lily, you are asking me to heal my mother's murderer."

"What do you mean?"

"My mother was murdered by a death squad in Guadalupe. By men just like him. I was there. I remember it now."

"Then you have a link with him."

"I have no link with him! I'm not a candidate for sainthood; I'm not fixated on forgiveness. I'm not even a mind-healer. Why don't you find one of them—there must be some of them left in this city—and let me go back to my germs and broken bones?"

"The mind-healers have failed with him. You are our last hope. You've been in that world he comes out of."

"That's why I tell you it's hopeless. I know these guys. They're not like us, Lily. They're lacking something. It's a different breed of human being, and I mean that literally."

"Is it? Are you telling me that you could not kill?"

Madrone sat down in the chair opposite Lily's, tipping it back so it leaned against the wall. "I don't know. I had opportunities, down south, to kill. I couldn't do it then. Except once. I had to hurt somebody to save Katy. I didn't kill him, but it was just luck. At the moment I didn't care. But that's different from what he did, Lily!"

"Is it? Was he, too, not acting out of what his life and training had taught him to believe and defend? Imagine the inner wrenching it must have taken for him to stop, to let all of that collapse when he found himself violating something that ran deeper, some instinct perhaps he never knew he had. Can't you find some compassion for him in your heart?"

"Maybe one drop."

Lily smiled. The strain eased from her face; it returned to its habitual calm mask, which Madrone suddenly found irritating. "We will have victory only if we are stronger healers than they are warriors."

"But nobody can heal somebody else. You know that, Lily. We heal ourselves or not at all."

"Nevertheless you do work as a healer. You shift energies. You change the climate to one in which healing can occur."

"But I can't change his past or his history. You're not talking about healing, you're talking about making him someone other than he is."

"Who says you cannot heal the past? Time is only a construct. Everything that ever was exists now."

"I don't like to think that. I like to think that some things are over and done with, for good."

"But how can they be? The slave trade and the slaughter of the tribes of this land and the burning of the Witches live on in you, and somewhere in me lives a child starving in the potato famine and a young girl from China kept in a cage off Stockton Street and sold to passersby. All that is part of who we are in this moment."

"Then nothing really gets any better!" Madrone protested.

"On the contrary. If you can heal something in this moment now, you in some measure heal all the pain that ever was."

"That's too big for me, Lily."

"Try it this way. If you can somehow heal yourself, you help to redeem your ancestors. Who were, of course, also the torturers, the murderers, the rapists. We are none of us completely pure. If you can heal this young man, if in this present moment your compassion can create for him a new channel for his mind and heart and self, then you do in some sense heal his history."

"Lily, I caught two of the Johnson kids when they were born. How can I heal their murderer?"

"Try."

o o o

Madrone squatted beside the figure huddled in the corner. I don't know what to do here, she thought. I'm not a mind-healer, I don't even want to begin to probe his *ch'i* or taste his energy. All I can do is sit, ground, breathe, maybe.

She shifted her body to sit cross-legged and took some deep breaths. Compassion. Goddess, if you were trying to evolve creatures of compassion, you should have stuck with dogs. Dogs are better, kinder, sometimes vicious but never methodically cruel.

"You promised to be my instrument," a voice whispered.

How do I become the instrument of compassion when I am so blazing, raging mad?

"Sit. Sit until the energy changes."

Madrone sat. An hour passed, and another hour. Lily brought her tea, in silence. Once she stood and went to relieve herself in Lily's bathroom, but she returned to sit again.

Compassion. No, she could not find it in herself, only grief and anger at the waste. What could her mother have done with the years that were taken from her? She could have been there for me, to place the cowrie necklace around my throat when my moon blood first came, to hear about my visions, my first love affairs, to comfort me when Bird went away, to have visions and lovers and sorrows of her own. The waste, the waste! Madrone looked at the soldier's dull eyes and thought about blood. Coatlicue, you gave me your knife, and from all I know you were not a gentle Goddess. Didn't you demand sacrifice, the heart ripped from the chest, or was that just a story the priests told about you? But I could do that. If your knife were more than an energy form, if it were made of steel, I could plunge it into this man's chest and rip out that cold, cold heart. If we could do that, Mama, rip out all the cold hearts, remove them, remove scum from the earth. Who said that? One of the Angels, wasn't it? I understand them now. Goddess, keep me out of the bee mind because I would sense this man's disease and sting him to death to protect the hive.

Rage churned in her, lit a fire in her belly, burst into flame on her breath. Oh, I am tired of being the Healer! I want to be the Destroyer, to rend and tear with my nails, to eat human flesh, to say no! no! no! until it all stops and starts over again, soft and new. I have not killed and I will not kill, not with Lily in the next room, but, *Diosa,* I do want to kill, to cleanse, to exact some payment for all the suffering, some justice, some revenge.

Madrone felt her body come alive. She could hardly stay still, she wanted to dance and let her feet tumble civilizations, wave her hands in the air to cause thunder and hurricanes, drip sweat from her breasts to drown the fields. Don't talk to me about compassion, talk to me about forest fires, volcanic eruptions, the whirlwind that clears its own path. Goddess, you have not made the world correctly; what you have birthed has sickened and poisoned itself. Knock it down and begin again.

Her hands felt hot. She was the volcano, hot lava poured from her palms. If I touch him now, I'll scorch him, I'll change him, it will serve him right. She reached out and took the soldier's hand. An aura, red as flame, enveloped their clasped hands.

His flesh was cold, but it felt familiar, like touching a part of herself, like remembering something she had always known. We are alike, she thought, in some way, flesh of one flesh. How can that be?

The flame changed. It grew until it surrounded her with still pure color, red at the corona and gold within and in the very center blue, like one drop of water.

Then she fell into the water, and it grew until it became an ocean she floated on.

The waves carried her, supported her, soaked her lungs and her brain. The room seemed to open out, white and gold and filled with a light that rang and quivered. The room, the wall, the man dissolved and there was only the play of color and harmony, beautiful as the ice road but warm now. Yes, everything was warm, her own hands, her own heart; her rage was a fire set adrift on the water, a flaming boat of offerings.

His hand warmed under her touch. She began to heal, which was only to reach and offer, without judgment, to let this power flow.

They sat in silence throughout the night, holding hands. Outwardly, nothing moved. Inwardly, Madrone poured colors down gray dust roads, kindled rain on mud-cracked fields, cried over corpses, and excavated a long-buried stone that began to pulse and beat like a heart.

Night turned to dawn. The patch of sky framed by Lily's window changed to indigo, then hazy blue.

Finally the man looked up. His head rose slowly, like the tip of a bulb risking an emergence into light. His eyes unfolded like uncertain petals and slowly focused on Madrone. Quickly he looked away.

"My name's Madrone," she said softly. "What's your name?"

"Don't got one." His voice was low and toneless; he spoke reluctantly, as if words were rationed.

"You don't have a name?"

"Number's Ohnine fivethirtythree sixteenhundred, Unit Five."

"Oh. What do people call you?"

"Ohnine."

Color flamed between them. He seemed pitiful to her suddenly, a man without even a name to call his own. How could she fear him?

"What you gonna do to me?"

He feared her. Madrone pitched her own voice low, to match his, and spoke slowly. "We're going to keep you here, in isolation, for another week or two, until your immune system has a chance to regenerate from booster withdrawal. And then—it depends."

She saw terror flicker over his face, and his eyes shut down again.

"We're not going to hurt you, Ohnine."

He looked at her suspiciously. "Why not?"

"That's not how we operate."

"That's how everybody operates."

"Not us."

"What you gonna do, then?"

"If you can heal yourself, if you can work with us, you could help us."

"Help you how?"

"Help us understand you, all of you."

"What for?"

"So we can save ourselves, and you all too, maybe."

"What you mean?"

"I mean that there is truly a place for you at our table, if you choose to join us. That you could live in this city, the rest of your unit too, with enough to eat and drink and nobody giving you orders to kill people. There'd be work to do, but it'd be worthwhile work, making things, growing things. And you could have a name of your own, not just a number, and respect, if you earn respect."

"Don't believe you."

"You have to believe me, because I am going to give you a name."

"I come from the pens. We don't got names. Only the white boys get to earn them."

"But now you're part of us. All of us in this city, we're like a unit too. All of us together. And everybody has a name."

"What name you gonna give me?"

She thought for a moment, looking at him, his dark eyes round and suddenly almost childlike. This is my week for naming, she thought, first the baby, now him. He should have a strong name, not something Spanish, that he wouldn't be able to pronounce, a simple name that would mean something. Maybe she should name him after Rio, who had also killed and, according to Maya, often been out of control. And Rio had changed. Maybe this man could, too.

"Rio" was too associated with her grandfather. She couldn't name him that. But in translation . . . ?

"River. Your name will be River. That means a big stream of water that flows free above the ground."

"River? That's my name?"

"It fits you," Madrone said.

"You gave me a name."

"It's yours now. Nobody can take it from you."

"River," he said again. His lips curved in a tentative smile, and he looked young for a moment, like a small boy. Then his smile faded. His eyes were open, anguished, vulnerable.

"How do you know who to stand with?" he asked.

"What do you mean?"

"How do you know who your people are? Bird—you know Bird?"

"He was my lover," Madrone admitted.

"That Bird, he talk a lot about his people, about this city. Lotta bullshit, maybe."

"Maybe not."

"But it sound good. I like to picture what it be like, if what he say was true. Then that day, you know the day I mean?" Madrone nodded, and he went on. "We had our orders to kill—kill any people come at us like that. Didn't think nothing about it. We in the army, we do what they say to do. I shoot one, shoot another one. They keep on coming. Stupid, man, I think, stupidest fucking thing I ever seen. I shoot again. I can feel Bird behind me— he don't like it. Well, they his people, I think, and then this thought come to me: Who my people? I never asked that before, and I have to stop to think about it. I see that girl, the little one, and I think, how do I know who she is? I don't even know who I am. Never even thought before that I might be somebody, but maybe I am. She look like me, kind of—maybe she my people and I don't even know? I couldn't kill her."

"No," Madrone said softly. "I'm glad."

"Maybe I already kill my people—maybe they gonna haunt me for it. How do I know? I never thought about it before, but now I can't stop thinking about it. Where did I come from? What happened to me?"

"You found your immortal soul," Madrone said. "The bigsticks said you didn't have one. But they were wrong."

"And now you gave me a name," River said. "You must be my people, now."

"We will be your people," Madrone said. "Will you help us?"

"What you want?"

"I want to save Bird."

"Yeah. He one tough demonfucker, but they gonna break him down."

"And the others too. There's a girl, a young girl, a friend of mine and Bird's."

"That skinny little girl they bring him to see?"

"Where are they keeping her?"

"I don't know. They move her all the time. Sometimes they keep her close by, down the hall. Sometimes in another building."

"Could you find her? I think they're using her to threaten Bird, to make him do what they want."

"They using her, all right. Maybe I can find her. Have to make contact with the unit, first. See what they know."

Madrone sighed. "I guess the first step is to get you well. Then we'll see." There was one thing more left to do, to seal his trust. She stood and went into Lily's kitchen where the old woman sat at the table sound asleep. When Madrone entered, she stirred.

"I've got him talking," Madrone said, as she filled a bowl with honey from a jar on the counter.

"That's wonderful!"

"You were right, Lily. I can't hate him anymore. I feel for him."

Lily smiled. "We may win, you know. This morning I can believe in miracles again."

Lily followed her into the living room but squatted down by the doorway, leaving the room's breadth between her and River.

Madrone sat again before River, holding the bowl of honey in her hands. Can I really do this? she wondered. Do I have enough power? She closed her eyes, and suddenly she felt as if a pair of hands covered her own. Power flooded through her, augmenting her own. My mother's hands. She is no longer severed from me, and now my own power is complete. Breathing deep, she triggered her bee mind and then let herself sink even deeper into trance, so deep she could read River's chemistry from his smell. Fear, and pain, and an immune system that was barely functional. She could see the patterns in the *ch'i* worlds, she could taste what he lacked and will her own body to provide it, brewed out of her own hormones and proteins, exuded in the bead of sweat that formed in her bee spot. She let it drop into the honey, placed her hand above the bowl to charge it with *ch'i,* and let it transform. There, it was done. She had brewed him up an elixir of life.

River had watched her, transfixed with fear and fascination. Now she took the breaths that called her back to herself, and looked into his eyes, and smiled.

"Don't be afraid," she said. "I'm going to give you another gift."

"What?"

"Your freedom. Taste this honey. See, it's harmless, I'll taste it myself." She dipped a finger in, let the sweetness coat her tongue and send a rush of energy down her spine. "But it will change you. It's magic, good magic. Eat this honey, and you will never need the boosters again."

Cautiously, River dipped a finger in and licked it off.

"Tastes good."

"It is good. Go ahead, eat more. Eat as much as you can."

"We have a machine to help with that," Lily said from the far end of the room. "It's called a spoon. Also I could provide some bread. Perhaps some toast? Would you like that, soldier?"

"River," Madrone said. "He has a name now, and it's River."

River nodded, and Lily went off to fix a meal.

"If this shit works," River said to Madrone, "I get you an army."

"It's a deal."

35

"I cannot stand this," Maya said to herself. She was wandering the house, unable to settle anywhere, unable to cook or clean or tend to the sick soldiers. Anyway, between Mary Ellen and Sara, they didn't really need her. She was old and useless. Sam had work, Madrone was off somewhere healing, but all she had was the consciousness that they were losing, and her own vision was at the root of their failure. Maybe compassion could not overcome cruelty. Maybe she had been wrong, to believe in that possibility, but now it was being put to the test and here she sat, doing nothing. Nothing but sitting in stupid Council meetings, listening to her grandson being attacked by idiots. No, she could not—would not—stand for it.

She made her way to her own room, which was free of wounded soldiers. Sam had fallen asleep on the downstairs cot, and Maya hoped he wouldn't wake or look for her. Madrone had been gone all night, and Nita was working up in the ritual room. Sara and Mary Ellen were in the kitchen; Lou and Aviva had not yet arrived. Yes, she could do it. Now was the time, and today was the day. She closed her door.

Maya put on a white dress that she had worn years before to ceremonies for the orishas. It was very old, a thick white cotton skirt, a crushed cotton blouse that dipped to a slenderizing point at the waistline. Not that she needed slenderizing anymore. She brushed out her long silver hair and let it hang down. She wrapped a white cloak around her and took down from its peg her silver-handled walking stick, which seemed the appropriate prop, in every sense of the word. She scribbled a note to Sam, another to Madrone, and left them on the bed.

She peeked carefully out of her doorway. Nobody was in the hall. This was fun, in a way, like sneaking out of her mother's house when she was a kid. Quietly she tiptoed down the stairs, tucking her cane under her arm and gripping the handrail to steady herself. Out the front door and there, she had done it. She was free.

For a moment Maya stood looking at the door of the house after she closed it behind her. Up these steps she had come, so many years before, to find a home with Johanna when she had tired of Mexico, of being on the run. Here she had brought Rio home. Inside these walls she had told stories to Rachel, Madrone's mother, and held tiny Brigid's hand on the steps as she first learned to maneuver her own way up and down. Maybe I will return and walk back through that door, she thought. Maybe I will not. In any case, you've been a good house. You've sheltered me a long, long time. But you cannot shelter me now.

She walked on. The summer gardens were parched from lack of rain, and the streambed was dry. The soldiers must have rebuilt the dam again. Oh, whatever came of this, there would be hunger. No children played among the dry brown sticks. No one moved on the walkways, except, here and there, an armed khaki-dressed figure or a ghost in white like her, on a mission of haunting.

The Transport Collective had immobilized the gondolas, and the soldiers so far had ignored the aerial transport system. Maya would have to walk downtown. That was okay, the exercise would do her good. She would take one last slow look at the city she had loved for so many years. It still shone in her imagination as a place of magic, of gingerbread houses and green-topped hills and fairy spires. Goodbye, labyrinth of winding pathways. Farewell, streams and fruit trees and gardens. *Adiosa,* you cheerful and confident children who now scurry into your houses, afraid. Perhaps you are waiting for me to free you. Perhaps you already suspect I will fail.

The morning had passed by the time she reached the old stone mansion atop Nob Hill where the General made his headquarters. The house had been built as a monument to the private wealth of one of the gold barons back in the nineteenth century, had become an exclusive men's club in the twentieth, and after the Uprising a home for the very old, where they could be cared for in peace and dignity. Maya wondered what had happened to them, who had taken them in, whether any of them were as old as she was, why she was still alive.

The garden in the grounds was still green and flourishing, she noted. The gracious steps of the house were lined with ghosts, silent and patient in their white cloaks. Maya could discern that in some of the watchers patience had hardened into apathy and desolation. Still they waited. No one emerged.

She would not wait.

She mounted the steps, leaning heavily on her cane. The ghosts made way for her, one young woman leaping up and offering her arm. Maya looked into her eyes for a moment, startled, thinking they were her daughter Brigid's eyes. But no, not Brigid, just another dark-eyed, dark-haired young woman. Brigid was dead anyway, but ghosts should be dead, and Maya was wandering in the confusion of the old.

The heavy front door was locked. She raised her cane and pounded on it. Silence. She pounded again, harder. The door opened a crack and a dark face peered out at her.

"Get off the steps, or we'll clear you off! You can't come in here!"

"You cannot keep me out," Maya said, sliding her cane into the crack and butting against the door with her shoulder. But really it was her eyes that gave her entrance. For now she had slipped out of herself and something larger had slipped in, the Reaper, *La Segadora,* the Old Crone, the Death Hag. She had become the Implacable One. No boy soldier could withstand her. She pushed the guard out of the way and strode down the hall. He followed after her and tried to grab her arm, but she dangled her cane between his feet and he tripped and fell hard on the marble floor. I'm skirting the edge of nonviolence, she admitted, but while he was gathering himself up again she pushed through a pair of imposing double doors and found herself in the General's office.

The sunny room was lined with bay windows facing the north, looking out over the water to Mount Tamalpais across the Bay. The General sat behind a large oak desk, his feet on a faded but still beautiful oriental rug. Three of his staff stood at loose attention around him.

Maya pounded her cane on the floor, and the General turned and stared. With his soft belly hidden behind the desk, he appeared to be a solid edifice of muscular flesh, topped by straw-colored hair cropped short. He peered up at her with eyes small and hard as buckshot.

"What in Satan's name is this? How the hell did she get in here?"

"Sir—" the breathless soldier from the hallway began, but the General motioned him to be silent. He rose from his desk and came over to Maya, towering above her.

"Who the Jesus are you?"

Maya opened her mouth to say something reasonable, but what came out seemed to come through her from somewhere else.

"Your death," Maya said. "I am what you have always resisted and what you come to in the end. I am your fate."

"My fate is to exterminate the sinners who corrupt this world."

He was much taller than she, but suddenly her eyes seemed on a level with his. A voice poured through her, spilling out over him. "Your fate is in your blood and bones, where every person's fate lies. Your fate is right here, arisen before your very eyes. I stand face to face with you."

"Who are you?" the General said again.

"I am what you cannot escape, the gray in your hair, the lines on the back of your hand. I am the Reaper, the reckoning, the consequences of your actions. Clench tight your hopes and I will pry loose your grip. I am your destination."

She was a vessel for the voice as a streambed channels water that comes from some greater source, high and far away.

"I am fate, and chance, your chance to rise to the great opportunity you have here. Yes, I see who you are, and who you might be. Your ancestors cluster around you. One of them is a small boy who watches as the Inquisitors drag his mother off, strip her naked in the public square, prick her with needles searching for devil's marks, rape her, burn her alive. Yes, I see his eyes as he watches the flesh that meant his comfort and food crackle and char, as the hands that soothed him blacken. I see him wear that pain as armor, grow into it until it becomes his skin.

"And now he is a grown man in a faraway place, Africa. Here he is on *La Gorée,* do you know that name? The Last Door, they called it, an island through which all slaves passed on their way out of the continent. And here he is, your illustrious forefather, in the rape room, violating a black woman while her own small boy is forced to watch. Maybe he leaves his seed in her, seed of pain that grows in her belly and somehow survives the Middle Passage through hell to be born. Not your ancestor, that one, but the father of fathers of someone else, one of these men here, maybe, or my own grandson. And the woman is able to love the child, as women do love, because she understands that what has been planted in her is the pain of a child, until this one too is torn away from her. Oh, it is awesome what human beings are capable of doing to each other and surviving. So many women harboring seeds of pain, nurturing, bringing them to birth so those offspring can enact their pain on some other woman's body, and always, always with one hope—that somehow, someday, this will change. Someone will refuse to pass the pain on any longer. Who knows? Maybe you are that person?"

The General was staring at her, transfixed. "Pain forms a man," he said.

"Or breaks him."

"A man is not made until he has been broken." Then he seemed to shake himself awake again. "What is your name?"

Maya took a deep breath. The Reaper deserted her, and she was just a woman again, old and small. She drew herself up to her full height and spoke with dignity.

"Maya Greenwood."

"Aha. The writer?"

"I wasn't aware my reputation still survived in the Southlands."

"I once had the pleasure of burning a number of your books."

"A fan," Maya said. "I'm flattered."

"You intrigue me," the General said. "What did you hope to achieve, coming to me like this? Did you expect to win me over with your blasphemous babbling? I would have thought Maya Greenwood was smarter than that."

"I came to warn you," Maya said, although her voice felt old and tremulous. "You cannot win here."

The General laughed. "Your grandson wouldn't agree with you. He seems to think we can't lose."

Now, Old Bitch, now would be a good moment for Divine Possession to strike. But Maya remained empty. Still, I won't beg him or plead with him to let me see my grandson. "I have come to share his ordeal," Maya said.

"That can be arranged." The General gestured to his guards. "Lock her up. But don't work her over. Her heart might go out on us, and I've got a special use for her."

Maya sat down on the rug. "There is a place set for you at our table, if you will choose to join us," she said as the soldiers dragged her away.

∘ ∘ ∘

The room they locked Maya in had once been an office. It still held a desk, if not a bed or a chair, and she perched on it, swinging her legs. There was no toilet but perhaps she would use one of the drawers as a waste bucket, when the need arose. They had left her water and a hunk of bread, but she would not touch their food. No, she would just close her eyes, and drift. She was close to Bird now; surely she would reach him now.

But she did not reach Bird, only Johanna, who stood with her hands on her hips, observing Maya disapprovingly. "This is a fine predicament you've landed yourself in," Johanna said.

"I had to do it," Maya said.

"No, you didn't have to. You wanted to, Goddess only knows why. Some unresolved Jewish guilt complex, maybe."

"You just can't wait to come on over to our side, can you?" asked Rio, who appeared behind her.

"I'm sorry you made them tear down the jail after the Uprising," Maya told him. "I could have been locked up in a real cell that had a bunk bed and a toilet."

"If it's creature comforts you were interested in, you should have stayed home, where you had a nice comfy bed and someone to warm it for you," Rio said.

"Jealous?" Maya asked.

"Hah."

"Anyway, you know how it is," Maya said, "when you get all fired up to commit some brave political act, and you feel invulnerable for a while, like you'll never care about food or sleep again. But then it wears off, leaving you mourning for your bathtub and a hot teakettle."

"Maya, we're with you," Rio said. "Whatever happens."

Suddenly she was very afraid. Really, I've been afraid all along, she admitted, but what a good job I've done convincing myself that I wasn't. Goddess, what have I done to myself? What have I done to Bird?

"What's going to happen?" she wailed. "What's going to happen to me?"

"Oh, you're going to die, of course," Johanna said. "Eventually."

"I mean now. What's going to happen now?"

"Now you're going to get some sleep," Johanna said. "See if you can curl up on that desk, and don't let your Gandhi complex keep you from drinking some of that water."

        ° ° °

"What do you mean, she's gone?" Sam said. "Where did she go?" Suddenly he looked every bit of his eighty-some years. His face crumpled, and he gripped Madrone's shoulder with a shaky hand.

"She left us notes," Madrone said, trying to keep her own voice calm. "I guess she slipped out this morning, while I was over at Lily's and you were asleep on the cot."

"But that was hours ago!" Sam protested. "How could I have not noticed that she wasn't here?"

They were standing in the kitchen, where Mary Ellen continued chopping greens for supper.

"I didn't notice either," Madrone admitted. "I came home and fell asleep. There were dozens of people here; I didn't realize she wasn't one of them. It wasn't until I went to get her for dinner that I saw the notes."

"Let me see," Sam said. He grabbed his note from Madrone, but his hand was shaking and his eyes were tearing. "Read it to me."

"Dear Sam," Madrone read. *"I've gone to haunt the General. Don't get in a flap—it's what I'm called to do, for better or worse. And the worst will be that they kill me, and really, Sam, at my age death can scarcely be seen as premature. I do love you. You've been a great comfort to me in a terrible time, and whatever world I'm in, I will always thank you. I regret leaving you alone. Forgive me, and please try to understand. Love, Maya."*

"It's suicide! Sheer bloody stupid suicide!" Sam began to cry. Madrone held him and soothed him, but she was crying herself. "I loved her, Madrone. I really loved her!"

"I know. I know, Sam."

"And if they find out Bird's her grandson—"

"Don't think about it, Sam. There's no point in torturing yourself. She's gone, now, and we're just going to have to let her go. Or follow her with magic, not with worries." Oh, she could sound so wise and cool. "Lie down a bit, Sam. Rest until supper. I'll do some magic for her."

"Will you?"

"I will, right now. You rest."

        ° ° °

Madrone went out into the back garden of Black Dragon House. Unlike the front gardens, the back was still mostly green, although weeds choked the vegetable beds. Honeybees buzzed around the blue stars of prickly borage. Only the lawn was dead, and she lay down on the brown dry grass and closed her eyes.

Concentrating on her breath, she slipped back into her bee mind. She saw, not the world of visual form as she knew it, but a multifaceted prism of light and shade intertwined with streaks of color. Traces of scent bombarded her, the heady clarity of borage, the perfume of the rose, the pungent pineapple sage. She could get lost in the twining, trailing scents, drifting in for miles —how tempting to pick one and follow it, track a particular sweetness to its source, return to the hive to dance directions.

Nothing happened in words or even pictures, exactly, but more as an overlay of images and smells and movements and feelings, like the body sense of magnetic north, feelings of rightness or wrongness. And yes, as she approached the hive, disturbance. A buzz of fear and alarm; this was nothing they had ever known. Madrone exuded a calming smell, not the queen smell, which might trigger competition with their own queen, but something just enough akin to it that the bees relaxed. She was not a threat.

Under their immediate distress was a deeper sense of alarm. Things were not right. Gardens they counted on were dying. So many of the flowers were gone, withered up early, dried on the vine. Everywhere they smelled fear and pain.

Madrone let the honey of her body well up into the bee spot and began to speak to them, a speech of projected visions and pheromones, molecular scents on the air. Slowly they gathered, touching, tasting, until her body was covered with crawling bees. Help us, she said, and we will grow the green well-watered gardens again, let the borage run rampant, dance for you in summertime. You are part of our powers, our forgotten powers. Help us, please, sisters, help.

○ ○ ○

Bird had been alone in the dark with the dead for so long that he was no longer sure he was alive. They had taken him back to this dark bare room, where time no longer passed but left him marooned in a vacuum, without gravity. Occasionally his body intruded itself with its pain, its hungers, its need to relieve itself. At intervals the door was opened, something resembling food was pushed in, the bucket of his wastes was replaced. Once in a while, he tried to remember his muscles, to keep them functioning and exercised, but he was too weak to sustain activity for long. Mostly he drifted, conversing with ghosts until the slender cord of vital energy that held him to his body stretched thin and fragile and frayed.

He was lost not only in his own pain but the shadowy pain of multitudes of others, awash in guilt and fear and despair that he could no longer separate. Ghosts spoke to him, telling tales of their suffering. "You conjured us up," they seemed to say. "Now listen, listen. This is how it was, when the slavers came to my village, when the Nazis broke down the door and took us off to the camps, when the whites broke our temples and sent us to the mines, when everything we knew and cared about was destroyed. Listen to us, feed us, carry our pain."

No, I have nothing to feed you, I can't carry my own pain, let alone the weight of all of yours. *Diosa,* I have too many ancestors, one history of oppression would be enough to inherit. Leave me alone!

"Then listen, listen to us, we are your ancestors too. I sold my daughter to the slavers, I loaded the cattle cars, I smashed the temples of the heathens, I applied the lash, I raped. We are your ancestors, we are the unquiet dead. Feed us, heal us, listen to our stories. Or we will feed on you."

Go ahead. Eat me, kill me, let me have some peace.

Maybe he was already dead, caught in the hell the Millennialists warned of. Familiar, it was so familiar, this place, as if he had already spent years and years here, eternity. Often he couldn't clearly remember who he was and what he had done to merit this punishment. He had been weak, he had betrayed something, he thought, but he was not clear what or how or why or if he could have resisted or whose nightmare he was trapped in. And there were hell worlds after hell worlds to be lost in, too many of them, the underside of the last five thousand years of history, and he could find no way out because he had given in and accepted the power of the killers.

"No, we want you to sing for us, speak for us, redeem our lives," the ghosts clamored, victims and victimizers, their voices intertwined.

But I can't even redeem my own. I have no voice left, and I am going to die defeated.

"Then we have no hope."

No hope, no hope, buzzed around his brain like a tuneless song. Having no hope, he felt no fear, and that was a small relief. Even when he thought of Rosa, what did it matter, ultimately, what happened to her? She would be just one more victim among legions of the dead.

I tried, I wasn't strong enough. You see, Maya, it's not the Good Reality or the Bad Reality, it's *El Mundo de la Fuerza,* the reality of brute force, that is stronger than all our magic. Oh, Lily, it was a noble attempt. Fight on the landscape of consciousness, you said, but the body is too damn vulnerable, and we cannot win. We cannot win.

36

"Yºou got to eat, ma'am," the soldier said, distressed, picking up the platter of bread Maya had left untouched.

"No, young man, there you're wrong," Maya replied. "I'm ninety-nine years old. I don't got to do nothing. Anything."

"For real?" he breathed. He looked very young to Maya; perhaps they drafted them at fifteen or sixteen in the South. His eyes were wide and round in his copper face. "You really ninety-nine years old?"

"Just had my birthday, back in June. Fog-Rolls-In Moon, we call it. Not that we were much in the mood to celebrate."

"Maybe you like some soup? Bring you some," he offered.

"I am a wild bird. I do not eat in captivity."

"You don't eat, you die, ma'am."

"Call me Maya. It's my name. What's your name?"

"Don't got one. They took it when they took me for the army."

"Ridiculous. Nobody can take your name. You still remember it, don't you?"

He glanced quickly around the dark room, as if worried that someone might overhear them, and then nodded.

"What is it?"

"Tom," he whispered. He looked around again. "*Tomás,* my mother used to say."

"Tomás, that's a fine name. *Mucho gusto,* Tomás. Pleased to meet you. There, that was your name, and now you have it back. So you have a mother? You weren't bred for the army?"

He shook his head no. "Our unit, we come off the streets. Soup, ma'am? What you say?"

"Why are you so worried about me?"

"You die, you haunt me."

"I'd consider it. Intermittently, at least. Why does that bother you?"

He shuddered. "Come out to the guardroom, ma'am. I need to clean this place."

"You'll have to carry me."

"You hurt?"

"No, I'm refusing to cooperate. It's a time-honored political tactic."

"Okay, I carry you"—he hesitated, and then said her name—"Maya." He set down the bread, slid his hands under her body, and lifted her, holding her out from his body as if afraid to allow too much contact. He carried her into the hallway, where a number of soldiers were stationed. They were all bronze-skinned, with dark straight hair; they all reminded her of Carlos, who had seduced her long ago and gotten her pregnant with Brigid, Bird's mother. Three of them were playing cards at a desk they'd set up facing a bank of elevators. Tomás set her down on an empty chair beside the desk.

"Watch her," he said to the card players. "I got to clean her cell."

"Tie her," suggested the soldier closest to Tomás, a big man with forearms so muscular they bulged out of his sleeves.

"I ain't gonna tie her. She's ninety-nine years old."

"No shit?" The soldier turned and looked at Maya.

"On my honor, as a Witch and a former Girl Scout."

The soldiers shifted their chairs away from her. Tomás took a bucket of cleaning materials out of a closet and disappeared into the room where Maya had been held.

"You gonna put a spell on us?" asked another of the men. He had lost several of his front teeth, and his gums were nearly black.

"I don't need to," Maya said. "You are already under a spell, a spell I'd like to free you from."

"Who got us under a spell?" asked the man Maya thought of as Muscles.

"The General, of course. He's got you under a spell of obedience. Otherwise, why are you here? You don't want to be here, do you? When you could sit with us at our table, at the place we have ready for you?"

"What you people mean by that?" asked the third soldier, whom Maya nicknamed Tiny to herself. "You mean we should come on over to your side, win the war for you? Then what? We die from no boosters?"

"No fucking boosters half the time anyway, man, long as they keep losing trains," Teeth said.

"We're on the edge of a solution to the booster problem," Maya said, wondering if that were really true. "We've almost got it licked."

"Say you do," Muscles said. "Say we come over, say we even win. Then what? What you do with us? How you feed an army?"

"We don't want an army," Maya said. "We can't feed an army. But we can offer you ways to feed yourselves. Land, if you want to farm. Work here in the City, if you prefer. A house to live in—a big one if you share it, a small place or an apartment if you want to live on your own."

"What kind of work?" Teeth asked suspiciously.

"What kind of work would you like to do? We can train you for anything you like or apprentice you to one of the work groups. You could build transport towers, or help maintain the water systems, or raise silkworms. Some of you might even want to study at the university. We're short-handed here in the North; we've got more that needs doing than people to do it. So we all work hard, I won't lie to you. You'd have to work hard too. But you'd never lack for food or water."

"Why should we believe you?" Tiny asked. "What's the catch?"

"You've seen our city," Maya said. "Have you found any slums? Any ghettos? You've seen who our leaders were, before you murdered most of them. You've seen that they come from all races, that no one group rules us. It's true there are some things we won't tolerate here. Rape, for one. Violence. But we're offering you a chance at freedom. Isn't that worth taking a gamble on?"

They were silent. Behind the masks of their faces, thoughts were churning, even if Maya couldn't read what they were. You see, Johanna? Rio, do you understand, now? This is what I was sent to do.

Tomás emerged with the cleaning bucket. "The room's clean, now. I can put her back."

Muscles shook his head. "Let her stay out here with us."

"Yeah," said Teeth. "I like to hear her talk."

"I never thought it would come to this," Sam said. "All those years I spent training: Stanford, Johns Hopkins. Those names meant something in my day. Who would ever have thought I'd come to depend on a Witch brewing potions from honey and sweat?"

"Bitch, bitch, bitch!" Madrone said. They were making rounds in Black Dragon House, where, after a week of her new treatment, almost all the deserters showed marked improvement.

"Don't complain, Sam," Lou said. He held the wrist of one of the men who had been the sickest, taking his pulses in the Chinese medical tradition. "Just pray it continues working."

"Witches don't pray, we incant," Madrone said.

Lou ignored her. "You're doin' fine," he said to his patient.

"I feel better."

"You'll be well enough to get up in a day or two." Lou stood. "That about covers it for today."

They went into the kitchen, where Lily sat drinking tea at the big round table. She rose and greeted them. At the counter, River was helping Mary Ellen chop vegetables for dinner. He had taken to following Madrone around, like a big Labrador puppy, but she would not allow him on rounds. Really, she was surprised at how well he seemed to adjust. He was used to following orders and was still most comfortable doing what he was told, either by her, because he trusted her, or by Sam, the oldest, whitest man around. And he delighted in helping Mary Ellen.

"I understand him and his kind," Mary Ellen said. "I know how to handle them. Firmly, and don't turn your back until you sure they're going to be loyal to you. Then let your enemies watch out!"

Rations were getting scarce, but people all over the City contributed to feeding the sick soldiers, even when they had to go short themselves. Still, they often ate odd things. Today, Madrone noted, Mary Ellen appeared to have harvested the lovage, an herb that grew prolifically and tasted like a bitter form of celery.

"He's still looking good," Sam said, jerking his chin at River. "How do you feel? Still no fevers or pains?"

"I feel good," River said. "Don't worry. She fixed me. When we gonna tell the rest of the army?"

"How long has it been?" Sam asked.

"It's been ten days, for him," Madrone said.

"I still think we should wait at least a full two weeks. Six would be better. Just to be sure there aren't any side effects or relapses."

"We don't have six weeks, Sam," Madrone said.

"I know that. Fourteen days was our compromise."

"At this juncture, every day counts," Lily put in. "The people are falling into despair. There've been so many deaths and losses. They haven't yet turned to violence, but unless we can give them some hope soon—"

"But if we announce that we have a cure for booster withdrawal, we've got to be damn sure we really do," Sam said. "Otherwise, we're going to end up with an army of ex-soldiers, sick, mean, desperate, and believing we betrayed them."

"Bird hasn't been seen in the Plaza for a long time now," Madrone said in a low voice. "Rosa can't be found. Goddess knows what's happening to them. And Maya—"

Sam put his arm around her. "I know, I know. But it's just a few more days. It's looking good, Madrone. Let's not spoil it by rushing."

"And Council?" Lily said. "Last night they almost approved a policy legitimizing assassination. Several of us blocked it, of course, but how long can we hold them back?"

"Can't you tell them we're on the verge of something?" Sam asked. "Get them to hold out just a little longer."

"I've been saying that to them for weeks, long before it was remotely true. Sooner or later, they're going to stop believing me."

"You're probably right, Sam," Madrone said, suddenly close to tears, "but I'm not sure I can bear it. I have horrible dreams about Bird every night, but when I wake up I can't remember them."

Sam squeezed her shoulders. "Four more days, that's all. Can't you do some magic with your bees and find Rosa? Then you'd feel better, knowing what's happening to her."

"Or worse," Lou said, "as the case may be."

"*Dream* to her," Lily suggested.

"Nothing comes clear to me. I just have nightmares. Maybe I'm just losing it, running on too much adrenaline and not enough sleep."

"Tell me something new," Lou said.

"Three days, Sam?" Lily said. "Can we compromise on that? If you're certain it's necessary, we'll wait. But no longer. One way or another, a change is coming. We can't go on like this forever."

"We have, back where I come from," Mary Ellen said, looking up from the chopping board.

"No," Lily said. "Even there, this can't go on forever."

○ ○ ○

The bees were searching. Madrone lay in the garden in the warm sun, following their flight. Through narrow cracks they squeezed, up and down cold halls of stucco and cement, behind the locks of closed doors and into the grates of ventilation systems, winging swiftly through any opened door. Back they came, eager to escape the dead air and the chemical smell and the odors of pain. They had not found Rosa. No scent, no taste of a young girl's fear or hope. Nothing. Only hints of Bird, something in their humming that sang of despair, a reek of decay. Follow that, she told them, changing something in her sweat so that the stink of rot and fear was scent-tagged as something desirable, a field of pollen-laden blossoms, a new source of honey. Find it, stay with it, cherish it like a precious larva to be tended and cleaned and fed. It is our hope, little sisters. Yours and mine.

○ ○ ○

Without meetings, without consensus, without formalized strategies, people began to fill the streets. By day small groups sat down in the major roadways, impeding the movements of troops. When they were cleared, with blows or shots, others took their places. By night, spontaneous marches assembled, hundreds and finally thousands of people, dressed in white, roaring and chanting and marching through the streets while drums beat. Madrone joined them when her work for the day was done. It assuaged some deep need in her, to walk in company with others, voices raised. The soldiers just stood and watched. Whether they had been ordered not to fire or were afraid of ghosts, nobody knew. At times it seemed to Madrone as if the dead marched with them. Voices whistled in the atmosphere, and feet echoed off pavements where no living feet trod. Wraiths of fog hovered low to the ground and moved against the wind.

A day passed, and another day. River was still well. He asked to march with her, stopping her on the front steps as she was on her way out, but she was afraid he might be recognized by someone from his unit.

"Give it one more day," she said. "Then we can decide how to let them know that they don't have to fear withdrawal if they come over to us."

River shook his head. "What we waiting for? I'm not gonna have no relapse. I'm telling you, I feel good. I can feel the change. It's like my body belong to me in a way it never did."

"I'm glad, River."

The drumbeat pulled her along, driving them all to the same rhythm; they sang chants in one hoarse voice, as if they had become one organism, one animal incandescent with rage. Something was about to break, here. Some tide was about to turn.

o o o

The Council meeting was small, and one of the Voices was missing. Coyote, in his unmasked everyday form, had been shot the night before, trying to block a squadron of soldiers from destroying one of the transport towers.

"We can't meet with one of the Voices missing," a young woman protested.

"We're going to have to," said Joseph wearily. "I'm Crow for the day; I've made the decision. We don't have a choice. There's no time to choose a successor, and we've got things we have to decide."

"I don't like it," murmured a second woman. "It's bad luck to ignore the Trickster. But I guess we've got to live with it."

"It's a sign," Cress said, standing up. "We've let them destroy too much, even one of the Four Sacred Things. When are we going to fight back?"

"We are fighting back," Lily said. "We're on the verge of winning. Soldiers are coming over to our side every day."

"A few," Cress admitted. "And some of us are defecting to their side."

"I don't want to discuss Bird again," Lily said. "We've had that debate."

"I didn't say anything about Bird," Cress protested. "You're the one who brought him up. The point is, a few soldiers puking in makeshift hospitals on our side aren't going to win this for us. They can bring up thousands of soldiers, hundreds of thousands."

"Yet another reason why we can't win if we fight on their terms," Lily said.

"Lily, you don't seem to understand that people are tired of your mystical bullshit. We've gone along with you so far, and what has it gotten us? Bullets in the head, the streams dammed, people dying in the streets!" Now Cress was up and shouting. Joseph jumped up and called for order, but Cress ignored him. "We've had it, Lily! One more massacre, one more round of deaths, and some of us are going to take action, Council or no Council!"

"Then they will win!" Lily said, rising to her feet and raising her voice in response. "You're threatening the very heart of what we're fighting for! What keeps us together in this city, what allows us to build what we have built, is respect for this Council, for our mutual consensus. If you violate that, the Stewards won't have to bother taking over. We will already be destroyed!"

"When consensus blocks the will of the majority, it becomes tyranny!" Cress yelled.

"You don't have a majority! You have a vocal bloc!"

"No, you have a vocal bloc, which is blocking what the majority wants to do!"

"Process!" Joseph thundered. "Both of you, shut up! I will take comments only from those who have not yet spoken today."

Madrone stood. She was tired, tired, tired of all the arguments. One of these meetings was more exhausting than ten hours of healing. "I have good news," she said in a flat voice. Try to sound a little cheerful, then. "We've developed a protocol for booster withdrawal that appears to be effective. We're ready to start leaking that news to the army."

Cress opened his mouth to speak, but a look from Joseph silenced him.

Sachiko stood up. "That's wonderful, Madrone. So maybe more soldiers will defect now?"

"We hope so," Madrone said.

"That's speculation," said the woman sitting beside Cress. "We don't know for sure."

"But can't we give it a little time?" Madrone pleaded. "A week or two, at least, to see what happens, before we go splintering off into factions and breaking the Council? It would be a shame to start shooting at the soldiers just when they might be about to come over to our side."

"If we're going to mount an offensive, we have to do it while we still have some resources," Cress said. Joseph glared at him.

"We will never have enough resources to defeat them with guns," Lily countered quietly.

"I said I wanted to hear from those who have not spoken yet," Joseph said.

Silence fell on the room. Sachiko looked at Joseph. "I did speak once, but I wasn't really finished," she said.

"Go ahead."

"I think Madrone is right. We've got so much invested in this strategy, so many lives already lost. It only makes sense to give it a little more time to work, now that we have some real hope to offer the soldiers. I'd like to make that a proposal. But, Cress, I do hear your concerns. We can't hold people back forever from taking actions they want to take."

"They're not concerns," Cress said. "They're not threats. I'm simply going to state here, once and for all, what Water Council and our allies intend to do. Unless there's some radical change in the situation in the next few days, we intend to take autonomous action. We won't block your proposal, but we won't bind ourselves to abide by it either."

"Then you will do our enemies' work for them," Lily said.

"Process!" Joseph said again. But the process had broken down.

∘   ∘   ∘

In the dark, Bird felt a flicker of motion. By reflex, he opened his eyes. He thought he was awake now and had been asleep before, but he didn't know for sure. It didn't matter. Bad dreams haunted his sleeping, ghosts plagued his waking.

The darkness around him was vibrating and humming, alive with a sound that was strange and yet not strange. He had heard it before; it reminded him of something: sunlight, and flowers, which he had forgotten existed. Then he recognized the sound as the buzzing of a bee.

"What?" Bird said, and jumped at the sound of his own voice. Had he spoken aloud, for the first time in how long? "What?" he said again, just to test if he really existed, if his lips made sounds that his ears could hear. He wasn't sure, but he thought they did.

It was too dark for even his long-accustomed eyes to see much, but in his mind's eye he pictured a honeybee, furred and golden. Something landed on his forehead; he closed his eyes as it walked delicately over his face. Its touch was so soft, so gentle, like the feather touch of a lover's hand, like Madrone's fingers tracing his cheekbones and eyelids, like forgiveness. He almost cried—it was so long since he had been touched that way, and it seemed miraculous, the Goddess herself reaching out to him to remind him of life. The dark unfolded and blossomed, a black rose, a night lily. He felt warm, as if someone were holding his hands.

The bee stayed with him, and when it left another came. He still had no sense of time but he began to trust the bees, that their comings and goings measured intervals. They seemed to take shifts, perhaps no one of them could stand the stench and the darkness very long, but they never left him alone again. He was grateful. Their buzzing chased the ghosts out of his head; their feet on his skin reminded him that the body could feel not only pain but pleasure. He had nothing to offer them in return; the thin and slimy soup that appeared periodically was not something that would nourish them. But he spoke to them and praised them and sang them little songs, which they seemed to like, although how he knew that he couldn't say. Most likely he was just out of his mind, talking to insects, but he no longer cared. His voice croaked at first, but as he used it the tones improved. He sang them all the songs he knew, and when he was done he made up new ones, songs that fit the hell worlds, songs of the unquiet dead, their losses, their betrayals, their defeats. The bees didn't care. Listen, spirits, I am singing for you, like you wanted. Are you happy now? No one will ever hear these songs, but I'm singing.

The guards came for him without warning. The opening of the door, the sound of their heavy boots, and their hands grabbing him and jerking him up to his feet sent such a rush of physical terror through Bird's body that he almost vomited. The bees deserted him, and he felt jealous. He wanted to fly away too. His hands were cuffed behind his back, and he was marched on unsteady legs down a long corridor toward a new ordeal. You little winged fuckers, he thought. I was past fear, and then you made me come alive again, and where are you now?

In the room they brought him to, Rosa waited, tied and shivering.

"We're giving you a choice tonight," the guard said. "We can work on her while you watch, or let her watch while we work on you. Who will it be, you or her?"

He had just barely enough will left to open his lips and force out one word: "Me."

He promised himself he wouldn't scream in front of her, but he screamed and groveled and shit in his pants. They were going to work on him until he begged them to work on her instead. How long would that take? And would it matter anyway? If he held out this time, would he give way the next? Already he was beginning to hate her, to hate her screaming that hurt his ears, to want her silent, dead, ended, to want to see her suffer as he was suffering.

Then the General himself came in.

"Is he ready?"

"Not quite, sir. He's holding out longer than we expected."

"We're out of time. Give him a shot—not too much. I don't want him to appear drugged. Then clean him up. I've got a use for him."

∘ ∘ ∘

All day long, people had been converging in the Central Plaza. Some had gathered early in the morning; others arrived in contingents that formed spontaneously in the outlying neighborhoods and made their way chanting and singing through the streets, picking up others along the way. Now it seemed that the whole of the city had grouped together in this one spot. The crowd kept shifting, weaving and circling, restless as a brew coming to boil.

The sound system installed after the Uprising still worked perfectly, fueled by the solar cells high in the tops of trees. When a speaker stood on the raised platform in the center of the square, her or his voice was carried easily to the outer boundaries, clear and audible. Now it was the soldiers who took advantage of it, massing on the platform in the center, warning the people to disperse and go home. The crowd responded with chants and pounding drums and howls like ghost cries on the wind.

A phalanx of soldiers approached from the street in front of the old library, clubbing and beating a path through the crowds. There was a moment of confusion when they reached the platform, then they cleared a space.

Madrone looked up. Isis and Nita were on either side of her, and River stood at her back. He was still healthy, and the three days they had promised Sam to wait had passed. He had insisted on coming with them to the Plaza. "Maybe be a chance to talk to the army," he'd said, and Madrone had nodded and accepted his reasoning. If they could gain the central platform, he could speak to the whole crowd at once.

From where they stood, they could see the General, surrounded by the white faces of his Private Guard. He stood on the east side of the platform. A squadron of copper-brown soldiers carrying a white bundle climbed the steps and stood on the west side. They set their burden down by the flagpole where the starred cross of the Southlands flapped above their heads.

"What are they doing?" Nita asked. Shorter than Madrone, she could see little but the backs of the people in front of her.

"They tying something to the flagpole. Or somebody," River told her.

The soldiers moved back, revealing Maya, pale and frail in her tattered white dress, bound to the pole, a gag stretched across her mouth.

"Oh, Goddess," Nita murmured. Madrone gripped her hand.

Isis nudged them. "Let's get up there, closer to her. Maybe we can do something."

They began worming their way through the crowd but stopped as a new group of soldiers pushed their way through the massed people and mounted the platform in the center. They were molasses dark, with coiled African hair, like River.

"Do they color-coordinate all the squadrons?" Nita asked.

"Keeps the races from mixing," Isis said. "Also, it looks good on parade."

"That's my unit," River said. "I got to talk to them." He plunged into the crowd in the wake of the soldiers. Madrone moved to follow him but Isis held her back.

"Let him go. He can take care of himself."

River's unit arranged themselves in two lines on the north and south sides of the platform. One lone figure was left standing in the center. It was Bird. Madrone recognized him, even though in his uniform he appeared as one more dark, anonymous soldier. He gave off a red glow of pain, surrounded by a dull gauzy film that seemed to wrap him up in a separate bubble of air. Still, he seemed to be standing and walking.

General Alexander stepped forward. His voice was boomed out over the crowd.

"I didn't call you here," he said. "Nevertheless, it is opportune that you have come. The Fourth Expeditionary Force of the Stewardship has claimed this land in the name of the Four Purities. We are charged with the cleansing of this land from all forms of Witchcraft and demon worship. Before you stands the chief Witch and demoness. You have come to witness her execution." He motioned to the west, where Maya stood bound.

I should be afraid, Maya thought. *I should feel something. But nothing seemed quite real to her. She was already halfway gone, why bother to hurry the inevitable?*

Girlfriend, I always knew you would come to a bad end, but shot in the public square? Really!

Shut up, Johanna, or do something.

What is there to do? This has gone beyond your doing or mine. All we can do is wait.

Bird stood in the center of the square, not sure how he'd gotten there, not clear what was happening around him. Everything looked fuzzy, his eyes wouldn't focus, and the back of his throat was dry and hurting. It was like a hangover, a pain hangover, but there was something that kept him from quite feeling it, from quite being able to focus his eyes.

One of the General's Private Guard approached him. A white face loomed up before his face, spoke. "One wrong move from you, slimecrawler, and we'll fire into the crowd."

He felt something cold in his hands. They seemed very far away, like somebody else's hands. He looked down. The soldiers had handed him a laser rifle.

"One of your number has abandoned the ways of evil and joined us to receive the blessings of Our Lord," the General went on. "Cadet Fivefour Threethreefour, once known as Bird, we honor you today by choosing you as the executioner."

It took him a long time before he understood. There, across the way, stood Maya. She faced him, her old eyes steady. She had shrunk and aged in these weeks, she had lost that timeless quality and now simply looked old, frail, ready to die.

They wanted him to kill her.

Here it was, then, the end of the road. He had been led along it step by step, and now here was the unthinkable thing they wanted from him. If he refused, what would they do? Kill her themselves, slowly, with torture, while he watched? Or work on him until he broke again, and pleaded with them to allow him to kill her? Oh, Goddess, he had done this to her, he had told them about her, told them her name. His own weakness had already murdered her.

If he could only make contact, make her understand and forgive. He stared through the empty air between them. Maya seemed calm but he was sweating, his breath coming in stifled gasps. If he closed his eyes, he was still falling, weightless, unable to strike ground. His hands shook. But he was the one with the gun. He could, if he chose, turn and train it on the General, but before he could pivot and shoot other guns would fire. How many of the crowd would they kill in retaliation? And if they killed him, who would stand between Rosa and Maya and their fate?

I have been burned before, Maya's eyes seemed to say, it is not new to me, this death. What are you afraid of?

Not death, *abuelita,* not for me. Death is an act of grace, he tried to tell her. If only I could administer it to myself, I would. But I don't dare, not with these guns behind me, ready to turn and fire on people who don't want to die yet.

But death is a gift I can offer you. I can release you. I can restore your lost loves. I can make you safe.

Think, Bird. He heard Rio's voice. Think it out carefully. But he couldn't think. His head was too heavy; he could hardly hold it up. His eyes refused to see clearly.

Maya stood looking calmly at her own death in Bird's face. She was afraid, not for her own life, which she had held on to far too long, but for him, for what this act would do to him. He would never be free of it. There was nothing she could do to help him. She couldn't even speak. What would she say? Bird, your failing is that you are simply mortal, susceptible to pressure and fear and capable of making great mistakes. I have failed you, Bird. Good feminist that I was, I always said yes, men should feel, should cry, should not be afraid to show their vulnerability. But in my secret heart, what I really wanted from you was the impermeable courage of the warrior. I wanted you to be invincible, larger than life. I did not raise you to accept less of yourself.

Madrone stood still, hardly breathing. If she could meet Bird's eyes or touch him or speak with him, even flash him a sign—but he was shut off, his eyes focused only on Maya, who one way or another was now going to die. She wanted to scream, to throw her own body between them, to beg him not to do this. Because if you do, Bird, you will destroy us all. We will never again be able to believe in our power to resist.

Across the Plaza, she caught a glimpse of Cress, who was standing surrounded by a knot of his supporters. *Diosa,* what were they going to do? If Bird shoots, he'll confirm their worst accusations. They'll break our unity, shatter the Council, and run riot, sniping at soldiers from rooftops, ambushing troops on the street. And the soldiers won't come to us, the ones who might have wanted to sit at our table. They'll shoot back, and we will lose.

But if he refused? Was she about to see him die now, right in front of her, without ever having a chance to greet him one more time? Oh, Bird, Bird, I love you and I can't help you, I don't even know what to hope for. All she could do was reach for him, reach and reach with her uncaught love.

Bird felt a breath of wind caressing his cheek like the touch of a hand, like a spirit, like the memory of rain. He sensed a presence, not a voice, not a ghost, just a sense of someone standing there with him.

Whoever you are, go away, he whispered. No one can stand with me here. I have walked here on my own two feet. I won't find any way back. They are too strong for us, and I can't think anymore. My brain hurts, and my ears are ringing.

Madrone waited. Bird didn't see her, he wouldn't turn to look at her, and maybe that was just as well, yet she couldn't help but believe that if he would look at her, she could save him. Maybe that was an illusion, like so many others. With all her power and all her skills, she could only watch, and not shield herself from the pain, as she no longer hid from her own memories. Watching, she took a long, deep breath and began to open.

Layer by layer, peeling away everything she had ever constructed to tell her who she was and separate what was not, she opened. She felt she was holding Maya's hand, not an old hand but a smooth-skinned hand with bitten nails seventeen years old, and in her other hand, Johanna's fingers pressed her, and touched through her, and then it all came crowding in, pain and hate and ugliness and emptiness and fear, she swallowed it all until her own belly ached, and she moaned, and swelled, and cried with rage, but it came on, on and on, moving through the spirits in the crowd. It was all here, thousands of years of the lash and the stake and the bomb. Could she take that into herself to heal it as she had taken other sorts of disease? Could she heal not just the pain of the wound but the pleasure in hurting and the worse and deeper pain behind that?

The ghosts of the dead were swarming, hovering over this square like bees, hordes of them, millions of them, legions of victims, legions of victimizers. She was stretched like a live wire between two ghost hands, light and dark, and she could not bear any more, could not heal this with either her love or her rage, could not transform the magnitude of this history. They would be lost, lost forever, she and Bird and all of them. She stared at him; he was so far away and so closed to her, he who had had the power to make her happy just with a touch, a meeting of eyes. Yet that was not in him but in her own openness, in their opening together. How were we made that we could do this for each other and to each other, so much beauty, so much pain? There was always a choice, to hurt or to heal, but she no longer knew what healing was, or what it meant to be whole if wholeness included all of this. She felt rain beating on her face, and wind on her naked flesh, and she heard a song that was carried not so much to her ears but directly through her skin, like a current. As if she had, indeed, become an instrument in some larger hand, a spoon to stir the cauldron, a knife to cut through the fabric of this world and reveal world after world of possibilities and forms. She closed her eyes and began to sweat honey.

Bird felt a stirring around him. Dimly he heard the voice of the General, yelling an order. "You've got ten seconds, boy. Ten . . ."

He couldn't think, and anyway his body seemed to have a will of its own. His arms responded to commands; his slow brain had lost its influence.

"Nine . . ."

He lifted the rifle. It was heavy in his arms, heavy as a sleeping child. He looked down the sights.

"Eight . . ."

Everything swam and rocked. He felt seasick.

"Seven . . ."

Steady. Hold the rifle steady. Maya's face was outlined in a circle, marked by the cross hairs, the cross in the circle, the mandala, the four sacred directions, the Four Sacred Things.

"Six . . ."

Air, I cannot breathe, I am falling past the limits of what I can resist.

"Five . . ."

Fire, this burns; *abuela,* my soul has been burned away, forgive me, forgive me.

"Four . . ."

Water, the rains will never come again.

"Three . . ."

Earth, this is hard, hard as rock, hard as banging out broken chords for Madrone so she would have a song to take with her when she went. I am tumbling and tumbling and there is no earth under me.

"Two . . ."

He began to hear that song in his mind; it filled him with a sense of her presence, and the memory of loving her, a memory that hurt terribly because he was no longer who he had been, and even she could not heal him of this.

"One . . ."

Abuelita, this is a gift I give you. Isn't it? If only my head would clear.

"Ready!"

But he was not ready, would never be ready.

"Aim . . ."

My aim is to save you suffering what I have suffered.

"Fire!"

A bee circled, landed on his forehead, and stung him between the eyes.

Bird let out a small cry. A golden pain, a good pain, shot through him like a shaft of sunlight breaking through the fog. A myriad of Mayas swam and danced before his eyes, but each one was clear and perfect. Bees walked his murderous wrists with thread feet, and he wanted to caress them. They had reached for him; they had not abandoned him. Not because he deserved compassion, but because by their very nature they were emissaries of a power that was always and everywhere offering itself, asking nothing in return, a force that set the bees in motion and colored the blossoms and made them sweet. That was the real gift, the true grace: not death, but love, the fifth sacred thing.

"Fire!" the General repeated, louder.

Bee venom trickled through his veins, dissolving the drugs, dissolving the haze of pain. Suddenly everything became very clear. Each separate face in the crowd seemed to have a firm outline drawn around it. Maya's eyes glowed, big as moons. He would not put out their light. No, what happened to Maya, to Rosa, was not under his control, never had been. He could not save them. He could not redeem the choices he had made before, he could not guarantee that he'd have the strength to resist again. But none of that mattered. What mattered was only to gather the courage for this one moment, to step off the road.

Slowly, as if he were laying a child down to sleep, Bird lowered the rifle and placed it on the platform.

"I won't kill for you," he said to the General.

"Then you'll die."

"It's a better choice," Bird said. "There's more hope in it." He raised his hands above his head and waited for the noise and the blast of pain. But he wasn't afraid. He could feel the ground under him again.

The song he had made for Madrone echoed in his ears. He'd thought he'd lost the music that was in him, but now it worked his lips and pried his mouth open and forced its way out of him in croaks and gasps. He tried to sing for the people as he had sung for the bees, hoarsely at first, but gradually his voice strengthened, and the sound rose and swelled above the crowd. His upraised arms became a gesture not of surrender but invoking, for he had never loved his life more than at this moment, loved his own breath and the movement of blood in his veins and the touch of air on his skin and his own voice reverberating.

That was all he had to do, to sing—to his grandmother and his lover and his enemies and his executioners. He had found his ground to stand on, and, yes, there was a bottom place, a place where who he was and what he could not do was stronger than fear and stronger even than hope. He understood now that he could never lose the music. It grew in him as the silence grew around him. They had broken his hands, but they had not broken his voice, they had broken his will but they had not broken his ears, and if they took his ears they could never take the inner ear, the inner voice. And even when his voice was silenced, some voice would still continue to sing. For he realized now that he was wrong in thinking the music was in him.

He was in the music, and it would always find an instrument.

"Unit Five, fire!" the General ordered. "Kill him."

Ghosts wheeled and circled like gulls.

Now, Bird thought. Now I will die and join you.

He looked out at the men who had their guns trained on him. It was his own unit, and that seemed comforting, somehow, to die at the hands of friends, not strangers. For they were his friends. He had grown into them, become one of them, as they now shared some part of him. He smiled and sang louder.

But he did not die. One by one, the soldiers lowered their guns.

"Fire!" the General ordered again. They remained standing, silent, impassive, disobedient.

Go ahead, Bird almost wanted to shout at them. Get it over with, do it, I cannot maintain this tension any longer.

He stopped singing. Complete and utter silence gripped the square. He could hear only ghost wings in the air and a drumbeat, like a heart, pulsing.

"He's in our unit, man," Threetwo said. "We don't kill our own."

"Fire!" the General roared a third time. "Fire, you slimecrawlers, or I'll have every soulless one of you taken out and shot!"

River sprang up onto the platform. "Unit Five," he cried out, and everyone in the Plaza could hear him. "We in the wrong army! Follow me, and fight for ourselves! The Witches, they can fix us so we don't need the boosters. They our true people. Stand with them—we got nothing to fear. Come on!"

"Shoot to kill!" the General ordered his Private Guard.

River knocked Bird down and grabbed his discarded rifle as gunfire rang out. The soldiers of Unit Five returned fire, leaping off the platform and into the panicked crowd. Lasers flared, shots rang out, and people began screaming and desperately trying to push through the press of bodies. The squadron around Maya melted away to join the scattered soldiers of River's unit.

"Get down!" Madrone screamed, pushing Nita to the ground, for they were caught between Unit Five and the General's Guards. Shots were flying around her. Up on the platform, Maya was still tied to the pole, exposed, lasers streaking by her calm eyes.

"Madrina," Madrone screamed, but her words were lost in the chaos. A wild laser struck something electrical under the platform, and black smoke began to rise.

"Come on," Isis called to her, and began crawling toward the west side of the platform. Madrone followed, wriggling on her belly through the chaos of shots and smoke and stampeding feet. Nita was lost behind them.

Bird lay on the platform in shock, trying to decide if he were alive or dead. War had erupted around him. The General's army was fighting itself. He knew he should move, but his body wouldn't seem to obey his mind. Clouds of smoke billowed around him, full of ghosts. Cleis and Zorah and Tom passed by; his brother Marley played a drumbeat that brought clouds gathering and drops of rain down from the sky; Rio stood over him; there were warriors and ancestors and flocks of extinct birds. Every battered child, every bruised slave, every starved peasant, every woman raped and murdered, every soldier who'd died for somebody else's ends, legions and legions of the dead came marching, howling, screaming, whipping cold wind fingers across the nape of his neck, ruffling his hair so it stood on end. He opened his mouth and tried to sing to them, but the acrid smoke choked him. Still he thought the dead took up the chorus, whining and whistling and shrieking until he had to move, crawling down the length of the platform while the spot he'd been lying on burst into flame.

Air. He could breathe again. The wind whipped the smoke aside and he caught a glimpse of Maya, still tied to the pole. He had to reach her. Bent over, crouching, he ran.

Isis and Madrone reached the edge of the platform near Maya just in time to see Bird dive at her feet as a sheet of laser fire went streaking above his head. Maya's dress was singed, but she looked unharmed.

"Are you okay?" Bird had to shout to be heard. She nodded. He fumbled with the ropes that held her, but the knots were so tight he wondered how he would ever get her loose. Suddenly he felt someone tugging at his leg, reaching up from the side of the platform to place a pocketknife in his hand. He opened the blade and cut the cords that bound Maya to the pole.

Released, she slumped forward but he caught her and eased her down.

"Give her here," a voice called from below. He handed her down to the strong pair of arms that reached up for her. Isis picked Maya up, slung her over her shoulder, and ran. Amidst the bullets and the streaks of laser fire, he half jumped, half fell, off the platform to the ground. Familiar arms enfolded him; he remembered them from somewhere as he recognized the body that pressed close to his. He blinked his eyes to clear his vision and saw Madrone.

"You're alive!" he said.

"So are you!" For one long moment they clung together, while fire engulfed the platform and the crowd fled. Wrapped in her arms, he felt whole again, redeemed, forgiven. Holding his miraculously still-living body, she was finally home.

He pulled back, although he still held tight to her hands.

"Rosa," he said.

"Are you okay? Can you walk?"

"Rosa, now, while the power is here."

She nodded, and they made their way through the thinning crowd, calling out to people as they ran.

"The prisoners! We've got to free the prisoners!"

The crowd surged behind them, as they ran out the north side of the Plaza, down the street that faced the Old Library. Their following grew as they continued down the block, rising like a tide that broke on the glass doors of the old Federal building, where five armed soldiers stood guard.

"Who goes first?" Madrone asked, looking warily at the soldiers.

"The dead," Bird said, and sang again. Gray wraiths swirled up from the crowd and bore down on the waiting soldiers. Madrone closed her eyes, sent out a call. Within moments, they were surrounded by a cloud of bees, humming and buzzing and making forays at the soldiers, flying into their eyes. The soldiers dropped their guns and fled.

○ ○ ○

They found Rosa locked in a room in the basement. Her eyes were closed, her head thrown back at an odd angle, and for one terrible moment Madrone was sure she was dead.

Another one, Madrone thought. Mama, I have tried so hard to stop all this, and failed and failed.

Bird went to her and picked her up in his arms. Her skin was cold but she stirred, as he touched her, and flinched.

"She's alive," he whispered. "Thank the Goddess."

She opened her eyes, and looked up at him, and then shrank away.

"It's okay, *querida*. I'm okay now," he murmured. He didn't want to think about how she had last seen him and what she might be remembering. "You're safe now. Look, Madrone is here."

"Madrone?"

Bird transferred Rosa into Madrone's arms. She held the girl tight, crooning to her, stroking her tangled hair. "It's okay, baby. It's going to be all right. *Diosa,* I am so very glad to find you alive."

Bird sank back against the gray stucco wall. His energy was leaking away, tears streamed down his face, the ghosts were leaving him now. It was dark here and his eyes were at ease, his whole body felt oddly comfortable, like an animal returned to a familiar cage. In a moment he was going to be sick on the floor.

"Let's get out of here," he said.

They carried Rosa up into the open air and sat next to her, keeping vigil on the steps. The crowd had moved off, they were marching to the hospital, someone said, and the soldiers were battling one another. River had led a squadron to take the armory. Many were fleeing back down the highway to the South or turning over their guns and asking for asylum. The Plaza and the surrounding streets were littered with the dead. Groups of volunteers were searching the building, battering down doors to free the prisoners they found within.

The steps were cold and cement and solid under Bird. The sun was warm, and Madrone's hand that clung to his was warm too. Rosa nestled into Madrone's shoulder, unable to speak. People passed them by, waving banners and singing songs of victory.

"I guess we're winning," Madrone said. "I can hardly believe it. We should feel happy."

"In a moment I will," Bird said. "It's got to run a long way to catch up with me."

Inside he felt cold as the vacuum of space. The light hurt his eyes so badly. He wanted to hold Madrone, but he couldn't even turn to her.

"I was giving her piano lessons," Bird said. "Do you remember, Rosa? Maybe now you'll learn to play that Mozart piece."

Then he was crying and Madrone slipped an arm around his shoulders.

"You'll heal," she said. "You'll both heal. We all will."

He looked up at her, wiping his eyes on the back of his sleeve. "I'll probably have to go live with the Wild Boar People. Does the whole city think I'm a traitor?"

"After today, they'll think you're a hero."

"No. I don't want to be a hero."

"What do you want to be, *querido*? This is victory; you can be anything you want."

"A piano teacher," he said, and laughed. Suddenly happiness hit him. He was alive, and Rosa had survived, and Madrone too, and before them a boy hoisted a banner on the flagpole, the double spiral in the quartered circle on a rainbow ground. "Even if I'm a very bad one."

Madrone laughed. Rosa looked up and smiled.

"How am I going to get you two home?" Madrone asked. "Goddess knows if there's any transport going. I don't think I can carry Rosa so far, and Bird, you look like hell."

"I've been there."

"But we're out, now, aren't we?" Rosa said.

"Yes," Madrone said. "Out of hell, and free, and safe as anybody can be in this world. That's real. We've made it back into *El Mundo Bueno*."

"Hold me, and I'll try to remember that," Bird said.

She wrapped her arms around him, hugging Rosa between them. He was warm and alive, as was she, against all odds, and they had come back to each other from terrible places. Pain and joy wrapped around them. Bird's eyes still hurt, but when he closed them suddenly his ears were filled with music. In time, he knew, he would sing it and struggle to play it and write it down. Well or badly, it didn't matter, only that he sang what was in him. Songs for the living, songs for the dead. He began to hum. Madrone felt the music through his skin, humming like the bees, ringing like the voice for which she too was an instrument. A victory song. Today, she remembered suddenly, was the first of August, or Third Foggy Moon, the Day of the Reaper, the twenty-first anniversary of the Uprising. Soon they could climb the hill, make the offerings, say to the Reaper, "See, Goddess, this is what we have made of our city. This is how we have preserved it, defended it, saved our own lives." The streams would soon flow again. And this winter, the rains would come.

37

They lit bonfires on the tops of all the hills in the city. All night, drummers pounded out rhythms and people cried and danced. The army was gone. Some had fled down the old highway, others had died in the crossfire of mutinies, many had simply laid down their guns and asked to be taken in. The streets were thronged with people, the streams flowed again, and lights moved on the bay as boats sailed home.

o o o

The General lay in a hospital room, and Maya sat beside him, still dressed in white. She had been fed some clear broth and a piece of toast; she felt more alive now, almost substantial, even though Sam had yelled at her and told her to stay home. But she was not tired, only a little light-headed from her long fast. When they heard that Alexander had been found wounded in the Central Plaza, a laser burn piercing his chest and lung, she had known she had to come and see him for herself.

"So you're dying and I'm not," Maya said to him. The General's eyes were closed; he did not respond. "How ironic. You get shot by your own men and I get carried off by a gorgeous Amazon pirate. Not bad for a woman of my mature years."

The General moaned.

"You're in pain. Maybe you should have let Madrone work on you. She pulls off miracles, from time to time."

They had offered him healing, but when Madrone came, her hands extended toward him, he shook his head and whispered with labored breath, "No Witchcraft!"

"I'm offering you some healing," Madrone had said. "Pure and simple, no ideology attached." But he shook his head again, and she shrugged her shoulders and left, not reluctantly. For she was tired too. She'd managed to find a wagon to take Bird and Rosa home, but that was hours and hours ago, and since then she hadn't sat down or stopped to eat a meal. There were so many wounded to tend, and too many dead. And this was the man responsible, the man who'd tortured Bird and Rosa and murdered Marie and so many more.

But I would have healed him nevertheless, or tried, she thought, and so there is a loss here, loss of the possibility of some opening. Maybe I've had it backward all along. I thought healing was pouring energy out, but it's not. It's opening, refining each receptor to any possibility of hope and comfort and change, taking in and taking in until you overflow. She felt rich, even in her exhaustion. She would go home now to Bird, who had stripped off his uniform and bathed and put on his own clothes, and they would touch, his touch would sing to her, and she in her own way would sing to him.

"I don't mind dying," the General whispered, his voice so low that Maya had to lean close to his mouth to hear. "Better than living in defeat."

"That happy philosophy, throughout history, has killed more men than gonorrhea," Maya said. "Still, I have to admire your consistency, if not your ideals. In spite of all the suffering you've caused, I would ease your pain if I could."

The General groaned. He was silent for a long time. Maya sat and waited. She didn't mind waiting with the nearly dead, she was that way herself. Why am I here? she asked herself. Is this an act of compassion, or do I just need to see with my own eyes that the man is really dead?

"You made your own defeat," Maya went on, speaking as much to herself as to the limp form on the bed. "With your own fear, and with the hatred you yourselves have sown. So that even though you seemed so much more powerful than us, you could not win in the end. Although I have to admit there were more than a few moments when I doubted that."

The General gasped and strained and finally managed to spit out a few words. "Others will replace me."

"Maybe. Maybe not. Perhaps you have taught us the lessons we need to know to resist those others too."

A bright bubble of blood burst between the General's lips. "War never ends," he gasped, in a voice so low she had to lean down to hear it.

She took his hand, cold even as she lifted it. "There was a place for you at our table, General, if only you could have believed us." He closed his eyes and died.

°　°　°

"Well, Lily, now what?" Sam asked. The kitchen was crowded and warm with the smell of simmering soup and noisy with five conversations going on at once.

"Come to Council tomorrow," she said. "It will all be debated. What to do with the deserters. How to rebuild. Whether or not we should anticipate further attacks."

"Tomorrow?" Madrone said. It already was tomorrow, wasn't it? She had worked through the night and lost count of time. "Don't we get a day off?"

"You're tired, I know. But these are pressing issues; we should at least begin the discussions. Of course, nothing will be resolved immediately. But you will come, won't you? All of you—you from the South too. We need the information you can give us."

"I'll be happy to come," Katy said, shifting Lucia to her other breast. "I've been wishing I could see how one of your Councils functions."

"I suppose I should go," Maya said. She was ensconced in the big easy chair, tucked under an afghan that Johanna had crocheted long ago. She was still eating very little; really, it seemed a shame, now that she was halfway discarnate, to interrupt the process of dissolution. Everything she looked at wavered and shimmered. At the edge of her vision, ghost forms danced. Now, for instance, Johanna's arms were wrapped around her. Rio sat at her feet, his hand resting lightly on her thigh.

"I suppose you should stay home in bed," Sam said decisively.

"Is that a proposition?"

"It's an order."

"Then for sure I'll go. I never obey orders."

"Does Defense think there's a chance of further attacks?" Nita asked.

"Nobody knows for sure," Lily said. "We think not, not soon anyway. They'll need some time to recover from this defeat and consider what they can learn from it. But as long as the Southlands continue in their present system, we can expect attacks. That's why we especially want you who have been down there, Madrone and Bird too, to be part of this discussion. We need to consider more active aid for their Web."

Bird sat silent on the couch, huddled in the corner. He was having a hard time shaking the ghosts; they seemed to follow him everywhere. From time to time he had to leave the room to check on Rosa, who was sleeping in Maya's bed, and reassure himself that she was really alive. When he closed his eyes, Marie and Lan and Roberto stared at him. They vanished only when Madrone touched him or when he sat at the piano, as he had done for an hour that morning, picking out the music he heard in his ears, writing it down. Now he noticed that Lily's eyes were fixed on him.

"No, Lily, I'm not going. Don't look for me at Council. You all can condemn me better when I'm not there."

"We aren't going to condemn you, Bird. People understand a little better now. They think you're very brave."

"Well, I'm not. I'm no hero any more than I was a villain before. None of you understands the least thing about what happened to me!"

"We know you did the best you could, Bird," Lily said softly.

"Of course I did the best I could. Maybe I did the best anybody could. That's not the point. The problem is, it wasn't good enough. Consider that before you go rushing off to liberate the Southlands."

"Maybe it was, Bird. Maybe it was exactly what had to happen. Because if you hadn't worked for them, if you hadn't in some way become part of them, there might have been no opening for your unit to become just the smallest bit more like us. Enough like us to shift the balance and change everything."

"That's a nice rationalization," Bird said. "I wish I believed it. Do you, really?"

"I believe that you never stopped resisting them, in every way you could. Those ways were imperfect, true, but you can't blame yourself for what you couldn't do. Defense Council is planning to ask you to join us."

"You're crazy. Cress'll have you drummed out of the city, unless he got shot yesterday."

"He has a bad laser burn in his shoulder," Madrone said, "but he'll survive."

"Besides, I'm not old, and I'm not a woman," Bird said.

"Defense agrees that the time has come to change our policy. We're the only Council restricted by gender, and that's not right. It leaves us open to attacks by such as Cress. But you, Bird, know more than anyone here what we're fighting against. We can learn so much from your experiences, even the worst of them. Especially the worst of them. We need you to help us plan how to deal with the Southlands."

Bird wasn't sure he believed her. Nevertheless, something gray and clinging lifted from his shoulders and partially dissolved. He looked up at Madrone, who sat across the room. She was worn and dry and wizened and aged. That was what the Southlands did to you. But she was beautiful to him, maybe more so than before, maybe because they were more alike now, both wounded, both survivors. Both strong, he realized. I am strong. Even if other forces are sometimes stronger.

"And how was it in the Southlands?" he asked Madrone.

"Hard," Madrone said. Why, she realized, I have yet to tell my story to anyone back here. "Very hard. But I'm glad I went. I learned a lot. I don't know how much good I did, or if I'd go back."

"But you'd consider it?" Katy asked eagerly.

"You ask me that, after you've threatened never to move from the Sisters' garden?"

"I will go back," Katy said. "Maybe not right away, because of the baby. But it's my home, it's my struggle. Hers, too."

Madrone looked at Bird. "Would you?"

He looked around the room. It was warm and bright and smelled of good food, filled with his family and friends. He was safe now; nobody would hurt him or face him with impossible choices. He had his music back, if not the skill of his hands, and Madrone, alive and soft-eyed. Would he risk all that again?

"After I rest up," he said, "I'd consider it. With you."

"Come back with the unit, man," said River, looking up from the soup he was eagerly downing. "Raise an army down there, free from the boosters, and we could take over."

"I can't singlehandedly free every soldier in the Southlands from the need for the boosters," Madrone said.

"We'll have the labs back in service soon, though, and we'll run them through a complete analysis," Sam said. "I'm sure we can find a drug protocol that'll be effective."

"If so, you'll shift the odds for the Web," Katy said. "You may make our victory possible."

"Consider this, too," Lily said. "We are no longer being held under radio silence. The jamming of the airwaves has stopped. We've got short-wave operators right now searching for others out there, trying to talk to other parts of the world. The time for isolation is over. There may be a lot of places to go."

"What kind of places?" Isis asked, sitting up alert.

"All kinds of places. Over the mountains to the east, over the ocean to the western islands, maybe even Asia and Japan. It's a big world. Once it was all connected, and still the tides and the currents and the air streams link us."

"I'll go west," Isis said. "Sail off over the ocean, find those places. With you, baby." She fondled Sara's arm.

"I'm not going back to the Southlands," Sara said. "But I'd go to Hawaii. Think you could find it?"

"Don't mind looking. That appeals to me. Who else?" Isis winked at Maya. "How about you, Great-Grandmama? Maybe a beautiful pirate steal you away from that old hairy man?"

Maya smiled. Yes, everything was fading, dreamy. Already she could feel herself rocking aboard ship. She was tired, so tired, and yet the thought of that journey appealed to her. They would set sail over the steel-gray dying ocean, in zigzag courses against the prevailing winds. They would search out the old lands, the wild lands and the islands, and there she would do what she had always done: talk to anyone who would listen, tell stories, pull the tail of the beast and, when it growled, stand her ground. There she would serve what she had always served, what was truly sacred: air and fire, water and earth, and in that service she believed she would always find companions.

And maybe on the way they would find the old sea, the clean sea, where the dream poems of whales still resounded in the deep places, where dolphins arched and ran near the secret rendezvous grounds of the golden seal. Oh, the world was a very big place; she had traveled enough when she was young to know that anything might still hide in the vast spaces of the west. There might be islands of summer where she would find the disappearing songbirds, and schools of deep-sea salmon massing to return up great rivers and spawn in mountain streams. Oh yes. Oh yes. She would believe, she had always needed to believe, that at daybreak in some warm ocean, seahorses still rose to greet their mates with a circular dance, their spiral tails twined around spires of sea grass. She had never seen them but she would go and find them, stranger than any mythical beast, the living creatures of the ancient, unwounded earth.

She would find them, going west, flanked by ghosts, accompanied by her beloved dead, by fallen heras and heros and villains and the ranks of the extinct, west against the wind to bring them home, west toward the moon and the evening star, west against the bright slanting rays of the sun and the turning clock of the earth, until west became east, until sunset became sunrise, until time swallowed its own tail and the day that was ending became a day that was just beginning to dawn.

ACKNOWLEDGMENTS

Many people have lent me their help and support as I worked on this book. Isis Coble read draft after draft of original material, offering insightful criticism and heartening enthusiasm. Marie Cantlon, who edited my three previous books, was also invaluable to me in helping me conceive and structure this story. Linda Gross at Bantam was a delight to work with; her questions and suggestions helped refine and clarify the story. In fact, everyone at Bantam has been a joy to work with, and I deeply appreciate their support and professionalism.

My agent, Ken Sherman, also cheered me on through the early drafts. Wendy Williams thought up the title. Susan Sedon-Boulet created the beautiful cover art. David Abram went prowling about the Santa Monica Mountains with me and suggested I use bees in the story. Arisika Raszak, Marina Alzugaray, and Arachne helped with information about midwifery and suggestions in the birth scenes. Patricia Witt gave me background on biology and the workings of the immune system, and Rafael Jesús González deepened my understanding of Coatlicue. Charles Dabo spoke Spanish with me daily and was unfailingly willing to translate. Michael Shapiro of *Libros Sin Fronteras* also consulted on the Spanish. William Doub provided the Chinese phrases quoted here.

Many of the chants and songs quoted in this story are actually used in rituals. The chant "Free the heart, let it go" on page 19 was created in a ritual class I taught in a summer workshop in Creation Spirituality at Omega Institute, by a woman whose name I am sorry to say I've forgotten. "If we have courage" on page 24 was written by myself and Rose May Dance. The chant "The earth is our mother" used as a password by the Web is Native American. The chant "Silver Shining Wheel" on page 97 is by Sparky T. Rabbit. "Yemaya Asesu," sung by Madrone on page 182, is a traditional Yoruba chant taught to me by Luisah Teish. The invocation on page 96 that begins: "By the earth that is her body" comes from the Faery tradition of Witchcraft and was taught me by Victor Anderson. The song to Elijah sung on page 216 is from the Jewish Seder.

"I wish I was a tiny sparrow" on page 61 is an old English folk song. "My mama makes counterfeit whiskey," on page 109, is a variation of the old tune, "My Bonnie Lies Over the Ocean." I have no idea where it comes from, but Rose May Dance taught it to me and it is excellent for calming fussy babies.

The quotation from Diane Di Prima on page 238 is from a poem I heard her read at An Evening of Music and Poetry for an End to Nuclear Testing, Dec. 5, 1990, at the First Unitarian Church in San Francisco. All other chant lyrics and poems are by me.

Ch'i, the Chinese word for subtle energy, is more properly written *qi* in today's revised phonetic spelling, but I have stayed with the older version as it is easier for the reader to hear correctly.

In inventing the future, I've drawn on many sources. Mark Shoenbeck offered me hospitality at the New Alchemy Institute on Cape Cod, where much of the food-growing techniques in this book had their inspiration. The Voices in the Council were inspired by a practice begun at the Fifth North American Bioregional Congress in 1989. The permaculture movement has also been a rich source of ideas. Many of the rituals strongly resemble those created by Reclaiming, the collective I work and teach with, and especially the Celebrations for the Ancestors of Many Cultures we have begun to do every Halloween season. I thank the members of the planning group for bringing to life a multicultural vision like that expressed here. The phrase "May you never hunger; may you never thirst," is part of our ritual blessing of food and drink. Many of the political and social structures were inspired by years of organizing and participating in nonviolent direct actions against various wars and weapons.

This is a work of fiction, and all of the characters in it are my own inventions. As the saying goes, any resemblance to persons living or dead is pure coincidence. I do, however, really live in a collective house, which in physical structure resembles Black Dragon House. I thank my housemates for providing me with just the proper mix of affection, stimulation, irritation, entertainment, and humor. My *compañero,* David Miller, walked into my life in the middle of this work and sustained me with more love and support than I had imagined was possible. Florence Ida Dabo Kemp is my daily reminder of what is at stake. This book is dedicated to her, to her brand new sister, Aminatou Kaira Dabo Kemp, to my newest Goddesschildren, Casey Cooper Quirke and Emily Sunrise Iverson, and to all the new ones who must live in the future that we create or destroy with our choices today.

ABOUT THE AUTHOR

*S*TARHAWK *is the author of* The Spiral Dance: A Rebirth of the Ancient Religion of the Great Goddess, Dreaming the Dark: Magic, Sex, and Politics, *and* Truth or Dare: Encounters with Power, Authority and Mystery.

A feminist and peace activist, she is one of the foremost voices of ecofeminism, and travels widely in North America and Europe giving lectures and workshops. She holds an M.A. in Psychology from Antioch West University and since 1983 has been a lecturer at the Institute for Culture and Creation Spirituality at Holy Names College in Oakland. She consulted on the films Goddess Remembered *and* The Burning Times, *directed by Donna Read and produced by the National Film Board of Canada, and co-wrote the commentary for* Full Circle, *a third film forthcoming in the same Women's Spirituality series.* The Fifth Sacred Thing *is her first novel.*

She lives in San Francisco, where she works with the Reclaiming collective, which offers classes, workshops, and public rituals in earth-based spirituality.